The Diary and Letters of Madame D'Arblay

Madame D'Arblay is the married name of Frances 'Fanny' Burney

Volume III (1792-1840) of III

Frances Burney was born on June 13th, 1752 in Lynn Regis (now King's Lynn). By the age of 8 Frances had still not learned the alphabet and couldn't read. She now began a period of self-education, which included devouring the family library and to begin her own 'scribblings', these journal writings would document her life and cover the next 72 years.

Her journal writing was accepted but writing novels was frowned upon by her family and friends. Feeling that she had been improper, she burnt her first manuscript, The History of Caroline Evelyn, which she had written in secret.

It was only in 1778 with the anonymous publication of Evelina that her talents were available to the wider world. She was now a published and admired author.

Despite this success and that of her second novel, Cecilia, in 1785, Frances travelled to the court of King George III and Queen Charlotte and was offered the post of "Keeper of the Robes". Frances hesitated. She had no wish to be separated from her family, nor to anything that would restrict her time in writing. But, unmarried at 34, she felt obliged to accept and thought that improved social status and income might allow her greater freedom to write.

The years at Court were fruitful but took a toll on her health, writing and relationships and in 1790 she prevailed upon her father to request her release from service. He was successful.

The ideals of the French Revolution had brought support from many English literates for the ideals of equality and social justice. Frances quickly became attached to General Alexandre D'Arblay, an artillery officer who had fled to England. In spite of the objections of her father they were married on July 28th, 1793.

On December 18th, 1794, Frances gave birth to their only child, a son, Alexander.

Frances's third novel, Camilla, in 1796 earned her £2000 and was enough for them to build a house in Westhumble; Camilla Cottage.

In 1801 D'Arblay was offered service with the government of Napoleon in France, and in 1802 Frances and her son followed him to Paris, where they expected to remain for a year. The outbreak of the war between France and England meant their stay extended for ten years.

In August 1810 Frances developed breast cancer and underwent a mastectomy performed by "7 men in black". Frances was later able to write about the operation in detail, being conscious through most of it, anesthetics not yet being in use.

With the death of D'Arblay, in 1818, of cancer, Frances moved to London to be near her son. Tragically he died in 1837. Frances, in her last years, was by now retired but entertained many visits from younger members of the Burney family, who gathered to listen to her fascinating accounts and her talents for imitating the people she described.

Frances Burney died on January 6th, 1840.

Index of Contents

THE FRENCH POLITICAL EMIGRANTS: MISS BURNEY MARRIES M. D'ARBLAY.

[The following section must be pronounced, from the historical point of view, one of the most valuable in the " Diary." It gives us authentic glimpses of some of the actors in that great Revolution, "the Death-Birth of a new order," which was getting itself transacted, with such terrible accompaniments, across the channel. The refugees with whom Fanny grew acquainted, and who formed the little colony at juniper Hall, near Dorking, were not the men of the first emigration—princes and nobles who fled their country, like cowards, as soon as they found themselves in danger, and reentered it like traitors, in the van of a foreign invasion. Not such were the inmates of Juniper Hall. These were constitutional monarchists, men who had taken part with the people in the early stage of the Revolution, who had been instrumental in making the Constitution, and who had sought safety in flight only when the Constitution was crushed and the monarchy abolished by the triumph of the extreme party. To the grands seigneurs of the first emigration, these constitutional royalists, were scarcely less detestable than the jacobins themselves.

A few leading facts and dates will perhaps assist the reader to a clearer understanding of the situation. September 1791, the French Assembly, having finished its work of Constitution-making, and the said [Constitution being accepted by the king, retires gracefully, and the new Assembly, constitutionally elected, meets, October 1. But the Constitution, ushered in with such rejoicings, proves a failure. The king has the right to veto the acts of the Assembly, and he exerts that right with a vengeance:—vetoes their most urgent decrees: decree against the emigrant noblesse, plotting, there at Coblenz, the downfall of their country; decree against nonjuring priests, intriguing endlessly against the Constitution. Patriot-Minister Roland remonstrates with his majesty, and the patriotic ministry is forthwith dismissed. Meanwhile distress and disorder are everywhere, and emigration is on the increase Abroad, Austria and Prussia are threatening invasion, and the emigrants at Coblenz are clamorous for war. War with Austria is declared, April 20, 1792; war with Prussia follows three months later; England remaining still neutral. One of our friends of juniper Hall, Madame de Staël's friend, Count Louis de Narbonne, has been constitutional minister of war, but had to retire in March, when the popular ministry—Roland's—came into office. It is evident that the king and the Assembly cannot act together; nay, the king himself feels the impossibility of it, and is already setting his hopes on foreign interference, secretly corresponding with Austria and Prussia. The people of Paris, too, feel the impossibility, and are setting their hopes on something very different. The monarchy must go; jacobins' club (1) and men of the Gironde, afterwards at death- grapple with one another, are now united on this point; they, and not a constitutional government, are the true representatives of Paris and of France.

A year ago, July 1791, the people of Paris, demanding the deposition of the king, were dispersed by General Lafayette with volleys of musketry. But Lafayette's popularity and power are now gone. "The hero of two worlds," as he was called, was little more than a boy when he fought under Washington, in the cause of American independence. Animated by the same love of liberty which had carried him to America, Lafayette took part in the early movements of the French Revolution. In 1789, after the fall of the Bastille, he was commander of the national guard, and one of the most popular men in France. A high-minded man, full of sincerity, of enthusiasm: "Cromwell Grandison," Mirabeau nicknamed him. Devoted to the Constitution, Lafayette was no friend to the extreme party, to the jacobins, with their Danton, their Robespierre. He had striven for liberty, but for liberty and monarchy combined; and the two things were fast becoming irreconcilable. And now, in July 1792, distrusted alike by the Court and the people, Lafayette sits sad at Sedan, in the midst of his army. War has already commenced, with a desultory and unsuccessful attack by the French upon the Austrian Netherlands. But the real struggle is now approaching. Heralded by an insolent proclamation, the Duke of Brunswick is marching from Coblenz with more than a hundred thousand Prussians, Austrians, and emigrants; and General Lafayette, alas! appears more bent upon denouncing jacobinism than upon defending the frontier.

The country is indeed in danger. With open hostility advancing from without, doubt and suspicion fermenting within, Paris at last rises in good earnest, August 10, 1792. This is the answer to Brunswick's insolent proclamation. Paris attacks the Tuileries, King Louis and his family taking refuge in the Assembly; captures the Tuileries, not without terrible loss, the brave Swiss guard standing steadfast to their posts, and getting, the greater part of them, massacred. Yielding to the demands of the people, the Assembly passes decrees suspending the king, dismissing the ministers, and convoking a National Convention. This was the work of the famous 10th of August, the birthday of the French Republic. on the 13th August the royal family is sent to the prison of the Temple from whence the king and the queen, unhappy Marie Antoinette, will come forth only to trial and execution. A new patriotic ministry is formed—Rolan again minister of the interior, Danton, the soul of the insurrection, minister of justice; a tribunal is appointed) and the prisons of Paris are filled with persons suspect. Executions follow; but the tribunal makes not quick enough work. Austrians and Prussians are advancing towards Paris; in Paris itself thousands of aristocrats, enemies to their country, are lying hid, ready to join the foreign foes.

In these desperate straits, Paris, at least sansculotte Paris, frenzied and wild for vengeance, falls upon the mad expedient of massacring the prisoners: more than a thousand suspected royalists are slaughtered, after brief improvised Trial or pretence of trial; or even without trial at all. This butchery is known as the "September massacres" (Sept. 2-6, 1792), infamous in history, heartily approved by few, perhaps, even of the more violent Republicans; indignantly denounced by Rowland and the less violent, powerless, nevertheless, to interfere, Paris being "in death-panic, the enemy and gibbets at its door."(2) Sept. 22, the Legislative Assembly having Dissolved, the National Convention holds its first meeting and proclaims the Republic: royalty for ever abolished in France.

Among the feelings, with which the news of these events are received in England, horror predominates. Still the Government takes no decisive step. The English ambassador in Paris, Lord Gower, is indeed recalled, in consequence of the events of August 10, but the French ambassador, Chauvelin, yet remains in London, although unrecognised in an official capacity after the deposition of Louis. War is in the wind, and, although Fox and many members of the opposition earnestly deprecate any hostile interference in the affairs of the Republic, a strong contingent of the Whig party, headed by Burke, is not less earnest in their efforts to make peace with France impossible. Pitt, indeed, is in favour of neutrality, but Pitt is forced to give way at last. Meanwhile, the popular feeling in favour of the royalists is being heightened and extended by the constant influx of French refugees. Thousands of the recalcitrant clergy, especially, with no king's veto now to protect them, are seeking safety, in England. Many adherents of the Constitution, too, ex-members of the Assembly and others, are fleeing hither from a country intolerant of monarchists, even constitutional; establishing themselves at juniper Hall and elsewhere. Among them we note the Duke de Liancourt, whose escape the reader will find related in the following pages; Count de Lally-Tollendal and M. de jaucourt, saved, both, by good fortune, from the September massacres; Vicomte de Montmorency, or call him citoyen, who voted for the abolition of titles; ex-minister of war Narbonne, concealed after August 10 by Madame de Stael, and escaping disguised as a servant; and presently, too, Madame de Stael herself; and last, but not least interesting to readers of the Diary, General Alexandre dArblay, whom Fanny will before long fall in love with and marry. One person, too, there is, more noteworthy, or at least more prominent in history, than any of these, whom

Fanny meets at Mickleham, whom she dislikes instinctively at first sight, but whose plausible speech and ingratiating manners soon make a convert of her.

This is citizen Talleyrand—Charles Maurice de Talleyrand-P,rigord, Bishop of Autun. He, too, is now an emigrant, although he came to England in a far different character, as secret ambassador from the Constitutional Government of France; citizen Chauvelin being the nominal ambassador. On the whole, Talleyrand's diplomacy has not been productive of much good, to himself or others. Back in Paris before the 10th of August, he returned to London in September with a passport from Danton. A questionable man; some think him a jacobin, others a royalist in disguise. And now, while he is in London, there is talk of him in the Convention: citizen Talleyrand, it seems, has professed himself " disposed to serve the king;" whereupon (December 5, 1792) citizen Talleyrand is decreed accused, and his name is inscribed on the list of emigrants.

We must turn once again to France. At Sedan, in a white heat of indignation on the news of that 10th of August, constitutional (sic) Lafayette emits a proclamation: the Constitution is destroyed, the king a prisoner: let us march for Paris and restore them! There is hope at first, that the army will follow Lafayette, but hope tells a flattering tale: the soldiers, it seems, care more for their country than for the Constitution. Lafayette sees that all is lost; rides (August 18) for Holland with a few friends, of whom General d'Arblay is one; intends to take passage thence for America, but falls, instead, into the hands of the Austrians, and spends the next few years imprisoned in an Austrian fortress. General d'Arblay, after a few days, is allowed to proceed to England.

Lafayette gone, the command of the army falls to General Dumouriez. Brunswick with his Prussians and emigrants, Clairfait with his Austrians, are now in France; advancing upon Paris. They take Longwy and Verdun; try to take Thonville and Lille, but cannot; and find Dumouriez and his sansculottes, there in the passes of Argonne, the "Thermopylae of France," an unexpectedly hard nut to crack. In fact, the nut is not to be cracked at all: Dumouriez, " more successful than Leonidas," flings back the invasion; compels the invaders to evacuate France; and in November, assuming the offensive, conquers the whole Austrian Netherlands. Meantime, in the south-east, the war in which the Republic is engaged with the King of Sardinia progresses also favourably, and Savoy and Nice are added to the French territory. Europe may arm, but a people fighting for an ideal is not to be crushed. France has faith in her ideal of liberty and fraternity, questionable or worse though some of the methods are by which she endeavours to realise it. But Danton is right: "il nous faut de l'audace, et encore de l'audace, et toujours de l'audace;" and with superb audacity the Republic defies the armed powers of Europe, decrees (November 19) assistance to every nation that will strike a blow for freedom, and cast off its tyrants. A yet more daring act of defiance follows—tragic to all men, unspeakably horrible to Fanny Burney and all friends of monarchy, constitutional or other. In December 1792, poor King Louis is tried before the National Convention, found guilty of "conspiring against liberty;" condemned to death by a majority of votes; in January, executed January 21. It is even as Danton said in one of his all-too gigantic figures 'the coalesced kings threaten us; we hurl at their feet, as gage of battle, the Head of a King."' (3) Louis's kinsman, profligate Philippe Egalit, ci-devant Duc d'Orleans, votes for death; before another year has passed he himself will have perished by the guillotine. In England, war is resolved upon; even Pitt sees not how it can be avoided. January 24, ambassador Chauvelin is ordered to quit England within eight days; Talleyrand remaining yet another year. Spain, too, is arming, and Holland is England's ally. War being inevitable, the Republic determines to be first in the field; declares war on England and Holland, February 1, 1793, and on Spain, March 7. ED.]

ARRIVAL OF FRENCH EMIGRANTS AT JUNIPER HALL.

August 1792. Our ambassador is recalled from France Russia has declared war against that wretched kingdom. But it may defy all outward enemies to prove in any degree destructive in comparison with its lawless and barbarous inmates. We shall soon have no authentic accounts from Paris, as no English are expected to remain after the ambassador, and no French will dare to write, in such times of pillage, what may carry them à la lanterne. (4)

(Mrs. Phillips to Fanny Burney.) Mickleham, September 1792. We shall shortly, I believe, have a little colony of unfortunate (or rather) fortunate, since here they are safe) French noblesse in our neighbourhood. Sunday evening Ravely informed Mr. Locke that two or three families had joined to take Jenkinson's house, Juniper Hall, and that another family had taken a small house at Westhamble, which the people very reluctantly let, upon the Christian-like supposition that, being nothing but French papishes, they would never pay. Our dear Mr. Locke, while this was agitating, sent word to the landlord that he would be answerable for the rent; however, before this message arrived, the family were admitted. The man said they had pleaded very hard indeed, and said, if he did but know the distress they had been in, he would not hesitate.

This house is taken by Madame de Broglie, daughter of the mareschal, who is in the army with the French princes; (5) or, rather, wife to his son, Victor Broglie, till very lately general of one of the French armies, and at present disgraced, and fled nobody knows where. This poor lady came over in an open boat, with a son younger than my Norbury, and was fourteen hours at sea. She has other ladies with her, and gentlemen, and two little girls, who had been sent to England some weeks ago; they are all to lodge in a sort of cottage, containing only a kitchen and parlour on the ground floor.

I long to offer them my house, 'and have been much gratified by finding Mr. Locke immediately determined to visit them; his taking this step will secure them the civilities, at least, of the other neighbours.

At Jenkinson's are-la Marquise de la Chattre, whose husband is with the emigrants; her son; M. de Narbonne, lately ministre de la guerre; (6) M. de Montmorency; Charles or Theodore Lameth; Jaucourt; and one or two more, whose names I have forgotten, are either arrived to-day, or expected. I feel infinitely interested for all these persecuted persons. Pray tell me whatever you hear of M. de Liancourt, etc. Heaven bless you!

THE DOCTOR'S FIVE DAUGHTERS.

(Fanny Burney to Dr. Burney.) Halstead, October 2, '92. My dearest padre, I have just got your direction, in a letter from my mother, and an account that you seem to be in health and spirits; so now I think it high time to let you know a little about some of your daughters, lest you should forget you have any such incumbrances.

In the first place, two of them, Esther and F. B., had a safe and commodious journey hither, in the midst of pattering showers and cloudy skies, making up as well as they could for the deficiencies of the elements by the dulcet recreation of the concord of sweet sounds; not from tabrets and harps, but from the harmony of hearts with tongues.

In the second place, a third of them, Charlotte F., writes word her caro sposo has continued very tolerably well this last fortnight, and that she still desires to receive my visit according to the first appointment.

In the third place, a fourth of them, Sarah, is living upon French politics and with French fugitives, at Bradfield, (7) where she seems perfectly satisfied with foreign forage.

In the fourth place, Susanna, another of them, sends cheering histories of herself and her tribe, though she concludes them with a sighing ejaculation of "I wish I did not know there was such a country as France!"

A VISIT TO ARTHUR YOUNG. (8)

Oct. 5. I left Halstead, and set off, alone, for Bradfield Hall, which was but one stage of nineteen miles distant. Sarah, (9) who was staying with her aunt, Mrs. Young, expected me, and came running out before the chaise stopped at the door, and Mr. Young following, with both hands full of French newspapers. He welcomed me with all his old spirit and impetuosity, exclaiming his house never had been so honoured since its foundation, nor ever could be again, unless I re-visited it in my way back, even though all England came in the meantime!

Do you not know him well, my Susan, by this opening rodomontade?

"But where," cried he, "is Hetty? O that Hetty! Why did you not bring her with you? That wonderful creature! I have half a mind to mount horse, and gallop to Halstead to claim her! What is there there to merit her? What kind of animals have you left her with? Anything capable of understanding her?"

During this we mounted up-stairs, into the dining-room. Here all looked cold and comfortless, and no Mrs. Young appeared. I inquired for her, and heard that her youngest daughter, Miss Patty, had just had a fall from her horse, which had bruised her face, and occasioned much alarm.

The rest of the day we spoke only of French politics. Mr. Young is a severe penitent of his democratic principles, and has lost even all pity for the constituans revolutionnaires, who had "taken him in" by their doctrines, but cured him by their practice, and who "ought better to have known what they were about before they presumed to enter into action."

Even the Duc de Liancourt, (11) who was then in a small house at Bury, merited, he said, all the personal misfortunes that had befallen him. "I have real obligations to him," he added, "and therefore I am anxious to show him respect, and do him any service, in his present reverse of fortune; but he has brought it all on himself, and, what is worse; on his country."

He wrote him, however, a note to invite him to dinner the next day. The duke wrote an answer, that lamented excessively being engaged to meet Lord Euston, and dine with the Bury aldermen.

THE DUKE DE LIANCOURT'S ABORTIVE EFFORTS AT ROUEN.

I must now tell you the history of this poor duke's arriving in England, for it involves a revival of loyalty, an effort to make some amends to his unhappy sovereign for the misery into which he had largely contributed to plunge him; which, with me, has made his peace for ever.

But first I should tell, he was the man who almost compelled the every-way- deluded Louis to sanction the National Assembly by his presence when first it resisted his orders. The queen and all her party were strongly against the measure, and prophesied it would be the ruin of his authority; but the duke, highly ambitious of fame, as Mr. Young describes him, and willing to sacrifice everything to the new systems then pervading all France, suddenly rushed into his closet, upon the privilege of being one of the five or seven pairs de France (12) who have that licence, and, with a strong and forcible eloquence, declared nothing but his concession would save the nation from a civil war; while his entering, unarmed, into the National Assembly, would make him regarded for ever as the father and saviour of his people, and secure him the powerful sovereignty of the grateful hearts of all his subjects.

He succeeded, and the rest is public.

This incident has set all the Coblenz (13) party utterly and for ever against the duke. He had been some time in extreme anguish for the unhappy king, whose ill-treatment on the 20th of June 1792, (14) reached him while commandant at Rouen. He then first began to see, that the monarch or the jacobins must inevitably fall, and he could scarce support the prospect of ultimate danger threatening the former. When the news reached him of the bloody 10th of August, a plan which for some time he had been forming, of gaining over his regiment to the service of the king, was rendered abortive. Yet all his officers except One had promised to join in any enterprise for their insulted master. He had hoped to get the king to Rouen under this protection, as I gather, though this matter has never wholly transpired, But the king could not be persuaded to trust any one. How should he?—especially a revolutionnaire?

No time now was to be lost, and, in his first impetuosity of rage and despair, he instantly summoned his officers and his troops; and, in the midst of them all, upon the parade or place of assembling, he took off his hat, and called out aloud, "Vive le roi!"

His officers echoed the sound, all but one!—yet not a soldier joined. Again be waved his hat, and louder and louder called out, "Vive le roi!" And then every soldier repeated it after him.

Enchanted with hope, he felt one exulting moment, when this single dissentient officer called out aloud, as soon as the loyal cry was over, "As an officer of the nation I forbid this!—Vive la nation!"

The duke instantly had the man arrested, and retired to his apartment to compose his excess agitation, and consider how to turn this promise of loyalty to the service of his now imprisoned king; but, in a short time, an officer strongly attached to him entered the room hastily, and cried, "Sauvez vous, M. de Liancourt! (15)—be speedy! the jacobin party of Rouen have heard of your indiscretion and a price is this moment set upon your head!"

The duke knew too well with whom he had to act for a moment's hesitation. To serve the king was now impossible, as he had but to appear in order to be massacred. He could only save his own life by flight.

THE DUKE'S ESCAPE TO ENGLAND: "POT PORTERE."

In what manner he effected his escape out of Rouen he has never mentioned. I believe he was assisted by those who, remaining behind, could only be named to be torn in pieces for their humanity. M. Jamard, a French priest, tells me no human being knows when or how he got away, and none suspected him to be gone for two days. He went first to Abbeville there, for two days, he appeared everywhere, walking about in his regimentals, and assuming an air of having nothing to apprehend. This succeeded, as his indiscretion had not yet spread at Abbeville; but, meanwhile, a youth whom he had brought up from a child, and on whose fond regard and respect he could rely, was employed in seeking him the means of passing over to England. This was infinitely difficult, as he was to leave France without any passport.

How he quitted Abbeville I know not; but he was in another town, near the coast, three days, still waiting for a safe conveyance; and here, finding his danger increased greatly by delay, he went to some common house, without dress or equipage or servants that could betray him, and spent his whole time in bed, under pretence of indisposition, to avoid being seen.

At length his faithful young groom succeeded; and he got, at midnight, into a small boat, with only two men. He had been taken for the King of France by one, who had refused to convey him; and some friend, who assisted his escape, was forced to get him off, at last, by holding a pistol to the head of his conductor, and protesting he would shoot him through and through, if he made further demur, or spoke aloud. It was dark, and midnight.

Both he and his groom planted themselves in the bottom of the boat, and were covered with fagots, lest any pursuit should ensue: and thus wretchedly they were suffocated till they thought themselves at a safe distance from France. The poor youth then, first looking up, exclaimed, "Ah! nous sommes perdus! (16) they are carrying us back to our own country!" The duke started up; he had the same opinion, but thought opposition vain; he charged him to keep silent and quiet; and after about another league, they found this, at least, a false alarm, owing merely to a thick fog or mist.

At length they landed—at Hastings, I think. The boatman had his money, and they walked on to the nearest public-house. The duke, to seem English, called for "pot portere." It was brought him, and he drank it off in two draughts, his drought being extreme; and he called for another instantly. That also, without any suspicion or recollection of consequences, was as hastily swallowed; and what ensued he knows not. He was intoxicated, and fell into a profound sleep. His groom helped the people of the house to carry him upstairs and put him to bed. How long he slept he knows not, but he woke in the middle of the night without the smallest consciousness of where he was, or what had happened. '

France alone was in his head. France and its horrors, which nothing—not even English porter and intoxication and sleep—could drive away.

He looked round the room with amaze at first, and soon after with consternation. It was so unfurnished, so miserable, so lighted with only one small bit of a candle, that it occurred to him he was in a maison de force (17) thither conveyed in his sleep. The stillness of everything confirmed this dreadful idea. He arose, slipped on his clothes, and listened at the door. He heard no sound. He was scarce, yet, I suppose, quite awake, for he took the candle, and determined to make an attempt to escape.

Down-stairs he crept, neither hearing nor making any noise and he found himself in a kitchen ' he looked round, and the brightness of a shelf of pewter plates struck his eye under them were pots and kettles shining and polished. "Ah! "? cried he to himself, "je suis en Angleterre."(18) The recollection came all at once at sight of a cleanliness which, in these articles, he says, is never met with in France.

He did not escape too soon, for his first cousin, the good Duc de la Rochefoucault, another of the first revolutionnaires, was massacred the next month. (19) The character he has given of this murdered relation is the most affecting, in praise and virtues, that can possibly be heard. Sarah has heard him till she could not keep the tears from her eyes. They had been eleves (20) together, and loved each other as the tenderest brothers.

MADAME DE GENLIS'S HASTY RETREAT.

You will all be as sorry as I was myself to hear that every ill story of la Comtesse de Genlis was confirmed by the duke.

She was resident at Bury, when he arrived, with Mlle. Egalit,, Pamela, Henrietta Circe, and several others, who appeared in various ways, as artists, gentlemen, domestics, and equals, on various occasions. The history of their way of life is extraordinary, and not very comprehensible, probably owing to the many necessary difficulties which the new 'system of equality produces. (21)

A lady of Bury, a sister of Sir Thomas Gage, had been very much caught by Madame Brulard, (22) who had almost lived at the house of Sir Thomas. Upon the arrival of the duke he was invited to Sir Thomas Gage's immediately; and Miss G, calling upon Madame Brulard, mentioned him, and asked if she knew him?—No, she answered; but she had seen him. This was innocently repeated to the duke, who then, in a transport of rage, broke out with "Elle M'a vu! (23) and is that all?—Does she forget that she has spoke to me? that she has heard me too? " And then he related, that when all was wearing the menacing aspect of anarchy, before it broke out, and before he was ordered to his regiment at Rouen, he had desired an audience of Madame Brulard, for the first time, having been always a friend of Madame d'Orl,ans, and consequently her enemy. She was unwilling to see him, but he would not be refused. He then told her that France was upon the point of ruin, and that the Duc d'Orl,ans, who had been its destruction, and "the disgrace of the Revolution," could alone now prevent the impending havoc. He charged her therefore, forcibly and peremptorily, to take in charge a change of measures, and left her with an exhortation which he then flattered himself would have some chance of averting the coming dangers. But quickly, after she quitted France voluntarily, and settled in England. "And can she have forgot all this?" cried he.

I know not if this was repeated to Madame de Brulard but certain it is she quitted Bury with the utmost expedition. She did not even wait to pay her debts, and left the poor Henrietta Circe behind, as a sort of hostage, to prevent alarm. The creditors, however, finding her actually gone, entered the house, and poor Henrietta was terrified into hysterics. Probably she knew not but they were jacobins, or would act upon jacobin principles. Madame Brulard then sent for her, and remitted money, and proclaimed her intention of returning to Suffolk no more.

A NOBLEMAN OF THE ANCIEN REGIEM.

The duke accepted the invitation for to-day, and came early, on horseback. He had just been able to get over some two or three of his horses from France. He has since, I hear, been forced to sell them.

Mrs. Young was not able to appear; Mr. Young came to my room door to beg I would waste no time; Sarah and I, therefore, proceeded to the drawing-room. The duke was playing with a favourite dog, the thing probably the most dear to him in England; for it was just brought him over by his faithful groom, whom he had sent back upon business to his son.

He is very tall, and, were his figure less, would be too fat, but all is in proportion. His face, which is very handsome, though not critically so, has rather a haughty expression when left to itself, but becomes soft and spirited in turn, according to whom he speaks, and has great play and variety. His deportment is quite noble, and in a style to announce conscious rank even to the most sedulous equaliser. His carriage is peculiarly upright, and his person uncommonly well made. His manners are such as only admit of comparison with what We have read, not what we have seen; for he has all the air of a man who would wish to lord over men, but to cast himself at the feet of women.

He was in mourning for his barbarously murdered cousin the Duc de la Rochefoucault. His first address was of the highest style. I shall not attempt to recollect his words, but they were most elegantly expressive of his satisfaction in a meeting he had long, he said, desired.

With Sarah he then shook hands. She had been his interpretess here on his arrival, and he seems to have conceived a real kindness for her; an honour of which she is extremely sensible, and with reason.

A little general talk ensued, and he made a point of curing Sarah of being afraid of his dog. He made no secret of thinking it affectation, and never rested till he had conquered it completely. I saw here, in the midst of all that at first so powerfully struck me of dignity, importance, and high-breeding, a true French Polisson; for he called the dog round her, made it jump on her shoulder, and amused himself as, in England, only a schoolboy or a professed fox-hunter would have dreamt of doing.

This, however, recovered me to a little ease, which his compliment had rather overset. Mr. Young hung back, nearly quite silent. Sarah was quiet when reconciled to the dog, or, rather, subdued by the duke; and then, when I thought it completely out of his head, he tranquilly drew a chair next mine, and began a sort of separate conversation, which he suffered nothing to interrupt till we were summoned to dinner.

His subject was 'Cecilia;' and he seemed not to have the smallest idea I could object to discussing it, any more than if it had been the work of another person. I answered all his demands and interrogatories with a degree of openness I have never answered any other upon this topic; but the least hope of beguiling the misery of an emigre tames me.

Mr. Young listened with amaze, and all his ears, to the many particulars and elucidations which the duke drew from me; he repeatedly called out he had heard nothing of them before, and rejoiced he was at least present when they were communicated.

This proved, at length, an explanation to the duke himself, that, the moment he understood, made him draw back, saying, "Peut-etre que je suis indiscret?" (24) However, he soon returned to the charge - and when Mr. Young made any more exclamations, he heeded them not: he smiled, indeed, when Sarah also affirmed he had procured accounts she had never heard before; but he has all the air of a man not new to any mark of more than common favour. At length we were called to dinner, during which he spoke of general things.

DUCAL VIVACITY AND SADNESS.

The French of Mr. Young, at table, was very comic; he never hesitates for a word, but puts English wherever he is at a loss, with a mock French pronunciation. "Monsieur Duc," as he calls him, laughed once or twice, but clapped him on the back, called him "un brave homme," and gave him instruction as well as encouragement in all his blunders.

When the servants were gone, the duke asked me if anybody might write a letter to the king? I fancy he had some personal idea of this kind. I told him yes, but through the hands of a lord of the bedchamber, or some state officer, or a minister. He seemed pensive, but said no more.

He inquired, however, if I had not read to the queen and seemed to wish to understand my office; but here he was far more circumspect than about 'Cecilia.' He has lived so much in a Court, that he knew exactly how far he might inquire with the most scrupulous punctilio.

I found, however, he had imbibed the jacobin notion that our beloved king was still disordered; for, after some talk upon his illness, and very grave and proper expressions concerning the affliction and terror it produced in the kingdom, he looked at me very fixedly, and, with an arching brow, said, "Mais, mademoiselle—apres tout—le roi—est il bien gueri?"(25)

I gave him such assurances as he could not doubt, from their simplicity, which resulted from their truth.

Mr. Young would hardly let Sarah and me retreat; however, we promised to meet soon to coffee. I went away full of concern for his injuries, and fuller of amazement at the vivacity with which he bore them.

When at last we met in the drawing-room, I found the duc all altered. Mr. Young had been forced away by business, and was but just returned, and he had therefore been left a few minutes by himself; the effect was visible, and extremely touching. Recollections and sorrow had retaken possession of his mind; and his spirit, his vivacity, his power of rallying were all at an end. He was strolling about the room with an air the most gloomy, and a face that looked enveloped in clouds of sadness and moroseness. There was a fiert, almost even fierce in his air and look, as, wrapped in himself, he continued his walk. I felt now an increasing compassion:—what must he not suffer when he ceases to fight with his calamities! Not to disturb him we talked with one another; but he soon shook himself and joined us; though he could not bear to sit down, or stand a moment in a place.

"CETTE COQUINE DE BRULARD."

Sarah spoke of Madame Brulard, and, in a little malice, to draw him out, said her sister knew her very well. The duke with eyes of fire at the sound, came up to me: "Comment, mademoiselle! vous avez connu cette coquine de Brulard?" (26) And then he asked me what I had thought of her.

I frankly answered that I had thought her charming; gay, intelligent, well-bred, well-informed, and amiable.

He instantly drew back, as if sorry he had named her so roughly, and looked at Sally for thus surprising him; but I immediately continued that I could now no longer think the same of her, as I could no longer esteem her; but I confessed my surprise had been inexpressible at her duplicity.

'He allowed that, some years ago, she might have a better chance than now of captivation, for the deeper she had immersed in politics, the more she had forfeited of feminine attraction. "Ah!" he cried, " with her talents-her knowledge-her parts-had she been modest, reserved, gentle, what a blessing might she have proved to her country! but she is devoted to intrigue and cabal, and proves its curse." He then spoke with great asperity against all the femmes de lettres now known; he said they were commonly the most disgusting of their sex, in France, by their arrogance, boldness, and mauvais moeurs.

GRACEFUL OFFERS OF HOSPITALITY.

I inquired if Mr. Young had shown him a letter from the Duke of Grafton, which he had let me read in the morning. It was to desire Mr. Young would acquaint him if the Duc de Liancourt was still in Bury, and, if so, to wait upon him, in the Duke of Grafton's name, to solicit him to make Euston his abode while in England, and to tell him that he should have his apartments wholly unmolested, and his time wholly unbroken; that he was sensible, in such a situation of mind, he must covet much quiet and freedom from interruption and impertinence; and he therefore promised that, if he would honour his house with his residence, it should be upon the same terms as if he were in an hotel-that he would never know if he were at home or abroad, or even in town or in the country, and he hoped the Duc de Liancourt would make no more scruple of accepting such an asylum and retreat at his house than he would himself have done of accepting a similar one from the duke in France, if the misfortunes of his own country had driven him to exile.

I was quite in love with the Duke of Grafton for this kindness. The Duc de Liancourt bowed to my question, and seemed much gratified with the invitation; but I see he cannot brook obligation; he would rather live in a garret, and call it his own. He told me, however, with an air of some little pleasure, that he had received just such another letter from Lord Sheffield. I believe both these noblemen had been entertained at Liancourt some years ago.

I inquired after Madame la duchesse, and I had the satisfaction to hear she was safe in Switzerland. The duke told me she had purchased an estate there.

He inquired very particularly after your juniper colony, and M. de Narbonne, but said he most wished to meet with M. d'Arblay, who was a friend and favourite of his eldest son.

THE EMIGRANTS AT JUNIPER HALL DESCRIBED.

[It is hoped that some pages from Mrs. Phillips's journalizing letters to her sister, written at this period, may not be unacceptable, since they give particulars concerning several distinguished actors and sufferers in the French Revolution, and also contain the earliest description of M. d'Arblay. (27))

(Mrs. Philips to Fanny Burney.) Mickleham, November, 1792. It gratifies me very much that I have been able to interest you for our amiable and charming neighbours.

Mrs. Locke had been so kind as to pave the way for my introduction to Madame de la Chattre, and carried me on Friday to juniper Hall, where we found M. de Montmorency, a ci-devant duc, (28) and one who gave some of the first great examples of sacrificing personal interest to what was then considered the public good. I know not whether you will like him the better when I tell you that from him proceeded the motion for the abolition of titles in France; but if you do not, let me, in his excuse, tell you he was scarcely one-and- twenty when an enthusiastic spirit impelled him to this, I believe, ill-judged and mischievous act. My curiosity was greatest to see M. de Jaucourt, because I remembered many lively and spirited speeches made by him during the time of the Assembl,e L,gislalive, and that he was a warm defender of my favourite hero, M. Lafayette.

Of M. de Narbonne's abilities we could have no doubt from his speeches and letters whilst ministre de la guerre, which post he did not quit till last May. (29) By his own desire, he then joined Lafayette's army, and acted under him; but on the 10th of August, he was involved, with perhaps nearly all the most honourable and worthy of the French nobility, accused as a traitor by the jacobins, and obliged to fly from his country M. d'Argenson was already returned to France, and Madame de Broglie had set out the same day, November 2nd, hoping to escape the decree against the emigrants. (30)

Madame de la Chattre received us with great politeness. She is about thirty-three; an elegant figure, not pretty, but with an animated and expressive countenance; very well read, pleine d'esprit, and, I think, very lively and charming.

A gentleman was with her whom Mrs. Locke had not yet seen, M. d'Arblay. She introduced him, and when he had quitted the room, told us he was adjutant-general to M. Lafayette, mar,chal de camp, and in short the first in military rank of those who had accompanied that general when he so unfortunately fell into the hands of the Prussians; but, not having been one of the Assembl,e Constituante, he was allowed, with four others, to proceed into Holland, and there M. de Narbonne wrote to him. "Et comme il l'aime infiniment," said Madame de la Chàtre, "il l'a prié de venir vivre avec lui."(31)

He had arrived only two days before. He is tall, and a good figure, with an open and manly countenance; about forty, I imagine.

It was past twelve. However, Madame de la Chàtre owned she had not breakfasted—ces messieurs were not yet ready. A little man, who looked very triste indeed, in an old- fashioned suit of clothes, with long flaps to a waistcoat embroidered in silks no longer very brilliant, sat in a corner of the room. I could not imagine who he was, but when he spoke was immediately convinced he was no Frenchman. I afterwards heard he had been engaged by M. de Narbonne for a year, to teach him and all the party English. He had had a place in some college in France at the beginning of the Revolution, but was now driven out and destitute. His name is Clarke. He speaks English with an accent tant soit Peu Scotch.

Madame de la Chàtre, with great franchise entered into details of her situation and embarrassment, whether she might venture, like Madame de Broglie, to go over to France, in which case she was dans le cas où elle pouvoit toucher sa fortune (32) immediately. She said she could then settle in England, and settle comfortably. M. de la Chàtre, it seems, previous to his joining the king's brothers, had settled upon her her whole fortune. She and all her family were great favourers of the original Revolution and even at this moment she declares herself unable to wish the restoration of the old r,gime, with its tyranny and corruptions—persecuted and ruined as she and thousands more have been by the unhappy consequences of the Revolution,

M. de Narbonne now came in. He seems forty, rather fat, but would be handsome were it not for a slight cast of one eye. He was this morning in great spirits. Poor man! It was the only time I have ever seen him so. He came up very courteously to me, and begged leave de me faire Sa Cour (33) at Mickleham, to which I graciously assented.

Then came M. de jaucourt, whom I instantly knew by Mr. Locke's description. He is far from handsome, but has a very intelligent countenance, fine teeth, and expressive eyes. I scarce heard a word from him, but liked his appearance exceedingly, and not the less for perceiving his respectful and affectionate manner of attending to Mr. Locke but when Mr. Locke reminded us that Madame de la Chàtre had not breakfasted, we took leave, after spending an hour in a manners so pleasant and so interesting that it scarcely appeared ten minutes.

MONSIEUR D'ARBLAY.

Nov. 7. Phillips was at work in the parlour, and I had just stepped into the next room for some papers I wanted, when I heard a man's voice, and presently distinguished these words: "Je ne parle pas trop bien l'Anglois, monsieur." (34) I came forth immediately to relieve Phillips, and then found it was M. d'Arblay.

I received him de bien bon coeur, as courteously as I could. The adjutant of M. Lafayette, and one of those who proved faithful to that excellent general, could not but be interesting to me. I was extremely pleased at his coming, and more and more pleased with himself every moment that passed. He seems to me a true militaire, franc et loyal—open as the day; warmly affectionate to his friends; intelligent, ready, and amusing in conversation, with a great share of gaiete de coeur, and, at the same time, of naivete and bonne foi. He was no less flattering to little Fanny than M. de Narbonne had been.

We went up into the drawing-room with him, and met Willy on the stairs, and Norbury capered before us. "Ah, madame," cried M. d'Arblay, "la jolie petite maison que vous avez, et les jolis petits hôtes!" (35) looking at the children, the drawings, etc. He took Norbury on his lap and played with - him. I asked him if he was not proud of being so kindly noticed by the adjutant-general of M. Lafayette? "Est-ce qu'il sait le nom de M. Lafayette?" (36) said he, smiling. I said he was our hero, and that I was thankful to see at least one of his faithful friends here. I asked if M. Lafayette was allowed to write and receive letters. He said yes, but they were always given to him open.

Norbury now (still seated on his lap) took courage to whisper him, "Were you, sir, put in prison with M. Lafayette?" "Oui, mon ami," "And—was it quite dark?" I was obliged, laughing, to translate this curious question. M. d'Arblay laughed too: "Non, mon ami," said he, "on nous amis abord dans une assez jolie chambre." (37)

I lamented the hard fate of M. Lafayette, and the rapid and wonderful reverse he had met with, after having been, as he well merited to be, the most popular man in France. This led M. d'Arblay to speak of M. de Narbonne, to whom I found him passionately attached. Upon my mentioning the sacrifices made by the French nobility, and by a great number of them voluntarily, he said no one had made more than M. de Narbonne; that, previous to the Revolution, he had more wealth and more power than almost any except the princes of the blood.

For himself, he mentioned his fortune and his income from his appointments as something immense, but 1 never remember the number of hundred thousand livres, nor can tell what their amount is without some consideration. . . .

The next day Madame de la Chattre was so kind as to send me the French papers, by her son, who made a silent visit of about five minutes.

M. DE JAUCOURT. MADAME DE STAEL.

Friday morning. I sent Norbury with the French papers, desiring him to give them to M. d'Arblay. He stayed a prodigious while, and at last came back attended by M. de Narbonne, M. de Jaucourt, and M. d'Arblay. M. de Jaucourt is a delightful man—as comic, entertaining, unaffected, unpretending, and good-humoured as dear Mr Twining, only younger, and not quite so black. He is a man likewise of first-rate abilities—M. de Narbonne says, perhaps superior to Vaublanc (38) and of very uncommon firmness and integrity of character.

The account Mr. Batt gave of the National Assembly last summer agrees perfectly with that of M. de Jaucourt, who had the misfortune to be one of the deputies, and who, upon some great occasion in support of the king and constitution, found only twenty-four members who had courage to support him, though a far more considerable number gave him secretly their good wishes and prayers. It was on this that he regarded all hope of justice and order as lost, and that he gave in sa d,mission (39) from the Assembly. In a few days he was seized, and sans forme de process (40) having lost his inviolability as a member, thrown into the prison of the Abbaye, where, had it not been for the very extraordinary and admirable exertions of Madame de Stael (M. Necker's daughter, and the Swedish ambassador's wife), he would infallibly have been massacred.

I must here tell you that this lady, who was at that time seven months gone with child, was indefatigable in her efforts to save every one she knew from this dreadful massacre. She walked daily (for carriages were not allowed to pass in the streets) to the H6tel de Ville, and was frequently shut up for five hours together with the horrible wretches that composed the Comit, de Surveillance, by whom these murders were directed; and by her eloquence, and the consideration demanded by her rank and her talents, she obtained the deliverance of above twenty unfortunate prisoners, some of whom she knew but slightly. . . .

Madame de la Chattre and M. de Jaucourt have since told me that M. de Narbonne and M. d'Arblay had been treated with singular ingratitude by the king, whom they nevertheless still loved as well as forgave. They likewise say he wished to get rid of M. de Narbonne from the ministry, because he could not trust him with his projects of contre revolution.

M. d'Arblay was the officer on guard at the Tuileries the night on which the king, etc, escaped to Varennes, (41) and ran great risk of being denounced, and perhaps massacred, though he had been kept in the most perfect ignorance of the king's intention.

SEVERE DECREES AGAINST THE EMIGRANTS.

The next Sunday, November 18th, Augusta and Amelia came to me after church, very much grieved at the inhuman decrees just passed in the Convention, including as emigrants, with those who have taken arms against their country, all who have quitted it since last July; and adjudging their estates to confiscation, and their persons to death should they return to France.

" Ma'am," said Mr. Clarke, " it reduces this family to nothing: all they can hope is, by the help of their parents and friends, to get together wherewithal to purchase a cottage in America, and live as they can."

I was more shocked and affected by this account than I could very easily tell you. To complete the tragedy, M. de Narbonne had determined to write an offer—a request rather—to be allowed to appear as a witness in behalf of the king, upon his trial; and M. d'Arblay had declared he would do the same, and share the fate of his friend, whatever it might be.

MONSIEUR GIRARDIN.

On Tuesday, the 20th, I called to condole with our friends on these new misfortunes. Madame de la Chattre received me with politeness, and even cordiality: she told me she was a little recovered from the first shock—that she should hope to gather together a small débris of her fortune, but never enough to settle in England—that, in short, her parti était pris (42)—that she must go to America. It went to my heart to hear her say so. Presently came in M. Girardin. He is son to the Marquis de Girardin d'Ermenonville, the friend of Rousseau, whose last days were passed, and whose remains are deposited, in his domain. This M. Girardin was a pupil of Rousseau; he was a member of the Legislative Assembly, and an able opponent of the jacobins.

It was to him that M. Merlin, après bien de gestes menaçans, (43) had held a pistol, in the midst of the Assembly. His father was a mad republican, and never satisfied with the rational spirit of patriotism that animated M. Girardin; who, witnessing the distress of all the friends he most esteemed and honoured, and being himself in personal danger from the enmity of the jacobins, had, as soon as the Assembly Legislative broke up, quitted Paris, I believe, firmly determined never to re-enter it under the present regime.

I was prepossessed very much in favour of this gentleman, from his conduct in the late Assembly and all we had heard of him. I confess I had not represented him to myself as a great, fat, heavy-looking man, with the manners of a somewhat hard and morose Englishman: he is between thirty and forty, I imagine; he had been riding as far as to the cottage Mr. Malthouse had mentioned to him—l'asile de jean Jacques (44)—and said it was very near this place (it is at the foot of Leith Hill, Mr. Locke has since told me).

They then talked over the newspapers which were come that morning. M. de St. Just, (45) who made a most fierce speech for the trial and condemnation of the king, they said had before only been known by little madrigals, romances, and heures tendres, published in the 'Almanac des Muses.' "A cette heure," said M. de jaucourt, laughing, "c'est un fier republicain."(46)

THE PHILLIPSES AT JUNIPER HALL.

Nov. 27. Phillips and I determined at about half-past one to walk to "junipre" together. M. d'Arblay received us at the door, and showed the most flattering degree of pleasure at our arrival. We found with Madame de la Chattre another French gentleman, M. Sicard, who was also an officer of M. de Lafayette's.

M. de Narbonne said he hoped we would be sociable, and dine with them now and then. Madame de la Chattre made a speech to the same effect, "Et quel jour, par exemple," said M. de Narbonne, "feroit wieux qu'aujourd'hui?" (47) Madame de la Chattre took my hand instantly, to press in the most pleasing and gratifying manner imaginable this proposal; and before I had time to answer, M. d'Arblay, snatching up his hat, declared he would run and fetch the children.

I was obliged to entreat Phillips to bring him back, and entreated him to entendre raison.(48) . . . I pleaded their late hour of dinner, our having no carriage, and my disuse to the night air at this time of the year; but M. de Narbonne said their cabriolet (they have no other carriage) should take us home, and that there was a top to it, and Madame de la Chattre declared she would cover me well with shawls, etc. . . . M. d'Arblay scampered off for the little ones, whom all insisted upon having, and Phillips accompanied him, as it wanted I believe almost four hours to their dinner time. . . .

Then my dress: Oh, it was parfaite, and would give them all the courage to remain as they were, sans toilette: in short, nothing was omitted to render us comfortable and at our ease, and I have seldom passed a more pleasant day—never, I may fairly say, with such new acquaintance. I was only sorry M. de jaucourt did not make one of the party.

MYSTERY ATTENDING M. DE NARBONNE'S BIRTH.

Whilst M. d'Arblay and Phillips were gone, Madame de la Chattre told me they had that morning received M. Necker's "Defense du Roi," and if I liked it that M. de Narbonne would read it out to us. (49) You may conceive my answer. It is a most eloquent production, and was read by M. de Narbonne with beaucoup d'ame. Towards the end it is excessively touching, and his emotion was very evident, and would have struck and interested me had I felt no respect for his character before.

I must now tell you the secret of his birth, which, however, is, I conceive, no great secret even in London, as Phillips heard it at Sir Joseph Banks's. Madame Victoire, daughter of Louis XV, was in her youth known to be attached to the Comte de Narbonne, father of our M. de Narbonne. The consequence of this attachment was such as to oblige her to a temporary retirement, under the pretence of indisposition during which time la Comtesse de Narbonne, who was one of her attendants, not only concealed her own chagrin, but was the means of preserving her husband from a dangerous situation, and the princess from disgrace. She declared herself with child, and, in short, arranged all so well as to seem the mother of her husband's son; though the truth was immediately suspected, and rumoured about the Court, and Madame de la Chattre told me, was known and familiarly spoken of by all her friends, except in the presence of Narbonne, to whom no one would certainly venture to hint it. His father is dead, but la Comtesse de Narbonne, his reputed mother, lives, and is still an attendant on Madame Victoire, at Rome. M. de Narbonne's wife is likewise with her, and he himself was the person fixed on by Mesdames to accompany them when they quitted France for Italy. An infant daughter was left by him at Paris, who is still there with some of his family, and whom he expressed an earnest wish to. bring over, though the late decree may perhaps render his doing so impossible. He has another daughter, of six years old, who is with her mother at Rome, and whom he told me the pope had condescended to embrace. He mentioned his mother once (meaning la Comtesse de Narbonne) with great respect and affection.

REVOLUTIONARY SOCIETIES IN NORFOLK. DEATH OF MR. FRANCIS.

(Fanny Burney to Mrs. Philips.) Aylsham, Norfolk, November 27, '92. My dearest Susanna's details of the French colony at juniper are truly interesting. I hope I may gather from them that M. de Narbonne, at least, has been able to realise some property here. I wish much to hear that poor Madame de Broglie has been permitted to join her husband.

Who is this M. Malouet (50) who has the singular courage and feeling to offer to plead the cause of a fallen monarch in the midst of his ferocious accusers? And how ventures M. de Chauvelin to transmit such a proposal? I wish your French neighbours could give some account of this. I hear that the son for whom the Duc de Liancourt has been trembling, has been reduced to subscribe to all jacobin lengths, to save his life, and retain a little property. What seasons are these for dissolving all delicacy of internal honour!

I am truly amazed, and half alarmed, to find this county with little revolution societies, which transmit their notions of things to the larger committee at Norwich, which communicates the whole to the reformists of London. I am told there is scarce a village in Norfolk free from these meetings. . . .

My good and brilliant champion in days of old, Mr. Windham, has never been in Norfolk since I have entered it. He had a call to Bulstrode, to the installation of the Duke of Portland, just as I arrived, and he has been engaged there and at Oxford ever since. I regret missing him at Holkham: I bad no chance of him anywhere else, as I have been so situated, from the melancholy circumstances of poor Mr. Francis's illness, that I have been unable to make acquaintance where he visits.

(Miss Burney's second visit at Aylsham proved a very mournful one. Soon after her arrival, Mr. Francis, her brother-in-law, was seized with an apoplectic fit, which terminated in his death; and Miss Burney remained with her widowed sister, soothing and assisting her, till the close of the year, when she accompanied the bereaved family to London.]

DEPARTURE OF MADAME DE LA CHATRE.

(Mrs. Philips to Fanny Burney.) December 16, '92. . . . Everything that is most shocking may, I fear, be expected for the unfortunate King of France, his queen, and perhaps all that belong to him. M. d'Arblay said it would indeed scarce have been possible to hope that M. de Narbonne could have escaped with life, had the sauf-conduit requested been granted him, for attending as a witness at the king's trial. . . .

M. de Narbonne had heard nothing new from France, but mentioned, with great concern, the indiscretion of the king, in having kept all his letters since the Revolution; that the papers lately discovered in the Tuileries would bring ruin and death on hundreds of his friends; and that almost every one in that number "s'y trouvoient compliqués" (51) some way or other. A decree of accusation had been lanc, against M. Talleyrand, not for anything found from himself, but because M. de Laporte, long since executed, and from whom, of course, no renseignemens or explanations of any kind could be gained, had written to the king that l'Eveque d'Autun (52) was well disposed to serve him. Can there be injustice more flagrant?

M. Talleyrand, it seems, had proposed returning, and hoped to settle his affairs in France in person, but now he must be content with life; and as for his property (save what he may chance to have in other countries), he must certainly lose all.

Monday, December 17, In the morning, Mr. and Mrs. Locke called, and with them came Madame de la Chattre, to take leave.

She now told us, perfectly in confidence, that Madame de Broglie had found a friend in the Mayor of Boulogne, that she was lodged at his house, and that she could answer for her (Madame de la Chattre) being received by him as well as she could desire (all this must be secret, as this good mayor, if accused of harbouring or befriending des émigrés, would no doubt pay for it with his life). Madame de la Chattre said, all her friends who had ventured upon writing to her entreated her not to lose the present moment to return, as, the three months allowed for the return of those excepted in the decree once past, all hope would be lost for ever. Madame de Broglie, who is her cousin, was most excessively urgent to her to lose not an instant in returning, and had declared there would be no danger. Madame de la Chattre was put in spirits by this account, and the hope of becoming not destitute of everything; and I tried to hope without fearing for her, and, indeed, most sincerely offer up my petitions for her safety.

Heaven prosper her! Her courage and spirits are wonderful. M. de Narbonne seemed, however, full of apprehensions for her. M. de Jaucourt seemed to have better hopes; he, even he, has now thoughts of returning, or rather his generosity compels him to think of it. His father has represented to him that his sister's fortune must suffer unless he appears in France again, and although he had resisted every other consideration, on this he has given way.

ARRIVAL OF M. DE LA CHATRE.

Friday, December 21st, we dined at Norbury Park, and met our French friends: M. d'Arblay came in to coffee before the other gentlemen. We had been talking of Madame de la Chattre, and conjecturing conjectures about her sposo: we were all curious, and all inclined to imagine him old, ugly, proud, aristocratic, a kind of ancient and formal courtier; so we questioned M. d'Arblay, acknowledging our curiosity, and that we wished to know, enfin, if M. de la Chattre was "digne d'etre, poux d'une personne si aimable et si charmante que Madame de la Chattre."(53) He looked very drolly, scarce able to meet our eyes; but at last, as he is la franchise mˆme, he answered, "M. de la Chattre est un bon homme—parfaitement bon homme: au reste, il est brusque comme un cheval de carrosse."(54)

We were in the midst of our coffee when St. jean came forward to M. de Narbonne, and said somebody wanted to speak to him. He went out of the room; in two minutes he returned, followed by a gentleman in a great-coat, whom we had never seen, and whom he introduced immediately to Mrs. Locke by the name of M. de la Chattre. The appearance of M. de la Chattre was something like a coup de theatre; for, despite our curiosity, I had no idea we should ever see him, thinking that nothing could detach him from the service of the French princes.

His abord and behaviour answered extremely well the idea M. d'Arblay had given us of him, who in the word brusque rather meant unpolished in manners than harsh in character. He is quite old enough to be father to Madame de la Chattre, and, had he been presented to us as such, all our wonder would have been to see so little elegance in the parent of such a woman.

After the first introduction was over, he turned his back to the fire, and began sans faton, a most confidential discourse with M. de Narbonne. They had not met since the beginning of the Revolution, and, having been of very different parties, it was curious and pleasant to see them now, in their mutual misfortunes, meet en bons amis. They rallied each other sur leurs disgraces very good-humouredly and comically; and though poor M. de la Chattre had missed his wife by only one day, and his son by a few hours, nothing seemed to give him de phumeur. (55) He gave the account of his disastrous journey since he had quitted. the princes, who are themselves reduced to great distress, and were unable to pay him his arrears: he said he could not get a sou from France, nor had done for two years. All the money he had, with his papers and clothes, were contained in a little box, with which he had embarked in a small boat—I could not hear whence: but the weather was tempestuous, and he, with nearly all the passengers, landed, and walked to the nearest town, leaving his box and two faithful servants (who had never, he said, quitted him since he had left France) in the boat: he had scarce been an hour at the auberge (56) when news was brought that the boat had sunk,

At this, M. de Narbonne threw himself back on his seat, exclaiming against the hard fate which pursued all ses malheureux amis! (57) "Mais attendez donc," cried the good humoured M. de la Chattre, "Je n'ai pas encore fini: on nous a assurés que personne n'a péri et que même tout ce qu'il y avait sur le bateau a été sauvé!'(58) He said, however, that being now in danger of falling into the hands of the French, he dared not stop for his box or servants; but, leaving a note of directions behind him, he proceeded incognito, and at length got on board a packet-boat for England, in which though he found several of his countrymen and old acquaintance, he dared not discover himself till they were en pleine mer. (59) He went on gaily enough, laughing at ses amis les constitutionnaires, (60) and M. de Narbonne, with much more wit, and not less good humour, retorting back his raillery on the parti de Brunswick.. . .

M. de la Chattre mentioned the quinzaine (61) in which the princes' army had been paid up, as the most wretched he had ever known. Of 22,000 men who formed the army of the emigrants, 16,000 were gentlemen, men of family and fortune: all of whom were now, with their families, destitute. He mentioned two of these who had engaged themselves lately in some orchestra, where they played first and second flute. The princes, he said, had been twice arrested for debt in different places—that they were now so reduced that they dined, themselves, the Comte d'Artois, children, tutors, etc.—eight or nine persons in all—upon one single dish.

ENGLISH FEELING AT THE REVOLUTIONARY EXCESSES.

(Fanny Burney to Mrs. Locke.) Chelsea, December 20, '92. ..... God keep us all safe and quiet! All now wears a fair aspect; but I am told Mr. Windham says we are not yet out of the wood though we see the path through it. There must be no relaxation. The Pretended friends of the people, pretended or misguided, wait but the stilling of the present ferment of loyalty to come forth. Mr. Grey has said so in the House. Mr. Fox attended the St. George's meeting, after keeping back to the last, and was nobody there!

The accounts from France are thrilling. Poor M. d'Arblay's speech should be translated, and read to all English imitators of French reformers. What a picture of the now reformed! Mr. Burke's description of the martyred Duc de la Rochefoucault should be read also by all the few really pure promoters of new systems. New systems, I fear, in states, are always dangerous, if not wicked. Grievance by grievance, wrong by wrong, must only be assailed, and breathing time allowed to old prejudices, and old habits, between all that is done. . . .

I had fancied the letters brought for the King of France's trial were forgeries. One of them, certainly, to M. Bouill,, had its answer dated before it was written. If any have been found, others will be added, to serve any evil purposes. Still, however, I hope the king and his family will be saved. I cannot but believe it, from all I can put together. If the worst of the jacobins hear that Fox has called him an "unfortunate monarch,"—that Sheridan has said "his execution would be an act of injustice,"—and Grey, "that we ought to have spared that one blast to their glories by earlier negotiation and an ambassador,"—surely the worst of these wretches will not risk losing their only abettors and palliators in this kingdom? I mean publicly; they have privately and individually their abettors and palliators in abundance still, wonderful as that is.

I am glad M. d'Arblay has joined the set at "Junipre." What miserable work is this duelling, which I hear of among the emigrants, after such hair-breadth 'scapes for life and existence!—to attack one another on the very spot they seek for refuge from attacks! It seems a sort of profanation of safety.

LOUIS XVI'S EXECUTION.

(Fanny Burney to Dr. Burney.) Norbury Park, January 28, '93. My dearest padre, I have been wholly without spirit for writing, reading, working, or even walking or conversing, ever since the first day of my arrival. The dreadful tragedy (62) acted in France has entirely absorbed me. Except the period of the illness of our own inestimable king, I have never been so overcome with grief and dismay, for any but personal and family calamities. O what a tragedy! how implacable its villainy, and how severe its sorrows! You know, my dearest father, how little I had believed such a catastrophe possible: with all the guilt and all the daring already shown, I had still thought this a height of enormity impracticable. And, indeed, without military law throughout the wretched city, it had still not been perpetrated. Good heaven!—what must have been the sufferings of the few unhardened in crimes who inhabit that city of horrors!—if I, an English person, have been so deeply afflicted, that even this sweet house and society—even my Susan and her lovely children—have been incapable to give me any species of pleasure, or keep me from a desponding low-spiritedness, what must be the feelings of all but the culprits in France?

M. de Narbonne and M. d'Arblay have been almost annihilated: they are for ever repining that they are French, and, though two of the most accomplished and elegant men I ever saw, they break our hearts with the humiliation they feel for their guiltless birth in that guilty country!

We are all here expecting war every day. This dear family has deferred its town journey till next Wednesday. I have not been at all at Mickleham, nor yet settled whether to return to town with the Lockes, or to pay my promised visit there first. All has been so dismal, so wretched, that I have scarce ceased to regret our living at such times, and not either Sooner or later. These immediate French sufferers here interest us, and these alone have been able to interest me at all. We hear of a very bad tumult in Ireland, and near Captain Phillips's property: Mr. Brabazon writes word it is very serious.

Heaven guard us from insurrections! What must be the feelings at the queen's house? how acute, and how indignant!

A GLOOMY CLUB MEETING.

(Dr. Burney to Fanny Burney and Mrs. Phillips.) Chelsea College, January 31, 1793. . . . At the Club, (63) on Tuesday, the fullest I ever knew, consisting of fifteen members, fourteen seemed all of one mind, and full of reflections on the late transaction in France; but, when about half the company was assembled, who should come in but Charles Fox! There were already three or four bishops arrived, hardly one of whom could look at him, I believe, without horror, After the first bow and cold salutation, the conversation stood still for several minutes. During dinner Mr Windham, and Burke, jun., came in, who were obliged to sit at a side table. All were boutonn,s, (64) and not a word of the martyred king or politics of any kind was mentioned; and though the company was chiefly composed of the most eloquent and loquacious men in the kingdom, the conversation was the dullest and most uninteresting I ever remember at this or any such large meeting. Mr Windham and Fox, civil-young Burke and he never spoke. The Bishop of Peterborough as sulky as the devil; the Bishop of Salisbury, more a man of the world, very cheerful; the Bishop of Dromore (65) frightened as much as a barn-door fowl at the sight of a fox; Bishop Marlow preserved his usual pleasant countenance. Steevens in the chair; the Duke of Leeds on his right, and Fox on his left, said not a word. Lords Ossory and Lucan, formerly much attached, seemed silent and sulky.

MADAME DE STAEL AT JUNIPER HALL.

(Fanny Burney to Dr. Burney.) Norbury Park, Monday, February 4, '93. . . . Madame de Stael, daughter of M. Necker, is now at the head of the colony of French noblesse, established near Mickleham. She is one of the first women I have ever met with for abilities and extraordinary intellect. She has just received, by a private letter, many particulars not yet made public, and which the Commune and Commissaries of the Temple had ordered should be suppressed. It has been exacted by those cautious men of blood that nothing should be printed that could attendrir le peuple. (66)

Among other circumstances, this letter relates that the poor little dauphin supplicated the monsters who came with the decree of death to his unhappy father, that they would carry him to the Convention, and the forty-eight Sections of Paris, and suffer him to beg his father's life. This touching request was probably suggested to him by his miserable mother or aunt....

M. de Narbonne has been quite ill with the grief of this last enormity: and M. d'Arblay is now indisposed. This latter is one of the most delightful characters I have ever met, for openness, probity, intellectual knowledge, and unhackneyed manners.

(Madame de Stael to Fanny Burney. (67)) Written from juniper Hall, Dorking, Surrey, 1793. When I learned to read English I begun by Milton, to know all or renounce at all in once. I follow the same system in writing my first English letter to Miss Burney; after such an enterprize nothing can affright me. I feel for her so tender a friendship that it melts my admiration, inspires my heart with hope of her indulgence, and impresses me with the idea that in a tongue even unknown I could express sentiments so deeply felt.

My servant will return for a french answer. I intreat Miss Burney to correct the words but to preserve the sense of that card.

Best compliments to my dear protectress, Madame Phillipe.

(Madame de Stael to Fanny Burney.) Your card in french, my dear, has already something of Your grace in writing English: it is cecilia translated. My, only correction is to fill the interruptions of some sentences, and I put in them kindnesses for me. I do not consult my master to write to you; a fault more or less is nothing in such an occasion. What may be the perfect grammar of Mr. Clarke, it cannot establish any sort of equality between you and I. then I will trust with my heart alone to supply the deficiency. let us speak upon a grave subject: do I see you that morning? What news from Captain phillip? when do you come spend a large week in that house? every question requires an exact answer; a good, also. my happiness depends on it, and I have for pledge your honour.

Good morrow and farewell.

Pray Madame Phillips, recollecting all her knowledge in french, to explain that card to you.

(Madame de Stael to Fanny Burney.) January, 1793. tell me, my dear, if this day is a charming one, if it must be a sweet epoch in my life?—do you come to dine here with your lovely sister, and do you stay night and day till our sad separation? I rejoice me with that hope during this week do not deceive my heart. I hope that card very clear, mais, pour plus de certitude, je vous dis en françois que votre chambre, la maison, les habitants de juniper, tout est prêt á recevoir la première femme d'angleterre. (68) Janvier.

MISS BURNEY'S ADMIRATION OF MADAME DE STAEL.

(Fanny Burney to Dr. Burney.) Mickleham, February 29, 1793. Have you not begun, dearest sir, to give me up as a lost sheep? Susanna's temporary widowhood, however, has tempted me on, and spelled me with a spell I know not how to break. It is long, long since we have passed any time so completely together; her three lovely children only knit us the closer. The widowhood, however, we expect now quickly to expire, and I had projected my return to my dearest father for Wednesday next, which would complete my fortnight here but some circumstances are intervening that incline me to postpone it another week. Madame de Stal, daughter of M. Necker, and wife of the Swedish ambassador to France, is now head of the little French colony in this neighbourhood. M. de Stael, her husband, is at present suspended in his embassy, but not recalled and it is yet uncertain whether the regent Duke of Sudermania will send him to Paris, during the present horrible Convention, or order him home. He is now in Holland, waiting for commands. Madame de Stal, however, was unsafe in Paris, though an ambassadress, from the resentment owed her by the commune, for having received and protected in her house various destined victims of the 10th August and of the 2nd September. She was even once stopped in her carriage, which they called aristocratic, because of its arms and ornaments, and threatened to be murdered, and only saved by one of the worst wretches of the Convention, Tallien, who feared provoking a war with Sweden, from such an offence to the wife of its ambassador. She was obliged to have this same Tallien to accompany her, to save her from massacre, for some miles from Paris, when compelled to quit it.

She is a woman of the first abilities, I think, I have ever seen; she is more in the style of Mrs. Thrale than of any other celebrated character, but she has infinitely more depth, and seems an even profound politician and metaphysician. She has suffered us to hear some of her works in MS., which are truly wonderful, for powers both of thinking and expression. She adores her father, but is much alarmed at having had no news from him since he has heard of the massacre of the martyred Louis; and who can wonder it should have overpowered him?

Ever since her arrival she has been pressing me to spend some time with her before I return to town. She wanted Susan and me to pass a month with her, but, finding that impossible, she bestowed all her entreaties upon me alone, and they are grown so urgent, upon my preparation for departing, and acquainting her my furlough of absence was over, that she not only insisted upon my writing to you, and telling why I deferred my return, but declares she will also write herself, to ask your permission for the visit. She exactly resembles Mrs. Thrale in the ardour and warmth of her temper and partialities. I find her impossible to resist, and therefore, if your answer to her is such as I conclude it must be, I shall wait upon her for a week. She is only a short walk from hence, at juniper Hall.

FAILING RESOURCES.

There can be nothing imagined more charming, more fascinating, than this colony; between their sufferings and their argr,mens they occupy us almost wholly. M. de Narbonne, alas, has no thousand pounds a year! he got over only four thousand pounds at the beginning, from a most splendid fortune; and, little foreseeing how all has turned out, he has lived, we fear, upon the principal; for he says, if all remittance is withdrawn, on account of the war, he shall soon be as ruined as those companions of his misfortunes with whom as yet he has shared his little all. He bears the highest character for goodness, parts, sweetness of manners, and ready wit. You could not keep your heart from him if you saw him only for half an hour. He has not yet recovered from the black blow of the king's death, but he is better, and less jaundiced; and he has had a letter which, I hear, has comforted him, though at first it was almost heart-breaking, informing him of the unabated regard for him of the truly saint-like Louis. This is communicated in a letter from M. de Malesherbes. (69)

THE BEGINNING OF THE END.

M. d'Arblay is one of the most singularly interesting characters that can ever have been formed. He has a sincerity, a frankness, an ingenuous openness of nature, that I had been unjust enough to think could not belong to a Frenchman. With all this, which is his military portion, he is passionately fond of literature, a most delicate critic in his own language, welL versed in both Italian and German, and a very elegant poet. He has just undertaken to become my French master for pronunciation, and he gives me long daily lessons in reading. Pray expect wonderful improvements! In return, I hear him in English; and for his theme, this evening he has been writing an English address "Mr. Burney," (ie. M. le Docteur), joining in Madame de Stael's request.

I hope your last club was more congenial? M. de Talleyrand insists on conveying this letter for you. He has been on a visit here, and returns again on Wednesday. He is a man of admirable conversation, quick, terse, fin, and yet deep, to the extreme of those four words. They are a marvellous set for excess of agreeability.

"THIS ENCHANTING MONSIEUR D'ARBLAY."

(Fanny Burney to Mrs. Locke.) Mickleham. Your kind letter, my beloved Fredy, was most thankfully received, and we rejoice the house and situation promise so much local comfort; but I quite fear with you that even the bas bleu will not recompense the loss of the "Junipre" society. It is, indeed, of incontestable superiority. But you must burn this confession, or my poor effigy will blaze for it. I must tell you a little of our proceedings, as they all relate to these people of a thousand.

M. d'Arblay came from the melancholy sight of departing Norbury to Mickleham, and with an air the most triste, and a sound of voice quite dejected, as I learn from Susanna for I was in my heroics, and could not appear till the last half hour. A headache prevented my waiting upon Madame de Stal that day, and obliged me to retreat soon after nine o'clock in the evening, and my douce compagne would not let me retreat alone. We had only robed ourselves in looser drapery, when a violent ringing at the door startled us; we listened, and heard the voice of M. d'Arblay, and Jerry answering, "They're gone to bed." "Comment? What?" cried he: "C'est impossible! what you say?" Jerry then, to show his new education in this new colony, said "Allec coucheé" It rained furiously, and we were quite grieved, but there was no help. He left a book for "Mlle. Burnet," and word that Madame de Stael could not come on account of the bad weather. M. Ferdinand was with him and has bewailed the disaster and M. Sicard says he accompanied them till he was quite wet through his redingote; but this enchanting M. d'Arblay will murmur at nothing.

The next day they all came, just as we had dined, for a morning visit, Madame de Stael, M. Talleyrand, M. Sicard, and M. d'Arblay; the latter then made "insistance" upon commencing my "master of the language," and I think he will be almost as good a one as the little don. (70)

M. de Talleyrand opened, at last, with infinite wit and capacity. Madame de Stael whispered me, "How do you like him?" "Not very much," I answered, "but I do not know him." "Oh, I assure you," cried she, "he is the best of the men."

I was happy not to agree; but I have no time for such minute detail till we meet. She read the noble tragedy of "Tancrrède," (71) till she blinded us all round. She is the most charming person, to use her own phrase, "that never I saw."

We called yesterday upon Madame de Stael, and sat with her until three o'clock, only the little don being present. She was delightful; yet I see much uneasiness hanging over the whole party, from the terror that the war may stop all remittances. Heaven forbid!

TALLEYRAND IS FOUND CHARMING.

(Fanny Burney to Mrs Locke.) Thursday, Mickleham. I have no heart not to write, and no time to write. I have been scholaring all day, and mastering too: for our lessons are mutual, and more entertaining than can easily be conceived. My master of the language says he dreams of how much more solemnly he shall write to charming Mrs. Locke after a little more practice. Madame de Stael has written me two English notes, quite beautiful in ideas, and not very reprehensible in idiom. But English has nothing to do with elegance such as theirs—at least, little and rarely. I am always exposing myself to the wrath of John Bull, when this coterie come in competition; It is inconceivable what a convert M. de Talleyrand has made of me; I think him now one of the first members, and one of the most charming, of this exquisite set: Susanna is as completely a proselyte.

His powers of entertainment are astonishing, both in information and in raillery. We know nothing of how the rest of the world goes on. They are all coming to-night. I have yet avoided, but with extreme difficulty, the change of abode. Madame de Stael, however, will not easily be parried, and how I may finally arrange I know not. Certainly I will not offend or hurt her, but otherwise I had rather be a visitor than a guest

Pray tell Mr. Locke that "the best of the men" grows upon us at every meeting. We dined and stayed till midnight at "junipre" on Tuesday, and I would I could recollect but the twentieth part of the excellent things that were said. Madame de Stael read us the opening of her work "Sur le Bonheur:" it seems to me admirable. M. de Talleyrand avowed he had met with nothing better thought or more ably expressed; it contains the most touching allusions to their country's calamities.

A PROPOSED VISIT TO MADAME DE STAEL DISAPPROVED OF.

(Doctor Burney to Fanny Burney.) Chelsea College, February 19, 1793. Why, Fanny, what are you about, and where are you? I shall write at you, not knowing how to write to you, as Swift did to the flying and romantic Lord Peterborough. I had written the above, after a yesterday's glimmering and a feverish night as usual, when behold! a letter of requisition for a further furlough! I had long histories ready for narration de vive voix, but my time is too short and my eyes and head too -weak for much writing this morning. I am not at all surprised at your account of the captivating powers of

Madame de Stael. It corresponds with all I had heard about her, and with the opinion I formed of her intellectual and literary powers, in reading her charming little "Apologie de Rousseau." But as nothing human is allowed to be perfect, she has not escaped censure. Her house was the centre of revolutionists Previous to the 10th of August, after her father's departure, and she has been accused of partiality to M. de N. (72) But Perhaps all may be jacobinical malignity. However, unfavourable stories of her have been brought hither, and the Burkes and Mrs. Ord have repeated them to me. But you know that M. Necker's administration, and the conduct of the nobles who first joined in the violent measures that subverted the ancient establishments by the abolition of nobility and the ruin of the church, during the first National Assembly, are held in greater horror by aristocrats than even the members of the present Convention. I know this will make you feel uncomfortable, but it seemed to me right to hint it to You. If you are not absolutely in the house of Madame do Stael when this arrives, it would perhaps be possible for you to waive the visit to her, by a compromise, of having something to do for Susy, and so make the addendum to your stay under her roof. . .

(Fanny Burney to Dr. Burney.) Mickleham, February 22, '03, What a kind letter is my dearest father's, and how kindly speedy! yet it is too true it has given me very uncomfortable feelings. I am both hurt and astonished at the acrimony of malice; indeed, I believe all this Party to merit nothing but honour, compassion, and praise. Madame de Stael, the daughter of M. Necker—the idolising daughter—of course, and even from the best principles, those of filial reverence, entered into the opening of the Revolution just as her father entered into it; but as to her house having become the centre of revolutionists before the 10th of August, it was so only for the constitutionalists, who, at that period, were not only members of the then established government, but the decided friends of the king. The aristocrats were then already banished, or wanderers from fear, or concealed and silent from cowardice; and the jacobins—I need not, after what I have already related, mention how utterly abhorrent to her must be that fiend-like set. The aristocrats, however, as you well observe, and as she has herself told me, hold the constitutionalists in greater horror than the Convention itself. This, however, is a violence against justice which cannot, I hope, be lasting; and the malignant assertions which persecute her, all of which she has lamented to us, she imputes equally to the bad and virulent of both these parties. The intimation concerning M. de N. was, however, wholly new to us, and I do firmly believe it a gross calumny. M. de N. was of her society, which contained ten or twelve of the first people in Paris, and, occasionally, almost all Paris! she loves him even tenderly, but so openly, so simply, so unaffectedly, and with such utter freedom from all coquetry, that, if they were two men, or two women, the affection could not, I think, be more obviously undesigning. She is very plain, he is very handsome; her intellectual endowments must be with him her sole attraction. M. de Talleyrand was another of her society, and she seems equally attached to him. M. le Viscomte de Montmorenci she loves, she says, as her brother: he is another of this bright constellation, and esteemed of excellent capacity. She says, if she continues in England he will certainly come, for he loves her too well to stay away. In short, her whole coterie live together as brethren. Madame la Marquise de la Chattre, who has lately returned to France, to endeavour to obtain de quoi vivre en Angleterre, (73) and who had been of this colony for two or three months since the 10th of August, is a bosom friend of Madame de Stael and of all this circle: she is reckoned a very estimable as well as fashionable woman; and a daughter of the unhappy Montmorin, who was killed on the 1st of September (74) is another of this set. Indeed, I think you could not spend a day with them and not see that their commerce is that of pure, but exalted and most elegant, friendship.

I would, nevertheless, give the world to avoid being a guest under their roof, now I have heard even the shadow of such a rumour; and I will, if it be possible without hurting or offending them. I have waived and waived acceptance almost from the moment of Madame de Stael's arrival. I prevailed with her to let my letter go alone to you, and I have told her, with regard to your answer, that you were sensible of the honour her kindness did me, and could not refuse to her request the week's furlough; and then followed reasons for the Compromise you pointed out, too diffuse for writing. As

Yet they have succeeded, though she is surprised and disappointed. She wants us to study French and English together, and nothing could to me be more desirable, but for this invidious report.

M. d'Arblay as well as M. de Narbonne, sent over a declaration in favour of the poor king. M. d'A. had been the commandant at Longwy, and had been named to that post by the king himself. In the accusation of the infernals, as Mr. Young justly calls them, the king is accused of leaving Longwy undefended, and a prey to the Prussians. M. d'Arblay, who before that period had been promoted into the regiment of M. de Narbonne, and thence summoned to be adjutant-general of Lafayette, wrote therefore, on this charge, to M. de Malesherbes, and told him that the charge was utterly false, that the king had taken every precaution for the proper preservation of Longwy, and that M. d'Arblay, the king's commandant, had himself received a letter of thanks and approbation from Duniouriez, who said, nothing would have been lost had every commandant taken equal pains, and exerted equal bravery. This original letter M. d'Arblay sent to M. Malesherbes, not as a vindication of himself, for he had been summoned from Longwy before the Prussians assailed it, but as a vindication of the officer appointed by the king, while he had yet the command. M. de Malesherbes wrote an answer of thanks, and said he should certainly make use of this information in the defence, However, the fear of Dumouriez, I suppose, prevented his being named. M. d'Arblay, in quitting France with Lafayette, upon the deposition of the king, had only a little ready money in his pocket, and he has been décrété, (75) I since, and all he was worth in the world is sold and seized by the Convention. M. de Narbonne loves him as the tenderest of brothers, and, while one has a guinea in the world, the other will have half. "Ah!" cried M. d'Arblay, upon the murder of the king, which almost annihilated him, "I know not how those can exist who have any feelings of remorse, when I scarce can endure my life, from the simple feeling of regret that ever I pronounced the word liberty in France!"

M. DE LALLY TOLENDAL AND HIS TRAGEDY.

(Mrs. Phillips to Mrs. Locke.) Mickleham, April 2, 1793..... I must, however, say something of juniper, whence I had an irresistible invitation to dine, etc, yesterday, and M. de Lally Tolendal(76) read his "Mort de Strafford," which he had already recited once, and which Madame do Stael requested him to repeat for my sake.

I had a great curiosity to see M. de Lally. I cannot say that feeling was gratified by the sight of him, though it was satisfied, insomuch that it has left me without any great anxiety to see him again. He is the very reverse of all that my imagination had led me to expect in him: large, fat, with a great head, small nose, immense cheeks, nothing distingu, in his manner and en fait d'esprit, and of talents in conversation, so far, so very far, distant from our juniperians, and from M. de Talleyrand, who was there, as I could not have conceived, his abilities as a writer and his general reputation considered. He seems un bon garçon, un trés honnéte garçon, as M. Talleyrand says of him, et non de plus. (77)

He is extremely absorbed by his tragedy, which he recites by heart, acting as well as declaiming with great energy, though seated, as Le Texier is. He seemed, previous to the performance, occupied completely by It, except while the dinner lasted, which he did not neglect; but he was continually reciting to himself till we sat down to table, and afterwards between the courses.

M. Talleyrand seemed much struck with his piece, which appears to me to have very fine lines and passages in it, but which, altogether, interested me but little. I confess, indeed, the violence of ses gestes, and the alternate howling and thundering of his voice in declaiming, fatigued me excessively. If our Fanny had been present, I am afraid I should many times have been affected as one does not expect to be at a tragedy. We sat down at seven to dinner, and had half finished before M. d'Arblay appeared, though repeatedly sent for; he was profoundly grave and silent, and disappeared after the dinner, which was very gay. He was sent for, after coffee and Norbury were gone, several times, that the tragedy might be begun; and at last Madame de S. impatiently proposed beginning without him. "Mais cela lui fera de la peine,"(78) said M. d'Autun (Talleyrand), good-naturedly; and, as she persisted, he rose up and limped out of the room to fetch him he succeeded in bringing him.

M Malouet has left them. La Princesse d'Henin is a very pleasing, well-bred woman: she left juniper the next morning with M. de Lally.

CONTEMPLATED DISPERSION OF THE FRENCH COLONY.

(Mrs. Phillips to Fanny Burney) Mickleham, April 3. After I had sent off my letter to you on Monday I walked on to juniper, and entered at the same moment with Mr. Jenkinson (79) and his attorney—a man whose figure strongly resembles some of Hogarth's most ill-looking, personages, and who appeared to me to be brought as a kind of spy, or witness of all that was passing. I would have retreated, fearing to interrupt business, but I was surrounded, and pressed to stay, by Madame de Stael with great empressement, and with much kindness by M. d'Arblay and all the rest. Mr. Clarke was the spokesman, and acquitted himself with great dignity and moderation; Madame de S. now and then came forth with a little coquetterie pour adoucir ce sauvage jenkinson. (80) "What will you, Mr. Jenkinson? tell to me, what will you?" M. de Narbonne, somewhat indign, de la mauvaise foi, and exceed, des longueurs de son adversaire, (81) was not quite so gentle with him, and I was glad to perceive that he meant to resist, in some degree at least, the exorbitant demands of his landlord.

Madame de Stael was very gay, and M. de Talleyrand very comique, this evening; he criticised, amongst other things, her reading of prose, with great sang froid. . . . They talked over a number of their friends and acquaintances with the utmost unreserve, and sometimes with the most comic humour imaginable,—M. de Lally, M. de Lafayette, la Princesse d'Henin, la Princesse de Poix, a M. Guibert, an author. and one who was, Madame de Stael told me, passionately in love with her before she married; and innumerable others.

M. d'Arblay had been employed almost night and day since he came from London in Writing a memoire, which Mr Villiers had wished to have, upon the 'Artillerie Cheval,' and he had not concluded it till this morning.

(Mrs. Philips to Fanny Burney.) Tuesday, May 14. Trusting to the kindness of chance, I begin in at the top of my paper. Our Juniperians went to see Paine's hill yesterday, and had the good-nature to take my little happy Norbury. In the evening came Miss F— to show me a circular letter, sent by the Archbishop of Canterbury to all the parishes in England, authorising the ministers of those parishes to raise a subscription for the unfortunate French clergy. She talked of our neighbours, and very shortly and abruptly said, "So, Mrs. Phillips, we hear you are to have Mr. Norbone and the other French company to live with you—Pray is it so?"

I was, I confess, a little startled at this plain inquiry, but answered as composedly as I could, setting out with informing this bˆte personnage that Madame de Stael was going to Switzerland to join her husband and family in a few days, and that of all the French company none would remain but M. de Narbonne and M. d'Arblay, for whom the captain and myself entertained a real friendship and esteem, and whom he had begged to make our house their own for a short time, as the impositions they had had to support from their servants, etc, and the failure of their remittances from abroad, had obliged them to resolve on breaking up housekeeping.

I had scarcely said thus much when our party arrived from Paine's hill; the young lady, though she had drunk tea, was so obliging as to give us her company for near two hours, and made a curious attack on M. de N., upon the first pause, in wretched French, though we had before, all of us, talked no other language than English:—"Je vous prie, M. Gnawbone, comment se porte la reine?"(82)

Her pronunciation was such that I thought his understanding her miraculous: however, he did guess her meaning, and answered, with all his accustomed douceur and politeness, that he hoped well, but had no means but general ones of information.

"I believe," said she afterwards, "nobody was so hurt at the king's death as my papa! he couldn't ride on horseback next day!"

She then told M. de Narbonne some anecdotes (very new to him, no doubt), which she had read in the newspapers, of the Convention; and then spoke of M. Egalit,. "I hope," said she, flinging her arms out with great violence, "he'll come to be gullytined. He showed the king how he liked to be gullytined, so now I hope he'll be gullytined himself!—So shocking! to give his vote against his own nephew!"

If the subject of her vehemence and blunders had been less just or less melancholy, I know not how I should have kept my face in order.

Our evening was very pleasant when she was gone, Madame de Stael is, with all her wildness and blemishes, a delightful companion, and M. de N. rises upon me in esteem and affection every time I see him: their minds in some points ought to be exchanged, for he is as delicate as a really feminine woman, and evidently suffers when he sees her setting les bienséances (83) aside, as it often enough befalls her to do.

Poor Madame de Stael has been greatly disappointed and hurt by the failure of the friendship and intercourse she had wished to maintain with you,—of that I am sure; I fear, too, she is on the point of being offended. I am not likely to be her confidant if she is so, and only judge from the nature of things, and from her character, and a kind of dépit (84) in her manner once or twice in speaking of you. She asked me If you would accompany Mrs. Locke back into the country? I answered that my father would not wish to lose you for so long a time at once, as you had been absent from him as a nurse so many days.

After a little pause, "Mais est-ce qu'une femme est en tutelle pour la vie dans ce pays?" she said. "Il me paroit que votre soeur est comme une demoiselle de quatorze ans." (85) I did not oppose this idea, but enlarged rather on the constraints laid upon females, some very unnecessarily, in England,—hoping to lessen her d,pit; it continued, however, visible in her countenance, though she did not express it in words.

[The frequency and intimacy with which Miss Burney and M. d'Arblay now met, ripened into attachment the high esteem which each felt for the other; and, after many struggles and scruples, occasioned by his reduced circumstances and clouded prospects, M. d'Arblay wrote her an offer of his hand; candidly acknowledging, however, the slight hope he entertained of ever recovering the fortune he had lost by the Revolution.

At this time Miss Burney went to Chesington for a short period; probably hoping that the extreme quiet of that place would assist her deliberations, and tranquillise her mind during her present perplexities.]

MADAME DE STAEL'S WORDS OF FAREWELL. M. D'ARBLAY.

(Mrs. Philips to Fanny Burney at Chesington.)

Sunday, after church, I walked up to Norbury; there unexpectedly I met all our juniperians, and listened to one of the best conversations I ever heard: it was on literary topics, and the chief speakers Madame de Stael, M. de Talleyrand, Mr. Locke, and M. Dumont, a gentleman on a visit of two days at juniper, a Genevois, homme d'esprit et de lettres. I had not a word beyond the first " how d'yes " with any one, being obliged to run home to my abominable dinner in the midst of the discourse.

On Monday I went, by invitation, to juniper to dine, and before I came away at night a letter arrived express to Madame de Stael. On reading it, the change in her countenance made me guess the contents. It was from the Swedish gentleman who had been appointed by her husband to meet her at Ostend; he wrote from that place that he was awaiting her arrival. She had designed walking home with us by moonlight, but her spirits were too much oppressed to enable her to keep this intention. M. d'Arblay walked home with Phillips and me. Every moment of his time has been given of late to transcribing a MS. work of Madame de Stael, on 'L'Influence des Passions.' It is a work of considerable length, and written in a hand the most difficult possible to decipher.

On Tuesday we all met again at Norbury, where we spent the day. Madame de Stael could not rally her spirits at all, and seemed like one torn from all that was dear to her. I was truly concerned. After giving me a variety of charges, or rather entreaties, to watch and attend to the health, spirits, and affairs of the friends she was leaving, she said to me, "Et dites á Mlle. Burney que je ne lui en veux pas du tout—que je quitte le pays l'aimant bien sincérement et sans rancune."(86)

I assured her earnestly, and with more words than I have room to insert, not only of your admiration, but affection, and sensibility of her worth and chagrin at seeing no more of her. I hope I exceeded not your wishes; mais il n'y avoit pas moyen de resister. (87)

She seemed pleased, and said, "Vous ˆtes bien bonne de me dire cela,"(88) but in a low and faint voice, and dropped the subject.

Before we took leave, M. d'Arblay was already gone, meaning to finish transcribing her MS. I came home with Madame de Stael and M. de Narbonne. The former actually sobbed in saying farewell to Mrs. Locke, and half way down the hill; her parting from me was likewise very tender and flattering.

I determined, however, to see her again, and met her near the school, on Wednesday morning with a short note and a little offering which I was irresistibly tempted to make her. She could not speak to me, but kissed her hand with a very speaking and touching expression of countenance.

it was this morning, and just as I was setting out to meet her, that Skilton arrived from Chesington. I wrote a little, walked out, and returned to finish as I could.

At dinner came our Tio—(89) very bad indeed. After it we walked together with the children to Norbury; but little Fanny was so well pleased with his society that it was impossible to get a word on any particular subject. I, however, upon his venturing to question me whereabouts was the campagne ou se trouvoit Mlle. Burney, (90) ventured de mon côte, (91) to speak the name of Chesington, and give a little account of its inhabitants, the early love we had for the spot, our excellent Mr. Crisp, and your good and kind hostesses. He listened with much interest and pleasure, and said, "Mais, ne pourroit-on pas faire ce petit voyage-I?" (92)

I ventured to say nothing encouraging, at least, decisively, in a great measure upon the children's account, lest they should repeat; and, moreover, your little namesake seemed to me surprisingly attentive and ,veillee, as if elle se doutoit de quelque chose. (93)

When we came home I gave our Tio so paper to write to you; it was not possible for me to add more than the address, much as I wished it.

REGRETS RESPECTING MADAME DE STAEL.

(Fanny Burney to Mrs. -Locke.) Chesington, 1793. I have been quite enchanted to-day by my dear Susan's intelligence that my three convalescents walked to the wood. Would I had been there to meet and receive them. I have regretted excessively the finishing so miserably an acquaintance begun with so much spirit and pleasure, and the depit I fear Madame de Stael must have experienced. I wish the world would take more care of itself, and less of its neighbours. I should have heen very safe, I trust, without such flights, and distances, and breaches. But there seemed an absolute resolution formed to crush this acquaintance, and compel me to appear its wilful renouncer. All I did also to clear the matter, and soften to Madame de Stael any pique or displeasure, unfortunately served only to increase them. Had I understood her disposition better, I should certainly have attempted no palliation, for I rather offended her pride than mollified her wrath. Yet I followed the golden rule, for how much should I prefer any acknowledgment of regret at such an apparent change, from any one I esteemed, to a seeming unconscious complacency in an unexplained caprice! I am vexed, however, very much vexed, at the whole business. I hope she left Norbury Park with full satisfaction in its steady and more comfortable connection. I fear mine will pass for only a fashionable one.

Miss Kitty Cooke still amuses me very much by her incomparable dialect; and by her kindness and friendliness. I am taken the best care of imaginable. My poor brother, who will carry this to Mickleham, is grievously altered by the loss of his little girl. It has affected his spirits and his health, and he is grown so thin and meagre, that he looks ten years older than when I saw him last. I hope he will now revive, since the blow is over; but it has been a very, very hard one, after such earnest pains to escape it.

Did the wood look very beautiful? I have figured it to myself with the three dear convalescents wandering in its winding paths, and inhaling its freshness and salubrity, ever since I heard of this walk. I wanted prodigiously to have issued forth from some little green recess, to have hailed your return. I hope Mr. Locke had the pleasure of this sight. Is jenny capable of such a mounting journey?

Do you know anything of a certain young lady, who eludes all my inquiries, famous for having eight sisters, all of uncommon talents? I had formerly some intercourse with her, and she used to promise she would renew it whenever I pleased but whether she is offended that I have slighted her offers so long, or whether she is fickle, or only whimsical, I know not all that is quite undoubted is that she has concealed herself so effectually from my researches, that I might as well look for justice and clemency in the French Convention, as for this former friend in the plains and lanes of Chesington where, erst, she met me whether I would or no.

M. D'ARBLAY'S VISIT TO CHESINGTON.

(Fanny Burney to Mrs. Locke.) Chesington, 1793. How sweet to me was my dearest Fredy's assurance that my gratification and prudence went at last hand in hand! I had longed for the sight of her writing, and not dared wish it.

I shall now long Impatiently till I can have the pleasure of saying "Ma'am, I desire no more of your letters."

I have heard to-day all I can most covet of all my dear late malades. I take it for granted this little visit was made known to my dearest sister confidant. I had prepared for it from the time of my own expectation, and I have had much amusement in what the preparation produced. Mrs Hamilton ordered half a ham to be boiled ready; and Miss Kitty trimmed up her best cap, and tried it on, on Saturday, to get it in shape to her face. She made chocolate also, which we drank up on Monday and Tuesday, because it was spoiling. "I have never seen none of the French quality," she says, "and I have a purdigious curosity; though as to dukes and dukes' sons, and these high top captains, I know they'll think me a mere country bumpkin. Howsever, they can't call me worse than 'Fat Kit Square,' and that's the worst name I ever got from any of our English petite bears, which I suppose these petite French quality never heard the like of."

Unfortunately, however, when all was prepared above, the French top captain entered while poor Miss Kitty was in dishabill, and Mrs. Hamilton finishing washing up her china from breakfast. A maid who was out at the pump, and first saw the arrival, ran in to give Miss Kitty time to escape, for she was in her round dress night-cap, and without her roll and curls. However, he followed too quick, and Mrs. Hamilton was seen in her linen gown and mob, though she had put on a silk one in expectation for every noon these four or five days past; and Miss Kitty was in such confusion, she hurried out of the room. She soon, however, returned with the roll and curls, and the forehead and throat fashionably lost, in a silk gown. And though she had not intended to speak a word, the gentle quietness of her guest so surprised and pleased her, that she never quitted his side while he stayed, and has sung his praises ever since.

Mrs. Hamilton, good soul! in talking and inquiring since of his history and conduct, shed tears at the recital. She says now she, has really seen one of the French gentry that has been drove out of their country by the villains she has heard of, she shall begin to believe there really has been a Revolution! and Miss Kitty says, "I purtest I did not know before but it was all a sham."

THE MATRIMONIAL PROJECT IS DISCUSSED.

(Fanny Burney to Mrs. Phillips.) Friday, May 31, Chesington. My heart so smites me this morning with making no answer to all I have been requested to weigh and decide, that I feel I cannot with any ease return to town without at least complying with one demand, which first, at parting yesterday, brought me to write fully to you, my Susan, if I could not elsewhere to my satisfaction.

in the course of last night and this morning Much indeed has occurred to me, that now renders my longer silence as to prospects and proceedings unjustifiable to myself. I will therefore now address myself to both my beloved confidants, and open to them all my thoughts, and entreat their own with equal plainness in return.

M. d'Arblay's last three letters convince me he is desperately dejected when alone, and when perfectly natural. It is not that he wants patience, but he wants rational expectation of better times, expectation founded on something more than mere aerial hope, that builds one day upon what the next blasts; and then has to build again, and again to be blasted.

What affects me the most in this situation is, that his time may as completely be lost as another's peace, by waiting for the effects of distant events, vague, bewildering, and remote, and quite as likely to lead to ill as to good. The very waiting, indeed, with the mind in such a state, is in itself an evil scarce to be recompensed. . . .

My dearest Fredy, in the beginning of her knowledge of this transaction, told me that Mr. Locke was of opinion that one hundred pounds per annum (94) might do, as it does for many a curate. M. d'A. also most solemnly and affectingly declares that le simple necessaire is all he requires and here, in your vicinity, would unhesitatingly be preferred by him to the most brilliant fortune in another séjour. If he can say that, what must I be not to echo it? I, who in the bosom of my own most chosen, most darling friends—

I need not enter more upon this; you all must know to me a crust of bread, with a little roof for shelter, and a fire for warmth, near you, would bring me to peace, to happiness, to all that My heart holds dear, or even in any situation could prize. I cannot picture such a fate with dry eyes; all else but kindness and society has to me so always been nothing.

With regard to my dear father, he has always left me to myself; I will not therefore speak to him while thus uncertain what to decide.

it is certain, however, that, with peace of mind and retirement, I have resources that I could bring forward to amend the little situation; as well as that, once thus undoubtedly established and naturalised, M. d'A. would have claims for employment.

These reflections, with a mutual freedom from ambition might lead to a quiet road, unbroken by the tortures of applications, expectations, attendance, disappointment, and time-wasting hopes and fears; if there were not apprehensions the one hundred pounds might be withdrawn. I do not think it likely, but it is a risk too serious in its consequences to be run. M. d'A. protests he could not answer to himself the hazard.

How to ascertain this, to clear the doubt, or to know the fatal certainty before it should be too late, exceeds my powers of suggestion. His own idea, to write to the queen, much as it has startled me, and wild as it seemed to me, is certainly less wild than to take the chance of such a blow in the dark. Yet such a letter could not even reach her. His very name is probably only known to her through myself. In short, my dearest friends, you will think for me, and let me know what occurs to you, and I will defer any answer till I hear your opinions. Heaven ever bless you! And pray for me at this moment.

DR. BURNEY'S OBJECTIONS TO THE MATCH.

(Dr. Burney to Fanny Burney.) May, 1793, Dear Fanny, I have for some time seen very plainly that you are ,prise, and have been extremely uneasy at the discovery. YOU must have observed my silent gravity, surpassing that of mere illness and its consequent low spirits. I had some thoughts of writing to Susan about it, and intended begging her to do what I must now do for myself—that is, beg and admonish you not to entangle yourself in a wild and romantic attachment, which offers nothing in prospect but poverty and distress, with future inconvenience and unhappiness. M. d'Arblay is certainly a very amiable and accomplished man, and of great military abilities I take for granted; but what employment has he for them of which the success is not extremely hazardous? His property, whatever it was, has been confiscated—décrété—by the Convention—and if a counter-revolution takes place, unless it be exactly such a one as suits the particular political sect in which he enlisted, it does not seem likely to secure to him an establishment in France. And as to an establishment in England, I know the difficulty which very deserving natives find in procuring one, with every appearance of interest, friends, and probability; and, to a foreigner, I fear the difficulty will be more than doubled.

As M. d'Arblay is at present circumstanced, an alliance with anything but a fortune sufficient for the support of himself and partner would be very imprudent. He is a mere soldier of fortune, under great disadvantages. Your income, if it was as certain as a freehold estate, is insufficient for the purpose; and if the queen should be displeased and withdraw her allowance, what could you do?

I own that, if M. d'Arblay had an establishment in France sufficient for him to marry a wife with little or no fortune, much as I am inclined to honour and esteem him, I should wish to prevent you from fixing your residence there; not merely from selfishness, but for your own sake, I know your love for your family, and know that it is reciprocal; I therefore cannot help thinking that you would mutually be lost to each other. The friends, too, which you have here, are of the highest and most desirable class. To quit them, in order to make new friendships in a strange land, in which the generality of its inhabitants at present seem incapable of such virtues as friendship is built upon, seems wild and visionary.

If M. d'Arblay had a sufficient establishment here for the purposes of credit and comfort, and determined to settle here for life, I should certainly think ourselves honoured by his alliance; but his situation is at present so very remote from all that can satisfy prudence, or reconcile to an affectionate father the idea of a serious attachment, that I tremble for your heart and future happiness. M. d'Arblay must have lived too long in the great world to accommodate himself contentedly to the little. his fate seems so intimately connected with that of his miserable country, and that country seems at a greater distance from peace, order, and tranquillity now than it has done at any time since the Revolution.

These considerations, and the uncertainty of what party will finally prevail, make me tremble for you both. You see, by what I have said, that my objections are not personal, but wholly prudential. For heaven's sake, my dear Fanny, do not part with your heart too rapidly, or involve yourself in deep engagements which it will be difficult to dissolve; and to the last degree imprudent, as things are at present circumstanced, to fulfil.

As far as character, merit, and misfortune demand esteem and regard, you may be sure that M. d'Arblay will be always received by me with the utmost attention and respect, but, in the present situation of things, I can by no means think I ought to encourage (blind and ignorant as I am of all but his misfortunes) a serious and solemn union with one whose unhappiness would be a reproach to the facility and inconsiderateness of a most affectionate father.

THE MARRIAGE TAKES PLACE.

Memorandum, this 7th May, 1825.

In answer to these apparently most just, and, undoubtedly, most parental and tender apprehensions, Susanna, the darling child of Dr. Burney, as well as first chosen friend of M, d'Arblay, wrote a statement of the plans, and means, and purposes of M. d'A. and F. B.—so clearly demonstrating their power of happiness, with willing economy, congenial tastes, and mutual love of the country, that Dr. B. gave way, and sent, though reluctantly, a consent - by which the union took place the 31st Of July, 1793, in Mickleham church, In presence of Mr. and Mrs. Locke, Captain and Mrs. Phillips, M. de Narbonne, and Captain Burney, who was father to his sister, as Mr. Locke was to M. d'A.; and on the 1st of August the ceremony was re-performed in the Sardinian chapel, according to the rites of the Romish Church; and never, never was union more blessed and felicitous; though after the first eight years of unmingled happiness, it was assailed by many calamities, chiefly of separation or illness, yet still mentally unbroken. F. D'ARBLAY.

ANNOUNCEMENT OF THE MARRIAGE TO A FRIEND.

(Madame d'Arblay to Mrs.—.) August 2, 1793. How in the world shall I begin this letter to my dearest M—! how save her from a surprise almost too strong for her weak nerves and tender heart!

After such an opening, perhaps any communication may be a relief but it is surprise only I would guard against; my present communication has nothing else to fear; it has nothing in it sad, melancholy, unhappy, but it has everything that is marvellous and unexpected.

Do you recollect at all, when you were last in town, my warm interest for the loyal part of the French exiles? do you remember my ,loge of a French officer, in particular, a certain M. d'Arblay?

Ah, my dear M—, you are quick as lightning; your sensitive apprehension will tell my tale for me now, without more aid than some details of circumstance.

The ,loge I then made, was with design to prepare you for an event I had reason to expect: such, however, was the uncertainty of my situation, from prudential obstacles, that I dared venture at no confidence, though my heart prompted it strongly, to a friend so sweetly sympathising in all my feelings and all my affairs—so constantly affectionate- so tenderly alive to all that interests and concerns me.

My dearest M—, you will give me, I am sure, your heart-felt wishes—your most fervent prayers. The choice I have made appears to me all you could yourself wish to fall to my lot—all you could yourself have formed to have accorded best with your kind partiality.

I had some hope you would have seen him that evening when we went together from Mrs. M. Montagu to Mrs. Locke's, for he was then a guest in Portland Place; but some miserable circumstances, of which I knew nothing till after had just fallen out, and he had shut himself up in his room. He did not know we were there.

Many, indeed, have been the miserable circumstances that have, from time to time, alarmed and afflicted in turn, and seemed to render a renunciation indispensable. The difficulties, however, have been conquered; and last Sunday Mr. and Mrs. Locke, my sister and Captain Phillips, and my brother Captain Burney, accompanied us to the altar, in Mickleham church; since which the ceremony has been repeated in the chapel of the Sardinian ambassador, that if, by a counter-revolution in France, M. d'Arblay recovers any of his rights, his wife may not be excluded from their participation.

You may be amazed not to see the name of my dear father upon this solemn occasion - but his apprehensions from the smallness of our income have made him cold and averse and though he granted his consent, I could not even solicit his presence. I feel satisfied, however, that time will convince him I have not been so imprudent as he now thinks me. Happiness is the great end of all our worldly views and proceedings, and no one can judge for another in what will produce it. To me, wealth and ambition would always be unavailing; I have lived in their most centrical possessions, and I have always seen that the happiness of the richest and the greatest has been the moment of retiring from riches and from power. Domestic comfort and social affection have invariably been the sole as well as ultimate objects of my choice, and I have always been a stranger to any other species of felicity.

M. d'Arblay has a taste for literature, and a passion for reading and writing, as marked as my own; this is a sympathy to rob retirement of all superfluous leisure, and insure to us both occupation constantly edifying or entertaining. He has seen so much of life, and has suffered so severely from its disappointments, that retreat, with a chosen companion, is become his final desire.

Mr. Locke has given M. d'Arblay a piece of ground in his beautiful park, upon which we shall build a little neat and plain habitation. We shall continue, meanwhile, in his neighbourhood, to superintend the little edifice, and enjoy the Society of his exquisite house, and that of my beloved sister Phillips. We are now within two miles of both, at a farm-house, where we have what apartments we require, and no more, in a most beautiful and healthy situation, a mile and a half from any town. The nearest is Bookham; but I beg that MY letters may be directed to me at Captain Phillips's, Mickleham, as the post does not come this way, and I may else miss them for a week. AS I do not correspond with Mrs Montagu, and it would be awkward to begin upon such a theme, I beg that when you write you will say something for me.

One of my first pleasures, in our little intended home, will be, finding a place of honour for the legacy of Mrs. Delany. Whatever may be the general wonder, and perhaps blame, of general people, at this connexion, equally indiscreet in pecuniary points for us both, I feel sure that the truly liberal and truly intellectual judgment of that most venerated character would have accorded its sanction, when acquainted with the worthiness of the object who would wish it.

Adieu, my sweet friend. Give my best compliments to Mr. —, and give me your kind wishes, your kind prayers, my ever dear M—.

(1) So called from the convent where their meetings were held.

(2) Carlyle.

(3) Carlyle.

(4 "To the lamp;" the street lamp-irons being found, by the French sansculottes, a handy substitute for the gallows. ED.

(5) The old Marshal Duke de Broglie was one of the early emigrants. He quitted France in July 1789, after the fall of the Bastille. ED.

(6) "Minister of War."

(7) Bradfield Hall, near Bury St. Edmund's, Suffolk, the house of Arthur Young, See infra. ED.

(8) "Arthur Young, the well-known writer of works on agriculture, still in high repute. He was a very old friend of the Burneys; connected with them also, by marriage, Mrs. Young being a sister of Dr. Burney's second wife. His "Travels in France" (from 1769 to 1790), published in 1794, gives a most valuable and interesting account of the state of that country just before the Revolution. Arthur Young was appointed Secretary to the Board of Agriculture, established by Act of Parliament in 1793. He died in 1820, in his seventy-ninth year, having been blind for some years previous to his death. ED.

(9) Fanny's half-sister, Sarah Harriet Burney, ED.

(10) " Minister of war."

(11) *One memorable saying is recorded of the Duke de Liancourt. He brought the news to the king of the capture of the Bastille by the people of Paris, July 14, 1789. "Late at night, the Duke de Liancourt, having official right of entrance, gains access to the royal apartments unfolds, with earnest clearness, in his constitutional way, the Job's-news. 'Mais,' said poor Louis, 'c'est une r,volte, Why, that is a revolt!'—'Sire,' answered Liancourt, 'it is not a revolt,—it is a revolution.'" (Carlyle.) ED.*

(12) *"Peers of France."*

(13) *Coblenz was the rallying-place of the emigrant noblesse. ED.*

(14) *On the 20th of June 1792, sansculotte Paris, assembling in its thousands, broke into the Tuileries, and called upon the king to remove his veto upon the decree against the priests, and to recall the ministry—Roland's—which he had just dismissed. For three hours the king stood face to face with the angry crowd, refusing to comply. In the evening, the Mayor of Paris, Petion, arrived, with other popular leaders from the Assembly, and persuaded the people to disperse. ED.*

(15) *"Save Yourself, M. de Liancourt!"*

(16) *"Ah! we are lost!"*

(17) *"prison."*

(18) *" I am in England.*

(19) *The Duke de la Rochefoucault, "journeying, by quick stages, with his mother and wife, towards the Waters of Forges, or some quieter country, was arrested at Gisors; conducted along the streets, amid effervescing multitudes, and killed dead ' by the stroke of a paving-stone hurled through the coach-window.' Killed as a once Liberal, now Aristocrat; Protector of Priests, Suspender of virtuous P,tions, and most unfortunate Hot-grown-cold, detestable to Patriotism. He dies lamented of Europe; his blood spattering the cheeks of his old mother, ninety-three years old." (Carlyle, Erench Aevolulion, Part III, Book I, ch. vi.) ED.*

(20) *School-boys.*

(21) *See note 361 ante, vol. ii. p. 449. ED.*

(22) *The name under which Madame de Genlis was now passing.*

(23) *" She has seen me!"*

(24) *"Perhaps I am indiscreet?"*

(25) *"But, mademoiselle—after all—the king—is he quite cured? "*

(26) *"What, mademoiselle! you knew that infamous woman?"*

(27) *These "journalizing letters" of Mrs. Phillips continue without interruption from the present page to page 37. ED.*

(28) *Not yet duke, but viscount. He was created duke by Louis XVIII, in 1822. ED.*

(29) It should be March. "The portfolio of war was withdrawn from him, by a very laconic letter from the king, March 10, 1792; he had held it three months and three days." (Nouvelle Biographie G,n,rale: art. Narbonne.) ED.

(30) Severe decrees against the emigrants were passed in the Convention shortly afterwards. See infra, P. 33. ED.

(31) "And as he is extremely attached to him, he has begged him to come and live with him."

(32) In a position to realise her fortune."

(33) "To pay his respects to me."

(34) "I do not speak English very well."

(35) "What a pretty little house you have, and what pretty little hosts."

(36) "Does he know the name of M. Lafayette?"

(37) "They put us at first into a pretty enough room."

(38) A constitutionalist and member of the Legislative Assembly, who narrowly escaped with his life on the 10th of August. He lived thenceforward in retirement until after the fall of Robespierre and the jacobins, and came again to the fore under Napoleon. ED.

(39) "His resignation."

(40) "Without form of law."

(41) The night of June 20-21, 1791, King Louis fled disguised from Paris, with his family; got safely as far as Varennes, but was there discovered, and obliged to return. ED.

(42) "Resolution was taken."

(43) "After many threatening gestures."

(44) The asylum of Jean jacques (Rousseau).

(45) St. just was one of the most notable members of the National Convention. "Young Saint-just is coming, deputed by Aisne in the North; more like a Student than a Senator; not four-and-twenty yet (Sept. 1792); who has written Books; a youth of slight stature, with mild mellow voice, enthusiast olive-complexion and long black hair." (Carlyle.) He held with Robespierre, and was guillotined with him, July 28, 1794. ED.

(46) ' "And now he is a proud republican."

(47) "What day better than the present?"

(48) "Listen to reason."

(49) M. de Necker was father of Madame de Stael, and at one time the most popular minister of France. Controller-general of finances from 1776 to 1781, and again in 1788. In July 1789, he was dismissed, to the anger of indignant Paris; had to he recalled before many days, and returned in triumph, to be, it was hoped, "Saviour of France." But his popularity gradually declined, and at last "'Adored Minister' Necker sees good on the 3rd of September, 1790, to withdraw softly, almost privily—with an eye to the 'recovery of his health.' Home to native Switzerland; not as he last came; lucky to reach it alive!" (Carlyle) ED.

(50) Malouet was a member of the Assembly, and one of the constitutional royalists who took refuge in England in September, 1792. Hearing of the intended trial of the king, 'Malouet wrote to the Convention, requesting a passport, that he might go to Paris to defend him. He got no passport, however; only his name put on the list of emigrants for an answer. ED.

(51) "Were mixed up in it."

(52) The Bishop of Autun:—Talleyrand. ED.

(53) "Worthy to be the husband of so amiable and charming a person as Madame de la Chattre."

(54) "M. de la Chattre is a capital fellow; but as rough as a cart-horse."

(55) The spleen.

(56) Inn.

(57) "His unfortunate friends."

(58) "But wait a bit; I have not yet finished: we were assured that no one was lost, and even that everything on the vessel was saved."

(59) "Out at sea."

(60) "His friends the constitutionalists."

(61) Fortnight.

(62) The execution of Louis XVI.

(63) The Literary Club.

(64) Guarded: circumspect.

(65) Dr. Percy, editor of the "Reliques of Ancient English Poetry." ED.

(66) "Move the people to compassion."

(67) As literary curiosities, the subjoined notes from Madame de Stael, have been printed verbatim et literatim: they are probably her earliest attempts at English writing.

(68) "But, to make more sure, I tell you in French that your room, the house, the inmates of Juniper, everything is ready to receive the first woman in England."

(69) Malesherbes was one of the counsel who defended Louis at his trial. The Convention, after debate, has granted him Legal Counsel, of his own choosing. Advocate Target feels himself 'too old,' being turned of fifty-four - and declines. . . . Advocate Tronchet, some ten years older, does not decline. Nay behold, good old Malesherbes steps forward voluntarily; to the last of his fields , the good old hero! He is gray with seventy years; he says, 'I was twice called to the Council of him who was my Master, When all the world coveted that honour; and I owe him the same service now, when it has become one which many reckon dangerous!"—(Carlyle). Malesherbes was guillotined in 1794, during "the Reign of Terror." ED.

(70) Mr. Clarke.

(71) Voltaire's. ED.

(72) Narbonne. ED.

(73) "Something to live on in England."

(74) September 2, it should be. ED.

(75) i.e, Decret, d'accusation, accused. ED.

(76) Lally Tolendal was the son of the brave Lally, Governor of Pondicherry, whose great services in India were rewarded by the French government with four years' imprisonment, repeated torture, and finally ignominious death, in 1760. The infliction of torture on criminals was not put a stop to in France until the Revolution. ED.

(77) "A very good fellow, and nothing more."

(78) "But he will be hurt at that."

(79) The owner of Juniper Hall. ED.

(80) "Coquetry to soften that barbarous jenkinson."

(81) "Indignant at the bad faith, and tired with the tediousness of his opponent."

(82) "Pray, Mr. Gnawbone, how is the queen?"

(83) Punctiliousness: propriety.

(84) Pet: Vexation.

(85) "Is a woman in leading strings all her life in this country? It seems to me that your sister is like a child of fourteen."

(86) "And tell Miss Burney that I don't desire it of her-that I leave the Country loving her sincerely, and bearing her no grudge."

(87) "There was no way out of it."

(88) "You are very good to say SO."

(89) M. d'Arblay. "When Lieutenant [James] Burney accompanied captain Cook to otaheite, each of the English sailors was adopted as a brother by some one of the natives. The ceremony consisted in rubbing noses together, and exchanging the appellation Tyo or Toio, which signified 'chosen friend.' This title was sometimes playfully given to Miss Burney by Mrs. Thrale." note to the original edition of the "Diary", vol. ii. page 38. ED.

(90) "Country place where Miss Burney was."

(91) "On my part."

(92) "Could not one make that little journey?"

(93) "Wide awake, as if she suspected something."

(94) The amount of Fanny's pension from the queen. ED.

SECTION 20. (1793-6)

LOVE IN A COTTAGE: THE D'ARBLAYS VISIT WINDSOR.

[Never, probably, did Fanny enjoy greater happiness than during the first few years of her married life, "Love in a cottage" on an income of one hundred pounds a year, was exactly suited to her retiring and affectionate nature. The cottage, too, was within easy walking distance of Mickleham, where resided her favourite sister, Susanna, and of Norbury Park, the home of her dearest friends, the Lockes. Here, then, in this beautiful part of Surrey, with a devoted husband by her side, and, in due time, a little son (her only child) to share with him her tenderness and care. Did Fanny lead, for some time, a tranquil and, in the main, a happy life. Her chief excursions were occasional visits to the queen and princesses-delightful visits now that she was out of harness. Towards the end, however, of the period of which the following 'Section contains the history, two melancholy events, happening in quick succession, brought sorrow to the little household at Book'ham. The departure for Ireland of Susan Phillips left a grievous gap in the circle of Fanny's best-loved friends. We gather from the "Diary" that Captain (now Major) Phillips had gone to Ireland, with his little son, Norbury, to superintend the management of his estate at Belcotton, some months before his wife left Mickleham. In the autumn of 1796 he returned to fetch his wife and the rest of his family. An absence of three years was intended. The parting was rendered doubly distressing by the evidently declining state of Susan's health. Shortly afterwards, in October 1796, died Fanny's step-mother, who had been, for many years, more or less an invalid. Fanny hastened to Chelsea on receiving the news, and spent some time there with her father and his Youngest daughter. The following extract from a memorandum of Dr. Burney's will be read, we think, not without Interest.

"On the 26th of October, she [his second wife] was interred in the burying-ground of Chelsea College. On the 27th, I returned to my melancholy home, disconsolate and stupified, Though long expected, this calamity was very severely felt; I missed her counsel, converse, and family regulations; and a companion of thirty years, whose mind was cultivated, whose intellects were above the general level of her sex, and whose curiosity after knowledge was insatiable to the last. These were losses that caused a vacuum in my habitation and in my mind, that has never been filled up.

"My four eldest daughters, all dutiful, intelligent, and affectionate, were married, and had families of their own to superintend, or they might have administered comfort. My youngest daughter, Sarah Harriet, by my second marriage, had quick intellects, and distinguished talents; but she had no experience in household affairs. However, though she had native spirits of the highest gaiety, she became a steady and prudent character, and a kind and good girl. There is, I think, considerable merit in her novel, 'Geraldine,' particularly in the conversations; and I think the scene at the emigrant cottage really touching. At least it drew tears from me, when I was not so prone to shed them as I am at present." (95)

During these years Fanny did not suffer her pen to lie idle. Her tragedy, "Edwy and Elgiva," was produced, though without success, at Drury Lane. On the other hand, the success of her third novel, "Camilla, or a Picture of Youth, " published by subscription in 1796, was, at least from a financial point of view, conspicuous and immediate. Out of an edition of four thousand, three thousand five hundred copies were sold within three months.

Were we to attempt to rank Madame d'Arblay's novels in order of merit, we should perhaps feel compelled to place "Camilla" at the bottom of the list, yet without intending to imply any considerable inferiority. But it is full of charm and animation the characters—the female characters especially-are drawn with a sure hand, the humour is as diverting, the satire as spirited as ever. Fanny"s fops and men of the ton are always excellent in their kind, and "Camilla" contains, perhaps, her greatest triumph in this direction, in the character of Sir Sedley Clarendal. Lovel. in "Evelina," and Meadows, in "Cecilia," are mere blockheads, whose distinction is wholly due to the ludicrousness of their affectations; but in Sir Sedley she has attempted, and succeeded in the much more difficult task of portraying a man of naturally good parts and feelings, who, through idleness and vanity, has allowed himself to sink into the position of a mere leader of the ton, whose better nature rises at times, in spite of himself, above the flood of affectation and folly beneath which he endeavours to drown it. Camilla herself, the light-hearted, unsuspicious Camilla, however she may differ, in some points of character, from Fanny's other heroines, possesses one quality which is common to them all, the power of fascinating the reader. Perhaps the least satisfactory character in the book is that of the hero, Edgar Mandlebert, whose extreme caution in the choice of a wife betrays him into ungenerous suspicions, as irritating to the impatient reader as they are distressing to poor Camilla. In fine, whatever faults, as occasionally of style, the book may have the interest never for One moment flags from the first page to the last of the entire five volumes.

The subscription-price of "Camilla" was fixed at one guinea. Fanny's friends, Mrs. Crewe, Mrs. Boscawen, and Mrs. Locke, exerted themselves with the utmost zeal and success in procuring subscribers, and the printed lists prefixed to the first volume contains nearly eleven hundred names. Among them we notice the name of Edmund Burke, whose great career was closing in a cloud of domestic trouble. Early in 1794 he lost his brother, Richard, and in August of the same year a far heavier blow fell upon him in the death, at the age of thirty-six, of his only and promising son, "the pride and ornament of my existence," as he called him in a touching letter to Mrs. Crewe. The desolate father, already worn with the thankless toils of statesmanship, in which his very errors had been the outcome of a noble and enthusiastic temperament, never recovered from this blow. But when Mrs. Crewe sent him, in 1795, the proposals for publishing "Camilla," Burke roused himself to do a new kindness to an old friend. He forwarded to Mrs. Crewe a note for twenty pounds, desiring in return one copy of the book, and justified his generous donation in a letter of the most delicate Courtesy. "As to Miss Burney," he wrote, "the subscription ought to be, for certain persons, five guineas; and to take but a single copy each. The rest as it is. I am sure that it is a disgrace to the age and nation, if this be not a great thing for her, if every person in England who has received pleasure and instruction from 'Cecilia,' were to rate its value at the hundredth part of their satisfaction, Madame d'Arblay would be one of the richest women in the kingdom.

"Her scheme was known before she lost two of her most respectful admirers from this house; and this, with Mrs. Burke's' subscription and mine, make the paper I send you. One book is as good as a thousand: one of hers is certainly as good as a thousand others."

The book, on its Publication was sent to Bath, where Burke was lying ill-too ill to read it. To Mrs. Crewe, who visited him at the time, he said: "How ill I am you will easily believe, when a new work of Madame d'Arblay's lies on my table, unread!"(96)

Meanwhile the retirement of the "hermits" at Bookham was now and again disturbed by echoes of the tumult without. The war was progressing, and the Republic was holding its own against the combined powers of Europe. Dr. Burney refers to the "sad news" from Dunkirk. In August, 1793, an English army, commanded by the Duke of York, had invested that important stronghold: on the night of September 8, thanks to the exertions of the garrison and the advance of General Houchard to its relief, the siege was urriedly abandoned and his royal highness had to beat a retreat, leaving behind him' his siege-artillery and a large quantity of aggage and ammunition. Another siege—that of Toulon-seemed likely to prove a matter of nearer concern to Fanny. The inhabitants of Toulon, having royalist, or at least anti-jacobin, sympathies, and stirred by the fate of Marseilles, had determined, in an unhappy hour, to defy the Convention and to proclaim the dauphin by the title of Louis XVII. They invoked the protection of the English fleet under Admiral Hood, who accordingly took possession of the harbour and of the French ships of war stationed therein, while a force of English and Spanish soldiers was sent on shore to garrison the forts. In the course of these proceedings the admiral issued to the townspeople two proclamations, by the second of which, dated August 28, 1793, after noticing the declaration of the inhabitants in favour of monarchy, and Their desire to re-establish the constitution as it was accepted by the late king, he explicitly declared that he took possession of Toulon and should keep it solely as a deposit for Louis XXIII, and that only until the restoration of peace. This hopeful intelligence did not escape General d'Arblay, busied among his cabbages at Bookham. A blow to be struck for Louis XVII. and the constitution! The general straightway flung aside the "Gardener's Dictionary," and wrote an offer to Mr. Pitt of his services as volunteer at Toulon, in the sacred cause of the Bourbons. Happily for Fanny, his offer was not accepted, for some reason unexplained. (97) In the meantime, General Dugommier and the republicans, a young artillery-officer named Napoleon Buonaparte among them, were using their best endeavours to reduce Toulon, with what result we shall presently see. ED.]

THE FRENCH CLERGY FUND. THE TOULON ExPEDITION.

(Dr. Burney to Madame d'Arblay.) September 12, 1793. Dear Fanny—In this season of leisure I am as fully occupied as ever your friend Mr. DelVile (98) was. So many people to attend, so many complaints to hear, and so many grievances to redress, that it has been impossible for me to write to you sooner. I have been out of town but one Single day, I believe, since you were here: that was spent at Richmond with my sisters. But every day produces business for other people, which occupies me as much as ever I found myself in days of hurry about my own affairs.

I have had a negotiation and correspondence to carry on for and with Charlotte Smith, (99) of which I believe I told you the beginning, and I do not see the end myself. Her second son had his foot shot off before Dunkirk, and has undergone a very dangerous amputation, which, it is much feared, will be fatal.

Mrs. Crewe, having seen at Eastbourne a great number of venerable and amiable French clergy suffering all the evils of banishment and beggary with silent resignation, has for some time had in meditation a plan for procuring some addition to the small allowance the committee at Freemasons' hall is able to allow, from the residue of the subscriptions and briefs in their favour. Susan will show you the plan. . . .

You say that M. d'Arblay is not only his own architect, but intends being his own gardener. I suppose the ground allotted to the garden of your maisonnette is marked out, and probably will be enclosed and broken up before the foundation of your mansion is laid; therefore, to encourage M. d'Arblay in the study of horticulture, I have the honour to send him Miller's 'Gardeners' Dictionary,'—an excellent book, at least for the rudiments of the art. I send you, my dear Fanny, an edition of Milton, which I can well spare, and which you ought not to live without; and I send you both our dear friend Dr. Johnson's 'Rasselas.'

This is sad news from Dunkirk, at which our own jacobins will insolently triumph. Everything in France seems to move in a regular progression from bad to worse. After near five years' struggle and anarchy, no man alive, with a grain of modesty, would venture to predict how or when the evils of that country will be terminated. In the meantime the peace and comfort of every civilised part of the globe is threatened with similar calamities.

(Madame dArblay to Dr. Burney) Bookham, September 29, 1793. When I received the last letter of my dearest father, and for some hours after, I was the happiest of all human beings. I make no exception, for I think none possible: not a wish remained to me; not a thought of forming one.

This was just the period—is it not always so?—for a blow of sorrow to reverse the whole scene: accordingly, that evening M. d'Arblay communicated to me his desire of going to Toulon. He had intended retiring from public life; his services and his sufferings in his severe and long career, repaid by exile and confiscation, and for ever embittered to his memory by the murder of his sovereign, had justly satisfied the claims of his conscience and honour; and led him, without a single self-reproach, to seek a quiet retreat in domestic society: but the second declaration of Lord Hood no sooner reached this little obscure dwelling, no sooner had he read the words Louis XVII. and the constitution to which he had sworn united, than his military ardour rekindled, his loyalty was all up in arms, and every sense of duty carried him back to wars and dangers.

I dare not speak of myself, except to say that I have forborne to oppose him with a single solicitation; all the felicity of this our chosen and loved retirement would effectually be annulled by the smallest suspicion that it was enjoyed at the expense of any duty, and therefore, since he is persuaded it is right to go, I acquiesce. He is now writing an offer of his services, which I am to convey to Windsor, and which he means to convey himself to Mr. Pitt. As I am sure it will interest my dear father, I will copy it for him. . . .

My dearest father, before this tremendous project broke into our domestic economy, M, d'Arblay had been employed in a little composition, which, being all in his power, he destined to lay at your feet, as a mark of his pleasure in your attention to his horticultural pursuit. He has just finished copying it for you, and to-morrow it goes by the stage.

Your hint of a book from time to time enchanted him: it seems to me the only present he accepts entirely without pain. He has just requested me to return to Mrs. Locke herself a cadeau she had brought us. If it had been an old Courtcalendar, or an almanac, or anything in the shape of a brochure, he would have received it with his best bow and smile.

This Toulon business finally determines our deferring the maisonnette till the spring. Heaven grant it may be deferred no longer! (100) Mr Locke says it will be nearly as soon ready as if begun in the autumn, for it will be better to have it aired and inhabited before the winter seizes it, If the memoire which M. d'Arblay is now writing is finished in time, it shall accompany the little packet; if not, we will send it by the first opportunity.

Meanwhile, M. d'Arblay makes a point of our indulging ourselves with the gratification of subscribing one guinea to your fund, (101) and Mrs. Locke begs you will trust her and insert her subscription in your list, and Miss Locke and Miss Amelia Locke. Mr. Locke is charmed with your plan. M. d'Arblay means to obtain you Lady Burrel and Mrs. Berm. If you think I can write to any purpose, tell me a little hint how and of what, dearest sir; for I am in the dark as to what may remain yet unsaid. Otherwise, heavy as is my heart just now, I could work for them and Your plan. (102)

(Dr. Burney to Madame d'Arblay.) October 4, 1793. Dear Fanny, This is a terrible coup, so soon after your union; but I honour M, d'Arblay for offering his service on so great an occasion, and you for giving way to what seems an indispensable duty. Common-place reflections on the vicissitudes of human affairs would afford you little consolation. The stroke is new to your situation, and so will be the fortitude necessary on the occasion. However, to military men, who, like M. d'Arblay, have been but just united to the object of their choice, and begun to domesticate, it is no uncommon tbing for their tranquillity to be disturbed by " the trumpet's loud clangor." Whether the offer is accepted or not, the having made it will endear him to those embarked in the same cause among his countrymen, and elevate him in the general opinion of the English public. This consideration I am sure will afford you a satisfaction the most likely to enable you to support the anxiety and pain of absence.

I have no doubt of the offer being taken well at Windsor, and of its conciliating effects. If his majesty and the ministry have any settled plan for accepting or rejecting similar offers I know not; but it seems very likely that Toulon will be regarded as the rallying point for French royalists of all sects and denominations. . . .

I shall be very anxious to know how the proposition of M. d'Arblay has been received; and, if accepted, on what conditions, and when and how the voyage is to be performed, I should hope in a stout man of war; and that M. de Narbonne will be of the party, being so united in friendship and political principles.

Has M. d'Arblay ever been at Toulon? It is supposed to be so well fortified, both by art and nature, on the land side, that; if not impregnable, the taking it by the regicides will require so much time that it is hoped an army of counterrevolutionists will be assembled from the side of Savoy, sufficient to raise the siege, if unity of measures and action prevail between the Toulonnais and their external friends. But even if the assailants should make such approaches as to render it necessary to retreat, with such a powerful fleet as that of England and Spain united, it will not only be easy to carry off the garrison and inhabitants in time, but to destroy such ships as cannot be brought away, and ruin the harbour and arsenal for many years to come.'

I have written to Mrs. Crewe all you have said on the subject of writing something to stimulate benevolence and commiseration in favour of the poor French ecclesiastics, amounting to six thousand now in England, besides four hundred laity here and eight hundred at Jersey, in utter want. The fund for the laity was totally exhausted the 27th of last month, and the beginning of the next that raised by former subscriptions and briefs will be wholly expended!

The expense, in only allowing the clergy 8 shillings a week, amounts to about 7500 pounds a-month, which cannot be supported long by private subscriptions, and must at last be taken up by Parliament; but to save the national disgrace of suffering these excellent people to die of hunger, before the Parliament meets and agrees to do something for them, the ladies must work hard. You and M. d'Arblay are very good in wishing to contribute your mite; but I did not intend leading you into this scrape. If you subscribe your pen, and he his sword, it will best answer Mr. Burke's idea, who says, "There are two ways by which people may be charitable-the one by their money, the other by their exertions."

(Madame d'Arblay to Dr. Burney.) Sunday noon, October 21, 1793. My dearest father will think I have been very long in doing the little I have done; but my mind is so anxiously discom-fited by the continued suspense with regard to M. d'Arblay's proposition and wish, that it has not been easy to me to weigh completely all I could say, and the fear of repeating what had already been offered upon the subject has much restrained me, for I have seen none of the tracts that may have appeared. However, it is a matter truly near my heart; and though I have not done it rapidly, I have done it with my whole mind, and, to own the truth, with a species of emotion that has greatly affected me, for I could not deeply consider the situation of these venerable men without feeling for them to the quick. If what I have written should have power to procure them one more guinea, I shall be paid.

If you think what I have drawn up worth printing, I should suppose it might make a little sixpenny paper, and be sold for the same purpose it is written. Or will it only do to be printed at the expense of the acting ladies, and given gratis? You must judge of this.

(Madame d'Arblay to Dr. Burney.) Bookham, October 27, 1793. My most dear father,—The terrible confirmation of this last act of savage hardness of heart(104) has wholly overset us again. M. d'Arblay had entirely discredited its probability, and, to the last moment, disbelieved the report not from milder thoughts of the barbarous rulers of his unhappy country, but from seeing that the death of the queen could answer no purpose, helpless as she was to injure them, while her life might answer some as a hostage with the emperor. Cruelty, however, such as theirs, seems to require no incitement whatever; its own horrible exercise appears sufficient both to prompt and to repay it. Good heaven! that that wretched princess should so finish sufferings so unexampled!

With difficulties almost incredible, Madame de Stael has contrived, a second time, to save the lives of M. de Jaucourt and M, de Montmorenci, who are just arrived in Switzerland. We know as yet none of the particulars; simply that they are saved is all: but they write in a style the most melancholy to M. de Narbonne, of the dreadful fanaticism of licence, which they dare call liberty, that still reigns unsubdued in France, and they have preserved nothing but their persons! of their vast properties they could secure no more than pocket-money, for travelling in the most penurious manner. They are therefore in a state the most deplorable. Switzerland is filled with gentlemen and ladies of the very first families and rank, who are all starving, but those who have had the good fortune to procure, by disguising their quality, some menial office!

No answer comes from Mr. Pitt; and we now expect none till Sir Gilbert Elliot makes his report of the state of Toulon and of the Toulonnese till which, probably, no decision will be formed whether the constitutionals in England will be employed or not.

[M. d'Arblay's offer of serving in the expedition to Toulon was not accepted, and the reasons for which it was declined do not appear.]

MADAME D'ARBLAY ON HER MARRIAGE.

(Madame d'Arblay to Mrs.—.)

The account of your surprise, my sweet friend, was the last thing to create mine: I was well aware of the general astonishment, and of yours in particular. My own, however, at my very extraordinary fate, is singly greater than that of all my friends united. I had never made any vow against marriage, but I had long, long been firmly persuaded it was for me a state of too much hazard and too little promise to draw me from my individual plans and purposes. I remember, in playing -at questions and commands, when I was thirteen, being asked when I intended to marry? and surprising my playmates by solemnly replying) "When I think I shall be happier than I am in being single." It is true, I imagined that time would never arrive - and I have pertinaciously adhered to trying no experiment upon any other hope - for, many and mixed as are the ingredients which form what is generally considered as happiness, I was always fully convinced [hat social sympathy of character and taste could alone have any chance with me; all else I always thought, and now know, to be immaterial. I have only this peculiar, that what many contentedly assert or adopt in theory, I have had the courage to be guided by in practice.

We are now removed to a very small house in the suburbs of a very small village called Bookham. We found it rather inconvenient to reside in another person's dwelling, though our own apartments were to ourselves. Our views are not so beautiful as from Phenice farm, but our situation is totally free from neighbours and intrusion. We are about a mile and a half from Norbury Park, and two miles from Mickleham. I am become already so stout a walker, by use, and with the help of a very able supporter, that I go to those places and return home on foot without fatigue, when the weather is kind. At other times I condescend to accept a carriage from Mr. Locke; but it is always reluctantly, I so much prefer walking where, as here, the country and prospects are inviting.

I thank you for your caution about building: we shall certainly undertake nothing but by contract - however, it would be truly mortifying to give up a house in Norbury Park we defer the structure till the spring, as it is to be so very slight, that Mr. Locke says it will be best to have it hardened in its first stage by the summer's sun. It will be very small, merely a habitation for three people, but in a situation truly beautiful, and within five minutes of either Mr. Locke or my sister Phillips: it is to be placed just between those two loved houses.

My dearest father, whose fears and drawbacks have been my Sole subject of regret, begins now to see I have not judged rashly, or with romance, in seeing my own road to my own felicity. And his restored cheerful concurrence in my constant principles, though new station, leaves me, for myself, without a wish. L'ennui, which could alone infest our retreat, I have ever been a stranger to, except in tiresome company, and my companion has every possible resource against either feeling or inspiring it.

As my partner is a Frenchman, I conclude the wonder raised by the connexion may spread beyond my own private circle; but no wonder upon earth can ever arrive near my own in having found such a character from that nation. This is a prejudice certainly, impertinent and very John Bullish, and very arrogant but I only share it with all my countrymen, and therefore must needs forgive both them and myself. I am convinced, however, from your tender solicitude for me in all ways, that you will be glad to hear that the queen and all the royal family have deigned to send me wishes for my happiness through Mrs. Schwellenberg, who has written me what you call a very kind congratulation.

[In the year 1794, the happiness of the "Hermitage" was increased by the birth of a son, (105) who was christened Alexander Charles Louis Piochard d'Arblay; receiving the names of his father, with those of his two godfathers, the Comte de Narbonne and Dr. Charles Burney.]

MR. CANNING.

(Madame d'Arblay to Doctor Burney) Bookham, February 8, 1794. The times are indeed, as my dearest father says, tremendous, and reconcile this retirement daily more and more to my chevalier—chevalier every way, by birth, by his order, and by his character; for to-day he has been making his first use of a restoration to his garden in gathering snowdrops for his fair Dulcinea—you know I must say fair to finish the phrase with any effect.

I am very sorry for the sorrow I am sure Mr. Burke will feel for the loss of his brother, announced in Mr. Coolie's paper yesterday. Besides, he was a comic, good-humoured, entertaining man, though not bashful. (106)

What an excellent opening Mr. Canning has made at last! Entre nous soit dit, I remember, when at Windsor, that I Was told Mr. Fox came to Eton purposely to engage to himself that young man, from the already great promise of his rising abilities - and he made dinners for him and his nephew, Lord Holland, to teach them political lessons. It must have had an odd effect upon him, I think, to hear such a speech from his disciple. (107)

Mr. Locke now sends us the papers for the debates every two or three days; he cannot quicker, as his own household readers are so numerous. I see almost nothing of Mr. Windham in them; which vexes me: but I see Mr. Windham in Mr. Canning.

TALLEYRAND'S LETTERS OF ADIEU. (108)

(M. de Talleyrand to Mrs. Philips.) Londres, 1794. Madame,—Il faut qu'il y ait eu de l'impossibilit, pour que ce matin je n'aie pas eu l'honneur de vous voir; mais l'im-possibilit, la plus forte m'a priv, du dernier plaisir que je pouvois avoir en Europe. Permettez moi, madame, de vous remercier encore une fois do toutes vos bont,s, de vous demander un peu de part dans votre souvenir, et laissez moi vous dire que mes voeux se porteront dans tous les terns de ma vie vers vous, vers le capitaine, vers vos enfants. Vous allez avoir en Amerique un serviteur bien zélé; je ne reviendrai pas en Europe sans arriver dans le Surrey: tout ce qui, pour mon esprit et pour mon coeur, a quelque valeur, est l.

Voulez-vous bien presenter tous mes complimens au capitaine? (109)

(M. de Talleyrand to M. and Madame d'Arblay.) Londres, 2 Mars, 1794. Adieu, mon cher D'Arblay: je quitte votre pays jusqu'au moment o— il n'appartiendra plus aux petites passions des hommes. Alors j'y reviendrai; non, en verite, pour m'occuper d'affaires, car il y a long tems que je les ai abandonn,es pour jamais; mais pour voir les excellens habitans du Surrey, J'espere savoir assez d'Anglais pour entendre Madame d'Arblay; d'ici quatre mois je ne vais faire autre chose que l'etudier: et pour apprendre le beau et bon langage, c'est "Evelina" et "Cecilia" qui sont mes livres d'etude et de plaisir. Je vous souhaite, mon cher ami, toute espece de bonheur, et vous ^tes on position de remplir tous mes souhaits.

Je ne sais combien de tems je resterai en Amérique: s'il se référoit quelque chose de raisonnable et de stable pour notre malheureux pays, je reviendrois; si l'Europe s'abieme dans la campagne prochaine, je preparerai en Amerique des asyles tous nos amis.

Adieu: mes hommages Madame d'Arblay et Madame phillips, je vous en prie: je vous demande et vous promets amiti, pour la vie. (110)

M. D'ARBLAY'S HORTICULTURAL PURSUITS.

(Madame d'Arblay to Doctor Burney.) Bookham, March 22, 1794. My dear father. I am this Moment returned from reading your most welcome and kind letter at our Susanna's. The account of your better health gives me a pleasure beyond all words; and it is the more essential to my perfect contentment on account of your opinion of our retreat. I doubt not, my dearest father, but you judge completely right, and I may nearly say we are both equally disposed to pay the most implicit respect to your counsel. We give up, therefore, all thoughts of our London excursion for the present, and I shall write to that effect to our good intended hostess very speedily. I can easily conceive far more than you enlarge upon in this counsel: and, indeed, I have not myself been wholly free from apprehension of possible embarras, should we, at this period, visit London; for though M. d'Arblay not only could stand, but would court, all personal scrutiny, whether retrospective or actual, I see daily the extreme susceptibility which attends his very nice notions of honour, and how quickly and deeply his spirit is wounded by whatever he regards as injustice. Incapable, too, of the least trimming or disguise, he could not, at a time such as this, be in London without suffering or risking perhaps hourly, something unpleasant. Here we are tranquil, undisturbed and undisturbing. Can life, he often says, he more innocent than ours, or happiness more inoffensive? He works in his garden, or studies English and mathematics, while I write. When I work at my needle, he reads to me; and we enjoy the beautiful country around us in long and romantic strolls, during which he carries under his arm a portable garden chair, lent us by Mrs. Locke, that I may rest as I proceed. He is extremely fond, too, of writing, and makes, from time to time, memorandums of such memoirs, poems, and anecdotes as he recollects, and I wish to have preserved. These resources for sedentary life are certainly the first blessings that can be given to man, for they enable him to be happy in the extremest obscurity, even after tasting the dangerous draughts of glory and ambition.

The business of M. de Lafayette (111) has been indeed extremely bitter to him. It required the utmost force he could put upon himself not to take some public part in it. He drew up a short but most energetic defence of that unfortunate general, in a letter, which he meant to print and send to the editors of a newspaper which had traduced him, with his name at full length. But after two nights' sleepless deliberation, the hopelessness of serving his friend, with a horror and disdain of being mistaken as one who would lend any arms to weaken government at this crisis, made him consent to repress it. I was dreadfully uneasy during the conflict, knowing, far better than I can make him conceive, the mischiefs that might follow any interference at this moment, in matters brought before the nation, from a foreigner. But, conscious of his own integrity, I plainly see he must either wholly retire, or come forward to encounter whatever he thinks wrong. Ah—better let him accept your motto, and cultiver son jardin! He is now in it, notwithstanding our long walk to Mickleham, and working hard and fast to finish some self-set task that to-morrow, Sunday, must else impede.

M. d'Arblay, to my infinite satisfaction, gives up all thoughts of building, in the present awful state of public affairs. To show you, however, how much he is "of your advice" as to son jardin, he has been drawing a plan for it, which I intend to beg, borrow, or steal (all one), to give you some idea how seriously he studies to make his manual labours of some real utility.

This sort of work, however, is so totally new to him, that he receives every now and then some of poor Merlin's "disagreeable compliments" for, when Mr. Locke's or the captain's gardeners favour our grounds with a visit, they commonly make known that all has been done wrong. Seeds are sowing in some parts when plants ought to be reaping, and plants are running to seed while they are thought not yet at maturity. Our garden, therefore, is not yet quite the most profitable thing in the world; but M. d'A. assures me it is to be the staff of our table and existence.

A little, too, he has been unfortunate; for, after immense toil in planting and transplanting strawberries round our hedge, here at Bookham, he has just been informed they will bear no fruit the first year, and the second we may be "over the hills and far away!" Another time, too, with great labour, he cleared a considerable compartment of weeds, and, when it looked clean and well, and he showed his work to the gardener, the man said he had demolished an asparagus-bed! M. d'A. protested, however, nothing could look more like des mauvaises herbes.

His greatest passion is for transplanting. Everything we possess he moves from one end of the garden to another, to produce better effects. Roses take place of jessamines, jessamines of honeysuckles, and honeysuckles of lilacs, till they have all danced round as far as the space allows; but whether the effect may not be a general mortality, summer only can determine.

Such is our horticultural history. But I must not omit that we have had for one week cabbages from our own cultivation every day! O, you have no idea how sweet they tasted! We agreed they had a freshness and a go–t we had never met with before. We had them for too short a time to grow tired of them, because, as I have already hinted, they were beginning to run to seed before we knew they were eatable. . .

April. Think of our horticultural shock last week, when Mrs. Bailey, our landlady, "entreated M. d'Arblay not to Spoil her fruit-trees!"—trees he had been pruning with his utmost skill and strength. However, he has consulted your "Millar" thereupon, and finds out she is very ignorant, which he has gently intimated to her.

MRS. PIOZZI.

(Madame d'Arblay to Dr. Burney.) Bookham, April, 1794. What a charming letter was your last, my dearest father How full of interesting anecdote and enlivening detail! The meeting with Mrs. Thrale, so surrounded by her family, made me breathless; and while you were conversing with the Signor, and left me in doubt whether you advanced to her or not, I almost gasped with impatience and revived old feelings, which, presently, you reanimated to almost all their original energy How like my dearest father to find all his kindness rekindled when her ready hand once more invited it! I heard her voice in, "Why here's Dr. Burney, as young as ever!" and my dear father in his parrying answers. (112) No scene could have been related to me more interesting or more welcome. My heart and hand, I am sure, would have met her in the same manner. The friendship was too pleasant in its first stage, and too strong in its texture, to be ever obliterated, though it has been tarnished and clouded. I wish few things more earnestly than again to meet her.

M. D'ARDLAY AS A GARDENER.

(Madame d'Arblay to Dr. Burney.) (113) Bookham, August, '94. It is just a week since I had the greatest gratification of its kind I ever, I think, experienced:—so kind a thought, so sweet a surprise as was my dearest father's visit! How softly and soothingly it has rested upon my mind ever since!

"Abdolomine"(114) has no regret but that his garden was not in better order; he was a little piqu,, he confesses, that you said it was not very neat—and, to be shor! O but his passion is to do great works: he undertakes with pleasure, pursues with energy, and finishes with spirit; but, then, all is over! He thinks the business once done always done; and to repair, and amend, and weed, and cleanse—O, these are drudgeries insupportable to him!

However, you should have seen the place before he began his operations, to do him justice; there was then nothing else but mauvaises herbes; now, you must at least allow there is a mixture of flowers and grain! I wish you had seen him yesterday, mowing down our hedge—with his sabre, and with an air and attitudes so military, that, if he had been hewing down other legions than those he encountered—ie, of spiders—he could scarcely have had a mien more tremendous, or have demanded an arm more mighty. Heaven knows, I am "the most contente personne in the world" to see his sabre so employed!

A NOVEL AND A TRAGEDY.

You spirited me on in all ways; for this week past I have taken tightly to the grand ouvrage. (115) If I go on so a little longer, I doubt not but M. d'Arblay will begin settling where to have a new shelf for arranging it! which is already in his rumination for Metastasio; (116) I imagine you now. Seriously resuming that work; I hope to see further sample ere long.

We think with very great pleasure of accepting my mother's and your kind invitation for a few days. I hope and mean, if possible, to bring with me also a little sample of something less in the dolorous style than what always causes your poor shoulders a little Shrug. (117) . . .

How truly grieved was I to hear from Mr. Locke of the death of young Mr. Burke! (118) What a dreadful blow upon his father and mother! to come at the instant of the son's highest and most honourable advancement, and of the father's retreat to the bosom of his family from public life! His brother, too, gone so lately! I am most sincerely sorry, indeed, and quite shocked, as there seemed so little suspicion of such an event's approach, by your account of the joy caused by Lord Fitzwilliam's kindness. Pray tell me if you hear how poor Mr. Burke and his most amiable wife endure this calamity, and how they are. . . .

(Madame d'Arblay to Mrs.—.) Bookham, April 15, 1795. So dry a reproof from so dear a friend! And do you, then, measure my regard of heart by my remissness of hand? Let me give you the short history of my tragedy, (119) fairly and frankly. I wrote it not, as your acquaintance imagined, for the stage, nor yet for the press. I began it at Kew palace, and, at odd moments, I finished it at Windsor; without the least idea of any species of publication.

Since I left the royal household, I ventured to let it be read by my father, Mr. and Mrs. Locke, my sister Phillips, and, of course, M. d'Arblay, and not another human being. Their opinions led to what followed, and my brother, Dr. Charles, showed it to Mr. Kemble while I was on my visit to my father last October. He instantly and warmly pronounced for its acceptance, but I knew not when Mr. Sheridan would see it, and had not the smallest expectation of its appearing this year. However, just three days before my beloved little infant came into the world, an express arrived from my brother, that Mr. Kemble wanted the tragedy immediately, in order to show it to Mr. Sheridan, who had just heard of it, and had spoken in the most flattering terms of his good will for its reception.

Still, however, I was in doubt of its actual acceptance till three weeks after my confinement, when I had a visit from my brother, who told me he was, the next morning, to read the piece in the green-room. This was a precipitance for which I was every way unprepared, as I had never made but one copy of the play, and had intended divers corrections and alterations. Absorbed, however, by my new charge and then growing ill, I had a sort of indifference about the matter, which, in fact, has lasted ever since.

The moment I was then able to hold a pen I wrote two short letters, to acknowledge the state of the affair to my sisters - and to one of these epistles I had an immediate laughing answer, informing me my confidence was somewhat of the latest, as the subject of it was already in all the newspapers! I was extremely chagrined at this intelligence; but, from that time, thought it all too late to be the herald of my own designs. And this, added to my natural and incurable dislike to enter upon these egotistical details unasked, has caused my silence to my dear M—, and to every friend I possess. Indeed, speedily after, I had an illness so severe and so dangerous, that for full seven weeks the tragedy was neither named nor thought of by M. d'Arblay or myself.

The piece was represented to the utmost disadvantage, save only Mrs. Siddons and Mr. Kemble - for it was not written with any idea of the stage, and my illness and weakness, and constant absorbment, at the time of its preparation, occasioned it to appear with so many undramatic effects, from my inexperience of theatrical requisites and demands, that, when I saw it, I myself perceived a thousand things I wished to change. The performers, too, were cruelly imperfect, and made blunders I blush to have pass for mine, added to what belong to me. The most important character after the hero and heroine had but two lines of his part by heart! He made all the rest at random, and such nonsense as put all the other actors out as much as himself; so that a more wretched Performance, except Mrs. Siddons, Mr. Kemble, and Mr. Bensley, could not be exhibited in a barn. All this concurred to make it very desirable to withdraw the piece for alterations, which I have done.

(Dr. Burney to Madame d'Arblay.) May 7, 1795. One of my dinners, since my going out, was at Charlotte's, with the good Hooles. After dinner Mr. Cumberland came in, and was extremely courteous, and seemingly friendly, about you and your piece. He took me aside from Mrs. Paradise, who had fastened on me and held me tight by an account of her own and Mr. paradise's complaints, so circumstantially narrated, that not a stop so short as a comma occurred in more than an hour, while I was civilly waiting for a full period. Mr. Cumberland expressed his sorrow at what had happened at Drury-lane, and said that, if he had had the honour of knowing you sufficiently, he would have told you d'avance what would happen, by what he had heard behind the scenes. The players seem to have given the play an ill name. But, he says, if you would go to work again, by reforming this, or work with your best powers at a new plan, and would submit it to his inspection, he would, from the experience he has had, risk his life on its success. This conversation I thought too curious not to be mentioned. . . .

HASTINGS' ACQUITTAL. DR. BURNEY'S METASTASIO.

Well, but how does your Petit and pretty monsieur do? 'Tis pity you and M. d'Arblay don't like him, poor thing! And how does horticulture thrive? This is a delightful time of the year for your Floras and your Linnaei: I envy the life of a gardener in spring, particularly in fine weather.

And so dear Mr. Hastings is honourably acquitted! (120) and I visited him the next morning, and we cordially shook hands. I had luckily left my name at his door as soon as I was able to go out, and before it was generally expected that he would be acquitted. . . .

The young Lady Spencer and I are become very thick, I have dined with her at Lady Lucan's, and met her at the blue parties there. She has invited me to her box at the opera, to her house in St James's Place, and at the Admiralty, whither the family removed last Saturday, and she says I must come to her the 15th, 22nd, and 29th of this month, when I shall see a huge assembly. Mrs. Crewe says all London will be there. She is a pleasant, lively, and comical creature, with more talents and discernment than are expected from a character si folftre. My lord is not only the handsomest and the best intentioned man in the kingdom, but at present the most useful and truly patriotic. And then, he has written to Vienna for Metastasio's three inedited volumes, which I so much want ere I advance too far in the press for them to be of any use.

I am halooed on prodigiously in my Metastasio mania. All the critics—Warton, Twining, Nares, and Dr. Charles—say that his "Estratto dell' Arte Poetica d'Aristotile," which I am now translating, is the best piece of dramatic criticism that has ever been written. "Bless my heart!" says Warton, "I, that have been all my life defending the three unities, am overset." "Ay," quoth I, "has not he made you all ashamed of 'em? You learned folks are only theorists in theatrical matters, but Metastasio had sixty years' successful practice. There!—Go to." My dear Fanny, before you write another play, you must read Aristotle and Horace, as expounded by my dear Metastasio. But, basta. You know when I take up a favourite author, as a Johnson, a Haydn, or a Metastasio, I do not soon lay him down or let him be run down. . . .

Here it strikes three o'clock: the post knell, not bell, tolls here, and I must send off my scrib: but I will tell you, though I need not, that, now I have taken up Metastasio again, I work at him in every uninterrupted moment. I have this morning attempted his charming pastoral, in "il Re Pastore." I'll give you the translation, because the last stanza is a portrait:—

To meadows, woods, and fountains
Our tender flocks I'll lead;
In meads beneath the mountains
My love shall see them feed.

Our simple narrow mansion
Will suit our station well;
There's room for heart expansion
And peace and joy to dwell.

BABY D'ARBLAY. THE WITHDRAWN TRAGEDY.

(From Madame d'Arblay to Dr. Burney) Hermitage, Bookham, May 13, 1795. As you say, 'tis pity M. d'A, and his rib should have conceived such an antipathy to the petit monsieur! O if you could see him now! My mother would be satisfied, for his little cheeks are beginning to favour of the trumpeter's, and Esther would be satisfied, for he eats like an embryo alderman. He enters into all we think, say, mean, and wish! His eyes are sure to sympathise in all our affairs and all our feelings. We find some kind reason for every smile he bestows upon us, and some generous and disinterested Motive for every grave look.

If he wants to be danced, we see he has discovered that his gaiety is exhilarating to us; if he refuses to be moved, we take notice that he fears to fatigue us. If he will not be quieted without singing, we delight in his early go—t for les beaux arts. If he is immovable to all we can devise to divert him, we are edified by the grand sirieux of his dignity and philosophy: if he makes the house ring with loud acclaim because his food, at first call, does not come ready warm into his mouth, we hold up our hands with admiration at his vivacity.

Your conversation with Mr. Cumberland astonished me. I certainly think his experience of stage effect, and his interest with players, so important, as almost instantly to wish putting his sincerity to the proof. How has he got these two characters—one, of Sir Fretful Plagiary, detesting all works but those he owns, and all authors but himself—the other, of a man too perfect even to know or conceive the vices of the world, such as he is painted by Goldsmith in "Retaliation?" And which of these characters is true? (121)

I am not at all without thoughts of a future revise of "Edwy and Elgiva," for which I formed a plan on the first night, from what occurred by the representation. And let me own to you, when you commend my "bearing so well a theatrical drubbing," I am by no means enabled to boast I bear it with conviction of my utter failure. The piece was certainly not heard, and therefore not really judged. The audience finished with an unmixed applause on hearing it was withdrawn for alterations, and I have considered myself in the publicly accepted situation of having at my own option to let the piece die, or attempt its resuscitation, its reform, as Mr. Cumberland calls it. However, I have not given one moment to the matter since my return to the Hermitage. F. D'A.

PS—I should he very glad to hear good news of the revival of Mr. Burke. Have you ever seen him since this fatality in his family? I am glad, nevertheless with all my heart, of Mr. Hastings's honourable acquittal.

"CAMILLA."

(Madame d'Arblay to Mrs.—.) Bookham, June 15, '95, Let me hasten to tell you something of myself that I shall be very sorry you should hear from any other, as your too susceptible mind would be hurt again, and that would grieve me quite to the heart.

I have a long work, which a long time has been in hand, that I mean to publish soon—in about a year. Should it succeed, like 'Evelina' and 'Cecilia,' it may be a little portion to our Bambino. We wish, therefore, to print it for ourselves in this hope; but the expenses of the press are so enormous, so raised by these late Acts, that it is out of all question for us to afford it. We have, therefore, been led by degrees to listen to counsel of some friends, and to print it by subscription. This is in many—many ways unpleasant and unpalatable to us both; but the real chance of real use and benefit to Our little darling overcomes all scruples, and therefore, to work we go!

You will feel, I dare believe, all I could write on this Subject; I once rejected such a plan, formed for me by Mr. Burke, where books were to be kept by ladies, not booksellers, the Duchess of Devonshire, Mrs. Boscawen, and Mrs. Crewe; but I was an individual then, and had no cares of times to come: now, thank heaven! this is not the case;—and when I look at my little boy's dear, innocent, yet intelligent face, I defy any pursuit to be painful that may lead to his good.

(Madame d'Arblay to Dr. Burney.) Bookham, June 18, '95. All our deliberations made, even after your discouraging calculations, we still mean to hazard the publishing by subscription. And, indeed, I had previously determined, when I. changed my state, to set aside all my innate and original abhorrences, and to regard and use as resources, myself, what had always been considered as such by others. Without this idea, and this resolution, our hermitage must have been madness. . . .

I like well the idea of giving no name at all, why should not I have my mystery as well as "Udolpho?" (122) but, " now, don't fly, Dr. Burney! I own I do not like calling it a novel; it gives so simply the notion of a mere love-story, that I recoil a little from it. I mean this work to be sketches of characters and morals put in action, not a romance. I remember the word "novel" was long in the way of 'Cecilia,' as I was told at the queen's house; and it was not permitted to be read by the princesses till sanctioned by a bishop's recommendation, the late Dr. Ross of Exeter.

Will you then suffer mon amour Propre to be saved by the proposals running thus?—Proposals for printing by subscription, in six volumes duodecimo, a new work by the author of "Evelina" and "Cecilia."

How grieved I am you do not like my heroine's name! (123) the prettiest in nature! I remember how many people did not like that of "Evelina," and called it "affected" and "missish," till they read the book, and then they got accustomed in a few pages, and afterwards it was much approved. I must leave this for the present untouched; for the force of the name attached by the idea of the character, in the author's mind, is such, that I should not know how to sustain it by any other for a long while. In "Cecilia" and "Evelina" 'twas the same: the names of all the personages annexed, with me, all the ideas I put in motion with them. The work is so far advanced, that the personages are all, to me, as so many actual acquaintances, whose memoirs and opinions I am committing to paper. I will make it the best I can, my dearest father. I will neither be indolent, nor negligent, nor avaricious. I can never half answer the expectations that seem excited. I must try to forget them, or I shall be in a continual quivering.

Mrs. Cooke, my excellent neighbour, came in Just now to read me a paragraph of a letter from Mrs. Leigh, of Oxfordshire, her sister. . . . After much of civility about the new work and its author, it finishes thus:—"Mr. Hastings I saw just now: I told him what was going forward; he gave a great jump, and exclaimed, 'Well, then, now I can serve her, thank Heaven, and I will! I will write to Anderson to engage Scotland, and I will attack the East Indies myself!'" F. D'A.

P.S. The Bambino is half a year old this day. N.B. I have not heard the Park or Tower guns. I imagine the wind did not set right.

AN INVITATION TO THE HERMITAGE.

(Madame d"Arblay to the Comte de Narbonne. (124)] Bookham, 26th December, 1795. What a letter, to terminate so long and painful a silence! It has penetrated us with sorrowing and indignant feelings. Unknown to M. d'Arblay whose grief and horror are upon point of making him quite ill, I venture this address to his most beloved friend; and before I seal it I will give him the option to burn or underwrite it. I shall be brief in what I have to propose: sincerity need not be loquacious, and M. de Narbonne is too kind to demand phrases for ceremony.

Should your present laudable but melancholy plan fail, and should nothing better offer, or till something can be arranged, will you dear Sir, condescend to share the poverty of our hermitage? Will you take a little cell under our rustic roof, and fare as we fare? What to us two hermits is cheerful and happy, will to you, indeed, be miserable but it will be some solace to the goodness of your heart to witness our contentment;—to dig with M. d'A. in the garden will be of service to your health; to muse sometimes with me in the parlour will be a relaxation to your mind. You will not blush to own your little godson. Come, then, and give him your blessing; relieve the wounded feelings of his father—oblige his mother—and turn hermit at Bookham, till brighter suns invite you elsewhere. F. D'ARBLAY.

You will have terrible dinners, alas!—but your godson comes in for the dessert. (125)

PRESENTATION OF "CAMILLA" AT WINDSOR.

[During the years 1794 and 1795, Madame d'Arblay finished and prepared for the press her third novel, "Camilla," which was published partly by subscription in 1796 the dowager Duchess of Leinster, the Hon. Mrs. Boscawen, Mrs. Crewe, and Mrs. Locke, kindly keeping lists, and receiving the names of subscribers.

This work having been dedicated by permission to the queen, the authoress was desirous of presenting the first copy to her majesty, and made a journey to Windsor for that honour.)

(Madame d'Arblay to Dr. Burney.) Bookham, July 10, 1796. If I had as much of time as of matter, my dear father, what an immense letter should I write you! But I have still so many book oddments of accounts, examinations, directions, and little household affairs to arrange, that, with baby-kissing, included, I expect I can give you to-day only part the first of an excursion which I mean to comprise in four parts: so here begins.

The books were ready at eleven or twelve, but not so the tailor! The three Miss Thrales came to a short but cordial hand-shaking at the last minute, by appointment; and at about half-past three we set forward. I had written the day before to my worthy old friend Mrs. Agnew, the housekeeper, erst, of my revered Mrs. Delany, to secure us rooms for one day and night, and to Miss Planta to make known I could not set out till late.

When we came into Windsor at seven o'clock, the way to Mrs. Agnew's was so intricate that we could not find it, till one of the king's footmen recollecting me, I imagined, came forward, a volunteer, and walked by the side of the chaise to show the postilion the house.—N.B. No bad omen to worldly augurers.

Arrived, Mrs. Agnew came forth with faithful attachment, to conduct us to our destined lodgings. I wrote hastily to Miss Planta, to announce to the queen that I was waiting the honour of her majesty's commands; and then began preparing for my appearance the next morning, when I expected a summons, but Miss Planta came instantly herself from the queen, with orders of immediate attendance, as her majesty would see me directly! The king was just gone upon the Terrace, but her majesty did not walk that evening.

Mrs. Agnew was my maid, Miss Planta my arranger; my landlord, who was a hairdresser, came to my head, and M. d'Arblay was general superintendent. The haste and the joy went hand in hand, and I was soon equipped, though shocked at my own precipitance in sending before I was already visible. Who, however, could have expected such prompt admission? and in an evening?

M. d'Arblay helped to carry the books as far as to the gates. My lodgings were as near to them as possible. At our first entry towards the Queen's lodge we encountered Dr. Fisher and his lady: the sight of me there, in a dress announcing indisputably whither I was hieing, was such an Astonishment, that they looked at me rather as a recollected spectre than a renewed acquaintance. When we came to the iron rails poor Miss Planta, in much fidget, begged to take the books from M. d'Arblay, terrified, I imagine, lest French feet should contaminate the gravel within!—while he, innocent of her fears, was insisting upon carrying them as far as to the house, till he saw I took part with Miss Planta, and he was then compelled to let us lug in ten volumes as we could.

The king was already returned from the Terrace, the page told us." O, then," said Miss Planta, "you are too late!" However, I went into my old dining-parlour; while she said she would see if any one could obtain the queen's commands for another time. I did not stay five minutes ruminating upon the dinners, "gone where the chickens," etc, when Miss Planta return and told me the queen would see me instantly.

The queen was in her dressing-room, and with only the Princess Elizabeth. Her reception was the Most gracious. yet, when she saw my emotion in thus meeting her again; she herself was by no means quite unmoved. I presented my little—yet not small— offering, upon one knee placing them, as she directed, upon a table by her side, and expressing, as well as I could, my devoted gratitude for her invariable goodness to me. She then began a conversation, in her old style, upon various things and people, with all her former graciousness of manner, which soon, as she perceived my strong sense of her indulgence, grew into even all its former kindness. Particulars I have now no room for; but when in about half an hour, she said, "How long do you intend to stay here, Madame d'Arblay?" and I answered, "We have no intentions, ma'am," she repeated, laughing, "You have no intentions!—Well, then, if you can come again to-morrow Morning, you shall see the princesses."

She then said she would not detain me at present; encouraged by all that had passed, I asked if I might presume to put at the door of the king's apartment a copy of MY little work. She hesitated, but with smiles the most propitious; then told me to fetch the books - and whispered something to the Princess Elizabeth, who left the room by another door at the same moment that I retired for the other set. Almost immediately upon my return to the queen and the Princess Elizabeth, the king entered the apartment, and entered it to receive himself my little offering.

"Madame d'Arblay," said her majesty, "tells me that Mrs. Boscawen is to have the third set; but the first—Your majesty will excuse me—is mine."

This was not, you will believe, thrown away upon me. The king, smiling, said, "Mrs Boscawen, I hear, has been very zealous."

I confirmed this. and the Princess Elizabeth eagerly called out, "Yes, sir! and while Mrs. Boscawen kept a copy for Madame d'Arblay, the Duchess of Beaufort kept one for Mrs. Boscawen."

This led to a little discourse upon the business, in which the king's countenance seemed to speak a benign interest; and the queen then said, "This book was begun here, sir." Which already I had mentioned.

"And what did you write of it here?" cried he. "How far did You go?—Did You finish any part? or only form the skeleton?"

"Just that, sir," I answered; "the skeleton was formed here, but nothing was completed. I worked it up in my little cottage."

"And about what time did You give to it?"

"All my time, sir; from the Period I planned publishing it, I devoted myself to it wholly. I had no episode but a little baby. My subject grew Upon me, and increased my materials to a bulk that I am afraid will be more laborious to wade through for the reader than for the writer."

"Are you much frightened cried he, smiling, "as much frightened as you were before?"

"I have hardly had time to know yet, sir. I received the fair sheets of the last volume only last night. I have, therefore, had no leisure for fear. And sure I am, happen what May to the book from the critics, it can never cause me pain in any proportion with the pleasure and happiness I owe to it." I am sure I spoke most sincerely and he looked kindly to believe me.

He asked if Mr. Locke had seen it; and when I said no, he seemed comically pleased, as if desirous to have it in its first state. He asked next if Dr. Burney had overlooked it; and, upon the same answer, looked with the same satisfaction. He did not imagine how it would have passed Current with my dearest father: he appeared Only to be glad it would be a genuine work: but, laughingly, said, "So you kept it quite snug?"

"Not intentionally, sir, but from my situation and my haste; I should else have been very happy to have consulted my father and Mr. Locke; but I had so much, to the last moment, to write, that I literally had not a moment to hear what could be said. The work is longer by the whole fifth Volume than I had first planned; and I am almost ashamed to look at its size, and afraid my readers would have been more obliged to me if I had left so much out than for putting So much in."

He laughed and inquired who corrected my proofs? 'Only myself," I answered.

"Why, some authors have told me," cried he, "that they are the last to do that work for themselves. They know so well by heart what ought to be, that they run on without seeing what is. They have told me, besides, that a mere plodding head is best and surest for that work; and that the livelier the imagination, the less it should be trusted to."

I must not go on thus minutely, or my four parts will be forty. But a full half-hour of graciousness, I could almost call kindness, was accorded me, though the king came from the concert to grant it; and it broke up by the queen saying, "I have told Madame d'Arblay that, if she can come again to-morrow, she shall see the princesses."

The king bowed gently to my grateful obeisance for this offer, and told me I should not know the Princess Amelia, she was so much grown, adding, "She is taller than you!"

I expressed warmly my delight in the permission of Seeing their royal highnesses, and their majesties returned to the concert-room. The Princess Elizabeth stayed, -and flew up to me, crying, "How glad I am to see you here again, my dear Miss Burney!—I beg your pardon,—Madame d'Arblay I mean, but I always call all my friends by their maiden names when I first see them after they are married."

I warmly now opened upon my happiness in this return to all their sights, and the condescension and sweetness with which it was granted me - and confessed I could hardly behave prettily and properly at my first entrance after so long an absence. "O, I assure you I felt for you!" cried she; "I thought you must be agitated; it was so natural to you to come here-to mamma!"

You will believe, my dearest father, how light-hearted and full of glee I went back to my expecting companion: Miss Planta accompanied me, and stayed the greatest part of the little remaining evening, promising to let me know at what hour I should wait upon their royal highnesses.

A CONVERSATION WITH THE QUEEN.

The next morning, at eight or nine o'clock, my old footman, Moss, came with Mlle, Jacobi's compliments to M. and Madame d'Arblay, and an invitation to dine at the Queen's lodge.

Miss Planta arrived at ten, with her majesty's commands that I should be at the Queen's lodge at twelve. I stayed meanwhile, with good Mrs. Agnew, and M. d'Arblay made acquaintance with her worthy husband, who is a skilful and famous botanist, and lately made gardener to the queen for Frogmore, so M. d'Arblay consulted him about our cabbages! and so, if they have not now a high flavour, we are hopeless.

At eleven M. d'Arblay again ventured to esquire me to the rails round the lodge, whence I showed him my ci-devant apartment, which he languished to view nearer. I made a visit to Mlle. Jacobi, who is a very good creature, and with whom I remained very comfortably till her majesty and the princesses returned from Frogmore, where they had passed two or three hours. Almost immediately I was summoned to the queen by one of the pages.

She was just seated to her hair-dresser. She conversed upon various public and general topics till the friseur was dismissed, and then I was honoured with an audience, quite alone, for a full hour and a half. During this, nothing could be more gracious than her whole manner, and The particulars, as there was no pause, would fill a duodecimo volume at least. Among them was Mr. Windham, whom she named with great favour; and gave me the opportunity of expressing my delight upon his belonging to the government. We had so often conversed about him during the accounts I had related of Mr. Hastings's trial, that there was much to say upon the acquisition to the administration, and my former round assertions of his goodness of heart and honour. She inquired how you did, my dearest father, with an air of great kindness and, when I said well, looked pleased, as she answered, "I was afraid he was ill, for I saw him but twice last year at our music."

She then gave me an account of the removal of the concert to the Haymarket since the time I was admitted to it. She then talked of some books and authors, but found me wholly in the Clouds as to all that is new. She then said, "What a very pretty book Dr. Burney has brought out upon Metastasio! I am very much pleased with it. Pray (smiling) what will he bring out next?"

"As yet, madam, I don't know of any new plan."

"But he will bring out something else?"

"Most probably, but he will rest a little first, I fancy."

"Has he nothing in hand?"

"Not that I now know of, madam."

"O but he soon will!" cried she, again smiling.

"He has so active a mind, ma'am, that I believe it quite impossible to him to be utterly idle, but, indeed, I know of no present design being positively formed."

We had then some discourse upon the new connexion at Norbury park—the Fitzgeralds, etc.; and from this she led to various topics of our former conferences, both in persons and things, and gave me a full description of her new house at Frogmore, its fitting up, and the share of each princess in its decoration. She spoke with delight of its quiet and ease, and her enjoyment of its complete retirement. "I spend," she cried, "there almost constantly all my mornings. I rarely come home but just before dinner, merely to dress, but to-day I came sooner."

This was said in a manner so flattering, I could scarce forbear the air of thanking her, however, I checked the expression, though I could not the inference which urged it.

WITH THE PRINCESS ROYAL AND PRINCESS AUGUSTA.

At two o'clock the Princess Elizabeth appeared. "Is the princess royal ready?" said the queen. She answered, "Yes:" and her majesty then told me I might go to her, adding, "You know the way, Madame d'Arblay." And, thus licensed, I went to the apartment of her royal highness up stairs. She was just quitting it. She received me most graciously, and told me she was going to sit for her picture, if I would come and stay with her while she sat. Miss Bab Planta was in attendance, to read during this period. The princess royal ordered me a chair facing her; and another for Miss Bab and her book, which, however, was never opened. The painter was Mr. Dupont. (126) She was very gay and very charming, full of lively discourse and amiable condescension.

In about an hour the Princess Augusta came in: she addressed me with her usual sweetness, and, when she had looked at her sister's portrait, said, "Madame d'Arblay, when the princess royal can spare you, I hope you will come to me," as she left the room. I did not flout her; and when I had been an hour with the princess royal, she told me she would keep me no longer from Augusta, and Miss Planta came to conduct me to the latter. This lovely princess received me quite alone; Miss Planta only shut me in, and she then made me sit by her, and kept me in most bewitching discourse more than an hour. She has a gaiety, a charm about her, that is quite resistless: and much of true, genuine, and very original humour. She related to me the history of all the feats, and exploits, and dangers, and escapes of her brothers during last year; rejoicing in their safety, yet softly adding, "Though these trials and difficulties did them a great deal of good."

We talked a little of France, and she inquired of me what I knew of the late unhappy queen, through M. d'Arblay; and spoke of her with the most virtuous discrimination between her foibles and her really great qualities, with her most barbarous end. She then dwelt upon Madame Royale, saying, in her unaffected manner, "It's very odd one never hears what sort of girl she is." I told her all I had gathered from M. d'Arblay. She next spoke of my Bambino, indulging me in recounting his faits et gestes; and never moved till the princess royal came to summon her. They were all to return to Frogmore to dinner. "We have detained Madame d'Arblay between us the whole morning," said the princess royal, with a gracious smile. "Yes," cried Princess Augusta, "and I am afraid I have bored her to death; but when once I begin upon my poor brothers, I can never stop without telling all my little bits of glory." She then outstayed the princess royal to tell me that, when she was at Plymouth, at church, she saw so many officers' wives, and sisters, and mothers, helping their maimed husbands, or brothers, or sons, that she could not forbear whispering to the queen, "Mamma, how lucky it is Ernest is just come so seasonably with that wound in his face! I should have been quite shocked, else, not to have had one little bit of glory among ourselves!"

When forced away from this sweet creature, I went to Mlle. Jacobi, who said, "But where is M. d'Arblay?" Finding it too late for me to go to my lodging to dress before dinner I wrote him a word, which immediately brought him to the Queen's lodge: and there I shall leave my dear father the pleasure of seeing us, mentally, at dinner, at my ancient table, both invited by the queen's commands. Miss Gomme was asked to meet me, and the repast was extremely pleasant.

A PRESENT FROM THE KING AND QUEEN.

just before we assembled to dinner Mlle. Jacobi desired to speak with me alone, and, taking me to another room, presented me with a folded little packet, saying, "The queen ordered me to put this into your hands, and said, 'Tell Madame d'Arblay it is from us both.'" It was a hundred guineas. I was confounded, and nearly sorry, so little was such a mark of their goodness in my thoughts. She added that the king, as soon as he came from the chapel in the morning, went to the queen's dressing-room just before he set out for the levee, and put into her hands fifty guineas, saying, "This is for my set!" The queen answered, "I shall do exactly the same for mine," and made up the packet herself. "'Tis only,' she said, 'for the paper, tell Madame d'Arblay, nothing for the trouble!'" meaning she accepted that.

The manner of this was so more than gracious, so kind, in the words us both, that indeed the money at the time was quite nothing in the scale of my gratification; it was even less, for it almost pained me. However, a delightful thought that in a few minutes occurred made all light and blithesome. "We will come, then," I cried, "once a year to Windsor, to walk the Terrace, and see the king, queen, and sweet princesses. This will enable us, and I shall never again look forward to so long a deprivation of their sight." This, with my gratitude for their great goodness, was what I could not refrain commissioning her to report.

CURIOSITY REGARDING M. D'ARBLAY.

Our dinner was extremely cheerful; all my old friends were highly curious to see M. d'Arblay, who was in spirits, and, as he could address them in French, and at his ease, did not seem much disapproved of by them. I went to my lodging afterwards to dress, where I told my monsieur this last and unexpected stroke, which gave him exactly my sensations, and we returned to tea. We had hopes of the Terrace, as my monsieur was quite eager to see all this beloved royal House. The weather, however, was very unpromising. The king came from the lodge during our absence; but soon after we were in the levee three royal coaches arrived from Frogmore: in the first was the queen, the Princesses Royal and Augusta, and some lady in waiting. M. d'Arblay stood beside me at a window to see them; her majesty looked up and bowed to me, and, upon her alighting, she looked up again. This, I am sure, was to see M. d'Arblay, who could not be doubted, as he wore his croix the whole time he was at Windsor. The princesses bowed also, and the four younger, who followed, all severally kissed their hands to me, and fixed their eyes on my companion with an equal expression of kindness and curiosity; he therefore saw them perfectly.

THE KING APPROVES THE DEDICATION OF "CAMILLA."

In a few minutes a page came to say, "The princesses desire to see Madame d'Arblay," and he conducted me to the apartment of the Princess Elizabeth, which is the most elegantly and fancifully ornamented of any in the lodge, as she has most delight and most taste in producing good effects.

Here the fair owner of the chamber received me, encircled with the Princesses Mary and Amelia, and no attendant. They were exactly as I had left them—kind, condescending, open, and delightful; and the goodness of the queen, in sparing them all to me thus, without any allay of ceremony, or géne of listening Mutes, I felt most deeply.

They were all very gay, and I not very sad, so we enjoyed A perfectly easy and even merry half-hour in divers discourses, in which they recounted to me who had been most anxious about "the book," and doubted not its great success, as everybody was so eager about it. "And I must tell you one thing," Cried the Princess Elizabeth; "the king is very much pleased with the dedication."

This was, you will be sure, a very touching hearing to me; And Princess Mary exclaimed, "And he is very difficult!"

"O, yes, he's hardly ever pleased with a dedication," cried one of the princesses. "He almost always thinks them so fulsome."

"I was resolved I would tell it you," cried Princess Elizabeth.

Can you imagine anything more amiable than this pleasure in giving pleasure?

A DELICIOUS CHAT WITH THE PRINCESSES.

Soon after the Princess Augusta came in, smiling and lovely. Princess royal next appeared Princess Augusta sat down, and charged me to take a chair next her. Princess royal did not stay long, and soon returned to summon her sister Augusta downstairs, as the concert was begun: but she replied she could not come yet: and the princess royal went alone. We had really a most delicious chat then.

They made a thousand inquiries about my book, and when and where it was written, etc, and how I stood as to fright and fidget. I answered all with openness, and frankly related my motives for the publication. Everything of housekeeping, I told them, was nearly doubled in price at the end of the first year and half of our marriage, and we found it impossible to continue so near our friends and the capital with our limited income, though M. d'A. had accommodated himself completely, and even happily, to every species of economy, and though my dearest father had capitally assisted us; I then, therefore, determined upon adopting a plan I had formerly rejected, of publishing by subscription. I told them the former history of that plan, as Mr. Burke's, and many particulars that seemed extremely to interest them. My garden, our way of life, our house, our Bambino, all were inquired after and related. I repeatedly told them the strong desire M. d'Arblay had to be regaled with a sight of all their House -a House to which I stood so every way indebted, and they looked kindly concerned that the weather admitted no prospect of the Terrace.

I mentioned to the Princess Augusta my recent new obligation to their majesties, and my amaze and even shame at their goodness.

"O, I am sure," cried she, "they were very happy to have it in their power."

"Yes, and we were so glad!"

"So glad!" echoed each of the others.

"How enchanted should I have been," cried I, "to have presented my little book to each of your royal highnesses if I had dared! or if, after her majesty has looked it over, I might hope for such a permission, how proud and how happy it would make me!"

"O, I daresay you may," cried the Princess Augusta, eagerly. I then intimated how deeply I should feel such an honour, if it might be asked, after her majesty had read it - and the Princess Elizabeth gracefully undertook the office. She related to me, in a most pleasant manner, the whole of her own recent transaction, its rise and cause and progress, in "The Birth of Love:" (127) but I must here abridge, or never have done. I told them all my scheme for coming again next July, which they sweetly seconded. Princess Amelia assured me she had not forgotten me; and when another summons came for the concert, Princess Augusta, comically sitting still and holding me by her side, called out, "Do you little ones go!"

But they loitered also, and we went on, on, on, with our chat,—they as unwilling as myself to break it up, till staying longer was impossible; and then, in parting, they all expressed the kindest pleasure in our newly-adopted plan of a yearly visit.

"And pray," cried Princess Elizabeth, "write again immediately!"

"O, no," cried Princess Augusta, "wait half a year—to rest; and then—increase your family—all ways!"

"The queen," said Princess Elizabeth, "consulted me which way she should read 'Camilla-' whether quick, at once, or comfortably at Weymouth: so I answered, 'Why, mamma, I think, as you will be so much interested in the book, Madame d'Arblay would be most pleased you should read it now at once, quick, that nobody may be mentioning the events before You come to them, and then again at Weymouth, slow and comfortably.'"

In going, the sweet Princess Augusta loitered last but her youngest sister, Amelia, who came to take my hand when the rest were departed, and assure me she should never forget Me.

We spent the remnant of Wednesday evening with my old friends, determining to quit Windsor the next day, if the weather did not promise a view of the royal family upon the Terrace for M. d'Arblay.

THE KING NOTICES M. D'ARBLAY.

Thursday morning was lowering, and we determined upon departing, after only visiting some of my former acquaintances. 'We met Miss Planta in our way to the lodge, and took leave; but when we arrived at Mlle. Jacobi's we found that the queen expected we should stay for the chance of the Terrace, and had told Mlle. Jacobi to again invite us to dinner. . . .

We left the friendly Miss Goldsworthy for other visits; first to good old Mrs. Planta; next to the very respectable Dr. Fisher and his wife. The former insisted upon doing the honours himself of St. George's cathedral to M. d'Arblay which occasioned his seeing that beautiful antique building to the utmost advantage. Dr. Fisher then accompanied us to a spot to show M. d'Arblay Eton in the best view.

Dinner passed as before, but the evening lowered, and hopes of the Terrace were weak, when the Duke and Duchess of York arrived. This seemed to determine against us, as they told us the duchess never went upon the Terrace but in the finest weather, and the royal family did not choose to leave her. We were hesitating therefore whether to set off for Rose Dale, when Mlle. Jacobi gave an intimation to me that the king, herself, and the Princess Amelia, would walk on the Terrace. Thither instantly we hastened, and were joined by Dr. and Mrs. Fisher. The evening was so raw and cold that there was very little company, and scarce any expectation of the royal family and when we had been there about half an hour the musicians retreated, and everybody was preparing to follow, when a messenger suddenly came forward, helter skelter, running after the horns and clarionets, and hallooing to them to return. This brought back the straggling parties, and the King, Duke of York, and six princesses soon appeared.

I have never yet seen M. d'Arblay agitated as at this moment; he could scarce keep his steadiness, or even his ground. The recollections, he has since told me, that rushed upon his mind of his own king and royal House were so violent and so painful as almost to disorder him. His majesty was accompanied by the duke, and Lord Beaulieu, Lord Walsingham, and General Manners; the princesses were attended by Lady Charlotte Bruce, some other lady, and Miss Goldsworthy: The king stopped to speak to the Bishop of Norwich and some others at the entrance, and then walked on towards us, who were at the further end. As he approached, the princess royal said, loud enough to be heard by Mrs. Fisher, "Madame d'Arblay, sir;" and instantly he came on a step, and then stopped and addressed me, and, after a word or two of the weather, he said, "Is that M. d'Arblay?" and most graciously bowed to him and entered into a little conversation; demanding how long he had been in England, how long in the country, etc, and with a sweetness, an air of wishing us well, that will never, never be erased from our hearts.

M. d'Arblay recovered himself immediately Upon this address, and answered with as much firmness as respect.

Upon the king's bowing and leaving US, the commander-in-chief (128) most courteously bowed also to M. d'Arblay, and the princesses all came up to speak to me, and to curtsy to him; and the Princess Elizabeth cried, "I've got leave! and mamma says she won't wait to read it first!"

After this the king and duke never passed without taking off their hats, and the princesses gave me a smile and a curtsy at every turn: Lord Walsingbam came to speak to me, and Mr. Fairly, and General Manners, who regretted that more of our old tea-party were not there to meet me once more.

THE KING AND QUEEN ON "CAMILLA."

As soon as they all re-entered the lodge we followed to take leave of Mlle. Jacobi; but, upon moving towards the passage, the princess royal appeared, saying, "Madame d'Arblay, I come to waylay you!" and made me follow her to the dressing-room, whence the voice of the queen, as the door opened, called out, in mild accents, "Come in, Madame d'Arblay!"

Her majesty was seated at the upper end of the room, with the Duchess of York (129) on her right, and the Princesses Sophia and Amelia on her left. She made me advance, and said, "I have just been telling the Duchess of York that I find her royal highness's name the first Upon this list,"—producing "Camilla."

"Indeed," said the duchess, bowing to me, "I was so very impatient to read it, I could not but try to get it as early as possible. I am very eager for it, indeed!"

"I have read," said the queen, "but fifty pages yet; but I am in great uneasiness for that Poor little girl that I am afraid will get the small-pox! and I am sadly afraid that sweet little other girl will not keep her fortune! but I won't Peep! I read quite fair. But I must tell Madame d'Arblay I know a country gentleman, in Mecklenburg, exactly the very character of that good old man the Uncle!" She seemed to speak as if delighted to meet him upon paper.

The king now came in, and I could not forbear making up to him, to pour forth some part of my full heart for his goodness! He tried to turn away, but it was smilingly; and I had courage to pursue him, for I could not help it. He then slightly bowed it off, and asked the queen to repeat what she had said upon the book.

"O, your majesty," she cried, "I must not anticipate!" yet told him of her pleasure in finding an old acquaintance.

"Well!" cried the king archly, " and what other characters have you seized?"

"None," I protested, "from life."

"O!" cried he, shaking his head, "you must have some!"

"Indeed your majesty will find none!" I cried.

"But they may be a little better, or a little worse," he answered, "but still, if they are not like somebody, how can they play their parts?"

"O, yes, sir," I cried, "as far as general nature goes, or as characters belong to classes, I have certainly tried to take them. But no individuals!"

My account must be endless if I do not now curtail. The Duke of York, the other princesses, General Manners, and all the rest of the group, made way to the room soon after, upon hearing the cheerfulness of the voice of the king, whose graciousness raised me into spirits that set me quite at my ease. He talked much upon the book, and then of Mrs. Delany, and then of various others that my sight brought to his recollection, and all with a freedom and goodness that enabled me to answer without difficulty or embarrassment, and that produced two or three hearty laughs from the Duke of York.

ANECDOTE OF THE DUCHESS OF YORK.

After various other topics, the queen said, "Duchess, Madame d'Arblay is aunt of the pretty little boy (130) you were so good to."

The duchess understood her so immediately that I fancy this was not new to her. She bowed to me again, very smilingly, upon the acknowledgments this encouraged me to offer; and the king asked an explanation.

"Sir," said the duchess, "I was upon the road near Dorking, and I saw a little gig overturned, and a little boy was taken out, and sat down upon the road. I told them to stop and ask if the little boy was hurt, and they said yes, and I asked where he was to go, and they said to a village just a few miles off; so I took him into my coach, Sir, and carried him home."

"And the benedictions, madam," cried I, "of all his family have followed you ever since!"

"And he said your royal highness called him a very pretty boy," cried the queen, laughing, to whom I had related it.

"Indeed, what he said is very true," answered she, nodding.

"Yes; he said," quoth I, again to the queen, "that he saw the duchess liked him."

This again the queen repeated and the duchess again nodded, and pointedly repeated, "It is very true."

"He was a very fine boy-a very fine boy indeed!" cried the king; "what is become of him?"

I was a little distressed in answering, "He is in Ireland, sir."

"In Ireland! What does he do in Ireland? what does he go there for?"

"His father took him, Sir," I was forced to answer.

"And what does his father take him to Ireland for?"

"Because-he is an Irishman, Sir!" I answered, half laughing.

When at length, every one deigning me a bow of leavetaking, their majesties, and sons and daughters, retired to the adjoining room, the Princess Amelia loitered to shake hands, and the Princess Augusta returned for the same condescension, reminding me of my purpose for next year. While this was passing, the princess royal had repaired to the apartment of Mlle. Jacobi, where she had held a little Conversation with M. d'Arblay.

A VISIT TO MRS. BOSCAWEN.

We finished the evening very cheerfully with Mlle. Jacobi and Mlle. Montmoulin, whom she invited to meet us, and the next morning left Windsor and visited Rose Dale. (131) Mrs. Boscawen received us very sweetly, and the little offering as if not at all her due, Mrs. Levison Gower was with her, and showed us Thomson's temple. Mrs. Boscawen spoke of my dearest father with her Usual true sense of how to Speak of him. She invited us to dinner, but we were anxious to return to our Bambino, and M. d'Arblay had, all this time, only fought off being ill with his remnant of cold. Nevertheless, when we came to Twickenham, my good old friend Mr. Cambridge was so cordial and so earnest that we could not resist him, and were pressed in to staying dinner. . . .

At a little before eleven we arrived at our dear cottage, and to our sleeping Bambino.

THE RELATIVE SUCCESS OF MADAME D'ARBLAY'S NOVELS.

(Madame d'Arblay to Dr. Burney.) Bookham, Friday, October, 1796. I meant to have begun with our thanks for my dear kind father's indulgence of our extreme curiosity and interest in the sight of the reviews. I am quite happy in what I have escaped of greater severity, though my mate cannot bear that the palm should be contested by "Evelina" and "Cecilia;" his partiality rates the last as so much the highest; so does the newspaper I have mentioned, of which I long to send you a copy. But those immense men, whose single praise was fame and security—who established, by a word, the two elder sisters-are now silent, Johnson and Sir Joshua are no more, and Mr. Burke is ill, or otherwise engrossed; yet, even without their powerful influence, to which I owe such unspeakable obligation, the essential success of "Camilla" exceeds that of the elders. The sale is truly astonishing. Charles has just sent to me that five hundred only remain of four thousand, and it has appeared scarcely three months.

The first edition of "Evelina" was of eight hundred, the second of five hundred, and the third of a thousand. What the following have been I have never heard. The sale from that period became more flourishing than the publisher cared to announce. Of "Cecilia" the first edition was reckoned enormous at two thousand and as a part of payment Was reserved for it, I remember our dear Daddy Crisp thought it very unfair. It was printed, like this, in July, and sold in October, to every one's wonder. Here, however, the sale's increased in rapidity more than a third. Charles says,—

"Now heed no more what critics thought 'em. Since this you know, all people bought 'em."

A CONTEMPLATED COTTAGE.

We have resumed our original plan, and are going immediately to build a little cottage for ourselves. We shall make it as small and as cheap as will accord with its being warm and comfortable. We have relinquished, however, the very kind offer of Mr. Locke, which he has renewed, for his park. We mean to make this a property saleable or letable for our Alex, and in Mr. Locke's park we could not encroach any tenant, if the Youth's circumstances, profession, or inclination should make him not choose the spot for his own residence. M. dArblay, therefore, has fixed upon a field of Mr. Locke's, which he will rent, and of which Mr. Locke will grant him a lease of ninety years. By this means, we shall leave the little Alex a little property, besides what will be in the funds, and a property likely to rise in value, as the situation of the field is remarkably beautiful. It is in the valley, between Mr. Locke's park and Dorking, and where land is so scarce, that there is not another possessor within many miles who would part, upon any terms, with half-an-acre. My kindest father will come and give it, I trust, his benediction. I am now almost jealous of Bookham for having received it.

Imagine but the ecstasy of M. d'Arblay in training, all his own way, an entire new garden. He dreams now of cabbage-walks, potato-beds, bean-perfumes, and peas-blossoms. My mother should send him a little sketch to help his flower-garden, which will be his second favourite object.

THE PRINCESS ROYAL'S FIRST INTERVIEW WITH HER FIANCE.

(Madame d'Arblay to Mrs. Locke.) 1796. A private letter from Windsor tells me the Prince of Wurtemberg has much pleased in the royal House, by his manner and address upon his interview, but that the poor Princess royal was almost dead with terror, and agitation, and affright, at the first meeting. (132) She could not utter a word. The queen was obliged to speak her answers. The prince said he hoped this first would be the last disturbance his presence would ever occasion her. She then tried to recover, and so far conquered her tumult as to attempt joining in a general discourse from time to time. He paid his court successfully, I am told, to the sisters, who all determine to like him; and the princess royal is quite revived in her spirits again, now this tremendous opening sight is over.

You will be pleased, and my dearest Mr. Locke, at the style of my summons: 'tis so openly from the queen herself, Indeed, she has behaved like an angel to me, from the trying time to her of my marriage with a Frenchman. "So odd, you know," as Lady Inchiquin said.

OPINIONS OF THE REVIEWS ON "CAMILLA."

(Dr. Burney to Madame d'Arblay.) November, 1796. . . . The "Monthly Review" has come in to-day, and it does not satisfy me, or raise my spirits, or anything but my indignation. James has read the remarks in it on "Camilla," and we are all dissatisfied. Perhaps a few of the verbal criticisms may be worth your attention in the second edition; but these have been picked out and displayed with no friendly view, and without necessity, in a work of such length and intrinsic sterling worth. J'enrage! Morbleu!

(Madame d'Arblay to Dr. Burney.) Bookham, November, 1796. I had intended writing to my dearest father by a return of goods, but I find it impossible to defer the overflowings of my heart at his most kind and generous indignation with the reviewer. What censure can ever so much hurt as such compensation can heal? And, in fact, the praise is so strong that, were it neatly put together, the writer might challenge my best enthusiasts to find it insufficient. The truth, however, is, that the criticisms come forward, and the panegyric is entangled, and so blended with blame as to lose almost all effect. The reviews, however, as they have not made, will not, I trust, mar me. "Evelina" made its way all by itself; it was well spoken of, indeed, in all the reviews, compared with general novels, but it was undistinguished by any quotation, and only put in the Monthly Catalogue, and only allowed short single paragraph. It was circulated only by the general public till it reached, through that unbiassed medium, Dr. Johnson and Mr. Burke, and thence it wanted no patron.

Nov. 14. Upon a second reading of the Monthly Review upon "Camilla," I am in far better humour with it, and willing to confess to the criticisms, if I may claim by that concession any right to the eulogies. They are stronger and more important, upon re-perusal, than I had imagined, in the panic of a first survey and an unprepared-for disappointment in anything like severity from so friendly an editor. The recommendation, at the conclusion, of the book as a warning guide to youth, would recompense me, upon the least reflection, for whatever strictures Might precede it. I hope my kind father has not suffered his generous—and to me most cordial—indignation against the reviewer to interfere with his intended answer to the affectionate letter of Dr. Griffiths. (133)

DEATH OF MADAME D'ARBLAY'S STEPMOTHER.

(Madame d'Arblay to Mrs. Phillips.) Bookham, November 7, 1796. Yes, my beloved Susan safe landed at Dublin was indeed all-sufficient for some time; nor, indeed, could I even read any more for many minutes. That, and the single sentence at the end, "My Norbury is with me"—completely overset ne, though only with joy. After your actual safety, nothing could so much touch me as the picture I Instantly viewed of Norbury in Your arms. Yet I shall hope for more detail hereafter.

The last letter I had from you addressed to myself shows me your own sentiment of the fatal event (134) which so speedily followed your departure, and which my dear father has himself announced to you, though probably the newspapers will anticipate his letter. I am very sorry, now, I did not write sooner; but while you were still in England, and travelling so slowly, I had always lurking ideas that disqualified me from writing to Ireland.

The minute I received, from Sally, by our dearest father's desire the last tidings I set out for Chelsea. I was much Shocked by the news, long as it has been but natural to look forward to it. My better part spoke even before myself upon the propriety of my instant journey, and promised me a faithful nursing attendance during my absence.

I went in a chaise, to lose no time - but the uncertainty how I might find my poor father made me arrive with a nervous seizure upon my voice that rendered it as husky as Mr. Rishton's.

While I settled with the postilion, Sally, James, Charlotte, and Marianne, came to me. Esther and Charles had been there the preceding day; they were sent to as soon as the event had happened. My dearest father received me with extreme kindness, but though far, far more calm and quiet than I could expect, he was much shaken, and often very faint. However, in the course of the evening, he suffered me to read to him various passages from various books, such as conversation introduced; and as his nature is as pure from affectation as from falsehood, encouraged in himself, as well as permitted in us, whatever could lead to cheerfulness.

Let me not forget to record one thing that was truly generous in my poor mother's last voluntary exertions. She charged Sally and her maid both not to call my father when she appeared to be dying; and not disturb him if her death should happen in the night, nor to let him hear it till he arose at his usual time. I feel sensibly the kindness of this sparing consideration.

Yet not so would I be used! O never should I forgive the misjudged prudence that should rob me of one little instant of remaining life in one who was truly dear to me'; Nevertheless, I shall not be surprised to have his first shock succeeded by a sorrow it did not excite, and I fear he will require much watching and vigilance to be kept as well as I have quitted him.

THE FRENCH EMIGRES AT NORBURY.

(Madame d'Arblay to Mrs. Phillips.) Bookham, December 25, 1796. You will have heard that the Princesse d'Henin and M. de Lally have spent a few days at Norbury Park. We went every evening regularly to meet them, and they yet contrive to grow higher and higher in our best opinions and affections; they force that last word; none other is adequate to such regard as they excite.

M. de Lally read us a pleading for émigrés of all descriptions, to the people and government of France, for their re-instalment in their native land, that exceeds in eloquence, argument, taste, feeling, and every power of oratory and truth united, anything I ever remember to have read. It is so affecting in many places, that I was almost ill from restraining My nearly convulsive emotions. My dear and honoured partner gives me, perhaps, an interest in such a subject beyond what is mere natural due and effect, therefore I cannot be sure such will be its universal success; yet I shall be nothing less than Surprised to live to see his statue erected in his own country, at the expense of his own restored exiles. 'Tis, indeed, a wonderful performance. And he was so easy, so gay, so unassuming, yet free from condescension, that I almost worshipped him. M. d'Arblay cut me off a bit of the coat in which he read his pleading, and I shall preserve it, labelled!

The princess was all that was amiable and attractive, and she loves my Susanna so tenderly, that her voice was always caressing when she named her. She would go to Ireland, she repeatedly said, on purpose to see you, were her fortune less miserably cramped. The journey, voyage, time, difficulties, and sea-sickness, would be nothing for obstacles. You have made, there, that rare and exquisite acquisition-an ardent friend for life.

DR. BURNEY'S DEPRESSED STATE.

I have not heard very lately of my dearest father; all accounts speak of his being very much lower in spirits than When I left him. I sometimes am ready to return to him, for my whole heart yearns to devote itself to him - but the babe, and the babe's father—and there is no going en famille uninvited—and my dear father does not feel equal to making the invitation.

One of the Tichfield dear girls seems to be constantly with Sally, to aid the passing hours, but Our poor father wants something more than cheerfulness and affection, though nothing without them could do; he wants some one to find out pursuits—to entice him into reading, by bringing books, or starting subjects; some one to lead him to talk of what he thinks, or to forget what he thinks of, by adroitly talking of what may catch other attention. Even where deep sorrow is impossible, a gloomy void must rest in the total breaking up such a long and such a fast connexion.

I must always grieve at your absence at such a period. our Esther has SO much to do in her own family, and fears so much the cold of Chelsea, that she can be only of day and occasional use, and it is nights and mornings that call for the confidential companion that might best revive him, He is more amiable, more himself, if possible, than ever. God long preserve him to bless us all!

COVETOUS OF PERSONAL DISTINCTION.

Your old acquaintance, Miss —, has been passing ten days in this neighbourhood. She is become very pleasingly formed in manners, wherever she wishes to oblige, and all her roughnesses and ruggednesses are worn off. I believe the mischief done by her education, and its wants, not cured, if curable au fond; but much amended to all, and apparently done away completely to many. What really rests is a habit of exclusively consulting just what she likes best, not what would be or prove best for others. She thinks, indeed, but little of anything except with reference to herself, and what gives her an air, and will give her a character, for inconstancy, that is in fact the mere result of seeking her own gratification alike in meeting or avoiding her connexions. If she saw this, she has understanding sufficient to work it out of her; but she weighs nothing sufficiently to dive into her own self. She knows she is a very clever girl, and she is neither well contented with others, nor happy in herself, but where this is evidently acknowledged.

We spent an evening together at Norbury Park; she was shown all Mr. William's pictures and drawings. I knew her expectations of an attention she had no chance of exciting and therefore devoted myself to looking them over with her yet, though Mr. Locke himself led the way to see them, and explained several, and though Amelia addressed her with the utmost sweetness, and Mrs. Locke with perfect good breeding, I could not draw from her one word relative to the evening, or the family, except that she did not think she had heard Mr. William's voice once. A person so young, and with such good parts, that can take no pleasure but in personal distinction, which is all her visit can have wanted, will soon cut all real improvement short, by confining herself to such society alone as elevates herself. There she will always make a capital figure, for her conversation is sprightly and entertaining, and her heart and principles are both good: she has many excellent qualities, and various resources in herself; but she is good enough to make me lament that she is not modest enough to be yet better.

BABY D'ARBLAY AGAIN; AND OTHER MATTERS.

(Madame d'Arblay to Dr. Burney.) Bookham, Nov. 29, 1796. My little man waits for your lessons to get on in elocution: he has made no further advance but that of calling out, as he saw our two watches hung on two opposite hooks over the chamber chimney-piece, "Watch, papa,—watch, mamma;" so, though his first speech is English, the idiom is French. We agree this is to avoid any heartburning in his parents. He is at this moment so exquisitely enchanted with a little penny trumpet, and finding he can produce such harmony his own self, that he is blowing and laughing till he can hardly stand. If you could see his little swelling cheeks you would not accuse yourself of a misnomer in calling him cherub. I try to impress him with an idea of pleasure in going to see grandpapa, but the short visit to Bookham is forgotten, and the permanent engraving remains, and all his concurrence consists in pointing up to the print over the chimney-piece, and giving it one of his concise little bows.

Are not people a little revived in the political world by this unexampled honour paid to Mr. Pitt? (135) Mr. Locke has subscribed 3000 pounds.

How you rejoiced me by what you say of poor Mr. Burke for I had seen the paragraph of his death with most exceeding great concern.

The Irish reports, are, I trust, exaggerated; few things come quite plainly from Hibernia: yet what a time, in all respects, to transport thither, as you too well term it, our beloved Susan! She writes serenely, and Norbury seems to repay a world of sufferings: it is delightful to see her SO satisfied there, at least; but they have all, she says, got the brogue.

Our building is to be resumed the 1st of March; it will then soon be done, as it is only of lath and plaster, and the roof and wood-work are already prepared.' My indefatigable superintendent goes every morning for two, three, or four hours to his field, to work at a sunk fence that 'IS to protect his garden from our cow. I have sent Mrs. Boscawen, through Miss Cambridge, a history of our plan. The dwelling is destined by M. d'Arblay to be called the Camilla cottage.

(95) "Memoires of Dr. Burney," vol. iii. pp. 224-5.

(96) "Memoirs of Dr. Burney," vol. iii, pp. 210-11.

(97) In the "Memoirs of Dr. Burney" Madame d'Arblay writes that "Before the answer of Mr. Pitt to the memorial could be returned, the attempt upon Toulon proved abortive." Mr, Pitt must certainly have been in no hurry to reply; for the memorial was sent to him about the commencement of October, and Toulon was not evacuated by the English until the 18th of December. ED.

(98) A character in "Cecilia." ED.

(99) The well-known novelist. ED.

(100) The cottage which Fanny and her husband contemplated building, was not actually commenced until after the publication of "Camilla," in 1796. ED.

(101) The fund which Mrs. Crewe was exerting herself to raise for the benefit of the French emigrant clergy. ED.

(102) Mrs. Crewe had been urging Dr. Burney to engage his daughter to contribute, by her pen, to the relief of the emigrant clergy. Fanny accordingly wrote an "Address to the Ladies of Great Britain," in the form of a short pamphlet, which was published by Cadell, and which appears to have had the desired effect. ED.

(103) Alas for Dr. Burney's hopes! Toulon was successfully defended until the middle of December, when the vigorous measures of the besiegers, inspired by the genius of Young Buonaparte, resulted in the complete triumph of the Republicans. On the 17th of December they carried by storm Fort Eguillette and the heights of Faron. From these positions their artillery commanded the harbour, and, further defence of the town being thereby rendered impracticable, its instant evacuation was resolved upon by the allies. An attempt to burn the French war-ships in the harbour, before abandoning the place, was only partially successful. On the 18th and 19th the troops embarked. Vast numbers of fugitives were taken on board the retreating fleet, but a large proportion of the unfortunate Toulonnais remained, to experience the cruel vengeance of the Republicans. ED.

(104) The execution of Marie Antoinette, October 16, 1793. ED.

(105) He was born on the 18th of December 1794. ED.

(106) Goldsmith has drawn the character of Richard Burke in "Retaliation," as follows:—

"Here lies honest Richard, whose fate I must Sigh at; Alaq, that such frolic should now be so quiet! What spirits were his! what wit and what whim! Now breaking a jest, and now breaking a limb; Now wrangling and grumbling to keep up the ball; Now teasing and vexing, yet laughing at all. In short, so provoking a devil was Dick, that we wish'd him full ten times a day at old Nick, But, missing his mirth and agreeable vein, As often we wish'd to have Dick back again." ED.

(107) George Canning, who was not yet twenty-four years of age, had just entered Parliament as member for Newport. He had formerly been a Whig and an associate of Fox and Sheridan, but the excesses of the French Revolution appear to have driven him, as they had driven Burke and Windham, over to the opposite camp. He took his seat as a Tory and a supporter of Mr. Pitt, and a Tory he remained to the end of his days. Canning's maiden speech, to which Fanny refers, was delivered January 31, in a debate on the treaty between Great Britain and the King of Sardinia. By this treaty, which was signed April 25, 1793, it was agreed that the two contracting parties should make common cause in the war against the French Republic; that England should pay to the King of Sardinia an annual subsidy of 200,000 pounds, to enable him to maintain the war; and that England should not conclude peace without providing for the restoration to Sardinia of the territories which had been torn from it by the Republic. In the debate of January 31, 1794, Fox vigorously attacked the treaty, while Canning, who spoke later, defended it in an able and well-received maiden speech. ED.

(108) Talleyrand's intrigues had made him an object of suspicion to both parties. He was detested by the royalists of the first emigration, had been d,cr,t, d'accusation by the Convention, and was regarded by the English government as a dangerous person. In January 1794, he received an order from the government to quit England within five days, and he embarked in consequence, for the United States, February 3. ED.

(109) "London, 1794. Madame,—Had it been possible I would have had the honour of seeing you this morning , but the utter impossibility of doing so has deprived me of the last pleasure that I might have had in Europe. Permit me, madame, to thank you again for all your kindness, and to ask a little place in your memory, and let me tell you, I shall never cease, while I live, to offer my vows for your

welfare, and for that of the captain and your children. You will have a very zealous servant in America; I shall not return to Europe without coming to Surrey: everything of value to my intellect or my heart is there.

"Kindly present my compliments to the captain."

(110) "London, March 2, 1794. Farewell, my dear d'Arblay: I leave your country till the time when it will no longer be governed by the petty passions of men. Then I will return; not, indeed, to busy myself with public affairs, for I have long since abandoned them for ever; but to see the excellent inhabitants of Surrey. I hope to know enough English to understand Madame d'Arblay; for the next four months, I shall do nothing but study it: and, to acquaint myself with the beauties of the language, I take 'Evelina' and 'Cecilia,' both for study and pleasure. I wish You, my dear friend, all kinds of happiness, and you are in the way to fulfil all my wishes.

"I do not know how long I shall remain in America. If there were a prospect of the re-establishment of reason and stability in our unhappy country, I should return; if Europe goes to pieces in the coming campaign, I will prepare a refuge in America for all our friends.

"Farewell. My respects to Madame d'Arblay and Mrs. Phillips. I ask of you and I promise you a lifelong friendship."

(The date at the head of this letter Is evidently incorrect—probably a slip of the writer's. Talleyrand embarked February 3. ED.

(111) Lafayette's brilliant services in the cause of liberty had not secured him from the usual fate of moderate revolutionists at this period. In the early days of the Revolution, he was the hero of the French people; in 1792, denounced by Robespiérre and the jacobins, he was compelled to seek safety in flying from France. He escaped the guillotine, indeed, but fell into the hands of the Austrians, was cast into prison, and did not gain his liberty till September, 1797. ED.

(112) This was Dr. Burney's first meeting with Mrs. Piozzi since her marriage. It occurred at one of Salomon's celebrated concerts, where the doctor, with surprise, perceived Piozzi among the audience, not knowing that he had returned from Italy. He entered into a cordial conversation with the Signor, and inquired after his wife. "Piozzi, turning round, pointed to a sofa, on which, to his infinite joy, Dr. Burney beheld Mrs. Thrale Piozzi, seated in the midst of her daughters, the four Miss Thrales," those young ladies (at least, the three elder, for Cecilia had been abroad with Mr. and Mrs. Piozzi) having made up their minds by this time to accept the inevitable, and to be reconciled to their mother." See "Memoirs of Dr. Burney," vol. iii. p. 198. ED.

(113) Written after the Doctor's first visit to Bookham.

(114) Name of a gardener in a drama of Fontenelle's.

(115) The novel of "Camilla," then lately begun.

(116) "Memoirs of the Life and Writings of Metastasio," a work which Dr. Burney was then engaged upon, and which was published in three Volumes, 8vo in 1796. ED.

(117) "Edwy and Elgiva," a tragedy by Madame d'Arblay.

(118) Edmund Burke's only son, Richard, died August 2, 1794. ED

(119) "Edwy and Elgiva," produced by Sheridan at Drury-lane, March 21, 1795; it was acted but once, and never printed. ED.

(120) Warren Hastings was acquitted of all the charges, April 23, 1795.

(121) Both characters, to some extent, were true. Goldsmith's portrait of Cumberland, though flattering, is not, we fancy, without a slight undercurrent of irony. Here are the lines from "Retaliation."

"Here Cumberland lies, having acted his parts, The Terence of England, the mender of hearts; A flattering painter, who made it his care to draw men as they ought to be, not as they are. His gallants are all faultless, his women divine, And Comedy wonders at being so fine: Like a tragedy-queen he has dizen'd her out, or rather like Tragedy giving a rout. His fools have their follies so lost in a crowd of virtues and feelings, that Folly grows proud and coxcombs, alike in their failings atone: Adopting his portraits, are pleas'd with their own, Say, where has our poet this malady caught? Or wherefore his characters thus without fault? Say, was it that, mainly directing his view to find out men's virtues, and finding them few, quite sick of pursuing each troublesome elf, He grew lazy at last, and drew from himself?" ED.

(122) The novels of Mrs. Radcliffe were now at the height of their popularity. "The Mysteries of Udolpho," perhaps the most powerful of her works, had recently been published, to the intense delight of all lovers of the thrilling and romantic. ED.

(123) The name was then "Ariella," changed afterwards to "Camilla."

(124) Written during his embarrassments from the French Revolution, and answer to a letter expressing bitter disappointment from repeated losses.

(125) M. de Narbonne, in reply, expressed, in lively terms, his gratitude for Madame d'Arblay's invitation, and his pleasure in receiving it. But he declined the proposal. He was not, he said, wholly without resources, or without hopes for the future, and circumstances made it desirable that he should reside at present near the French frontier. ED.

(126) Gainsborough Dupont, a nephew of the great Gainsborough. He was a portrait-painter of some merit, and an excellent mezzo- tint engraver. some of his best plates were engraved after paintings by Gainsborough. Mr Dupont died in 1797. ED.

(127) "The Birth of Love;" a poem: with engravings, from designs by her royal highness the Princess Elizabeth.

(128) i.e, the Duke of York, second son of the king. He had been appointed field-marshal and commander-in-chief early in 1795. ED.

(129) The Duchess of York was daughter to the King of Prussia. ED.

(130) Susan's little son, Norbury Phillips. ED.

(131) Rose Dale, Richmond, Surrey. This place was formerly the residence of the poet Thomson, and afterwards became the property of the Honourable Mrs. Boscawen.

(132) The princess royal was married, May 18, 1797, to Frederick William, hereditary prince of Wurtemberg. ED.

(133) Editor and proprietor of the "Monthly Review."

(134) The death of Dr. Burney's second wife.

(135) Fanny alludes to the so-called "loyalty loan," proposed and carried by Mr Pitt, to meet the expenses of the war. "Pitt evinced his own Public spirit, when he relied on and appealed to the public spirit of the People. He announced a loan of 18,000,000 pounds, at five per cent., to be taken at 112 pounds, 10 shillings, for every 100 pounds stock, and with an option to the proprietors to he paid off at par within two years after a treaty of peace." (Stanhope's "Life of Pitt," vol. ii, P. 389.) The loan was taken up by the Public with extraordinary eagerness, 5,000,000 pounds being subscribed on the first day of issue (December 1, 1796). ED.

(136) They had commenced building the cottage in October. Fanny writes, November 29: "Our cottage building stops now, from the shortness of the days, till the beginning of March. The foundation is laid, and it will then be run up with great speed. The well, at length, is finished, and it is a hundred and odd feet deep. The water is said to be excellent, but M. d'Arblay has had it now stopped to prevent accidents from hazardous boys, who, when the field is empty of owners, will be amusing themselves there. He has just completed his grand plantations; part of which are in evergreens, part in firewood for future time, and part in an orchard." ED.

SECTION 21. (1797-8)

"CAMILLA" COTTAGE. SUNDRY VISITS TO THE ROYAL FAMILY.

[Fanny's pen portraits of the princesses are as fascinating as Gainsborough's paintings of them. Their truly amiable characters and sweet dispositions are nowhere more pleasantly illustrated than in the following section of the "Diary." A list of their names, with the dates of their births and deaths, may be useful to the reader.

1. Charlotte, princess royal. Born 1767: Queen of Wirtemburg: died 1828.

2. Augusta, Fanny's favourite, as she well deserved to be. Born 1768: never married: died 1840.

3. Elizabeth, the artist of the family. Born 1770: married the hereditary prince (afterwards, in 1820, Landgrave) of Hesse-Homburg in 1818, and settled in Germany: died 1840.

4. Mary. Born 1776: married her cousin, William Frederick, Duke of Gloucester, in 1816: died 1857.

5. Sophia, born 1777: died 1848.

6. Amelia, born 1783. Her health first gave way in 1798 (see p. 180): she died, unmarried, at Windsor, in 1810. A few days before her death she gave her poor blind, old father, a ring containing a scrap of her hair; saying only, as she pressed it into his hand, "Remember me!" The poor king's anguish brought on a fresh attack of insanity, from which he never recovered. ED.]

A DISAGREEABLE JOURNEY HOME.

(Madame d'Arblay to Dr. Burney.) Bookham, January 3, '97. Was extremely vexed at missing our uncertain post yesterday, and losing, unavoidably, another to-day, before I return my dearest father our united thanks for the kind and sweet fortnight passed under his roof. Our adventures in coming back were better adapted to our departure than our arrival, for they were rather rueful. One of the horses did not like his business, and wanted to be off, and we were stopped by his gambols continually , and, if I had not been a soldier's wife, I should have been terribly alarmed; but my soldier does not like to see himself disgraced in his other half, and so I was fain to keep up my courage, till, at length, after we had passed Fetcham, the frisky animal plunged till he fastened the shaft against a hedge, and then, little Betty beginning to scream, I inquired of the postilion if we had not better alight. If it were not, he said, for the dirt, yes. The dirt then was defied, and I prevailed, though with difficulty, upon my chieftain to consent to a general dismounting. And he then found it was not too soon, for the horse became inexorable to all menace, caress, chastisement, or harangue, and was obliged to be loosened.

Meanwhile, Betty, Bab, and I trudged on, vainly looking back for our vehicle, till we reached our little home—a mile and a half. Here we found good fires, though not a morsel of food; this however, was soon procured, and our walking apparel changed for drier raiment; and I sent forth our nearest cottager, and a young butcher, and a boy, towards Fetcham, to aid the vehicle, or its contents, for my chevalier had stayed on account of our chattels: and about two hours after the chaise arrived, with one horse, and pushed by its hirer, while it was half dragged by its driver. But all came safe; and we drank a dish of tea, and ate a mutton chop, and kissed our little darling, and forgot all else of our journey hut the pleasure we had had at Chelsea with my dearest father and dear Sally.

And just now I received a letter from our Susanna, which tells me the invasion (137) has been made in a part of Ireland where all is so loyal there can be no apprehension from any such attempt; but she adds, that if it had happened in the north everything might have been feared. Heaven send the invaders far from all the points of the Irish compass! and that's an Irish wish for expression, though not for meaning. All the intelligence she gathers is encouraging, with regard to the spirit and loyalty of all that surround her. But Mr. Brabazon is in much uneasiness for his wife, whose situation is critical, and he hesitates whether or not to convey her to Dublin, as a place of more security than her own habitation. What a period this for the usual journey of our invaluable Susan!

BURKE'S FUNERAL AT BEACONSFIELD.

(Dr. Burney to Madame d'Arblay.) Saturday Night, July 22, 1797. I was invited to poor Mr. Burke's funeral, (138) by Mrs. Crewe and two notes from Beaconsfield. Malone and I went to Bulstrode together in my car, this day sevennight, with two horses added to mine. Mrs. Crewe had invited me thither when she went down first. We found the Duke of Portland there; and the Duke of Devonshire and Windham came to dinner. The chancellor and speaker of the House of Commons could not leave London till four o'clock, but arrived a little after seven. We all set off together for Beaconsfield, where we found the rest of the pall-bearers—Lord Fitzwilliam, Lord Inchiquin, and Sir Gilbert Eliot, with Drs. King and Lawrence, Lord North, Dudley North, and many of the deceased's private friends, though by his repeated injunction the funeral was to be very private. We had all hatbands, scarfs, and gloves; and he left a list to whom rings of remembrance are to be sent, among whom my name occurred, and a jeweller has been here for my measure. I went back to Bulstrode, by invitation, with the two dukes, the chancellor, and speaker, Windham, Malone, and Secretary King. I stayed there till Sunday evening, and got home just before the dreadful storm. The duke was extremely civil and hospitable, pressed me much to stay longer and go with them, the chancellor, speaker, Windham, and Mrs. Crewe, to Pinn, to see the school, founded by Mr. Burke, for the male children of French emigrant nobles; but I could not with prudence stay, having a couple of ladies waiting for me in London, and two extra horses with me.

So much for poor Mr. Burke, certainly one of the greatest men of the present century; and I think I might say the best orator and statesman of modern times. He had his passions and prejudices to which I did not subscribe - but I always admired his great abilities, friendship, and urbanity - and it would be ungrateful in you and me, to whom he was certainly partial, not to feel and lament his loss.

(Madame d'Arblay to Dr. Burney.) Bookham, July 27, '97. I was surprised, and almost frightened, though at the same time gratified, to find you assisted in paying the last honours to Mr. Burke. How sincerely I sympathise in all you say of that truly great man! That his enemies say he was not perfect is nothing compared with his immense superiority over almost all those who are merely exempted from his peculiar defects. That he was upright in heart, even where he acted wrong, I do truly believe; and that he asserted nothing he had not persuaded himself to be true, from Mr. Hastings's being the most rapacious of villains, to the king's being incurably insane. He was as generous as kind, and as liberal in his sentiments as he was luminous in intellect and extraordinary in abilities and eloquence. Though free from all little vanity, high above envy, and glowing with zeal to exalt talents and merit in others, he had, I believe a consciousness of his own greatness, that shut out those occasional and useful self-doubts which keep our judgment in order, by calling our motives and our passions to account.

DEATH OF M. D'ARBLAY'S BROTHER.

(Madame d'Arblay to Dr. Burney.) Bookham, August 10, '97. You know, I believe, with what cruel impatience and uncertainty my dear companion has waited for some news of his family; no tidings, however, could be procure, nor has ever heard from any part of it till last Saturday morning, when two letters arrived by the same post, with information of the death of his only brother.

Impossible as it has long been to look back to France without fears amounting even to expectation of horrors, he had never ceased cherishing hopes some favourable turn would, in the end, unite him with this last branch of his house; the shock, therefore, has been terribly severe, and has cast a gloom upon his mind and spirits which nothing but his kind anxiety to avoid involving mine can at present suppress. He is now the last of a family of seventeen, and not one relation of his own name now remains but his own little English son. His father was the only son of an only son, which drives all affinity on the paternal side into fourth and fifth kinsmen.

On the maternal side, however, he has the happiness to hear that an uncle, who is inexpressibly dear to him, who was his guardian and best friend through life, still lives, and has been permitted to remain unmolested in his own house, at Joigny, where he is now in perfect health, save from rheumatic attacks, which though painful are not dangerous. A son, too, of this gentleman, who was placed as a commissaire-de-guerre by M. d'Arblay during the period of his belonging to the war committee, still holds the same situation, which is very lucrative, and which M. d'A. had concluded would have been withdrawn as soon as his own flight from France was known.

The little property of which the late Chevalier d'Arblay died possessed, this same letter says, has been "vendu pour la nation,"(139) because his next heir was an emigré; though there is a little niece, Mlle. Girardin, daughter of an only sister, who is in France, and upon whom the succession was settled, if her uncles died without immediate heirs.

Some little matter, however, what we know not, has been reserved by being bought in by this respectable uncle, who sends M. d'Arblay word he has saved him what he may yet live upon, if he can find means to return without personal risk, and who solicits to again see him with urgent fondness, in which he is joined by his aunt with as much warmth as if she, also, was his relation by blood, not alliance.

The late chevalier, my M. d'A. says, was a man of the softest manners and most exalted honour; and he was so tall and so thin, he was often nicknamed Don Quixote, but he was so completely aristocratic with regard to the Revolution, at its very commencement, that M. d'A. has heard nothing yet with such unspeakable astonishment as the news that he died, near Spain, of his wounds from a battle in which he had fought for the Republic. "How strange," says M. d'A., "is our destiny! that that Republic which I quitted, determined to be rather an hewer of wood and drawer of water all my life than serve, he should die for." The secret history of this may some day come out, but it is now inexplicable, for the mere fact, without the smallest comment, is all that has reached us, In the period, indeed, in which M. d'A. left France, there were but three steps possible for those who had been bred to arms-flight, the guillotine, or fighting for the Republic, "The former this brother," M. d'A. says, "had not energy of character to undertake in the desperate manner in which he risked it himself, friendless and fortuneless, to live in exile as he could. The guillotine no one could elect; and the continuing in the service, though in a cause he detested, was, probably, his hard compulsion."

Our new habitation will very considerably indeed exceed our first intentions and expectations. I suppose it has ever been so, and so ever must be; for we sought as well as determined to keep within bounds, and M. d'A. still thinks he has done it, however, I am more aware of our tricks upon travellers than to enter into the same delusion.

The pleasure, however, he has taken in this edifice is my first joy, for it has constantly shown me his heart has invariably held to those first feelings which, before our union, determined him upon settling in England. O! if you knew how he has been assailed, by temptations of every sort that either ambition, or interest, or friendship could dictate, to change his plan, and how his heart sometimes yearns towards those he yet can love in his native soil, while his firmness still remains unshaken,— you would not wonder I make light of even extravagance in a point that shows him thus fixed to make this object a part of the whole system of his future life.

FROM CREWE HALL TO CHELSEA.

(Dr. Burney to Madame d'Arblay.) Friday Night, September 13, 1797. My dear Fanny, Where did I leave off?—hang me if I know!—I believe I told you, or all when with YOU, Of the Chester and Liverpool journey and voyage. On Saturday 26th August, the day month from leaving London, M. le pr,sident de Frondeville and I left Crewe Hall on our way back. The dear Mrs. Crewe kindly set us in our way as far as Etruria. We visited Trentham Hall, in Staffordshire, the famous seat of the Marquis of Stafford,—a very fine place—fine piece of water—fine hanging woods,—the valley of Tempe— and the river Trent running through the garden. Mrs C. introduced us to the marchioness, who did us the honour of showing us the house herself; it has lately been improved and enlarged by Wyatt:— fine pictures, library, etc.

After a luncheon here, we went to Etruria, which I had never seen. Old Mr. Wedgwood is dead, and his son and successor not at home; but we went to the pottery manufacture, and saw the whole process of forming the beautiful things which are dispersed all over the universe from this place. Mrs. C. offered to send you a little hand churn for your breakfast butter; but I should have broke it to pieces, and durst not accept of it. But if it would be of any use, when you have a cow, I will get you one at the Wedgwood ware-house in London. Here we parted.

The president and I got to Lichfield by about ten o'clock that night. In the morning, before my companion was up, I strolled about the city with one of the waiters, in search of Frank Barber,' who I had been told lived there; but on inquiry I was told his residence was in a village three or four miles off. I however soon found the house where dear Dr. Johnson was born, and his father's shop. The house is stuccoed, has five sash-windows in front, and pillars before it. It is the best house thereabouts, near St. Mary's Church, in a broad street, and is now a grocer's shop.

I went next to the Garrick house, which has been lately repaired, stuccoed, enlarged, and sashed. Peter Garrick, David's eldest brother, died about two years ago, leaving all his Possessions to the apothecary that had attended him. But the will was disputed and set aside not long since, it having appeared at a trial that the testator was insane at the time the will was made; so that Mrs. Doxie, Garrick's sister, a widow with a numerous family, recovered the house and £30,000, She now lives in it with her family, and has been able to set up a carriage. The inhabitants of Lichfield were so pleased with the decision of the court on the trial, that they illuminated the streets, and had public rejoicings on the occasion.

After examining this house well, I tried to find the residence of Dr. James, inventor of the admirable fever powders, which have so often saved the life of our dear Susey, and others without number. But the ungrateful inhabitants knew nothing about him. . . .

The cathedral, which has been lately thoroughly repaired internally, is the most complete and beautiful Gothic building I ever saw. The outside was trés mal trait, by the fanatics of the last century; but there are three beautiful spires still standing, and more than fifty whole-length figures of saints in their original niches. The choir is exquisitely beautiful. A fine new organ is erected, and was well played, and I never heard the cathedral service so well performed to that instrument only before. The services and anthems were middle-aged music, neither too old and dry, nor too modern and light; the voices subdued, and exquisitely softened and sweetened by the building,

While the lessons were reading, which I could not hear, I looked for monuments, and found a beautiful one to Garrick, and another just by it to Johnson; the former erected by Mrs. Garrick, who has been daily abused for not erecting one to her husband in Westminster Abbey; but sure that was a debt due to him from the public, and that due from his widow best paid here. (141) Johnson's has been erected by his friends:—both are beautiful, and alike in every particular.

There is a monument here to Johnson's first patron, Mr. Walmsley, whose amplitude of learning and copiousness of communication were such, that our revered friend said, "it might be doubted whether a day passed in which he had not some advantage from his friendship." There is a monument likewise to Lady M. W. Montagu, and to the father of Mr. Addison, etc.

We left Lichfield about two o'clock, and reached Daventry that night, stopping a little at Coventry to look at the great church and Peeping Tom. Next day got to St. Albans time enough to look 'It the church and neighbouring ruins. Next morning breakfasted at Barnet, where my car met me, and got to Chelsea by three o'clock, leaving my agreeable compagnon de voyage, M. le président, at his apartments in town. . . .

AT DR. HERSCHEL'S.

(Dr. Burney to Madame d'Arblay.) Chelsea College, Thursday, September 28. My dear Fanny,—I read your letter pen in hand, and shall try to answer it by to-day's post. But first let me tell you that it was very unlikely to find me at home, for on Tuesday I went to Lord Chesterfield's at Bailie's, and arrived there in very good time for a four o'clock dinner - when, behold! I was informed by the porter that "both my lord and lady were in town, and did not return till Saturday!" Lord Chesterfield had unexpectedly been obliged to go to town by indisposition. Though I was asked to alight and take refreshment, I departed immediately, intending to dine and lie at Windsor, to be near Dr. Herschel, with whom a visit had been arranged by letter. But as I was now at liberty to make that visit at any time of the day I pleased, I drove through Slough in my way to Windsor, in order to ask at Dr. Herschel's door when my visit would be least inconvenient to him—that night or next morning. The good soul was at dinner, but came to the door himself, to press me to alight immediately and partake of his family repast - and this he did so heartily that I could not resist. I was introduced to the family at table, four ladies, and a little boy about the age and size of Martin. (142) I was quite shocked at seeing so many females: I expected (not knowing Herschel was married) only to have found Miss Herschel. . . . I expressed my concern and shame at disturbing them at this time of the day; told my story, at which they were so cruel as to rejoice, and went so far as to say they rejoiced at the accident which had brought me there, and hoped I would send my carriage away, and take a bed with them. They were sorry they had no stables for my horses. I thought it necessary, You may, be sure, to faire la petite bouche, but in spite of my blushes I was obliged to submit to my trunk being taken in and the car sent to the inn just by. . . .

Your health was drunk after dinner (put that int.) your pocket); and after much social conversation and a few hearty laughs, the ladies proposed to take a walk, in order, I believe, to leave Herschel and me together. We walked and talked round his great telescopes till it grew damp and dusk, then retreated into his study to philosophise. I had a string of questions ready to ask, and astronomical difficulties to solve, which, with looking at curious books and instruments, filled up the time charmingly till tea, which being drank with the ladies, we two retired again to the starry. Now having paved the way, we began to talk of my poetical plan, and he pressed me to read what I had Done. (143) Heaven help his head! my eight books, of from four hundred to eight hundred and twenty lines, would require two or three days to read.

He made me unpack my trunk for my MS., from which I read him the titles of the chapters, and begged he would choose any book or character of a great astronomer he pleased. "Oh, let us have the beginning." I read him the first eighteen or twenty lines of the exordium, and then said I rather wished to come to modern times - I was more certain of my ground in high antiquity than after the time of Copernicus, and began my eighth chapter, entirely on Newton and his system. He gave me the greatest encouragement said repeatedly that I perfectly understood what I was writing' about - and only stopped me at two places: one was at a word too strong for what I had to describe, and the other at one too weak. The doctrine he allowed to be quite orthodox, concerning gravitation, refraction, reflection, optics, comets, magnitudes, distances, revolutions, etc, but made a discovery to me which, had I known sooner, would have overset me, and prevented my reading any part of my work: he said he had almost always had an aversion to poetry, which he regarded as the arrangement of fine words, without any useful meaning or adherence to truth; but that, when truth and science were united to these fine words, he liked poetry very well; and next morning, after breakfast, he made me read as much of another chapter on Descartes, etc, as the time would allow, as I had ordered my carriage at twelve. I read, talked, asked questions, and looked at books and instruments, till near one, when I set off for Chelsea.

HOSPITALITY UNDER DIFFICULTIES.

(Madame d'Arblay to Mrs. Francis.) Westhamble, November 16, 1797. Your letter was most welcome to me, my dearest Charlotte, and I am delighted Mr. Broome (144) and my dear father will so speedily meet. If they steer clear of politics, there can be no doubt of their immediate exchange of regard and esteem. At all events, I depend upon Mr. B.'s forbearance of such subjects, if their opinions clash. Pray let me hear how the interview went off.

I need not say how I shall rejoice to see you again, nor how charmed we shall both be to make a nearer acquaintance with Mr. Broome; but, for heaven's sake, my dear girl, how are we to give him a dinner?—unless he will bring with him his poultry, for ours are not yet arrived from Bookham; and his fish, for ours are still at the bottom of some pond we know not where, and his spit, for our jack is yet without clue; and his kitchen grate, for ours waits for Count Rumford's (145) next pamphlet;—not to mention his table-linen;—and not to speak of his knives and forks, some ten of our poor original twelve having been massacred in M. d'Arblay's first essays in the art of carpentering;-and to say nothing of his large spoons, the silver of our plated ones having feloniously made off under cover of the whitening-brush—and not to talk of his cook, ours being not yet hired;-and not to start the subject of wine, ours, by some odd accident, still remaining at the wine-merchant's! With all these impediments, however, to convivial hilarity, if he will eat a quarter of a joint of meat (his share, I mean), tied up by a packthread, and roasted by a log of wood on the bricks,—and declare no potatoes so good as those dug by M. d'Arblay out of our garden,—and protest our small beer gives the spirits of champagne,—and make no inquiries where we have deposited the hops he will conclude we have emptied out of our table-cloth,— and pronounce that bare walls are superior to tapestry,—and promise us the first sight of his epistle upon visiting a new-built cottage,—we shall be sincerely happy to receive him in our hermitage; where I hope to learn, for my dearest Charlotte's sake, to love him as much as, for his own I have very long admired him.

WAR TAXES. "CAMILLA" COTTAGE.

(Madame d'Arblay to Mrs. Phillips.) Westhamble, December, '97. The new threefold assessment of taxes has terrified us rather seriously; though the necessity, and therefore justice, of them, we mutually feel. My father thinks his own share will amount to eighty pounds a year! We have, this very morning, decided upon parting with four of our new windows, —a great abatement of agr,mens to ourselves, and of ornament to our appearance; and a still greater sacrifice to the amour Propre of my architect, who, indeed,—his fondness for his edifice considered,—does not ill deserve praise that the scheme had not his mere consent, but his own free proposition. . . .

We quitted Bookham with one single regret—that of leaving our excellent neighbours the Cookes. . . . we languished for the moment of removal with almost infantine fretfulness at every delay that distanced it; and when at last the grand day came, our final packings, with all their toil and difficulties and labour and expense, were mere acts of pleasantry; so bewitched were we with the impending change, that, though from six o'clock to three we were hard at work, without a kettle to boil the breakfast, or a knife to cut bread for a luncheon, we missed nothing, wanted nothing, and were as insensible to fatigue as to hunger.

M. d'Arblay set out on foot, loaded with remaining relics of things, to us precious, and Betty afterwards with a remnant of glass or two; the other maid had been sent two days before. I was forced to have a chaise for my Alex and me, and a few looking-glasses, a few folios, and not a few other oddments and then, with dearest Mr. Locke, our founder's portrait, and my little boy, off I set, and I would my dearest Susan could relate to me as delicious a journey.

My mate, striding over hedge and ditch, arrived first, though he set out after' to welcome me to our new dwelling; and we entered our new best room, in which I found a glorious fire of wood, and a little bench, borrowed of one of the departing carpenters: nothing else. We contrived to make room for each other, and Alex disdained all rest. His spirits were so high upon finding two or three rooms totally free for his horse (alias any stick he can pick up) and himself, unencumbered by chairs and tables and such-like lumber, that he was as merry as a little Andrew and as wild as twenty colts. Here we unpacked a small basket containing three or four loaves, and, with a garden-knife, fell to work;

some eggs had been procured from a neighbouring farm, and one saucepan had been brought. We dined, therefore, exquisitely, and drank to our new possession from a glass of clear water out of our new well.

At about eight o'clock our goods arrived. We had our bed put up in the middle of our room, to avoid risk of damp walls, and our Alex had his dear Willy's crib at our feet.

We none of us caught cold. We had fire night and day in the maids' room, as well as Our own -or rather in my Susan's room; for we lent them that, their own having a little inconvenience against a fire, because it is built without a chimney. We Continued making fires all around us the first fortnight, and then found wood would be as bad as an apothecary's bill, so desisted; but we did not stop short so soon as to want the latter to succeed the former, or put our calculation to the proof.

Our first week was devoted to unpacking, and exulting in Our completed plan. To have no one thing at hand, nothing to eat, nowhere to sit—all were trifles, rather, I think, amusing than incommodious. The house looked so clean, the distribution of the rooms and closets is so convenient, the prospect everywhere around is so gay and so lovely, and the park of dear Norbury is so close at hand, that we hardly knew how to require anything else for existence than the enjoyment of our own situation.

At this period I received my summons. I believe I have already explained that I had applied to Miss Planta for advice whether my best chance of admission would be at Windsor, Kew, or London. I had a most kind letter of answer, importing my letter had been seen, and that her majesty would herself fix the time when she could admit me. This was a great happiness to me, and the fixture was for the Queen's house in town.

VISITORS ARRIVE INOPPORTUNELY.

The only drawback to the extreme satisfaction of such graciousness as allowing an appointment to secure me from a fruitless journey, as well as from impropriety and all fear of intrusion, was, that exactly at this period the Princess d'Henin and M. de Lally were expected at Norbury. I hardly could have regretted anything else, I was so delighted by my summons; but this I indeed lamented. They arrived to dinner on Thursday: I was involved in preparations, and unable to meet them, and my mate would not be persuaded to relinquish aiding me.

The next morning, through mud, through mire, they came to our cottage. The poor princess was forced to change shoes and stockings. M. de Lally is more accustomed to such expeditions. Nothing could be more sweet than they both were, nor indeed, more grateful than I felt for my share in their kind exertion. The house was re-viewed all over, even the little pot au feu was opened by the princess, excessively curious to see our manner of living in its minute detail.

I have not heard if your letter has been received by M. de Lally; but I knew not then you had written, and therefore did not inquire. The princess talked of nothing so much as you, and with a softness of regard that quite melted me. I always tell her warmly how you feel about her. M. de Lally was most melancholy about France; the last new and most alas! barbarous revolution (146) has disheartened all his hopes—alas! whose can withstand it? They made a long and kind visit, and in the afternoon we went to Norbury Park, where we remained till near eleven o'clock, and thought the time very short.

Madame d'Henin related some of her adventures in this second flight from her terrible country, and told them with a spirit and a power of observation that would have made them interesting if a tale of old times; but now, all that gives account of those events awakens the whole mind to attention.

M. de Lally after tea read us a beginning of a new tragedy, composed upon an Irish story, but bearing allusion so palpable to the virtues and misfortunes of Louis XVI. that it had almost as strong an effect upon our passions and faculties as if it had borne the name of that good and unhappy prince. It is written with great pathos, noble sentiment, and most eloquent language. I parted from them with extreme reluctance—nay, vexation.

ANOTHER VISIT TO THE ROYAL FAMILY.

I set off for town early the next day, Saturday. My time was not yet fixed for my royal interview, but I had various preparations impossible to make in this dear, quiet, obscure cottage. Mon ami could not accompany me, as we had still two men constantly at work, the house without being quite unfinished but I could not bear to leave his little representative, who, with Betty, was my companion to Chelsea. There I was expected, and Our dearest father came forth with open arms to welcome us. He was in delightful spirits, the sweetest humour, and perfectly good looks and good health. My little rogue soon engaged him in a romp, which conquered his rustic shyness, and they became the best friends in the world.

Thursday morning I had a letter from Miss Planta, written with extreme warmth of kindness, and fixing the next day at eleven o'clock for my royal admission.

I went up-stairs to Miss Planta's room, where, while I waited for her to be called, the charming Princess Mary passed by, attended by Mrs. Cheveley. She recollected me and turned back, and came up to me with a fair hand graciously held out to me. "How do you do, Madame d'Arblay?" she cried: "I am vastly glad to see you again and how does your little boy do?"

I gave her a little account of the rogue, and she proceeded to inquire about my new cottage, and its actual state. I entered into a long detail of its bare walls, and unfurnished sides, and the gambols of the little man unencumbered by cares of fractures from useless ornaments, that amused her good-humoured interest in my affairs very much, and she did not leave me till Miss Planta came to usher me to Princess Augusta.

That kind princess received me with a smile so gay, and a look so pleased at my pleasure in again seeing her, that I quite regretted the etiquette which prevented a chaste embrace. She was sitting at her toilette having her hair dressed. The royal family were all going at night to the play. She turned instantly from the glass to face me, and insisted upon my being seated immediately. She then wholly forgot her attire and ornaments and appearance, and consigned herself wholly to conversation, with that intelligent animation which marks her character. She inquired immediately how my little boy did, and then with great sweetness after his father, and after my father.

My first subject was the princess royal, and I accounted for not having left my hermitage in the hope of once more seeing her royal highness before her departure. It would have been, I told her, so melancholy a pleasure to have come merely for a last view, that I could not bear to take my annual indulgence at a period which would make it leave a mournful impression upon my mind for a twelvemonth to come. The princess said she could enter into that, but said it as if she had been surprised I had not appeared. She then gave me some account of the ceremony; (147) and when I told her I had heard that her royal highness the bride had never looked so lovely, she confirmed the praise warmly, but laughingly added, "'Twas the queen dressed her! You know what a figure she used to make of herself, with her odd manner of dressing herself; but mamma said, 'Now really, princess royal, this one time is the last, and I cannot suffer you to make such a quiz of yourself; so I will really have you dressed such a quiz of yourself, properly.' And indeed the queen was quite in the right, for everybody said she had never looked so well in her life."

The word "quiz," you may depend, was never the queen's. I had great comfort, however, in gathering, from all that passed on that subject, that the royal family is persuaded this estimable princess is happy. From what I know of her disposition I am led to believe the situation may make her so. She is born to preside, and that with equal softness and dignity; but she was here in utter subjection, for which she had neither spirits nor inclination. She adored the king, honoured the queen, and loved her sisters, and had much kindness for her brothers; but her style of life was not adapted to the royalty of her nature, any more than of her birth; and though she only wished for power to do good and to confer favours, she thought herself out of her place in not possessing it.

I was particularly happy to learn from the Princess Augusta that she has already a favourite friend in her new Court, in one of the princesses of Wurtemberg, wife of a younger brother of the hereditary prince, and who is almost as a widow, from the prince, her husband, being constantly with the army. This is a delightful circumstance, as her turn of mind, and taste, and employments, accord singularly with those of our princess.

I have no recollection of the order of our conversation, but will give you what morsels occur to me as they arise in my memory.

The terrible mutiny occupied us some time. (148) She told me many anecdotes that she had learnt in favour of various sailors, declaring, with great animation, her security in their good hearts, however drawn aside by harder and more cunning heads. The sweetness with which she delights to get out of all that is forbidding in her rank is truly adorable. In speaking of a sailor on board the St. Fiorenzo, when the royal family made their excursion by sea from Weymouth, she said, "You must know this man was a great favourite of mine, for he had the most honest countenance you can conceive, and I have often talked with him, every time we have been at Weymouth, so that we were good friends; but I wanted now in particular to ask him concerning the mutiny, but I knew I should not get him to speak out while the king and queen and my sisters were by; so I told Lady Charlotte Bellasyse to watch an opportunity when he was upon deck, and the rest were in the cabin, and then we went up to him and questioned him; and he quite answered my expectations, for, instead of taking any merit to himself from belonging to the St. Fiorenso, which was never in the mutiny, the good creature said he was sure there was not a sailor in the navy that was not sorry to have belonged to it, and would not have got out of it as readily as himself, if he had known but how."

The Princess Elizabeth now entered, but she did not stay. She came to ask something of her sister relative to a little f^te she was preparing, by way of a collation, in honour of the Princess Sophia, who was twenty this day. She made kind inquiries after my health, etc, and, being mistress of the birthday f^te, hurried off, and I had not the pleasure to see her any more.

I must be less minute, or I shall never have done. My charming Princess Augusta renewed the conversation. Admiral Duncan's noble victory (149) became the theme, but it was interrupted by the appearance of the lovely Princess Amelia, now become a model of grace, beauty and sweetness, in their bud. She gave me her hand with the softest expression of kindness, and almost immediately began questioning me concerning my little boy and with an air of interest the most captivating. But again Princess Augusta declined any interruptors: "You shall have Madame d'Arblay all to yourself, my dear, soon," she cried, laughingly; and, with a smile a little serious, the sweet Princess Amelia retreated.

It would have been truly edifying to young ladies living in the great and public world to have assisted in my place at the toilette of this exquisite Princess Augusta. Her ease, amounting even to indifference, as to her ornaments and decoration, showed a mind so disengaged from vanity, so superior to personal appearance, that I could with difficulty forbear manifesting my admiration. She let the hair-dresser proceed upon her head without comment and without examination, just as if it was solely his affair; and when the man, Robinson, humbly begged to know what ornaments he was to prepare the hair for, she said, "O, there are my feathers, and my gown is blue, so take what you think right." And when he begged she would say whether she would have any ribbons or other things mixed with the feathers and jewels, she said, "You understand all that best, Mr. Robinson, I'm sure; there are the things, so take just what you please." And after this she left him wholly to himself, never a moment interrupting her discourse or her attention with a single direction.

INTERVIEW WITH THE QUEEN.

Princess Augusta had just begun a very interesting account of an officer that had conducted himself singularly well in the mutiny, when Miss Planta came to summon me to the queen. I begged permission to return afterwards for my unfinished narrative, and then proceeded to the white closet.

The queen was alone, seated at a table, and working. Miss Planta opened the door and retired without entering. I felt a good deal affected by the sight of her Majesty again, so graciously accorded to my request; but my first and instinctive feeling was nothing to what I experienced when, after my profoundly respectful reverence, I raised my eyes, and saw in hers a look of sensibility so expressive of regard, and so examining, so penetrating into mine, as to seem to convey, involuntarily, a regret I had quitted her. This, at least, was the idea that struck me, from the species of look which met me; and it touched me to the heart, and brought instantly, in defiance of all struggle, a flood of tears into my eyes. I was some minutes recovering; and when I then entreated her forgiveness, and cleared up, the voice with which she Spoke, in hoping I was well, told me she had caught a little of my sensation, for it was by no means steady. Indeed, at that moment, I longed to kneel and beseech her pardon for the displeasure I had felt in her long resistance of my resignation, for I think, now, it was from a real and truly honourable wish to attach me to her for ever. But I then suffered too much from a situation so ill adapted to my choice and disposition, to do justice to her opposition, or to enjoy its honour to myself. Now that I am so singularly, alas! nearly singularly happy, though wholly from my perseverance in that resignation, I feel all I owe her, and I feel more and more grateful for every mark of her condescension, either recollected or renewed.

She looked ill, pale, and harassed. The king was but just returned from his abortive visit to the Nore, and the inquietude she had sustained during that short separation, circumstanced many ways alarmingly, had evidently shaken her: I saw with much, with deep concern, her sunk eyes and spirits. I believe the sight of me raised not the latter. Mrs. Schwellenberg had not long been dead, and I have some reason to think she would not have been sorry to have had me supply the vacancy; for I had immediate notice sent me of her death by Miss Planta, so written as to persuade me it was a letter by command. But not all my duty, all my gratitude, could urge me, even one short fleeting moment, to weigh any interest against the soothing serenity, the unfading felicity, of a hermitage such as mine.

We spoke of poor Mrs. Schwelly, and of her successor, Mlle. Backmeister, and of mine, Mrs. Bremyere; and I could not but express my concern that her majesty had again been so unfortunate, for Mlle. Jacobi had just retired to Germany, ill and dissatisfied with everything in England. The Princess Augusta had recounted to me the whole narrative of her retirement, and its circumstances.

The queen told me that the king had very handsomely taken care of her. But such frequent retirements are heavy weights upon the royal bounty.

I felt almost guilty when the subject was started; but not from any reproach, any allusion, not a word was dropped that had not kindness and goodness for its basis and its superstructure at once.

"How is your little boy?" was one of the earliest questions. "is he here?" she added.

"O yes," I answered, misunderstanding her, "he is my shadow; I go nowhere without him."

"But here, I mean?"

"O no! ma'am, I did not dare presume—"

I stopped, for her look said it would be no presumption. And Miss Planta had already desired me to bring him to her next time; which I suspect was by higher order than her own suggestion.

She then inquired after my dear father, and so graciously, that I told her not only of his good health, but his occupations, his new work, a "Poetical History of Astronomy," and his consultations with Herschel.

She permitted me to speak a good deal of the Princess of Wurtemberg, whom they still all call princess royal. She told me she had worked her wedding garment, and entirely, and the real labour it had proved, from her steadiness to have no help, well knowing that three stitches done by any other would make it immediately said it was none of it by herself. "As the bride of a widower," she continued, "I know she ought to be in white and gold; but as the king's eldest daughter she had a right to white and silver, which she preferred."

A little then we talked of the late great naval victory, and she said it was singularly encouraging to us that the three great victories at sea had been "against our three great enemies, successively: Lord Howe against the French, Lord St. Vincent against the Spaniards, and Lord Duncan against the Dutch." (150)

She spoke very feelingly of the difficult situation of the Orange family, now in England, upon this battle; and she repeated me the contents of' a letter from the Princess of Orange, whose character she much extolled, upon the occasion, to the Princess Elizabeth, saying she could not bear to be the only person in England to withhold her congratulations to the king upon such an occasion, when no one owed him such obligations; but all she had to regret was that the Dutch had not fought with, not against, the English, and that the defeat had not fallen upon those who ought to be their joint enemies. She admired and pitied, inexpressibly, this poor fugitive princess.

I told her of a note my father had received from Lady Mary Duncan, in answer to his wishing her joy of her relation's prowess and success, in which he says, "Lady Mary has been, for some days past, like the rest of the nation drunk for joy." This led to more talk of this singular lady: and reciprocal stories of her oddities.

She then deigned to inquire very particularly about our new cottage, its size, its number of rooms, and its grounds. I told her, honestly, it was excessively comfortable, though unfinished and unfitted up, for that it had innumerable little contrivances and conveniences, just adapted to our particular use and taste, as M. d'Arblay had been its sole architect and surveyor. "Then I dare say," she answered, "it is very commodious, for there are no people understand enjoyable accommodations more than French gentleman, when they have the arranging them themselves."

This was very kind, and encouraged me to talk a good deal of my partner, in his various works and employments; and her manner of attention was even touchingly condescending, all circumstances considered. And she then related to me the works of two French priests, to whom she has herself been so good as to commit the fitting up of one of her apartments at Frogmore. And afterwards she gave me a description of what another French gentleman—elegantly and feelingly avoiding to say emigrant—had done in a room belonging to Mrs. Harcourt, at Sophia farm, where he had the sole superintendence of it, and has made it beautiful. When she asked about our field, I told her we hoped in time to buy it, as Mr. Locke had the extreme kindness to consent to part with it to us, when it should suit our convenience to purchase instead of renting it. I thought I saw a look of peculiar satisfaction at this, that seemed to convey pleasure in the implication thence to be drawn, that England was our decided, not forced or eventual residence. And she led me on to many minute particulars of our situation and way of living, with a sweetness of interest I can never forget. Nor even here stopped the sensations of gratitude and pleasure she thus awoke. She spoke then of my beloved Susan; asked if she were still in Ireland, and how the "pretty Norbury" did. She then a little embarrassed me by an inquiry "why Major Phillips went to Ireland?" for my answer, that he was persuaded he should improve his estate by superintending the agriculture of it himself, seemed dissatisfactory; however, she pressed it no further. But I cannot judge by what passed whether she concludes he is employed in a military way there, or whether she has heard that he has retired. She seemed kindly pleased at all I had to relate of my dear Norbury, and I delighted to call him back to her remembrance.

She talked a good deal of the Duchess of York, who continues the first favourite of the whole royal family. She told me of her beautiful works, lamented her indifferent health, and expatiated upon her admirable distribution of her time and plan of life, and charming qualities and character.

But what chiefly dwells upon me with pleasure is, that she spoke to me upon some subjects and persons that I know she would not for the world should be repeated, with just the same confidence, the same reliance upon my grateful discretion for her openness, that she honoured me with while she thought me established in her service for life. I need not tell my Susan how this binds me more than ever to her.

Very short to me seemed the time, though the whole conversation was serious, and her air thoughtful almost to sadness, when a page touched the door, and said something in German. The queen, who was then standing by the window, turned round to answer him, and then, with a sort of Congratulatory smile to me, said, "Now you will see what you don't expect—the king!"

I could indeed not expect it, for he was at Blackheath at a review, and he was returned only to dress for the levee. . .

THE KING AND HIS INFANT GRAND-DAUGHTER.

The king related very pleasantly a little anecdote of Lady —. "She brought the little Princess Charlotte,"(151) he said "to me just before the review. 'She hoped,' she said, 'I should not take it ill, for, having mentioned it to the child, she built so upon it that she had thought of nothing else.' Now this," cried he, laughing heartily, "was pretty strong! How can she know what a child is thinking of before it can speak?"

I was very happy at the fondness they both expressed for the little princess, "A sweet little creature," the king called her; "A most lovely child," the queen turned to me to add and the king said he had taken her upon his horse, and given her a little ride, before the regiment rode up to him. "'TIS very odd," he added, "but she always knows me on horseback, and never else." "Yes," said the queen, "when his majesty comes to her on horseback, she claps her little bands, and endeavours to say 'Gampa!' immediately." I was much pleased that she is brought up to such simple and affectionate acknowledgment of relationship.

The king then inquired about my father, and with a look of interest and kindness that regularly accompanies his mention of that most dear person. He asked after his health, his spirits, and his occupations, waiting for long answers to each inquiry. The queen anticipated my relation of his astronomic work, and he seemed much pleased with the design, as well as at hearing that his prot,g, Dr. Herschel, had been consulted.

I was then a little surprised by finding he had heard of "Clarentine."(152) He asked me, smilingly, some questions about it, and if it were true, what he suspected, that my young sister had a mind to do as I had done, and bring out a work in secret? I was very much pleased then when the queen said, "I have seen it, sir, and it is very pretty." . . .

ADMIRAL DUNCAN'S VICTORY. THE PRINCE AND PRINCESS OF ORANGE.

I then, by her majesty's kind appointment, returned to my lovely and loved Princess Augusta. Her hairdresser was just gone, and she was proceeding in equipping herself "If you can bear to see all this work," cried she, "pray come and sit with me, my dear Madame d'Arblay."

Nothing could be more expeditious than her attiring herself, nothing more careless than her examination how it succeeded. But judge my confusion and embarrassment, when, upon my saying I came to petition for the rest of the Story, she had just begun, and her answering by inquiring what it was about, I could not tell! It had entirely escaped my memory; and though I sought every way I could suggest to recall it, I so entirely failed, that after her repeated demands, I was compelled honestly to own that the commotion I had been put in by my interview with their majesties had really driven it from my mind.

She bore this with the true good humour of good sense but I was most excessively ashamed.

She then resumed the reigning subject of the day, Admiral Duncan's victory and this led to speak again of the Orange family; but she checked what seemed occurring to her about them, till her wardrobe-woman had done and was -dismissed; then, hurrying her away, while she sat down by me, putting on her long and superb diamond earrings herself, and without even turning towards a glass, she said, "I don't like much to talk of that family before the servants, for I am told they already think the king too good to them."

The Princess of Orange is, I find, a great favourite with them all; the Prince Frederick also, I believe, they like very much; but the prince himself, she said, " has never, in fact, had his education finished. He was married quite a boy, but, being married, concluded himself a man, and not only turned off all his instructors, but thought it unnecessary to ask, or hear, counsel or advice of any one. He is like a fallow field, that is, not of a soil that can't be improved; but one that has been left quite to itself, and therefore has no materials put in it for improvement."

She then told me that she had hindered him, with great faculty, from going to a great dinner, given at the Mansion House. upon the victory of Admiral Duncan. It was not, she said, that he did not feel for his country in that defeat, but that he never weighed the impropriety of his public appearance upon an occasion of rejoicing at it, nor the Ill effect the history of his so doing would produce in Holland. She had the kindness of heart to take upon herself preventing him "for no one," says she, "that is about him dares ever speak to him, to give him any hint of advice; which is a great "Misfortune: to him, poor man, for it makes him never know what is said or thought of him." She related with a great deal of humour her arguments to dissuade him, and his naŒve manner of combating them. But though she conquered at last, she did not convince, The Princess of Orange, she told me, had a most superior understanding and might guide him sensibly and honourably, but he was so jealous of being thought led by her counsel' that he never listened to it at all. She gave me to understand that this unhappy princess had had a life of uninterrupted indulgence and prosperity till the late revolution - and that the suddenness of such adversity had rather soured her mind, which, had it met sorrow and evil by any gradations, would have been equal to bearing them even nobly - but so quick a transition from affluence, and power, and wealth, and grandeur, to a fugitive and dependent state, had almost overpowered her.

A door was now opened from an inner apartment, where, I believe, was the grand collation for the Princess Sophia's birthday, and a tall thin young man appeared at it, peeping and staring, but not entering.

"O! How do you do, Ernest?" cried the princess; "I hope you are well; only pray do shut the door."

He did not obey, nor move, either forwards or backwards, but kept peering and peeping. She called to him again, beseeching him to shut the door- but he was determined to first gratify his curiosity, and, when he had looked as long as he thought pleasant, he entered the apartment; but Princess Augusta, instead of receiving and welcoming him, only said, "Good-bye, my dear Ernest; I shall see you again at the play."

He then marched on, finding himself so little desired, and only saying, "No, you won't; I hate the play."

I had risen when I found it one of the princes, and with a motion of readiness to depart - but my dear princess would not let me. When we were alone again, "Ernest," she said, "has a very good heart; only he speaks without taking time to think." She then gave me an instance. The Orange family by some chance were all assembled with our royal family when the news of the great victory at sea arrived; or at least upon the same day. "We were all," said she, " distressed for them upon SO trying an occasion and at supper we talked, of' course, of every other subject; but Ernest, quite uneasy at the forbearance, said to me, 'You don't think I won't drink Duncan's health to-night?' 'Hush!' cried I. 'That's very hard indeed!' said he, quite loud. I saw the princess of

orange looking at him, and was sure she had heard him; I trod upon his foot, and made him turn to her. She looked so disturbed, that he saw she had understood him, and he coloured very high. The Princess of Orange then said, 'I hope my being here will be no restraint upon anybody: I know what must be the subject of everybody's thoughts, and I beg I may not prevent its being so of their discourse.' Poor Ernest now was so sorry, he was ready to die, and the tears started into his eyes; and he would not have given his toast after this for all the world."

SOME NOTABLE ACTRESSES.

The play they were going to was "The Merchant of Venice," to see a new actress, just now much talked of—Miss Betterton; and the king, hearing she was extremely frightened at the thoughts of appearing before him, desired she might choose her own part for the first exhibition in his presence. She fixed upon Portia.

In speaking of Miss Farren's marriage with the Earl of Derby, she displayed that sweet mind which her state and station has so wholly escaped sullying; for, far from expressing either horror, or resentment, or derision at an actress being elevated to the rank of second countess of England, she told me, with an air of satisfaction, that she was informed she had behaved extremely well since her marriage, and done many generous and charitable actions.

She spoke with pleasure, too, of the high marriage made by another actress, Miss Wallis, who has preserved a spotless character, and is now the wife of a man of fortune and family Mr Campbell.

In mentioning Mrs. Siddons, and her great and affecting powers, she much surprised me by intelligence that she had bought the proprietorship of Sadler's-wells. I could not hear it without some amusement it seemed, I said, so extraordinary a combination—so degrading a one, indeed, that of the first tragic actress, the living Melpomene, and something so burlesque as Sadler's-wells. She laughed, and said it offered her a very ludicrous image, for Mrs. Siddons and Sadler's-wells," said she, " seems to me as ill-fitted as the dish they call a toad in a hole which I never saw, but always think of with anger, putting a noble sirloin of beef into a poor, paltry batter-pudding!

THE DUKE OF CLARENCE.

The door now again opened, and another royal personage put in his head - and upon the princess saying, "How d'ye do, William?" I recollected the Duke of Clarence.

I rose, of course, and he made a civil bow to my curtsey The princess asked him about the House of Lords the preceding evening, where I found he had spoken very handsomely and generously in eulogium of Admiral Duncan. Finding he was inclined to stay, the princess said to me,

"Madame d'Arblay, I beg you will sit down."

"Pray, madam," said the duke, with a formal motion of his hand, "let me beg you to be seated."

"You know—you recollect Madame d'Arblay, don't you, William?" said the princess. He bowed civilly an affirmative, and then began talking to me of Chesington. How I grieved poor dear Kitty was gone! How great would have been her gratification to have heard that he mentioned her, and with an air of kindness, as if he had really entered into the solid goodness of her character. I was much Surprised and much pleased, yet not without some perplexity and some embarrassment, as his knowledge of the excellent Kitty was from her being the dupe of the mistress of his aide-de-camp.

The princess, however, saved me any confusion beyond apprehension, for she asked not one question. He moved on towards the next apartment, and we were again alone.

She then talked to me a great deal of him, and gave me, admirably, his character. She is very partial to him, but by no means blindly. He had very good parts, she said, but seldom did them justice. "If he has something of high importance to do," she continued, "he will exert himself to the utmost, and do it really well; but otherwise, he is so fond of his ease, he lets everything take its course. He can just do a great deal or nothing. However, I really think, if he takes pains, he may make something of a speaker by and by in the House."

She related a visit he had made at Lady Mary Duncan's, at Hampton Court, upon hearing Admiral Duncan was there and told me the whole and most minute particulars of the battle, as they were repeated by his royal highness from the admiral's own account. But You will dispense with the martial detail from me. "Lady Mary," cried she, "is much enchanted with her gallant nephew. 'I used to look,' says she, 'for honour and glory from my other side, the T—s; but I receive it only from the Duncans! As to the T—s, what good do they do their country?—why, they play all day at tennis, and learn with vast skill to notch and scotch and go one! And that's what their country gets from them!'"

I thought now I should certainly be dismissed, for a page came to the door to announce that the Duke of York was arrived: but she only said, "Very well; pray shut the door," which seemed her gentle manner of having it understood she would not be disturbed, as she used the same words when messages were brought her from the Princesses Elizabeth and Mary.

She spoke again of the Duchess of York with the same fondness as at Windsor. "I told you before," she said, "I loved her like one of my own sisters, and I can tell you no more: and she knows it; for one day she was taken ill, and fainted, and we put her upon one of our beds, and got her everything we could think of ourselves, and let nobody else wait upon her; and when she revived she said to my brother, 'These are my sisters—I am sure they are! they must be my own!"

PRINCESS SOPHIA OF GLOUCESTER.

Our next and last interruption, I think, was from a very gentle tap at the door, and a "May I come in?" from a soft voice, while the lock was turned, and a youthful and very lovely female put in her head.

The princess immediately rose, and said, " "O yes," and held out her two hands to her; turning at the same time to me, and saying, "Princess Sophia."

I found it was the Duke of Gloucester's (154) daughter. She is very fat, with very fine eyes, a bright, even dazzling bloom, fine teeth, a beautiful skin, and a look of extreme modesty and sweetness. She curtseyed to me so distinguishingly, that I was almost confused by her condescension, fearing she 'Might imagine, from finding me seated with the Princess 'Augusta, and in such close conference, I was somebody.

"You look so fine and so grand," cried she, examining the princess's attire, which was very superb in silver and diamonds, "that I am almost afraid to come near you!" Her own dress was perfectly simple, though remarkably elegant.

O!—I hate myself when so fine cried Princess Augusta; "I cannot bear it but there is no help—the people at the play always expect it."

They then conversed a little while, both standing; and then Princess Augusta said, "Give my love to the duke (meaning of Gloucester), "and I hope I shall see him bye and bye; and to William." (155) (meaning the duke's son). And this, which was not a positive request that she would prolong her visit, was understood; and the lovely cousin made her curtsey and retired.

To me, again, she made another, so gravely low and civil, that I really blushed to receive it, from added fear of being mistaken. I accompanied her to the door, and shut it for her; and the moment she was out of the room, and out of sight of the Princess Augusta, she turned round to me, and with a smile of extreme Civility, and a voice very soft, said, "I am so happy to see you!—I have longed for it a great, great while—for I have read you with such delight and instruction, so often."

I was very much surprised indeed; I expressed my sense of her goodness as well as I could; and she curtseyed again, and glided away. "How infinitely gracious is all your royal highness's House to me!" cried I, as I returned to my charming princess; who again made me take my seat next her own, and again renewed her discourse.

I stayed on with this delightful princess till near four o'clock, when she descended to dinner. I then accompanied her to the head of the stairs, saying, "I feel quite low that this is over! How I wish it might be repeated in half a year instead of a year!"

"I'm sure, and so do I!" were the last kind words she condescendingly uttered.

I then made a little visit to Miss Planta, who was extremely friendly, and asked me why I should wait another year before I came. I told her I had leave for an annual visit, and could not presume to encroach beyond such a permission. However, as she proposed my calling upon her when I happened to be in town, I begged her to take some opportunity to hint my wish of admission, if possible, more frequently.

Very soon afterwards I had a letter from Miss Planta, saying she had mentioned to her majesty my regret of the long intervals of annual admissions; and that her majesty had most graciously answered, "She should be very glad to see me whenever I came to town."

DIARY RESUMED: (Addressed to Mrs. Phillips.)

INDIGNATION AGAINST TALLEYRAND.

Westhamble, Jan. 18, 1798. I am very impatient to know if the invasion threat affects your part of Ireland. Our 'Oracle' is of opinion the French soldiers will not go to Ireland, though there flattered with much help, because they can expect but little advantage, after all the accounts spread by the Opposition of its starving condition; but that they will come to England, though sure of contest, at least, because there they expect the very road to be paved with gold.

Nevertheless, how I wish my heart's beloved here! to share with us at least the same fears, instead of the division of apprehension we must now mutually be tormented with. I own I am sometimes affrighted enough. These sanguine and sanguinary wretches will risk all for the smallest hope of plunder; and Barras assures them they have only to enter England to be lords of wealth unbounded.

But Talleyrand!—how like myself must you have felt at his conduct! indignant—amazed—ashamed! Our first prepossession against him was instinct—he conquered it by pains indefatigable to win us, and he succeeded astonishingly, for we became partial to him almost to fondness. The part he now acts against England may be justified, perhaps, by the spirit of revenge; but the part he submits to perform of coadjutor with the worst of villains—with Barras—Rewbel—Merlin—marks some internal atrocity of character that disgusts as much as disappoints me. And now, a last stroke, which appears in yesterday's paper, gives the finishing hand to his portrait in my eyes. He has sent (and written) the letter which exhorts the King of Prussia to order the Duke of Brunswick to banish and drive from his dominions all the emigrants there in asylum —and among these are the Archbishop of Rennes (his uncle) and—his own mother!

Poor M. de Narbonne! how will he be shocked and let down! where he now is we cannot conjecture: all emigrants are exiled from the Canton of Berne, where he resided; I feel extremely disturbed about him. If that wretch Talleyrand has not given him some private Intimation to escape, and where to be safe, he must be a monster.

THE D'ARBLAY MAISONNETTE.

This very day, I thank God! we paid the last of our work men. Our house now is our own fairly —that it is our own madly too you will all think, when I tell you the small remnant of our income that has outlived this payment. However, if the Carmagnols do not seize our walls, we despair not of enjoying, in defiance of all straitness and strictness, our dear dwelling to our hearts' content. But we are reducing our expenses and way of life, in order to go on, in a manner you would laugh to see, though almost cry to hear. But I never forget Dr. Johnson's words. When somebody said that a certain person "had no turn for economy," he answered, "Sir, you might as well say that he has no turn for honesty."

We know nothing yet of our taxes—nothing—of our assessments; but we are of good courage, and so pleased with our maisonnette, we think nothing too dear for it, provided we can but exist in it. I should like much to know how you stand affected about the assessment, and about the invasion. O that all these public troubles would accelerate Your return! private blessings they would then, at least, prove. Ah, my Susan, how do I yearn for some little ray upon this subject!

Charles and his family are at Bath, and Charlotte is gone to them for a fortnight. All accounts that reach me of all the house and race are well. Mr. Locke gives us very-frequent peeps indeed, and looks with such benevolent pleasure at our dear cottage and its environs! and seems to say, "I brought all this to bear," and to feel happy in the noble trust he placed in our self-belief that he might venture to show that kind courage without which we could never have been united. All this retrospection is expressed by his penetrating eyes it every visit. He rarely alights; but I frequently enter the phaeton, and take a conversation in an airing. And when he comes without his precious Amelia, he indulges my Alex in being our third.

INTERVIEW WITH THE QUEEN AND THE PRINCESSES.

And now I have to prepare another Court relation for MY dearest Susanna. I received on Wednesday morn a letter from our dearest father, telling me he feared he should be forced to quit his Chelsea apartments, from a new arrangement among the officers, and wishing me to represent his difficulties, his books, health, time of life, and other circumstances, through Miss Planta, to the queen. M. d'Arblay and I both thought that, if I had any chance of being of the smallest use, it would be by endeavouring to obtain an audience-not by letter; and as the most remote hope of success was sufficient to urge -every exertion, we settled that I should set out instantly for Chelsea; and a chaise, therefore, we sent for from Dorking, and I set off at noon. M. d'A. would not go, as we knew not what accommodation I might find; and I could not, uninvited and unexpected, take my little darling boy; so I went not merrily, though never more willingly.

My dear father was at home, and, I could see, by no means surprised by my appearance, though he had not hinted at desiring it. Of course he was not very angry nor sorry, and we communed together upon his apprehensions, and settled our plan. I was to endeavour to represent his case to the queen, in hopes it might reach his majesty, and procure some order in his favour.

I wrote to Miss Planta, merely to say I was come to pass three days at Chelsea, and, presuming upon the gracious permission of her majesty, I ventured to make known my arrival, in the hope it might possibly procure me the honour of admittance. The next morning, Thursday, I had a note from Miss

Planta, to say that she had the pleasure to acquaint me, her majesty desired I would be at the Queen's house next day at ten o'clock.

Miss Planta conducted me immediately, by order, to the Princess Elizabeth, who received me alone, and kept me téte a téte till I was summoned to the queen, which was nearly an hour. She was all condescension and openness, and inquired into my way of life and plans, with a sort of kindness that I am sure belonged to a real wish to find them happy and prosperous. When I mentioned how much of our time was mutually given to books and writing, M. d'Arblay being as great a scribbler as myself, she good-naturedly exclaimed, "How fortunate he should have so much the same taste!"

"It was that, in fact," I answered, "which united us for our acquaintance began, in intimacy, by reading French together, and writing themes, both French and English, for each other's correction."

"Pray," cried she, "if it is not impertinent, may I ask to what religion you shall bring up your son?"

"The Protestant," I replied; telling her it was M. d'Arblay's own wish, since he was an Englishman born, he should be an Englishman bred,—with much more upon the subject that my Susan knows untold.

She then inquired why M. d'Arblay was not naturalised. This was truly kind, for it looked like wishing our permanently fixing in this his adopted country. I answered that he found he could not be naturalised as a catholic, which had made him relinquish the plan; for though he was firmly persuaded the real difference between the two religions was trifling, and such as even appeared to him, in the little he had had opportunity to examine, to be in favour of Protestantism, he could not bring himself to study the matter with a view of changing that seemed actuated by interest; nor could I wish it, earnest as I was for his naturalisation. But he hoped, ere long, to be able to be naturalised as an Irishman, that clause of religion not being there insisted upon, or else to become a denizen, which was next best, and which did not meddle with religion at all. She made me talk to her a great deal of my little boy, and my father, and M. d'Arblay; and when Miss Planta came to fetch me to her majesty, she desired to see me again before my departure.

The queen was in her White closet, working at a round table, with the four remaining princesses, Augusta, Mary, Sophia, and Amelia. She received me most sweetly, and with a look of far better spirits than upon my last admission. She permitted me, in the most gracious manner, to inquire about the princess royal, now Duchess of Wirtemberg, and gave me an account of her that I hope is not flattered; for it seemed happy, and such as reconciled them all to the separation. When she deigned to inquire, herself, after my dear father, you may be sure of the eagerness with which I seized the moment for relating his embarrassment and difficulties. She heard me with a benevolence that assured me, though she made no speech, my history would not be forgotten, nor remembered vainly. I was highly satisfied with her look and manner. The Princesses Mary and Amelia had a little opening between them, and when the queen was conversing with some lady who was teaching the Princess Sophia some work, they began a whispering conversation with me about my little boy. How tall is he?—how old is he?—Is he fat or thin?—is he like you or M. d'Arblay? etc.—with sweet vivacity of interest, -the lovely Princess Amelia finishing her listening to my every answer with a "dear little thing!" that made me long to embrace her as I have done in her childhood. She is now full as tall as princess royal, and as much formed; she looks seventeen, though only fourteen, but has an innocence, a Hebe blush, an air of modest candour, and a gentleness so caressingly inviting, of voice and eye, that I have seldom seen a more captivating young creature.

Then they talked of my new house, and inquired about every room it contained; and then of our grounds, and they were mightily diverted with the mixtures of roses and cabbages, sweet briars, and potatoes, etc.

The queen, catching the domestic theme, presently made inquiries herself, both as to the building and the child, asking, with respect to the latter, "Is he here?" as if she meant in the palace. I told her I had come so unexpectedly myself upon my father's difficulties, that I had not this time brought my little shadow. I believed, however, I should fetch him, as, if I lengthened my stay, M. d'Arblay would come also. "To be sure!" she said, as if feeling the trio's full objections to separating.

She asked if I had seen a play just come out, called "He's much to Blame;" and, on my negative, began to relate to me its plot and characters, and the representation and its effect; and, warming herself by her own account and my attention, she presently entered into a very minute history of each act, and a criticism upon some incidents, with a spirit and judiciousness that were charming. She is delightful in discourse when animated by her subject, and speaking to auditors with whom, neither from circumstance nor suspicion, she has restraint. But when, as occasionally she deigned to ask my opinion of the several actors she brought in review, I answered I had never seen them, neither Mrs. Pope, Miss Betterton, Mr. Murray, etc,—she really looked almost concerned. She knows my fondness for the theatre, and I did not fear to say my inability to indulge it was almost my only regret in my hermit life. "I, too," she graciously said, "prefer plays to all other amusements."

By degrees all the princesses retired, except the Princess Augusta. She then spoke more openly upon less public matters, in particular upon the affair, then just recent, of the Duke of Norfolk, who, you may have heard, had drunk, at the Whig Club, "To the majesty of the people," in consequence of which the king had erased his name from the privy council. His grace had been caricatured drinking from a silver tankard with the burnt bread still in flames touching his mouth, and exclaiming, "Pshaw! my toast has burnt my mouth."

This led me to speak of his great brick house, which is our immediate vis-a-vis. And much then ensued upon Lady—concerning whom she opened to me very completely, allowing all I said of her uncommon excellence as a mother, but adding, "Though she is certainly very clever, she thinks herself so a little too much, and instructs others at every word. I was so tired with her beginning everything with 'I think,' that, at last, just as she said so, I stopped her, and cried, 'O, I know what you think, Lady —!' Really, one is obliged to be quite sharp with her to keep her in her place." . . .

Lady C—, she had been informed, had a considerable sum in the French funds, which she endeavoured from time to time to recover, but upon her last effort, she had the following query put to her agent by order of the Directory: how much she would have deducted from the principal, as a contribution towards the loan raising for the army of England? If Lady C— were not mother-in-law to a minister who sees the king almost daily, I should think this a made story.

When, after about an hour and a half's audience, she dismissed me, she most graciously asked my stay at Chelsea, and desired I would inform Miss Planta before I returned home. This gave me the most gratifying feeling, and much hope for my dearest father.

ROYAL CONTRIBUTIONS TOWARDS THE WAR.

Returning then, according to my permission, to Princess Elizabeth, she again took up her netting, and made me sit by her. We talked a good deal of the new-married daughter of Lady Templetown, and she was happy, she said, to hear from me that the ceremony was performed by her own favourite Bishop of Durham, for she was sure a blessing would attend his joining their hands. She asked me much of my little man, and told me several things of the Princess Charlotte, her niece, and our future queen; she seems very fond of her, and says 'tis a lovely child, and extremely like the Prince of Wales. "She is just two years old," said she, "and speaks very prettily, though not plainly. I flatter myself Aunt Liby, as she calls me, is a great favourite with her."

My dearest Princess Augusta soon after came in, and, after staying a few minutes, and giving some message to her sister, said, "And when you leave Elizabeth, my dear Madame d'Arblay, I hope you'll come to me."

This happened almost immediately, and I found her hurrying over the duty of her toilette, which she presently despatched, though she was going to a public concert of Ancient Music, and without scarcely once looking in the glass, from haste to have done, and from a freedom from vanity I never saw quite equalled in any young woman of any class. She then dismissed her hairdresser and wardrobe-woman, and made me sit by her.

Almost immediately we began upon the voluntary contributions to the support of the war; and when I mentioned the queen's munificent donation of five thousand pounds a-year for its support, and my admiration of it, from my peculiar knowledge, through my long residence under the royal roof, of the many claims which her majesty's benevolence, as well as state, had raised upon her powers, she seemed much gratified by the justice I did her royal mother, and exclaimed eagerly "I do assure you, my dear Madame d'Arblay, people ought to know more how good the queen is, for they don't know it half." And then she told me that she only by accident had learnt almost all that she knew of the queen's bounties. "And the most I gathered," she continued, laughing, "was, to tell you the real truth, by my own impertinence - for when we were at Cheltenham, Lady Courtown (the queen's lady-in-waiting for the country) put her pocket-book down on the table, when I was alone with her, by some chance open at a page where mamma's name was written: so, not guessing at any secret commission, I took it up, and read; Given by her majesty's commands—so much, and so much, and so much. And I was quite surprised. However, Lady Courtown made me promise never to mention it to the queen; so I never have. But I long it should be known, for all that; though I would not take such a liberty as to spread it of my own judgment."

I then mentioned my own difficulties formerly, when her Majesty, upon my ill state of health's urging my resigning the honour of belonging to the royal household, so graciously settled upon me a pension, that I had been forbidden to name it. I had been quite distressed in not avowing what I so gratefully felt, and hearing questions and surmises and remarks I had no power to answer. She seemed instantly to comprehend that my silence might do wrong, on such an occasion, to the queen, for she smiled, and with great quickness cried, "O, I dare say you felt quite guilty in holding your tongue." And she was quite pleased with the permission afterwards granted me to be explicit.

When I spoke of her own and her royal sisters' contributions, one hundred pounds per annum, she blushed, bat seemed ready to enter upon the subject, even confidentially, and related its whole history. No one ever advised or named it to them, as they have none of them any separate establishment, but all hang upon the queen, from whose pin-money they are provided for till they marry, or have a household of their own granted by Parliament. "Yet we all longed to subscribe," cried she, "and thought it quite right, if other young ladies did, not to be left out. But the difficulty was, how to do what would not be improper for us, and yet not to be generous at mamma's expense, for that would only have been unjust. So we consulted some of our friends, and then fixed upon one hundred pounds a-piece; and when we asked the queen's leave, she was so good as to approve it. So then we spoke to the king, and he said it was but little, but he wished particularly nobody should subscribe what would really distress them; and that, if that was all we could conveniently do, and regularly continue, he approved it more than to have us make a greater exertion, and either bring ourselves into difficulties or not go on. But he was not at all angry."

She then gave me the history of the contribution of her brothers. The Prince of Wales could not give in his name without the leave of his creditors. "But Ernest," cried she, "gives three hundred pounds a-year, and that's a tenth of his income, for the king allows him three thousand pounds."

All this leading to discourse upon loyalty, and then its contrast, democracy, she narrated to me at full length a lecture of Therwall's, which had been repeated to her by M. de Guiffardiére. It was very curious from her mouth. But she is candour in its whitest purity, wherever it is possible to display it, in discriminating between good and bad, and abstracting rays of light even from the darkest shades. So she did even from Therwall.

She made me, as usual, talk of my little boy, and was much amused by hearing that, imitating what he heard from me, he called his father "mon ami," and tutoyed him, drinking his health at dinner, as his father does to me—"la santé."

When at length the Princess Augusta gave me the bow of cong, she spoke of seeing me again soon: I said I should therefore lengthen my stay in town, and induce M. d'Arblay to come and bring my boy.

"We shall see you then certainly," said she, smiling, "and do pray, my dear Madame d'Arblay, bring your little boy with you. And don't say anything to him," cried she, as I was departing; "let us see him quite natural."

I understood her gracious, and let me say rational, desire, that the child should not be impressed with any awe of the royal presence. I assured her I must obey, for he was so young, so wild, and so unused to present himself, except as a plaything, that it would not be even in my power to make him orderly. . . .

My dear father was extremely pleased with what I had to tell him, and hurried me back to Westhamble, to provide myself with baggage for sojourning with him. My two Alexanders, you will believe, were now warmly invited to Chelsea, and we all returned thither together, accompanied by Betty Nurse.

INVITATION TO THE PLAY. MRS SCHWELLENBERG'S SUCCESSOR.

I shall Complete my next Court visit before I enter upon aught else. I received, very soon, a note from Madame Bremyere, who is my successor. [I have told you poor Mlle. Jacobi is returned to Germany, I think; and that her niece, La Bettina, is to marry a rich English merchant and settle in London.] This note says Mrs Bremyere has received the queen's commands to invite Madame d'Arblay to the play tomorrow night "-with her own desire I would drink coffee in her apartment before we went to the theatre. Could anything More sweetly mark the real kindness of the queen than this remembrance of my fondness for plays?

My dear father lent me his carriage, and I was now introduced to the successor of Mrs. Schwellenberg, Mlle. Bachmeister, a German, brought over by M. de Luc, who travelled to Germany to accompany her hither. I found she was the lady I had seen with the queen and princesses, teaching some work. Not having been to the so-long-known apartments since the death of Mrs. Schwellenberg, I knew not how they were arranged, and had concluded Madame Bremyere possessed those of Mrs. Schwellenberg. Thither, therefore, I went, and was received, to my great surprise, by this lady, who was equally surprised by my entrance, though without any doubt who I might be, from having seen me with the queen, and from knowing I was to join the play-party to my ci-devant box. I inquired if I had made any mistake, but though she could not say no, she would not suffer Me to rectify it, but sent to ask Madame Bremyere to meet me in her room.

Mlle. Bachmeister is extremely genteel in her figure, though extremely plain in her face; her voice is gentle and penetrating; her manners are soft, yet dignified, and she appears to be both a feeling and a cultivated character. I could not but lament such had not been the former possessor of an apartment I had so often entered with the most cruel antipathy. I liked her exceedingly; she is a marked gentlewoman in her whole deportment, though whether so from birth, education, or only mind, I am ignorant.

Since she gave me so pleasant a prejudice in her favour, you will be sure our acquaintance began with some spirit. We talked much of the situation she filled; and I thought it my duty to cast the whole of my resignation of one so similar upon ill health. Mrs. Bremyere soon joined us, and we took up Miss Barbara Planta in our way to the theatre.

When the king entered, followed by the queen and his lovely daughters, and the orchestra struck up "God save the king," and the people all called for the singers, who filled the stage to sing it, the emotion I was suddenly filled with so powerfully possessed me, that I wished I could, for a minute or two, have flown from the box, to have sobbed; I was so gratefully delighted at the sight before me, and so enraptured at the continued enthusiasm of the no longer volatile people for their worthy, revered sovereign, that I really suffered from the restraint I felt of being forced to behave decorously.

The play was the "Heir at Law," by Colman the younger. I liked it extremely. It has a good deal of character, a happy plot, much interest in the under parts, and is combined, I think, by real genius, though open to innumerable partial criticisms. I heard a gentleman's voice from the next box call softly to Miss Barbara Planta, "Who is that lady?" and heard her answer my name, and him rejoin, "I thought so." I found it was Lord Aylesbury, who also has resigned, and was at the play only for the pleasure of sitting opposite his late royal mistress. . . .

MADAME D'ARBLAY'S LITTLE BOY AT COURT.

About a week after this theatrical regale, I went to the Queen's house, to make known I had only a few more days to remain at Chelsea. I arrived just as the royal family had set out for Windsor; but Miss Bacbmeister, fortunately, had only ascended her coach to follow. I alighted, and went to tell my errand. Mrs. Bremyere, Mrs. Cheveley, and Miss Planta were her party. The latter promised to speak for me to the queen; but, gathering I had my little boy, in my father's carriage, she made me send for him. They took him in, and loaded him with bonbons and admiration, and would have loaded him with caresses to boot, but the little wretch resisted that part of the entertainment. Upon their return from Windsor, you will not suppose me made very unhappy to receive the following billet:—

March 8th, 1798. My dear friend, the queen has commanded me to acquaint you that she desires you will be at the Queen's house on Thursday morning at ten o'clock, with your lovely boy. You are desired to come upstairs in Princess Elizabeth's apartments, and her majesty will send for you as soon as she can see you. Adieu! Yours most affectionately, M. Planta.

A little before ten, you will easily believe, we were at the Queen's house, and were immediately ushered into the apartment of the Princess Elizabeth, who, to show she expected my little man, had some playthings upon one of her many tables; for her royal highness has at least twenty in her principal room. The child, in a new muslin frock, sash, etc.' did not look to much disadvantage, and she examined him with the most good-humoured pleasure, and, finding him too shy to be seized, had the graciousness, as well as sense, to play round and court him by sportive wiles, instead of being offended at his insensibility to her royal notice. She ran about the room, peeped at him through chairs, clapped her hands, half caught without touching him, and showed a skill and a sweetness that made one almost sigh she should have no call for her maternal propensities.

There came in presently Miss D—, a young lady about thirteen, who seems in some measure under the protection of her royal highness, who had rescued her poor injured and amiable mother, Lady D-, from extreme distress, into which she had been involved by her unworthy husband's connexion with the infamous Lady W-, who, more hardhearted than even bailiffs, had forced certain of those gentry, in an execution she had ordered in Sir H. D—'s house, to seize even all the children's playthings! as well as their clothes, and that when Lady D— had but just lain in, and was nearly dying! This charming princess, who had been particularly acquainted with Lady D— during her own illness at Kew Palace, where the queen permitted the intercourse, came forward upon this distress, and gave her a small independent house in the neighbourhood of Kew, with every advantage she could annex to it. But she is now lately no more, and, by the sort of reception given to her daughter, I fancy the princess transfers to her that kind benevolence the mother no longer wants.

just then, Miss Planta came to summon us to the Princess Augusta. She received me with her customary sweetness, and called the little boy to her. He went fearfully and cautiously, yet with a look of curiosity at the state of her head, and the operations of her friseur, that seemed to draw him on more powerfully than her commands. He would not, however, be touched, always flying to my side at the least attempt to take his hand. This would much have vexed me, if I had not seen the ready allowance she made for his retired life, and total want of use to the sight of anybody out of our family, except the Lockes, amongst whom I told her his peculiar preference for Amelia. "Come then," cried she, "come hither, my dear, and tell me all about her,—is she very good to you?—do you like her very much?"

He was now examining her fine carpet, and no answer was to be procured. I would have apologised, but she would not let me. "'Tis so natural," she cried, "'that he should be more amused with those shapes and colours than with my stupid questions."

Princess Mary now came in, and, earnestly looking at him, exclaimed, "He's beautiful!—what eyes!—do look at his eyes!"

"Come hither, my dear," again cried Princess Augusta, "come hither;" and, catching him to her for a Moment, and, holding up his hair. to lift up his face and made him look at her, she smiled very archly, and cried, "O! horrid eyes! shocking eyes!—take them away!"

Princess Elizabeth then entered, attended by a page, who was loaded with playthings which she had been sending for. You may suppose him caught now! He seized upon dogs, horses, chaise, a cobbler, a watchman, and all he could grasp but would not give his little person or cheeks, to my great confusion, for any of them.

I was fain to call him a little savage, a wild deer, a creature just caught from the woods, and whatever could indicate his rustic life, and apprehension of new faces,—to prevent their being hurt; and their excessive good nature helped all my excuses, nay, made them needless, except to myself. .

Princess Elizabeth now began playing upon an organ she had brought him, which he flew to seize. "Ay, do! that's right, my dear," cried Princess Augusta, stopping her ears at some discordant sounds; "take it to mon ami, to frighten the cats out of his garden."

And now, last of all, came in Princess Amelia, and, strange to relate! the child was instantly delighted with her! She came first up to me, and, to my inexpressible surprise and enchantment, she gave me her sweet beautiful face to kiss!—an honour I had thought now for ever over, though she had so frequently gratified me with it formerly. Still more touched, however, than astonished, I would have kissed her hand, but, withdrawing it, saying, "No, no,—you know I hate that!" she again presented me her ruby lips, and with an expression of -such ingenuous sweetness and innocence as was truly captivating. She is and will be another Princess Augusta.

She then turned to the child, and his eyes met hers with a look of the same pleasure that they were sought. She stooped down to take his unresisting hands, and, exclaiming "Dear little thing!" took him in her arms, to his own as obvious content as hers.

"He likes her!" cried Princess Augusta, "a little rogue! see how he likes her!"

"Dear little thing!" with double the emphasis, repeated the young princess, now sitting down and taking him upon her knee; "and how does M. d'Arblay do?"

The child now left all his new playthings, his admired carpet, and his privilege of jumping from room to room, for the gentle pleasure of sitting in her lap and receiving her caresses. I could not be very angry, you will believe, yet I would have given the world I could have made him equally grateful to the Princess Augusta. This last charming personage, I now found, was going to sit for her picture—I fancy to send to the Duchess of Wurtemberg. She gave me leave to attend her with my bantling. The other princesses retired to dress for Court.

It was with great difficulty I could part my little love from his grand collection of new playthings, all of which he had dragged into the painting-room, and wanted now to pull them down-stairs to the queen's apartment. I persuaded him, however, to relinquish the design without a quarrel, by promising we would return for them.

HIS PRESENTATION TO THE QUEEN.

I was not a little anxious, you will believe, in this presentation of my unconsciously honoured rogue, who entered the White closet totally unimpressed with any awe, and only with a sensation of disappointment in not meeting again the gay young party, and variety of playthings, he had left above. The queen, nevertheless, was all condescending indulgence, and had a Noah's ark ready displayed upon the table for him.

But her look was serious and full of care, and, though perfectly gracious, none of her winning smiles brightened her countenance, and her voice was never cheerful. I have since known that the Irish conspiracy with France was just then discovered, and O'Connor that very morning taken. (156) No wonder she should have felt a shock that pervaded her whole mind and manners! If we all are struck with horror at such developments of treason, danger, and guilt, what must they prove to the royal family, at whom they are regularly aimed? How my heart has ached for them in that horrible business!

"And how does your papa do?" said the queen.

"He's at Telsea," answered the child.

"And how does grandDapa do?"

"He's in the toach," he replied.

"And what a pretty frock you've got on! who made it you, mamma, or little aunty?"

The little boy now grew restless, and pulled me about, with a desire to change his situation. I was a good deal embarrassed, as I saw the queen meant to enter into conversation as usual; which I knew to be impossible, unless he had some entertainment to occupy him. She perceived this soon, and had the goodness immediately to open Noah's ark herself, which she had meant he should take away with him to examine and possess at once. But he was now soon in raptures: and, as the various animals were produced, looked with a delight that danced in all his features; and when any appeared of which he knew the name, he capered with joy; such as, "O! a tow [cow]!" But at the dog, he clapped his little hands, and running close to her Majesty; leant upon her lap, exclaiming, "O, it's bow wow!"

"And do you know this, little man?" said the queen, showing him a cat.

"Yes," cried he, again jumping as he leant upon her, "its name is talled pussey!"

And at the appearance of Noah, in a green mantle, and leaning on a stick, he said, "That's the shepherd's boy!"

The queen now inquired about my dear father, and heard all I had to say relative to his apartments, with an air of interest, yet not as if it was new to her. I have great reason to believe the accommodation then arranging, and since settled, as to his continuance in the College, has been deeply influenced by some royal hint. . . .

I imagined she had just heard of the marriage of Charlotte, for she inquired after my sister Frances, whom she never had mentioned before since I quitted my post. I was obliged briefly to relate the transaction, seeking to adorn it by stating Mr. Broome's being the author of "Simkin's Letters." She agreed in their uncommon wit and humour.

My little rebel, meanwhile, finding his animals were not given into his own hands, but removed from their mischief, was struggling all this time to get at the Tunbridge-ware of the queen's work-box, and, in defiance of all my efforts to prevent him, he seized one piece, which he called a hammer, and began violently knocking the table with it. I would fain have taken it away silently - but he resisted such grave authority, and so continually took it back, that the queen, to my great confusion, now gave it him. Soon, however, tired also of this, he ran away from me into the next room, which was their majesties' bedroom, and in which were all the jewels ready to take to St. James's, for the Court attire. I was excessively ashamed, and obliged to fetch him back in my arms, and there to keep him. "

"Get down, little man," said the queen; "you are too heavy for your mamma."

He took not the smallest notice of this admonition. The queen, accustomed to more implicit obedience, repeated it but he only nestled his little head in my neck, and worked' about his whole person, so that I with difficulty held him.

The queen now imagined he did not know whom she meant, and said, "What does he call you? Has he any particular name for you?"

He now lifted up his head, and, before I could answer, called out, in a fondling manner, "Mamma, mamma!"

"O!" said she, smiling, "he knows who I mean!"

His restlessness still interrupting all attention, in defiance of my earnest whispers for quietness, she now said, "Perhaps he is hungry?" and rang her bell, and ordered a page to bring some cakes.

He took one with great pleasure, and was content to stand down to eat it. I asked him if he had nothing to say for it; he nodded his little head, and composedly answered, "Sanky, queen!" This could not help amusing her, nor me, neither, for I had no expectation of quite so succinct an answer.

The carriages were now come for St. James's, and the Princesses Augusta and Elizabeth came into the apartment. The little monkey, in a fit of renewed lassitude after his cake, had flung himself on the floor, to repose at his ease. He rose, however, upon their appearance, and the sweet Princess Augusta said to the queen, "He has been so good, up-stairs, mamma, that nothing could be better behaved." I could have kissed her for this instinctive kindness, excited by a momentary view of my embarrassment at his little airs and liberties.

The queen heard her with an air of approving, as well as understanding, her motive, and spoke to me with the utmost condescension of him, though I cannot recollect how, for I was a good deal fidgeted lest he should come to some disgrace, by any actual mischief or positive rebellion. I escaped pretty well, however, and they all left us with smiles and graciousness. . . .

You will not be much surprised to hear that papa came to help us out of the coach, at* our return to Chelsea, eager to know how our little rebel had conducted himself, and how he had been received. The sight of his playthings, you will believe, was not very disagreeable. The ark, watchman, and cobbler, I shall keep for him till he may himself judge their worth beyond their price.

MLLE. BACHMEISTER PRODUCES A FAVOURABLE IMPRESSION.

I returned to the Queen's house in the afternoon to drink coffee with Mlle. Bachmeister, whom I found alone, and spent a half-hour with very pleasantly, though very seriously, for her character is grave and feeling, and I fear she is not happy. Afterwards we were joined by Madame Bremyere, who is far more cheerful.

The play was called "Secrets Worth Knowing;" a new piece. In the next box to ours sat Mrs. Ariana Egerton, the bed-chamber-woman to her majesty, who used so frequently to visit me at Windsor. She soon recollected me, though she protested I looked so considerably in better health, she took me for my own Younger sister - and we had a great deal of chat together, very amicable and cordial. I so much respect her warm exertions for the emigrant ladies, that I addressed her with real pleasure, in pouring forth my praises for her kindness and benevolence.

When we returned to the Queen's house my father's carriage was not arrived, and I was obliged to detain Mlle. Bachmeister in conversation for full half an hour, while I waited; but it served to increase my good disposition to her. She is really an interesting woman. Had she been in that place while I belonged to the queen, heaven knows if I had so struggled for deliverance, for poor Mrs. Schwellenberg so wore, wasted, and tortured all my little leisure, that my time for repose was, in fact, my time of greatest labour. So all is for the best! I have escaped offending lastingly the royal mistress I love and honour, and I live at Westhamble with my two precious Alexanders.

(137) The most interesting account of the unfortunate expedition to Bantry Bay is to be found in Wolfe Tone's " Memoirs." Wolfe Tone, one of the leading members of the Irish Revolutionary party, had been for some time resident in Paris, engaged in negotiations with the Directory, with the view of obtaining French support for the Irish in their intended attempt to throw off the yoke of England. About the middle of December, 1796, a large French fleet, under the Admiral Villaret-Joyeuse, sailed from Brest, having on board an army of f twenty-five thousand men, commanded by General Hoche, one of the ablest officers of the Republic. Wolfe Tone accompanied the troops in the capacity of adjutant to the general, But the fleet was dispersed by storms. The vessel which had General Hoche on board was obliged to put into the harbour of Rochelle, and comparatively few of the ships, with about six thousand troops on board, actually cast anchor in Bantry Bay. Even there, the wind was so 'Violent as to render landing impossible, and after a few days' delay the expedition returned to France. ED.

(138) Edmund Burke died, at his house at Beaconsfield, half an hour after midnight on the morning of Sunday, July 9, 1797. He was buried, July 15, in the parish church of Beaconsfield. ED.

(139) Sold for the benefit of the nation.

(140) Dr. Johnson's negro servant. Johnson left him a comfortable annuity, on which he retired to Lichfield. He died in the infirmary at Stafford, February 13, 1801. ED.

(141) The Garrick family resided in Lichfield. David Garrick was born in Hereford, but educated at Lichfield. ED.

(142) Dr. Burney's little grandson, and the son of Captain James BAR Burney. after years, as readers of "Elia" will remember, Martin Burney was the friend of Charles Lamb. ED.

(143) Since the death of his second wife, Dr. Burney had been engaged upon a "historical and didactic poem on astronomy." He had been urged to the undertaking by Fanny, who hoped that the interest of this new occupation might prove a relief to his sorrow. Astronomy Was a favourite subject with Dr. Burney, and he made great progress with the poem, which was for years his favourite recreation. At a later period, however, for some reason which his daughter never discovered, he relinquished the task and destroyed the manuscript. ED.

(144) Ralph Broome, who married Charlotte Francis in 1798, wasthe author of "The Letters of Simpkin the Second, poetic recorder of all the proceedings upon the trial of Warren Hastings, Esq, in Westminster Hall," published by Stockdale, 1789. These letters, which had already appeared separately in "The World," form, as the title implies, a burlesque report of the trial, in rhymed verse. The author is very severe upon the managers, and proportionately favourable to Mr. Hastings. The letters are amusing and not without Wit, although in these respects "Simpkin the Second" falls decidedly short of "Simpkin the First," who is, of course, the Simple Simkin of Anstey's "New Bath Guide." upon which clever satire Broome had modelled his performance. ED.

(145) Benjamin Thompson, Count Rumford, was a very singular character—a compound of experimental philosopher, practical philanthropist, soldier and statesman. He was born at Woburn, Massachusetts, in 1753. A Tory during the struggle for American independence, he embarked for England before the close of the war. There he was well received by the government, but shortly afterwards he went to Bavaria, where he entered into the service of the Elector. He soon attained a high reputation by the reforms which he introduced in various departments, and was created a Count of the Holy Roman Empire, by the title of Count Rumford. Among his principal achievements in

Bavaria were the reforms which he brought about in the army, and the measures which he instituted for the relief of the poor and the suppression of beggary. To Fanny, at present, Count Rumford was more interesting as the inventor of an improved Cooking range, by which the consumption of fuel was greatly reduced. See his "Life" by James Renwick, in Sparks's "Library of American Biography," Boston, 1845. ED.

(146) The insurrection of the 18th of Fructidor (September 4, 1797). In 1795, on the dissolution of the Convention, the government of France was entrusted to a Directory of five persons, assisted by two councils—the Council of Ancients, and the Council of Five hundred. In course of time, the reactionary, or anti-revolutionary, party obtained a large majority in the councils, which were thus involved in continual disputes with the Directory. The army supported the Directory, and on the 4th of September a large body of troops surrounded the Tuileries, and arrested a number of the most obnoxious members of the councils; many of these Were afterwards—not guillotined, but transported to South America. ED.

(147) The marriage of the princess royal and the hereditary prince of Wurtemberg, May 18, 1797. ED.

(148) In April, 797, a serious mutiny broke out in the fleet at Spithead. The sailors demanded increased pay and better food. Their demands were finally conceded, and they returned to their duty, May 14. A few days later, a still more alarming mutiny broke out in the fleet at the Nore. The mutineers hoisted the red flag, May 23, and, being joined by vessels from other squadrons, found themselves presently masters of eleven ships of the line, and thirteen frigates. With this powerful fleet they blocked the Thames, and put a stop to the river trade of London. Their demands were more extensive than those of the Spithead Mutineers, but government firmly refused further concessions, and in June the want of union and resolution among the men brought about the collapse of the mutiny. Ship after ship deserted the red flag, until the last vessel was steered into Sheerness harbour, and given up to the authorities. Several of the leaders were tried by court-martial and hanged; the rest of the mutineers were pardoned. ED.

(149) The decisive victory gained by Admiral Duncan over the Dutch fleet, off Camperdown, October 11, 1797. in January, 1795, the French army under General Pichegru had conquered Holland with little difficulty, meeting, indeed, with much sympathy from the inhabitants. The Prince of Orange and his family were forced to take refuge in England and the representatives of the Dutch people immediately assembling, proclaimed Holland a republic, under the protection of France. From that time Holland had been in alliance with France, and at war with England. Duncan was rewarded for his victory with a pension and a peerage—Viscount Duncan of Camperdown henceforward. ED.

(150) Duncan's victory we have already noted. Lord Howe's was the great victory of June 1, 1794, over the French fleet commanded by Admiral Villaret-joyeuse. It was in this battle that the Vengeur went down, out of which incident Barrere manufactured, for the benefit of the French people, that rousing story of the disabled ship refusing to strike its colours, and sinking while every man of the crew, with his last breath, shouted "Vive la Republique!" Magnificent, had it not been pure fiction! Lord St. Vincent (then Admiral Jervis) gained a complete victory over the Spanish fleet off Cape St. Vincent, February 14, 1797. Spain, as well as Holland, was now in alliance with France: had made peace with France in 1795, and declared war against England in the following year. Admiral Jervis received the title of Earl St. Vincent and a pension in consequence of his victory. ED.

(151) Only child of the Prince and Princess of Wales, born January 7, 1796. ED.

(152) A novel by Sarah Harriet Burney. ED.

(153) The Duke of Cumberland, afterward, King of Hanover; fifth son of George III.; born 1771, died 1851. ED.

(154) William Henry, Duke of Gloucester, and brother of George III. ED.

(155) William Frederick, afterwards Duke of Gloucester, and husband of the Princess Mary. He was born in 1776, and died in 1836. ED.

(156) Arthur O'Connor, nephew and heir of Lord Longueville, was one of the Irish leaders, who took part in the negotiations between the Revolutionary party in Ireland and the French Directory. He and two or three of his associates were arrested at Margate (February 28, 1798), where they were attempting to hire a boat to take them to France. They were tried at Maidstone (May 21), and one of the party, on whom were found some compromising papers, including an address to the Directory, was convicted and hanged. O'Connor was acquitted, but immediately rearrested and detained in custody during the rising in Ireland. ED.

SECTION 22. (1798-1802)

VISITS TO OLD FRIENDS: WESTHAMBLE: DEATH OF MRS. PHILLIPS: SOJOURN IN FRANCE.

[From the "Memoirs of Dr. Burney" we extract the following details respecting the death of Fanny's favourite sister, Susan Phillips.

"Winter now was nearly at hand, and travelling seemed deeply dangerous, in her sickly state, for the enfeebled Susanna. Yet she herself, panting to receive again the blessing of her beloved father, concentrated every idea of recovery in her return. She declined, therefore, though with exquisite sensibility, the supplicating desire of this Editor [Madame d'Arblay] to join and to nurse her at Belcotton, her own cottage; and persevered through every impediment in her efforts to reach the parental home. . . . Every obstacle, at length, being finally vanquished, the journey was resolved upon, and its preparations were made;— when a fearful new illness suddenly confined the helpless invalid to her bed. There she remained some weeks - after which, with the utmost difficulty, and by two long days' travelling, though for a distance of only twenty-six miles, she reached Dublin where, exhausted, emaciated, she was again forced to her bed; there again to remain for nearly as long a new delay! " Every hour of separation became now to the Doctor Dr. Burney] an hour of grief, from the certainty that, the expedition once begun, it could be caused only by suffering malady, or expiring strength.

"It was not till the very close of the year 1799, amidst deep snow, fierce frost, blighting winds, and darksome days, that, scarcely alive, his sinking Susanna was landed at Park Gate. There she was joined by her affectionate brother, Dr. Charles, who hastened to hail her arrival, that he might convey her in his own warm carriage to her heart-yearning father, her fondly impatient brethren, and the tenderest of friends. But he found her in no state to travel: further feeble, drooping, wasted away, scarcely to be known, shrunk, nearly withered!—yet still with her fair mind in full possession of its clearest powers; still with all the native sweetness of her looks, manners, voice, and smiles; still with all her desire to please; her affecting patience of endurance; her touching sensibility for every species of attention; and all her unalterable loveliness of disposition, that sought to console for her own afflictions, to give comfort for her own sufferings!

"During the space of a doubtful week, her kind brother Dr. Charles, awaited the happy moment when she might be able to move on. But on—save as a corpse,—she moved no more! *

Gentle was her end! gentle as the whole tenor of her life but as sudden in its conclusion as it had been lingering in its approach."

She died at Park Gate, January 6, 1800, and was buried in Neston Churchyard, near Park Gate. ED.

The latter portion of the following section introduces the reader to new scenes and new acquaintances. During the summer of 1801 negotiations for peace between France and England were carried on in London, between lord Hawkesbury, on the part of the English government, and M. Otto, the French plenipotentiary. The preliminary treaty was signed in London, October 1, 1801, and ratified a few days later on the part of Napoleon Bonaparte, then First Consul, and de facto ruler of France, by a special envoy from Paris—General Lauriston. The definitive treaty, by which the details of mutual concessions, etc, were finally arranged, was signed at Amiens, March 25, 1802. In England the peace was received with rapture: General Lauriston was drawn in triumph in his carriage through the streets of London by the people. The "mutual concessions," however, showed a large balance in favour of France. As Sheridan observed, it was a peace of which every one was glad, but no one proud.

The establishment of peace determined M. d'Arblay to revisit France, and to endeavour to obtain from the First Consul the half-pay pension to which his former services in the army had entitled him. In this project he was warmly encouraged by his old friend and comrade, General Lauriston, whom he had called upon in London, and who had received him with open arms. The result of his journey may be read in the following pages. His wife and son joined him in France, in April, 1802, with the intention of returning to England after a year's absence. But their return was prevented by the renewal of the war between the two countries in the following year, and ten years elapsed before Fanny saw again her father and her native country. Her first impressions of France are recorded in the "Diary" with very pleasant minuteness, but of her life during the greater part of these years of exile a few letters, written at long intervals, give us all the information which we possess. ED.)

A VISIT TO MRS. CHAFONE.

March 1798. I have not told you of my renewed intercourse with Mrs. Chapone, who had repeatedly sent me kind wishes and messages, of her desire to see me again. She was unfortunately ill, and I was sent from her door without being named; but she sent me a kind note to Chelsea, which gave me very great pleasure. Indeed, she had always behaved towards me with affection as well as kindness, and I owe to her the blessing of my first acquaintance with my dear Mrs Delany. It was Mrs. Chapone who took me to her first, whose kind account had made her desire to know me, and who always expressed the most generous pleasure in the intimacy she had brought about, though it soon took place of all that had preceded it with herself. I wrote a very long answer, with a little history of our way of life, and traits of-M. d'Arblay, by which her quick discernment might judge both of that and my state of mind.

When we came again to Chelsea at this period, our Esther desired, or was desired by Mrs. Chapone, to arrange a meeting. I was really sorry I could not call upon her with my urchin; but I could only get conveyed to her one evening, when I went with our Esther, but was disappointed of M. d'Arblay, who had been obliged to go to Westhamble. This really mortified me, and vexed Mrs. Chapone.

We found her alone, and she received me with the most open affection. Mrs. Chapone knew the day I could be with her too late to make any party, and would have been profuse in apologies if I had not truly declared I rejoiced in seeing her alone, Indeed, it would have been better If we had been so completely, for our dearest Esther knew but few of the old connexions concerning whom I wished to inquire and to talk, and she knew too much of all about myself and my situation of which Mrs. Chapone wished to ask and to hear. I fear, therefore, she was tired, though she would not: say so, and though she looked and conducted herself with great sweetness.

Mrs. Chapone spoke warmly of "Camilla," especially of Sir Hugh, but told me she had detected me in some Gallicisms, and pointed some out. She pressed me in a very flattering manner to write again; and dear Hetty, forgetting our relationship's decency, seconded her so heartily you must have laughed to hear her hoping we could never furnish our house till I went again to the press. When Mrs. Chapone heard of my father's difficulties about Chelsea, and fears of removal, on account of his twenty thousand volumes,—"Twenty thousand volumes!" she repeated; "bless me! why, how can he so encumber himself? Why does he not burn half? for how much must be to spare that never can be worth his looking at from such a store! And can he want to keep them all? I should not have suspected Dr. Burney, of all men, of being such a Dr. Orkborne!" (157)

MRS. BOSCAWEN, LADY STRANGE, AND MR. SEWARD.

The few other visits which opportunity and inclination united for my making during our short and full fortnight were—

To Mrs. Boscawen, whither we went all three, for I knew she wished to see our little one, whom I had in the coach with Betty, ready for a summons. Mrs. Boscawen was all herself,—that is, all elegance and good-breeding. Do you remember the verses on the blues which we attributed to Mr. Pepys?—

Each art of conversation knowing, High-bred, elegant boscawen.

To Miss Thrale's, where I also carried my little Alex.

To Lady Strange (158) whom I had not seen for more years than I know how to count. She was at home, and alone, except for her young grandchild, another Bell Strange, daughter of James, who is lately returned from India, with a large fortune, is become member of Parliament, and has married, for his second wife, a niece of Secretary Dundas's. Lady Strange received me with great kindness, and, to my great surprise, knew me instantly. I found her more serious and grave than formerly; I had not seen her since Sir Robert's death, and many events of no enlivening nature; but I found, with great pleasure, that all her native fire and wit and intelligence were still within, though less voluntary and quick in flashing out, for every instant I stayed she grew brighter and nearer her true self.

Her little grandchild is a delightful little creature, the very reverse of the other Bell (159) in appearance and disposition, for she is handsome and open and gay; but I hope, at the same time, her resemblance in character, as Bell is strictly principled and upright.

Lady Strange inquired if I had any family, and, when she gathered I had a little one down-stairs in the carriage, desired to see it, for little Bell was wild in the request. "But have nae mair!" cried she; "the times are bad and hard;—ha' nae mair! if you take my advice, you'll ha' nae mair! you've been vary discreet, and, faith, I commend you!"

Little Bell had run down-stairs to hasten Betty and the child, and now, having seized him in her arms, she sprang into the room with him. His surprise, her courage, her fondling, her little form, and her prettiness, had astonished him into consenting to her seizure; but he sprang from her to me the moment they entered the drawing-room. I begged Lady Strange to give him her blessing. She looked at him with a strong and earnest expression of examining interest and pleasure, and then, with an arch smile, turning suddenly about to me, exclaimed, "Ah! faith and troth, you mun ha' some mair! if you can make 'em so pratty as this, you mun ha' some mair! sweet bairn! I gi' you my benediction! be a comfort to your papa and mamma! Ah, madam!" (with one of her deep sighs) "I must gi' my consent to your having some mair! if you can make 'em so pratty as this, faith and troth, I mun let you have a girl!"

I write all this without scruple to my dearest Susan, for prattiness like this little urchin's is not likely to spoil either him or ourselves by lasting. 'Tis a juvenile flower, yet one my Susan will again, I hope, view while still in its first bloom. . . .

I was extremely pleased in having an interview again with my old, and I believe very faithful, friend Mr. Seward, whom I had not seen since my marriage, but Whom I had heard, through the Lockes, was indefatigable in inquiries and expressions of good-will upon every occasion. He had sent me his compilation of anecdotes of distinguished characters, and two little letters have passed between us upon them. I was unluckily engaged the morning he was at Chelsea, and obliged to quit him before we had quite overcome a little awkwardness which our long absence and my changed name had involuntarily produced at our first meeting; and I was really sorry, as I have always retained a true esteem for him, though his singularities and affectation of affectation always struck me. But both those and his spirit of satire are mere quizziness: his mind is all solid benevolence and worth.

A MYSTERIOUS BANK-NOTE.

And now I must finish this Chelsea narrative, with its most singular, though brief, adventure. One morning at breakfast, my father received a letter, which he opened, and found to be only a blank cover with a letter enclosed, directed "A Madame, Madame d'Arblay." This, upon opening, produced a little bank-note of five pounds, and these words:—

"Madame d'Arblay need not have any scruple in accepting the enclosed trifle, as it is considered only as a small tribute of gratitude and kindness, so small, indeed, that every precaution has been taken to prevent the least chance of discovery; and the person who sends it even will never know whether it was received or not. Dr. Burney is quite ignorant of it."

This is written evidently in a feigned hand, and I have not the most remote idea whence it can come. But for the word gratitude I might have suggested many; but, upon the whole, I am utterly unable to suggest any one creature upon earth likely to do such a thing. I might have thought of my adorable princess, but that it is so little a sum. Be it as it may, it is certainly done in great kindness, by some one who knows five pounds is not so small a matter to us as to most others; and after vainly striving to find out or conjecture whence it came, we determined to devote it to our country. There's patriotism! we gave it in voluntary subscription for the war and it was very seasonable to us for this purpose.

This magnificent patriotic donation was presented to the Bank of England by Mr. Angerstein, through Mr. Locke, and we have had thanks from the committee which made us blush. Many reasons have prevented my naming this anecdote, the principal of which were fears that, if it should be known such a thing was made use of, and, as it chanced when we should otherwise have really been distressed how to come forward or hold back, any other friend might adopt the same method, which, gratefully as I feel the kindness that alone could have instigated it, has yet a depressing effect, and I would not have it become current. Could I, or should I ever trace it, I must, in some mode or other, attempt retaliation.

THE NEW BROTHER-IN-LAW: A CORDIAL PROFESSOR.

(Madame d'Arblay to Mrs. Phillips.) After sundry abortive proposals of our new brother-in-law, Mr. Broome, for our meeting, he and Charlotte finally came, with little Charlotte, to breakfast and spend a day with us. He has by no means the wit and humour and hilarity his "Simkin's Letters" prepare for; but the pen and the tongue are often unequally gifted. He is said to be very learned, deeply skilled in languages, and general erudition and he is full of information upon most subjects that can be mentioned. We talked of India, and he permitted me to ask what questions I pleased upon points and things of which I was glad to gather accounts from so able a traveller.

Another family visit which took place this Summer gave us pleasure of a far more easy nature, because unmixed with watchful anxiety; this was from Charles and his son, who, by an appointment for which he begged our consent, brought with him also Mr. Professor Young, of Glasgow, a man whose learning sits upon him far lighter than Mr. Broome's! Mr. Young has the bonhonlie of M. de Lally, with as much native humour as he has acquired erudition: he has a face that looks all honesty and kindness, and manners gentle and humble; an enthusiasm for whatever he thinks excellent, whether in talents or character, in art or in nature; and is altogether a man it seems impossible to know, even for a day, and not to love and wish well. This latter is probably the effect of his own cordial disposition to amity. He took to us, all three, so evidently and so warmly, and was so smitten with our little dwelling, its situation and simplicity, and so much struck with what he learned and saw of M. d'Arblay's cultivating literally his own grounds, and literally being his own gardener, after finding by conversation, what a use he had made of his earlier days in literary attainments, that he seemed as if he thought himself brought to a vision of the golden age,—such was the appearance of his own sincere and upright mind in rejoicing to see happiness where there was palpably no luxury, no wealth. It was a most agreeable surprise to me to find such a man in Mr. Professor Young, as I had expected a sharp though amusing satirist, from his very comic but sarcastic imitation of Dr. Johnson's "Lives," in a criticism upon Gray's "Elegy."

Charles was all kind affection, and delighted at our approbation of his friend, for the professor has been such many years, and very essentially formerly, a circumstance Charles is now gratefully and warmly returning. It is an excellent part of Charles's character that he never forgets any kind office he has received.

I learned from them that Mr. Rogers, author of the "Pleasures of Memory," that most sweet poem, had ridden round the lanes about our domain to view it, and stood—or made his horse stand,—at our gate a considerable time, to examine our Camilla cottage,—a name I am sorry to find Charles, or some one, had spread to him; and he honoured all with his good word. I should like to meet with him.

PRECOCIOUS MASTER ALEX.

Lady Rothes (160) constant in every manifestation of regard, came hither the first week of our establishment, and came three times to denials, when my gratitude forced open my doors. Her daughter, Lady Harriet, was with her: she is a pretty and pleasing young woman. Sir Lucas came another morning, bringing my old friend Mr. Pepys. Alex was in high spirits and amused them singularly. He had just taken to spelling; and every word he heard, of which he either knew or could guess the orthography, he instantly, in a little concise and steady manner, pronounced all the letters of, with a look of great but very grave satisfaction at his own performances, and a familiar nod at every word so conquered, as thus:—

Mr. Pepys. You are a fine boy, indeed!

Alex. B. o. y. boy. (Every letter articulated with strong, almost heroic emphasis.)

Mr. P. And do you run about here in this pleasant place all day long?

Alex. D, a, y; day.

Mr. P. And can you read your book, You Sweet little fellow?

Alex. R, e, a, d; read. Etc.

He was in such good looks that all this nonsense won nothing but admiration, and Mr. Pepys could attend to nothing else, but only charged me to let him alone. "For mercy's sake, don't make him study," cried Sir Lucas also; "he is so well disposed that you must rather repress than advance him, or his health may pay the forfeit of his application."

"O, leave him alone! cried Mr. Pepys: "take care only of his health and strength; never fear such a boy as that wanting learning."

THE BARBAULDS.

I was extremely surprised to be told by the maid a gentleman and lady had called at the door, who sent in a card and begged to know if I could admit them; and to see the names on the card were Mr. and Mrs. Barbauld. (161) I had never seen them more than twice; the first time, by their own desire, Mrs. Chapone carried me to meet them at Mr. Burrows's: the other time, I think, was at Mrs. Chapone's. You must be sure I could not hesitate to receive, and receive with thankfulness, this civility from the authoress of the most useful books, next to Mrs. Trimmer's, that have been yet written for dear little children; though this with the world is probably her very secondary merit, her many pretty Poems, and particularly songs, being generally esteemed. But many more have written those as well, and not a few better; for children's books she began the new walk, which has since been so well cultivated, to the great information as well as utility of parents.

Mr. Barbauld is a dissenting minister—an author also, but I am unacquainted with his works. They were in our little dining-parlour-the only one that has any chairs in it—and began apologies for their visit; but I interrupted and finished them with my thanks. She is much altered, but not for the worse to me, though she is for herself, since the flight of her youth, which is evident, has taken also with it a great portion of an almost set smile, which had an air of determined complacence and prepared acquiescence that seemed to result from a sweetness which never risked being off guard. I remember Mrs. Chapone's saying to me, after our interview, "She is a very good young woman, as well as replete with talents; but why must one always smile so? It makes my poor jaws ache to look at her."

We talked, of course, of that excellent lady; and you will believe I did not quote her notions of smiling. The Burrows family, she told me, was quite broken up; old Mrs. Amy alone remaining alive. Her brother, Dr. Aiken, (162) with his family, were passing the summer at Dorking, on account of his ill-health, the air of that town having been recommended for his complaints. The Barbaulds were come to spend some time with him, and would not be so near without renewing their acquaintance. They had been walking in Norbury Park, which they admired very much; and Mrs. Barbauld very elegantly said, "If there was such a public officer as a legislator of taste, Mr. Locke ought to be chosen for it."

They inquired much about M. d'Arblay, who was working in his garden, and would not be at the trouble of dressing to appear. They desired to see Alex, and I produced him; and his orthographical feats were very well-timed here, for as soon as Mrs. Barbauld said, "What is your name, you pretty creature?" he sturdily answered "B, o, y; boy."

Almost all our discourse was upon the Irish rebellion. Mr. Barbauld is a very little, diminutive figure, but well-bred and sensible.

I borrowed her poems, afterwards, of Mr. Daniel, who chanced to have them, and have read them with much esteem of the piety and worth they exhibit, and real admiration of the last amongst them, which is an epistle to Mr. Wilberforce in favour of the demolition of the slave-trade, 1 'n which her energy seems to spring from the real spirit of virtue, suffering at the luxurious depravity which can tolerate, in a free land, so unjust, cruel, and abominable a traffic.

We returned their visit together in a few days, at Dr. Aiken's lodgings, at Dorking, where, as she permitted M. d'Arblay to speak French, they had a very animated discourse upon buildings, French and English, each supporting those of their own country with great spirit, but my monsieur, to own the truth, having greatly the advantage both in manner and argument. He was in spirits, and came forth with his best exertions. Dr. Aiken looks very sickly, but is said to be better: he has a good countenance.

PRINCESS AMELIA AT JUNIPER HALL.

(Madame d'Arblay to Mrs. Phillips.) Westhamble, 1798. And now, my beloved Susan, I will sketch my last Court history of this year.

The Princess Amelia, who had been extremely ill since My last royal admittance, of some complaint in her knee which caused spasms the most dreadfully painful, was now returning from her sea-bathing at Worthing, and I heard from all around the neighbourhood that her royal highness was to rest and stop one night at juniper Hall, whither she was to be attended by Mr. Keate the surgeon, and by Sir Lucas Pepys, who was her physician at Worthing.

I could not hear of her approaching so near our habitation, and sleeping within sight of us, and be contented without an effort to see her; yet I would not distress Lady Rothes by an application she would not know how either to refuse or grant, from the established etiquette of bringing no one into the presence of their royal highnesses but by the queen's permission. So infinitely sweet, however, that young love of a princess always is to me, that I gathered courage to address a petition to her majesty herself, through the medium of Miss Planta, for leave to pay my homage. I will copy my answer, sent by return of post...

"My dear friend, I have infinite pleasure in acquainting you that the queen has ordered me to say that you have her leave to see dear Princess Amelia, provided Sir Lucas Pepys and Dr. Keate permit it, etc."

With so complete and honourable a credential, I now scrupled not to address a few lines to Lady Rothes, telling her My authority, to prevent any embarrassment, for entreating her leave to pay my devoirs to the young princess on Saturday morning,—the Friday I imagined she would arrive too fatigued to be seen. I intimated also my wish to bring my boy, not to be presented unless demanded, but to be Put into some closet where he might be at hand in case of that honour. The sweet princess's excessive graciousness to him gave me courage for this request. Lady Rothes sent me a kind note which made me perfectly comfortable.

It was the 1st of December, but a beautifully clear and fine day. I borrowed Mr. Locke's carriage. Sir Lucas came to us immediately, and ushered us to the breakfast-parlour, giving me the most cheering accounts of the recovery of the princess. Here I was received by Lady Rothes, who presented me to Lady Albinia Cumberland, widow of Cumberland the author's only son, and one of the ladies of the princesses. I found her a peculiarly pleasing woman, in voice, manner, look, and behaviour.

This introduction over, I had the pleasure to shake hands with Miss Goldsworthy, whom I was very glad to see, and who was very cordial and kind; but who is become, alas! so dreadfully deaf, there is no conversing with her, but by talking for a whole house to hear every word! With this infirmity, however, she is still in her first youth and brightness, compared with her brother, who, though I knew him of the party, is so dreadfully altered, that I with difficulty could venture to speak to him by the name of General Goldsworthy. He has had three or four more strokes of apoplexy since I saw him. I fancy he had a strong consciousness of his alteration, for he seemed embarrassed and shy, and only bowed to me, at first, without speaking. but I wore that off afterwards, by chatting over old stories with him. The princess breakfasted alone, attended by Mrs. Cheveley. When this general breakfast was over, Lady Albinia retired. But in a very few minutes she returned, and said, "Her royal highness desires to see Madame d'Arblay and her little boy."

The princess was seated on a sofa, in a French gray riding-dress, with pink lapels, her beautiful and richly flowing and shining fair locks unornamented. Her breakfast was still before her, and Mrs. Cheveley in waiting. Lady Albinia announced me, and she received me with the brightest smile, calling me up to her, and stopping my profound reverence, by pouting out her sweet ruby lips for me to kiss.

She desired me to come and sit by her; but, ashamed of so much indulgence, I seemed not to hear her, and drew a chair at a little distance. "No, no," she cried, nodding, "come here; come and sit by me here, my dear Madame d'Arblay." I had then only to say 'twas my duty to obey her, and I seated myself on her sofa. Lady Albinia, whom she motioned to sit, took an opposite chair, and Mrs. Cheveley, after we had spoken a few words together, retired.

Her attention now was bestowed upon my Alex, who required not quite so much solicitation to take his part of the sofa. He came jumping and skipping up to her royal highness, with such gay and merry antics, that it was impossible not to be diverted with so sudden a change from his composed and quiet behaviour in the other room. He seemed enchanted to see her again, and I was only alarmed lest he should skip upon her poor knee in his caressing agility.

I bid him, in vain, however, repeat Ariel's "Come unto these yellow sands," which he can say very prettily; he began, and the princess, who knew it, prompted him to go on —but a fit of shame came suddenly across him-or of capriciousness-and he would not continue.

Lady Albinia soon after left the room - and the princess, then, turning hastily and eagerly to me, said, "Now we are alone, do let me ask you one question, Madame d'Arblay. Are you—are you—[looking with strong expression to discover her answer] writing anything?"

I could not help laughing, but replied in the negative.

"Upon your honour?" she cried earnestly, and looking disappointed. This was too hard an interrogatory for evasion; and I was forced to say—the truth—that I was about nothing I had yet fixed if or not I should ever finish, but that I was rarely without some project. This seemed to satisfy and please her.

I told her of my having seen the Duke of Clarence at Leatherhead fair. "What, William?" she cried, surprised. This unaffected, natural way of naming her brothers and sisters is infinitely pleasing. She took a miniature from her pocket, and said, "I must show you Meney's picture," meaning Princess Mary, whom she still calls Meney, because it was the name she gave her when unable to pronounce Mary—a time she knew I well remembered. It was a very sweet miniature, and extremely like. "Ah! what happiness," I cried, "your royal highness will feel, and give, upon returning to their majesties and their royal highnesses, after such an absence, and such sufferings!" "O! yes!—I shall be SO glad!" she cried, and then Lady Albinia came in and whispered her it was time to admit Lady Rothes, who then entered with Lady Harriet and the Miss Leslies. When she was removing, painfully lifted from her seat between Sir Lucas and Mr. Keate, she stopped to pay her compliments and thanks to Lady Rothes with a dignity and self- command extremely striking. .

DEATH OF MR. SEWARD.

(Madame d'Arblay to Mrs. Locke.) Westhamble, May 2, 1799. Poor Mr. Seward! I am indeed exceedingly concerned—nay, grieved—for his loss to us: to us I trust I may say; for I believe he was so substantially good a creature, that he has left no fear or regret merely for himself. He fully expected his end was quickly approaching. I saw him at my father's at Chelsea, and he spent almost a whole morning with me in chatting of other times, as he called it; for we travelled back to Streatham, Dr. Johnson, and the Thrales. But he told me he knew his disease incurable. Indeed he had passed a quarter of an hour in recovering breath, in a room with the servants, before he let me know he had mounted the college stairs. My father was not at home. He had thought himself immediately dying, he said, four days before, by certain sensations that he believed to be fatal, but he mentioned it with cheerfulness; and though active in trying all means to lengthen life, declared himself perfectly calm in suspecting they would fail. TO give me a proof, he said he had been anxious to serve Mr. Wesley, the methodist musician, and he had recommended him to the patronage of the Hammersleys, and begged my father to meet him there to dinner; but as this was arranged, he was seized himself with a dangerous attack, which he believed to be mortal. And during this belief, "willing to have the business go on," said he, laughing, "and not miss me, I wrote a letter to a young lady, to tell her all I wished to be done upon the occasion, to serve Wesley, and to show him to advantage. I gave every direction I should have given in person, in a complete persuasion at the moment I should never hold a pen in my hand again."

This letter, I found, was to Miss Hammersley.

I had afterwards the pleasure of introducing M. d'Arblay to him, and it seemed a gratification to him to make the acquaintance. I knew he had been curious to see him, and he wrote my father word afterwards he had been much pleased.

My father says he sat with him an hour the Saturday before he died - and though he thought him very ill, he was so little aware his end was so rapidly approaching, that, like my dearest friend, he laments his loss as if by sudden death.

I was sorry, too, to see in the newspapers, the expulsion of Mr. Barry from the Royal Academy. I suppose it is from some furious harangue. (163) His passions have no restraint though I think extremely well of his heart, as well as of his understanding.

DR. BURNEY AGAIN VISITS DR. HERSCHEL.

(Dr. Burney to Madame d'Arblay.) Slough, Monday morning, July 22, 1799, in bed at Dr. Herschel's, half-past five, where I can neither sleep nor lie idle.

My dear Fanny, I believe I told you on Friday that I was going to finish the perusal of my astronomical verses to the great astronomer on Saturday. Here I arrived at three o'clock, neither Dr. nor Mrs. H. at home. This was rather discouraging, but all was set to rights by the appearance of Miss Baldwin, a sweet, timid, amiable girl, Mrs. Herschel's niece.....When we had conversed about ten minutes, in came two other sweet girls, the daughters of Dr. Parry of Bath, on a visit here. More natural, obliging, charming girls I have seldom seen; and, moreover, very pretty. We soon got acquainted. I found they were musical, and in other respects very well educated. It being a quarter past four, and the lord and lady of the mansion not returned, Miss Baldwin would have dinner served, according to order, and an excellent dinner it was, and our chattation no disagreeable sauce.

After an admirable dessert, I made the Misses Parry sing and play, and sang and played with them so delightfully, "you can't think!"

Mr. and Mrs. H. did not return till between seven and eight; but when they came, apologies for being out on pressing business, cordiality and kindness, could not be more liberally bestowed.

After tea Dr. H. proposed that we two should retire into a quiet room, in order to resume the perusal of my work, in which no progress had been made since last December. The evening was finished very cheerfully; and we went to our bowers not much out of humour with each other, or with the world.

DR. BURNEY AND THE KING.

We had settled a plan to go to the chapel at Windsor in' the morning, the king and royal family being there, and the town very full. Dr. H. and Mrs. H. stayed at home, and I was accompanied by the three Graces. Dr. Goodenough, the successor of Dr. Shepherd, as canon, preached. I had dined with him at Dr. Duval's. He is a very agreeable man, and passionately fond of music, with whom, as a professor, a critic, and an historian of the art; I seem to stand very high; but I could not hear a single sentence of his sermon, on account of the distance. After the service I got a glimpse of the good king, in his light-grey farmer-like morning Windsor uniform, in a great crowd, but could not even obtain that glance of the queen and princesses. The day was charming. The chapel is admirably repaired, beautified, and a new west window painted on glass. All was cheerfulness, gaiety, and good humour, such as the subjects of no other monarch, I believe, i on earth enjoy at present; and except return of creepings now and then, and a cough, I was as happy as the best.

At dinner we all agreed to go to the Terrace,—Mr, Mrs and Miss H, with their nice little boy, and the three young ladies. This plan we put in execution, and arrived on the Terrace a little after seven. I never saw it more crowded or gay. The park was almost full of happy people—farmers, servants, and tradespeople,—alt In Elysium. Deer in the distance, and dears unnumbered near. Here I met with everybody I wished and expected to see previous to the king's arrival in the part of the Terrace where I and my party were planted. .....

Chelsea, Tuesday, three o'clock. Not a moment could I get to write till now; and I am afraid of forgetting some part of my history, but I ought not, for the events of this visit are very memorable.

When the king and queen, arm in arm, were approaching the place where the Herschel family and I had planted ourselves, one of the Misses Parry heard the queen say to his majesty, "There's Dr. Burney," when they instantly came to me, so smiling and gracious that I longed to throw myself at their feet. "How do you, Dr. Burney?" said the king, "Why, you are grown fat and young."

"Yes, indeed," said the queen; "I was very glad to hear from Madame d'Arblay how well you looked."

"Why, you used to be as thin as Dr. Lind," says the king. Lind was then in sight—a mere lath; but these few words were accompanied with such Very gracious smiles, and seemingly affectionate good-humour—the whole royal family, except the Prince of Wales, standing by in the midst of a crowd of the first people in the kingdom for rank and office—that I was afterwards looked at as a sight. After this the king and queen hardly ever passed by me without a smile and a nod. The weather was charming; the park as full as the Terrace, the king having given permission to the farmers, tradesmen, and even livery servants, to be there during the time of his walking.

Now I must tell you that Herschel proposed to me to go with him to the king's concert at night, he having permission to go when he chooses, his five nephews (Griesbachs) making a principal part of the band. "And," says he, "I know you will be welcome." But I should not have presumed to believe this if his majesty had not formerly taken me into his concert-room himself from your apartments. This circumstance, and the gracious notice with which I had been just honoured, emboldened me. A fine music-room in the Castle, next the Terrace, is now fitted up for his majesty's evening concerts, and an organ erected. Part of the first act had been performed previous to our arrival. There were none but the performers in the room, except the Duchesses of Kent and cumberland, with two or three general officers backwards. The king seldom goes into the music-room after the first act; and the second and part of the third were over before we saw anything of him, though we heard his majesty, the queen, and princesses talking in the next room. At length he came directly up to me and Herschel, and the first question his majesty asked me was,—"How does Astronomy go on?" I, pretending to suppose he knew nothing of my poem, said, "Dr. Herschel will better inform your majesty than I can." "Ay, ay," says the king, "but you are going to tell us something with your pen;" and moved his hand in a writing manner. "What—what—progress have you made?" "Sir, it is all finished, and all but the last of twelve books have been read to my friend Dr. Herschel." The king, then, looking at Herschel, as who would say, "How is it?" "It is a very capital work, sir," says H. "I wonder how you find time?" said the king. "I make time, Sir." "How, how?" "I take it out of my sleep, sir." When the considerate good king, "But you'll hurt your health. How long," he adds, "have you been at it?" "Two or three years, at odd and stolen moments, Sir." "Well," said the king (as he had said to you before), "whatever you write, I am sure will be entertaining." I bowed most humbly, as ashamed of not deserving so flattering a speech. "I don't say it to flatter you," says the king; "if I did not think it, I would not say it."

OVERWHELMED WITH THE ROYAL GRACIOUSNESS.

(Madame d'Arblay to Dr. Burney.) "Fore George, a more excellent song than t'other!" Westhamble, July 25, '99. Why, my dearest padre, your subjects rise and rise, till subjects, in fact, are no longer in question. I do not wonder you felt melted by the king's goodness. I am sure I did in its perusal. And the queen! Her naming me so immediately went to my heart. Her speeches about me to Mrs. Locke in the drawing-room, her interest in my welfare, her deigning to say she had "never been amongst those who had blamed my marriage,"though she lost by it my occasional attendances, and her remarking "I looked the picture of happiness," had warmed me to the most fervent gratitude, and the more because her saying she had never been amongst those who had blamed me shows there were people who had not failed to do me ill offices in her hearing; though probably, and I firmly believe, without any personal enmity, as I am unconscious of my having any owed me; but merely from a cruel malice with which many seize every opportunity, almost involuntarily, to do mischief and most especially to undermine at Court any one presumed to be in any favour. And, still further, I thought her words conveyed a confirmation of what her conduct towards me in my new capacity always led me to conjecture, namely, that my guardian star had ordained it so that the real character and principles of my honoured and honourable mate had, by some happy chance, reached the royal ear "before the news of our union. The dear king's graciousness: to M. d'Arblay upon the Terrace, when the commander-in-chief, just then returned from the Continent, was by his side, made it impossible not to suggest this: and now, the queen's again naming me so in, public puts it, in my conception, beyond doubt. My kindest father will be glad, I am sure, to have added to the great delight of his recital a strength to a notion I so much love to cherish.

WAR RUMOURS.

(Madame d'Arblay to Mrs. Phillips.) Aug. 14, '99. People here are very sanguine that Ireland is quiet, and will remain so; and that the combined fleets can never reach it. How are your own politics upon that point? Mine will take their colour, be it what it may. Our dear father is Visiting about, from Mr. Cox's to Mrs. Crewe, with whom be is now at Dover, where Mr. Crewe has some command. We are all in extreme disturbance here about the secret expedition. Nothing authentic is arrived from the first armament; and the second is all prepared for sailing. . . . Both officers and men are gathered from all quarters. - Heaven grant them speedy safety, and ultimate peace! God bless my own dearest Susan, and strengthen and restore her. Amen! Amen.

ILLNESS AND DEATH OF MRS. PHILLIPS.

(Madame d'Arblay to Dr. Burney.) Westhamble, October 1, '99. Whether gaily or sadly to usher what I have to say I know not, but your sensations, like mine, will I am sure be mixed. The major has now written to Mrs. Locke that he is anxious to have Susan return to England. She is "in an ill state of health," he says, and he wishes her to try her native air; but the revival of coming to you and among us all, and the tender care that will be taken of her, is likely to do much for her; therefore, if we get her but to this side the channel, the blessing is comparatively so great, that I shall feel truly thankful to heaven.

(Madame d'Arblay to Mrs. Phillips.) Westhamble, December 10, '99. O my Susan, my heart's dear sister! with what bitter sorrow have I read this last account! With us, with yourself, your children, all, you have trifled in respect to health, though in all things else you are honour and veracity personified; but nothing had prepared me to think you in such a grave state as I now find you. Would to God I could get to you! If Mr. Keirnan thinks you had best pass the winter in Dublin, stay, and let me come to you. Venture nothing against his opinion, for mercy's sake! Fears for your health take place of all impatience to expedite your return; only go not back to Belcotton, where you cannot be under his direction, and are away from the physician he thinks of so highly.

I shall write immediately to Charles about the carriage. I am sure of his answer beforehand,—so must you be. Act, therefore, with regard to the carriage, as if already it were arranged. But I am well aware it must not set out till you Are well enough to nearly fix your day of sailing. I say nearly, for we must always allow for accidents. I shall write to our dear father, and Etty, and James, and send to Norbury Park - but I shall wait till to-morrow, not to infect them with what I am infected.. . .

O my Susan! that I could come to you! But all must depend on Mr. Keirnan's decision. If you can come to us with perfect safety, however slowly, I shall not dare add to your embarrassment of persons and package. Else Charles's carriage—O, what a temptation to air it for you all the way! Take no more large paper, that you may write with less fatigue, and, if possible, oftener;—to any one will suffice for all.

(Madame d'Arblay to Doctor Burney.) 9th January, 1800. My most dear padre, my mate will say all, so I can only offer up my earnest prayers I may soon be allowed the blessing—the only one I sigh for—of embracing my dearest Susan in your arms and under your roof. Amen. F. D'A.

These were the last written lines of the last period—unsuspected as such—of my perfect happiness on earth; for they were stopped on the road by news that my heart's beloved sister, Susanna Elizabeth Phillips, had ceased to breathe. The tenderest of husbands—the most feeling of human beings—had only reached Norbury Park, on his way to a believed meeting with that angel, when the fatal blow was struck; and he came back to West Hamble— to the dreadful task of revealing the irreparable loss which his own goodness, sweetness, patience, and sympathy could alone have made supported.

(Madame d'Arblay to Mrs. Locke.) 9th January, 1800. "As a guardian angel!"—Yes, my dearest Fredy, as such in every interval of despondence I have looked up to the sky to see her, but my eyes cannot pierce through the thick atmosphere, and I can only represent her to me seated on a chair of sickness, her soft hand held partly out to me as I approach her; her softer eyes so greeting me as never welcome was expressed before; and a smile of heavenly expression speaking the tender gladness of her grateful soul that God at length should grant our re-union. From our earliest moments, my Fredy, when no misfortune happened to our dear family, we wanted nothing but each other. Joyfully as others were received by us—loved by us—all that was necessary to our happiness was fulfilled by our simple junction. This I remember with my first remembrance; nor do I recollect a single instance of being affected beyond a minute by any outward disappointment, if its result was leaving us together.

She was the soul of my soul! and 'tis wonderful to me, my dearest Fredy, that the first shock did not join them immediately by the flight of mine-but that over-that dreadful, harrowing, never-to be-forgotten moment of horror that made me wish to be mad—the ties that after that first endearing period have shared with her my heart, come to my aid. Yet I was long incredulous; and still sometimes I think it is not—and that she will come— and I paint her by my side—by my father's—in every room of these apartments, destined to have chequered the woes of her life with rays of comfort, joy, and affection.

O, my Fredy! not selfish is the affliction that repines her earthly course of sorrow was allowed no shade!—that at the instant soft peace and consolation awaited her she should breathe her last! You would understand all the hardship of resignation for me were you to read the joyful opening of her letter, on her landing, to my poor father, and her prayer at the end to be restored to him. O, my Fredy! could you indeed think of me—be alarmed for me on that dreadful day?—I can hardly make that enter my comprehension; but I thank you from my soul; for that is beyond any love I had thought possible, even from Your tender heart.

Tell me you all keep well, and forgive me my distraction. I write so fast I fear you can hardly read; but you will See I am conversing with you, and that will show you how I turn to you for the comfort of your tenderness. Yes, you have all a loss, indeed!

A PRINCESS'S CONDESCENSION.

(Madame d'Arblay to Mrs. Locke). Greenwich, Friday, February, 1800. Here we are, my beloved friend. We came yesterday. All places to me are now less awful than my own so dear habitation. My royal interview took place on Wednesday. I was five hours with the royal family, three of them alone with the queen, whose graciousness and kind goodness I cannot express. And each of the princesses saw me with a sort of concern and interest I can never forget. I did tolerably well, though not quite as steadily as I expected but with my own Princess Augusta I lost all command. She is still wrapt up, and just recovering from a fever herself- and she spoke to me in a tone—a voice so commiserating—I could not stand it—I was forced to stop short in my approach, and hide my face with my muff. She came up to me immediately, put her arm upon my shoulder, and kissed me—I shall never forget it. How much more than thousands of words did a condescension so tender tell me her kind feelings!—She is one of the few beings in this world that can be, in the words of M. de Narbonne, "all that is douce and all that is sbirituelle,"—his words upon my lost darling!

It is impossible more of comfort or gratification could be given than I received from them all.

HORTICULTURAL MISFORTUNES.

(Madame d'Arblay to Dr. Burney). Westhamble, March 22, 1800. Day after day I have meant to write to my dearest father 'but I have been unwell ever since our return, and that has not added to my being sprightly. I have not once crossed 'the threshold since I re-entered the house till to-day, when Mr. and Mrs. Locke almost insisted upon taking me an airing. I am glad of it, for it has done me good, and broken a kind of spell that made me unwilling to stir.

M. d'Arblay has worked most laboriously in his garden but his misfortunes there, during our absence, might melt a heart of stone. The horses of our next neighbouring farmer broke through our hedges, and have made a kind of bog of our mead ow, by scampering in it during the wet; the sheep followed, who have eaten up all our greens, every sprout and cabbage and lettuce, destined for the winter; while the horses dug up our turnips and carrots; and the swine, pursuing such examples, have trod down all the young plants besides devouring whatever the others left of vegetables. Our potatoes, left, from our abrupt departure, in the ground, are all rotten or frostbitten, and utterly spoilt; and not a single thing has our whole ground produced us since we came home. A few dried carrots, which remain from the in-doors collection, are all we have to temper our viands.

What think you of this for people who make it a rule to owe a third of their sustenance to the garden? Poor M, d'A.'s renewal of toil, to supply future times, is exemplary to behold, after such discouragement. But he works as if nothing had failed; such is his patience as well as industry.

My Alex, I am sure you will be kindly glad to hear, is entirely well; and looks so blooming—no rose can be fresher. I am encouraging back his spouting propensity, to fit him for his royal interview with the sweet and gay young princess who has demanded him, who will, I know, be diverted with his speeches and gestures. We must present ourselves before Easter, as the Court then adjourns to Windsor for ten days. My gardener will not again leave his grounds to the fourfooted marauders; and our stay, therefore, will be the very shortest we can possibly make it; for though we love retirement, we do not like solitude.

I long for some further account of you, dearest: sir, and how you bear the mixture of business and company, of "fag and frolic," as Charlotte used to phrase it.

Westhamble, April 27, 1800. My Alex improves in all that I can teach, and my gardener is laboriously recovering from his winter misfortunes. He is now raising a hillock by the gate, for a view of NorbUry Park from our grounds, and he has planted potatoes upon almost every spot where they can grow. The dreadful price of provisions makes this our first attention. The poor people about us complain they are nearly starved, and the children of the journeymen of the tradesmen at Dorking come to our door to beg halfpence for a little bread. What the occasion of such universal dearth can be we can form no notion, and have no information. The price of bread we can conceive from the bad harvest; but meat, butter, and shoes!—nay, all sorts of nourriture or clothing seem to rise in the same proportion, and without any adequate cause. The imputed one of the war does not appear to me sufficient, though the drawback from all by the income-tax is severely an underminer of comfort. What is become of the campaign? are both parties incapacitated from beginning? or is each waiting a happy moment to strike some definitive stroke? We are strangely in the dark about all that is going on, and unless you will have the compassion to write us some news, we may be kept so till Mr. Locke returns.

A WITHDRAWN COMEDY.

[Towards the close of the preceding year Dr. Charles Burney had placed in the hands of Mr. Harris, the manager of Covent Garden-theatre, a comedy by Madame d'Arblay, called "Love and Fashion." Mr. Harris highly approved the piece, and early in the spring put it into rehearsal; but Dr. Burney was seized with a panic concerning its success, and, to oblige him, his daughter and her husband withdrew it. The following letter announced their generous compliance with his wishes.]

(Madame d'Arblay to Doctor Burney.) Monday. I hasten to tell you, dearest sir, Mr. H. has at length listened to our petitions, and has returned me my poor ill-fated —, wholly relinquishing all claim to it for this season. He has promised also to do his utmost, as far as his influence extends, to keep the newspapers totally silent in future. We demand, therefore, no contradictory paragraph, as the report must needs die when the reality no more exists. Nobody has believed it from the beginning, on account of the premature moment when it was advertised.

This release gives me present repose, which, indeed, I much wanted; for to combat your, to me, unaccountable but most afflicting displeasure, in the midst of my own panics and disturbance, would have been ample punishment to me had I been guilty of a crime, in doing what I have all my life been urged to, and all my life intended, writing a comedy. Your goodness, your kindness, your regard for my fame, I know have caused both your trepidation, which doomed me to certain failure, and your displeasure that I ran, what you thought, a wanton risk. But it is not wanton, my dearest father. My imagination is not at my own control, or I would always have continued in the walk YOU approved. The combinations for another long work did not occur to me; incidents and effects for a drama did. I 'thought the field more than open—inviting to me. The chance held out golden dreams. The risk could be only our own; for, permit me to say, appear when it will, you will find nothing in the principles, the moral, or the language that will make you blush for me. A failure upon those points only, can bring disgrace; Upon mere cabal or want of dramatic powers, it can only cause disappointment.

I hope, therefore, my dearest father, in thinking this over you will cease to nourish such terrors and disgust at an essay so natural, and rather say to yourself, with an internal smile, "After all, 'tis but like father like child; for to what walk do I confine myself? She took my example in writing—she takes it in ranging. Why then, after all, should I lock her up in one paddock, well as she has fed there, if she says she finds nothing more to nibble; while I find all the earth unequal to my ambition, and mount the skies to content it? Come on, then, poor Fan! the world has acknowledged you my offspring, and I will disencourage you no more. Leap the pales of your paddock—let us pursue our career; and, while you frisk from novel to comedy, I, quitting music and prose, will try a race with poetry and the stars."

I am sure my dear father will not infer, from this appeal, I mean to parallel our works. No one more truly measures her own inferiority, which, with respect to yours, has always been my pride. I only mean to show, that if my muse loves a little variety, she has an hereditary claim to try it.

M. D'ARBLAY's FRENCH PROPERTY.

(Madame d'Arblay to Doctor Burney.) Westhamble, November 7, 1800. I think it very long not to hear at least of YOU, my dearest padre. My tranquil and happy security, alas! has been broken in upon by severe conflicts since I wrote to My dearest father last, which I would not communicate while yet pending, but must now briefly narrate. My partner, the truest of partners, has been erased from the list of emigrants nearly a year; and in that period has been much pressed and much blamed by his remaining friends in France, by every opportunity through which they could send to him, for not immediately returning, and seeing if anything could be yet saved from the wreck of his own and family's fortune; but he held steady to his original purpose never to revisit his own country till it was at peace with this; till a letter came from his beloved uncle himself, conveyed to him through Hambro', which shook all the firmness of his resolution, and has kept him, since its receipt, in a state of fermentation, from doubts and difficulties, and crossing wishes and interests, that has much affected his health as well as tranquillity.

All, however, now, is at least decided; for a few days since he received a letter from M. Lajard, who is returned to Paris, with information from his uncle's eldest son, that some of his small property is yet unsold, to about the amount of 1000 pounds, and can still be saved from sequestration if he will immediately go over and claim it; or, if that is impossible, if he will send his procuration to his uncle, from some country not at war with France.

This ended all his internal contest; and he is gone this very morning to town to procure a passport and a passage in some vessel bound to Holland.

So unused are we to part, never yet for a week having been separated during the eight years of our union, that our first idea was going together, and taking our Alex; and certain I am nothing would do me such material and mental good as so complete a change of scene; but the great expense of the voyage and journey, and the inclement season for our little boy, at length finally settled us to pray only for a speedy meeting. But I did not give it up till late last night, and am far from quite reconciled to relinquishing it even now.

He has no intention to go to France, or he would make an effort to pass by Calais, which would delightfully shorten the passage; but he merely means to remain at the Hague while he sends over his procuration, and learns how soon he may hope to reap its fruits.

Westhamble, 16th December, 1800. He is returned, my dearest father, already! MY joy and surprise are so great I seem in a dream. I have just this moment a letter from him, written at Gravesend. What he has been able to arrange as to his affairs, I know not; and just now cannot care, so great is my thankfulness for his safety and return. He waits in the river for his passport, and will, when he obtains it, hasten, I need not say, to Westhamble.

HOME MATTERS.

(Madame d'Arblay to Dr. Burney.) Westhamble, September i, 1801. A carpet we have-though not yet spread, as the chimney is unfinished, and room incomplete. Charles brought us the tapis-so that, in fact, we have yet bought nothing for our best room—and meant,—for our own share—to buy a table . . . and if my dearest father will be so good—and so naughty at once, as to crown our salle d'audience with a gift we shall prize beyond all others, we can think only of a table. Not a dining one, but a sort of table for a little work and a few books, en gala—without which, a room looks always forlorn. I need not say how we shall love it; and I must not say how we shall blush at it; and I cannot say how we feel obliged at it—for the room will then be complete in love-offerings. Mr. Locke finished glazing or polishing his impression border for the chimney on Saturday. It will be, I fear, his last work of that sort, his eyes, which are very longsighted, now beginning to fail and weaken at near objects.

My Alex intends very soon, he says, to marry-and, not long since, with the gravest simplicity, he went up to Mr William Locke, who was here with his fair bride, and said, "How did you get that wife, William? because I want to get such a one—and I don't know which is the way." And he is now actually employed in fixing sticks and stones at convenient distances, upon a spot very near our own, where he means to raise a suitable structure for his residence, after his nuptials. You will not think he has suffered much time to be wasted before he has begun deliberating upon his conjugal establishment.

We spent the greatest part of last week in visits at Norbury Park, to meet M. de Lally, whom I am very sorry you missed.

He is delightful in the country full of resources, of gaiety, of intelligence, of good humour and mingling powers of instruction. with entertainment. He has read us several fragments of works of his own, admirable in eloquence, sense, and feeling. chiefly parts of tragedies, and all referring to subjects next his heart, and clearest in his head; namely, the French Revolution and its calamities, and filial reverence and enthusiasm for injured parents.

CONTEMPLATED JOURNEY TO FRANCE.

(Madame d'Arblay to Dr. Burney.) Westhamble, October 3, 1801. God avert mischief from this peace, my dearest father! For in our hermitage you may imagine, more readily than I can express, the hopes and happiness it excites. M. d'Arblay now feels paid for his long forbearance, his kind patience, and compliance with my earnest wishes not to revisit his native land while we were at war with it. He can now go with honour as well as propriety - for every body, even the highest personages, will rather expect he should make the journey as a thing of course, than hear of it as a proposition for deliberation. He will now have his heart's desire granted, in again seeing his loved and respectable uncle, and many relations, and more friends, and his own native town, as well as soil; and he will have the delight of presenting to that uncle, and those friends, his little pet Alex. With all this gratification to one whose endurance of such a length of suspense, and repetition of disappointment, I have observed with gratitude, and felt with sympathy, must not I, too, find pleasure? Though, on my side, many are the drawbacks - but I ought not, and must not, listen to them. We shall arrange our affairs with all the speed in our power, after the ratification is arrived, for saving the cold and windy weather; but the approach of winter is unlucky, as it will lengthen our stay, to avoid travelling and voyaging during its severity - unless, indeed, any internal movement, or the menace of any, should make frost and snow secondary fears, and induce us to scamper off. But the present is a season less liable in all appearance to storms, than the seasons that may follow. Fates, joy, and pleasure, will probably for some months occupy the public in France - and it will not be till those rejoicings are past, that they will set about weighing causes of new commotion, the rights of their governors, or the means, or desirability of changing them. I would far rather go immediately, than six months hence.

[The projected journey of Madame d'Arblay with her husband did not take place this year; the season being already advanced, and their little boy not strong enough to bear the fatigue of such an expedition. Monsieur d'Arblay went alone to France.]

M. D'ARBLAY's ROUGH SEA PASSAGE.

(Madame d'Arblay to Dr. Burney.) Westhamble, November 11, 1801. I did not purpose writing to my dearest father till my suspense and inquietude were happily removed by a letter from France; but as I find he is already anxious himself, I will now relate all I yet know of my dearest traveller's history. On Wednesday the 28th of October, he set off for Gravesend. A vessel, he was told, was ready for sailing and would set off the following day. He secured his passage, and took up his abode at an inn, whence he wrote me a very long letter, in full hope his next would be from his own country. But Thursday came, and no sailing—though the wind was fair, and the weather then calm: he amused his disappointment as well as he could by visiting divers gardeners, and taking sundry lessons for rearing and managing asparagus. Friday, also, came-and still no sailing! He was more and more vexed; but had recourse then to a chemist, with whom he revised much of his early knowledge. Saturday followed—no sailing! and he found the people waited on and on, in hopes of more passengers, though never avowing their purpose, His patience was now nearly exhausted, and he went and made such vifs remonstrances that he almost startled the managers. They pretended the ballast was all they stayed for: he offered to aid that himself; and actually went to work, and never rested till the vessel was absolutely ready: orders, enfin, were given for sailing next morning, though he fears, with all his skill, and all his eloquence, and all his aiding, they were more owing to the arrival of four passengers than to his exertions. That night, October the 31st, he went on board; and November the 1st he set sail at five o'clock in the morning.

You know how high a wind arose on Sunday the 1st, and how dreadful a storm succeeded, lasting all night, all Monday, and all night again. How thankful, how grateful am I to have heard of his safety since so terrifying a period. They got on, with infinite difficulty and danger, as far as Margate; they there took anchor, and my kind voyager got a letter for me sent on shore, "moyennant un schelling." (164) To tell you my gratitude in knowing him safe after that tempest—no I cannot! Your warm affections, my dearest father, will easily paint to you my thankfulness.

Next, they got on to Deal, and here anchored again, for the winds, though they abated on shore, kept violent and dangerous near the coast. Some of the passengers went on shore, and put two letters for me in the post, assuring me all was safe. These two passengers, who merely meant to dine on shore, and see the town, were left behind. The sea rose so high, no boat could put off to bring them back; and, though the captain hoisted a flag to announce he was sailing, there was no redress. They had not proceeded a league before the sea grew yet more rough and perilous, and the captain was forced to hoist a flag of distress. Everything in the vessel was overset; my poor M. d'Arblay's provision-basket flung down, and its contents demolished; his bottle of wine broken by another toss, and violent fall, and he was nearly famished. The water now began to get into the ship, all hands were at work that could work, and he, my poor voyager, gave his whole noble strength to the pump, till he was so exhausted, so fatigued, so weakened, that with difficulty he could hold a pen to repeat that still—I might be tranquille, for all danger was again over. A pilot came out to them from Dover, for seven guineas, which the higher of the passengers subscribed for (and here poor M. d'A. was reckoned of that class], and the vessel was got into the port at Dover, and the pilot, moyennant un autre schelling, put me again a letter, with all these particulars, into the post.

This was Thursday the 5th. The sea still so boisterous, the vessel was unable to cross the water. The magistrates at Dover permitted the poor passengers all to land; and M. d'Arblay wrote to me again, from the inn, after being regaled with an excellent dinner, of which he had been much in want. Here they met again the two passengers lost at Deal, who, in hopes of this circumstance, had travelled post from thence to Dover. Here, too, M. d'A. met the Duke de Duras, an hereditary officer of the crown, but who told him, since peace was made, and all hope seemed chased of a proper return to his country, he was going, incognito, to visit a beloved old mother, whom he had not seen for eleven years. "I have no passport," he said, "for France, but I mean to avow myself to the commissary at Calais, and tell him I know I am not erased, nor do I demand to be so. I only solicit an interview with a venerable parent. Send to Paris, to beg leave for it. You may put me in Prison till the answer arrives; but, for mercy, for humanity's sake, suffer me to wait in France till then! guarded as you please!" This is his Purposed address—which my M. d'A. says he heard, avec les larmes aux yeux. (165) I shall long to hear the event.

On Friday, November 6th, M. d'A. wrote me two lines:"Nov. 6, 1801. Je pars! the wind is excellent—au revoir." This is dated ten o'clock in the morning. I have not had a word since.

[in the original edition here follow three letters, in French, from M. d'Arblay to his wife. From these letters we translate the following extracts. ED.

"Paris. "I do not yet know positively when it will be possible for me to go to see my uncle. The settlement of my claim of half-pay is anything but advanced. . . . To-morrow morning I have an appointment with Du Taillis, aide-de-camp to Berthler (the French minister of war). When I leave him, I hope to see Talleyrand; but what I most particularly desire is, not to depart without having at least a glimpse of the first Consul (Napoleon), that man so justly celebrated. . . . In reference to the obligation which we, formerly on the list of emigrants, have to him, Narbonne said to me to-day, 'He has set all our heads on our shoulders.' I like this expression."

"Paris, November 16, 1801. "La Tour Maubourg, one of the companions of General Lafayette, wished to marry his daughter to an emigrant whose name was not yet struck off the list. He obtained an interview with the first Consul, at which he entered into details on the matter, without attempting to conceal the objections which might be taken to the requested erasement of the young man's name from the list of emigrants. Bonaparte interrupted him and said, 'Is the young man agreeable to your daughter?' 'Yes, General.'-' 'Is he agreeable to you, M. de Maubourg?' 'Very much so, General.'—'Well then, the man whom you judge worthy to enter into such a family as yours, is surely worthy also to be a French citizen.'"

"15th Frimaire (December 6), 1801. "According to all appearance, my dearest, I shall not obtain the settlement I ask for. Everybody says that nothing could be more just than my demand, but so many persons who have served all through the war are at present on half-pay, that I am desperately afraid it will be the same with my past services as with my property, and for the same reason-the impossibility of satisfying all demands, however well founded. Meanwhile, my dearest, it is impossible to conceal from ourselves that we have been living, for some years, with all our economy, on resources which are now either exhausted, or very nearly so. The greater part of our income [Fanny's pension] is anything but certain, yet what should we do if that were to fail us The moral of this discourse is, that while I am fit for something, it is my duty, as a husband and a father, to try what can be done to secure for us, if possible, an old age of absolute independence; and for our little one a position which may prevent his being a burden to us. . . .

". . . The consuls in England have not yet been nominated. The consulship in London will be well worth having, and perhaps, although there will be plenty of candidates, it might not be impossible for me to obtain it. It is at least probable that I could get appointed to one of the sea-ports. . . .

"... Answer me at once, I beg of you. Think if this plan is opposed to any of your tastes; for you know there is only one possible happiness for me. Need I say more?")

SUGGESTED ABANDONMENT' OF CAMILLA COTTAGE.

(Madame d'Arblay to M. d'Arblay.) Westhamble, December 15, 1801. The relief, the consolation of your frequent letters I can never express, nor my grateful sense of your finding time for them, situated as you now are, and yet that I have this moment read, of the 15 Frimaire, has made my heart ache heavily. Our hermitage is so dear to me-our book-room, 'so precious, and in its retirement, its beauty of prospect, form, convenience, and comforts, so impossible to replace, that I sigh, and deeply, in thinking of relinquishing it. Your happiness, however, is now all mine; if deliberately therefore, you wish to try a new system, I will surely try it, with you, be it what it may. I will try any thing but what I try now—absence! Think, however, well, mon tres cher ami, before you decide upon any occupation that robs you of being master of your own time, leisure, hours, gardening, scribbling, and reading.

In the happiness you are now enjoying, while it Is SO new to you, you are perhaps unable to appreciate your own value of those six articles, which, except in moments of your bitter regret at the privation of your first friends and beloved country, have made your life so desirable. Weigh, weigh it well in the detail. I cannot write.

Should you find the sum total preponderate in favour of your new scheme, I will say no more. All schemes will to me be preferable to seeing you again here, without the same fondness for the place, and way of life, that has made it to me what it has been. With regard to the necessity or urgency of the measure, I could say much that I cannot write. You know now I can live with you, and you know I am not without views, as well as hopes, of ameliorating our condition.

I will fully discuss the subject with our oracle. (166) His kindness, his affection for you! Yesterday, when I produced your letter, and the extracts from M. Necker, and was going to read some, he said, in that voice that is so penetratingly sweet, when he speaks from his heart—"I had rather hear one line of d'Arblay's than a volume of M. Necker's,"—yet at the same time begging to peruse the MS. when I could spare it. I wish you could have heard the tone in which he pronounced those words: it vibrated on my ears all day.

I have spent near two hours upon this theme with our dearest oracle and his other half He is much affected by the idea of any change that may remove us from his daily sight; but, with his unvarying disinterestedness, says he thinks such a place would be fully acquitted by you. If it is of consul here, in London, he is sure you would fill up all its functions even admirably. I put the whole consideration into your own hands, what, upon mature deliberation, you judge to be best, I will abide by. Heaven guide and speed your determination!

M. D'ARBLAY'S PROPOSED RETIREMENT FROM MILITARY SERVICE.

1802.

[The beginning of this year was attended with much anxiety to Madame d'Arblay. Her husband, disappointed in the hopes suggested by his friends, of his receiving employment as French commercial consul in London, directed his efforts to obtaining his half-pay on the retired list of French officers. This was promised, on condition that he should previously serve at St. Domingo, where General Leclerc was then endeavouring to put down Toussaint's insurrection. He accepted the appointment conditionally on his being allowed to retire as soon as that expedition should be ended. This, he was told, was impossible, and he therefore hastened back to his family towards the end of January.

In February, a despatch followed him from General Berthier, then minister at war, announcing that his appointment was made out, and on his own terms. 'To this M. d'Arblay wrote his acceptance, but repeated a stipulation he had before made, that while he was ready to fight against the enemies of the Republic, yet, should future events disturb the peace lately established between France and England, it was his unalterable determination never to take up arms against the British government. As this determination had already been signified by M. d'Arblay, he waited not to hear the result of its repetition, but set off again for Paris to receive orders, and proceed thence to St. Domingo.

After a short time he was informed that his stipulation of never taking up arms against England could not be accepted, and that his military appointment was in consequence annulled. Having been required at the Alien office, on quitting England, to engage that he would not return for the space of one year, he now proposed that Madame d'Arblay, with her little boy, should join him in France: and among the following letters will be found several in which she describes her first impressions on reaching that country, and the society to which she was introduced.]

(Madame d'Arblay to Miss Planta.) Camilla Cottage, Westhamble, February 11, 1802. A most unexpected, and, to me, severe event, draws from me now an account I had hoped to have reserved for a far happier communication, but which I must beg you to endeavour to seek some leisure moment for making known, with the utmost humility, to my royal mistress. . . .

Upon the total failure of every effort M. d'Arblay could make to recover any part of his natural inheritance, he was advised by his friends to apply to the French government for half pay, upon the claims of his former military services. He drew up a memoir, openly stating his attachment and loyalty to his late king, and appealing for this justice after undeserved proscription. His right was admitted, but he was informed it could only be made good by his re-entering the army; and a proposal to that effect was sent him by Berthier, the minister of war.

The disturbance of his mind at an offer which so many existing circumstances forbade his foreseeing, was indescribable. He had purposed faithfully retiring to his hermitage, with his fellow-hermit, for the remainder of his life: and nothing upon earth could ever induce him to bear arms against the country which had given him asylum, as well as birth to his wife and child;—and yet a military spirit of honour, born and bred in him, made it repugnant to all his feelings to demand even retribution from the government of his own country, yet refuse to serve it. Finally, therefore, he resolved to accept the offer conditionally—to accompany the expedition to St. Domingo, for the restoration of order in the French colonies, and then, restored thus to his rank in the army, to claim his retraite. This he declared to the minister of war, annexing a further clause of receiving his instructions immediately from the government.

The minister's answer to this was, that these conditions were impossible. Relieved rather than resigned-though dejected to find himself thus thrown out of every promise of prosperity, M. d'Arblay hastened back to his cottage, to the inexpressible satisfaction of the- recluse he had left there.

short, however, has been its duration! A packet has just followed him, containing a letter from Berthier, to tell him that his appointment was made out according to his own demands! and enclosing another letter to the commander-in-chief, Leclerc, with the orders of government for employing him, delivered in terms, the most distinguished, of his professional character.

All hesitation, therefore, now necessarily ends, and nothing remains for M. d'Arblay but acquiescence and despatch,— while his best consolation is in the assurance he has universally received, that this expedition has the good wishes and sanction of England. And, to avert any misconception or misrepresentation, he has this day delivered to M. Otto (167) a letter, addressed immediately to the first Consul, acknowledging the flattering manner in which he has been called forth, but decidedly and clearly repeating what he had already declared to the war minister, that though he would faithfully fulfil the engagement into which he was entering, it was his unalterable resolution never to take up arms against the British government.

I presume to hope this little detail may, at some convenient moment, meet her majesty's eyes-with every expression of my profoundest devotion.

M. D'ARBLAY's DISAPPOINTMENT.

(Madame d'Arblay to M. d'Arblay.) Westhamble, March 14, 1802. O my dearest friend, can the intelligence I have most desired come to me in a form that forbids my joy at it? What tumultuous sensations your letter of the 8th has raised! (168) Alas! that to relinquish this purpose should to you be as great unhappiness as to me was its suggestion! I know not how to enter upon the subject—how to express a single feeling. I fear to seem ungrateful to providence, or to you ungenerous. I will only, therefore, say, that as all your motives have been the most strictly honourable, it is not possible they should not, ultimately, have justice done them by all.

That I feel for your disappointment I need not tell you, when you find it has power to shake to its foundation what would else be the purest satisfaction of my soul. Let us—let us hope fairer days will ensue and do not let the courage which was so prompt to support you to St. Domingo fail you in remaining at Paris.

What you say of the year's probation I knew not before. Would you have me make any inquiry if it be irreversible?' I should think not; and am most ready and eager to try by every means in my power, if you will authorize me. If not, to follow you, whithersoever you will, is much less my duty than my delight! You have only to dictate whither, and how, and every doubt, every fear, every difficulty, will give way to my eager desire to bring your little boy to you. Would I not have left even Kin to have followed you and your fate even to St. Domingo? 'Tis well, however, you did not listen to me, for that poor little susceptible soul could not, as yet lose us both at once, and be preserved himself He has lived' so singularly alone with us, and for us, that he does not dream of any possible existence in which we should be both separated from him.

But of him—our retreat—our books—our scribbling—our garden—our unique mode of life—I must not talk to you now, now that your mind, thoughts, views, and wishes are all distorted from themes of peace, domestic life, and literary pursuits; yet time, I hope, reflection, your natural philosophy of accommodating yourself to your fate, and your kindness for those who are wholly devoted to you, will bring you back to the love of those scenes, modes, and sentiments, which for upwards of eight years have sufficed for our mutual happiness.

I had been negotiating for apartments at Twickenham, opposite Richmond, ever since you went, and on Friday I wrote to close with the engagement. This very morning I have two letters, full of delight at our approaching neighbourhood. Miss C. (169) herself writes in tears, she says, of joy, that I should be so near her, and that you should have wished it, and blesses you for your confidence in her warm friendship.   It is quite impossible to read of such affection and zeal and goodness with dry eyes. I am confounded how to disenchant her— yet so generous and disinterested she is, that, however disappointed, she will be sure to rejoice for me in our re-union; for you, my dearest friend!

ah! who can rejoice? Your mind was all made up to the return of its professional pursuits, and I am frightened out of all my own satisfaction by MY dread of the weight of this chagrin upon your spirits. What you can do to avert depression, that cruel underminer of every faculty that makes life worth sustaining, I beseech you to call forth. Think how I have worked for fortitude since Feb. 11th. Alas! vainly I have tried what most I wished—my poor pen!—but now "occupe-toi pour r,aliser l'esp,rance." Those words will operate like magic, I trust; and I will not close my eyes this night till I have committed to paper some opening to a new essay. Be good, then, and don't let me be as unhappy this way as I have been the other. Direct always to me, Norbury Park, Dorking. Heaven bless—bless you

[Here follows, in the original edition, another letter in French, from M. d'Arblay to his wife. We translate the following passage. ED.

"At Ventose, year 10, (March 12, 1802). "You have doubtless communicated to our friends at Norbury Park, the letters which I have sent you. Did I tell you that I sent a copy of those letters to M. de Lafayette? (170) M. de Lafayette came at once to Paris, and requested an interview with Bonaparte, who granted it immediately. Addressing him, M. de Lafayette said, ' I have come to speak to you of one of my friends and companions—d'Arblay.' 'I know that business,' said the first Consul, in a tone which expressed more good-will than I ventured to hope for, at least, more than I had been given reason to expect. 'I assure you,' said M. de Lafayette to me, the next day, 'you have some good friends with the first Consul, who had already spoken to him on your business. He seemed to me, from the first instant, rather disposed in your favour than angry with you. . . . When I told him of your fear lest this business should have excited his displeasure, he replied positively, that it should do you no injury whatever, and that he would regard, in the step you had taken, only the husband of Cecilia.'

"I hope you will not be very displeased at the way this business, which has caused me much vexation, has terminated. I think I may even add, in confidence, that I am, perhaps, not without a near prospect of getting my retiring pension. Come to me, then, my dearest.

ON THE EVE OF MADAME D'ARBLAY'S JOURNEY TO FRANCE.

(Madame d'Arblay to Doctor Burney.) March 30, 1802. Now, indeed, my dearest father, I am in an excess of hurry not to be exceeded by even any of yours. I have a letter from M. d'Arblay, to tell me he has already taken us an apartment, and he dates from the 5th of April, in Paris, where he has reasons for remaining some time, before we go to his good uncle, at Joigny. I am to take the little sweet child with me you saw here one day, Mlle. de Chavagnac, whose father, le Comte de Chavagnac, has desired her restoration. My kind Mrs: Locke is almost in affliction at parting with her though glad of an opportunity of sending her with friends the poor thing knows and loves. I fear, I have so very much to do here, that I shall have a very, very short enjoyment of my beloved father at Chelsea but I shall get there as soon as possible, and stay there to my last moment. I have a thousand things, and very curious ones, to tell you; but I must defer them for vive voix. I am really bewildered and almost trembling with hurry, and with what I am going to undertake! Yet through all, i bless God every moment of my life that M. d'Arblay went not to that pestilential climate I do all— all I can to keep up my courage—or rather to make up; and when I feel faltering, I think of St Domingo! Every body that knows St Domingo now owns that he had hardly a chance for safety, independent of tempests in the voyage, and massacres in the mountains. May I but be able to console him for all he has sacrificed to my peace and happiness! and no privation will be severe, so that at our stated period, Michaelmas twelvemonth, we return to my country, and to my dearest father, whom heaven bless and preserve, prays his dutiful, affectionate and grateful, and devoted daughter, F. d'A.

DIARY: (Addressed to Dr. Burney).

IN FRANCE DURING THE PEACE AND SUBSEQUENTLY.

April, 1802. I seize, at length, upon the largest paper I can procure, to begin to my beloved father some account of our journey, and if I am able, I mean to keep him a brief journal of my proceedings during this destined year or eighteen months' separation, secure of his kindest interest in all that I may have to relate, and certain he will be anxious to know how I go on in a strange land: 'tis my only way now of communicating with him, and I must draw from it one of my dearest worldly comforts, the hopes of seeing his loved hand with some return.

April 15. William and John conducted my little boy and me in excellent time to the inn in Piccadilly, where we met my kind Mrs. Locke and dear little Adrienne de Chavagnac. The parting there was brief and hurried; and I set off on my grand expedition, with my two dear young charges, exactly at five o'clock. . . .

Paris, April 15, 1802. The book-keeper came to me eagerly, crying "vite, vite, madame, prenez votre place dans la diligence, car voici un Monsieur Anglais, qui surement va prendre la meileure!" En effet, ce Monsieur Anglais did not disappoint his expectations, or much raise mine, for he not only took the best place, but contrived to ameliorate it by the little scruple with which he made every other worse, from the unbridled expansion in which he indulged his dear person, by putting out his elbows against his next, and his knees and feet against his opposite neighbour. He seemed prepared to look upon all around-him with a sort of sulky haughtiness, pompously announcing himself as a commander of distinction who had long served at Gibraltar and various places, who had travelled thence through France, and from France to Italy, who was a native of Scotland, and -of proud, though unnamed genealogy '; and was now going to Paris purposely to behold the first Consul, to whom he meant to claim an introduction through Mr. Jackson. His burnt complexion, Scotch accent, large bony face and figure, and high and distant demeanour, made me easily conceive and believe him a highland chief. I never heard his name, but I think him a gentleman born, though not gently bred.

The next to mention is a Madame Raymond or Grammont, for I heard not distinctly which, who seemed very much a gentlewoman, and who was returning to France, too uncertain of the state of her affairs to know whether she might rest there or not. She had only one defect to prevent my taking much interest in her; this was, not merely an avoidance, but a horror of being touched by either of my children; who, poor little souls, restless and fatigued by the confinement they endured, both tried to fling themselves upon every passenger in turn; and though by every one they were sent back to their sole prop, they were by no one repulsed with such hasty displeasure as by this old lady, who seemed as fearful of having the petticoat of her gown, which was stiff, round, and bulging, as if lined with parchment, deranged, as if she had been attired in a hoop for Court.

The third person was a Madame Blaizeau, who seemed an exceeding good sort of a woman, gay, voluble, good humoured, and merry. All we had of amusement sprung from her sallies, which were uttered less from a desire of pleasing others, her very natural character having none of the high polish bestowed by the Graces, than from a jovial spirit of enjoyment which made them produce pleasure to herself. She soon and frankly acquainted us she had left France to be a governess to some young ladies before the Revolution, and under the patronage, as I think, of the Duke of Dorset, she had been courted, she told us, by an English gentleman farmer, but he would not change his religion for her, nor she for him, and so, when every thing was bought for her wedding, they broke off the connexion; and she afterwards married a Frenchman. She had seen a portrait, set richly in diamonds, of the king, prepared for a present to the first Consul; and described its superb ornaments and magnificence, in a way to leave no doubt of the fact. She meant to stop at St. Denis, to inquire if her mother yet lived, having received no intelligence from or of her, these last ten eventful years!

At Canterbury, while the horses were changed, my little ones and I went to the cathedral; but dared merely seize sufficient time to view the outside and enter the principal aisle. I was glad even of that much, as its antique grandeur gave me a pleasure which I always love to cherish in the view of fine old cathedrals, those most permanent monuments of what our ancestors thought reverence to God, as manifested in munificence to the place dedicated to his worship.

At Dover we had a kind of dinner-supper in one, and my little boy and girl and I retired immediately after it, took some tea in our chamber, and went to rest.

April 16. As we were not to sail till twelve, I had hoped to have seen the castle and Shakspeare's cliff, but most unfortunately it rained all the morning, and we were confined to the inn, except for the interlude of the custom-house, where, however, the examination was so slight, and made with such civility, that we had no other trouble with it than a wet walk and a few shillings. Our passports were examined; and we then ' went to the port, and, the sea being perfectly smooth, were lifted from the quay to the deck of our vessel with as little difficulty as we could have descended from a common chair to the ground.

ARRIVAL AT CALAIS.

The calm which caused our slow passage and our sickness, was now favourable, for it took us into the port of Calais so close and even with the quay, that we scarcely accepted even a hand to aid us from the vessel to the shore.

The quay was lined with crowds of people, men, women, and children, and certain amphibious females, who might have passed for either sex, or anything else in the world, except what they really were, European women! Their men's hats, men's jackets, and men's shoes - their burnt skins, and most savage-looking petticoats, hardly reaching, nay, not reaching their knees, would have made me instantly believe any account I could have heard of their being just imported from the wilds of America.

The vessel was presently filled with men, who, though dirty and mean, were so civil and gentle, that they could not displease, and who entered it so softly and quietly, that, neither hearing nor seeing their approach, it seemed as if they had availed themselves of some secret trap-doors through which they had mounted to fill the ship, without sound or bustle, in a single moment. When we were quitting it, however, this tranquillity as abruptly finished, for in an instant a part of them rushed round me, one demanding to carry Alex, another Adrienne, another seizing my ,critoire, another my arm, and some one, I fear, my parasol, as I have never been able to find it since.

We were informed we must not leave the ship till Monsieur le commissaire arrived to carry us, I think, to the Municipality of Calais to show our passports. Monsieur le commisSaire in white with some red trappings, soon arrived, civilly hastening himself quite out of breath to save us from waiting' We then mounted the quay, and I followed the rest of the passengers, who all followed the commissary, accompanied by two men carrying the two children, and two more carrying one my ,critoire, and the other insisting on conducting its owner. The quantity of people that surrounded and walked with us, surprised me; and their decency, their silence their quietness astonished me. To fear them was impossible: even in entering France with all the formed fears hanging upon its recent though past horrors. But on coming to the municipality, I was, I own, extremely ill at ease, when upon our gouvernante's desiring me to give the commissary my passport, as the rest of the passengers had done, and my answering it was in my ,critoire, she exclaimed, "Vite! Vite! cherchez-le, ou vous serez arrêtee!"(172) You may be sure I was quick enough, or at least tried to be so, for my fingers presently trembled, and I could hardly put in the key.

In the hall to which we now repaired, our passports were taken and deposited, and we had new ones drawn up and given us in their stead. On quitting this place we were accosted by a new crowd, all however as gentle, though not as silent, as our first friends, who recommended various hotels to us, one begging we would go to Grandsire, another to Duroc, another to Meurice—and this last prevailed with the gouvernante, whom I regularly followed, not from preference, but from the singular horror my otherwise worthy and wellbred old lady manifested, when, by being approached by the children, her full round coats risked the danger of being modernised into the flimsy, falling drapery of the present day.

At Meurice's our goods were entered, and we heard that they would be examined at the custom-house in the afternoon. We breakfasted, and the crowd of fees which were claimed by the captain, steward, sailors, carriers, and heaven knows who, besides, are inconceivable. I gave whatever they asked, from ignorance of what was due, and from fear of offending those of whose extent, still less of whose use, of power I could form no judgment. I was the only one in this predicament; the rest refusing or disputing every demand. They all, but us, went out to walk, but I stayed to write to my dearest father, to Mrs. Locke, and my expecting mate.

"GOD SAVE THE KING!" ON FRENCH SOIL.

We were all three too much awake by the new scene to try for any repose, and the hotel windows sufficed for our amusement till dinner; and imagine, my dearest sir, how my repast was seasoned, when I tell you that, as soon as it began, a band "of music came to the window and struck up "God save the king." I can never tell you what a pleased emotion was excited in my breast by this sound on a shore so lately hostile, and on which I have so many, so heartfelt motives for wishing peace and amity perpetual!

A RAMBLE THROUGH THE TOWN.

This over, we ventured out of the hotel to look at the street. The day was fine, the street was clean, two or three people who passed us, made way for the children as they skipped out of my hands, and I saw such an unexpected appearance of quiet, order and civility, that, almost without knowing it, we strolled from the gate, and presently found ourselves in the market-place, which was completely full of sellers, and buyers, and booths, looking like a large English fair.

The queer, gaudy jackets, always of a different colour from the petticoats of the women, and their immense wing-caps, which seemed made to double over their noses, but which all flew back so as to discover their ears, in which I regularly saw large and generally drop gold ear-rings, were quite as diverting ...to myself as to Alex and Adrienne. Many of them, also, had gold necklaces chains, and crosses; but ear-rings all: even maids who were scrubbing or sweeping, ragged wretches bearing burdens on their heads or shoulders, old women selling fruit or other eatables, gipsy-looking creatures with children tied to their backs—all wore these long, broad, large, shining ear-rings.

Beggars we saw not—no, not one, all the time we stayed or sauntered; and for civility and gentleness, the poorest and most ordinary persons we met or passed might be compared with the best dressed and best looking walkers in the streets of our metropolis, and still to the disadvantage of the latter. I cannot say how much this surprised me, as I had conceived a horrific idea of the populace of this country, imagining em all transformed into bloody monsters.

Another astonishment I experienced equally pleasing, though not equally important to my ease; I saw innumerable pretty women and lovely children, almost all of them extremely fair. I had been taught to expect nothing but mahogany complexions and hideous features instantly on crossing the strait of Dover. When this, however, was mentioned in our party afterwards, the Highlander exclaimed, "But Calais was in the hands of the English so many years, that the English race there is not yet extinct."

The perfect security in which I now saw we might wander about, induced us to walk over the whole town, and even extend our excursions to the ramparts surrounding it. It is now a very clean and pretty town, and so orderly that there was no more tumult or even noise in the market-place, where the people were so close together as to form a continual crowd, than in the by-streets leading to the country, where scarcely a passenger was to be seen. This is certainly a remark which, I believe, could never be made in England.

When we returned to the hotel, I found all my fellow travellers had been to the custom house! I had quite forgotten, or rather neglected to inquire the hour for this formality, and was beginning to alarm myself lest I was out of rule, when a young man, a commissary, I heard, of the hotel, came to me and asked if I had anything contraband to the laws of the Republic. I answered as I had done before, and he readily undertook to go through the ceremony for me without my appearing. I was so much frightened, and so happy not to be called upon personally, that I thought myself very cheaply off in his after-demand of a guinea and a half. I had two and a half to pay afterwards for additional luggage.

We found reigning through Calais a general joy and satisfaction at the restoration of Dimanche and abolition of decade. (173) I had a good deal of conversation with the maid of the inn, a tall, fair, extremely pretty woman, and she talked much upon this subject, and the delight it occasioned, and the obligation all France was under to the premier Consul for restoring religion and worship.

SUNDAY ON THE ROAD TO PARIS.

Sunday, April 18. We set off for Paris at five o'clock in the morning. The country broad, flat, or' barrenly steep—without trees, without buildings, and scarcely inhabited—exhibited a change from the fertile fields, and beautiful woods, band gardens, and civilisation of Kent, so sudden and unpleasant that I only lamented the fatigue of my position, which regularly impeded my making use of this chasm of pleasure and observation for repose. This part of France must certainly be the least frequented, for we rarely met a single carriage, and the villages, few and distant, seemed to have no intercourse with each other. Dimanche, indeed, might occasion this stiffness, for we saw, at almost all the villages, neat and clean peasants going to or coming from mass, and seeming indescribably elated and happy by the public permission of divine worship on its originally appointed day.

I was struck with the change in Madame Raymond, who joined us in the morning from another hotel. Her hoop was no more visible; her petticoats were as lank, or more so, than her neighbours'; and her distancing the children was not only at an end, but she prevented me from renewing any of my cautions to them, of not incommoding her, and when we were together a few moments, before we were joined by the rest, she told me, with a significant smile, not to tutor the children about her any more, as she only avoided them from having something of consequence to take care of, which was removed. I then saw she meant some English lace or muslin, which she had carried in a petticoat, and, since the customhouse examination was over, had now packed in her trunk.

Poor lady! I fear this little merchandise was all her hope of succour on her arrival! She is amongst the emigrants who have twice or thrice returned, but not yet been able to rest in their own country.

What most in the course of this journey struck me, was the satisfaction of all the country people, with whom I could converse at the restoration of the Dimanche; and the boasts they now ventured to make of having never kept the decade, except during the dreadful reign of Robespierre, when not to oppose any of his severest decrees was insufficient for safety, it was essential even to existence to observe them with every parade of the warmest approval.

The horrible stories from every one of that period of wanton as well as political cruelty, I must have judged exaggerated, either through the mist of fear or the heats of resentment but that, though the details had innumerable modifications there was but one voice for the excess of barbarity.

At a little hamlet near Clermont, where we rested some time, two good old women told us that this was the happiest day (twas Sunday) of their lives; that they had lost le bon Dieu for these last ten years, but that Bonaparte had now found him! In another cottage we were told the villagers had kept their own cur, all this time concealed, and though privately and with fright, they had thereby saved their souls through the whole of the bad times! And in another, some poor creatures said they were now content with their destiny, be it what it might, since they should be happy, at least, in the world to come, but that while denied going to mass, they had all their sufferings aggravated by knowing that they must lose their souls hereafter, besides all that they had to endure here!

O my dearest father! that there can have existed wretches of such diabolical wickedness as to have snatched, torn, from the toiling indigent every ray even of future hope! Various of these little conversations extremely touched me nor was I unmoved, though not with such painful emotion, on the sight of the Sunday night dance, in a little village through which we passed, where there seemed two or three hundred peasants engaged in that pastime all clean and very gaily dressed, yet all so decent and well behaved, that, but for the poor old fiddlers, we might have driven on, and not have perceived the rustic ball.

Here ends the account of my journey, and if it has amused my dearest father, it will be a true delight to me to have scribbled it. My next letter brings me to the capital, and to the only person who can console me for my always lamented absence from himself.

ENGAGEMENTS, OCCUPATIONS, AND FATIGUE

(Madame d'Arblay to Miss Planta.) Paris, April 27, 1802. A week have I been here, my dear Miss Planta, so astonishingly engaged, so indispensably occupied, or so suffering from fatigue, that I have not been able till now to take up pen, except to satisfy my dear father of our safe arrival.

To give you some idea of these engagements, occupations, and fatigues, I must begin with the last. We were a whole long, languid day, a whole restless, painful night, upon the sea; my little Alex sick as death, suffering if possible yet more than myself, though I had not a moment of ease and comfort. My little Adrienne de Chavagnac was perfectly well all the time, singing and skipping about the cabin, and amusing every one by her innocent enjoyment of the novelty of the scene. . . .

As to my occupations; my little apartment to arrange, my trunks and baggage to unpack and place, my poor Adrienne to consign to her friends, my Alex to nurse from a threatening malady; letters to deliver, necessaries to buy; a femme de chambre to engage; and, most important of all! my own sumptuous wardrobe to refit, and my own poor exterior to reorganise! I see you smile, methinks, at this hint; but what smiles would brighten the countenance of a certain young lady called Miss Rose, who amused herself by anticipation, when I had last the honour of seeing her, with the changes I might have to undergo, could she have heard the exclamations which followed the examination of my attire: "This won't do! That YOU can never wear! This you can never be seen in! That would make you stared at as a curiosity!— Three petticoats! no one wears more than one!— Stays? everybody has left off even corsets!—Shift sleeves? not a soul now wears even a chemise!" etc. In short, I found all I possessed seemed so hideously old fashioned, or so comically rustic, that as soon as it was decreed I must make appearance in the grand monde, hopeless of success in exhibiting myself in the' costume Francais, I gave over the attempt, and ventured to come forth as a gothic Anglaise, who never heard of, or never heeded the reigning metamorphosis.

As to my engagements;—when should I finish, should I tell all that have been made or proposed, even in the short space of a single week? The civilities I have met with, contrary to all my expectations, have not more amazed me for myself, than gratified me for M. d'Arblay, who is keenly alive to the kind, I might say distinguished, reception I have been favoured with by those to whom my arrival is known.

Your favourite hero is excessively popular at this moment from three successive grand events, all occurring within the short time of my arrival, the ratification of the treaty of peace—the restoration of Sunday, and Catholic worship—and the amnesty of the emigrants. At the Opera buffa, the loge in which I sat was exactly opposite to that of the first Consul but he and his family are all at Malmaison.

DIARY RESUMED: (Addressed to Dr. Burney.)

ARISTOCRATIC VISITORS.

Paris, April 1, 1802. (174) Almost immediately after my arrival in Paris, I was much surprised by a visit from the ci-devant Prince de Beauvau, madame his wife, and Mademoiselle de Mortemar her sister, all brought by Madame d'Henin. if gratified in the first instance by a politeness of attention so little my due and so completely beyond my expectations, how was my pleasure enhanced when I found they all three spoke English with the utmost ease and fluency, and how pleased also at the pleasure I was able to give them in reward of their civility, by a letter I had brought from Mrs. Harcourt, which was received with the warmest delight by Mademoiselle de Mortemar and a message from a young lady named Elizabeth, with the profoundest gratitude.

April 24. This morning Madame d'Henin was so kind as to accompany us, in making our visit to Madame de Beauvau her niece, and Mademoiselle de Mortemar. We found them at home with M. de Beauvau, and they indulged me with the sight of their children, who are the most flourishing and healthy possible, and dressed and brought up with English plainness and simplicity. The visit was very pleasant, and Madame d'Henin made a party for us all to meet again the next day, and go to the Opera buffa.

ANXIETY TO SEE THE FIRST CONSUL.

I have heard much of the visit of Mrs. Damer and the Miss Berrys to Paris, and their difficulty to get introduced to the first Consul. (175) A lady here told us she had been called upon by Miss Berry, who had complained with much energy upon this subject, saying, "We have been everywhere—seen everything—heard every body—beheld such sights! listened to such discourse! joined such society! and all to obtain his notice! Don't you think it very extraordinary that he should not himself desire to see Mrs. Damer?

"Madame," replied the lady, "perhaps if you had done but half this, the first Consul might have desired to see you both."

"But you don't imagine," answered she, laughing, "we came over from England to see you ci-devants? We can see such as you at home!"

She was gone before our arrival; and, as I understand, succeeded at last in obtaining an introduction. They were both, Mrs. Damer and Miss Berry, as I am told, very gay and agreeable, as well as enterprising, and extremely well répandues.

AT THE OPERA-BOUFFE.

April 25. I was not much better in the evening, but the party for the Opera buffa being formed by Madame d'Henin on my account, my going was indispensable. She had borrowed the loge of M. de Choiseul, which, being entailed upon the family perp,tuit,, has in a most extraordinary manner continued unalienated through the whole course of massacres and proscriptions to the present day, when the right owner possesses it. It is the largest and best box, except that which is opposite to it, in the theatre. . . .

The opera was "Le Nozze di Dorina," by Sarti, and extremely pretty; though I wished it had been as new to M. C— de P— as to myself, for then he would not have divided my attention by obligingly singing every note with every performer. In truth, I was still so far from recovered from the fatigue of my journey, that I was lulled to a drowsiness the most distressing before the end of the second act, which being but too obvious, Madame d'Henin and M. d'Arblay took me away before I risked a downright nap by waiting for the third.

DIFFICULTIES RESPECTING MADAME DE STAEL.

April 26. The assembly at Madame d'Henin's was one of the most select and agreeable at which I was ever present. Assembly, however, I ought not to call a meeting within the number of twenty. But I was uneasy for my poor Alex, and therefore stole away as soon as possible; not, however, till Madame de Tess, made a party for us for the following Thursday at her house, nor till I had held a private discourse with Mademoiselle de — upon my embarrassment as to Madame de Stael, from the character she held in England; which embarrassment was not much lightened by her telling me it was not held more fair in France! Yet, that everywhere the real evil is highly exaggerated by report, envy, and party-spirit, all allow. She gives, however, great assemblies at which all Paris assist, and though not solicited or esteemed by her early friends and acquaintance, she is admired, and pitied, and received by them. I would she were gone to Copet! (176)

What most perplexed me at this period was the following note from Madame de Stael.

"je voudrois vous te moigner mon empressement, madame, et je crains d'être indiscrette. j'espere que vous aurez la bont, de me faire dire quand vous serez assez remise des fatigues de votre voyage pour que je puisse avoir l'honneur de vous voir sans vous importuner. "Ce 4 florial. (177) "Necker Stael de H." (178)

How is it possible, when even the common civility of a card for her card is yet unreturned, that she can have brought herself thus to descend from her proud heights to solicit the renewal of an acquaintance broken so abruptly in England, and so palpably shunned in France? Is it that the regard she appeared to conceive for me in England was not only sincere but constant? If so, I must very much indeed regret a waste of kindness her character and conduct make it impossible for me to repay, even though, on this spot, I am assured all her misfortunes are aggravated, nay caricatured, by report, and that she exerts her utmost influence, and calls forth her best talents, upon every occasion which presents itself for serving those who have been her friends; and that, notwithstanding circumstances and disunion, either in politics or morals, may have made them become her enemies. Her generosity is cited as truly singular upon this head, and I have heard histories of her returning, personally, good for evil that would do honour to any character living.

After much deliberation and discussion, my French master composed the following answer:—

"Madame d'Arblay ne peut qu' étre infiniment flattée de l'extrême bonté, de Madame la Comtesse de Stael. Elle aura très certainement l'honneur de se présenter chez Madame de Stael aussitôt que possible." (179)

Cooler than this it was not easy to write, and the ne peut qu'être is a tournure that is far enough from flattering. I hope, however, it will prepare her for the frozen kind of intercourse which alone can have place between us.

MADAME DE LAFAYETTE.

As I wished much to see the parade, or review, which was to take place on the 5th, and is only once a month, we were forced to devote the preceding day to visits, as it was decreed in our council of etiquette that I could not appear in a place where I might be seen by those who had shown me the civility of beginning an acquaintance, till I had acknowledged my debt to them. . . . I was so thoroughly tired when I returned from all these visits, that I was forced to rest upon a bed for the remainder of the day, to my no small discomposure before the evening was closed; for, in a close cap, my feet in their native, undraperied state, hidden by a large, long, wrapping morning gown, your daughter, my dearest sir, lay reclined on a bed when, rather late in the evening, I was told Madame d'Henin was in the salon. I was going to send in my excuses, while I rose to get ready for waiting upon her - but Alex flung open the door, and seeing where I was, and how fatigued, she insisted on my keeping still, and came to my bedside, and sat in friendly converse, listening to the history of my morning excursion, till a ring at the bell of our ante-room made me desire to have nobody admitted. Alex again, however, frisking about, prevented Pauline, my little femme de chambre, from hearing me, and she announced Madame de Lafayette!

You may easily believe this name, and my present situation, put me into no small commotion. I was beseeching Madame d'Henin to go to the saloon with my apologies, when Alex, whose illness, though it has diminished his strength and his flesh, has left his spirits as wild as ever, called out to proclaim where I was, and while Madame Lafayette was gently moving on, flung the bedroom door wide open, saying, "Mamma is here!" Madame Lafayette, concluding, I suppose, that I received du monde in the French manner, immediately presented herself at the door, where I had no resource but to entreat Madame d'Henin, who is her intimate friend, to receive her, for I was wholly powerless, with my unsandaled feet, from rising. Madame d'Henin now brought her to my bedside, where nothing could have been more awkward than my situation: but that the real reverence I had conceived for her character and her virtues made the sight of so singular a person, her condescension in the visit, and her goodness, though lame, in mounting three pair of stairs, give me a sensation of pleasure, that by animating my spirits, endowed me with a courage that overcame all difficulties both of language and position, and enabled me to express my gratitude for her kindness and my respect for her person, with something far nearer to fluency and clearness than anything in speech I have yet attempted. My mind instantly presented her to me, torn from her beloved family, and thrown into the death-impending prison of Robespierre; and then saved by his timely destruction from the scaffold, and then using her hardly-recovered liberty only by voluntarily sacrificing it to be immured with her husband in the dungeon of Olmutz.(180) Various as may be the opinions of the politics of M. de Lafayette, all Europe, I believe, concur in admiration of the character and conduct of his virtuous and heroic wife. Indeed, nothing since my arrival has so sensibly gratified me, from without, as this visit.

Madame Lafayette is the daughter of the ci-devant Duc d'Ayen, and consequently niece of Madame de Tess,, the duke's sister. She was married to M. de Lafayette when she was only seventeen years of age. By some cold or mismanagement, and total want of exercise in the prison of Olmutz, some humour has fallen into one of her ankles, that, though it does not make her absolutely lame, causes walking to be so painful and difficult to her that she moves as little as possible, and is always obliged to have a stool for her foot. She now resides with M. de Lafayette and their three children entirely in the country, at a chateau which has descended to her since the revolutionary horrors and therefore has not been confiscated, called "La Grange." They never come to Paris but upon business of positive necessity. She had arrived only this morning on a visit to her aunt, Madame de Tess,, to make some preparations for the approaching marriage of her only son.

Her youngest daughter, Mademoiselle de Lafayette, accompanied her. She is a blooming young creature of English fairness-as we English choose to say-with a bright native colour, and beautiful light hair; otherwise with but indifferent features, and not handsome: yet her air, though modest even to the extreme that borders upon bashfulness, is distinguished, and speaks her to be both sensible and well brought up.

Madame de Lafayette, also, is by no means handsome; but has eyes so expressive, so large, and so speaking, that it is not easy to criticise her other features, for it is almost impossible to look at them. Her manner is calm and mild, yet noble. She is respected even by surrounding infidels for her genuine piety, which, in the true character of true religion, is severe only for herself, lenient and cheerful for all others. I do not say this from what I could see in the hour she was so good as to pass with me, but from all I have heard.

She warmly invited me to La Grange, and requested me to name an early day for passing some time there. I proposed that it might be after the marriage had taken place,"as till then all foreign people or subjects might be obtrusive. She paused a moment, and then said, "Après?—c'est vrai we could then more completely enjoy Madame d'Arblay' society; for we must now have continual interruptions, surrounded as we are by workmen, goods, chattels, and preparations; so that there would be a nail to hammer between almost every word; and yet, as we are going to Auvergne, after the ceremony, it will be so long before a meeting may be arranged, that I believe the less time lost the better."

I know M. d'Arblay desired this acquaintance for me too earnestly to offer any opposition; and I was too much charmed with its opening to make any myself: it was therefore determined we should go the following week to La Grange.

SIGHT-SEEING AT THE TULLERIES.

May 5-Again a full day. M. d'Arblay had procured us three tickets for entering the apartments at the Tuileries to see the parade of General Hulin, now high in actual rank and service, but who had been a sous-officier under M. d'Arblay's command; our third ticket was for Madame d'Henin, who had never been to this sight—nor, indeed, more than twice to any spectacle since her return to France—till my arrival; but she is so obliging and good as to accept, nay to seek, every thing that can amuse, of which I can profit. We breakfasted with her early, and were appointed to join the party of

M. le Prince de Beauvau, who had a general in his carriage, through whose aid and instructions we hoped to escape all difficulties.

Accordingly the coach in which they went was desired to stop at Madame d'Henin's door, so as to let us get into our fiacre, and follow it straight. This was done, and our precursor stopped at the gate leading to the garden of the Tuileries. The De Beauvaus, Mademoiselle de Mortemar, and their attending general, alighted, and we followed their example and joined them, which was no sooner done than their general, at the sight of M. d'Arblay, suddenly drew back from conducting Madame de Beauvau, and flew up to him. They had been ancient camarades, but had not met since M. d'A.'s emigration.

The crowd was great, but civil and well dressed; and we met with no impediment till we came to the great entrance. Alas, I had sad recollections of sad readings in mounting the steps! We had great difficulty, notwithstanding our tickets, in making our way—I mean Madame d'Henin and ourselves, for Madame de Beauvau and Mademoiselle de Mortemar having an officer in the existing military to aid them, were admitted and helped by all the attendants; and so forwarded that we wholly lost sight of them, till we arrived, long after, in the apartment destined for the exhibition. This, however, was so crowded that every place at the windows for seeing the parade was taken, and the row formed opposite to see the first Consul as he passes through the room to take horse, was so thick and threefold filled, that not a possibility existed of even a passing peep. Madame d'Henin would have retired, but as the whole scene was new and curious to me, I prevailed with her to stay, that I might view a little of the costume of the company; though I was sorry I detained her, when I saw her perturbed spirits from the recollections which, I am sure, pressed upon her on re-entering this palace: and that her sorrows were only subdued by her personal indignation, which was unconscious, but yet very prominent, to find herself included in the mass of the crowd in being refused all place and distinction, where, heretofore, she was amongst the first for every sort of courtesy. Nothing of this, however, was said and you may believe my pity for her was equally unuttered.

We seated ourselves now, hopeless of any other amusement than seeing the uniforms of the passing officers, and the light drapery of the stationary ladies, which, by the way, is not by any means so notorious nor so common as has been represented; on the contrary, there are far more who are decent enough to attract no attention, than who are fashionable enough to call for it.

During this interval M. d'Arblay found means, by a ticket lent him by M. de Narbonne, to enter the next apartment, and there to state our distress, not in vain, to General Hulin; and presently he returned, accompanied by this officer, who is, I fancy, at least seven feet high, and was dressed in one of the most showy uniforms I ever saw. M. d'Arblay introduced me to him. He expressed his pleasure in seeing the wife of his old comrade, and taking my hand, caused all the crowd to make way, and conducted me into the apartment adjoining to that where the first Consul receives the ambassadors, with a flourish of manners so fully displaying power as well as courtesy, that I felt as if in the hands of one of the seven champions who meant to mow down all before him, should any impious elf dare dispute his right to give me liberty, or to show me honour.

A GOOD PLACE IS SECURED.

He put me into the first place in the apartment which was sacred to general officers, and as many ladies as could be accommodated in two rows only at the windows. M. d'Arblay, under the sanction of his big friend, followed with Madame d'Henin, and we had the pleasure of rejoining Madame de Beauvau and Mademoiselle de Mortemar, who were at the same windows, through the exertions of General Songis.

The scene now, with regard to all that was present, was splendidly gay and highly animating. The room was full, but not crowded, with officers of rank in sumptuous rather than rich uniforms, and exhibiting a martial air that became their attire, which, however, generally speaking, was too gorgeous to be noble. Our window was that next to the consular apartment, in which Bonaparte was holding a levee, and it was close to the steps ascending to it; by which means we saw all the forms of the various exits and entrances, and had opportunity to examine every dress and every countenance that passed and repassed. This was highly amusing, I might say historic, where the past history and the present office were known.

Sundry footmen of the first Consul, in very fine liveries, were attending to bring or arrange chairs for whoever required them; various peace-officers, superbly begilt, paraded occasionally up and down the chamber, to keep the ladies to their windows and the gentlemen to their ranks, so as to preserve the passage or lane through which the first Consul was to walk upon his entrance, clear and open; and several gentlemanlike looking persons, whom in former times I should have supposed pages of the back stairs, dressed in black, with gold chains hanging round their necks, and medallions pending from them, seemed to have the charge of the door itself, leading immediately to the audience chamber of the first Consul.

M. D'ARPLAY'S MILITARY COMRADES.

But what was most prominent in commanding notice, was the array of the aides-de-camp of Bonaparte, which was so almost furiously striking, that all other vestments, even the most gaudy, appeared suddenly under a gloomy cloud when contrasted with its brightness. We were long viewing them before we could discover what they were to represent, my three lady companions being as new to this scene as myself; but afterwards M. d'Arblay starting forward to speak to one of them, brought him across the lane to me, and said "General Lauriston,"

His kind and faithful friendship to M. d'Arblay, so amiably manifested upon his late splendid embassy to England, made me see him with great pleasure. It was of course but for a moment, as he was amongst those who had most business upon their hands. General d'Hennezel also came to me for a few minutes, and three or four others, whom M. d'Arblay named, but whom I have forgotten. Indeed, I was amazed at the number of old friends by whom he was recognised, and touched far more than I can express, to see him in his old coat and complete undress, accosted by his fine (former) brethren, in all their new and beautiful costume, with an eagerness of regard that, resulting from first impulse, proved their judgment, or rather knowledge of his merits, more forcibly than any professions, however warm, could have done. He was indeed, after the aides-de-camp, the most striking figure in the apartment, from contrasting as much with the general herd by being the plainest and worst dressed, as they did by being the gayest and most showy.

General Lauriston is a very handsome man, and of a very pleasing and amiable countenance; and his manly air carried off the frippery of his trappings, so as to make them appear almost to advantage.

ARRIVAL OF THE TROOPS.

While this variety of attire, of carriage, and of physiognomy amused us in facing the passage prepared for the first Consul, we were occupied, whenever we turned round, by seeing from the window the garden of the Tuileries filling with troops.

In the first row of females at the window where we stood, were three ladies who, by my speaking English with Mademoiselle de Mortemar and Madame de Beauvau, discovered .my country, and, as I have since heard, gathered my name; and here I blush to own how unlike was the result to what "One of this nation might have experienced from a similar discovery in England; for the moment it was buzzed "C'est Une etrangere, c'est une Anglaise," (181) every one tried to Place, to oblige, and to assist me, and yet no one looked curious, or stared at me. Ah, my dear padre, do you not a little fear, in a contrasted situation, no one would have tried to place oblige, or assist, yet every one would have looked curious, and stared? Well, there are virtues as well as defects of all classes, and John Bull can fight so good a battle for his share of the former, that he need not be utterly cast down in acknowledging now and then a few of the latter.

AN IMPORTANT NEW ACQUAINTANCE.

The best view from the window to see the marching forwards of the troops was now bestowed upon me, and I vainly offered it to the ladies of my own party, to whom the whole of the sight was as new as to myself. The three unknown ladies began conversing with me, and, after a little general-talk, one of them with sudden importance of manner, in a tone slow but energetic, said,

"Avez-vous vu, madame, le premier Consul?"

"Pas encore, madame."

"C'est sans doute ce que vous souhaitez le plus, madame?"

"Oui, madame."

"Voulez-vous le voir parfaitement bien, et tout fait votre aise?"

"je le desire beaucoup, madame." (182)

She then told me to keep my eyes constantly upon her, and not an instant lose sight of her movements; and to suffer no head, in the press that would ensue when the first Consul appeared, to intervene between us. "Faites comme cela, madame," continued she; "et vous le verrez bien, bien; car," added she, solemnly, and putting her hand on her breast,—"moi—je vais lui parler!" (183)

I thanked her very much, but it was difficult to express as much satisfaction as she displayed herself. You may suppose, however, how curious I felt for such a conversation, and how scrupulously I followed her injunctions of watching her motions. A little squat good-humoured lady, with yellow flowers over a mob cap upon her hair - who had little sunken eyes, concise nose, and a mouth so extended by perpetual smiling, that, hardly leaving an inch for the cheek, it ran nearly into the ear, on my other side now demanded my attention also, and told me she came regularly every month to the great review, that she might always bring some friend who wanted to see it. I found by this she was a person of some power, some influence, at least, and not entirely averse to having it known. She was extremely civil to me - but as my other friend had promised me so singular a regale, I had not much voluntary time to spare for her, this, however, appeared to be no impediment to that she was so obliging as to determine to bestow upon me, and she talked satisfied with my acquiescence to her civility, till a sort of bustle just before us making me look a little sharp, she cried—

"Vous le voyez, madame!"

"Qui?" exclaimed I, "le premier Consul?"

"Mais non!—pas encore—mais—ce—ce monsieur ll!" (184)

MADAME, C'EST MON MARL.

I looked at her to see whom I was to remark, and her eyes led me to a tall, large figure, with a broad gold-laced hat, who was clearing the lane which some of the company had infringed, with a stentorian voice, and an air and manner of such authority as a chief constable might exert in an English riot.

"Oui, madame," I answered, not conceiving why I was to look at him; "je le vois, ce monsieur; il est bien grand." (185)

"Oui, madame," replied she, with a yet widened smile, and a look of lively satisfaction; "il est bien grand! Vous le voyez bien?"

"O, fort bien!" cried I, quite at a loss what she meant me to understand, till at last, fixing first him, and then me, she expressively said—

"Madame, c'est mon mari!" (186)

The grin now was distended to the very utmost limits of the stretched lips, and the complacency of her countenance forcibly said, "What do you think of me now?" My countenance, however, was far more clever than my head, if it made her any answer. But, in the plenitude of her own admiration of a gentleman who seemed privileged to speak roughly, and push violently whoever, by a single inch, passed a given barrier, she imagined, I believe, that to belong to him entitled her to be considered as sharing his prowess; she seemed even to be participating in the merits of his height and breadth, though be could easily have put her into his pocket.

Not perceiving, as I imagine, all the delight of felicitation in my countenance that she had expected, her own fell, in a disappointed pause, into as much of length as its circular form would admit of; it recovered, however, in another minute its full merry rotundity, by conjecturing, as I have reason to think, that the niggardliness of my admiration was occasioned by my doubt of her assertions; for, looking at me with an expression that demanded my attention, she poked her head under the arm of a tall grenadier, stationed to guard our window, and trying to catch the eye of the object of her devotion, called out in an accent of tenderness, "M'ami! M'ami!"

The surprise she required was now gratified in full, though what she concluded to be excited by her happiness, was simply the effect of so caressing a public address from so diminutive a little creature to so gigantic a big one. Three or four times the soft sound was repeated ere it reached the destined ear, through the hubbub created by his own loud and rough manner of calling to order; but, when at last he caught the gentle appellation, and looked down upon her, it was with an eyebrow so scowling, a mouth so pouting, and an air that so rudely said, "What the devil do you want?" that I was almost afraid he would have taken her between his thumb and finger, and given her a shake. However, be only grumbled out, "Qu'est-ce que c'est, donc?"(187) A little at a loss what to say, she gently stammered, "M'ami,—le—le premier Consul, ne vient-il pas?"(188) "Oui! oui!" was blustered in reply, with a look that completed the phrase by "you fool you!" though the voice left it unfinished.

Not disconcerted even yet, though rather abashed, she turned to me with a pleased grin that showed her proud of his noble ferociousness, and said, "C'est mon mari, madame!" as if still fearful I was not fully convinced of the grandeur of her connexion. "M'ami" having now cleared the passage by ranging all the company in two direct lines, the officers of highest rank were assembled, and went in a sort of procession into the inner apartment to the audience of the first Consul. During the time this lasted, some relaxation of discipline ensued, and the gentlemen from the opposite row ventured to approach and peep at the windows with the ladies; but as soon as the generals descended from the steps they had mounted, their short conference being over, "M'ami" again appeared, to the inexpressible gratification of his loving little mate, again furiously hustled every one to his post; and the flags, next, as I think, were carried in procession to the inner apartment, but soon after brought back.

ADVENT OF THE FIRST CONSUL.

The Prince of Orange then passed us to enter the audience chamber, with a look so serious, an air so depressed, that I have not been at all surprised to hear he was that very night taken very ill.

The last object for whom the way was cleared was the second Consul, Cambacérès, who advanced with a stately and solemn pace, slow, regular, and consequential; dressed richly in scarlet and gold, and never looking to the right or left, but wearing a mien of fixed gravity and importance. He had several persons in his suite, who, I think, but am not sure, were ministers of state.

At length the two human hedges were finally formed, the door of the audience chamber was thrown wide open with a commanding crash, and a vivacious officer-sentinel, or I know not what, nimbly descended the three steps into our apartment, and placing himself at the side of the door, with one hand spread as high as possible above his head, and the other extended horizontally, called out in a loud and authoritative voice, "Le premier Consul!"

You will easily believe nothing more was necessary to obtain attention; not a soul either spoke or stirred as he and his suite passed along, which was so quickly that, had I not been placed so near the door, and had not all about me facilitated my standing foremost, and being least crowd obstructed, I could hardly have seen him. As it was, I had a view so near, though so brief, of his face, as to be very much struck by it. It is of a deeply impressive cast, pale even to sallowness, while not only in the eye but in every feature—care, thought, melancholy, and meditation are strongly marked, with so much of character, nay, genius, and so penetrating a seriousness, or rather sadness, as powerfully to sink into an observer's mind.

Yet, though the busts and medallions I have seen are, in general, such good resemblances that I think I should have known him untold, he has by no means the look to be expected from Bonaparte, but rather that of a profoundly studious and contemplative man, who "o'er books consumes" not only the "midnight oil" but his own daily strength, "and wastes the puny body to decay" by abstruse speculation and theoretic plans or rather visions, ingenious but not practicable. But the look of the commander who heads his own army, who fights his own battles, who conquers every difficulty by personal exertion, who executes all he plans, who performs even all he suggests; whose ambition is of the most enterprising, and whose bravery is of the most daring cast:—this, which is the look to be expected from his situation, and the exploits which have led to it, the spectator watches for in vain. The plainness, also, of his dress, so conspicuously contrasted by the finery of all around him, conspires forcibly with his countenance, so "sicklied o'er with the pale hue of thought," to give him far more the air of a student than a warrior.

The intense attention with which I fixed him in this short but complete view made me entirely forget the lady who had promised me to hold him in conference. When he had passed, however, she told me it was upon his return she should address him, as he was too much hurried to be talked with at the moment of going to the parade. I was glad to find my chance not over, and infinitely curious to know what was to follow.

THE PARADE OF TROOPS.

The review I shall attempt no description of. I have no knowledge of the subject, and no fondness for its object. It was far more superb than anything I had ever beheld: but while all the pomp and circumstance of war animated others, it only saddened me; and all of past reflection, all of future dread, made the whole grandeur of the martial scene, and all the delusive seduction of martial music, fill my eyes frequently with tears, but not regale my poor muscles with one single smile.

Bonaparte, mounting a beautiful and spirited white horse, closely encircled by his glittering aides-de-camp, and accompanied by his generals, rode round the ranks, holding his bridle indifferently in either hand, and seeming utterly careless of the prancing, rearing, or other freaks of his horse, insomuch as to strike some who were near me with a notion of his being a bad horseman. I am the last to be a judge upon this subject, but as a remarker, he only appeared to me a man who knew so well he could manage the animal when he pleased, that he did not deem it worth his while to keep constantly in order what he knew, if urged or provoked, he could subdue in a moment.

Precisely opposite to the window at which I was placed, the chief Consul stationed himself after making his round and thence he presented some swords of honour, spreading out one arm with an air and mien which changed his look from that of scholastic severity to one that was highly military and commanding. . . .

A SCENE.

The review over, the chief Consul returned to the palace. The lines were again formed, and he re-entered our apartment with his suite. As soon as he approached our window, I observed my first acquaintance start a little forward. I was now all attention to her performance of her promise; and just as he reached us she stretched out her hand to present him a petition!

The enigma of the conference was now solved, and I laughed at my own wasted expectation. Lui parler, however, the lady certainly did; so far she kept her word; for when he had taken the scroll, and was passing on, she rushed out of the line, and planting herself immediately before him so as to prevent his walking on, screamed, rather than spoke, for her voice was shrill with impetuosity to be heard and terror of failure, "C'est pour mon fils! vous me l'avez promis!" (189) The first Consul stopped and spoke; but not loud enough for me to hear his voice: while his aides-de-camp and the attending generals surrounding him more closely, all in a breath rapidly said to the lady, "Votre nom, madame, votre nom!"(190) trying to disengage the Consul from her importunity, in which they succeeded, but not with much ease, as she seemed purposing to cling to him till she got his personal answer. He faintly smiled as he passed on, but looked harassed and worn; while she, turning to me, with an exulting face and voice, exclaimed, "Je l'aurai! je l'aurai!" meaning what she had petitioned for—"car . . . tous ces g,n,raux m'ont demand,s mon nom!" (191) Could any inference be clearer?

The moment the chief Consul had ascended the steps leading to the inner apartment, the gentlemen in black with gold chains gave a general hint that all the company must depart, as the ambassadors and the ministers were now summoned to their monthly public audience with the chief Consul. The crowd, however, was so great, and Madame d'Henin was so much incommoded, and half ill, I fear, by internal suffering, that M. d'Arblay procured a pass for us by a private door down to a terrace leading to a quiet exit from the palace into the Tuileries garden.

WITH M. D'ARBLAY'S RELATIVES AT JOIGNY.

(Madame d'Arblay to Mrs. Burney.) (192) Paris, 1802. .....With the nearest relatives now existing of M. d'Arblay I am myself more pleased than I can tell you. We have spent a fortnight at Joigny, (193) and found them all awaiting us with the most enthusiastic determination to receive with open arms and open heart the choice and the offspring of their returned exile. Their kindness has truly penetrated me; and the heads of the family, the uncle and the aunt, are so charming as well as so worthy, that I could have remained with them for months had not the way of life which their residence in a country town has forced them to adopt, been utterly at war with all that, to me, makes peace, and happiness, and cheerfulness, namely, the real domestic life of living with my own small but all-sufficient family. I have never loved a dissipated life, which it is no virtue in me, therefore, to relinquish; but I now far less than ever can relish it, and know not how to enjoy anything away from home, except by distant intervals; and then with that real moderation, I am so far from being a misanthrope or sick of the world, that I have real pleasure in mixed society. It is difficult, however, in the extreme, to be able to keep to such terms. M. d'Arblay has so many friends, and an acquaintance so extensive, that the mere common decencies of established etiquettes demand, as yet, nearly all my time; and this has been a true fatigue both to my body and my spirits.

M. d'Arblay is related, though very distantly, to a quarter of the town, and the other three-quarters are his friends or acquaintance; and all of them came, first, to see me; next, to know how I did after the journey; next, were all to be waited upon in return; next, came to thank me for my visit; next, to know how the air of Joigny agreed with me - next, to make a little further acquaintance; and, finally, to make a visit of cong,. And yet all were so civil, so pleasant, and so pleased with my monsieur's return, that could I have lived three lives, so as to have had some respite, I could not have found fault for it was scarcely ever with the individual intruder, but with the continuance or repetition of interruption.

SOME JOIGNY ACQUAINTANCES.

(Madame d'Arblay to Miss Planta, for the queen and princesses.) Passy, December 19, 1802. .....Rarely, indeed, my dear Miss Planta, I have received more pleasure than from your last most truly welcome letter, with assurances so unspeakably seasonable. I had it here at Passy the 5th day after its date. I thank you again and again, but oh! how I thank God!

Permit me now to go back to Joigny, for the purpose of giving some account of two very interesting acquaintances we made there. The first was Colonel Louis Bonaparte, (194) youngest brother but one, (Jerome) of the first Consul. His regiment was quartered at Joigny, where he happened to be upon our last arrival at that town, and where the first visit he made was to M. MBazille, the worthy maternal uncle of M. d'Arblay. He is a young man of the most serious demeanour, a grave yet pleasing countenance, and the most reserved yet gentlest manners. His conduct in the small town (for France) of Joigny was not merely respectable, but exemplary; he would accept no distinction in consequence of his powerful connexions, but presented himself everywhere with the unassuming modesty of a young man who had no claims beyond what he might make by his own efforts and merits. He discouraged all gaming, to which the inhabitants are extremely prone, by always playing low himself; and he discountenanced parade, by never suffering his own servant to wait behind his chair where he dined. He broke up early both from table and from play - was rigid in his attentions to his military duties, strict in the discipline of is officers as well as men, -and the first to lead the way in every decency and regularity. When to this I add that his conversation is sensible, and well bred, yet uncommonly diffident, and that but twenty-three summers have yet rolled over his head, so much good sense, forbearance, and propriety, in a situation so open to flattery, ambition, or vanity, obtained, as they merited, high consideration and perfect good will.

I had a good deal of conversation with him, for he came to sit by me both before and after his card-party wherever I had the pleasure to meet him; and his quiet and amiable manners, and rational style of discourse, made him a great loss to our society, when he was summoned to Paris, upon the near approach of the event which gave him a son and heir. He was very kind to my little Alex, whom he never saw without embracing, and he treated M. d'Arblay with a marked distinction extremely gratifying to me.

The second acquaintance to which I have alluded is a lady, Madame de Souza.(195) She soon found the road to my good will and regard, for she told me that she, with another lady, had been fixed upon by M. del Campo, my old sea-visitor, for the high honour of aiding him in his reception of the first lady of our land and her lovely daughters, upon the grand f^te which he gave upon the dearest and most memorable of occasions (196) and she spoke with such pleasure and gratitude of the sweet condescension she then experienced, that she charmed and delighted me, and we struck up an intimacy without further delay. Our theme was always ready, and I only regretted that I could see her but seldom, as she lived two or three miles out of Joigny, at Cesy, in the small chateau of la ci-devant Princesse de Beaufremont, a lady with whom I had had the honour of making acquaintance in Paris, and who is one of those who suffered most during the horrors of the Revolution. At the dreadful period when all the rage was to burn the property and title-deeds of the rich and high-born, her noble chfteau, one of the most considerable in France, was. utterly consumed, and all her papers; that no record of her genealogy might remain, were committed, with barbarous triumph, to the flames: yet was this, such is her unhappy fate, the least of her misfortunes; her eldest daughter, a beautiful young creature, upon whom she doted, was in the chfteau at this horrible period, and forced to make her escape with such alarm and precipitance, that she never recovered from the excess of her terror, which robbed her of her life before she was quite seventeen years of age!

Around the small and modest chfteau de Cesy, in which Madame de Beaufremont and her youngest and now only daughter, Madame de Listenois, at present reside, the grounds have been cultivated in the English style; and the walks, now shady, now open, now rising, now descending, with water, bridges, cascades, and groves, and occasional fine picturesque views from the banks of the Yonne, are all laid out with taste and pretty effects. We strolled over them with a large party, till we came to a little recess. Madame de Beaufremont then took me by the arm, and we separated from the company to enter it together, and she showed me an urn surrounded with cypress trees and weeping willows, watered by a clear, small, running rivulet, and dedicated to the memory of her first-born and early-lost lamented daughter. Poor lady! she seems entirely resigned to all the rest of her deprivations, but here the wound is incurable! yet, this subject apart, she is cheerful, loves society, or rather social discourse, with a chosen few, and not only accepts with Pleasure whatever may enliven her, but exerts herself to contribute all that is in her power to the entertainment of others. She has still preserved enough from the wreck of her Possessions to live elegantly, though not splendidly; and her table is remarkably well served. She has a son-in-law, M. de Listenois, whom I did not see; but her remaining daughter Madame de Listenois, is a very fine young woman. Madame de Souza has spent the whole summer with these ladies. She told me she liked England so very much, and was so happy during the six weeks she passed there, that she wept bitterly on quitting it. She was received, she says, at Court in the most bewitching manner, and she delights in retracing her honours, and her sense of them. She is still so very handsome, though sickly and suffering, that I imagine she must then have been exquisitely beautiful. I am told, by a French officer who has served in Spain, M. de Meulan, that when she left that country she was reckoned the most celebrated beauty of Madrid.

I had another new acquaintance at Joigny, also, in a lady who came from Auxerre, as she was pleased to say, to see me, Madame La Villheurnois, widow of M. La Villheurnois, who was amongst the unhappy objects deports, by the order of the Directory, la Guiane. (197) As soon as the first civilities were over, she said, "Permettez, madame! connaisseZ-vous Sidney?" (198) I could not doubt who she meant, though there is no avoiding a smile at this drolly concise way of naming a man by his nom de baptême. (199) She was extremely surprised when I answered no; telling me she had concluded "que tout le monde en Angleterre"(200) must know Sidney! Yes, I said, by character certainly; but personally I had never the gratification of meeting with him. She told me she was intimately acquainted with him herself, from seeing him continually when he was confined in the Temple, as she attended there her "malheureux ,poux," (201) and she saw also, she said, "son valet et son jockey," (202) whom she never suspected to be disguised emigrants, watching to aid his escape. "Surtout," she added, "comme le jockey avait des trous aux bas terribles," (203) which induced her daughter to buy him a new pair of stockings for charity. A gentleman who accompanied her to Joigny, her secretary, told me he had played at ball with Sidney every day for six months, while he also attended upon poor M. La Vilheurnois......

THE INFLUENZA IN PARIS.

(Madame d'Arblay to Dr. Burney.) Passy, March 23, 1803. I have been anxious to write since I received your last kind inquiries, my dearest padre; but so tedious has been my seizure, that I have not yet got from its wraps or confinements. I feel, however, as if this were their last day, and that to-morrow would have the honour to see me abroad. I have had no fever, and no physician, and no important malady; but cold has fastened upon cold, so as utterly to imprison me. La gripe, (204) however, I escaped, so has Alex, and our maid and helpers—and M. d'Arblay, who caught it latterly in his excursions to Paris, had it so slightly that but for the fright attached to the seizure (which I thought would almost have demolished me at first, from the terror hanging on its very name at that fatal period) I should have deemed it a mere common cold. It is now universally over, but the mischief it has done is grievously irreparable. . . . It was a disastrous and frightful time. The streets of Paris were said to be as full of funerals as of cabriolets. For my own part, I have not once been able to enter that capital since I left it at the end of October. But I cannot help attributing much of the mortality which prevailed in consequence of this slight disease, to the unwholesome air occasioned by the dreadful want of cleanliness in that city, which, but for the healthiness of the beautiful and delicious walks around it, i.e, the Boulevards, must surely have proved pestilential. The air of our house at Passy is perfectly pure and sweet.

M. d'Arblay is now making a last effort with respect to his retraite, (205) which has languished in adjournment above a year. He has put it into the hands of a faithful and most amiable friend, now in high esteem with the premier Consul, General Lauriston, who so kindly renewed an ancient friendship with his former camarade when he was on his splendid short embassy in England. If through him it should fail, I shall never think of it more.

RUMOURS OF WAR.

(Madame dArblay to Mrs. Locke) No 54, Rue Basse, Passy, near Paris, April 30, 1803. How to write I know not, at a period so tremendous-nor yet how to be silent. My dearest, dearest friends! if the war indeed prove inevitable, what a heart-breaking position is ours! to explain it fully would demand folios, and yet be never so well done as you, with a little consideration, can do it for us. Who better than Mr. Locke and his Fredy-who so well can comprehend, that, where one must be sacrificed, the other will be yet more to be pitied? I will not go on. I will talk only of you, till our fate must be determined. And M. d'Arblay, who only in the wide world loves his paternal uncle as well (we always except ourselves at Westminster! how tenderly does he join in my every feeling! and how faithfully keep unimpaired all our best and happiest sympathies!

May 2. Better appearances in the political horizon now somewhat recruit my spirits, which have been quite indescribably tortured, rather than sunk, by the impossibility of any private arrangement for our mutual happiness in the dread event of war. God Almighty yet avert it! And should it fall to the lot of Lauriston to confirm the peace, what a guardian angel upon earth I shall deem him! How I wish he could meet with you! he is so elegant in his manners he would immediately give you pleasure; and his countenance is so true in announcing him amiable, that you might look at him with trust as well as satisfaction. . . .

May 13. Ah, my dearest friends—what a melancholy end to my hopes and my letter. I have just heard that Lord Whitworth (206) set off for Chantilly last night; war therefore seems inevitable; and my grief, I, who feel myself now of two countries, is far greater than I can wish to express. While posts are yet open, write to me, my beloved friend, and by Hamburg. I trust we may still and regularly correspond, long as the letters may be in travelling. As our letters never treat but of our private concerns, health and welfare neither country can object to our intercourse.

(Madame d'Arblay to Dr. Burney). Passy, May 6, 1803. if my dearest father has the smallest idea of the suspense and terror in which I have spent this last fortnight, from the daily menace of war, he will be glad, I am sure, of the respite allowed me-if no more—from a visit I have just received from Mrs. Huber, who assures me the Ambassador has postponed his setting off, and consented to send another courier. (207) To say how I pray for his success would indeed be needless. I have hardly closed my eyes many nights past. My dearest father will easily conceive the varying conflicts of our minds, and how mutual are our sufferings. . . .

We were buoyed up here for some days with the hope that General Lauriston was gone to England as plenipo, to end the dread contest without new effusion of blood: but Paris, like London, teems with hourly false reports, and this intelligence, unhappily, was of the number. The continued kindness and friendship of that gentleman for M. d'Arblay make me take a warm interest in whatever belongs to him. About ten days ago, when M. d'Arblay called upon him, relative to the affair so long impending of his retraite, he took his hand, and said "Fais-moi ton compliment!" (208) You are sure how heartily M. d'Arblay would be ready to comply-"but "what," he demanded, "can be new to you of honours?" "I have succeeded," he answered, "for you!—the first Consul has signed your m,moire." When such delicacy is joined to warm attachment, my dearest father will not wonder I should be touched by it. . . .

M. d'Arblay has now something in his native country, where all other claims are vain, and all other expectations completely destroyed. He had been flattered with recovering some portion, at least, of his landed property near Joigny; but those who have purchased it during his exile add such enormous and unaccountable charges to what they paid for it at that period, that it is become, to us, wholly unattainable.

"OUR LITTLE CELL AT PASSY."

(Madame d'Arblay to Dr. Burney.) Passy, April 11, 1804. We live in the most quiet, and, I think, enviable retired merit. Our house is larger than we require, but not a quarter furnished. Our view is extremely pretty from it, and always cheerful; we rarely go out, yet always are pleased to return. We have our books, our prate, and our boy—how, with all this, can we, or ought we to suffer ourselves to complain of our narrowed and narrowing income? If we are still able to continue at Passy, endeared to me now beyond any other residence away from you all, by a friendship I have formed here with one of the sweetest women I have ever known, Madame de Maisonneuve, and to M. d'Arblay by similar sentiments for all her family, our philosophy will not be put to severer trials than it can sustain. And this engages us to bear a thousand small privations which we might, perhaps, escape, by shutting ourselves up in some spot more remote from the capital. But as my deprivation of the society of my friends is what I most lament, so something that approaches nearest to what I have lost affords me the best reparation.

(Madame d'Arblay to Dr. Burney.) Passy, May 29, 1808. Before I expected it, my promised opportunity for again writing to my most dear father is arrived. I entirely forget whether, before the breaking out of the war stopt our correspondence, M. d'Arblay had already obtained his retraite: and, consequently, whether that is an event I have mentioned or not. Be that as it may, he now has it—it is 1500 livres, or 62 pounds, 10 shillings. per annum. But all our resources from England ceasing with the peace, we had so little left from what we had brought over, and M. d'Arblay has found so nearly nothing remaining of his natural and hereditary claims in his own province, that he determined upon applying for some employment that might enable him to live with independence, how ever parsimoniously. This he has, with infinite difficulty, etc, at length obtained, and he is now a redacteur in the civil department of les Batimens, etc. (209) This is no sinecure. He attends at his bureau from half-past nine to half-past four o'clock every day; and as we live so far off as Passy he is obliged to set off for his office between eight and nine, and does not return to his hermitage till past five. However, what necessity has urged us to desire, and made him solicit, we must not, now acquired, name or think of with murmuring or regret. He has the happiness to be placed amongst extremely worthy people; and those who are his chefs in office treat him with every possible mark of consideration and feeling. We continue steady to our little cell at Passy, which is retired, quiet, and quite to ourselves, with a magnificent view of Paris from one side, and a beautiful one of the country on the other. It is unfurnished-indeed, unpapered, and every way unfinished; for our workmen, in the indispensable repairs which preceded our entering it, ran us up bills that compelled us to turn them adrift, and leave every thing at a stand, when three rooms only were made just habitable.

THE PRINCE OF WALES EULOGIZED.

(Dr. Burney to Madame d'Arblay.) July 12, 1805. . . . Your brother, Dr. Charles, and I have had the honour last Tuesday of dining with the Prince of Wales at Lord Melbourne's at the particular desire of H.R.H. He is so good-humoured and gracious to those against whom he has no party prejudice, that it is impossible not to be flattered by this politeness and condescension. I was astonished to find him, amidst such constant dissipation, possessed of so much learning, wit, knowledge of books in general, discrimination of Character, as well as original humour. He quoted Homer to my son as readily as if the beauties of Dryden or Pope were under consideration. And as to music, he is an excellent critic; has an enlarged taste— admiring whatever is excellent in its kind, of whatever age or country the composers or performers may be; without, however, being insensible to the superior genius and learning necessary to some kinds of music more than others.

The conversation was general and lively, in which several of the company, consisting of eighteen or twenty, took a share, till towards the heel of the evening, or rather the toe of the morning; for we did not rise from table till one o'clock, when Lady Melbourne being returned from the opera with her daughters, coffee was ordered; during which H.R.H. took me outside and talked exclusively about music near half an hour, and as long with your brother concerning Greek literature. He is a most excellent mimic of well-known characters: had we been in the dark any one would have sworn that Dr. Parr and Kemble were in the room. Besides being possessed of a great fund of original humour, and good humour, he may with truth be said to have as much wit as Charles II, with much more learning—for his merry majesty could spell no better than the bourgeois gentilhomme.

DR. BURNEY AT BATH.

(Dr. Burney to Madame dArblay.) June 12, 1808. . . . Last autumn I had an alarming seizure in my left hand and, mine being pronounced a Bath case, on Christmas Eve I set out for that city, extremely weak and dispirited-put myself under the care of Dr. Parry, and after remaining there three months, I found my hand much more alive, and my general health considerably amended.

During my invalidity at Bath I had an unexpected visit from your Streatham friend, (210) of whom I had lost sight for more than ten years. I saw very few people, but none of an evening nor of a morning, on the days my hand was pumped on. When her name was sent in I was much surprised, but desired she might be admitted; and I received her as an old friend with whom I had spent much time very happily, and never wished to quarrel. She still looks well, but is grave, and candour itself; though still she says good things, and writes admirable notes and letters, I am told, to my granddaughters C. and M, of whom she is very fond. We shook hands very cordially, and avoided any allusion to our long separation and its cause; the Caro Sposo still lives, but is such an object from the gout that the account of his sufferings made me pity him sincerely; he wished, she told me, "to see his old and worthy friend," and, un beau matin, I could not refuse compliance with his wish. She nurses him with great affection and tenderness, never goes out or has company when he is in pain.

AFFECTIONATE GREETINGS TO DR. BURNEY.

(Madame d'Arblay to Dr. Burney.) September, 1808. After being so long robbed of all means of writing to my beloved father, I seize, with nearly as much surprise as gratitude, a second opportunity of addressing him almost before the first can have brought my hand to his sight. When will some occasion offer to bring me back-not my revenge, but my first and most coveted satisfaction? With how much more spirit, also, should I write, if I knew what were received of what already I have scrawled! Volumes, however, must have been told you, of what in other times I should have written, by Maria. For myself, when once a reunion takes place, I can scarcely conceive which will be hardest worked, my talking faculties or my listening ones. O what millions of things I want to inquire and to know! The rising generation, me thinks, at least, might keep me some letters and packets ready for occasional conveyances. I should be grateful beyond measure. M. d'Arblay writes—"how desired is, how happy shall be, the day, in which we shall receive your dearest blessing and embrace! Pray be so kind not to forget the mate always remembering your kindness for him and his. A thousand thousand loves to all."

(Madame d'Arblay to Dr. Burney.) No. 13, Rue d'Anjou, Paris, May 2, 1810. A happy May-day to my dearest father! Sweet-scented be the cowslips which approach his nostrils! lovely and rosy the milkmaids that greet his eyes, and animating as they are noisy the marrow-bones and cleavers that salute his ears! Dear, and even touching, are these anniversary recollections where distance and absence give them existence only in the memory! and, at this moment, to hear and see them I Would exchange all the Raphaels in our Museum, and the new and beautiful composition of Paesiello in the chapel.

Could you but send me a little food for the hope now in private circulation that the new alliance of the Emperor (211) may perhaps extend to a general alliance of all Europe, Oh, heaven! how would that brighten my faculties of enjoyment! I should run about to see all I have hitherto omitted to seek, with the ardent curiosity of a traveller newly arrived; and I should hasten to review and consider all I have already beheld, with an alertness of vivacity that would draw information from every object I have as yet looked at with undiscerning tameness. Oh, such a gleam of light would new-model or re-model me, and I should make you present to all my sights, and partake of all the wonders that surround me!

Were not this cruel obscurity so darkening to my views, and so depressing to my spirits, I could tell my dearest father many things that might amuse him, and detail to him, in particular, my great and rare happiness in a point the most essential, after domestic comforts, to peace of mind and cheerfulness, namely, my good fortune in my adopted friends in this my adopted country. The society in which I mix, when I can prevail with myself to quit my yet dearer fireside, is all that can be wished, whether for wit, wisdom, intelligence, gaiety, or politeness. The individuals with whom I chiefly mix, from being admired at first for their talents or amiability, are now sincerely loved for their kindness and goodness. Could I write more frequently, or with more security that I write not to the winds and the waves, I would characterize the whole set to you, and try to make us yet shake hands in the same Party. . . .

(Madame d'Arblay to Dr. Burney.) No. 13, Rue d'Anjou, Paris, 16 Sept. 1810. Can I tell you, my dearest father! oh, no! I can never tell you-the pleasure, the rapture with which I received your letter by Madame Solvyns. It had been so cruelly long since I had heard from you, so anxious and suffering a space since I had seen your handwriting, that, when at last it came, I might have seemed, to one who did not know me, rather penetrated by sudden affliction than by joy. But how different was all within to what appeared without! My partner-in-all received it at his bureau, and felt an impatience so unconquerable to communicate so extreme a pleasure that he quitted everything to hasten home; for he was incapable of going on with his business. How satisfactory, also, is all the intelligence! how gaily, with what spirit written! . . .

I do nothing of late but dream of seeing you, my most dear father. I think I dream it wide awake, too; the desire is so strong that it pursues me night and day, and almost persuades me it has something in it of reality: and I do not choose to discourage even ideal happiness.

DR. BURNEY's DIPLOMA.

(Madame d'Arblay to Dr. Burney.) No. 13, Rue d'Anjou, 14th April, 1811. .....Have you received the letter in which I related that your diploma has been brought to me by the perpetual secretary of the class of the Fine Arts of the Institute of France? (212) I shall not have it conveyed but by some very certain hand, and that, now, is most difficult to find. M. Le Breton has given me, also, a book of the list of your camarades, in which he has written your name. He says it will be printed in next year's register. He has delivered to me, moreover, a medal, which is a mark of distinction reserved for peculiar honour to peculiar select personages. Do you suppose I do not often—often—often think who would like, and be fittest to be the bearer to you of these honours? . . .

How kind was the collection of letters you made more precious by endorsing! I beseech you to thank all my dear correspondents, and to bespeak their patience for answers, which shall arrive by every wind that I can make blow their way; but yet more, beseech their generous attention to my impatience for more, should the wind blow fair for me before it will let me hail them in return. Difficultly can they figure to themselves my joy—my emotion at receiving letters from such dates as they can give me!

[During this year Madame d'Arblay's correspondence with her English connexions was interrupted not only by the difficulty of conveying letters, but also by a dangerous illness and the menace of a cancer, from which she could only be relieved by submitting to a painful and hazardous operation. The fortitude with which she bore this suffering, and her generous solicitude for Monsieur d'Arblay and those around her, excited the warmest sympathy in all who heard of her trial, and her French friends universally gave her the name of l'ange, (213) so touched were they by her tenderness and Magnanimity.]

(157) " Dr. Orkborne" is the name of one of the characters in "Camilla," a pedantic scholar, who lives only in his books. ED.

(158) Widow of Sir Robert Strange, the celebrated engraver, and a very old friend of the Burney family. She was a Scotchwoman (her maiden name, Isabel Lumisden), and in her younger days an enthusiastic Jacobite. She obliged her lover, Strange, to join the young Pretender in 1745, and afterwards married him against her father's wish. ED.

(159) "The other Bell" was the daughter of Sir Robert and Lady Strange. ED.

(160) Wife of Sir Lucas Pepys, the physician. ED.

(161) Anna Letitia Barbauld, the well-known author, and editor of Richardson's Correspondence, etc. ED.

(162) John Aiken, M.D, brother to Mrs. Barbauld, and, like his sister, an author and editor. His "Evenings at Home" is still a well-known book: many of our readers will probably have pleasant reminiscences of it, connected with their childhood. ED.

(163) Barry had published a furious attack upon his fellow-Academicians in a "Letter to the Dilettanti Society." He was already, owing chiefly to his own violent temper, on ill terms with nearly all of them, and the "Letter" prove (I to be the last straw. Various charges were drawn up against the Professor of Painting, and he was expelled forthwith from the Academy, without being permitted to speak in his own defence.

(164) "By the help of a shilling."

(165) "With tears in his eyes."

(166) i.e, Mr. Locke. ED.

(167) The French minister in England. ED.

(168) A letter in which M. d'Arblay had acquainted his wife with the withdrawal of his commission in the French army, in consequence of his refusal, under any circumstances, to bear arms against England. ED.

(169) Miss Cambridge. ED.

(170) Lafayette was then living in retirement, with his wife and family, at is chateau of La Grange. - ED.

(171) "Quick, quick, madam, take your seat in the diligence, for here is an English gentleman who is sure to take the best place!"—There is evidently some mistake here, in making the book-keeper in Piccadilly speak French and talk about the diligence. That the paragraph relates to Fanny's departure from London is evident from several passages in the text: the mention, later, of changing horses at Canterbury, the references to her fellow-travellers at Calais. The date to the above paragraph is also clearly wrong, as it will be seen that on the 18th of April they were still on the road to Paris. ED.

(172) "Quick! quick! look for it, or you will be arrested!"

(173) In the new calendar adopted by the Republic in 1793, a division of the month into decades, or periods of ten days, was substituted for the old division into weeks. Every tenth day (d,cadi) was a day of rest, instead of every seventh day, (Sunday, Dimanche). The months were of thirty days each, with five odd festival days (Sansculottades) in the year, and a sixth (Festival of the Revolution) in Leap Year. Napoleon restored the Sunday in place of d,cadi. The new calendar was discontinued altogether, January 1, 1806. ED.

(174) The date is again wrong—probably a misprint for April 21. ED.

(175) Mrs. Damer, the sculptor, as an ardent Whig and supporter of Charles Fox, professed herself at this time an enthusiastic admirer of the first Consul. She had known Jos,phine de Beauharnais before her marriage with Napoleon, and, after the peace of Amiens, visited Paris on Jos,phine's invitation. She was there introduced to Napoleon, to whom she afterwards presented a bust of Charles Fox, executed by herself. Mrs. Damer's companions on this excursion were Mary Berry, the author (born 1763, died 1852), and her younger sister, Agnes Berry. These two ladies were prodigious favourites with Horace Walpole, who called them his "twin wives," and was, it is said, even desirous, in his old age, of marrying the elder Miss Berry. One of his valued possessions was a marble bust of Mary Berry, the work of his kinswoman, Mrs. Damer. At his death in 1797 he bequeathed to the Miss Berrys a house for their joint lives, besides a legacy of 4000 pounds to each sister. Mary Berry published an edition of her old admirer's works the year after his death. ED.

(176) The Swiss home of her father, 'M. Necker, on the shore of the lake, and some ten miles north of the town of Geneva. Necker retired thither after his fall in 1790, and spent there, in retirement, the remaining years of his life. He died at Geneva, in April, 1804. ED.

(177) Madame de Stael's orthography is here preserved.

"I should like to prove to you my zeal, madam, and I am afraid of being indiscreet. I hope you will have the goodness to let me know when you are sufficiently recovered from the fatigue of your journey, that I might have the honour of seeing you without being tiresome to you."

(178) The 4th Floria (April 23).

(179) "Madame d'Arblay can only be infinitely flattered by the extreme goodness of Madame the Countess de Stael. She will very certainly have the honour of calling upon Madame de Stael as soon as possible."

(180) Madame de Lafayette was thrown into prison after the flight of her husband; released in February, 1795, more than six months after the death of Robespierre. She then journeyed to Austria, and obtained leave to share, with her two daughters, her husband's captivity at Olmutz. Lafayette was released in September, 1797; returned to France in 1800, Napoleon not forbidding, though not quite approving. Madame de Lafayette's constitution was permanently impaired by the confinement which she suffered at Olmutz. She died December 24, 1807. ED.

(181) "It's a foreigner, it's an Englishwoman."

(182) "Have you seen the first Consul, madam?"

"Not yet, madam."

"It is doubtless what you most wish for, madam?"

"Yes, madam."

"Do you wish to have an excellent view of him, and to see him quite at your ease?"

"I am particularly desirous of it, madam."

(183) "Do thus, madam, and you will see him well, well; for I-am going to speak to him! "

(184) "You see him, madam!"

"Whom?" exclaimed I, "the first Consul?"

"Oh no!—not yet;—but—that—that gentleman!"

(185) "yes, madam, I see that gentleman; he is very tall!"

(186) "Madam, it is my husband!"

(187) "What is the matter?"

(188) "M'ami, the—the first Consul, is he not coming?"

(189) "'Tis for my son! you promised it me!"

(190) "Your name, madam, your name!"

(191) "I shall have it! I shall have it! for all those generals asked my name!"

(192) Fanny's eldest sister, Esther, who married (1770) her cousin, Charles Rousseau Burney. ED.

(193) Joigny was the birth-place of M. d'Arblay. ED.

(194) Louis Bonaparte was born in 1778, and, young as he was, had already served with distinction in the campaign in Italy. He was subsequently king of Holland from 1806 to 1810, when that country was annexed by Napoleon to the French Empire. He married Hortense de Beauharnais, daughter, by her first marriage, of Napoleon's wife, Josephine, and was the father of the Emperor Napoleon III. ED.

(195) Authoress of "Adéle de Senange," etc.

(196) On the king's recovery, in the spring of 1789. ED.

(197) Many of the leading members of the Councils of "Ancients" and of "Five Hundred " had been transported to Guiana after the coup d',tat of September 4, 1797. See note (146) ante, p. 136. ED.

(198) "Excuse me, madam! do you know Sidney? Sidney" is Sir Sidney Smith, whose gallant and successful defence of Acre against the French, in the spring of 1799, obliged Napoleon to relinquish the invasion of Syria. ED.

(199) Christian name.

(200) "Every one in England."

(201) "Unfortunate husband."

(202) "His valet and his jockey, (groom)."

(203) "Especially as the jockey had terrible holes in his stockings."

(204) The influenza.

(205) Retiring pension.

(206) The English ambassador in Paris. All hopes of a satisfactory termination to the dispute between the English and French governments being now at an end, Lord Whitworth was ordered to return to England, and left Paris May 12, 1803. His return was followed by the recall of the French minister in London, and the declaration of war between the two countries. ED.

(207) The reader will have noticed that the date of this letter is earlier than that of the paragraph in the preceding letter, in which Fanny alludes to the departure of the Ambassador from Paris. ED.

(208) "Make me your compliments."

(209) "Or, as we might say, a clerk in the department of works." ED.

(210) Mrs. Piozzi. ED.

(211) Napoleon was crowned Emperor of the French, November 19, 1804. His "new alliance" was his marriage, in the spring of 1810, with the archduchess Maria Louisa, daughter of the Emperor of Austria. With this alliance in view he had been divorced from Jos,phine at the close of the preceding year. ED

(212) Dr. Burney had been elected a corresponding member of this section of the Institute. ED.

(213) The angel.

SECTION 23. (1812-14)

MADAME D'ARBLAY AND HER SON IN ENGLAND,

[At the commencement of the year 1814 was published "The Wanderer, or Female Difficulties," the fourth and last novel by the author of "Evelina," "Cecilia," and "Camilla." The five volumes were sold for two guineas-double the price of "Camilla,"—and we gather from Madame d'Arblay's own statement that she received at least fifteen hundred pounds for the work. She informs us also that three thousand six hundred copies were sold during the first six months. This pecuniary profit, however, was the only advantage which she derived from the book. It was severely treated by the critics; its popularity,— if it ever had any, for its large sale was probably due to the author's high reputation,—speedily declined; and the almost total oblivion into which it passed has remained unbroken to the present day. Yet "The Wanderer" was deserving of a better fate. In many respects it is not inferior to any of Madame d'Arblay's earlier works. Its principal defect is one of literary style, and its style, though faulty and unequal, is by no means devoid of charm and impressiveness. The artless simplicity and freshness of "Evelina" render that work, her first novel, the most successful of all in point of style. In "Cecilia" the style shows more of conscious art, and is more laboured. In "Camilla" and "The Wanderer" it is at once more careless and more affected than in the earlier novels; her English is at times slipshod, at times disfigured by attempts at fine writing. But, admitting all this, we must admit also that Fanny, even in "The Wanderer," proves herself mistress of what we may surely regard as the most essential part of style, its power of affecting the reader agreeably with the intentions of the author. She plays upon her reader's emotions with a sure touch; she excites or soothes him at her will; she arouses by turns his compassion, his mirth, his resentment, according as she strikes the keys of pathos, of humour, or of irony. A style which is capable of producing such effects is not rashly to be condemned on the score of occasional affectations and irregularities.

The question of style apart, we do not feel that "The Wanderer" shows the slightest decline in its author's powers. The plot is as ingeniously complicated as ever, the suspense as skilfully maintained; the characters seem to us as real as those in "Evelina," or "Cecilia," or in the "Diary" itself; the alternate pathos and satire of the book keep our attention ever on the alert. That it failed to win the suffrages of the public was certainly due to no demerit in the work. Many causes may have conspired against it. The public taste had long been debauched by novels of that nightmare school in which Mrs Radcliffe and "Monk" Lewis were the leaders. Moreover, in the very year in which "The Wanderer" was published, appeared the first of a series of works of fiction which, by their power and novelty, were to monopolise, for a time, the public attention and applause, and which were thereafter to secure for their author a high rank among the immortals of English literature. At the end of the fifth volume of "The Wanderer" were inserted a few leaves, containing a list of books recently published or "in the press;" and last on the list of the latter stands "Waverley, or 'Tis Sixty Years since."

Like "Evelina," "The Wanderer" is inscribed in a touching dedication (this time, however, in prose, and with his name prefixed) to Fanny's beloved father. The dedication is dated March 14, 1814: on the 12th of the following month Dr. Burney died at Chelsea College, in his eighty-seventh year. ED]

NARRATIVE OF MADAME D'ARBLAY'S JOURNEY TO LONDON.

ANXIETY TO SEE FATHER AND FRIENDS.

Dunkirk, 1812. There are few events of my life that I more regret not having committed to paper while they were fresher in my memory, than my police adventure at Dunkirk, the most fearful that I have ever experienced, though not, alas, the most afflicting, for terror, and even horror, are short of deep affliction; while they last they are, nevertheless, absorbers; but once past, whether ill or well, they are over, and from them, as from bodily pain, the animal spirits can rise uninjured: not so from that grief which has its source in irrelnediable calamity; from that there is no rising, no relief, save in hopes of eternity: for here on earth all buoyancy of mind that Might produce the return of peace, is sunk for ever. I will now, however, put down all that recurs to me of my first return home.

In the year 1810, when I had been separated from my dear father, and country, and native friends, for eight years, my desire to again see them became so anxiously impatient that my tender companion proposed my passing over to England alone, to spend a month or two at Chelsea. Many females at that period, and amongst them the young Duchesse de Duras, had contrived to procure passports for a short similar excursion; though no male was permitted, under any pretence, to quit France, save with the army.

Reluctantly—with all my wishes in favour of the scheme,—yet most reluctantly, I accepted the generous offer; for never did I know happiness away from that companion, no, not even out of his sight! but still, I was consuming with solicitude to see my revered father—to be again in his kind arms, and receive his kind benediction.

A MILD MINISTER OF POLICE.

For this all was settled, and I had obtained my passport, which was brought to me without my even going to the police office, by the especial favour of M. Le Breton, the Secretaire Perp,tuel

l'Institut. The ever active services of M. de Narbonne aided this peculiar grant; though, had not Bonaparte been abroad with his army at the time, neither the one nor the other would have ventured at so hardy a measure of assistance. But whenever Bonaparte left Paris, there was always an immediate abatement of severity in the police; and Fouch,, though he had borne a character dreadful beyond description in the earlier and most horrible times of the Revolution, was,'at this period, when minister of police, a man of the mildest manners, the most conciliatory conduct, and of the easiest access in Paris. He had least the glare of the new imperial court of any one of its administration; he affected, indeed, all the simplicity of a plain Republican. I have often seen him strolling in the most shady and unfrequented parts of the "Elysian Fields," muffled up in a plain brown rocolo, and giving le bras to his wife, without suite or servant, merely taking the air, with the evident design of enjoying also an unmolested téte a téte. On these occasions, though he was universally known, nobody approached him; and he seemed, himself, not to observe that any other person was in the walks. He was said to be remarkably agreeable in conversation, and his person was the best fashioned and most gentlemanly of any man I have happened to see, belonging to the government. Yet, such was the impression made upon me by the dreadful reports that were spread of his cruelty and ferocity at Lyons, (214) that I never saw him but I thrilled with horror. How great, therefore, was my obligation to M. de Narbonne and to M. Le Breton, for procuring me a passport, without my personal application to a man from whom I shrunk as from a monster.

EMBARKATION INTERDICTED.

I forget now for what spot the passport was nominated, perhaps for Canada, but certainly not for England and M. Le Breton, who brought it to me himself, assured me that no difficulty would be made for me either to go or to return, as I was known to have lived a life the most inoffensive to government, and perfectly free from all species of political intrigue, and as I should leave behind me such sacred hostages as my husband and my son. Thus armed, and thus authorized, I prepared, quietly and secretly, for my expedition, while my generous mate employed all his little leisure in discovering where and how I might embark - when, one morning, when I was bending over my trunk to press in its contents, I was abruptly broken in upon by M. de Boinville, who was in my secret, and who called upon me to stop! He had received certain, he said, though as yet unpublished information, that a universal embargo was laid upon every vessel, and that not a fishing-boat was permitted to quit the coast. Confounded, affrighted, disappointed, and yet relieved, I submitted to the blow, and obeyed the injunction. M. de Boinville then revealed to me the new political changes that occasioned this measure, which he had learned from some confiding friends in office; but which I do not touch upon, as they are now in every history of those times.

I pass on to my second attempt, in the year 1812.

Disastrous was that interval! All correspondence with England was prohibited under pain of death! One letter only reached me, most unhappily, written with unreflecting abruptness, announcing, without preface, the death of the Princess Amelia, the new and total derangement of the king, and the death of Mr. Locke. Three such calamities overwhelmed me, overwhelmed us both, for Mr. Locke, my revered Mr. Locke, was as dear to my beloved partner as to myself. Poor Mrs. C concluded these tidings must have already arrived, but her fatal letter gave the first intelligence, and no other letter, at that period, found its way to me. She sent hers, I think, by some trusty returned prisoner. She little knew my then terrible situation; hovering over my head was the stiletto of a surgeon for a menace of cancer yet, till that moment, hope of escape had always been held out to me by the Baron de Larrey— hope which, from the reading of that fatal letter, became extinct.

A CHANGE OF PLAN.

When I was sufficiently recovered for travelling, after a dreadful operation, my plan was resumed, but with an alteration which added infinitely to its interest, as well as to its importance. Bonaparte was now engaging in a new war, of which the aim and intention was no less than-the conquest of the world. This menaced a severity of conscription to which Alexander, who had now spent ten years in France, and was seventeen years of age, would soon become liable. His noble father had relinquished all his own hopes and emoluments in the military career, from the epoch that his king was separated from his country; though that career had been his peculiar choice, and was suited peculiarly to the energy of his character, the vigour of his constitution, his activity, his address, his bravery, his spirit of resource, never overset by difficulty nor wearied by fatigue—all which combination of military requisites—

"The eye could in a moment reach,
And read depicted in his martial air,"

But his high honour, superior to his interest, superior to his inclination, and ruling his whole conduct with unremitting, unalienable constancy, impelled him to prefer the hard labour and obscure drudgery of working at a bureau of the minister of the interior, to any and every advantage or promotion that could be offered him in his own immediate and favourite line of life, when no longer compatible with his allegiance and loyalty. To see, therefore, his son bear arms in the very cause that had been his ruin—bear arms against the country which had given himself as well as his mother, birth, would indeed have been heart-breaking. We agreed, therefore, that Alexander should accompany me to England, where, I flattered myself, I might safely deposit him, while I returned to await, by the side of my husband, the issue of the war, in the fervent hope that it would prove our restoration to liberty and reunion.

A NEW PASSPORT OBTAINED.

My second passport was procured with much less facility than the first. Fouch, was no longer minister of police, and, strange to tell, Fouch,, who, till he became that minister, had been held in horror by all France-all Europe, conducted himself with such conciliatory mildness to all ranks of people while in that office, evinced such an appearance of humanity, and exhibited such an undaunted spirit of justice in its execution, that at his dismission all Paris was in affliction and dismay! Was this from the real merit he had shown in his police capacity? Or was it from a yet greater fear of malignant cruelty awakened by the very name of his successor, Savary, Duke of Rovigo? (215)

Now, as before, the critical moment was seized by my friends to act for me when Bonaparte had left Paris to proceed towards the scene of his next destined enterprise; (216) and he was, I believe, already at Dresden when my application was made. My kind friend Madame de T— here took the agency which M. de Narbonne could no longer sustain, as he was now attending the emperor, to whom he had been made aide-de-camp, and through her means, after many difficulties and delays, I obtained a licence of departure for myself and for Alexander. For what place, nominally, my passport was assigned, I do not recollect; I think, for Newfoundland, but certainly for some part of the coast of America. Yet everybody at the police office saw and knew that England was my object. They connived, nevertheless, at the accomplishment of my wishes, with significant though taciturn consciousness.

COMMISSIONS FOR LONDON.

From all the friends whom I dared trust with my secret expedition, I had commissions for London; though merely verbal, as I was cautioned to take no letters. No one at that time could send any to England by the post. I was charged by sundry persons to write for them, and in their names, upon my arrival. Madame de Tracy begged me to discover the address of her sister-in-law, Madame de Civrac, who had emigrated into the wilds of Scotland, and of whom she anxiously wished for some intelligence. This occasioned my having a little correspondence with her, which I now remark because she is named as one of the principal dames de la societe by Madame de Genlis. Madame d'Astorre desired me to find out her father, M. le Comte de Cely, and to give him news of her and her children. This I did, and received from the old gentleman some visits, and many letters. Madame la Princesse de Chimay entrusted me with a petition—a verbal one, to the Prince of Wales, in favour of the Duc de Fitzjames, who, in losing his wife, had lost an English pension. This I was to transmit to his royal highness by means of the Duchess dowager of Buccleugh - who was also entreated to make known the duke's situation to M. d'Escars, who was in the immediate service of Louis XVIII; for M. d'Escars I had a sort of cipher from Madame de Chimay, to authenticate my account.

DELAY AT DUNKIRK.

Our journey—Alexander's and mine—from Paris to Dunkirk was sad, from the cruel separation which it exacted, and the fearful uncertainty of impending events; though I was animated at times into the liveliest sensations, in the prospect of again beholding my father, my friends, and my country. General d'Arblay, through his assiduous researches, aided by those of M. de Boinville and some others, found that a vessel was preparing to sail from Dunkirk to Dover, under American colours, and with American passports and licence and, after privately landing such of its passengers as meant but to cross the channel, to proceed to the western continents. M. d'Arblay found, at the same time, six or seven persons of his acquaintance who were to embark in this vessel.

We all met, and severally visited at Dunkirk, where I was compelled, through the mismanagement and misconduct of the captain of the vessel, to spend the most painfully wearisome six weeks of my life, for they kept me alike from all that was dearest to me, either in France or in England, save my Alexander. I was twenty times on the point of returning to Paris; but whenever I made known that design, the captain promised to sail the next morning. The truth is, he postponed the voyage from day to day and from week to week, in the hope of obtaining more passengers; and, as the clandestine visit he meant to make. to Dover, in his way to America, was whispered about, reinforcements very frequently encouraged his cupidity.

The ennui of having no positive occupation was now, for the first time, known to me; for though the first object of my active cares was with me, it was not as if that object had been a daughter, and always at my side; it was a youth of seventeen, who, with my free consent, sought whatever entertainment the place could afford, to while away fatigue. He ran, therefore, wildly about at his pleasure, to the quay, the dockyard, the sea, the suburbs, the surrounding country but chiefly, his time was spent in skipping to the "Mary Ann," our destined vessel, and seeing its preparations for departure. To stroll about the town, to call upon my fellow-sufferers, to visit the principal shops, and to talk with the good Dutch people while I made slight purchases, was all I could devise to do that required action.

THE MS. OF "THE WANDERER."

When I found our stay indefinitely protracted, it occurred to me that if I had the papers of a work which I had then in hand, they might afford me an occupation to while away my truly vapid and uninteresting leisure. I wrote this idea to my partner in all—as M. de Talleyrand had called M. d'Arblay; and, with a spirit that was always in its first youth where any service was to be performed, he waited on M. de Saulnier at the police office, and made a request that my manuscripts might be sent after me, with a permission that I might also be allowed to carry them with me on board the ship. He durst not say to England, whither no vessel was supposed to sail; but he would not, to M. de Saulnier, who palpably connived at my plan and purpose, say America. M. de Saulnier made many inquiries relative to these papers; but on being assured, upon honour, that the work had nothing in it political, nor even national, nor possibly offensive to the government, he took the single word of M. d'Arblay, whose noble countenance and dauntless openness of manner were guarantees of sincerity that wanted neither seals nor bonds, and invested him with the power to send me what papers be pleased, without demanding to examine, or even to see them, a trust so confiding and so generous, that I have regretted a thousand times the want of means to acknowledge it according to its merit.

This work was "The Wanderer, or Female Difficulties," of which nearly three volumes were finished. They arrived, nevertheless, vainly for any purpose at Dunkirk; the disturbance of my suspensive - state incapacitating me for any composition, save of letters to my best friend, to whom I wrote, or dictated by Alexander, every day; and every day was only supported by the same kind diurnal return. But when, at length, we were summoned to the vessel, and our goods and chattels were conveyed to the custom-house, and when the little portmanteau was produced, and found to be filled with manuscripts, the police officer who opened it began a rant of indignation and amazement at a sight so unexpected and prohibited, that made him incapable to inquire or to hear the meaning of such a freight. He sputtered at the mouth, and stamped with his feet, so forcibly and vociferously, that no endeavours of mine could induce him to stop his accusations of traitorous designs, till, tired of the attempt, I ceased both explanation and entreaty, and stood before him with calm taciturnity. Wanting, then, the fresh fuel of interruption or opposition, his fire and fury evaporated into curiosity to know what I could offer. Yet even then, though my account staggered his violence into some degree of civility, he evidently deemed it, from its very nature, incredible; and this fourth child of my brain had undoubtedly been destroyed ere it was born, had I not had recourse to an English merchant, Mr. Gregory, long settled at Dunkirk, to whom, happily, I had been recommended, as to a person capable, in any emergence, to afford me assistance; he undertook the responsibility; and the letter of M. d'Arblay, containing the licence of M. de Saulnier, was then all-sufficient for my manuscripts and their embarkation.

SPANISH PRISONERS AT DUNKIRK.

The second event I have to relate I never even yet recollect without an inward shuddering. In our walks out of the town, on the borders of the ocean, after passing beyond the dockyard or wharf, we frequently met a large party of Spanish prisoners, well escorted by gendarmes, and either going to their hard destined labour, or returning from it for repast or repose. I felt deeply interested by them, knowing they were men with and for whom our own English and the immortal Wellington were then fighting: and this interest induced me to walk on the bank by which they were paraded to and fro, as often as I could engage Alexander, from his other pursuits, to accompany me. Their appearance was highly in their favour, as well as their situation; they had a look calmly intrepid, of concentrated resentment, yet unalterable patience, They were mostly strong-built and vigorous; of solemn, almost stately deportment, and with fine dark eyes, full of meaning, rolling around them as if in watchful expectation of insult; and in a short time they certainly caught from my countenance an air of sympathy, for they gave me, in return, as we passed one another, a glance that spoke grateful consciousness. I followed them to the place of their labour; though my short-sightedness would not let me distinguish what they were about, whether mending fortifications, dykes, banks, parapets, or what not: and I durst not use my glass, lest I should be suspected as a spy. We only strolled about in their vicinity, as if merely visiting and viewing the sea.

The weather, it was now August-was so intensely hot, the place was so completely without shade, and their work was so violent, that they changed hands every two hours, and those who were sent off to recruit were allowed to cast themselves upon the burnt and straw-like grass, to await their alternate summons. This they did in small groups, but without venturing to solace their rest by any species of social intercourse. They were as taciturn with one another as with their keepers and taskmasters.

One among them there was who wore an air of superiority, grave and composed, yet decided, to which they all appeared to bow down with willing subserviency, though the distinction was only demonstrated by an air of profound respect whenever they approached or passed him, for discourse held they none. One morning, when I observed him seated at a greater distance than usual from his overseers, during his hour of release, I turned suddenly from my walk as if with a view to bend my way homewards, but contrived, while talking with Alexander and looking another way, to slant my steps close to where he sat surrounded by his mute adherents, and to drop a handful of small coin nearly under the elbow upon which, wearily, lie was reclining. We proceeded with alertness, and talking together aloud; but Alexander perceived this apparent chief evidently moved by what I had done, though forbearing to touch the little offering, which, however, his companions immediately secured.

After this I never met him that he did not make me a slight but expressive bow. This encouraged me to repeat the poor little tribute of compassion, which I soon found he distributed, as far as it would go, to the whole set, by the kindly looks with which every one thenceforward greeted me upon every meeting. Yet he whom we supposed to be some chief, and who palpably discovered it was himself I meant to distinguish, never touched the money, nor examined what was taken up by the others, who, on their part, nevertheless seemed but to take charge of it in trust. We were now such good friends, that this became more than ever my favourite walk and these poor unhappy captives never saw me without brightening up into a vivacity of pleasure that was to me a real exhilaration.

We had been at Dunkirk above five weeks, when one evening, having a letter of consequence to send to Paris, I begged Alexander to carry it to the post himself, and to deposit me upon the quay, and there to join me. As the weather was very fine I stood near the sea, wistfully regarding the element on which depended all my present hopes and views. But presently my meditations were interrupted, and my thoughts diverted from mere self by the sudden entrance, in a large body, of my friends the Spanish prisoners, who all bore down to the very place where I was stationed, evidently recognising me, and eagerly showing that it was not without extreme satisfaction. I saw their approach, in return, with lively pleasure, for, the quay being, I suppose, a place of certain security, they were unencumbered by their usual turnkeys, the gendarmes, and this freedom, joined to their surprise at my sight, put them also off their guard, and they flocked round though not near me, and hailed me with smiles, bows, and hands put upon their breasts. I now took courage to speak to them, partly in French, partly in English, for I found they understood a little of both those languages. I inquired whence they came, and whether they knew General Wellington. They smiled and nodded at his name, and expressed infinite delight in finding I was English; but though they all, by their head movements, entered into discourse, my friend the chief was the only one who attempted to answer me.

When I first went to France, being continually embarrassed for terms, I used constantly to apply to M. d'Arblay for aid, till Madame de Tess, charged him to be quiet, saying that my looks filled up what my words left short, "de sorte que," she added, "nous la devinons;" (217) this was the case between my Spaniards and myself, and we -devin-d one another so much to our mutual satisfaction, that while this was the converse the most to my taste of any I had had at Dunkirk, it was also, probably, most to theirs of any that had fallen to their lot since they had been torn from their native country.

SURPRISED BY AN OFFICER OF POLICE.

While this was going on I was privately drawing from my purse all that it contained of small money to distribute to my new friends - but at this same moment a sudden change in the countenance of the chief from looks of grateful feeling, to an expression of austerity, checked my purpose, and, sorry and alarmed lest he had taken offence, I hastily drew my empty hand from my reticule. I then saw that the change of expression was not simply to austerity from pleasure, but to consternation from serenity and I perceived that it was not to me the altered visage was directed; the eye pointed beyond me, and over my head startled, I turned round, and what, then, was my own consternation when I beheld an officer of the police, in full gold trappings, furiously darting forward from a small house at the entrance upon the quay, which I afterwards learnt was his official dwelling. When he came within two yards of us he stood still, mute and erect; but with an air of menace, his eyes scowling first upon the chief, then upon me, then upon the whole group, and then upon me again, with looks that seemed diving into some conspiracy.

My alarm was extreme—my imprudence in conversing with these unhappy captives struck me at once with foreboding terror of ill consequences. I had, however, sufficient presence of mind to meet the eyes of my antagonist with a look that showed surprise, rather than apprehension at his wrath.

This was not without some effect. Accustomed, probably, to scrutinize and to penetrate into secret plots, he might be an adept in distinguishing the fear of ill-treatment from the fear of detection. The latter I could certainly not manifest, as my compassion had shown no outward mark beyond a little charity but the former I tried, vainly, perhaps, to subdue: for I well knew that pity towards a Spaniard would be deemed suspicious, at least, if not culpable.

We were all silent, and all motionless; but when the man, having fixed upon me his eyes with intention to petrify me, saw that I fixed him in return with an open though probably not very composed face, he-spoke, and with a voice of thunder, vociferating reproach, accusation, and condemnation all in one. His words I could not distinguish; they were so confused and rapid from rage.

This violence, though it secretly affrighted me, I tried to meet with simple astonishment, making no sort of answer or interruption to his invectives. When he observed my steadiness, and that he excited none of the humiliation of discovered guilt, he stopped short and, after a pause, gruffly said,

"Qui êtes-vous?"

"Je me nomme d'Arblay."

"Etes-vous mariee?"

"Oui."

"O—est votre mari?"

"A Paris."

"Qui est-il?"

"Il travaille aux Bureaux de l'Interieur."

"Pourquoi le quittez-vous?" (218)

I was here sensibly embarrassed. I durst not avow I was going to England; I could not assert I was really going to America. I hesitated, and the sight of his eyes brightening up with the hope of mischief, abated my firmness; and, while he seemed to be staring me through, I gave an account, very imperfect, indeed, and far from clear, though true, that I came to Dunkirk to embark on board the "Mary Ann" vessel.

"Ah ha!" exclaimed he, "vous êtes Anglaise?" (219)

Then, tossing back his head with an air of triumphant victory, "suivez-moi!"(220) he added, and walked away, fast and fierce, but looking back every minute to see that I followed.

INTERROGATED AT THE POLICE OFFICE.

Never can I forget the terror with which I was seized at this command; it could only be equalled by the evident consternation and sorrow that struck me, as I turned my head around to see where I was, in my poor chief and his group. Follow I did, though not less per force than if I had been dragged by chains. When I saw him arrive at the gate of the little dwelling I have mentioned, which I now perceived to belong to him officially, I impulsively, involuntarily stopped. To enter a police office, to be probably charged with planning some conspiracy with the enemies of the state, my poor Alexander away, and not knowing what must have become of me; my breath was gone; my power of movement ceased; my head, or understanding, seemed a chaos, bereft of every distinct or discriminating idea; and my feet, as if those of a statue, felt riveted to the ground, from a vague but overwhelming belief I was destined to incarceration in some dungeon, where I might sink ere I could make known my situation to my friends, while Alex, thus unaccountably abandoned, might be driven to despair, or become the prey to nameless mischiefs.

Again the tiger vociferated a "suivez-moi!" but finding it no longer obeyed, he turned full round as he stood upon its threshold, and perceiving my motionless and speechless dismay, looked at me for two or three seconds in scornful, but investigating taciturnity. Then, putting his arms a-kimbo, he said, in lower, but more, taunting accents, "Vous ne le jugez donc pas   propos de me suivre?" (221)

This was followed by a sneering, sardonic grin that seemed anticipating the enjoyment of using compulsion. On, therefore, I again forced myself, and with tolerable composure I said, "Je n'ai rien, monsieur, je crois, faire ici?" (222)

"Nous verrons!"(223) he answered, bluffly, and led the way into a small hovel rather than parlour - and then haughtily seated himself at a table, on which were pen, ink, and paper, and, while I stood before him, began an interrogation, with the decided asperity of examining a detected criminal, of whom he was to draw up the proces verbal.

When I perceived this, my every fear, feeling, nay, thought, concentrated in Alexander, to whom I had determined not to allude, while I had any hope of self-escape, to avoid for us both the greatest of all perils, that of an accusation of intending to evade the ensuing conscription, for which, though Alex was yet too young, he was fast advancing to be amenable.

But now that I was enclosed from his sight, and there was danger every moment of his suddenly missing me, I felt that our only chance of safety must lie in my naming him before he should return. With all the composure, therefore, that I could assume, I said that I was come to Dunkirk with my son to embark in the "Mary Ann," an American vessel, with a passport from M. de Saulnier, secretary to the Duke de Rovigo, minister of police.

And what had I done with this son?

I had sent him to the post-office with a letter for his father.

At that instant I perceived Alexander wildly running past the window.

This moment was critical. I instantly cried, "Sir, there is my son!"

The man rose, and went to the door, calling Out, "Jeune homme!" (224)

Alex approached, and was questioned, and though much amazed, gave answers perfectly agreeing with mine.

I now recovered my poor affrighted faculties, and calmly said that if he had any doubt of our veracity, I begged he would send for Mr. Gregory, who knew us well. This, a second time, was a most happy reference. Mr. Gregory was of the highest respectability, and he was near at hand. There could be no doubt of the authenticity of such an appeal.

The brow of my ferocious assailant was presently unbent. I seized the favourable omen to assure him, with apparent indifference, that I had no objection to being accompanied or preceded to the Hotel Sauvage, where I resided, nor to giving him the key of my portmanteau and portfolio, if it were possible I had excited any suspicion by merely speaking, from curiosity, to the Spanish prisoners.

No, he answered, he would not disturb me; and then, having entered the name of Alexander by the side of mine, he let us depart. Speechless was my joy, and speechless was the surprise of Alexander, and we walked home in utter silence. Happily, this incident occurred but just before we set sail, for with it terminated my greatest solace at Dunkirk, the seeing and consoling those unhappy prisoners, and the regale of wandering by the sea-coast.

THE "MARY ANN" CAPTURED OFF DEAL.

Six weeks completely we consumed in wasteful weariness at Dunkirk; and our passage, when at last we set sail, was equally, in its proportion, toilsome and tedious. Involved in a sickening calm, we could make no way, but lingered two days and two nights in this long-short passage. The second night, indeed, might have been spared me, as it was spared to all my fellow voyagers. But when we cast anchor, I was so exhausted by the unremitting sufferings I had endured, that I was literally unable to rise from my hammock.

Yet was there a circumstance capable to have aroused me from any torpidity, save the demolishing ravage of sea-sickness for scarcely were we at anchor, when Alex, capering up to the deck, descended with yet more velocity than he had mounted to exclaim, "Oh, maman! there are two British officers now upon deck." But, finding that even this could not make me recover speech or motion, he ran back again to this new and delighting sight, and again returning 'cried out in a tone of rapture, "Maman, we are taken by the British! We are all captured by British officers!"

Even in my immovable, and nearly insensible state, this juvenile ardour, excited by so new and strange an adventure, afforded me some amusement. It did not, however, afford me strength, for I could not rise, though I heard that every other passenger was removed. With difficulty, even next morning, I crawled upon the deck, and there I had been but a short time, when Lieutenant Harford came on board to take possession of the vessel, not as French, but American booty, war having been declared against America the preceding week. Mr. Harford, hearing my name, most courteously addressed me, with congratulations upon my safe arrival in England. These were words to rewaken all the happiest purposes of my expedition, and they recovered me from the nerveless, sinking state into which my exhaustion had cast me, as if by a miracle. My father, my brothers, my sisters, and all my heart-dear friends, seemed rising to my view and springing to my embraces, with all the joy of renovating reunion. I thankfully accepted his obliging offer to carry me on shore in his own boat; but when I turned round, and called upon Alexander to follow us, Mr. Harford, assuming a commanding air, said, "No, madam, I cannot take that young man. No French person can come into my boat without a passport and permission from government." My air now a little corresponded with his own, as I answered, "He was born, Sir, in England!"

"Oh!" cried he, " "that's quite another matter; come along, Sir! we'll all go together."

I now found we were rowing to Deal, not Dover, to which town we had been destined by our engagement: but we had been captured, it seems, chemin fuisant, though so gently, and with such utter helplessness of opposition, that I had become a prisoner without any suspicion of my captivity.

JOY ON ARRIVING IN ENGLAND.

We had anchored about half a mile, I imagine, from the shore; which I no sooner touched than, drawing away my arm from Mr. Harford, I took up on one knee, with irrepressible transport, the nearest bright pebble, to press to my lips in grateful joy at touching again the land of my nativity, after an absence, nearly hopeless, of more than twelve years.

Of the happiness that ensued—my being again in the arms of my dearly loved father-in those of my dear surviving sisters—my brothers—my friends, some faint details yet remain in a few letters to my heart's confidant that he preserved: but they are truly faint, for my satisfaction was always damped in recording it to him who SO fondly wished to partake of it, and whose absence from that participation always rendered it incomplete.

And, on one great source of renovated felicity, I did not dare touch even by inference, even by allusion—that of finding my gracious royal mistress and her august daughters as cordial in their welcome, as trustingly confidential, and as amiably condescending, I had almost said affectionate, as if I had never departed from the royal roof under which, for five years, I had enjoyed their favour. To have spoken of the royal family in letters sent to France under the reign of Bonaparte, might have brought destruction on him for whom I would a thousand times sooner have suffered it myself.

(Madame d'Arblay to Mrs. Broome.) (225) Aug. 15, 1812. In a flutter of joy such as my tender Charlotte will feel in reading this, I write to her from England! I can hardly believe it; I look around me in constant inquiry and doubt I speak French to every soul, and I whisper still if I utter a word that breathes private opinion. . . .

We set off for Canterbury, where we slept, and on the 20th (226) proceeded towards Chelsea. While, upon some common, we stopped to water the horses, a gentleman on horseback passed us twice, and then, looking in, pronounced my name - and I saw it was Charles, dear Charles! who had been watching for us several hours and three nights following, through a mistake. Thence we proceeded to Chelsea, where we arrived at nine o'clock at night. I was in a state almost breathless. I could only demand to see my dear father alone: fortunately, he had had the same feeling, and had charged all the family to stay away, and all the world to be denied. I found him, therefore, in his library, by himself-but oh! my dearest, very much altered indeed—weak, weak and changed—his head almost always hanging down, and his hearing most cruelly impaired. I was terribly affected, but most grateful to God for my arrival. Our meeting, you may be sure, was very tender, though I roused myself as quickly as possible to be gay and cheering. He was extremely kind to Alex, and said, in a tone the most impressive, "I should have been very glad to have seen M. d'Arblay!" In discourse, however, he reanimated, and was, at times, all himself. But he now admits scarcely a creature but of his family, and will only see for a short time even his children. He likes quietly reading, and lies almost constantly upon the sofa, and will never eat but alone. What a change!

YOUNG D'ARBLAY SECURES A SCHOLARSHIP.

(Madame d'Arblay to Dr. Burney.) March 16, 1813. How will my kindest father rejoice for me! for my dear partner— for my boy! The election is gained, and Alexander has obtained the Tancred scholarship. He had all the votes: the opponent retired. Sir D— behaved handsomely, came forward, and speechified for us. Sir Francis Milman, who was chairman, led the way in the harangue. Dr. Davy, our supporter, leader, inspirer, director, heart and head, patron and guide, spoke also. Mr H— spoke, too; but nothing, they tell me, to our purpose, nor yet against it. He gave a very long and elaborate history of a cause which he is to plead in the House of Lords, and which has not the smallest reference whatsoever to the case in point. Dr. Davy told me, in recounting it, that he is convinced the good and wary lawyer thought this an opportunity not to be lost for rehearsing his cause, which would prevent loss of time to himself, or hindrance of business, except to his hearers: however, he gave us his vote. 'Tis a most glorious affair.

THE QUEEN ALARMED BY A MAD WOMAN.

(Madame d'Arblay to Dr. Burney.) May 11, 1813. My own inclination and intention kept in mind your charge, my dearest sir, that as soon as I was able I would wait upon Lady Crewe; (227) fortunately, I found her at home, and in her best style, cordial as well as good-humoured, and abounding in acute and odd remarks. I had also the good fortune to see my lord, who seems always pleasing, unaffected, and sensible, and to possess a share of innate modesty that no intercourse with the world, nor addition of years, can rob him of. I was much satisfied with my visit - but what I shall do for time, now once I have been launched from my couch, or sick chamber, I wot not.

What a terrible alarm is this which the poor tormented queen has again received! (228) I wrote my concern as soon as I heard of it, though I have not yet seen the printed account, my packet of papers reaching only to the very day before that event. My answer has been a most gracious summons to the Queen's house for to-morrow. Her majesty and two of the princesses come to town for four days. This robs me of my Chelsea visit for this week, as I keep always within call during the town residences, when I have royal notice of them, and, indeed, there is nothing I desire more than to see her majesty at this moment, and to be allowed to express what I have felt for her. My letter from Madame Beckersdorff says that such an alarm would have been frightful for anybody, but how much more peculiarly so for the queen, who has experienced such poignant horror from the effects of disordered intellects! who is always suffering from them, and so nearly a victim to the unremitting exercise of her duties upon that subject and these calls.

I have had a visit this morning from Mrs. Piozzi, who is in town only for a few days upon business. She came while I was out - but I must undoubtedly make a second tour, after my royal four days are passed, in order to wait upon and thank her.

I have been received more graciously than ever, if that be possible, by my dear and honoured queen and sweet Princesses Eliza and Mary. The queen has borne this alarm astonishingly, considering how great was the shock at the moment; but she has so high a character, that she will not suffer anything personal to sink her spirits, which she saves wholly for the calls upon them of others, and great and terrible have been those calls. The beloved king is in the best state possible for his present melancholy situation; that is, wholly free from real bodily suffering, or imaginary mental misery, for he is persuaded that he is always conversing with angels.

WEATHER COMPLAINTS. PROPOSED MEETING WITH LORD LANSDOWNE.

(Madame d'Arblay to Dr. Burney.) Chenies Street, Alfred-place, May 23, 1813. Oh, how teased I am, my dearest padre, by this eternal unwalkable weather! Every morning rises so fairly, that at every noon I am preparing to quit my conjuring, and repair, by your kind invitation, to prelude my promised chat by a repast with Sarah, when mizzling falls the rain, or hard raps the hail, and the day, for me, is involved in damps and dangers that fix me again to my dry, but solitary conjurations. I am so tired now of disappointments, that I must talk a little with my padre in their defiance, and in a manner now, thank God! out of their reach. Ah, how long will letters be any safer than meetings! The little world I see all give me hope and comfort from the posture of affairs but I am too deeply interested to dare be sanguine while in such suspense.

Lady Crewe invited me to her party that she calls Noah's ark; but I cannot yet risk an evening, and a dressed one too. She then said she would make me a small party with the Miss Berrys, and for a morning; and now she has written to Charles to make interest with me to admit Lord Lansdowne, at his own earnest request! I am quite non compos to know how I shall make my way through these honours, to my strength and re-establishment, for they clash with my private plan and adopted system of quiet. However, she says the meeting shall be in the country, at Brompton, and without fuss or ceremony. Her kindness is inexpressible, therefore I have not courage to refuse her. She has offered me her little residence at Brompton for my dwelling for a week or so, to restore me from all my influenzas: she may truly be called a faithful family friend. I hope dear Sarah and Fanny Raper will be of the party. If they are, charge them, dear sir, to let me hear their voices, for I shall never find out their faces.

What weather! what weather! when shall I get to Chelsea, and embrace again my beloved father?

This free-born weather of our sea-girt isle of liberty is very incommodious to those who have neither carriages for wet feet, nor health for damp shoulders. If the farmers, however, are contented, I must be patient. We may quarrel with all our wishes better than with our corn.

Adieu, my most dear father, till the sun shines drier.

A YOUNG GIRL'S ENTRY TO LONDON SOCIETY. MADAME DE STAEL.

(Madame d'Arblay to a friend.) London, August 20, 1813. . .Your charming girl, by what I can gather, has seen, upon the whole, a great deal of this vast town and its splendours,—a little more might, perhaps, have been better, in making her, with a mind such as hers, regret it a little less. Merit of her sort can here be known with difficulty. Dissipation is so hurried, so always in a bustle, that even amusement must be prominent, to be enjoyed. There is no time for development; nothing, therefore, is seen but what is conspicuous; and not much is heard but what is obstreperous. They who, in a short time, can make themselves known and admired now in London, must have their cupids, in Earl Dorset's phrase—

Like blackguard boys,
Who thrust their links full in your face.

I had very much matter that I meant and wished to say to you upon this subject; but in brief—I do not myself think it a misfortune that your dear girl cannot move in a London round, away from your own wing: you have brought her up so well, and she seems so good, gentle, and contented, as well as accomplished, that I cannot wish her drawn into a vortex where she may be imbued with other ideas, views, and wishes than those that now constitute her happiness—and happiness! what ought to be held more sacred where it is innocent—what ought so little to risk any unnecessary or premature concussion? With all the deficiencies and imperfections of her present situation, which you bewail but which she does not find out, it is, alas! a million to one whether, even in attaining the advantages and society you wish for her, she will ever again, after any change, be as happy as she is at this moment. A mother whom she looks up to and doats upon—a sister whom she so fondly loves—how shall they be replaced? The chances are all against her (though the world has, I know, such replacers), from their rarity.

I am truly glad you had a gratification you so earnestly coveted, that of seeing Madame de Stael: your account of her was extremely interesting to me. As to myself, I have not seen her at all. Various causes have kept me in utter retirement; and, in truth, with respect to Madame de Stael, my situation is really embarrassing. It is too long and difficult to write upon, nor do I recollect whether I ever communicated to you our original acquaintance, which, at first, was intimate. I shall always, internally, be grateful for the partiality with which she sought me out upon her arrival in this country before my- marriage: and still, and far more, if she can forgive my dropping her, which I could not help for none of my friends, at that time, would suffer me to keep up the intercourse! I had messages, remonstrances, entreaties, representations, letters, and conferences, till I could resist no longer; though I had found her so charming, that I fought the hardest battle I dared fight against almost all my best connections. She is now received by all mankind;—but that, indeed, she always was—all womankind, I should say—with distinction and pleasure. I wish much to see her "Essay on Suicide;" but it has not yet fallen in my way. When will the work come out for which she was, she says, chassée de la France? (229) Where did — hear her a whole evening? She is, indeed, most uncommonly entertaining, and animating as well as animated, almost beyond anybody, "Les Memoires de Madame de Stael" I have read long ago, and with singular interest and eagerness. They are so attaching, so evidently original and natural, that they stand very high, indeed, in reading that has given me most pleasure. My boy has just left me for Greenwich. (230) He goes in October to Cambridge; I wish to install him there myself. My last letter from Paris gives me to the end of October to stay in England.

ROGERS THE POET.

(Madame d'Arblay to Dr. Burney.) August 24, 1813. .....I was delighted by meeting Lady Wellington, not long since, at Lady Templetown's. Her very name electrified me with emotion. I dined at Mr. Rogers's, at his beautiful mansion in the Green Park, to meet Lady Crewe; and Mrs. Barbauld was also there, whom I had not seen many, many years, and alas, should not have known! Mr. Rogers was so considerate to my sauvagerie as to have no party, though Mr. Sheridan, he said, had expressed his great desire to meet again his old friend Madame d'Arblay! Lady Crewe told me she certainly would not leave town without seeking another chattery with her old friend, Dr. Burney, whom she always saw with fresh pleasure.

INTERVIEW WITH MR. WILBERFORCE.

(Madame d'Arblay to Dr. Burney.) Sandgate, Sept, 1813. Let me steal a moment to relate a singular gratification, and, in truth, a real and great honour I have had to rejoice in. You know, my padre, probably, that Marianne Francis was commissioned by Mr. Wilberforce (231) to bring about an acquaintance with your F. d'A., and that, though highly susceptible to such a desire, my usual shyness, or rather consciousness of inability to meet the expectations that must have made him seek me, induced my declining an interview. Eh bien—at church at Sandgate, the day after my arrival, I saw this justly celebrated man, and was introduced to him in the churchyard, after the service, by Charles. The ramparts and martellos around us became naturally our theme, and Mr. Wilberforce proposed showing them to me. I readily accepted the offer, and Charles and Sarah, and Mrs. Wilberforce and Mrs. Barrett, went away in their several carriages, while Mr. Barrett alone remained, and Mr. Wilberforce gave me his arm, and, in short, we walked the round from one to five o'clock! Four hours of the best conversation I have, nearly, ever enjoyed. He was anxious for a full and true account of Paris, and particularly of religion and infidelity, and of Bonaparte and the wars, and of all and everything that had occurred during my ten years' seclusion in France; and I had so much to communicate, and his drawing out and comments and episodes were all so judicious, so spirited, so full of information yet so unassuming, that my shyness all flew away and I felt to be his confidential friend, opening to him upon every occurrence and every sentiment, with the frankness that is usually won by years of intercourse. I was really and truly delighted and enlightened by him; I desire nothing more than to renew the acquaintance, and cultivate it to intimacy. But, alas! he was going away next morning.

INTENDED PUBLICATION OF "THE WANDERER."

(Madame d'Arblay to Dr. Burney.) Richmond Hill, Oct. 12, 1813. My most dear padre will, I am sure, congratulate me that I have just had the heartfelt delight of a few lines from M. d'Arblay, dated September 5th. I had not had any news since the 17th of August, and I had the melancholy apprehension upon my spirits that no more letters would be allowed to pass till the campaign was over. It has been therefore one of the most welcome surprises I ever experienced. He tells me, also, that he is perfectly well, and quite acabl, with business. This, for the instant, gives me nothing but joy; for, were he not essentially necessary in some department of civil labour and use, he would surely be included in some levée en masse. Every way, therefore, this letter gives me relief and pleasure.

I have had, also, this morning, the great comfort to hear that my Alexander is "stout and well at Cambridge, where his kind uncle Charles still remains.

I am indescribably occupied, and have been so ever since my return from Ramsgate, in giving more and more last touches to my work, about which I begin to grow very anxious. I am to receive merely 500 pounds upon delivery of the MS. The two following 500 by instalments from nine months to nine months, that is, in a year and a half from the day of publication. If all goes well, the whole will be 3000, but only at the end of the sale of eight thousand copies. Oh, my padre, if you approve the work, I shall have good hope.

GENERAL D'ARBLAY'S WOUNDED COMRADES.

(Madame d'Arblay to Mrs. Locke.) Dec. 16, 1813. Ah, my dearest friend, how is my poor cottage, how are my proofs, how is everything forced from my mind, except what necessity drives there, by this cruel stroke to my suffering partner! The world had power only in two instances to have given him quite so deadly a blow, dear to his heart of love as are some, nay, many others; but here—for M. de Narbonne, it was a passion of admiration, joined to a fondness of friendship, that were a part of himself. (232) How he will bear it, and in our absence, perpetually occupies my thoughts. And I have no means to hear from, or to write to him!—none, absolutely none!

Just before this wound was inflicted, I was already overwhelmed with grief for my poor Madame de Maisonneuve, for M. d'Arblay himself, and for my own personal loss, in the death—premature and dreadful, nay, inhuman—of the noble, perfect brother of that Madame de Maisonneuve; General Latour Maubourg, a man who, like my own best friend was—is signalized among his comrades by the term of a vrai Chevalier Français. He was without a blot; and his life has been thrown away merely to prevent his being made a prisoner! He had received a horrible wound on the first of the tremendous battles of Leipzic, and on the second he suffered amputation; and immediately after was carried away to follow the retreating army! In such a condition, who can wonder to hear that, a very few miles from Leipzic, he expired? (233)

DEATH OF DR. BURNEY.

[In the beginning of the year 1814, Madame d'Arblay published her fourth work, "The Wanderer," and nearly at the same time peace was declared between France and England. Her satisfaction at an event so long wished for, was deeply saddened by the death of her father, Dr. Burney; whom she nursed and attended to the last moment with dutiful tenderness.

Soon after the Restoration of the French royal family, Monsieur d'Arblay was placed by the Duke de Luxembourg in the French "gardes du corps." He obtained leave of absence towards the close of the year, and came to England for a few weeks; after which Madame d'Arblay returned with him to Paris, leaving their son to pursue his studies at Cambridge.]

(Madame d'Arblay to Mrs. —) March (234) 19, 1814. Be not uneasy for me, nay tender friend: my affliction is heavy, but not acute - my beloved father had been spared to us something beyond the verge of the prayer for his preservation, which you must have read, for already his sufferings had far surpassed his enjoyments. I could not have wished him so to linger, though I indulged almost to the last hour a hope he might yet recover, and be restored to comfort. I last of all gave him up, but never wished his duration such as I saw him on the last few days. Dear blessed parent! how blest am I that I came over to him while he was yet susceptible of pleasure—of happiness! My best comfort in my grief, in his loss, is that I watched by his side the last night, and hovered over him two hours after he breathed no more; for though much suffering had preceded the last hours, they were so quiet, and the final exit was so soft, that I had not perceived it though I was sitting by his bedside, and would not believe when all around announced it. I forced them to let me stay by him, and his revered form became stiff before I could persuade myself that he was gone hence for ever.

Yet neither then nor now has there been any violence, anything to fear from my grief; his loss was too indubitably to be expected, he had been granted too long to our indulgence to allow any species of repining to mingle with my sorrow; and it is repining that makes sorrow too hard to bear with resignation. Oh, I have known it!

FAVOURABLE NEWS OF M. D'ARBLAY.

(Madame d'Arblay to Mrs. Locke.) April 3, 1814. I hasten to impart to my kind and sympathising friend that I received-last night good tidings of my best friend of friends; they have been communicated to me, oddly enough, through the Alien office! Mr. Reeves wrote them to my reverend brother, (235) by the desire of an English lady now resident in Paris-Madame Solvyns (wife of a Frenchman), at the request of M. d'Arblay; they assure me of his perfect health...

Nothing could be so well timed as this intelligence, for my inquietude was beginning to be doubly restless from the accession of time that has fallen to me by having got rid of all my proofs, etc. it is only real and indispensable business that can force away attention from suspensive uneasiness. Another comfort of the very first magnitude, my sweet friend will truly, I know, participate in—my Alexander begins to listen to reason. He assures me he is now going on with very tolerable regularity; and I have given him, for this term, to soberize and methodize him a little, a private tutor; and this tutor has won his heart by indulging him in his problem passion. They work together, he says, with a rapidity and eagerness that makes the hour of his lesson by far the most delightful portion of his day. And this tutor, he tells me, most generously gives him problems to work at in his absence: a favour for which every pupil, perchance, would not be equally grateful, but which Alexander, who loves problems algebraic as another boy loves a play or an opera, regards as the height of indulgence.

"THE WANDERER."

[Soon after the publication of " The Wanderer," Madame d'Arblay wrote as follows to a friend:—]

I beseech you not to let your too ardent friendship disturb you about the reviews and critiques, and I quite supplicate you to leave their authors to their own severities or indulgence. I have ever steadily refused all interference with public opinion or private criticism. I am told I have been very harshly treated; but I attribute it not to what alone would affect me, but which I trust I have not excited, personal enmity. I attribute it to the false expectation, universally spread, that the book would be a picture of France, as well as to the astonishing ,clat of a work in five volumes being all bespoken before it was published. The booksellers, erroneously and injudiciously concluding the sale would so go on, fixed the rapacious price of two guineas, which again damped the sale. But why say damped, when it is only their unreasonable expectations that are disappointed? for they acknowledge that 3600 copies are positively sold and paid for in the first half year. What must I be, if not far more than contented? I have not read or heard one of the criticisms; my mind has been wholly occupied by grief for the loss of my dearest father, or the inspection of his MSS., and my harassing situation relative to my own proceedings. Why, then, make myself black bile to disturb me further? No; I will not look at a word till my spirits and time are calmed and quiet, and I can set about preparing a corrected edition. I will then carefully read all - and then, the blow to immediate feelings being over, I can examine as well as read, impartially and with profit, both to my future surveyors and myself.

MADAME D'ARBLAY'S PRESENTATION TO LOUIS XVIII AT GRILLON'S HOTEL.

1814. While I was still under the almost first impression of grief for the loss of my dear and honoured father I received a letter from Windsor Castle, written by Madame Beckersdorff, at the command of her majesty, to desire I would take the necessary measures for being presented to son altesse royale Madame Duchesse d'Angoulême, I who was to have a Drawing-room in London, both for French and English, on the day preceding her departure for France. The letter added, that I must waive all objections relative to my recent loss, as it would be improper, in the present state of things, that the wife of a general officer should not be presented; and, moreover, that I should be personally expected and well received, as I had been named to son altesse royale by the queen herself. In conclusion, I was charged not to mention this circumstance, from the applications or jealousies it might excite.

To hesitate was out of the question - and to do honour to my noble absent partner, and in his name to receive honour, were precisely the two distinctions my kind father would most have enjoyed for me.

I had but two or three days for preparation. Lady Crewe most amiably came to me herself, and missing me in person, wrote me word she would lend me her carriage, to convey me from Chelsea to her house in Lower Grosvenor Street, and thence accompany me herself to the audience. When the morning arrived I set off with tolerable courage.

Arrived, however, at Lady Crewe's, when I entered the room in which this dear and attached friend of my father received me, the heaviness of his loss proved quite overpowering to my spirits; and in meeting the two hands of my hostess, I burst into tears and could not, for some time, listen to the remonstrances against unavailing grief with which she rather chid than soothed me. But I could not contest the justice of what she uttered, though my grief was too fresh for its observance. Sorrow, as my dearest father was wont to say, requires time, as well as wisdom and religion, to digest itself, and till that time is both accorded and well employed, the sense of its uselessness serves but to augment, not mitigate, its severity.

Lady Crewe purposed taking this opportunity of paying her own respects, with her congratulations, to Madame la Duchesse d'Angoul^me. She had sent me a note from Madame de Gouvello, relative to the time, for presentation, which was to take place it Grillon's hotel in Albemarle Street.

We went very early, to avoid a crowd. But Albemarle Street was already quite full, though quiet. We entered the hotel without difficulty, Lady Crewe having previously demanded a private room of Grillon, who had once been cook to her lord. This private room was at the back of the house, with a mere yard or common garden for its prospect. Lady Crewe declared this was quite too stupid, and rang the bell for waiter after waiter, till she made M. Grillon come himself. She then, in her singularly open and easy manner, told him to be so good as to order us a front room, where we might watch for the arrival of the royals, and be amused ourselves at the same time by seeing the entrances of the mayor, aldermen, and common councilmen, and other odd characters, who would be coming to pay their court to these French princes and princesses.

M. Grillon gave a nod of acquiescence, and we were instantly shown to a front apartment just over the street door, which was fortunately supplied with a balcony.

I should have been much entertained by all this, and particularly with the originality, good humour, and intrepid yet intelligent odd fearlessness of all remark, or even consequence, which led Lady Crewe to both say and do exactly what she pleased, had my heart been lighter but it was too heavy for pleasure; and the depth of my mourning, and the little, but sad time that was yet passed since it had become my gloomy garb, made me hold it a matter even of decency, as well as of feeling, to keep out of sight. I left Lady Crewe, therefore, to the full enjoyment of her odd figures, while I seated myself, solitarily, at the further end of the room.

GRATTAN THE ORATOR.

In an instant, however, she saw from the window some acquaintance, and beckoned them up. A gentleman, middle-aged, of a most pleasing appearance and address, immediately obeyed her summons, accompanied by a young man with a sensible look; and a young lady, pretty, gentle, and engaging, with languishing, soft eyes; though with a smile and an expression of countenance that showed an innate disposition to archness and sport.

This uncommon trio I soon found to consist of the celebrated Irish orator, Mr. Grattan, (237) and his son and daughter. Lady Crewe welcomed them with all the alertness belonging to her thirst for amusement, and her delight in sharing it with those she thought capable of its participation. This she had sought, but wholly missed in me; and could neither be angry nor disappointed, though she was a little vexed. She suffered me not, however, to remain long in my seclusion, but called me to the balcony, to witness the jolting out of their carriages of the aldermen and common councilmen, exhibiting, as she said, "Their fair round bodies with fat capon lined;" and wearing an air of proudly hospitable satisfaction, in visiting a king of France who had found an asylum in a street of the city of Westminster.

The crowd, however, for they deserve a better name than mob, interested my observation still more. John Bull has seldom appeared to me to greater advantage. I never saw him en masse behave with such impulsive propriety. Enchanted to behold a king of France in his capital; conscious that le grand monarque was fully in his power; yet honestly enraptured to see that "The king would enjoy his own again," and enjoy it through the generous efforts of his rival, brave, noble old England; he yet seemed aware that it was fitting to subdue all exuberance of pleasure, which, else, might annoy, if not alarm, his regal guest. He took care, therefore, that his delight should not amount to exultation; it was quiet and placid, though pleased and curious: I had almost said it was gentlemanlike.

And nearly of the same colour, though from so inferior an incitement, were the looks and attention of the Grattans, particularly of the father, to the black mourner whom Lady Crewe called amongst them. My garb, or the newspapers, or both, explained the dejection I attempted not to repress, though I carefully forbade it any vent and the finely speaking face of Mr. Grattan seemed investigating the physiognomy, while it commiserated the situation of the person brought thus before him. His air had something foreign in it, from the vivacity that accompanied his politeness; I should have taken him for a well-bred man of fashion of France. Good breeding, in England, amongst the men, is ordinarily stiff, reserved, or cold. Among the exceptions to this stricture, how high stood Mr. Windham! and how high in gaiety with vivacity stood my own honoured father! Mr. Locke, who was elegance personified in his manners, was lively only in his own domestic or chosen circle.

A DEMONSTRATIVE IRISH LADY.

A new scene now both astonished and discomposed me. A lady, accompanied humbly by a gentleman, burst into the room with a noise, a self-sufficiency, and an assuming confidence of superiority, that would have proved highly offensive, had it not been egregiously ridiculous. Her attire was as flaunting as her air and her manner; she was rouged and beribboned. But English she was not - she was Irish, in its most flaunting and untamed nature, and possessed of so boisterous a spirit, that she appeared to be just caught from the woods—the bogs, I might rather say.

When she had poured forth a volley of words, with a fluency and loudness that stunned me, Lady Crewe, with a. smile that seemed to denote she intended to give her pleasure, presented me by name to Madame la Baronne de M—

She made me a very haughty curtsey, and then, turning rudely away, looked reproachfully at Lady Crewe, and screamed out, "Oh, fie! fie, fie, fie!" Lady Crewe, astonished and shocked, seemed struck speechless, and I stood still with my eyes wide open, and my mouth probably so also, from a sort of stupor, for I could annex no meaning nor even any idea to such behaviour. She made not, however, any scruple to develop her motives, for she vehemently inveighed against being introduced to such an acquaintance, squalling out, "She has writ against the émigrés!—she has writ against the Great Cause! O fie! fie! fie!"

When she had made these exclamations, and uttered these accusations, till the indulged vent to her rage began to cool it, she stopped of her own accord, and, finding no one spoke, looked as if she felt rather silly; while M. le Baron de M—, her very humble sposo, shrugged his shoulders. The pause was succeeded by an opening harangue from Lady Crewe, begun in a low and gentle voice, that seemed desirous to spare me what might appear an undue condescension, in taking any pains to clear me from so gross an attack. She gave, therefore, nearly in a whisper, a short character of me and of my conduct, of which I heard just enough to know that such was her theme; and then, more audibly, she proceeded to state, that far from writing against the emigrants, I had addressed an exhortation to all the ladies of Great Britain in their favour.

"Oh, then," cried Madame de M—, "it was somebody else—it was somebody else!"

And then she screamed out delightedly, "I'm so glad I spoke out, because of this explanation!—I'm so glad! never was so glad!" She now jumped about the room, quite crazily, protesting she never rejoiced so much at anything she had ever done in her life. But when she found her joy, like her assault, was all her own, she stopped short, astonished, I suppose, at my insensibility; and said to me, "How lucky I spoke out! the luckiest thing in the world! I'm so glad! A'n't you? Because of this éclaircissement."

"If I had required any ,claircissement," I drily began.

"O, if it was not you, then," cried she, "'twas Charlotte Smith."

Lady Crewe seemed quite ashamed that such a scene should pass where she presided, and Mr. Grattan quietly stole away.

Not quietly, nor yet by stealth, but with evident disappointment that her energies were not more admired, Madame la Baronne now called upon her attendant sposo, and strode off herself. I found she was a great heiress of Irish extraction and education, and that she had bestowed all her wealth upon this emigrant baron, who might easily merit it, when, besides his title, he gave her his patience and obsequiousness.

INQUIRIES AFTER THE DUCHESS D'ANGOULEME.

Some other friends of Lady Crewe now found her out, and she made eager inquiries amongst them relative to Madame la Duchesse d'Angoulˆme, but could gather no tidings. She heard, however, that there were great expectations of some arrivals down stairs, where two or three rooms were filled with company. She desired Mr. Grattan, junior, to descend into this crowd, and to find out where the duchess was to be seen, and when, and how.

He obeyed. But, when he returned, what was the provocation of Lady Crewe, what my own disappointment, to hear that the duchess was not arrived, and was not expected! She was at the house of Monsieur le Comte d'Artois, her father-in-law.

"Then what are we come hither for?" exclaimed her ladyship: "expressly to be tired to death for no purpose! Do pray, at least, Mr. Grattan, be so good as to see for my carriage, that we may go to the right house."

Mr. Grattan was all compliance, and with a readiness so obliging and so well bred that I am sure he is his father's true son in manners, though there was no opportunity to discover whether the resemblance extended also to genius. He was not, however, cheered when he brought word that neither carriage nor footman were to be found.

Lady Crewe then said he must positively go down, and make the Duc de Duras tell us what to do. In a few minutes he was with us again, shrugging his shoulders at his ill success. The king, Louis XVIII, (238) he said, was expected, and M. le Duc was preparing to receive him, and not able to speak or listen to any one.

Lady Crewe declared herself delighted by this information, because there would be an opportunity for having me presented to his majesty. "Go to M. de Duras," she cried, "and tell him Madame d'Arblay wishes it."

"For heaven's sake!" exclaimed I, "do no such thing! I have not the most distant thought of the kind! It is Madame la Duchesse d'Angoulˆme alone that I—"

"O, pho, pho!—it is still more essential to be done to the king—it is really important: so go, and tell the duke, Mr. Grattan, that Madame d'Arblay is here, and desires to be presented. Tell him 'tis a thing quite indispensable."

I stopped him again, and quite entreated that no such step might be taken, as I had no authority for presentation but to the duchess. However, Lady Crewe was only provoked at my backwardness, and charged Mr. Grattan not to heed me. "Tell the duke," she cried, "that Madame d'Arblay is our Madame de Stael! tell him we are as proud of our Madame d'Arblay as he can be of his Madame de Stael."

Off she sent him, and off I flew again to follow him and whether he was most amused or most teased by our opposing petitions, I know not - but he took the discreet side of not venturing again to return among us.

PREPARATIONS FOR THE PRESENTATIONS.

Poor Lady Crewe seemed to think I lost a place at Court, or perhaps a peerage, by my untamable shyness, and was quite vexed. Others came to her now, who said several rooms below were filled with expectant courtiers. Miss Grattan then earnestly requested me to descend with her, as a chaperon, that she might see something of what was going forwards.

I could not refuse so natural a request, and down we went, seeking one of the common, crowded rooms, that we might not intrude where there was preparation or expectation relative to the king.

And here, sauntering or grouping, meditating in silence or congratulating each other in coteries, or waiting with curiosity, or self-preparing for presentation with timidity, we found a multitude of folks in an almost unfurnished and quite unadorned apartment. The personages seemed fairly divided between the nation at home and the nation from abroad; the English and the French; each equally, though variously, occupied in expecting the extraordinary sight of a monarch thus wonderfully restored to his rank and his throne, after misfortunes that had seemed irremediable, and an exile that had appeared hopeless.

Miss Grattan was saluted, en passant, by several acquaintances, and amongst them by the son-in-law of her dear country's viceroy Lord Whitworth, the young Duke of Dorset; and Lady Crewe herself, too tired to abide any longer in her appropriated apartment, now descended.

We patrolled about, zig-zag, as we could; the crowd, though of very good company, having no chief or regulator, and therefore making no sort of avenue or arrangement for avoiding inconvenience. There was neither going up nor coming down; we were all hustled together, without direction and without object, for nothing whatsoever was present to look at or to create any interest, and our expectations were merely kept awake by a belief that we should know in time when and where something or somebody was to be seen.

For myself, however, I was much tormented during this interval from being named incessantly by Lady Crewe. My deep mourning, my recent heavy loss, and the absence and distance of my dear husband made me peculiarly wish to be unobserved. Peculiarly, I say; for never yet had the moment arrived in which to be marked had not been embarrassing and disconcerting to me, even when most flattering.

A little hubbub soon after announced something new, and presently a whisper was buzzed around the room of the "Prince de Cond,." His serene highness looked very much pleased—as no wonder—at the arrival of such a day; but he was so surrounded by all his countrymen who were of rank to claim his attention, that I could merely see that he was little and old, but very unassuming and polite. Amongst his courtiers were sundry of the French noblesse that were known to Lady Crewe and I heard her uniformly say to them, one after another; Here is Madame d'Arblay, who must be presented to the king.

Quite frightened by an assertion so wide from my intentions, so unauthorised by any preparatory ceremonies, unknown to my husband, and not, like a presentation to the Duchesse d'Angoulˆme, encouraged by my queen, I felt as if guilty of taking liberty the most presumptuous, and with a forwardness and assurance the most foreign to my character. Yet to control the zeal of Lady Crewe was painful from her earnestness, and appeared to be ungrateful to her kindness; I therefore shrunk back, and presently suffered the crowd to press between us so as to find myself wholly separated from my party. This would have been ridiculous had I been more happy - but in my then state of affliction, it was necessary to my peace.

ARRIVAL OF LOUIS XVIII.

Quite to myself, how I smiled inwardly at my adroit cowardice, and was contemplating the surrounding masses of people, when a new and more mighty hubbub startled me, and presently I heard a buzzing whisper spread throughout the apartment of "The king!—le roi!"

Alarmed at my strange situation, I now sought to decamp, meaning to wait for Lady Crewe up stairs: but to even approach the door was impossible. I turned back, therefore, to take a place by the window, that I might see his majesty alight from his carriage, but how great was my surprise when, just as I reached the top of the room, the king himself entered it at the bottom!

I had not the smallest idea that this was the chamber of audience; it was so utterly unornamented. But I now saw that a large fauteuil was being conveyed to the upper part, exactly where I stood, ready for his reception and repose.

Placed thus singularly, by mere accident, and freed from my fears of being brought forward by Lady Crewe, I felt rejoiced in so fair an opportunity of beholding the king of my honoured husband, and planted myself immediately behind, though not near to his prepared seat; and, as I was utterly unknown and must be utterly unsuspected, I indulged myself with a full examination. An avenue had instantly been cleared from the door to the chair, and the king moved along It slowly, slowly, slowly, rather dragging his large and weak limbs than walking; but his face was truly engaging; benignity was in every feature, and a smile beamed over them that showed thankfulness to providence in the happiness to which he was so suddenly arrived; with a courtesy, at the same time, to the spectators, who came to see and congratulate it, the most pleasing and cheering.

The scene was replete with motives to grand reflections and to me, the devoted subject of another monarch, whose melancholy alienation of mind was a constant source to me of sorrow, it was a scene for conflicting feelings and profound meditation.

THE PRESENTATIONS TO THE KING.

His majesty took his seat, with an air of mingled sweetness and dignity. I then, being immediately behind him, lost sight of his countenance, but saw that of every individual who approached to be presented. The Duc de Duras stood at his left hand, and was le grand maitre des cérémonies; Madame de Gouvello stood at his right side; though whether in any capacity, or simply as a French lady known to him, I cannot tell. In a whisper, from that lady, I learned more fully the mistake of the hotel, the Duchesse d'Angoulême never having meant to quit that of her beaupere, Monsieur le Comte d'Artois, in South Audley Street.

The presentations were short, and without much mark or likelihood. The men bowed low, and passed on; the ladies curtsied, and did the same. Those who were not known gave a card, I think, to the Duc de Duras, who named them; those of former acquaintance with his majesty simply made their obeisance.

M. de Duras, who knew how much fatigue the king had to go through, hurried every one on, not only with speed but almost with ill-breeding, to my extreme astonishment. Yet the English, by express command of his majesty, had always the preference and always took place of the French; which was an attention of the king in return for the asylum he had here found, that he seemed delighted to display,

Early in this ceremony came forward Lady Crewe, who being known to the king from sundry previous meetings, was not named; and only, after curtseying, reciprocated smiles with his majesty, and passed on. But instead of then moving off, though the duke, who did not know her, waved his hand to hasten her away, she whispered, but loud enough for me to hear, "Voici Madame d'Arblay; il faut qu'elle soit présentée." (239) She then went gaily off, without heeding me.

The duke only bowed, but by a quick glance recognised me, and by another showed a pleased acquiescence in the demand.

Retreat' now, was out of the question; but I so feared my position was wrong, that I was terribly disturbed, and felt hot and cold, and cold and hot, alternately, with excess of embarrassment. I was roused, however, after hearing for so long a time nothing but French, by the sudden sound of English. An address, in that language, was read to his majesty, which was presented by the noblemen and gentlemen of the county of Buckingham, congratulatory upon his happy restoration, and filled with cordial thanks for the graciousness of his manners, and the benignity of his conduct, during his long residence amongst them; warmly proclaiming their participation in his joy, and their admiration of his virtues. The reader was colonel Nugent, a near relation of the present Duke of Buckingham. But, if the unexpected sound of these felicitations delivered in English, roused and struck me, how much greater arose my astonishment and delight when the French monarch, in an accent of the most condescending familiarity and pleasure, uttered his acknowledgments in English also-expressing his gratitude for all their attentions, his sense of their kind interest in his favour, and his eternal remembrance of the obligations he owed to the whole county of Buckinghamshire, for the asylum and consolations he had found in it during his trials and calamities! I wonder not that Colonel Nugent was so touched by this reply, as to be led to bend the knee, as to his own sovereign, when the king held out his hand - for I myself, though a mere outside auditress, was so moved, and so transported with surprise by the dear English language from his mouth, that I forgot at once all my fears, and dubitations, and, indeed, all myself, my poor little self, in my pride and exultation at such a moment for my noble country. (240)

A FLATTERING ROYAL RECEPTION.

Fortunately for me, the Duc de Duras made this the moment for my presentation, and, seizing my hand and drawing me suddenly from behind the chair to the royal presence, he said, "Sire, Madame d'Arblay." How singular a change, that what, but the instant before, would have overwhelmed me with diffidence and embarrassment, now found me all courage and animation! and when his majesty took my hand—or, rather, took hold of my fist—and said, in very pretty English, "I am very happy to see you," I felt such a glow of satisfaction, that involuntarily, I burst forth with its expression, incoherently, but delightedly and irresistibly, though I cannot remember how. He certainly was not displeased, for his smile was brightened and his manner was most flattering, as he repeated that he was very glad to see me, and added that he had known me, "though without sight, very long: for I have read you—and been charmed with your books—charmed and entertained. I have read them often, I know them very well indeed; and I have long wanted to know you!"

I was extremely surprised, and not only at these unexpected compliments, but equally that my presentation, far from seeming, as I had apprehended, strange, was met by a reception of the utmost encouragement. When he stopped, and let go my hand, I curtsied respectfully, and was moving on; but he again caught my fist, and, fixing me, with looks of strong though smiling investigation, he appeared archly desirous to read the lines of my face, as if to deduce from them the qualities of my mind. His manner, however, was so polite and so gentle that he did not at all discountenance me: and though he resumed the praise of my little works, he uttered the panegyric with a benignity so gay as well as flattering, that I felt enlivened, nay, elevated, with a joy that overcame mauvaise honte.

The Duc de Duras, who had hurried on all others, seeing he had no chance to dismiss me with the same sans cérémonie speed, now joined his voice to exalt my satisfaction, by saying, at the next pause, "Et M. d'Arblay, sire, bon et brave, est un des plus devoués et fidèles serviteurs de votre majesté."(241)

The king with a gracious little motion of his head, and with eyes of the most pleased benevolence, expressively said, "Je le Crois." (242) And a third time he stopped my retiring curtsey, to take my hand.

This last stroke gave me such delight, for my absent best ami, that I could not again attempt to speak. The king pressed my hand—wrist I should say, for it was that he grasped, and then saying, "Bon jour, madame la comtesse," let me go.

My eyes were suffused with tears, from mingled emotions I glided nimbly through the crowd to a corner at the other end of the room, where Lady Crewe joined me almost instantly, and with felicitations the most amiably cordial and lively.

We then repaired to a side-board on which we contrived to seat ourselves, and Lady Crewe named to me the numerous personages of rank who passed on before us for presentation. But every time any one espied her and approached, she named me also; an honour to which I was very averse. This I intimated, but to no purpose; she went on her own way. The curious stares this produced, in my embarrassed state of spirits, from recent grief, were really painful to sustain; but when the seriousness of my representation forced her to see that I was truly in earnest in my desire to remain unnoticed, she was so much vexed, and even provoked, that she very gravely begged that, if such were the case, I would move a little farther from her; saying, "If one must be so ill-natured to people as not to name you, I had rather not seem to know who you are myself."

AN IMPORTANT LETTER DELAYED.

When, at length, her ladyship's chariot was announced, we drove to Great Cumberland-place, Lady Crewe being so kind as to convey me to Mrs. Angerstein. As Lady Crewe was too much in haste to alight, the sweet Amelia Angerstein came to the carriage to speak to her, and to make known that a letter had arrived from M. de la Chattre relative to my presentation, which, by a mistake of address, had not come in time for my reception. (244)

This note dispelled all of astonishment that had enveloped with something like incredulity my own feelings and perceptions in my unexpected presentation and reception. The king himself had personally desired to bestow upon me this mark of royal favour. What difficulty, what embarrassment, what confusion should I have escaped, had not that provoking mistake which kept back my letter occurred

M. D'ARBLAY ARRIVES IN ENGLAND.

Madame d"Arblay to Mrs. locke.) April 30, 1814. My own dearest friend must be the first, as she will be among the warmest, to participate in my happiness—M. d'Arblay is arrived. He came yesterday, quite unexpectedly as to the day, but not very much quicker than my secret hopes. He is extremely fatigued with all that has passed, yet well; and all himself, i.e, all that is calculated to fill my heart with gratitude for my lot in life. How would my beloved father have rejoiced in his sight, and in these glorious new events! (245)

A BRILLIANT ASSEMBLAGE.

(Madame d'Arblay to M. d'Arblay) June 18, 1814. Ah, mon ami! you are really, then, well?—really in Paris?— really without hurt or injury? What I have suffered from a suspense that has no name from its misery shall now be buried in restored peace, and hope, and happiness. With the most fervent thanks to providence that my terrors are removed, and that I have been tortured by only false apprehensions, I will try to banish from my mind all but the joy, and gratitude to heaven, that your safety and health inspire. Yet still, it is difficult to me to feel assured that all is well! I have so long been the victim to fear and anguish, that my spirits cannot at once get back their equilibrium. . . .

Hier j'ai quitt, ma retraite, très volontiers, pour (246) indulge myself with the sight of the Emperor of Russia. How was I charmed with his pleasing, gentle, and so perfectly unassuming air, manner, and demeanour! I was extremely gratified, also, by seeing the King of Prussia, who interests us all here, by a look that still indicates his tender regret for the partner of his hopes, toils, and sufferings, but not of his victories and enjoyments. It was at the queen's palace I saw them by especial and most gracious permission. The Prussian princes, six in number, and the young prince of Mecklenburg, and the Duchess of Oldenbourg, were of the party. All our royal dukes assisted, and the Princesses

Augusta and Mary. The Princess Charlotte looked quite beautiful. She is wonderfully improved. It was impossible not to be struck with her personal attractions, her youth, and splendour. The Duchess of York looked amongst the happiest; the King of Prussia is her brother.

M. D'ARBLAY ENTERS LOUIS XVIII.'S BODY-GUARD.

(Madame d'Arblay to Mrs. locke.) London, July, 1814. After a most painful suspense I have been at length relieved by a letter from Paris. It is dated the 18th of June, and has been a fortnight on the road. It is, he says, his fourth letter, and he had not then received one of the uneasy tribe of my own.

The consul-generalship is, alas, entirely relinquished, and that by M. d'Arblay himself, who has been invited into the garde du corps by the Duc de Luxembourg, for his own company an invitation he deemed it wrong to resist at such a moment; and he has since been named one of the officers of the garde du corps by the king, Louis XVIII, to whom he had taken the customary oath that very day—the 18th.

The season, however, of danger over, and the throne and order steadily re-established, he will still, I trust and believe, retire to civil domestic life. May it be speedily! After twenty years' lying by, I cannot wish to see him re-enter a military career at sixty years of age, though still young in all his faculties and feelings, and in his capacity of being as useful to others as to himself. There is a time, however, when the poor machine, though still perfect in a calm, is unequal to a storm. Private life, then, should be sought while it yet may be enjoyed; and M. d'Arblay has resources for retirement the most delightful, both for himself and his friends. He is dreadfully worn and fatigued by the last year; and he began his active services at thirteen years of age. He is now past sixty. Every propriety, therefore, will abet my wishes, when the king no longer requires around him his tried and faithful adherents. And, indeed, I am by no means myself insensible to what is so highly gratifying to his feelings as this mark of distinction bien plus honorable, cependant, (247) as he adds, than lucrative. . . . . .

(Madame d'Arblay to Mrs. Locke.) August 9, 1814. The friends of M. d'A. in Paris are now preparing to claim for him his rank in the army, as he held it under Louis XVI, of mareschal de Camp; and as the Duc de Luxembourg will present, in person, the demand au roi, there is much reason to expect it will be granted.

M. de Thuisy, who brought your letter from Adrienne, has given a flourishing account of M. d'A. in his new uniform, though the uniform itself, he says, is very ugly. But so sought is the company of the garde du corps du roi that the very privates, M. de T. says, are gentlemen. M. d'A. himself has only the place of sous-lieutenant; but it is of consequence sufficient, in that company, to be signed by the king, who had rejected two officers that had been named to him just before he gave his signature for M. d'A.

August 24, 1814. M. d'Arblay has obtained his rank, and the kind king has dated it from the aera when the original brevet was signed by poor Louis XVI in 1792.

[Here follows, in the original edition, a long letter in French from M. d'Arblay to his wife, dated "Paris, August 30, 1814." He records the enthusiasm manifested by the people of Paris on the arrival of the king and the Duchess of Angouleme, and the flattering reception given by the King to the Duke of Wellington. "After having testified his satisfaction at the sentiments which the duke had just expressed to him on the part of the prince regent, and told him that he infinitely desired to see the peace which had been so happily concluded, established on solid foundations, his majesty added, 'For

that I shall have need of the powerful co-operation of his royal highness. The choice which he has made of you, sir, gives me hope of it. He honours me. . . . I am proud to see that the first ambassador sent to me by England is the justly celebrated Duke of Wellington."' M. d'Arblay counts with certainty upon his wife's joining him in November, and ventures upon the unlucky assertion that " the least doubt of the stability of the paternal government, which has been so miraculously restored to us, is no longer admissible." ED.]

(214) Lyons rebelled against the Republic in the summer of 1793: against Jacobinism, in the first instance, and guillotined its jacobin leader, Chalier; later it declared for the king. After a long siege and a heroic defence, Lyons surrendered to the Republicans, October 9, 1793, and Fouch, was one of the commissioners sent down by the Convention to execute vengeance on the unfortunate town. A terrible vengeance was taken. "The Republic must march to liberty over corpses," said Fouch,; and thousands of the inhabitants were shot or guillotined. ED.

(215) The reputed assassin of the Duc d'Enghien. ["Assassin" is surely an unnecessarily strong term. The seizure of the Duke d'Enghien on neutral soil was illegal and indefensible: but he was certainly guilty of conspiring against the government of his country. He was arrested, by Napoleon's orders, in the electorate of Baden, in March, 1804; carried across the frontier, conveyed to Vincennes, tried by court-martial, condemned, and shot forthwith. ED.]

(216) The disastrous campaign in Russia. Napoleon left Paris on the 9th Of May, 1812. ED.

(217) "So that we divine her meaning."

(218) "Who are you?

"My name is d'Arblay."

"Are you married?"

"Yes."

"Where is your husband?"

"At Paris."

"Who is he?"

"He works in the Home Office."

"Why are you leaving him?"

(219) "You are English?"

(220) "Follow me!"

(221) "You do not think proper to follow me, then?"

(222) "I have nothing to do here, sir, I believe."

(223) "We shall see!" "

(224) "Young Man!"

(225) Her sister Charlotte, formerly Mrs. Francis. ED.

(226) The 20th of August. ED.

(227) Mrs Crewe's husband, John Crewe of Crewe Hall, cheshire, had been created a peer by the title of Baron Crewe of Crewe, in 1806. ED.

(228) An attempt to enter her apartment by a crazy woman.

(229) " Hunted out of France." The work in question was Madame de Stael's book on Germany (De l'Allemagne), which had been printed at Paris, and of which the entire edition had been seized by the police before its publication, on the plea that it contained passages offensive to the government. The authoress, moreover, was ordered to quit France, and joined her father at Coppet in Switzerland-ED.

(230) No doubt, for his uncle's school. Dr Charles Burney had left Hammersmith and established his school at Greenwich in 1793. ED.

(231) William Wilberforce, the celebrated philanthropist, was born at Htill in 1759. He devoted his life to the cause of the negro slaves; and to his exertions in Parliament were chiefly due the abolition of the slave trade in 1807, and the total abolition of slavery in the English colonies in 1833. He died in the latter year, thanking God that he "had seen the day in which England was willing to give twenty millions sterling for the abolition of slavery."ED.

(232) Narbonne was appointed by Napoleon, during the campaign of 1813, governor of the fortress of Torgau, on the Elbe. He defended the place with great resolution, even after the emperor had been obliged to retreat beyond the Rhine, but unhappily took the fever, and died there, November 17, 1813. ED.

(233) This proved to be a false report. General Victor de Latour Maubourg suffered the amputation of a leg at Leipzic, where he fought bravely in the service of the Emperor Napoleon. But he did not die of his wound, and we find him, in 1815, engaged in raising volunteers for the service of Louis XVIII. ED.

(234) Here is evidently a mistake as to the month: the date, no doubt, should be April 19. Dr. Burney died on the 12th of April, 1814. ED.

(235) Dr. Charles Burney. ED.

(236) Marie Thérése Charlotte, Duchess of Angouleme, was the daughter of Louis XVI and Marie Antoinette. She was born in 1778, and, after the execution of her father and mother she was detained in captivity in Paris until December, 1795, when she was delivered up to the Austrians in exchange for certain French prisoners of war. in 1799 she married her cousin, the Duke of Angouleme, son of Louis XVI's brother, the Count d'Artois, (afterwards Charles X. of France). On the return of Napoleon from Elba, the Duchess of Angoul^me so distinguished herself by her exertions and the spirit which she displayed in the king's cause, that Napoleon said of her "she was the only man in her family." ED.

(237) Henry Grattan, the Irish statesman, orator, and patriot. Already one of the most distinguished members of the Irish Parliament, he vigorously opposed the legislative union of Great Britain and Ireland in 1800. He sat in the Imperial Parliament as member for Dublin from 1806 until his death in 1820, in his seventy-fourth year. As an orator, Mr. Lecky writes of him, "He was almost unrivalled in crushing invective, in delineations of character, and in brief, keen arguments; carrying on a train of sustained reason he was not so happy." ED.

(238) Louis XVIII, formerly known as the Count of Provence, was the brother of the unfortunate Louis XVI. "Louis XVII" was the title given by the royalists to the young son of Louis XVI, who died, a prisoner, in June, 1795, some two years after the execution of his father. ED.

(239) "There is Madame d'Arblay; she must be presented."

(240) What a moment for her noble country, and what a subject for pride and exultation! Were we not very sure of Fanny's sincerity, it were scarcely possible to read with patience such passages as this and others similarly extravagant.

(241) Her common sense seems to take flight in the presence of royalty. ED.

(242) "And M. d'Arblay, Sire, good and brave, is one of your majesty's most devoted and faithful servants."

(243) "I believe it."

(244) This letter, addressed to Mrs. Angerstein, was to the effect that the Duchess of Angoulˆme would be very pleased to receive Madame d'Arblay, at 72 South Audley Street, between three and half-past three; and that the king (Louis XVIII.) also desired to see her, and would receive between four and five. ED.

(245) M. d'Arblay returned to France in the following June. ED.

(246) Yesterday I left my retreat, very willingly, to-"

(247) "Far more honorable, nevertheless—"

SECTION 24. (1815)

MADAME D'ARBLAY AGAIN IN FRANCE: BONAPARTE'S ESCAPE FROM ELBA.

[The two following sections contain Fanny's account of her adventures during the "Hundred Days " which elapsed between the return of Napoleon from Elba and his final downfall and abdication. This narrative may be recommended to the reader as an interesting supplement to the history of that period. The great events of the time, the triumphal progress of the emperor, the battles which decided his destiny and the fate of Europe, we hear of only at a distance, by rumour or chance intelligence; but our author brings vividly before us, and with the authenticity of personal observation, the disturbed state of the country, the suspense, the alarms, the distress occasioned by the war. To refresh our readers' memories, we give an epitome, as brief as possible, of the events to which Madame d'Arblay's narrative forms, as it were, a background.

When Napoleon abdicated the imperial throne, in April, 1814, the allied powers consented by treaty to confer upon him the sovereignty of the island of Elba, with a revenue of two million francs. To Elba he was accordingly banished, but the revenue was never paid. This disgraceful infringement of the treaty of Fontainebleau, joined to the accounts which he received of the state of public feeling in France, determined him to make the attempt to regain his lost empire. March 1, 1815, he landed at Cannes, with a few hundred men. He was everywhere received with the utmost enthusiasm. The troops sent to oppose him joined his standard with shouts of "Vive l'empereur!" March 20, he entered Paris in triumph, Louis XVIII having taken his departure the preceding evening, "amidst the tears and lamentations of several courtiers."(248)

The congress of the allied powers at Vienna proclaimed the emperor an outlaw, not choosing to remember that the treaty which they accused him of breaking, had been first violated by themselves. To his offers of negotiation, they replied not. The English army under the Duke of Wellington, the Prussian under Prince Blucher occupied Belgium; the Austrians and Russians were advancing in immense force towards the Rhine. Anxious to strike a blow before the arrival of the latter Napoleon left Paris for Belgium, June 12. His army amounted to about one hundred and twenty thousand men. On the 15th the fighting commenced, and the advanced guard of the Prussians was driven back. On the 16th, Blucher was attacked at Ligny, and defeated with terrible loss; but Marshal Ney was unsuccessful in an attack upon the combined English and Belgian army at Quatre Bras. Sunday, June 18, was the day of the decisive battle of Waterloo. After the destruction of his army, Napoleon hastened to Paris, but all hope was at an end. He abdicated the throne for the second time, proceeded to Rochefort, and voluntarily surrendered himself to Captain Maitland, of the English seventy-four, Bellerophon. He was conveyed to England, but was not permitted to land, and passed the few remaining years of his life a prisoner in the island of St. Helena. ED.]

AN INTERVIEW WITH THE DUCHESS OF ANGOULEME.

I come now to my audience with Madame, Duchesse d'Angoulême. (249) As I had missed, through a vexatious mistake, the honour she had herself intended me, of presentation in England, my own condescending royal mistress, Queen Charlotte, recommended my claiming its performance on my return to Paris. M. d'Arblay then consulted with the Vicomte d'Agoult, his intimate early friend, how to repair in France my English deprivation. M. d'Agoult was ,cuyer to her royal highness, and high in her confidence and favour. He advised me simply to faire ma cour as the wife of a superior officer in the garde du corps du roi, at a public drawing-room; but the great exertion and publicity, joined to the expense of such a presentation, made me averse, in all ways, to this proposal; and when M. d'Arblay protested I had not anything in view but to pay my respectful devoirs to her royal highness, M. d'Agoult undertook to make known my wish. It soon proved that this alone was necessary for its success, for madame la duchesse instantly recollected what had passed in England, and said she would name, with pleasure, the first moment in her power - expressing an impatience on her own part that an interview should not be delayed which had been desired by her majesty Queen Charlotte of England. . . .

I have omitted to mention that on the Sunday preceding, the Duchess d'Angoul^me, at Court, had deigned to tell my best friend that she was reading, and with great pleasure, Madame d'Arblay's last work. He expressed his gratification, and added that he hoped it was in English, as her altesse royale so well knew that language. No, she answered, it was the translation she read; the original she had not been able to procure. On this M. d'Arblay advised me to send a copy. I had none bound, but the set which had come back to me from my dear father. This, however, M. d'A. carried to the Vicomte d'Agoult, with a note from me in which, through the medium of M. d'Agoult, I supplicated leave from her royal highness to lay at her feet this only English set I possessed. In the most gracious manner possible, as the Vicomte told M. d'Arblay, her royal highness accepted the work, and deigned also to keep the billet. She had already, unfortunately, finished the translation, but she declared her intention to read the original.

Previously to my presentation, M. d'Arblay took me to the salon of the exhibition of pictures, to view a portrait of Madame d'Angouleme, that I might make some acquaintance with her face before the audience. This portrait was deeply interesting, but deeply melancholy.

ARRIVAL AT THE TUILERIES.

All these precautions taken, I went, at the appointed hour and morning, about the end of February, 1815, to the palace of the Tuileries, escorted by the most indulgent of husbands we repaired instantly to the apartment of the Duchesse de Serrent, who received us with the utmost politeness; she gave us our lesson how to proceed, and then delivered us over to some page of her royal highness.

We were next shown into a very large apartment. I communicated to the page a request that he would endeavour to make known to M. de Montmorency that I was arrived, and how much I wished to see him. In a minute or two came forth a tall, sturdy dame, who immediately addressed me by my name, and spoke with an air, that demanded my returning her compliment. I could not, however, recollect her till she said she had formerly met me at the Princess d'Henin's. I then recognised the dowager Duchesse de Duras, whom, in fact, I had seen last at the Princesse de Chimay's, in the year 1812, just before my first return to England; and had received from her a commission to acquaint the royal family of France that her son, the duke, had kept aloof from all service under Bonaparte, though he had been named in the gazettes as having accepted the place of chamberlain to the then emperor. Yet such was the subjection, at that time, of all the old nobility to the despotic power of that mighty ruler, that M. de Duras had not dared to contradict the paragraph.

She then said that her altesse royale was expecting me; and made a motion that I should pursue my way into the next room, M. d'Arblay no longer accompanying me. But before I disappeared she assured me that I should meet with a most gracious reception, for her altesse royale had declared she would see me with marked favour, if she saw no other English whatsoever; because Madame d'Arblay, she said, was the only English person who had been peculiarly recommended to her notice by the Queen of England.

In the next, which was another very large apartment, I was received by a lady much younger and more agreeable than Madame de Duras, gaily and becomingly dressed, and wearing a smiling air with a sensible face. I afterwards heard it was Madame de Choisy, who, a few years later, married the Vicomte d'Agoult.

Madame de Choisy instantly began some compliments, but finding she only disconcerted me, she soon said she must not keep me back, and curtsied me on to another room, into which she shut me.

A MISAPPREHENSION.

I here imagined I was to find M. de Montmorency, but I saw only a lady, who stood at the upper end of the apartment, and slightly curtsied, but without moving or speaking. Concluding this to be another dame de la cour, from my internal persuasion that ultimately I was to be presented by M. de Montmorency, I approached her composedly, with a mere common inclination of the head, and looked wistfully forward to the further door. She inquired politely after my health, expressing good-natured concern to hear it had been deranged, and adding that she was bien aise de me voir. (250) I thanked her, with some expression of obligation to her civility, but almost without looking at her, from perturbation lest some mistake had intervened to prevent my introduction, as I still saw nothing of M. de Montmorency.

She then asked me if I would not sit down, taking a seat at the same time herself. I readily complied; but was too much occupied with the ceremony I was awaiting to discourse, though she immediately began what was meant for a conversation. I hardly heard, or answered, so exclusively was my attention engaged in watching the door through which I was expecting a summons; till, at length, the following words rather surprised me (I must write them in English, for my greater ease, though they were spoken in French)—"I am quite sorry to have read your last charming work in French."

My eyes now changed their direction from the door to her face, to which I hastily turned my head, as she added,—"Puis-je le garder le livre que vous m'avez envoy,?"(251)

A DISCOVERY AND A RECTIFICATION.

Startled, as if awakened from a dream, I fixed her and perceived the same figure that I had seen at the salon. I now felt sure I was already in the royal presence of the Duchesse d'Angoulˆme, with whom I had seated myself almost cheek by jowl, without the smallest suspicion of my situation.

I really seemed thunderstruck. I had approached her with so little formality, I had received all her graciousness with so little apparent sense of her condescension, I had taken my seat, nearly unasked, so completely at my ease, and I had pronounced so unceremoniously the plain "vous," without softening it off with one single "altesse royale," that I had given her reason to think me either the most forward person in my nature, or the worst bred in my education, existing.

I was in a consternation and a confusion that robbed me of breath; and my first impulse was to abruptly arise, confess my error, and offer every respectful apology I could devise; but as my silence and strangeness produced silence, a pause ensued that gave me a moment for reflection, which represented to me that son altesse royale might be seriously hurt, that nothing in her demeanour had announced her, rank; and such a discovery might lead to increased distance and reserve in her future conduct upon other extra audiences, that could not but be prejudicial to her popularity, which already was injured by an opinion extremely unjust, but very generally spread, of her haughtiness. It was better, therefore, to be quiet, and to let her suppose that embarrassment, and English awkwardness and mauvaise honte, had occasioned my unaccountable manners. I preserved, therefore, my taciturnity, till, tired of her own, she gently repeated, "Puis-je le garder, cette copie que vous m'avez envoy?" civilly adding that she should be happy to read it again when she had a little forgotten it, and had a little more time.

I seized this fortunate moment to express my grateful acknowledgments for her goodness, with the most unaffected sincerity, yet scrupulously accompanied with all the due forms of profound respect.

What she thought of so sudden a change of dialect I have no means of knowing; hut I could not, for a long time afterwards, think of it myself with a grave countenance. From that time, however, I failed not to address her with appropriate reverence, though, as it was too late now to assume the distant homage pertaining, of course, to her very high rank, I insensibly suffered one irregularity to lead to, nay to excuse another; for I passed over all the etiquette d'usage, of never speaking but en r,ponse; and animated myself to attempt to catch her attention, by conversing with fullness and spirit upon every subject she began, or led to; and even by starting subjects myself, when she was silent. This gave me an opportunity of mentioning many things that had happened in Paris during my long ten years' uninterrupted residence, which were evidently very interesting to her. Had she become grave, or inattentive, I should have drawn back; but, on the contrary, she grew more and more ,veill,e, and her countenance was lighted up with the most encouraging approval.

CONVERSATION ON MADAME D'ARBLAY'S ESCAPE AND M. D'ARBLAY'S LOYALTY.

She was curious, she said, to know how I got over to England in the year 1812, having been told that I had effected my escape by an extraordinary disguise. I assured her that I had not escaped at all; as so to have done must have endangered the generous husband and father, who permitted mine and his son's departure. I had procured a passport for us both, which was registered in the ordinary manner, chez le ministre de police for foreign affairs; ches- one, I added, whose name I could not pronounce in her royal highness's hearing; but to whom I had not myself applied. She well knew I meant Savary, Duc de Rovigo, whose history with respect to the murdered Due d'Enghien has, since that period, been so variously related. I was then embarrassed, for I had owed my passport to the request of Madame d'A., who was distantly connected with Savary, and who had obtained it to oblige a mutual friend; I found, however, to my great relief, that the duchess possessed the same noble delicacy that renders all private intercourse with my own exemplary princesses as safe for others as it is honourable to myself; for she suffered me to pass by the names of my assistants, when I said they were friends who exerted themselves for me in consideration of my heavy grief, in an absence of ten years from a father whom I had left at the advanced age of seventy-five; joined to my terror lest my son should remain till he attained the period of the conscription, and be necessarily drawn into the military service of Bonaparte. And, indeed, these two points could alone, with all my eagerness to revisit my native land, have induced me to make the journey by a separation from my best friend.

This led me to assume courage to recount some of the prominent parts of the conduct of M. d'Arblay during our ten years' confinement, rather than residence, in France; I thought this necessary, lest our sojourn during the usurpation should be misunderstood. I told her, in particular, of three high military appointments which he had declined. The first was to be head of l',tat major of a regiment under a general whose name I cannot spell—in the army of Poland, a post of which the offer was procured for him by M. de Narbonne, then aide-de-camp to Bonaparte. The second was an offer, through General Gassendi, of being Commander of Palma Nuova, whither M. d'A. might carry his wife and son, as he was to have the castle for his residence, and there was no war with Italy at that time. The third offer was a very high one: it was no less than the command of Cherbourg, as successor to M. le Comte de la Tour Maubourg, who was sent elsewhere, by still higher promotion. Steady, however, invariably steady was M. d'Arblay never to serve against his liege sovereign, General Gassendi, one of the most zealous of his friends, contrived to cover up this dangerous rejection and M. d'Arblay continued in his humbler but far more' meritorious Office of sous Chef to one of the bureaux de l'interieur.

I had now the pleasure to hear the princess say, "Il a aqi bien noblement."(252) "For though he would take no part," I added, "la guerre, nor yet in the diplomatie, he could have no objection to making plans, arrangements, buildings, and so forth, of monuments, hospitals, and palaces; for at that period, palaces, like princes, were eleves tous les jours."(253)

She could not forbear smiling; and her smile, which is rare, is so peculiarly becoming, that it brightens her countenance into a look of youth and beauty.

"But why," I cried, recollecting myself, "should I speak French, when your royal highness knows English so well?"

"O, no!" cried she, shaking her head, "very bad!"

From that time, however, I spoke in my own tongue, and saw myself perfectly understood, though those two little words were the only English ones she uttered herself, replying always in French.

"Le roi," she said, "se rapelle tr s bien de vous avoir vu Londres."(254)

"O, je n'en doute nullement," (255) I replied, rather naŒvely, "for there passed a scene that cannot be forgotten, and that surprised me into courage to come forward, after I had spent the whole morning in endeavouring to shrink backward. And I could not be sorry—for I felt that his majesty could not he offended at a vivacity which his own courtesy to England excited."

The princess smiled, with a graciousness that assured me I had not mistaken the king's benevolence, of which she evidently partook.

THE PRINCE REGENT THE DUCHESS'S FAVOURITE.

The conversation then turned upon the royal family of England, and it was inexpressibly gratifying to me to hear her just appreciation of the virtues, the intellectual endowments, the sweetness of manner, and the striking grace of every one, according to their different character, that was mentioned. The prince regent, however, was evidently her favourite. The noble style in which he had treated her and all her family at his Carlton House fete, in the midst of their misfortunes, and while so much doubt hung against every chance of those misfortunes being ever reversed, did so much honour to his heart and proved so solacing to their woes and humiliation, that she could never revert to that public testimony of his esteem and goodwill without the most glowing gratitude.

"O!" she cried, "il a ét, parfait!" (256)

The Princesse Elise, (257) with whom she was in correspondence, seemed to stand next. "C'est elle," she said, "qui fait les honneurs de la famille royale, (258) and with a charm the most enlivening and delightful."

The conference was only broken up by a summons to the king's dinner. My audience, however, instead of a few minutes, for which the Duchesse de Duras had prepared me, was extended to three-quarters of an hour, by the watch of my kind husband, who waited, with some of his old friends whom he had joined in the palace, to take me home.

The princess, as she left me to go down a long corridor to the dining apartment, took leave of me in a manner the most gracious, honouring me with a message to her majesty the queen of England, of her most respectful homage, and with her kind and affectionate remembrance to all the princesses, with warm assurances of her eternal attachment. She then moved on, but again stopped when going, to utter some sentences most grateful to my ears, of her high devotion to the queen and deep sense of all her virtues. I little thought that this, my first, would prove also my last, meeting with this exemplary princess, whose worth, courage, fortitude, and piety are universally acknowledged, but whose powers of pleasing seem little known. After an opening such as this, how little could I foresee that this interview was to be a final one! . . . Alas! in a day or two after it had taken place, son altesse royale set out for Bordeaux. . . . And then followed the return of Bonaparte from Elba, and then the Hundred Days.

NARRATIVE OF MADAME D'ARBLAY'S FLIGHT FROM PARIS TO BRUSSELS

[The following Narrative was written some time after the events described took place. It is judged better to print it in a connected form: a few of the letters written on the spot being subsequently given.]

PREVAILING INERTIA ON BONAPARTE'S RETURN FROM ELBA.

I have no remembrance how I first heard of the return of Bonaparte from Elba. Wonder at his temerity was the impression made by the news, but wonder unmixed with apprehension. This inactivity of foresight was universal. A torpor indescribable, a species of stupor utterly indefinable, seemed to have enveloped the capital with a mist that was impervious. Everybody went about their affairs, made or received visits, met, and parted, without speaking, or, I suppose, thinking of this event as of a matter of any importance. My own participation in this improvident blindness is to myself incomprehensible. Ten years I had lived under the dominion of Bonaparte; I had been in habits of intimacy with many friends of those who most closely surrounded him; I was generously trusted, as one with whom information, while interesting and precious, would be inviolably safe-as one, in fact, whose honour was the honour of her spotless husband, and therefore invulnerable: well, therefore, by narrations the most authentic, and by documents the most indisputable, I knew the character of Bonaparte; and marvellous beyond the reach of my comprehension is my participation in this inertia. . . .

Thus familiar to his practices, thus initiated in his resources, thus aware of his gigantic ideas of his own destiny, how could I for a moment suppose he would re-visit France without a consciousness of success, founded upon some secret conviction that it was infallible, through measures previously arranged? I can only conclude that my understanding, such as it is, was utterly tired out by a long harass of perpetual alarm and sleepless apprehension. Unmoved, therefore, I remained in the general apparent repose which, if it were as real in those with whom I mixed as in myself, I now deem a species of infatuation. Whether or not M. d'Arblay was involved in the general failure of foresight I have mentioned, I never now can ascertain. To spare me any evil tidings, and save me from even the shadow of any unnecessary alarm, was the first and constant solicitude of his indulgent goodness.

At this period he returned to Paris to settle various matters for our Senlis residence. We both now knew the event that so soon was to monopolize all thought and all interest throughout Europe: but we knew it without any change in our way of life; on the contrary, we even resumed our delightful airings in the Bois de Boulogne, whither the general drove me every morning in a light calèche, of which he had possessed himself upon his entrance into the king's body-guard the preceding year.

Brief, however, was this illusion, and fearful was the light by which its darkness was dispersed. In a few days we hear that Bonaparte, whom we had concluded to be, of course, either stopped at landing and taken prisoner, or forced to save himself by flight, was, on the contrary, pursuing unimpeded his route to Lyons.

From this moment disguise, if any there had been, was over with the most open and frank of human beings, who never even transitorily practised it but to keep off evil, or its apprehension, from others. He communicated to me now his strong view of danger; not alone that measures might be taken to secure my safety, but to spare me any sudden agitation. Alas! none was spared to himself! More clearly than any one he anticipated the impending tempest, and foreboded its devastating effects. He spoke aloud and strenuously, with prophetic energy, to all with whom he was then officially associated but the greater part either despaired of resisting the torrent, or disbelieved its approach. What deeply interesting scenes crowd upon my remembrance, of his noble, his daring, but successless exertions! The king's body-guard immediately de service, (259) at that time, was the compagnie of the Prince de Poix, a man of the most heartfelt loyalty, but who had never served, and who was incapable of so great a command at so critical a juncture, from utter inexperience.

BONAPARTE'S ADVANCE: CONTEMPLATED MIGRATION FROM PARIS.

At this opening of the famous Hundred Days it seemed to occur to no one that Bonaparte would make any attempt upon Paris. It was calmly taken for granted he would speedily escape back to Elba, or remain in the south a prisoner, and it was only amongst deep or restless politicians that any inquietude was manifested with respect to either of these results. Madame la Princesse d'Henin, indeed, whom I was in the habit of frequently meeting, had an air and Manner that announced perturbation; but her impetuous spirit in politics kept her mind always in a state of energy upon public affairs.

But when Bonaparte actually arrived at Lyons the face of affairs changed. Expectation was then awakened—consternation began to spread; and report went rapidly to her usual work, of now exciting nameless terror, and now allaying even reasonable apprehension.

To me, every moment became more anxious. I saw General d'Arblay imposing upon himself a severity of service for which he had no longer health or strength, and imposing it only the more rigidly from the fear that his then beginning weakness and infirmities should seem to plead for indulgence. it was thus that he insisted upon going through the double duty of artillery officer at the barracks, and of officier superieur in the king's body-guards at the Tuileries. The smallest representation to M. le Duc de Luxembourg, who had a true value for him, would have procured a substitute: but he would not hear me upon such a proposition; he would sooner, far, have died at his post, He now almost lived either at the Tuileries or at the barracks. I only saw him when business or military arrangements brought him home; but he kindly sent me billets to appease my suspense every two or three hours.

The project upon Paris became at length obvious, yet its success was little feared, though the horrors of a civil war seemed inevitable. M. d'Arblay began to wish me away; he made various propositions for ensuring my safety; he even pressed me to depart for England to rejoin Alexander and my family: but I knew them to be in security, whilst my first earthly tie was exposed to every species of danger, and I besought him not to force me away. He was greatly distressed, but could not oppose my urgency. He procured me, however, a passport from M. le Comte de Jaucourt, his long attached friend, who was minister aux affaires étrangères (260) ad interim, while Talleyrand Perigord was with the Congress at Vienna.

I received it most unwillingly: I could not endure to absent myself from the seat of government, for I little divined how soon that government was to change its master. Nevertheless, the prudence of this preparatory measure soon became conspicuous, for the very following day I heard of nothing but purposed emigrations from Paris-retirement, concealment, embarrassments, and difficulties. My sole personal joy was that my younger Alexander was far away, and safely lodged in the only country of safety.

But, on the 17th, hope again revived. I received these words from my best friend, written on a scrap of paper torn from a parcel, and brought to me by his groom from the palace of the Tuileries, where their writer had passed the night mounting guard:—

"Nous avons de meilleures nouvelles. Je ne puis entrer dans aucun detail; mais sois tranquille, et aime bien qui t'aime uniquement. (261) God bless you."

This news hung upon the departure of Marshal Ney to meet Bonaparte and stop his progress, with the memorable words uttered publicly to the king, that he would bring him to Paris in an iron cage. The king at this time positively announced and protested that he would never abandon his throne nor quit his capital, Paris.

Various of my friends called upon me this day, all believing the storm was blowing over. Madame Chastel and her two daughters were calm, but, nevertheless, resolved to visit a small terre (262) which they possessed, till the metropolis was free from all contradictory rumours. Madame de Cadignan preserved her imperturbable gaiety and carelessness, and said she should stay, happen what might; for what mischief could befall a poor widow? Her sportive smiles and laughing eyes displayed her security in the power of her charms. Madame de Maisonneuve was filled with apprehensions for her brothers, who were all in highly responsible situations, and determined to remain in Paris to be in the midst of them. The Princesse d'Henin came to me daily to communicate all the intelligence she gathered from the numerous friends and connections through whom she was furnished with supplies. Her own plans were incessantly changing, but her friendship knew no alteration; and in every various modification of her intentions she always offered to include me in their execution, should my affairs reduce me, finally, to flight.

Flight, however, was intolerable to my thoughts. I weighed it not as saving me from Bonaparte - I could consider it only as separating me from all to which my heart most dearly clung. Madame d'Henin was undecided whether to go to the north or to the south-to Bordeaux or to Brussels; I could not, therefore, even give a direction to M. d'Arblay where I could receive any intelligence, and the body-guard of the king was held in utter suspense as to its destination. This, also, was unavoidable, since the king himself could only be guided by events.

The next day, the 18th of March, all hope disappeared. From north, from south, from east, from west, alarm took the field, danger flashed its lightnings, and contention growled its thunders: yet in Paris there was no rising, no disturbance, no confusion—all was taciturn suspense, dark dismay, or sullen passiveness. The dread necessity which had reduced the king, Louis XVIII, to be placed on his throne by foreigners, would have annihilated all enthusiasm of loyalty, if any had been left by the long underminings of revolutionary principles.

What a day was this of gloomy solitude! Not a soul approached me, save, for a few moments, my active Madame d'Henin, who came to tell me she was preparing to depart, unless a successful battle should secure the capital from the conqueror. I now promised that if I should ultimately be compelled to fly my home, I would thankfully be of her party; and she grasped at this engagement with an eagerness that gave proof of her sincere and animated friendship. This intimation was balm to the heart of my dearest partner, and he wished the measure to be executed and expedited; but I besought him, as he valued my existence, not to force me away till every other resource was hopeless.

GENERAL D'ARBLAY'S MILITARY PREPARATIONS.

He passed the day almost wholly at the barracks. When he entered his dwelling, in the Rue de Miromenil, it was only upon military business, and from that he could spare me scarcely a second. He was shut up in his library with continual comers and goers; and though I durst not follow him, I could not avoid gathering, from various circumstances, that he was now preparing to take the field, in full expectation of being sent out with his comrades of the guard, to check the rapid progress of the invader. I knew this to be his earnest wish, as the only chance of saving the king and the throne; but he well knew it was my greatest dread, though I was always silent upon the subject, well aware that while his honour was dearer to him than his life, my own sense of duty was dearer to me also than mine. While he sought, therefore, to spare me the view of his arms and warlike equipage and habiliments, I felt his wisdom as well as his kindness, and tried to appear as if I had no suspicion of his proceedings, remaining almost wholly in my own room, to avoid any accidental surprise, and to avoid paining him with the sight of my anguish. I masked it as well as I could for the little instant he had from time to time to spare me; but before dinner he left me entirely, having to pass the night cheval at the barracks, as he had done the preceding night at the Tuileries.

The length of this afternoon, evening, and night was scarcely supportable: his broken health, his altered looks, his frequent sufferings, and diminished strength, all haunted me with terror, in the now advancing prospect of his taking the field. And where? And how? No one knew! Yet he was uncertain whether he could even see me once more the next day! . . .

I come now to the detail of one of the most dreadful days of my existence, the 19th of March, 1815, the last which preceded the triumphant return of Bonaparte to the capital of France. Little, on its opening, did I imagine that return so near, or believe it would be brought about without even any attempted resistance. General d'Arblay, more in the way of immediate intelligence, and more able to judge of its result, was deeply affected by the most gloomy prognostics. He came home at about six in the morning, harassed, worn, almost wasted with fatigue, and yet more with a baleful view of all around him, and with a sense of wounded military honour in the inertia which seemed to paralyze all effort to save the king and his cause. He had spent two nights following armed on guard, one at the Tuileries, in his duty of garde du corps to the king; the other on duty as artillery captain at the barracks. He went to bed for a few hours; and then, after a wretched breakfast in which he briefly narrated the state of things he had witnessed and his apprehensions, be conjured me, in the most solemn and earnest manner, to yield to the necessity of the times, and consent to quit Paris with Madame d'Henin, should she ultimately decide to depart. I could not, when I saw his sufferings, endure to augment them by any further opposition; but never was acquiescence so painful! To lose even the knowledge whither he went, or the means of acquainting him whither I might go myself—to be deprived of the power to join him, should he be made prisoner—or to attend him, should he be wounded. . . . I could not pronounce my consent; but he accepted it so decidedly in my silence, that he treated it as arranged, and hastened its confirmation by assuring me I had relieved his mind from a weight of care and distress nearly intolerable. As the wife of an officer in the king's body-guard, in actual service, I might be seized, he thought, as a kind of hostage, and might probably fare all the worse for being also an Englishwoman.

He then wrote a most touching note to the Princesse d'Henin, supplicating her generous friendship to take the charge not only of my safety, but of supporting and consoling me.

After this, he hurried back to the Tuileries for orders, apparently more composed; and that alone enabled me to sustain my so nearly compulsory and so repugnant agreement. His return was speedy: he came, as he had departed, tolerably composed, for he had secured me a refuge, and he had received orders to prepare to march—to Melun, he concluded, to encounter Bonaparte, and to battle; for certain news had arrived of the invader's rapid approach. . . . at half-past two; at noon it was expected that the body-guard would be put in motion. Having told me this history, he could not spare me another moment till that which preceded his leaving home to join the Due de Luxembourg's company. He then came to me, with an air of assumed serenity, and again, in the most kindly, soothing terms, called upon me to give him an example of courage. I obeyed his injunction with my best ability-yet how dreadful was our parting! We knelt together in short but fervent prayer to heaven for each other's preservation, and then separated. At the door he turned back, and with a smile which, though forced, had inexpressible sweetness, he half gaily exclaimed, "Vive le roi!" I instantly caught his wise wish that we should part with apparent cheerfulness, and reechoed his words-and then he darted from my sight.

This had passed in an ante-room; but I then retired to my bedchamber, where, all effort over, I remained for some minutes abandoned to an affliction nearly allied to despair, though rescued from it by fervent devotion.

But an idea then started into my mind that yet again I might behold him. I ran to a window which looked upon the inward court-yard. There, indeed, behold him I did, but oh, with what anguish! just mounting his war-horse, a noble animal, of which he was singularly fond, but which at this moment I viewed with acutest terror, for it seemed loaded with pistols, and equipped completely for immediate service on the field of battle; while Deprez, the groom, prepared to mount another, and our cabriolet was filled with baggage and implements of war.

I could not be surprised, since I knew the destination of the general; but so carefully had he spared me the progress of his preparations, which he thought would be killing me by inches, that I had not the most distant idea he was thus armed and encircled with instruments of death-bayonets, lances, pistols, guns, sabres, daggers! what horror assailed me at the sight! I had only so much sense and self-control left as to crawl softly and silently away, that I might not inflict upon him the suffering of beholding my distress but when he had passed the windows, I opened them to look after him. The street was empty, the gay constant gala of a Parisian Sunday was changed into fearful solitude: no sound was heard, but that of here and there some hurried footstep, on one hand hastening for a passport to secure safety by flight; on the other, rushing abruptly from or to some concealment, to devise means of accelerating and hailing the entrance of the conqueror. Well in tune with this air of an impending crisis, was my miserable mind, which from grief little short of torture sunk, at its view, into a state of morbid quiet, that seemed the produce of feelings totally exhausted.

PREPARATIONS FOR FLIGHT: LEAVE-TAKINGS.

Thus I continued, inert, helpless, motionless, till the Princesse d'Henin came into my apartment. Her first news was, that Bonaparte had already reached Compiégne, and that to-morrow, the 20th of March, he might arrive in Paris, if the army of the king stopped not his progress. It was now necessary to make a prompt decision; my word was given, and I agreed to accompany her whithersoever she fixed to go. She was STILL hesitating; but it was settled I should join her in the evening, bag and baggage, and partake of her destination. . . .

I was now sufficiently roused for action, and my first return to conscious understanding was a desire to call in and pay every bill that might be owing, as well as the rent of our apartments up to the present moment, that no pretence might be assumed from our absence for disposing of our goods, books, or property of any description. As we never had any avoidable debts, this was soon settled; but the proprietor of the house was thunderstruck by the measure, saying, the king had reiterated his proclamation that he would not desert his capital. I could only reply that the general was at his majesty's orders, and that my absence Would be short. I then began collecting our small portion of plate, etc.; but while thus occupied, I received a message from Madame d'Henin, to tell me I must bring nothing but a small change of linen, and one band-box, as by the news she had just heard, she was convinced we should be back again in two or three days, and she charged me to be with her in an hour from that time. I did what she directed, and put what I most valued, that was not too large, into a hand-basket, made by some French prisoners in England, that had been given me by my beloved friend Mrs. Locke. I then swallowed, standing, my neglected dinner, and, with Madame Deprez, and my small allowance of baggage, I got into a fiacre, and drove to General Victor de la Tour Maubourg, to bid adieu to my dearest Madame de Maisonneuve, and her family.

It was about nine o'clock at night, and very dark. I sent on Madame Deprez to the princess, and charged her not to return to summon me till the last moment. The distance was small.

I found the house of the Marquis Victor de la Tour Maubourg in a state of the most gloomy dismay. No portier was in the way, but the door of the porte Cochère was ajar, and I entered on foot, no fiacre being ever admitted into les cours des hôtels. Officers and strangers were passing to and fro, some to receive, others to resign commissions, but all with quick steps, though in dead silence. Not a servant was in the way, and hardly any light; all seemed in disorder. I groped along till I came to the drawing-room, in which were several people, waiting for orders, or for an audience; but in no communication with each other, for here, also, a dismal taciturnity prevailed, from my own disturbance, joined to my short-sightedness, I was some time ere I distinguished Madame Victor de la Tour Maubourg, and when at last I saw her, I ventured not to address or to approach her. She was at a table, endeavouring to make some arrangement, or package, or examination, with papers and boxes before her, but deluged in tears, which flowed so fast that she appeared to have relinquished all effort to restrain them, and this was the more affecting to witness, as she is eminently equal and cheerful in her disposition. I kept aloof, and am not certain that she even perceived me. The general was in his own apartment, transacting military business of moment. But no sooner was I espied by my dearest Madame de Maisonneuve, than I was in her kind arms. She took me apart to reveal to me that the advance of the late emperor was still more rapid than its report. All were quitting Paris, or resigning themselves to passive submission. For herself, she meant to abide by whatever should be the destination of her darling brother Victor, who was now finishing a commission that no longer could be continued, of raising volunteers-for there was no longer any royal army for them to join! Whether the king would make a stand at the Tuileries, as he had unhappily promised, or whether he would fly, was yet unknown; but General Victor de Maubourg was now going to equip himself in full uniform, that he might wait upon his majesty in person, decidedly fixed to take his orders, be they what they might.

With danger thus before him, in his mutilated state, having undergone an amputation of the leg and thigh on the field of battle, who can wonder at the desolation of Madame Victor when he resolved to sustain the risk of such an offer? Presently, what was my emotion at the sudden and abrupt entrance into the room of an officer of the king's garde du corps! in the self-same uniform as that from which I had parted with such anguish in the morning! A transitory hope glanced like lightning upon my brain, with an idea that the body-guard was all at hand; but as evanescent as bright was the flash! The concentrated and mournful look of the officer assured me nothing genial was awaiting me - and when the next minute we recognized each other, I saw it was the Count Charles de la Tour Maubourg, the youngest brother of Madame de Maisonneuve; and he then told me he had a note for me from M. d'Arblay.

Did I breathe then? i think not! I grasped the paper in my hand, but a mist was before my eyes, and I could not read a word. Madame de Maisonneuve held a hurried conference with her brother, and then informed me that the body-guard was all. called out) the whole four companies, with their servants, equipage, arms and horses, to accompany and protect the king in his flight from Paris! But whither he would go, or with what intent, whether of battle or of escape, had not been announced. The Count Charles had obtained leave of absence for one hour to see his wife (Mademoiselle de Lafayette) and his children; but M. d'Arblay, who belonged to the artillery company, could not be spared even a moment. He had therefore seized a cover of a letter of M. de Bethizy, the commandant, to write me a few words.

I now read them, and found—

"Ma chère amie—Tout est perdu! je ne puis entrer dans aucun detail—de grèce, partez! le plutôt sera le mieux. A la vie et à la mort, A. D'A." (263)

Scarcely had I read these lines, when I was told that Madame d'Henin had sent me a summons. I now could but embrace my Madame de Maisonneuve in silence, and depart. . . .

ARISTOCRATIC IRRITABILITY.

Arrived at Madame la Princesse d'Henin's, all was in a perturbation yet greater than what I had left, though not equally afflicting. Madame d'Henin was so little herself, that every moment presented a new view of things, and urged her impatiently, nay imperiously, to differ from whatever was offered.

Now she saw instantly impending danger, and was for precipitate flight; now she saw fearless security, and determined not to move a step; the next moment all was alarm again, and she wanted wings for speed - and the next, the smallest apprehension awakened derision and contempt. I, who had never yet seen her but all that was elegant, rational, and kind, was thunderstruck by this effect of threatening evil upon her high and susceptible spirit. From manners of dignified serenity, she so lost all self-possession as to answer nearly with fury whatever was not acquiescent concurrence in her opinion: from sentiments of the most elevated nobleness she was urged, by every report that opposed her expectations, to the utterance of wishes and of assertions that owed their impulse to passion, and their foundation to prejudice; and from having sought, with the most flattering partiality, to attach me to her party, she gave me the severe shock of intimating that my joining her confused all er measures.

To change my plan now was impossible; my husband and my best friends knew me to be with her, and could seek me, or bestow information upon me, in no other direction; I had given up my own home, and to return thither, or to stay any where in Paris, was to constitute myself a prisoner: nevertheless, it was equally a sorrow and a violence to my feelings to remain with her another moment after so astonishing a reproach. Displeasure at it, however, subsided, when I found that it proceeded neither from weakened regard, nor a wanton abuse of power, but from a mind absolutely disorganized.

M. le Comte de Lally Tolendal, the Cicero of France, and most eloquent man of his day, and one of the most honourable, as well as most highly gifted, was, I now found, to be of our fugitive party. He was her admiring and truly devoted friend, and by many believed to be privately married to her. I am myself of that opinion, and that the union, on account of prior and unhappy circumstances, was forborne to be avowed. Certainly their mutual conduct warranted this conclusion. Nevertheless, his whole demeanour towards her announced the most profound respect as well as attachment; and hers to him the deepest consideration, with a delight in his talents amounting to an adoration that met his for her noble mind and winning qualities. She wanted, however, despotically to sway him; and little as he might like the submission she required, he commonly yielded, to avoid, as I conceive, the dangerous conjectures to which dissension might make them liable.

But at this moment, revolutionary terrors and conflicting sensations robbed each of them of that self-command which till now had regulated their public intercourse. She, off all guard, let loose alike the anxious sensibility and the arbitrary impetuosity of her nature: he, occupied with too mighty a trouble to have time or care for his wonted watchful attentions, heard alike her admonitions or lamentations with an air of angry, but silent displeasure; or, when urged too pointedly for maintaining his taciturnity, retorted her reproaches or remarks with a vehemence that seemed the echo of her own. Yet in the midst of this unguarded contention, which had its secret incitement, I doubt not, from some cruelly opposing difference of feelings—of ideas upon the present momentous crisis, nothing could be more clear than that their attachment to each other, though it could not subdue their violent tempers, was, nevertheless, the predominant passion of their souls.

THE COUNTESS D'AUCH'S COMPOSURE.

The turbulence of these two animated characters upon this trying occasion was strongly contrasted by the placid suffering and feminine endurance of Madame la Comtesse d'Auch, the daughter and sole heiress and descendant of M. de Lally. Her husband, like mine, was in the body-guard of Louis XVIII, and going, or gone, no one knew whither, nor with what intent; her estate and property were all near Bordeaux, and her little children were with her at Paris. The difficult task, in the great uncertainty of events, was now hers to decide, whether to seek the same refuge that her father and Madame Henin should resolve upon seeking, or whether to run every personal risk in trying to save her lands and fortune from confiscation, by traversing, with only her babies and servants, two or three hundred miles, to reach her chateau at Auch ere it might be seized by the conquering party. Quietly, and in total silence, she communed with herself, not mixing in the discourse, nor seeming to heed the disturbance around her; but, when at length applied to, her resolution, from her Own concentrated meditations, was fixedly taken, to preserve, if possible, by her exertions and courage, the property of her absent and beloved husband, for his hoped return and for her children. This steadiness and composure called not forth any imitation. M. de Lally breathed hard with absolute agony of internal debate; and Madame d'Henin now declared she was sure all would blow over in a false alarm, and that she would not hesitate any longer between Brussels and Bordeaux, but remain quietly in Paris, and merely sit up all night to be on the watch.

RUMOURS OF BONAPARTE'S NEAR APPROACH.

M. de Lally determined to go now in person to the Tuileries, to procure such information as might decide his shattered and irresolute friend. When he was gone, a total silence ensued. Madame d'Auch was absorbed in her fearful enterprise, and Madame d'Henin, finding no one opposed her (for my thoughts were with no one present), walked up and down the room, with hasty movement, as if performing some task. Various persons came and went, messengers, friends, or people upon business. She seized upon them all, impatiently demanding their news, and their opinions, but so volubly, at the same time, uttering her own, as to give them no time to reply, though as they left her, too much hurried themselves to wait her leisure for listening, she indignantly exclaimed against their stupidity and insensibility.

But what a new and terrible commotion was raised in her mind, in that of Madame d'Auch, and in mine, upon receiving a pencil billet from M. de Lally, brought by a confidential servant, to announce that Bonaparte was within a few hours' march of Paris! He begged her to hasten off, and said he would follow in his cabriolet when he had made certain arrangements, and could gain some information as to the motions of the king.

She now instantly ordered horses to her berlin, (264) which had long been loaded, and calling up all her people and dependants, was giving her orders with the utmost vivacity, when intelligence was brought her that no horses could now be had, the government having put them all in requisition. I was struck with horror. To be detained in Paris, the seat of impending conquest, and the destined capital of the conqueror—detained a helpless prisoner, where all would be darkly unknown to me, where Truth could find no entrance, Falsehood no detection—where no news could reach me, except news that was fatal—oh! what dire feelings were mine at this period!

Madame d'Auch, who had taken her precautions, instantly though sadly, went away, to secure her own carriage, and preserve her little babies.

DEPARTURE FROM PARIS AT NIGHT TIME.

Madame d'Henin was now almost distracted, but this dreadful prospect of indefinite detention, with all the horrors of captivity, lasted not long: Le Roy, her faithful domestic from his childhood, prevailed upon some stable friend to grant the use of his horses for one stage from Paris, and the berlin and four was at the porte Cochère in another moment, The servants and dependants of Madame d'Henin accompanied her to the carriage in tears; and all her fine qualities were now unmixed, as she took an affectionate leave of them, with a sweetness the most engaging, suffering the women to kiss her cheek, and smiling kindly on the men, who kissed her robe. Vivacity like hers creates alarm, but, in France, breeds no resentment; and where, like hers, the character is eminently noble and generous, it is but considered as a mark of conscious rank, and augments rather than diminishes personal devotion.

We now rushed into the carriage, averse, yet eager, between ten and eleven o'clock at night, 19th March, 1815. As Madame d'Henin had a passport for herself, et sa famille, we resolved to keep mine in reserve, in case of accidents or separation, and only to produce hers, while I should be included in its privileges. The decision for our route was for Brussels; the femme de chambre of Madame d'Henin-within, and the valet, Le Roy, outside the carriage, alone accompanied us, with two postilions for the four horses. Madame d'Henin, greatly agitated, spoke from time to time, though rather in ejaculations upon our flight, its uncertainties and alarms, than with any view to conversation; but if she had any answer, it was of simple acquiescence from her good and gentle femme de chambre; as to me . . . I could not utter a word—my husband on his war-horse—his shattered state of health—his long disuse to military service, yet high-wrought sense of military honour—all these were before me. I saw, heard, and was conscious of nothing else, till we arrived at Le Bourget, (265) a long, straggling, small town. And here, Madame d'Henin meant to stop, or at least change horses.

A HALT AT LE BOURGET.

But all was still, and dark, and shut up. It was the dead of night, and no sort of alarm seemed to disturb the inhabitants of the place. We knocked at the first inn: but after waiting a quarter of an hour, some stable-man came Out to say there was not a room vacant. The same reply was with the same delay given us at two other inns; but, finally, we were more successful, though even then we could obtain only a single apartment, with three beds. These we appropriated for Madame d'Henin, myself, and her maid; and the men-servants were obliged to content themselves with mattresses in the kitchen. The town, probably, was filled with fugitives from Paris.

A supper was directly provided, but Madame d'Henin, who now again repented having hurried off, resolved upon sending her faithful Le Roy back to the metropolis, to discover whether it were positively true that the king had quitted it, He hired a horse, and we then endeavoured to repose . . . but oh, how far from me was all possibility of obtaining it!

About three in the morning M. de Lally overtook us. His information was immediately conveyed to the Princesse d'Henin. It was gloomily affrighting. The approach of Bonaparte was wholly unresisted; all bowed before, that did not spring forward to meet him.

Le Roy returned about six in the morning. The king, and his guards, and his family, had all suddenly left Paris, but whither had not transpired. He was preceded, encircled, and followed by his four companies of body-guards.

Horror and distress at such a flight and such uncertainty were not mine only, though circumstances rendered mine the most poignant; but M. de Lally had a thousand fears for the excellent and loved husband of his daughter, M. le Comte d'Auch; and Madame d'Henin trembled, for herself and all her family, at the danger of the young Hombert La Tour du Pin.

THE JOURNEY RESUMED.

No longer easy to be so near Paris, we hastily prepared to get on for Brussels, our destined harbour. M. de Lally now accompanied us, followed by his valet in a cabriolet. Our journey commenced in almost total silence on all parts: the greatness of the change of government thus marvellously effecting, the impenetrable uncertainty of coming events, and our dreadful ignorance of the fate of those most precious to us, who were involved in the deeds and the consequences of immediate action, filled every mind too awfully for speech and our sole apparent attention was to the passengers we overtook, or by whom we were overtaken.

These were so few, that I think we could not count half a dozen on our way to Senlis, and those seemed absorbed in deadly thought and silence, neither looking at us, nor caring to encounter our looks. The road, the fields, the hamlets, all appeared deserted. Desolate and lone was the universal air. I have since concluded that the people of these parts had separated into two divisions; one of which had hastily escaped, to save their lives and loyalty, while the other had hurried to the capital to greet the conqueror, for this was Sunday, (266) the 20th of March.

Oh, what were my sensations on passing through Senlis Senlis, so lately fixed for my three months' abode with my general, during his being de service. When we stopped at a nearly empty inn, during the change of horses, I inquired after Madame Le Quint, and some other ladies who had been prepared to kindly receive me—but they were all gone! hastily they had quitted the town, which, like its environs, had an air of being generally abandoned.

The desire of obtaining intelligence made Madame d'Henin most unwilling to continue a straightforward journey, that must separate her more and more from the scene of action. M. de Lally wished to see his friend the young Duc d'Orleans, (267) who was at Peronne, with his sister and part of his family; and he was preparing to gratify this desire, when a discussion relative to the danger of some political misconstruction, the duke being at that time upon ill terms with Monsieur, Comte d'Artois, (268) made him relinquish his purpose. We wandered about, however, I hardly know where, save that we stopped from time to time at small hovels in which resided tenants of the Prince or of the Princess de Poix, who received Madame d'Henin with as much devotion of attachment as they could have done in the fullest splendour of her power to reward their kindness; though with an entire familiarity of discourse that, had I been new to French Customs, would have seemed to me marks of total loss of respect. But after a ten years' unbroken residence in France, I was too well initiated in the ways of the dependants Upon the great belonging to their own tenantry, to make a mistake so unjust to their characters. We touched, as I think, at Noailles, at St. just, at Mouchy, and at Poix—but I am only sure we finished the day by arriving at Roy, where still the news of that day was unknown. What made it travel so slowly I cannot tell; but from utter dearth of all the intelligence by which we meant to be guided, we remained, languidly and helplessly, at Roy till the middle of the following Monday, (269) the 21st March.

About that time some military entered the town and our inn. We durst not ask a single question, in our uncertainty to which side they belonged; but the four horses were hastily ordered, since to decamp seemed what was most necessary. But Brussels was no longer the indisputable spot, as the servants Overheard some words that implied a belief that Louis XVIII was quitting France to return to his old asylum, England. It was determined, therefore, though not till after a tumultuous debate between the princess and M. de Lally, to go straight to Amiens, where the prefect, M. Lameth, was a former friend, if not connection, of the princess.

We had now to travel by a cross-road, and a very bad one, and it was not till night that we arrived at the suburbs. It was here first we met with those difficulties that announced, by vigilance with disturbance, a kind of suspended government; for the officers of the police who demanded our passports were evidently at a loss whether to regard them as valid or not. Their interrogatories, meanwhile, were endless; and, finally, they desired us, as it was so late and dark, to find ourselves a lodging in the suburbs, and not enter the city of Amiens till the next morning.

Clouded as were alike our perceptions and our information, we could not but be aware of the danger of to-morrow, when our entrance might be of a sort to make our exit prohibited. Again followed a tumultuous debate, which ended in the hazardous resolve of appealing to the prefect and casting ourselves upon his protection. This appeal ended all inquisition: we were treated with deference, and accommodated in a decent room, while the passports of Madame d'Henin and of M. de Lally were forwarded to the prefecture. We remained here some time in the utmost stillness, no one pronouncing a word. We knew not who might listen, nor with what ears! But far from still was all within, because far from confident how the prefect might judge necessary to arrest, or to suffer our proceeding further. The answer was, at length, an order to the police officers to let us enter the city and be conducted to an hotel named by M. Lameth.

A SUPPER AT AMIENS WITH THE PREFECT.

We had an immensely long drive through the city of Amiens ere we came to the indicated hotel. But here Madame d'Henin found a note that was delivered to her by the secretary of the prefecture, announcing the intention of the prefect to have the honour of waiting upon her; and when M. Lameth was announced, M. de Lally and I retired to our several chambers.

Her téte a téte with him was very long, and ended in a summons to M. de Lally to make it a trio. This interview was longer still, and my anxiety for the news with which it might terminate relative to the king, the body-guard, and our detention or progression, was acute. At length I also was summoned.

Madame d'Henin came out to me upon the landing-place, hastily and confusedly, to say that the prefect did not judge proper to receive her at the prefecture, but that he would stay and sup with her, and that I was to pass for her premiere femme de chambre, as it would not be prudent to give in my name, though it had been made known to M. Lameth; but the wife of an officer so immediately in the service of the king must not be specified as the host of a prefect, if that prefect meant, to yield to the tide of a new government. Tide? Nay, torrent it was at this moment; and any resistance that had not been previously organized, and with military force, must have been vain. I made, however, no inquiry. I was simply acquiescent; and, distantly following Madame d'Henin, remained at the end of the room while the servants and the waiters adjusted matters for supper.

In a situation of such embarrassment I never before was placed. I knew not which way to look, nor what to do. Discovery at such a crisis might have been fatal, as far as might hang upon detention; and detention, which would rob me of all means of hearing of M. d'Arblay, should I gather what was his route, and be able to write to him, was death to my peace. I regretted I had not demanded to stay in another room; but, in such heart-piercing moments, to be in the way of intelligence is the involuntary first movement.

When all was arranged, and Madame d'Henin was seated M. de Lally set a chair for me, slightly bowing to me to take it. I complied, and supper began. I was helped, of course the last, and not once spoken to by any body. The repast' was not very gay, yet by no means dejected. The conversation was upon general topics, and M. de Lameth was entirely master of himself, seeming wholly without emotion.

I was afterwards informed that news had just reached him, but not officially, that Bonaparte had returned to Paris. Having heard, therefore, nothing from the new government he was able to act as if there were none such, and he kindly obliged Madame d'Henin by giving her new passports, which should the conquest be confirmed, would be safer than passports from the ministers of Louis XVIII. at Paris. . . .

M. Lameth could not, however, answer for retaining his powers, nor for what might be their modification even from hour to hour: he advised us, therefore, by no means to risk his being either replaced or restrained, but to get on as fast as possible with his passports while certain they were efficient. He thought it safer, also, to make a circuit than to go back again to the high-road we had quitted. Our design of following the king, whom we imagined gaining the sea-coast to embark for England, was rendered abortive from the number of contradictory accounts which had reached M. Lameth as to the route he had taken. Brussels, therefore, became again our point of desire; but M. Lameth counselled us to proceed for the moment to Arras, where M. — (I forget his name) would aid us either to proceed, or to change, according to circumstances, our destination. Not an instant, however, was to be lost, lest M. Lameth should be forced himself to detain us. Horses, therefore, he ordered for us, and a guide across the country for Arras.

I learnt nothing of this till we re-entered our carriage. The servants and waiters never quitted the room, and the prefect had as much his own safety to guard from ill construction or report as ours. Madame d'Henin, though rouged the whole time with confusion, never ventured to address a word to me. It was, indeed, more easy to be silent than to speak to me either with a tone of condescension or of command, and any other must have been suspicious. M. de Lally was equally dumb, but active in holding out every plat to me, though always looking another way. M. Lameth eyed me with curiosity, but had no resource against surmise save that adopted by Madame d'Henin. However, he had the skill and the politeness to name, in the course of the repast, M. d'Arblay, as if accidentally, yet with an expression of respect and distinction, carefully, as he spoke, turning his eyes from mine, though it was the only time that, voluntarily, he would have met them.

The horses being ready, M. Lameth took leave.

RECEPTION AT THE PREFECTURE AT ARRAS.

It was now about eleven at night. The road was of the roughest sort, and we were jerked up and down the ruts so as with difficulty to keep our seats: it was also very dark, and the drivers could not help frequently going out of their way, though the guide, groping on upon such occasions on foot, soon set them right. It was every way a frightful night. Misery, both public and private, oppressed us all, and the fear of pursuit and captivity had the gloomy effect of causing general taciturnity; so that no kind voice, nor social suggestion, diverted the sense of danger, or excited one of hope.

At what hour we arrived at Arras on Wednesday, the 22nd March, I cannot tell; but we drove straight to the prefecture, a very considerable mansion, surrounded with spacious grounds and gardens, which to me, nevertheless, had a bleak, flat, and desolate air, though the sun was brightly shining. We stopped at the furthest of many gates on the high road, while madame sent in to M. — (I forget his name) the note with which we had been favoured by M. Lameth. The answer was a most courteous invitation of entrance, and the moment the carriage stopped at the great door of the portico, the prefect, M. —, hastened out to give Madame d'Henin le bras. He was an old soldier and in full uniform, and he came to us from a battalion drawn out in array on one side the park. Tall, and with still a goodly port, though with a face worn and weather-beaten, he had the air of a gentleman as well as of a general officer and the open and hospitable smile with which he received the princess, while bareheaded and baldheaded he led her into his palace, diffused a welcome around that gave an involuntary cheeriness even to poor dejected me. How indescribably gifted is the human face. Yes, divine," in those who are invested with power, to transmit or to blight comfort even by a glance!

As Madame d'Henin demanded a private audience, I know not what passed; but I have reason to believe we were the first who brought news to Arras that approached to the truth of the actual position of Paris. M. Lameth, for Political reasons, had as studiously avoided naming M. de Lally as myself in his note, but M. de Lally was treated by the mistress of the house with the distinction due to a gentleman travelling with the princess; and as to me, some of the younger branches of the family took me under their protection, and very kind they were, showing me the garden, library, and views of the surrounding country.

A CHEERFUL DEJEUNER SOMEWHAT RUFFLED.

Meanwhile, an elegant breakfast was prepared for a large company, a review having been ordered for that morning, and several general officers being invited by the prefect. This repast had a cheerfulness that to me, an Englishwoman, was unaccountable and is indefinable. The king had been compelled to fly his capital, no one knew where he was seeking shelter; no one knew whether he meant to resign his crown in hopeless inaction, or whether to contest it in sanguinary civil war. Every family, therefore, with its every connection in the whole empire of the French, was involved in scenes upon which hung prosperity or adversity, reputation or disgrace, honour or captivity; yet at such a crisis the large assembled family met with cheerfulness, the many guests were attended to with politeness, and the goodly fare of that medley of refreshments called a dejeuner in France was met with appetites as goodly as its incitements.

This could not be from insensibility; the French are anything rather than insensible: it could not be from attachment to Bonaparte, the prefect loudly declaring his devotion to Louis XVIII. I can only, therefore, attribute it to the long revolutionary state of the French mind, as well as nation, which had made it so familiar to insurrection, change, and incertitude, that they met it as a man meets some unpleasant business which he must unavoidably transact, and which, since he has no choice to get rid of, he resolves to get through to the best of his ability.

We were still, however, smelling sweet flowers and regaled with fine fruits, when this serenity was somewhat ruffled by the arrival of the commander of the forces which had been reviewed, or destined for review, I know not which. He took the prefect aside, and they were some time together. He then, only bowing to the ladies of the house, hastened off. The prefect told us the news that imperfectly arrived was very bad, but he hoped a stand would be made against any obstinate revolt; and he resolved to assemble every officer and soldier belonging to his government, and to call upon each separately to take again, and solemnly, his oath of allegiance. While preparing for this ceremony the commander again returned, and told him he had positive information that the. defection was spreading, and that whole troops and' companies were either sturdily waiting in inaction, or boldly marching on to meet the conqueror.

A LOYAL PREFECT.

Our table was now broken up, and we were wishing to depart ere official intimation from the capital might arrest our further progress but our horses were still too tired, and no others were to be procured. We became again very uneasy, and uneasiness began to steal upon all around us. The prefect was engaged in perpetual little groups of consultation, chiefly with general officers, who came and went with incessant bustle, and occasionally and anxiously were joined by persons of consequence of the vicinity. The greater the danger appeared, the more intrepidly the brave old prefect declared his loyalty; yet he was advised by all parties to give up his scheme till he knew whether the king himself made a stand in his own cause.

He yielded reluctantly; and when Madame d'Henin found his steady adhesion to his king, she came up to him and said, that, finding the firmness of his devotion to Louis XVIII, she was sure it would give him pleasure to know he had at that moment under his roof the wife of a general officer in the actual escort of his majesty. He instantly came to me with a benevolent smile, and we had a conversation of deep Interest upon the present state of things. I had the heartfelt satisfaction to find that my honoured husband was known to him, not alone by reputation, but personally; and to find that, and to hear his praise, has always been one and the same thing. Alas! those sounds on these sad ears vibrate no more!.....At length, however, about noon, we set off, accompanied by the prefect and all his family to our carriage.

EMBLEMS OF LOYALTY AT DOUAY.

At Douay, we had the satisfaction to see still stronger outward marks of attachment to the king and his cause, for in every street through which we passed, the windows were decked with emblems of faithfulness to the Bourbon dynasty, white flags, or ribands, or, handkerchiefs. All, however, without commotion, all was a simple manifestation of respect. No insurrection was checked, for none had been excited—no mob was dispersed, for scarcely any one seemed to venture from his house.

Our intention was to quit the French territory that night, and sleep in more security at Tournay; but the roads became so bad, and our horses grew so tired, that it was already dark before we reached Orchies. M. de Lally went on from Douay in his cabriolet, to lighten our weight, as Madame d'Henin had a good deal of baggage. We were less at our ease, while thus perforce travelling slower, to find the roads, as we proceeded from Douay, become more peopled. Hitherto they had seemed nearly a blank. We now began, also, to be met, or to be overtaken, by small parties of troops. We naturally looked out with earnestness on each side, to discover to whom or to what they belonged: but the compliment of a similar curiosity on their part was all we gained. Sometimes they called out a "Vive—" but without finishing their wish; and we repeated—that is, we bowed to—the same hailing exclamation, without knowing or daring to inquire its purport.

STATE OF UNCERTAINTY AT ORCHIES.

At Orchies, where we arrived rather late in the evening, we first found decided marks of a revolutionary state of things. No orders were sent by either party. The king and his government were too imminently in personal danger to assert their rights, or retain their authority for directing the provinces; Bonaparte and his followers and supporters were too much engrossed by taking possession of the capital, and too uncertain of their success, to try a power which had as yet no basis, or risk a disobedience which they had no means to resent. The people, as far as we could see or learn seemed passively waiting the event; and the constituted authorities appeared to be self-suspended from their functions till the droit des plus fort (270) should ascertain who were their masters. Nevertheless, while we waited at Orchies for horses, news arrived by straggling parties which, though only whispered, created evidently some disturbance - a sort of wondering expectation soon stared from face to face, asking by the eye what no one durst pronounce by the voice; what does all this portend? and for what ought we to prepare?

A MISHAP ON THE ROAD.

it was past eleven o'clock, and the night was dark and damp, ere we could get again into our carriages but the increasing bustle warned us off, and a nocturnal journey had nothing to appal us equally with the danger of remaining. We eagerly, therefore, set off, but we were still in the suburbs of Orchies, when a call for help struck our ears, and the berlin stopped. It was so dark, we could not at first discern what was the matter, but we soon found that the carriage of M. de Lally had broken down. Madame d'Henin darted out of the berlin with the activity of fifteen. Her maid accompanied her, and I eagerly followed.

Neither M. de Lally nor his man had received any injury, but the cabriolet could no longer proceed without being repaired. The groom was sent to discover the nearest blacksmith, who came soon to examine the mischief, and declared that it could not be remedied before daylight. We were forced to submit the vehicle to his decree, but our distress what to do with ourselves was now very serious. We knew there was no accommodation for us at the inn we had 'just quitted, but that of passing the night by the kitchen fire, exposed to all the hazards of suspicious observation upon our evident flight. To remain upon the high road stationary in our berlin might, at such a period, encompass us with dangers yet more serious.

A KINDLY OFFER OF SHELTER.

We were yet unresolved, when a light from the windows of a small house attracted our attention, and a door was opened, at which a gentlewoman somewhat more than elderly stood, with a candle in her hand, that lighted up a face full of benevolence, in which was painted strong compassion on the view of our palpable distress. Her countenance encouraged us to approach her, and the smile with which she saw us come forward soon accelerated our advance; and when We reached her threshold, she waited neither for solicitation nor representation, but let us into her small dwelling without a single question, silently, as if fearful herself we might be observed, shutting the street door before she spoke. She then lamented, as we must needs, she said, be cold and comfortless, that she had no fire, but added that she and her little maid were in bed and asleep, when the disturbance on the road had awakened her, and made her hasten up, to inquire if any one were hurt. We told as much of our Story as belonged to our immediate situation, and she then instantly, assured us we should be welcome to stay in her house till the cabriolet was repaired.

Without waiting for our thanks, she then gave to each a chair, and fetched great plenty of fuel, with which she made an ample and most reviving fire, in a large stove that was placed in the middle of the room. She had bedding, she said, for two, and begged that, when we were warmed and comforted, we would decide which of us most wanted rest. We durst not, however, risk, at such a moment, either being separated or surprised; we entreated her, therefore, to let us remain together, and to retire herself to the repose her humanity had thus broken. But she would not leave us. She brought forth bread, butter, and cheese, with wine and some other beverage, and then made us each a large bowl of tea. And when we could no longer partake of her hospitable fare, she fetched us each a pillow, and a double chair, to rest our heads and our feet.

ALARMED BY POLISH LANCERS.

Thus cheered and refreshed, we blessed our kind hostess, and fell into something like a slumber, when we were suddenly roused by the sound of trumpets, and warlike instruments, and the trampling of many horses, coming from afar, but approaching with rapidity. We all started up alarmed, and presently the group, perceiving, I imagine, through the ill-closed shutters, some light, stopped before the house, and battered the door and the window, demanding admission. We hesitated whether to remain or endeavour to conceal ourselves but our admirable hostess bid us be still, while, calm herself, she opened the street door, where she parleyed with the party, cheerfully and without any appearance of fear, and told them she had no room for their accommodation, because she had given up even her own bed to some relations who were travelling, she gained from them an applauding huzza and their departure. She then informed us they were Polish lancers, and that she believed they were advancing to scour the country in favour of Bonaparte. She expressed herself an open 'and ardent loyalist for the Bourbons, but said she had no safety except in submitting, like all around her, to the stronger powers.

Again, by her persuasion, we sought to compose ourselves; but a second party soon startled us from our purpose, and from that time we made no similar attempt. I felt horrified at every blast of the trumpet, and the fear of being made prisoner, or pillaged, assailed me unremittingly.

At about five o'clock in the morning our carriages were at the door. We blessed our benevolent hostess, took her name and address, that we might seek some means of manifesting our gratitude, and then quitted Orchies. For the rest of our journey till we reached the frontiers, we were annoyed with incessant small military groups or horsemen; but though suspiciously regarded, we were not stopped. The fact is, the new government was not yet, in those parts, sufficiently organised to have been able to keep if they had been strong enough to detain us. But we had much difficulty to have our passports honoured for passing the frontiers; and if they had not been so recently renewed at Amiens, I think it most probable our progress would have been impeded till new orders and officers were entitled to make us halt.

ARRIVAL AT TOURNAY.

Great, therefore, was our satisfaction when, through all these difficulties, we entered Tournay, where, being no longer in the lately restored kingdom of France, we considered ourselves to be escaped from the dominion of Bonaparte, and where we determined therefore to remain till we could guide our further proceedings by tidings of the plan and the position of Louis XVIII. We went to the most considerable inn, and all retired to rest which, after so much fatigue, mental and bodily, we required, and happily obtained.

The next day we had the melancholy satisfaction of hearing that Louis XVIII also had safely passed the frontiers of his lost kingdom. As we were less fearful, now, of making inquiries, M. de Lally soon learnt that his majesty had halted at Lille, where he was then waiting permission and directions for a place of retreat from the King of Holland, or the Netherlands. But no intelligence whatsoever could we gain relative to the body-guards, and my disturbance increased, every moment.

There was far more commotion at Tournay than at any other town through which we passed; for as the people here were not under the French government, either old or new, they were not awed into waiting to know to which they should belong, in fearful passiveness: yet they had all the perplexity upon their minds of disquieting ignorance whether they were to be treated as friends or foes, since if Bonaparte prevailed they could not but expect to be joined again to his dominions. All the commotion, therefore, of divided interests and jarring opinions was awake, and in full operation upon the faculties and feelings of every Belgian at this critical moment.

FUTILE EFFORTS TO COMMUNICATE WITH M. D'ARBLAY.

The horror of my suspense relative to the safety and the fate of Monsieur d'Arblay reduced my mind to a sort of chaos, that makes it impossible to recollect what was our abode at Tournay. I can but relate my distress and my researches.

My first thought was to send a letter to my general at Lille, which if he was there would inform him of my vicinity, and if not, might perhaps find its way to his destination. At all events, I resolved only to write what would be harmless should it fall even into the hands of the enemy. I directed those few lines to M. le Chevalier d'Arblay, officier superieur du garde du corps de sa majest, Louis XVIII. But when I would have sent them to the post, I was informed there was no post then to Lille.

I then sought for a messenger, but was told that Lille was inaccessible. The few letters that were permitted to enter it were placed in a basket, the handle of which was tied to a long cord, that was hooked up to the top of the walls, and thence descended to appointed magistrates.

Vainly I made every effort in my power to avail myself of this method, no one of my party, nor at the inn, knew or could indicate any means that promised success, or even a trial. Worn at length by an anxiety I found insupportable, I took a resolution to go forth myself, stranger as I was to the place, and try to get my letter conveyed to the basket, however difficult or costly might be its carriage. Quite alone, therefore, I sallied forth, purposing to find, if possible, some sturdy boy who would be glad of such remuneration as I could offer, to pass over to Lille.

Again, however, vain was every attempt. I entered all decent poor houses; sauntered to the suburbs, and entered sundry cottages; but no inquiry could procure either a man or a boy that would execute my commission. French was so generally known that I commonly made myself understood, though I only received a shake of the head, or a silent walking off, in return to my propositions. But in the end, a lad told me he thought he had heard that Madame la Duchesse de St. Agnes had had some intercourse with Lille. Delighted, I desired him to show me the house she inhabited. We walked to it together, and I then said I would saunter near the spot while he entered, with my earnest petition to know whether madame could give me any tidings of the king's body-guard. He returned with an answer that madame would reply to a written note, but to nothing verbal. I bid the boy hie with me to the inn; but as I had no writing tackle, I sent him forward to procure me proper implements at the stationer's.

How it happened I know not, but I missed the boy, whom I could never regain and I soon after lost my way myself.

In much perplexity I was seeking information which way to steer, when a distant sound of a party of horse caught my attention. I stopped. The sound approached nearer; the boys and idle people in the street ran forward to meet it, and presently were joined or followed by the more decent inhabitants. I had not the temerity to make one among them, yet my anxiety for news of any sort was too acute to permit me to retire. I stood therefore still, waiting for what might arrive, till I perceived some outriders galloping forward in the royal livery of France. Immediately after, a chariot and four with the arms of France followed, encircled by horsemen, and nearly enveloped by a continually increasing crowd, whence, from time to time, issued a feeble cry of "Vive le roi!" while two or three other carriages brought up the rear. With difficulty now could I forbear plunging into the midst of them, for my big expectations painted to me Louis XVIII arrived at Tournay, and my bigger hopes pictured with him his loyal guard. They had soon however passed by, but their straggling followers showed me their route, which I pursued till I lost both sight and sound belonging to them.

I then loitered for my errand boy, till I found myself, by some indications that helped my remembrance, near the spot whence I had started. Glad, for safety's sake, to be so near my then home, though mourning my fruitless wandering, I hastened my footsteps; but what was my emotion on arriving within a few yards of the inn, to observe the royal carriage which had galloped past me, the horsemen, the royal livery and all the appearance that had awakened my dearest hopes. The crowd was dispersed, but the porter's lodge, or perhaps bookkeeper's, was filled with gentlemen, or officers in full uniform. I hurried on, and hastily inquired who it was that had just arrived. My answer was, the Prince de Cond.

A thousand projects now occurred to me for gaining intelligence from such high authority, but in the large courtyard I espied Madame d'Henin sauntering up and down, while holding by the arm of a gentleman I had never before seen. Anxious to avoid delay, and almost equally desirous to escape remonstrances on my enterprise, since I could listen only to my restless anxiety, I would have glided by unnoticed; but she called after me aloud, and I was compelled to approach her. She was all astonishment at my courage in thus issuing forth alone, I knew not where nor whither, and declared that I was m,connoissable; but I only answered by entreating her to inquire the names of some of the gentlemen just arrived, that I might judge whether any among them could give me the information for which I sighed.

No sooner did I hear that M. le Comte de Viomenil was of the number, than, recollecting his recent appointment at Paris, in conjunction with Victor de Maubourg, to raise volunteers for the king, I decided upon seeking him. Madame d'Henin would have given me some counsel, but I could not hear her; as I hurried off, however, the gentleman whose arm she held offered me his assistance in a tone and with a look of so much benevolence, that I frankly accepted it, and we sallied in search of a person known to me only by name. My stranger friend now saved me every exertion, by making every inquiry and led me from corridor to corridor, above, below, and to almost every apartment, asking incessantly if M. le Comte de Viomenil was not in the inn.

At length we learned that M. de Viomenil was dining quite alone in an upper chamber.

My kind-hearted conductor led me to the door of the room assigned, and then tapped at it; and on an answer of "entrez!" he let go my arm, and with a bow silently left me. I found M. de Viomenil at table: he said he could give no possible account of his majesty, save that he was at Gand, but that of the body-guard he knew positively nothing.

INTERVIEWS WITH M. DE CHATEAUBRIAND.

I afterwards learnt that my benevolent strange chevalier was no other than the celebrated M. de Chateaubriand. (271) I saw nothing more of him, save for a moment, when, in passing by a small staircase that led to my chamber, a door was suddenly opened, whence Madame d'Henin put out her head to invite me to enter, when she presented me to him and to Madame de Chateaubriand, a very elegant woman, but of a cold, reserved demeanour.

I expressed eagerly the pleasure I had experienced in seeing the author of "The Itinerary to Jerusalem," a work I had read in Paris with extraordinary interest and satisfaction; but I believe the "Genie du Christianisme," and perhaps the "Atala," were works so much more prized by that author as to make my compliment misplaced. However, I so much more enjoy the natural, pleasing, instructive, and simple, though ingenious style and matter of the "Itinerary" than I do the overpowering sort of heroic eloquence of those more popular performances, that the zest of dear hallowed truth would have been wanting had I not expressed my choice. The "Itinerary" is, indeed, one of the most agreeable books I know.

M. de Chateaubriand hung back, whether pleased or not, with an air of gentlemanly serenity. I had opportunity for further effort: we left Tournay to proceed to Brussels, and heavy was my heart and my will to quit, thus in ignorance, the vicinity of Lille.

At the town at which we stopped to dine which, I think, was Atot, we again met M. et Madame de Chateaubriand. This was a mutual satisfaction, and we agreed to have our meal in common. I now had more leisure, not of time alone, but of faculty, for doing justice to M. de Chateaubriand, whom I found amiable, unassuming, and, though somewhat spoilt by the egregious flattery to which he had been accustomed, wholly free from airs or impertinent self-conceit. Excessive praise seemed only to cause him excessive pleasure in himself, without leading to contempt or scorn of others. He is by no means tall, and is rather thickset - but his features are good, his countenance is very fine, and his eyes are beautiful, alike from colour, shape, and expression; while there is a striking benevolence in his look, tone of voice, and manner.

Madame de Chateaubriand also gained ground by farther acquaintance. She was faded, but not passe, and was still handsome, and of a most graceful carriage, though distant and uninviting. Her loftiness had in it something so pensive mixed with its haughtiness, that though it could not inspire confidence, it did not create displeasure. She possessed also a claim to sympathy and respect in being the niece of M. de Malesherbes, that wise, tender, generous, noble defender of Louis XVI.

The conversation during and after dinner was highly interesting. M. de Chateaubriand opened upon his situation with a trusting unreserve that impressed me with an opinion of the nobleness of his mind. Bonaparte had conceived against him, he said, a peculiar antipathy, for which various motives might be assigned: he enumerated them not, however, probably from the presence of his wife; as his marriage with a niece of that martyr to the service of the murdered king, Louis XVI, I conclude to be at their head. The astonishing and almost boundless success of his works, since he was dissatisfied with his principles, and more than suspicious of his disaffection to the imperial government, must have augmented aversion by mixing with it some species of apprehension. I know not what were the first publications of M. de Chateaubriand, but they were in such high estimation when first I heard him mentioned, that no author was more celebrated in France; when his "Martyres" came out, no other book was mentioned; and the famous critic Geoffroyq who guided the taste of Paris, kept it alive by criticisms of alternate praise and censure without end. "Atala," the pastoral heroic romance, bewitched all the reading ladies into a sort of idolatry of its writer, and scarcely a page of it remained unadorned by some representation in painting. The enthusiasm, indeed, of the draughtsmen and of the fair sex seemed equally emulous to place the author and the work at the head of celebrity and the fashion.

Of all this, of course, he spoke not but he related the story of his persecution by Napoleon concerning his being elected a member of the French Institute. I was in too much disturbance to be able to clearly listen to the narrative, but I perfectly recollect that the censor, to soften Napoleon, had sent back the manuscript to M. de Chateaubriand, with an intimation that no public discourse could be delivered that did not contain an ,loge of the Emperor. M. de Chateaubriand complied with the ordinance; but whether the forced praise was too feeble, or whether the aversion was too insuperable, I know not: all that is certain is, that Napoleon, after repeated efforts from the Institute of re-election, positively refused to ratify that of M. de Chateaubriand. (272)

Another time a cousin of this gentleman was reputed to be engaged in a conspiracy against the emperor. M. de Chateaubriand solemnly declared he disbelieved the charge; and, as his weight in public opinion was so great, he ventured to address a supplique to Napoleon in favour of his kinsman; but the answer which reached him the following day was an account of his execution!

(248) Horne's "History of Napoleon."

(249) This portion of the Diary is not dated, but the meeting with the Duchess of Angoulˆme must have taken place in January or February, 1815. Madame d'Arblay had joined her husband in France, her son remaining at Cambridge. ED.

(250) "Very glad to see me."

(251) "May I keep the book you sent me?"

(252) "He has acted very nobly."

(253) Raised every day."

(254) "The king recollects very well having seen you in London."

(255) "O, I don't doubt it at all."

(256) "He was perfect!"

(257) Princess Elizabeth.

(258) "'Tis she who does the honours of the royal family."

(259) On duty.

(260) Minister for foreign affairs.

(261) "We have better news. I can enter into no detail; but be calm, and love him who loves you alone.

(262) Country estate.

(263) "My dearest—All is lost! I cannot enter into details—pray, set out the sooner the better. Yours in life and death, A. d'A."

(264) A large travelling-coach. ED.

(265) Le Bourget was the scene of some desperate fighting during the siege of Paris in 1870. It was surprised and captured from the Prussians before daybreak of October 28, by a French force commanded by General de Bellemare, but, after a gallant defence of two days, it was retaken by the Prussians. December 21, an attempt was made by the French to recapture Le Bourget, but without success. ED.

(266) Monday, the 20th, it should be. ED.

(267) The son of Philippe Egalit,, afterwards King Louis Philippe. ED.

(268) Brother of Louis XVIII, whom he succeeded under the title of Charles X. ED.

(269) Should be Tuesday. ED.

(270) "Right of the strongest."

(271) Fran‡ois Ren, de Chateaubriand was born at Saint Malo in 1768 He visited the United States in 1789, and found, in the pathless forests of the new world, the scenery which he describes, with poetic fervour, in the pages of "Atala." The news of the king's flight to Varennes brought him back to Europe. He married (1792) 'Mlle. de la Vigne-Buisson, joined the emigrant army which marched with Brunswick to conquer France, got wounded at Thionville, and retired to England. After the appointment of Bonaparte to the office of first Consul, Chateaubriand returned to France, and published his heroic- sentimental romance of "Atala." Its success with the public was great, and it was followed by "The Genius of Christianity," and other works. Under the restored Bourbons, Chateaubriand filled high diplomatic posts. This most sentimental of men of genius died in July, 1848. ED.

(272) This occurred in the year 1811. ED.

SECTION 25. (1815)

AT BRUSSELS: WATERLOO: REJOINS M. D'ARBLAY.

SOJOURN AT BRUSSELS.

Arrived at Brussels, we drove immediately to the house in which dwelt Madame la Comtesse de Maurville. That excellent person had lived many years in England an emigrant, and there earned a scanty maintenance by keeping a French school. She had now retired upon a very moderate pension, but was surrounded by intimate friends, who only suffered her to lodge at her own home. She received us in great dismay, fearing to lose her little all by these changes of government. I was quite ill on my arrival: excessive fatigue, affright, and watchfulness overwhelmed me.

At Brussels all was quiet and tame. The Belgians had lost their original antipathy to Bonaparte, without having yet had time to acquire any warmth of interest for the Bourbons. Natively phlegmatic, they demand great causes or strong incitement to rouse them from that sort of passiveness that is the offspring of philosophy and timidity- philosophy, that teaches them to prize 'the blessings of safety; and timidity, that points out the dangers of enterprise. In all I had to do with them I found them universally worthy, rational, and kind-hearted; but slow, sleepy, and uninteresting, in the sickroom to which I was immediately consigned, I met with every sort of kindness from Madame de Maurville, whom I had known intimately at Paris, and who had known and appreciated my beloved, exemplary sister Phillips in London. Madame de Maurville was a woman that the Scotch would call long-headed; she was sagacious, penetrating, and gifted with strong humour. She saw readily the vices and follies of mankind, and laughed at them heartily, without troubling herself to grieve at them. She was good herself, alike in heart and in conduct, and zealous to serve and oblige; but with a turn to satire that made the defects of her neighbours rather afford her amusement than concern.

I was visited here by the highly accomplished Madame de la: Tour du Pin, wife to the favourite nephew of Madame d'Henin; a woman of as much courage as elegance, and who had met danger, toil, and difficulty in the Revolution with as much spirit, and nearly as much grace, as she had displayed in meeting universal admiration and homage at the court of Marie-Antoinette, of which she was one of the most brilliant latter ornaments. Her husband was at this time one of the French ministers at the Congress at Vienna; whence, as she learned a few days after my arrival at Brussels, he had been sent on an embassy of the deepest importance and risk, to La Vende or Bordeaux. She bore the term of that suspense with a heroism that I greatly admired, for I well knew she adored her husband. M. la Tour du Pin had been a prefect of Brussels under Bonaparte, though never in favour, his internal loyalty to the Bourbons being well known. But Bonaparte loved to attach great names and great characters to his government, conscious of their weight both at home and abroad, and he trusted in the address of that mental diving-machine, his secret police, for warding off any hazard he might run, from employing the adherents of his enemies. His greatly capacious, yet only half-formed mind, could have parried, as well as braved, every danger and all opposition, had not his inordinate ambition held him as arbitrarily under control as he himself held under control every other passion.

Madame de Maurville soon found us a house, of which we took all but the ground floor: the entresol was mine, the first floor was Madame d'Henin's, and that above it was for M. de Lally. It was near the cathedral, and still in a prolongation of Madame de Maurville's street, la Rue de la Montagne.

Nothing was known at Brussels, nothing at all, of the fate of the body-guard, or of the final destination of Louis XVIII. How circumstances of such moment, nay, notoriety, could be kept from public knowledge, I can form no idea; but neither in the private houses of persons of the first rank, in which, through Madame d'Henin, I visited, nor in any of the shops nor by any other sort of intercourse, either usual or accidental, could I gather any intelligence.

Madame la Duchesse de Duras, ci-devant Mademoiselle Kersaint, who had visited me in Paris, and who was now in hasty emigration at Brussels, with her youngest daughter, Mademoiselle Clara de Duras, seemed sincerely moved by my distress, and wrote to various of her friends, who were emigrating within her reach, to make inquiry for me. I visited her in a shabby hotel, where I found her without suite or equipage, but in perfect tranquillity at their loss, and not alone unmurmuring, but nearly indifferent to her privations; while Mademoiselle Clara ran up and down stairs on her mother's messages, and even brought in wood for the stove, with an alacrity and cheerfulness that seemed almost to enjoy the change to hardships from grandeur. Indeed, to very young people, such reverses, for a certain time, appear as a frolic. Novelty, mere novelty, during the first youth, can scarcely be bought too dear.

From M. de la Feronaye, Madame de Duras procured me intelligence that the body-guard had been dispersed and disbanded by the Duc de Berry, on the frontiers of La Belgique they were left at liberty to remain in France, or to seek other asylums, as his majesty Louis XVIII could not enter the kingdom of Holland with a military guard of his own. This news left me utterly in the dark which way to look for hope or information. Madame de Duras, however, said she expected soon to see the Duc de Richelieu, whose tidings might be more precise.

LETTERS FROM GENERAL D'ARBLAY.

Ten wretched days passed on in this ignorance, from the 19th to the 29th of March, 1815, when Madame de Maurville flew into my apartment, with all the celerity of fifteen, and all the ardour of twenty years of age, to put into my hands a letter from General d'Arblay, addressed to herself, to inquire whether she had any tidings to give him of my existence, and whether I had been heard of at Brussels, or was known to have travelled to Bordeaux, as Madame d'Henin, cousin to Madame de Maurville, had been uncertain, when M. d'Arblay left me in Paris, to which of those cities she should go.

The joy of that moment. Oh! the joy of that Moment that showed me again the handwriting that demonstrated the life and safety of all to which my earthly happiness clung, can never be expressed, and only by our meeting, when at last it took place, could be equalled. It was dated "Ypres, 27 Mars." I wrote directly thither, proposing to join him, if "there were any impediment to his coming on to Brussels. I had already written, at hazard, to almost every town in the Netherlands. The very next day, another letter from the same kind hand arrived to Madame la Duchesse d'Hurste. This was succeeded by news that the king, Louis XVIII, had been followed to Gand by his body-guard. Thither, also, I expedited a letter, under cover to the Duc de Luxembourg, capitaine of the company to which M. d'Arblay belonged.

I lived now in a hurry of delight that scarcely allowed me breathing-time, a delight that made me forget all my losses, my misfortunes-my papers, keepsakes, valuables of various sorts, with our goods, clothes, money-bonds, and endless et ceteras, left, as I had reason to fear, to seizure and confiscation upon the entry of the emperor into Paris—all, all was light, was nothing in the scale; and I wrote to my Alexander, and my dearest friends, to rejoice in my joy, and that they had escaped my alarm.

Next day, and again the next, came a letter from M. d'Arblay himself. The first was from Ypres, the second was from Bruges, and brought by the post, as my beloved correspondent had been assured of my arrival at Brussels by the Duc de Luxembourg, at Ghistelle, near Ostend, which M. d'Arblay was slowly approaching on horseback, when he met the carriage of Louis XVIII, as it stopped for a relay of horses, and the duke, espying him, descended from the second carriage of the king's suite, to fly to and embrace him, with that lively friendship he has ever manifested towards him. Thence they agreed that the plan of embarkation should be renounced, and, instead of Ostend M. d'Arblay turned his horse's head towards Gand, where he had a rendezvous with the duke.

There he remained, to renew the offer of his services to his king, and there he was most peculiarly distinguished by M. le Duc de Feltre (General Clarke), who was still occupying the Post assigned him on the restoration of Louis XVIII. of ministre de la guerre. (273)

Relieved now—or rather blest—I was no longer deaf to the kindness of those who sought to enliven my exile; I not only visited Madame la Duchesse de Duras, but also cultivated an intercourse with the charming Madame de la Tour du Pin whom I was the more glad to find delightful from her being of English origin; a Mademoiselle Dillon, Whose family was transplanted into France under James II, and who was descended from a nobleman whose eminent accomplishments she inherited with his blood; the famous Lord Falkland, on whose tomb in Westminster Abbey is carved

"Here lies the friend of Sir Philip Sidney."

Her sister, Miss Fanny Dillon, had been married by Bonaparte to General Bertrand; and thus, while one of them' was an emigrant following the fortunes of the Bourbons, the other was soon after destined to accompany Bonaparte himself into exile. Le Colonel de Beaufort, also, a warm, early friend of General d'Arblay, belonging to the garrison of Metz or of Toul, I forget which, had married a lady of great wealth in La Belgique; a woman rather unhappy in her person, but possessed of a generous and feeling heart: and this she instantly demonstrated by seeking and cultivating an acquaintance with the wandering wife of her husband's early camarade. I found her so amiable, and so soothing in her commiseration during my distress, that I warmly returned the partiality she showed me.

ARRIVAL OF GENERAL D'ARBLAY.

Four days passed thus serenely, when, on that which completed a fortnight's absence from my best friend, the Duc de Duras came to convoy his wife to Gand, where he was himself in waiting upon Louis XVIII, and shortly afterwards M. de Chateaubriand was made a privy counsellor and settled there also. And within a day or two after this my door was opened by General d'Arblay! Oh, how sweet was this meeting! this blessed reunion!— how perfect, how exquisite!

Here I must be silent.

General d'Arblay was only with me by the permission of the Duc de Luxembourg, and liable to receive orders daily to return to Gand; for I found to my speechless dismay, yet resistless approbation, that General d'Arblay had made a decision as noble as it was dangerous, to refuse no call, to abstain from no effort, that might bring into movement his loyalty to his king and his cause, at this moment of calamity to both. Yet such was the harassed, or rather broken state of his health, that his mental strength and unconquerable courage alone preserved the poor shattered frame from sinking into languor and inertion.

About this time I saw the entry of the new king, William Frederick, of the new kingdom of the Netherlands. (274) Tapestry, or branches of trees, were hung out at all the windows, or, in their failure, dirty carpets, old coats and cloaks, and even mats-a motley display of proud parade or vulgar poverty, that always, to me, made processions on the continent appear burlesque.

A MISSION ENTRUSTED TO GENERAL D'ARBLAY.

On the 22nd of April opened a new source, though not an unexpected one, of inquietude, that preyed the more deeply upon my spirits from the necessity of concealing its torments. . . . The military call for M. d'Arblay arrived from Gand. The summons was from M. le Comte de Roch. The immediate hope in which we indulged at this call was, that the mission to which it alluded need not necessarily separate us, but that I might accompany my honoured husband and remain at his quarters. But, alas! he set out instantly for Gand . . . . .

April 23rd brought me a letter: the mission was to Luxembourg. His adjoint was the Colonel Comte de Mazancourt, his aide-de-camp M. de Premorel, and also that gentleman's son. The plan was to collect and examine all the soldiers who were willing to return from the army of Bonaparte to that of Louis XVIII. Eleven other general officers were named to similar posts, all on frontier towns, for the better convenience of receiving the volunteers. On the 24th April M. d'Arblay again joined me revived by his natively martial spirit, and pleased to be employed!

April 26. We left the Rue de La Montague, after, on my part, exactly a month's residence. Our new apartments in the March, aux Bois were au premier, (275) and commodious and pleasant. One drawing-room was appropriated solely by M. d'Arblay for his military friends or military business; the other was mine.

Here we spent together seventeen days; and not to harass my recollections, I will simply copy what I find in MY old memorandum-book, as it was written soon after those days were no more:—"

Seventeen days I have passed with my best friend; and, alas! passed them chiefly in suspense and gnawing inquietude, covered over with assumed composure . but they have terminated, Heaven be praised! with better views, with softer calm, and fairer hopes. Heaven realize them! I am much pleased with his companions. M. le Comte de Mazancourt, his adjoint, is a gay, spirited and spirituel young man, remarkably well bred, and gallantly fond of his profession. M. de Premorel, the aide-de-camp, is a man of solid worth and of delicate honour, and he is a descendant of Godefroy de Bouillon. To this must be added, that he is as poor as he is noble, and bears his penury with the gentlemanly sentiment of feeling it distinct from disgrace. He is married, and has ten or eleven children: he resides with a most deserving wife, a woman also of family, on a small farm, which he works at himself, and which repays him by its produce. For many days in the year, potatoes, he told me, were the only food they could afford for themselves or their offspring! But they eat them with the proud pleasure of independence and of honour and loyalty, such as befits their high origins, always to serve, or be served, in the line of their legal princes. As soon as Louis XVIII. was established on his throne, M. de Premorel made himself known to the Duc de Luxembourg, who placed him in his own company in the garde du corps, and put his son upon the supernumerary list. . . . ."

This young man is really charming. He has a native noblesse of air and manner, with a suavity as well as steadiness of serene politeness, that announce the Godefroy blood flowing with conscious dignity and inborn courage through his youthful veins. He is very young, but tall and handsome, and speaks of all his brothers and sisters as if already he were chef de famille, and bound to sustain and protect them. I delighted to lead him to talk of them, and the conversation on that subject always brightened him into joy and loquacity. He named every one of them to me in particular repeatedly, with a desire I should know them individually, and a warm hope I might one day verify his representations.

This youth, Alphonse, and his father dined with us daily at this period. All the mornings were devoted to preparations for the ensuing expected campaign. When, however, all was prepared, and the word of command alone was waited for from the Marschal Duc de Feltre, my dearest friend indulged in one morning's recreation, which proved as 'agreeable as anything at such a period could be to a mind oppressed like mine. He determined that we should visit the Palais de Lachen, which had been the dwelling assigned as the palace for the Empress Josephine by Bonaparte at the time of his divorce. My dearest husband drove me in his cabriolet, and the three gentlemen whom he invited to be of the party accompanied us on horseback. The drive, the day, the road, the views, our new horses-all were delightful, and procured me a short relaxation from the foresight of evil.

The Palace of Lachen was at this moment wholly uninhabited, and shown to us by some common servant. It is situated in a delicious park d'Anglaise, and with a taste, a polish, and an elegance that clears it from the charge of frippery or gaudiness, though its ornaments and embellishments are all of the liveliest gaiety. There is in some of the apartments some Gobelin tapestry, of which there are here and there parts and details so exquisitely worked that I could have "hung over them enamoured."

"RULE BRITANNIA!" IN THE ALLEE VERTE.

Previously to this reviving excursion my dearest friend had driven me occasionally in the famous Allee Verte, which the inhabitants of Brussels consider as the first promenade in the world; but it by no means answered to such praise in my eyes: it is certainly very pretty, but too regular, too monotonous, and too flat to be eminently beautiful, though from some parts the most distant from the city there are views of cottages and hamlets that afford great pleasure.

Our last entertainment here was a concert in the public and fine room appropriated for music or dancing. The celebrated Madame Catalani had a benefit, at which the Queen of the Netherlands was present, not, however, in state, though not incognita; and the king of warriors, Marshal Lord Wellington, surrounded by his staff and all the officers and first persons here, whether Belgians, Prussians, Hanoverians, or English. I looked at Lord Wellington watchfully, and was charmed with every turn of his countenance, with his noble and singular physiognomy and his eagle eye. He was gay even to sportiveness all the evening, conversing with the officers around him. He never was seated, not even a moment, though I saw seats vacated to offer to him frequently. He seemed enthusiastically charmed with Catalani, ardently applauding whatsoever she sung, except the "Rule Britannia; and there, with sagacious reserve, he listened in utter Silence. Who ordered it I know not, but he felt it was injudicious in every country but -our own to give out a chorus of "Rule, Britannia! Britannia, rule the waves!"

And when an encore began to be vociferated from his officers, he instantly crushed it by a commanding air of disapprobation, and thus offered me an opportunity of seeing how magnificently he could quit his convivial familiarity for imperious' dominion when occasion might call for the transformation.

GENERAL D'ARBLAY LEAVES FOR LUXEMBOURG.

When the full order arrived from Gand, establishing the mission of M. d'Arblay at Luxembourg, he decided upon demanding an audience of the Duke of Wellington, with whom he thought it necessary to concert his measures. The duke received him without difficulty, and they had a conference of some length, the result of which was that his grace promised to prepare Blucher, the great Prussian general, then actually at Luxembourg, for aiding the scheme. M. d'Arblay himself also wrote to Blucher; but before any answer could be returned, a new ordonnance from the Duc de Feltre directed M. d'Arblay to hasten to his post without delay.

May 13, 1815. My best friend left me to begin his campaign; left me, by melancholy chance, upon his birthday. I could not that day see a human being—I could but consecrate it to thoughts of him who had just quitted me yet who from me never was, never can be, mentally absent, and to our poor Alexander, thus inevitably, yet severely cast upon himself.

AN EXCHANGE OF VISITS.

The next day the gentle and feeling Madame de Beaufort spent the morning with me, using the most engaging efforts to prevail with me to dine constantly at her table, and to accompany her in a short time to her villa. Without any charms, personal or even intellectual, to catch or fascinate, she seemed to have so much goodness of character, that I could not but try to attach myself to her, and accept her kindness as the "cordial drop" to make the cup of woe of my sad solitude go down; for Madame d'Henin, who, to equal sensibility, joined the finest understanding, was now so absorbed in politics that she had no time for any expansion of sympathy. She came, nevertheless, to see me in the evening, and to endeavour to draw me again into human life! And her kind effort so far conquered me, that I called upon her the next day, and met Madame de Vaudreuil, for whom I had a still unexecuted commission from the Duchess dowager of Buccleuch, upon whom I had waited at the request of the princesse de Chimay, to entreat the interest of her grace with the prince regent, that the English pension accorded to the Duchess of Fitzjames might be continued to the duke, her husband, who remained a ruined widower with several children. I failed in my attempt, the natural answer being, that there was no possibility of granting a pension to a foreigner who resided in his own country while that country was at open war with the land whence he aspired at its obtention, a word I make for my passing convenience.

I exchanged visits also with Madame de la Tour du Pin, the truly elegant, accomplished, and high-bred niece, by marriage, of Madame la Princesse d'Henin. Her husband, M. de la Tour du Pin, was at that time at Vienna, forming a part of the renowned Congress, by which he was sent to La Vende; to announce there the resolution of the assembled sovereigns to declare Bonaparte an outlaw, in consequence of his having broken the conditions of his accepted abdication, And I was discovered and visited by M. le Comte de Boursac, one of the first officers of the establishment of the Prince de Cond,, with whom he was then at Brussels; a man of worth and cultivation. At Paris he visited us so often, that he took up the name at the door of "Le Voisin," thinking it more safe to be so designated than to pronounce too frequently the name of a known adherent to the Bourbons. The good

Madame de Maurville I saw often, and the family of the Boyds, with which my general had engaged me to quit Brussels, should Brussels become the seat of War.

THE FETE DIEU.

Brussels in general was then inhabited by catholics, and catholic ceremonies were not unfrequent. In particular, la Fete Dieu was kept with much pomp, and a procession of priests paraded the streets, accompanied by images, pictures paintings, tapestry, and other insignia of outward and visible worship; and the windows were hung with carpets, and rugs, and mats, and almost with rags, to prove good will, at least, to what they deem a pious show. Ludicrous circumstances without end interrupted, or marred the procession, from frequent hard showers, during which the priests, decorated with splendid robes and petticoats, and ornaments the most gaudy, took sudden refuge at the doors of the houses by which they were passing, and great cloths, towels, or coarse canvas, were flung over the consecrated finery, and the relics were swaddled up in flannels, while dirt, splashes, running, scampering, and ludicrous wrappings up, broke at once and disfigured the procession.

THE ECCENTRIC LADY CAROLINE LAMB.

At Madame de la Tour du Pin's I kept the fete of Madame de Maurville, with a large and pleasant party; and I just missed meeting the famous Lady Caroline Lamb, (276) who had been there at dinner, and whom I saw, however, crossing the Place Royale, from Madame de la Tour du Pin's to the Grand Hotel; dressed, Or rather not dressed, so as to excite universal attention, and authorise every boldness of staring, from the general to the lowest soldier, among the military groups then constantly parading the Place, for she had one shoulder, half her back, and all her throat and neck, displayed as if at the call of some statuary for modelling a heathen goddess. A slight scarf hung over the other shoulder, and the rest of the attire was of accordant lightness. As her ladyship had not then written, and was not, therefore, considered as one apart, from being known as an eccentric authoress, this conduct and demeanour excited something beyond surprise, and in an English lady provoked censure, if not derision, upon the whole English nation.

A PROPOSED ROYAL CORPS.

Monsieur le Duc de Luxembourg came to inform me that he was on the point of negotiating with the Duke of Wellington and Prince Blucher, upon raising a royal corps to accompany their army into France, should the expected battle lead to that result; and he desired me to prepare M. d'Arblay, should such be the case, for a recall from Trèves, that he might resume his post in the body-guards belonging to the Compagnie de Luxembourg. He spoke of my beloved in terms of such high consideration, and with expressions so amiable of regard and esteem, that he won my heart. He could by no means, he said, be again under active military orders, and consent to lose so distinguished an officer from his corps. I had formerly met the duke in Paris, at Madame de Laval's, and he bad honoured me with a visit chez moi immediately after my return from England: and in consequence of those meetings, and of his real friendship for M. d'Arblay, he now spoke to me with the unreserved trust due to a tried confidant in case of peril and urgency. He stayed with me nearly two hours-for when once the heart ventured to open itself upon the circumstances, expectations, or apprehensions of. that eventful period, subjects, opinions, and feelings pressed forward with such eagerness for discussion, that those who upon such conditions met, found nothing so difficult as to separate.

I wrote instantly to M. d'Arblay; but the duke's plan proved abortive, as the Duke of Wellington and Prince Blucher refused all sanction to the junction of a French army with that of the allies. The thought, perhaps—and perhaps Justly, that by entering France with natives against natives, they might excite a civil war, more difficult to conduct than that of only foreigners against foreigners.

PAINFUL SUSPENSE.

Suspense, during all this period, was frightfully mistress of the mind; nothing was known, everything was imagined.

The two great interests that were at war, the Bourbonists and Bonapartists, were divided and sub-divided into factions, or rather fractions, without end, and all that was kept invariably and on both sides alive was expectation. Wanderers, deserters or captives from France, arrived daily at Brussels, all with varying news of the state of that empire, and of the designs of Bonaparte amongst them. The Chevalier d'Argy made me a visit, to deliver me a letter from M. de Premorel, for M. d'Arblay. This gentleman was just escaped from Sedan in the disguise of a paysan, and assisted by a paysanne, belonging to his family. She conducted him through by-paths and thick forests, that she knew to be least frequented by the troops, police, or custom-house officers of Bonaparte. He was going to offer his services to the king, Louis XVIII. I had much interesting public news from M. d'Argy: but I pass by all now except personal detail, as I write but for my nearest friends; and all that was then known of public occurrence has long been stale. . . .

During this melancholy period when leisure, till now a delight, became a burthen to me, I could not call my faculties into any species of intellectual service; all was sunk, was annihilated in the overpowering predominance of anxiety for the coming event. I endured my suspense only by writing to or hearing from him who was its object. All my next dear connections were well. I heard from them satisfactorily, and I was also engaged in frequent correspondence with the Princess Elizabeth, whose letters are charming, not only from their vivacity, their frankness, and condescension, but from a peculiarity of manner, the result of having mixed little with the world, that, joined to great fertility of fancy, gives a something so singular and so genuine to her style of writing, as to render her letters desirable and interesting, independent of the sincere and most merited attachment which their gracious kindness inspires.

INQUIETUDE AT BRUSSELS.

I come now to busier scenes, and to my sojourn at Brussels during the opening of one of the most famous campaigns upon record; and the battle of Waterloo, upon which, in great measure, hung the fate of Europe.

Yet upon reflection, I will write no account of these great events, which have been detailed so many hundred times, and so many hundred ways, as I have nothing new to offer upon them; I will simply write the narrative of my own history at that awful period.

I was awakened in the middle of the night by confused noises in the house, and running up and down stairs. I listened attentively, but heard no sound of voices, and soon all was quiet. I then concluded the persons who resided in the apartments on the second floor, over my head, had returned home later and I tried to fall asleep again.

I succeeded; but I was again awakened at about five o'clock in the morning Friday, 16th June, by the sound of a bugle in the March, aux Bois: I started up and opened the window. But I only perceived some straggling soldiers, hurrying in different directions, and saw lights gleaming from some of the chambers in the neighbourhood: all again was soon still, and my own dwelling in profound silence, and therefore I concluded there had been some disturbance in exchanging sentinels at the various posts, which was already appeased: and I retired once more to my pillow, and remained till my usual hour.

I was finishing, however, a letter for my best friend, when my breakfast was brought in, at my then customary time of eight o'clock; and, as mistakes and delays and miscarriages of letters had caused me much unnecessary misery, I determined to put what I was then writing in the post myself, and set off with it the moment it was sealed.

THE BLACK BRUNSWICKERS.

In my way back from the post-office, my ears were alarmed by the sound of military music, and my eyes equally struck with the sight of a body of troops marching to its measured time. But I soon found that what I had supposed to be an occasionally passing troop, was a complete corps; infantry, cavalry artillery, bag and baggage, with all its officers in full uniform, and that uniform was black. This gloomy hue gave an air so mournful to the procession, that, knowing its destination for battle, I contemplated with an aching heart. On inquiry, I learned it was the army of Brunswick. How much deeper yet had been my heartache had I foreknown that nearly all those brave men, thus marching on in gallant though dark array, with their valiant royal chief (277) at their head, the nephew of my own king, George III, were amongst the first destined victims to this dreadful contest, and that neither the chief, nor the greater part of his warlike associates, would within a few short hours, breathe again the vital air!

My interrogations were answered with brevity, yet curiosity was all awake and all abroad; for the procession lasted some hours. Not a door but was open; not a threshold but was crowded, and not a window of the many-windowed gothic modern, frightful, handsome, quaint, disfigured, fantastic, or lofty mansions that diversify the large' market-place of Brussels, but was occupied by lookers on. Placidly, indeed, they saw the warriors pass: no kind greeting welcomed their arrival; no warm wishes followed them to combat. Neither, on the other hand, was there the slightest symptom of dissatisfaction; yet even while standing thus in the midst of them, an unheeded, yet observant stranger, it was not possible for me to discern, with any solidity of conviction, whether the Belgians were, at heart, Bourbonists or Bonapartists. The Bonapartists, however, were in general the most open, for the opinion on both sides, alike with good will and with ill, was nearly universal that Bonaparte was invincible.

THE OPENING OF THE CAMPAIGN.

Still, I knew not, dreamt not, that the campaign was already opened—that Bonaparte had broken into La Belgique on the 15th, and had taken Charleroi; though it was news undoubtedly spread all over Brussels except to my lonely self. My own disposition, at this period, to silence and retirement, was too congenial with the taciturn habits of my hosts to be by them counteracted, and they suffered me, therefore, to return to my home as I had quitted it, with a mere usual and civil salutation; while themselves and their house were evidently continuing their common avocations with their common composure. Surely our colloquial use of the word phlegm must be derived from the character of the Flemings.

The important tidings now, however, burst upon me in sundry directions. The Princesse d'Henin, Colonel de Beaufort, Madame de Maurville, the Boyd family, all, with intelligence of the event, joined offers of service, and invitations to reside with them during this momentous contest, should I prefer such protection to remaining alone at such a crisis.

What a day of confusion and alarm did we all spend on the 17th! In my heart the whole time was Trèves! Trèves! Trèves! That day, and June 18th, I passed in hearing the cannon! Good heaven! what indescribable horror to be so near the field of slaughter! such I call it, for the preparation to the ear by the tremendous sound was soon followed by its fullest effect, in the view of the wounded, the bleeding martyrs to the formidable contention that was soon to terminate the history of the war. And hardly more afflicting was this disabled return from the battle, than the sight of the continually pouring forth ready-armed and vigorous victims that marched past my windows to meet similar destruction.

NEWS FROM THE FIELD OF BATTLE.

Accounts from the field of battle arrived hourly; sometimes directly from the Duke of Wellington to Lady Charlotte Greville, and to some other ladies who had near relations in the combat, and which, by their means, were circulated in Brussels; and at other times from such as conveyed those amongst the wounded Belgians, whose misfortunes were -inflicted near enough to the skirts of the spots of action, to allow of their being dragged away by their hovering countrymen to the city: the spots, I say, of action, for the far-famed battle of Waterloo was preceded by three days of partial engagements.

During this period, I spent my whole time in seeking and passing from house to house of the associates of my distress, or receiving them in mine. Ten times, at least, I crossed over to Madame d'Henin, discussing plans and probabilities, and interchanging hopes and fears. I spent a considerable part of the morning with Madame de la Tour du Pin, who was now returned from Gand, where Louis XVIII supported his suspense and his danger with a coolness and equanimity which, when the éclat surrounding the glory of his daring and great opponent shall no longer by its overpowering resplendence keep all around it in the shade, will carry him down to posterity as the monarch precisely formed, by the patient good sense, the enlightened liberality, and the immovable composure of his character, to meet the perilous perplexities of his situation, and, if he could not combat them with the vigour and genius of a hero, to sustain them at least with the dignity of a prince.

PROJECTS FOR QUITTING BRUSSELS.

Madame d'Henin and Madame de la Tour du Pin projected retreating to Gand, should the approach of the enemy be unchecked; to avail themselves of such protection as might be obtained from seeking it under the wing of Louis XVIII. M. de la Tour du Pin had, I believe, remained there with his majesty. M. de Lally and the Boyds inclined to Antwerp, where they might safely await the fate of Brussels, near enough for returning, should it weather the storm, yet within reach of vessels to waft them to the British shores should it be lost.

Should this last be the fatal termination, I, of course, had agreed to join the party of the voyage, and resolved to secure my passport, that, while I waited to the last moment, I might yet be prepared for a hasty retreat. I applied for a passport to Colonel Jones, to whom the Duke of Wellington had deputed the military command of Brussels in his absence but he was unwilling to sanction an evacuation of Brussels, which he deemed premature. It was not, he said, for us, the English, to spread alarm, or prepare for an overthrow: he had not sent away his own wife or children, and he had no doubt but victory would repay his confidence.

I was silenced, but not convinced; the event was yet uncertain, and my stake was, with respect to earthly happiness, my existence. A compromise occurred to me, which suggested my dispensing with a new passport, and contenting myself with obtaining his signature to my old one, accorded by

M. le Chevalier de Jaucourt. He could not refuse to sign it; and we then separated. I promised him, nevertheless, that I would remain to the last extremity; and I meant no other. I was now better satisfied, though by no means at ease.

Yet the motive of Colonel Jones was, that all should yield to the glory of the British arms and the Duke of Wellington. And I had the less right to be surprised, from the dreadful soldier's speech I had heard him utter when I first saw him, to the Princesse d'Henin: complaining of the length of time that was wasted in inaction, and of the inactivity and tameness of the Bourbons, he exclaimed, "We want blood, madam! what we want is blood!"

CALMLY AWAITING THE RESULT.

I found upon again going my rounds for information, that 'though news was arriving incessantly from the scene of action, and with details always varying, Bonaparte was always advancing. All the people of Brussels lived in the streets. Doors seemed of no use, for they were never shut. The individuals, when they re-entered their houses, only resided at the windows: so that the whole population of the city seemed constantly in public view. Not only business as well as society was annihilated, but even every species of occupation. All of which we seemed capable was, to inquire or to relate, to speak or to hear. Yet no clamour, no wrangling, nor even debate was intermixed with either question or answer; curiosity, though incessant, was serene; the faces were all monotony, though the tidings were all variety. I could attribute this only to the length of time during which the inhabitants had been habituated to change both of masters and measures, and to their finding that, upon an average, they neither lost nor gained by such successive revolutions. And to this must be joined their necessity of submitting, be it what it might, to the result. This mental consciousness probably kept their passions in order, and crushed all the impulses by which hope or fear is excited. No love of liberty buoyed up resistance; no views of independence brightened their imagination; and they bore even suspense with the calm of apparent philosophy, and an exterior of placid indifference.

The first intelligence Madame d'Henin now gave me was, that the Austrian minister extraordinary, M. le Comte de Vincent, had been wounded close by the side of the Duke of Wellington; and that he was just brought back in a litter to her hotel. As she was much acquainted with him, she desired me to accompany her in making her personal inquiries. No one now sent servants, cards, or messages, where there was any serious interest in a research. There was too much eagerness to bear delay, and ceremony and etiquette always fly from distress and from business.

Le Comte de Vincent, we had the pleasure to hear, had been hurt only in the hand; but this wound afterwards proved more serious than at first was apprehended, threatening for many weeks either gangrene or amputation. News, however, far more fatal struck our ears soon after: the gallant Duke of Brunswick was killed! and by a shot close also to the Duke of Wellington!

The report now throughout Brussels was that the two Mighty chiefs, Bonaparte and Wellington, were almost constantly in view of each other.

FLIGHT TO ANTWERP DETERMINED ON.

But what a day was the next—June 18th—the greatest, perhaps, in its result, in the annals of Great Britain!

My slumbers having been tranquillized by the close of the 17th, I was calmly reposing, when I was awakened by the sound of feet abruptly entering my drawing-room. I started, and had but just time to see by my watch that it was only six o'clock, when a rapping at my bedroom door so quick as to announce as much trepidation as it excited, made me slip on a long kind of domino always, in those times, at hand, to keep me ready for encountering surprise, and demanded what was the matter? "Open your door! there is not a moment to lose!" was the answer, in the voice of Miss Ann Boyd. I obeyed, in great alarm, and saw that pretty and pleasing young woman, with her mother, Mrs. Boyd, who remembered having known and played with me when we were both children, and whom I had met with at Passy, after a lapse of more than forty years. They both eagerly told me that all their new hopes had been overthrown by better authenticated news, and that I must be with them by eight o'clock, to proceed to the wharf, and set sail for Antwerp, whence we sail on for England, should the taking of Brussels by Bonaparte endanger Antwerp also.

To send off a few lines to the post, with my direction at Antwerp, to pack and to pay, was all that I could attempt, or even desire; for I had not less time than appetite for thinking of breakfast. My host and my maid carried my small package, and I arrived before eight in the Rue d'Assault. We set off for the wharf on foot, not a fiacre or chaise being procurable. Mr. and Mrs. Boyd, five or six of their family, a governess, and I believe some servants, with bearers of our baggage, made our party. Though the distance was short, the walk was long, because rugged, dirty, and melancholy. Now and then we heard a growling noise, like distant thunder, but far more dreadful. When we had got about a third part of the way, a heavy rumbling sound made us stop to listen. It was approaching nearer and nearer, and we soon found that we were followed by innumerable carriages, and a multitude of persons.

All was evidently military, but of so gloomy, taciturn, and forbidding a description, that when we were overtaken we had not courage to offer a question to any passer by. Had we been as certain that they belonged to the enemy as we felt convinced that, thus circumstanced, they must belong to our own interests, we could not have been awed more effectually into silent passiveness, so decisively repelling to inquiry was every aspect. In truth, at that period, when every other hour changed the current of expectation, no one could be inquisitive without the risk of passing for a spy, nor communicative without the hazard of being suspected as a traitor.

Arrived at the wharf, Mr. Boyd pointed out to us our barge, which seemed fully ready for departure; but the crowd already come and still coming so incommoded us, that Mr. Boyd desired we would enter a large inn, and wait till he could speak with the master, and arrange our luggage and places, We went, therefore, into a spacious room and ordered breakfast, when the room was entered by a body of military men of all sorts; but we were suffered to keep our ground till Mr, Boyd came to inform us that we must all decamp!

A CHECK MET WITH—.

Confounded, but without any interrogatory, we vacated the apartment, and Mr. Boyd conducted us not to the barge, not to the wharf, but to the road back to Brussels; telling us, in an accent of depression, that he feared all was lost-that Bonaparte was advancing-that his point was decidedly Brussels-and that the Duke of Wellington had sent orders that all the magazines, the artillery, and the warlike stores of every description, and all the wounded, the maimed, and the sick, should be immediately removed to Antwerp. For this purpose he had issued directions that every barge, every boat should be seized for the use of the army, and that everything of value should be conveyed away, the hospitals emptied, and Brussels evacuated.

If this intelligence filled us with the most fearful alarm, how much more affrighting still was the sound of cannon which next assailed our ears! The dread reverberation became louder and louder as we proceeded. Every shot tolled to our imaginations the death of myriads; and the conviction that the destruction and devastation were so near us, with the probability that if all attempt at escape should prove abortive, we might be personally involved in the carnage, gave us sensations too awful for verbal expression; we could only gaze and tremble, listen and shudder.

Yet, strange to relate! on re-entering the city, all seemed quiet and tranquil as usual! and though it was in this imminent and immediate danger of being invested, and perhaps pillaged, I saw no outward mark of distress or disturbance, or even of hurry or curiosity.

Having re-lodged us in the Rue d'Assault, Mr. Boyd tried to find some land carriage for our removal. But not only every chaise had been taken, and every diligence secured, the cabriolets, the calèches, nay, the waggons and the carts; and every species of caravan, had been seized for Military service. And, after the utmost efforts he could make, in every kind of way, he told us we must wait the chances of the day, for that there was no possibility of escape from Brussels either by land or water.

Remedy there was none; nor had we any other resource; we were fain, therefore, quietly to submit. Mr. Boyd, however, assured me that, though no land carriage was likely to find horses during this furious contest, he had been promised the return of a barge for the next morning, if he and his party would be at the wharf by six o'clock. We all therefore agreed that, if we were spared any previous calamity, we would set out for the wharf at five o'clock, and I accepted their invitation to be with them in the evening, and spend the night at their house. We then separated; I was anxious to get home, to watch the post, and to write to Trèves.

A CAPTURED FRENCH GENERAL.

My reappearance produced no effect upon my hosts: they saw my return with the same placid civility that they had seen my departure. But even apathy, or equanimity,—which shall I call it?—like theirs was now to be broken; I was seated at my bureau and writing, when a loud "hurrah!" reached my ears from some distance, while the daughter of my host, a girl of about eighteen, gently opening my door, said the fortune of the day had suddenly turned, and that Bonaparte was taken prisoner. At the same time the "hurrah!" came nearer. I flew to the window; my host and hostess came also, crying, "Bonaparte est pris! le voil! le Voil!" (278)

I then saw, on a noble war-horse in full equipinent, a general in the splendid uniform of France but visibly disarmed, and, to all appearance, tied to his horse, or, at least, held on, so as to disable him from making any effort to gallop it off, and surrounded, preceded, and followed by a. crew of roaring wretches, who seemed eager for the moment when he should be lodged where they had orders to conduct him, that they might unhorse, strip, pillage him, and divide the spoil.

His high, feathered, glittering helmet he had pressed down as low as he could on his forehead, and I could not discern his face; but I was instantly certain he was not Bonaparte, on finding the whole commotion produced by the rifling crew above mentioned, which, though it might be guided, probably, by some subaltern officer, who might have the captive in charge, had left the field of battle at a moment when none other could be spared, as all the attendant throng were evidently amongst the refuse of the army followers.

I was afterwards informed that this unfortunate general was the Count Lobau. He met with singular consideration during his captivity in the Low Countries, having thence taken to himself a wife. That wife I had met when last in Paris, at a ball given by Madame la Princesse de Beauvau. She was quite young and extremely pretty, and the gayest of the gay, laughing, chatting the whole evening, chiefly with the fat and merry, good-humoured Duchesse de Feltre (Madame la Mar,chale Clarke) and her husband, high in office, in fame, and in favour, was then absent on some official duty.

THE DEARTH OF NEWS.

The dearth of any positive news from the field of battle, even in the heart of Brussels, at this crisis, when everything that was dear and valuable to either party was at stake, was at one instant nearly distracting in its torturing suspense to the wrung nerves, and at another insensibly blunted them into a kind of amalgamation with the Belgic philosophy. At certain houses, as well as at public offices, news, I doubt not, arrived; but no means were taken to—promulgate it—no gazettes, as in London, no bulletins, as in Paris, were cried about the streets; we were all left at once to our conjectures and our destinies.

The delusion of victory vanished into a merely passing advantage, as I gathered from the earnest researches into which it led me; and evil only met all ensuing investigation; retreat and defeat were the words in every mouth around me!

The Prussians, it was asserted, were completely vanquished on the 15th, and the English on the 16th, while on the day just passed, the 17th, a day of continual fighting and bloodshed, drawn battles on both sides left each party proclaiming what neither party could prove—success.

It was Sunday; but church service was out of the question though never were prayers more frequent, more fervent, Form, indeed, they could not have, nor union, while constantly expecting the enemy with fire and sword at the gates, who could enter a place of worship, at the risk of making it a scene of slaughter? But who, also, in circumstances so awful, could require the exhortation of a priest or the example of a congregation, to stimulate devotion? No! in those fearful exigencies, where, in the full vigour of health, strength, and life's freshest resources, we seem destined to abruptly quit this mortal coil, we need no spur—all is spontaneous; and the soul is unshackled.

RUMOURS OF THE FRENCH COMING.

Not above a quarter of an hour had I been restored to my sole occupation of solace, before I was again interrupted and startled; but not as on the preceding occasion by riotous shouts; the sound was a howl, violent, loud, affrighting, and issuing from many voices. I ran to the window, and saw the March, aux Bois suddenly filling with a populace, pouring in from all its avenues, and hurrying on rapidly, and yet as if unconscious in what direction; while women with children in their arms, or clinging to their clothes, ran screaming out of doors - and cries, though not a word was ejaculated, filled the air, and from every house, I saw windows closing, and shutters fastening; all this, though long in writing, was presented to my eyes in a single moment, and was followed in another by a burst into my apartment, to announce that the French were come!

I know not even who made this declaration; my head was out of the window, and the person who made it scarcely entered the room and was gone.

How terrific was this moment! My perilous situation urged me to instant flight; and, without waiting to speak to the people of the house, I crammed my papers and money into a basket, and throwing on a shawl and bonnet, I flew down stairs and out of doors.

My intention was to go to the Boyds, to partake, as I had engaged, their fate, but the crowd were all issuing from the way I must have turned to have gained the Rue d'Assault, and I thought, therefore, I might be safer with Madame de Maurville, who, also, not being English, might be less obnoxious to the Bonapartists. To the Rue de la Montagne I hurried, in consequence, my steps crossing and crossed by an affrighted multitude; but I reached it in safety, and she received me with an hospitable welcome. I found her calm, and her good humour undisturbed. Inured to revolutions, under which she had smarted so as she could smart no more, from the loss of all those who had been the first objects of her solicitude, a husband and three sons! she was now hardened in her feelings upon public events, though her excellent heart was still affectionate and zealous for the private misfortunes of the individuals whom she loved.

What a dreadful day did I pass! dreadful in the midst of its glory! for it was not during those operations that sent details partially to our ears that we could judge of the positive state of affairs, or build upon any permanency of success. Yet here I soon recovered from all alarm for personal safety, and lost the horrible apprehension of being in the midst of a city that was taken, sword in hand, by an enemy-an apprehension that, while it lasted, robbed me of breath, chilled my blood, and gave me a shuddering ague that even now in fancy returns as I seek to commit it to paper.

FRENCH PRISONERS BROUGHT IN.

The alert (279) which had produced this effect, I afterwards learnt, though not till the next day, was utterly false; but whether it had been produced by mistake or by deceit I never knew. The French, indeed, were coming; but not triumphantly, they were prisoners, surprised and taken suddenly, and brought in, being disarmed, by an escort; and, as they were numerous, and their French uniform was discernible from afar, the almost universal belief at Brussels that Bonaparte was invincible, might perhaps, without any intended deception, have raised the report that they were advancing as conquerors.

NEWS OF WATERLOO.

I attempt no description of this day, the grandeur of which was unknown, or unbelieved, in Brussels till it had taken its flight, and could only be named as time past. The Duke of Wellington and Prince Blucher were too mightily engaged in meriting fame to spare an instant for either claiming or proclaiming it.

I was fain, therefore, to content myself with the intelligence that reached Madame de Maurville fortuitously. The crowds in the streets, the turbulence, the inquietude, the bustle the noise, the cries, the almost yells, kept up a perpetual expectation of annoyance. The door was never opened, but I felt myself pale and chill with fear of some sanguinary attack or military surprise. It is true that as Brussels was not fortified and could, in itself, offer no resistance, it could neither b' besieged nor taken by storm; but I felt certain that the Duke of Wellington would combat for it inch by inch, and that in a conflict between life and death, every means would be resorted to that could be suggested by desperation.

Madame de Maurville now told me that an English commissary was just arrived from the army, who had assured her that the tide of success was completely turned to the side of the Allies. She offered to conduct me to his apartment, which was in the same hotel as her own, and in which he was writing and transacting business gravely assuring me, and I really believe, herself, that he could not but be rejoiced to give me, in person, every particular I could wish to hear. I deemed it, however, but prudent not to put his politeness to a test so severe.

Urgent, nevertheless, to give me pleasure, and not easily set aside from following her own conceptions, she declared she would go down stairs, and inform Mr. Saumarez that she had a countrywoman of his in her room, whom he would be charmed to oblige. I tried vainly to stop her; good humour, vivacity, curiosity, and zeal were all against my efforts; she went, and to my great surprise returned escorted by Mr. Saumarez himself. His narration was all triumphant and his account of the Duke of Wellington might almost have seemed an exaggerated panegyric if it had painted some warrior in a chivalresque romance. . . . I could not but be proud of this account: independent from its glory; my revived imagination hung the blessed laurels of peace.

But though Hope was all alive, Ease and Serenity were not her companions: Mr. Saumarez could not disguise that there was still much to do, and consequently to apprehend; and he had never, he said, amongst the many he had viewed, seen a field of battle in such excessive disorder. Military carriages of all sorts, and multitudes of groups unemployed, occupied spaces that ought to have been left for manoeuvring or observation. I attribute this to the various nations who bore arms on that great day in their own manner; though the towering generalissimo of all cleared the ground, and dispersed what was unnecessary at every moment that was not absorbed by the fight.

When the night of this memorable day arrived, I took leave of Madame de Maurville to join the Boyds, according to my engagement: for though all accounts confirmed the victory of the Duke of Wellington, we had so little idea of its result, that we still imagined the four days already spent in the work of carnage must be followed by as many more, before the dreadful conflict could terminate.

Madame de Maurville lent me her servant, with whom I now made my way tolerably well, for though the crowd remained, it was no longer turbulent. A general knowledge of general success to the Allies was everywhere spread; curiosity therefore began to be satisfied, and inquietude to be removed. The concourse were composedly—for no composure is like that of the Flemings—listening to details of the day in tranquil groups, and I had no interruption to my walk but from my own anxiety to catch, as I could, some part of the relations. As all these have since been published, I omit them, though the interest with which I heard them was, at the moment, intense.

Three or four shocking sights intervened during my passage, of officers of high rank, either English or Belge, and either dying or dead, extended upon biers, carried by soldiers. The view of their gay and costly attire, with the conviction of their suffering, or fatal state, joined to the profound silence of their bearers and attendants, was truly saddening; and if my reflections were morally dejecting, what, oh what were my personal feelings and fears, in the utter uncertainty whether this victory were more than a passing triumph! In one place we were entirely stopped by a group that had gathered round a horse, of which a British soldier was examining one of the knees. The animal was a tall war-horse, and one of the noblest of his species. The soldier was enumerating to his hearers its high qualities, and exultingly acquainting them it was his own property, as he had taken it, if I understood right, from the fields He produced also a very fine ring, which was all he had taken of spoil. Yet this man gravely added that pillage had been forbidden by the commander-in-chief!

I found the Boyds still firm for departure. The news of the victory of the day, gained by the Duke of Wellington and Prince Blucher, had raised the highest delight; but further intelligence had just reached them that the enemy, since the great battle, was working to turn the right wing of the Duke of Wellington, who was in the most imminent danger; and that the capture of Brussels was expected to take place the next morning, as everything indicated that Brussels was the point at which Bonaparte aimed, to retrieve his recent defeat. Mr. Boyd used every possible exertion to procure chaises or diligence, or any sort of land conveyance, for Antwerp, but every horse was under military requisition, even the horses of the farmers, of the nobility and gentry, and of travellers. The hope of water-carriage was all that remained. We were to set off so early, that we agreed not to retire to rest.

THE VICTORY DECLARED TO BE COMPLETE.

A gentleman, however, of their acquaintance, presently burst into the room with assurances that the enemy was flying in all directions, his better news reanimated my courage for Brussels and my trust in the Duke of Wellington; and when the Boyd family summoned me the next morning at four or five o'clock to set off with them for Antwerp, I permitted my repugnance to quitting the only spot where I could receive letters from Trèves to conquer every obstacle, and begged them to excuse my changed purpose. They wondered at my temerity, and probably blamed it; but there was no time for discussion, and we separated.

It was not till Tuesday, the 20th, I had certain and satisfactory assurances how complete was the victory. At the house of Madame de Maurville I heard confirmed and detailed the matchless triumph of the matchless Wellington, interspersed with descriptions of scenes of slaughter on the field of battle to freeze the blood, and tales of woe amongst mourning survivors in Brussels to rend the heart. While listening with speechless avidity to these relations, we were joined by M. de la Tour du Pin, who is a cousin of Madame de Maurville, and who said the Duke of Wellington had galloped to Brussels from Wavre to see the Prince of Orange and inquire in person after his wounds. Prince Blucher was in close pursuit of Bonaparte, who was totally defeated, his baggage all taken, even his private equipage and personals, and who was a fugitive himself, and in disguise! The duke considered the battle to be so decisive, that while prince Blucher was posting after the remnant of the Bonapartian army, he determined to follow himself as convoy to Louis XVIII; and he told M. de la Tour du Pin and the Duke de Fitzjames, whom he met at the palace of the King of Holland, to acquaint their king with this his proposal, and to beg his majesty to set forward without delay to join him for its execution. The Duke de Fitzjames was gone already to Gand with his commission.

How daring a plan was this, while the internal state of France was so little known, while les places fortes (280) were all occupied, and while the corps of Grouchy was still intact, and the hidden and possible resources of Bonaparte were unfathomed!

The event, however, demonstrated that the Duke of Wellington had judged with as much quickness of perception as intrepidity of valour.

'Twas to Tournay he had desired that the King of France would repair.

THE WOUNDED AND THE PRISONERS.

The duke now ordered that the hospitals, invalids, magazines, etc, should all be stationed at Brussels, which he regarded as saved from invasion and completely secure. It is not near the scene of battle that war, even with victory, wears an aspect of felicity, no, not even in the midst of its highest resplendence of glory. A more terrific or afflicting sojourn than that of Brussels at this period can hardly be imagined. The universal voice declared that so sanguinary a battle as that which was fought almost in its neighbourhood, and quite within its hearing, never yet had spread the plains with slaughter; and though exultation cannot ever have been prouder, nor satisfaction more complete, in the brilliancy of success, all my senses were shocked in viewing the effects of its attainment. For more than a week from this time I never approached my window but to witness sights of wretchedness. Maimed, wounded, bleeding, mutilated, tortured victims of this exterminating contest passed by every minute: the fainting, the sick, the dying and the dead, on brancards, (281) In carts, in waggons, succeeded one another without intermission. There seemed to be a whole and a large army of disabled or lifeless soldiers! All that was intermingled with them bore an aspect of still more poignant horror; for the Bonapartian Prisoners who were now poured into the city by hundreds, had a mien of such ferocious desperation, where they were marched on, uninjured, from having been taken by surprise or overpowered by numbers - or faces of such anguish, where they were drawn on in open vehicles, the helpless victims of gushing wounds or horrible dislocations, that to see them without commiseration for their sufferings, or admiration for the heroic, however misled enthusiasm, to which they Were martyrs, must have demanded an apathy dead to all feeling but what is personal, or a rancour too ungenerous to yield even to the view of defeat.

Both the one set and the other of these unhappy warriors endured their calamities with haughty forbearance of complaint, The maimed and lacerated, while their ghastly visages spoke torture and death, bit their own clothes, perhaps their flesh! to save the loud utterance of their groans; while those of their comrades who had escaped these corporeal inflictions seemed to be smitten with something between remorse and madness that they had not forced themselves on to destruction ere thus they were exhibited in dreadful parade through the streets of that city they had been sent forth to conquer. Others of these wretched prisoners had, to me, as I first saw them, the air of the lowest and most disgusting of jacobins, in dirty tattered vestments of all sorts and colours, or soiled carters' frocks; but disgust was soon turned to pity, when I afterwards learnt that these shabby accoutrements had been cast over them by their conquerors after despoiling them of their own.

Everybody was wandering from home; all Brussels seemed living in the streets. The danger to the city, which had imprisoned all its inhabitants except the rabble or the military, once completely passed, the pride of feeling and showing their freedom seemed to stimulate their curiosity in seeking details on what had passed and was passing. But neither the pride nor the joy of victory was anywhere of an exulting nature. London and Paris render all other places that I, at least, have dwelt in, tame and insipid. Bulletins in a few shop-windows alone announced to the general public that the Allies had vanquished and that Bonaparte was a fugitive.

I met at the embassy an old English officer who gave me most interesting and curious information, assuring me that in the carriage of Bonaparte, which had been seized, there were proclamations ready printed, and even dated from the palace of Lachen, announcing the downfall of the Allies and the triumph of Bonaparte! But no satisfaction could make me hear without deadly dismay and shuddering his description of the field of battle. Piles of dead!—Heaps, masses, hills of dead bestrewed the plains!

I met also Colonel Jones; so exulting in success! so eager to remind me of his assurances that all was safe! And I was much interested in a narration made to me by a wounded soldier, who was seated in the courtyard of the embassy. He had been taken prisoner after he was severely wounded, on the morning of the 18th, and forced into a wood with many others, where he had been very roughly used, and stripped of his coat, waistcoat, and even his shoes; but as the fortune of the day began to turn, there was no one left to watch him, and he crawled on all-fours till he got out of the wood, and was found by some of his roving comrades.

Thousands, I believe I may say without exaggeration, were employed voluntarily at this time in Brussels in dressing wounds and attending the sick beds of the wounded. Humanity could be carried no further; for not alone the Belgians and English were thus nursed and assisted, nor yet the Allies, but the prisoners also; and this, notwithstanding the greatest apprehensions being prevalent that the sufferers, from their multitude, would bring pestilence into the heart of the city.

The immense quantity of English, Belgians, and Allies, who were first, of course, conveyed to the hospitals and prepared houses of Brussels, required so much time for carriage and placing, that although the carts, waggons, and every attainable or seizable vehicle were unremittingly in motion- now coming, now returning to the field of battle for more, it was nearly a week, or at least five or six days, ere the unhappy wounded prisoners, who were necessarily last served, could be accommodated. And though I was assured that medical and surgical aid was administered to them wherever it was possible, the blood that dried upon their skins and their garments, joined to the dreadful sores occasioned by this neglect, produced an effect so pestiferous, that, at every new entry, eau de Cologne, or vinegar, was resorted to by every inhabitant, even amongst the shopkeepers, even amongst the commonest persons, for averting the menaced contagion.

Even the churches were turned into hospitals, and every house in Brussels was ordered to receive or find an asylum for some of the sick.

The Boyds were eminently good in nursing, dressing wounds, making slops, and administering comfort amongst the maimed, whether friend or foe. Madame d'Henin sent her servants, and money, and cordials to all the French that came within her reach; Madame de la Tour du Pin was munificent in the same attentions; and Madame de Maurville never passed by an opportunity of doing good. M. de Beaufort, being far the richest of my friends at this place, was not spared; he had officers and others quartered upon him without mercy.

We were all at work more or less in making lint. For me, I was about amongst the wounded half the day, the British, s'entend! The rising in France for the honour of the nation now, and for its safety in independence hereafter, was brilliant and delightful, spreading in some directions from La Manche to La M,diterran,e: the focus of loyalty was Bordeaux. The king left Gand the 22nd. All Alost, etc, surrounded followed, or preceded him. The noble Blucher entered France at Mortes le Chateau.

HOSTILITIES AT AN END: TE DEUM FOR THE VICTORY,

It was not till June 26th that the blessed news reached me of the cessation of hostilities. Colonel Beaufort was the first who brought me this intelligence, smiling kindly himself at the smiles he excited. Next came la Princesse d'Henin, escorted by my and her highly valued M, de Lally Tolendal. With open arms that dear princess reciprocated congratulations. Madame de Maurville next followed, always cordial where she could either give or behold happiness. The Boyds hurried to me in a body to wish and be wished joy. And last, but only in time, not in kindness, came Madame la Vicomtesse de Laval, mother to the justly honoured philanthropist, or, as others—but not I—call him, bigot, M. Mathieu de Montmorency, who, at this moment, is M. le Duc de Montmorency.

Brussels now, which had seemed for so many days, from the unremitting passage of maimed, dying, or dead, a mere out-door hospital, revived, or, rather, was invigorated to something above its native state; for from uninteresting tameness it became elevated to spirit, consequence, and vivacity.

On the following Sunday I had the gratification of hearing, at the Protestant chapel, the Te Deum for the grand victory, in presence of the King and Queen of the Low Countries—or Holland, and of the Dowager Princess of Orange, and the young warrior her grandson. This prince looked so ill, so meagre, so weak, from his half-cured wounds, that to appear on this occasion seemed another, and perhaps not less dangerous effort of heroism, added to those which had so recently distinguished him in the field. What enthusiasm would such an exertion, with his pallid appearance, have excited in London or Paris! even here, a little gentle huzza greeted him from his carriage to the chapel, and for the same short passage, back again. After which, he drove off as tranquilly as any common gentleman might have driven away, to return to his home and his family dinner.

About the middle of July, but I am not clear of the date, the news was assured and confirmed of the brilliant re-enthronement of Louis XVIII, and that Bonaparte had surrendered to the English. Brussels now became an assemblage of all nations, from the rapturous enthusiasm that pervaded all to view the field of battle, the famous Waterloo, and gather upon the spot details of the immortal victory of Wellington.

MATERNAL ADVICE.

(Madame d'Arblay to her son.) April 26, 1815. At length, my long expecting eyes meet again your hand-writing, after a breach of correspondence that I can never 'recollect without pain. Revive it not in my mind by any repetition, and I will dismiss it from all future power of tormenting me, by considering it only as a dream of other times. Cry "Done!" my Alex, and I will skip over the subject, not perhaps as lightly, but as swiftly as you skip over the hills of Norbury Park. I delight to think of the good and pleasure that sojourn may do you; though easily, too easily, I conceive the melancholy reflections that were awakened by the sight of our dear, dear cottage; yet your expressions upon its view lose much of their effect by being overstrained, recherches, and designing to be pathetic. We never touch others, my dear Alex, where we study to show we are touched ourselves. I beg you, when you write to me, to let your pen paint your thoughts as they rise, not as you seek or labour to embellish them. I remember you once wrote me a letter so very fine from Cambridge, that, if it had not made me laugh, it would certainly have made me sick. Be natural, my dear boy, and you will be sure to please Your mother without wasting your time.

Let us know what you have received, what you have spent, what you may have still unpaid, and what you yet want. But for this last article, we both desire you will not wait our permission to draw upon your aunt, whom we shall empower to draw upon Mr. Hoare in our names. We know you to have no wanton extravagances, and no idle vanity, we give you, therefore, dear Alex, carte blanche to apply to your aunt, only consulting with her, and begging her kind, maternal advice to help your inexperience in regulating your expenses. She knows the difference that must be made between our fortune and that of Clement, but she knows our affection for our boy, and our confidence in his honour and probity, and will treat him with as much kindness, though not with equal luxury.

Your father charges you never to be without your purse, and never to let it be empty. Your aunt will counsel you about your clothes. About your books we trust to yourself. And pray don't forget, when you make sleeping visits, to recompense the trouble you must unavoidably give to servants. And if you join any party to any public place, make a point to pay for yourself. It will be far better to go seldom, and with that gentlemanly spirit, than often, with the air of a hanger-on. How infinitely hospitable has been your uncle James! But hospitality is his characteristic. We had only insisted upon your regularity at chapel and at lectures, and we hear of your attention to them comparatively, and we are fixed to be contented en attendant. Don't lose courage, dear, dear Alex, the second place is the nearest to the first. I love you with all my heart and soul! . . .

ABOUT THE GREAT BATTLE.

(Madame d'Arblay to General d'Arblay.) Monday, June 19, 1815. The sitting up all night, however little merrily, made me, I know not how, seem to have lived a day longer than real time, for I thought to-day the 20th when I finished my letter of this morning. I have now, therefore, to rectify that Mistake, and tell you that there is, therefore, no chasm in the known history of the Duke of Wellington. But, to my infinite regret, with all the great, nay marvellous feats he has performed, he is less, not more, in public favour, from not being approved, or rather, I think, comprehended, in the opening of this tremendous business. As I am sure the subject must be of deeper interest to you than any other, at such an instant, I will tell you all I know-all I have heard and gathered, for I know nothing, and add my own consequent conjectures, as soon as I have first acquainted you that I separated from the Boyds at about half past seven in the morning, too much satisfied with the news of Lord Wellington's victory to endure to distance myself still further from all I love most upon earth. They, therefore, still alarmed, went to Antwerp, and I am again at the little bureau, upon which my dearest ami has sometimes written in the March, aux Bois.

The first news the Duke of Wellington was known to receive of the invasion of les Pays Bas was at a ball at the Duchess of Richmond's. He would not break up the party, more than half of which was formed of his officers, nor suffer any interruption. Some time after, however, he went out, and when he returned distributed cards of orders to the several commanding officers. But he stayed to supper, after which fifty red-coats retired abruptly. Not so the duke—and he is now much—Ah, mon ami, two letters arrive at the same instant, that curtail all subjects but what belong to themselves. Nous allons commencer!—Heaven preserve and prosper the beloved partner of my soul. I dare enter upon nothing; I can only say the first of the two letters, written before the order of commencer was issued, is one of the fullest and dearest I have in my possession; and I shall read and re-read its interesting contents with heart-felt pleasure.

Tell, tell me, my beloved ami, where, when you would have me remove? I will not ask how—I will find that out. To be nearer to you—to hear more frequently—oh, what a solace!

The maimed, wounded, bleeding, fainting, arrive still every minute. There seems a whole, and a large army of mutilated Soldiers. Jerome is said to be killed, and Vandamme to have lost both legs. (282) Our loss is yet incalculable.

Every creature that was movable is gone to Antwerp, or England, but myself but my intense desire not to lose ground or time in my letters made me linger to the last, and now, thank heaven, all danger here is at an end, and all fugitives are returning.

The imperial guard is almost annihilated. They fought like demons. Napoleon cried out continually to them, the prisoners say, "A Bruxelles, mes enfans! Bruxelles! Bruxelles!" They were reported one day to be actually arrived here. I never saw, never, indeed, felt such consternation. Not only money, jewels, and valuables of pecuniary sorts were shut up, but babies from the arms of their terrified mothers and nurses. I flew out myself, to take refuge in the apartments of Madame de Maurville, and I never witnessed such horror and desolation.

I have left this for a word at the last minute. This is Wednesday, June 21st.... Mr Kirkpatrick tells me Murat is dead of his wounds; (283) Vandamme lost his two thighs, and is dead also; Jerome died of a cannon-ball at once. Poor M, de Vincent, the Austrian, has a ball still in his arm, which they cannot extract, Lord Fitzroy Somerset has an arm shot off; Lord Uxbridge a leg. Col. Hamilton is killed. Lobau is here a prisoner. I shall continue to write all the particulars I can gather. It has been the most bloody battle that ever was fought, and the victory the most entire.

AN ACCIDENT BEFALLS GENERAL D'ARBLAY.

On the 19th of July, 1815, during the ever memorable Hundred Days, I was writing to my best friend, when I received a visit from la Princesse d'Henin and Colonel de Beaufort, who entered the room with a sort of precipitancy and confusion that immediately struck me as the effect of evil tidings which they came to communicate. My ideas instantly flew to the expectation of new public disaster, when Madame d'Henin faintly pronounced the name of M. d'Arblay. Alarmed, I turned from one to the other in speechless trepidation, dreading to ask, while dying to know what awaited me. Madame d'Henin then said, that M. de Beaufort had received a letter from M. d'Arblay: and I listened with subdued, yet increasing terror, while they acquainted me that M. d'Arblay had received on the calf of his leg a furious kick from a wild horse, which had occasioned so bad a wound as to confine him to his bed - and that he wished M. de Beaufort to procure me some travelling guide, that I might join him as soon as it would be possible with safety and convenience.

But what was my agony when I saw that the letter was not in his own band! I conjured them to leave me, and let me read it alone. They offered, the one to find me a clever femme de chambre, the other to inquire for a guide to aid me to set out, if able, the next day; but I rather know this from recollection than from having understood them at the time: I only entreated their absence; and having consented to their return in a few hours, I forced them away.

No sooner were they gone, than, calming my spirits by earnest and devout prayer, which alone supports my mind, and even preserves my senses, in deep calamity, I ran over the letter, which was dated the fourth day after the wound, and acknowledged that three incisions had been made in the leg unnecessarily by an ignorant surgeon, which had so aggravated the danger, as well as the suffering, that he was now in bed, not only from the pain of the lacerated limb, but also from a nervous fever! and that no hope was held Out to him of quitting it in less than a fortnight or three weeks.

MADAME D'ARBLAY'S DIFFICULTIES IN REJOINING HER HUSBAND.

I determined not to wait, though the poor sufferer himself had charged that I should, either for the femme de chambe of Madame d'Henin or the guide of M. de Beaufort, which they could not quite promise even for the next day; and to me the next hour seemed the delay of an age. I went, therefore to order a chaise at six on the road to Luxembourg. The' answer was, that no horses were to be had!

Almost distracted, I flew myself to the inn; but the answer was repeated! The route to Luxembourg, they told me, was infested with straggling parties, first, from the wandering army of Grouchy, now rendered pillagers from want of food; and next, from the pursuing army of the Prussians, who made themselves pillagers also through the rights of conquest. To travel in a chaise would be impracticable, they assured me, without a guard.

I now resolved upon travelling in the diligence, and desired to secure a place in that for Trèves. There was none to that city!

"And what is the nearest town to Trèves, whence I might go on in a chaise?"

"Luxembourg."

I bespoke a place, but was told that the diligence had set off the very day before, and that none other would go for six days, as it only quitted Brussels once a week.

My friend the Baroness de Spagen next told me that, if travel I would, I had but to go by Liège, which, though not a direct, was the only safe road; that then she would put me under the protection of her brother-in-law, the Comte de Spagen, who was himself proceeding to that city by the ensuing night- coach.

I accepted this kindness with rapture. I flew myself to the book-keeper I had so abruptly quitted, and instantly secured a place in the Liège diligence for night; and I was taking leave of my hosts, a Brussels fiacre being at the door, laden with my little luggage, when I was told that Le Roi, the confidential servant of Madame d'Henin, besought to speak a word to me from his mistress. He told me that the Princesse 'was quite miserable at my hazardous plan, which she had gathered from Madame de la Tour du Pin, and that she supplicated me to postpone my purpose only till the next day, when I should have some one of trust to accompany me.

I assured him that nothing now could make me risk procrastination, but begged him to still the fears of the excellent Princesse by acquainting her I should be under the protection of the Comte de Spagen. I arrived at the inn after this last unprepared-for impediment, three or four minutes too late! What was the fermentation of my mind at this news! A whole week I must wait for the next diligence, and even then lose the aid and countenance of le Comte de Spagen.

Le Roi, who, through some short cut of footpaths and alleys, had got to the inn before me, earnestly pressed me, in the style of the confidential old servants of the French nobility, to go and compose myself chez la princesse. Even my host and hostess had pursued to wish me again good-bye, and now expressed their warm hopes I should return to them. But the book-keeper alone spoke a language to snatch me from despair, by saying my fiacre might perhaps catch the diligence two miles off, in the All,e Verte, where it commonly stopped for fresh passengers or parcels.

Eagerly I promised the coachman a reward if he could succeed, and off he drove. The diligence was at the appointed place, and that instant ready to proceed! I rushed into it with trepidation of hurry, and when more composed, I was eager to find out which of my fellow- travellers might be the Comte de Spagen; but I dared risk no question. I sat wholly silent. We arrived at Liège about nine in the morning I now advanced to the book-keeper, and made inquiries about the Comte de Spagen.

He had arrived in the earlier coach, and was gone on in some other to his estates.

As calmly as was in my power, I then declared my purpose to go to Trèves, and begged to be put on my way.

I was come wrong, the book-keeper answered; the road was by Luxembourg.

And how was I to get thither?

By Brussels, he said, and a week hence, the diligence having set off the day before.

Alas, I well knew that! and entreated some other means to forward me to Trèves,

He replied that he knew of none from Liège; but that if I would go to Aix, I might there, perhaps, though it was out of the road, hear of some conveyance; but he asserted it was utterly impossible I could leave Li ge without a passport from the Prussian police-office, where I should only and surely be detained if I had not one to show from whence I came. This happily, reminded me of the one I had from M. de jaucourt' in Paris, and which was fortunately, though accidentally, in my hand-basket.

Arrived at Aix, I earnestly inquired for a conveyance to Trèves; none existed! nor could I hear of any at all, save a diligence to juliers, which was to set out at four o'clock the next morning. To lose thus a whole day, and even then to go only more north instead of south, almost cast me into despair. But redress there was none, and I was forced to secure myself a place to Juliers, whence, I was told, I might get on.

At any more tranquil period I should have seized this interval for visiting the famous old cathedral and the tomb of Charlemagne; but now I thought not of them; I did not even recollect that Aix-la-Chapelle had been the capital of that emperor. I merely saw the town through a misty, mizzling rain, and that the road all around it was sandy and heavy, or that all was discoloured by my own disturbed view.

I laid down, in a scarcely furnished apartment, without undressing. I suffered no shutter or curtain to be closed, lest i should lose my vehicle; and such was my anxiety, that at three o'clock, by my own watch, I descended to inquire if we were not to set off. I wandered about by the twilight of a season that is never quite dark, but met no one. I returned to my chamber, but, always in terror of being forgotten, descended again in a quarter of an hour, though still without success. An hour, says Dr. Johnson, may be tedious, but it cannot be long: four o'clock at last struck, and I ran into a vehicle then ready in the courtyard of the auberge. (284)

I found myself alone, which, at first, was a great relief to my mind, that was overburthened with care and apprehension, and glad of utter silence. Ere long, however, I found it fed my melancholy, which it was my business rather to combat and I was not, therefore, sorry when a poor woman with a child was admitted from the outside through the charity of the coachman, as the rain grew heavier.

At Juliers we stopped at a rather large inn, at the head of an immensely long market-place. It was nearly empty, except where occupied by straggling soldiers, poor, lame, or infirm labourers, women, and children. The universal war of the Continent left scarcely a man unmaimed to be seen in civil life. The women who met my eyes were all fat, with very round and very brown faces. Most of them were barefooted, nay, barelegged, and had on odd small caps, very close round their visages. The better sort, I fancy, at that critical time, had hidden themselves or fled the town.

We entered Cologne through an avenue, said to be seven miles in length, of lime-trees. It was evening, but very light, and Cologne had a striking appearance, from its magnitude and from its profusion of steeples. The better sort of houses were white and looked neat, though in an old-fashioned style, and elaborately ornamented. But, between the ravages of time and of war, the greater part of them seemed crumbling away, if not tumbling down.

A FRIENDLY RECEPTION AT COLOGNE.

But while I expected to be driven on to some auberge, a police officer, in a Prussian uniform, came to the coach-door, and demanded our passports. My companion made herself known as a native, and was let out directly. The officer, having cast his eye over my passport, put his head through the window of the carriage, and, in a low whisper, asked me whether I were French?

French by marriage, though English by birth, I hardly knew which to call myself; I said, however, "Oui." He then, in a voice yet more subdued, gave me to understand that he could serve me. I caught at his offer, and told him I earnestly desired to go straight to Trèves, to a wounded friend. He would do for me what he could, he answered, for he was French himself, though employed by the Prussians. He would carry my passport for me to the magistrate of the place and get it signed without my having any further trouble though only, he feared, to Bonn, or, at farthest, to Coblenz, whence I might probably proceed unmolested. He knew also, and could recommend me to a most respectable lady and gentleman, both French, and under the Prussian hard gripe, where I might spend the evening en famille, and be spared entering any auberge. He conducted me, in silence, passing through the cloisters to a house not far distant, and very retired in its appearance'. Arrived at a door at which he knocked or rang, he still spoke not a word, but when an old man came to open it, in a shabby dress, but with a good and lively face, be gave him some directions in German and in a whisper, and then entrusted with my passport, he bowed to me and hurried away.

The old man led me to a very large room, scarcely at all furnished. He pulled out of a niche a sort of ebony armchair, very tottering and worn, and said he would call madame, for whom he also placed a fauteuil, at the head of an immense and clumsy table. I was then joined by an elderly gentlewoman, who was led in ceremoniously by a gentleman still more elderly. The latter made me three profound obeisances, which I returned with due imitation, while the lady approached me with good breeding, and begged me to take my seat.

The old man then, who I found was their domestic, served the tea. I know not whether this was their general custom, or a compliment to a stranger. But when we had all taken some, they opened into a little conversation. It was I, indeed, who began by apologising for my intrusion, and expressing at the same time my great relief in being spared going to an auberge, alone as I was; but I assured them that the gentleman who had brought me to their dwelling had acted entirely by his own uninfluenced authority.

They smiled or rather tried to smile, for melancholy was seated on their countenances in its most fixed colours and they told me that person was their best friend, and lost no opportunity to offer them succour or comfort. He had let them know my situation, and had desired they would welcome and cheer me. Welcome me, the lady added in French, they did gladly, since I was in distress; but they had little power to cheer me, involved as they were themselves in the depths of sorrow.

Sympathy of compassion soon led to sympathy of confidence; and when they heard to whom I belonged, and the nature of my terrible haste, they related their own sad history. Death, misfortune, and oppression had all laid on them their iron hands; they had lost their sons while forcibly fighting for a usurpation which they abhorred; they had lost their property by emigration; and they had been treated with equal harshness by the revolutionists because they were suspected of loyalty, and by the royalists because their children had served in the armies of the revolutionists. They were now living nearly in penury, and owed their safety and peace solely to the protection of the officer who had brought me to them.

With communications such as these, time passed so little heavily, however sadly, that we were ill-disposed to separate; and eleven o'clock struck, as we sat over their economical but well served and well cooked little supper, ere the idea of retiring was mentioned. They then begged me to go to rest, as I must be at the diligence for Coblenz by four o'clock the next morning.

To another large room, nearly empty except the old, high, and narrow bed, the domestic now conducted me, promising to call me at half-past three o'clock in the morning, and to attend me to the diligence. I did not dare undress; I tied my watch, which was a small repeater, round my wrist, and laid down in my clothes-but to strike my watch, and to pray for my beloved invalid, and my safe restoration to him, filled up, without, I believe, three minutes of repose, the interval to my conductor's return.

At half-past three we set out, after I had safely deposited all I durst spare, where my disinterested, but most poor host would inevitably find my little offering, which, if presented to him, he would probably have refused. I never heard his name, which he seemed studious to hold back; but I have reason to think he was of the ancient provincial noblesse. His manners, and those of his wife, had an antique etiquette in them that can only accord with that idea.

The walk was immensely long; it was through the scraggy and hilly streets I have mentioned, and I really thought it endless. The good domestic carried my luggage. The height of the houses made the light merely not darkness; we met not a creature; and the painful pavement and barred windows, and fear of being too late, made the walk still more dreary.

I was but just in time; the diligence was already drawn out of the inn-yard, and some friends of the passengers were taking leave. I eagerly secured my place - and never so much regretted the paucity of my purse as in my inability to recompense as I wished the excellent domestic whom I now quitted.

FROM COLOGNE TO COBLENZ AND TREVES.

I found myself now in much better society than I had yet been, consisting of two gentlemen, evidently of good education, and a lady. They were all, German, and spoke only that language one to another, though they addressed me in French as often as my absorption in my own ruminations gave any opening for their civility.

And this was soon the case, by my hearing them speak of the Rhine; my thoughts were so little geographical that it had not occurred to me that Cologne was upon that river - I had not, therefore, looked for or perceived it the preceding evening: but upon my now starting at the sound of its name and expressing my Strong -curiosity to behold it, they all began to watch for the first point upon which it became clearly visible, and all five with one voice called out presently after, "Ah, le voil!" (285) But imagination had raised expectations that the Rhine, at this part of its stream, would by no means answer. It seemed neither so wide, so deep, so rapid, nor so grand as my mind had depicted it nor yet were its waters so white or bright as to suit my ideas of its fame. At last my heart became better tuned. I was now on my right road; no longer travelling zig-zag, and as I could procure any means to get on, but in the straight road, by Coblenz, to the city which contained the object of all my solicitude.

And then it was that my eyes opened to the beauties of nature; then it was that the far-famed Rhine found justice in those poor little eyes, which hitherto, from mental preoccupation, or from expectations too high raised, had refused a cordial tribute to its eminent beauty, unless indeed its banks, till after Bonn, are of inferior loveliness. Certain it is, that from this time till my arrival at Coblenz, I thought myself in regions of enchantment.

From Coblenz to Trèves I was two days travelling, though it might with ease have been accomplished in less than half that time. We no longer journeyed in any diligence that may be compared with one of France or of England, but in a queer German carriage, resembling something mixed of a coach, a chaise, and a cart.

MEETING WITH GENERAL D'ARBLAY.

At Trèves, at length, on Monday evening, the 24th of July, 1815, I arrived in a tremor of joy and terror indescribable. But my first care was to avoid hazarding any mischief from surprise; and my first measure was to obtain some intelligence previously to risking an interview. It was now six days since any tidings had reached me. My own last act in leaving Brussels had been to write a few lines to M. de Premorel, my General's aide-de-camp, to announce my journey, and prepare him for my arrival.

I now wrote a few lines to the valet of Monsieur d'Arblay, and desired he would come instantly to the inn for the baggage of Madame d'Arblay, who was then on the road. Hardly five minutes elapsed before Francois, running like a race-horse, though in himself a staid and composed German, appeared before me. How I shook at his sight with terrific suspense! The good-natured creature relieved me instantly though with a relief that struck at my heart with a pang of agony—for he said that the danger was over, and that both the surgeons said so.

He was safe, I thanked God! but danger, positive danger had existed! Faint I felt, though in a tumult of grateful sensations: I took his arm, for my tottering feet would hardly support me; and M. de Premorel, hastening to meet me at the street-door, told me that the general was certain I was already at Trèves; I therefore permitted myself to enter his apartment at once.

Dreadfully suffering, but still mentally occupied by the duties of his profession, I found him. Three wounds had been inflicted on his leg by the kick of a wild horse, which he had bought at Trèves, with intent to train to military service. He was felled by them to the ground. Yet, had he been skilfully attended, he might have been completely cured! But all the best surgeons, throughout every district, had been seized upon for the armies and the ignorant hands into which he fell aggravated the evil, by incisions hazardous, unnecessary, and torturing.

WAITING FOR LEAVE TO RETURN TO FRANCE.

The adjoint of M. d'Arblay, M. le Comte de Mazancourt, had been sent to Paris by M. d'Arblay, to demand leave and passports for returning to France, the battle and peace of Waterloo having ended the purpose for which he had been appointed by Louis XVIII, through the orders of the Maréchal Duc de Feltre, minister at war, to raise recruits from the faithful who wished to quit the usurper.

My poor sufferer had been quartered upon M. Nell, a gentleman of Trèves; but there was no room for me at M. Nell's, and I was obliged—most reluctantly—to be conducted to an hotel at some distance. But the next day M. d'Arblay entered into an agreement with Madame de la Grange, a lady of condition who resided at Trèves, to admit me to eat and lodge at her house, upon the picnic plan, of paying the overplus of that expense I should cause her, with a proper consideration, not mentioned, but added by my dear general, for my apartment and incidental matters. This sort of plan, since their ruin by the Revolution, had become so common as to be called fashionable amongst the aristocratic noblesse, who were too much impoverished to receive their friends under their roofs but by community of fortune during their junction. Every morning after breakfast one of the family conducted me back to M. Nell's, where I remained till the hour of dinner, when M. Godefroy de Premorel commonly gave me le bras for returning, and Francois watched for me at the end of the repast. This was to me a cruel arrangement, forcing my so frequent absences; but I had no choice.

It was not till after reiterated applications by letter, and by MM. de Mazancourt and Premorel in person, that my poor general could obtain his letters of recall; though the re-establishment of Louis XVIII on his throne made the mission on the frontiers null, and though the hapless and helpless state of health of M. d'Arblay would have rendered him incapable of continuing to fulfil its duties if any yet were left to perform. The mighty change of affairs so completely occupied men's minds, as well as their hands, that they could work only for themselves and the present: the absent were utterly forgotten. The Duc de Luxembourg, however, at length interfered, and procured passports, with the ceremonies of recall.

DEPARTURE FOR PARIS.

On the morning of our departure from Trèves, all the families of Nell and La Grange filled the courtyard, and surrounded the little carriage in which we set out, with others, unknown to me, but acquainted with the general, and lamenting to lose sight of him—as who that ever knew him failed doing? M. de Mazancourt and the De Premorels had preceded us. The difficulty of placing the poor wounded leg was great and grievous, and our journey was anything but gay; the cure, alas, was so much worse than incomplete! The spirits of the poor worn invalid were sunk, and, like his bodily strength, exhausted; it was so new to him to be helpless, and so melancholy! After being always the most active, the most enterprising, the most ingenious in difficulty and mischance, and the most vivacious in conquering evils, and combating accidents; to find himself thus suddenly bereft not only of his powers to serve and oblige all around him, but even of all means of aiding and sufficing to himself, was profoundly dejecting; nor, to his patriot-heart, was this all: far otherwise. We re-entered France by the permission of foreigners, and could only re-enter at all by passports of all the Allies! It seemed as if all Europe had freer egress to that country than its natives!

Yet no one more rejoiced in the victory of Waterloo—no one was more elated by the prospect of its glorious results: for the restoration of the monarchy he was most willing to shed the last drop of his blood. But not such was the manner in which he had hoped to see it take place; he had hoped it would have been more spontaneous, and the work of the French themselves to overthrow the usurpation. He felt, therefore, severely shocked, when, at the gates of Thionville, upon demanding admittance by giving his name, his military rank, and his personal passport, he was disregarded and unheard by a Prussian sub-officer—a Prussian to repulse a French general, in the immediate service of his king, from entering France! His choler rose, in defiance of sickness and infirmity; but neither indignation nor representation were of any avail, till he condescended to search his portefeuille for a passport of All the Allies, which the Duc de Luxembourg had wisely forwarded to Trèves, joined to that of the minister at war. Yet the Prussian was not to blame. save for his uncourteous manners: the King of France was only such, at that moment, through Blucher and Wellington.

Three or four days, I think, we passed at Metz, where the general put himself into the hands of a surgeon of eminence, who did what was now to be done to rectify the gross mismanagement at Trèves.

In this time I saw all that was most worth remark in the old and famous city of Metz. But it looked drear and abandoned- as everywhere during my journey. Nothing was yet restored, for confidence was wanting in the state of things. Wellington and Blucher, the lords of the ascendant, seemed alone gifted with the Power of foreseeing, as they had been instrumentally of regulating, events.

A CHANCE VIEW OF THE EMPEROR OF RUSSIA.

Not long after, I forget exactly where, we came under new yet still foreign masters—the Russians; who kept Posts, like sentinels, along the high road, at stated distances. They were gentle and well-behaved, in a manner and to a degree that was really almost edifying. On the plains of Chalons there was a grand Russian encampment. We stopped half a day for rest at some small place in its neighbourhood and I walked about, guarded by the good Francois, to view it. But, on surveying a large old house, which attracted my notice by a group of Russian officers that I observed near its entrance, how was I struck on being told by Francois, that the Emperor of all the Russia's was at that moment its inhabitant! At the entrance of the little gate that opened the palisade stood a lady with two or three gentlemen. There was no crowd, and no party of guards, nor any sign of caution or parade of grandeur, around this royally honoured dwelling. And, in a few minutes, the door was quietly opened and the emperor came out, in an undress uniform, wearing no stars nor orders, and with an air of gay good humour, and unassuming ease. There was something in his whole appearance of hilarity, freedom, youthfulness, and total absence of all thought of state and power, that would have led me much sooner to suppose him a jocund young Lubin, or country esquire, than an emperor, warrior, or a statesman.

The lady curtsied low, and her gentlemen bowed profoundly as he reached the group. He instantly recognised them, and seemed enchanted at their sight. A sprightly conversation ensued, in which he addressed himself chiefly to the lady, who seemed accustomed to his notice, yet to receive it with a species of rapture. The gentlemen also had the easy address of conscious welcome to inspirit them, and I never followed up a conversation I could not hear, with more certainty of its being agreeable to all parties. They all spoke French, and I was restrained only by my own sense of propriety from advancing within hearing 'of every word; for no sentinel, nor guard of any kind, interfered to keep the few lookers on at a distance;

This discourse over, be gallantly touched his bat and leaped into his open carriage, attended by a Russian officer, and was out of sight in a moment. How far more happy, disengaged, and to his advantage, was this view of his imperial majesty, than that which I had had the year before in England, where the crowds that surrounded, and the pressure of unrestrained curiosity and forwardness, certainly embarrassed, if they did not actually displease him!

ENGLISH TROOPS IN OCCUPATION.

At Meaux I left again my captive companion for a quarter of an hour to visit the cathedral of the sublimely eloquent Bossuet. In happier moments I should not have rested Without discovering and tracing the house, the chamber, the library, the study, the garden which had been as it were sanctified by his virtues, his piety, his learning, and his genius and oh, how eagerly, if not a captive, would my noble-minded companion have been my conductor!

A new change again of military control soon followed, at which I grieved for my beloved companion. I almost felt ashamed to look at him, though my heart involuntarily, irresistibly palpitated with emotions which had little, indeed, in unison with either grief or shame; for the sentinels, the guards, the camps, became English.

All converse between us now stopped involuntarily, and as if by tacit agreement. M. d'Arblay was too sincere a loyalist to be sorry, yet too high-spirited a freeman to be satisfied. I could devise nothing; to say that might not cause some painful discussion or afflicting retrospection, and we travelled many miles in pensive silence-each nevertheless intensely observant of the astonishing new scene presented to our view, on re-entering the capital of France, to see the vision of Henry V. revived, and Paris in the hands of the English!

I must not omit to mention that notwithstanding this complete victory over Bonaparte, the whole of the peasantry and common people, converse with them when or where or how I might during our route, with one accord avowed themselves utterly incredulous of his defeat. They all believed he had only given way in order that he might come forward with new forces to extirpate all opposers, and exalt himself on their ashes to permanent dominion.

LEAVE-TAKING: M. DE TALLEYRAND.

On the eve of setting out for England, I went round to all I could reach of my intimate acquaintance, to make—as it has proved—a last farewell! M. de Talleyrand came in to Madame de Laval's drawing-room during my visit of leavetaking. He was named upon entering; but there is no chance he could recollect me, as I had not seen him since the first month or two after my marriage, when he accompanied M. de Narbonne and M. de Beaumetz to our cottage at Bookham. I could not forbear whispering to Madame de Laval, how many souvenirs his sight awakened! M. de Narbonne was gone, who made so much of our social felicity during the period of our former acquaintance; and Mr. Locke was gone, who made its highest intellectual delight; and Madame de Stael, (286) who gave it a zest of wit, deep thinking, and light speaking, of almost unexampled entertainment; and my beloved sister Phillips, whose sweetness, intelligence, grace, and sensibility won every heart: these were gone, who all, during the sprightly period in which I was known to M. Talleyrand, had almost always made our society. Ah! what parties were those! how select, how refined though sportive, how investigatingly sagacious though invariably well-bred!

Madame de Laval sighed deeply, without answering me, but I left M. de Talleyrand to Madame la Duchesse de Luynes, and a sister of A le Duc de Luxembourg, and another lady or two, while I engaged my truly amiable hostess, till I rose to depart: and then, in passing the chair of M. de Talleyrand, who gravely and silently, but politely, rose and bowed, I said, "M. de Talleyrand m'a oubli: mais on n'oublie pas M. de Talleyrand." (287) I left the room with quickness, but saw a movement of surprise by no means unpleasant break over the habitual placidity, the nearly imperturbable composure of his made-up countenance.

Our journey was eventless, yet sad; sad, not solely, though chiefly, from the continued sufferings of my wounded companion, but sad also, that I quitted so many dear friends, who had wrought themselves, by innumerable kindnesses, into my affections, and who knew not, for we could not bring ourselves to utter words that must have reciprocated so much pain, that our intended future residence was England. The most tender and generous of fathers had taken this difficult resolution for the sake of his son, whose earnest wish had been repeatedly expressed for permission to establish himself in the land of his birth. That my wishes led to the same point, there could be no doubt, and powerfully did they weigh with the most disinterested and most indulgent of husbands. All that could be suggested to compromise what was jarring in our feelings, so as to save all parties from murmuring or regret, was the plan of a yearly journey to France.

(273) Minister of war.

(274) About the close of the year 1813, when Napoleon's star was setting, and his enemies were pressing hard upon him, the Dutch threw off the yoke of France, recalled the Prince of Orange, and proclaimed him at Amsterdam King of the United Netherlands, by the title of William I. ED.

(275) On the first floor.

(276) Lady Caroline Lamb (born in 1785) was the wife of the Hon. William Lamb, afterwards Lord Melbourne and prime minister of England. A year or two before Fanny saw her, she was violently in love with Lord Byron: "absolutely besieged him," Rogers said. Byron was not unwilling to be besieged, though he presently grew tired of the lady, and broke off their correspondence, to her great distress, with an insulting and rather heartless letter. But it was more than a mere flirtation on Lady Caroline's part. She fainted away on meeting Byron's funeral (1824); "her mind became more affected; she was separated from her husband and died 26 January, 1828, generously cared for by him to the last."(Dict. of National Biography.) She was the author of two or three novel. ED.

(277) Son of the Duke of Brunswick who invaded France in 1792, and who died in 1806 of the wounds which he received in the battle of Jena. His son was killed at Quatre Bras, June 16, 1815. ED.

(278) "Bonaparte is taken! there he is!"

(279) Alarm.

(280) Fortresses.

(281) Litters.

(282) Both reports were false. Jerome Bonaparte, Napoleon's youngest brother, formerly King of Westphalia, was wounded in the groin at Quatre Bras, two days before the battle of Waterloo. His wound, however, was not so severe as to prevent him from serving at Waterloo, and, after the flight of the Emperor to Paris, Jerome remained to conduct the retreat and rally the fugitives. General Vandamme was not at Waterloo at all, nor was he wounded. He was attached to the army

commanded by Marshal Grouchy, and was engaged in a useless conflict with the Prussian rear-guard at Wavres on the day of the decisive battle. ED.

(283) Another false rumour. Murat was in France during the whole of the Waterloo campaign. This distinguished soldier had married Caroline Bonaparte, the youngest sister of Napoleon, by whom he was made King of Naples. In December, 1813, Murat was ungrateful enough to join the allied powers against the Emperor, but, after Napoleon's return from Elba, he threw himself into the war with characteristic precipitation. Marching from Naples with an army of 50,000 men, he occupied Rome and Florence, but was soon after totally defeated by the Austrians, and escaped with difficulty to France. The Emperor refused to see him. After the final abdication of Napoleon, Murat made a desperate attempt, with a handful of men, to regain his kingdom of Naples. He was taken prisoner, tried by a military commission, condemned to death, and immediately shot. At St. Helena Napoleon said of him, "It was his fate to ruin us every way; once by declaring against us, and again by unadvisedly taking our part." ED.

(284) Inn.

(285) "Ah! there it is!"

(286) This was a misapprehension. Madame de Stael died at Paris, July 14, 1817. The above narrative was written at a period some years later than that of the events to which it relates, and hence, in all probability, the mistake arose. ED.

(287) "M. de Talleyrand has forgotten me; but one does not forget M. de Talleyrand."

SECTION 26. (1815-8)

AT BATH AND ILFRACOMBE: GENERAL D'ARBLAY'S ILLNESS AND DEATH.

ARRIVAL IN ENGLAND.

(Madame d'Arblay to Mrs. Locke and Mrs. Angerstein.) Dover, Oct. 18, 1815. Last night, my ever dear friends, we arrived once more in old England.

I write this to send the moment I land in London. I cannot boast of our health, our looks, our strength, but I hope we may recover a part of all when our direful fatigues, mental and corporeal, cease to utterly weigh upon and wear us.

We shall winter in Bath. The waters of Plombiéres have been recommended to my poor boiteux, (288) but he has obtained a cong, that allows this change. Besides his present utter incapacity for military service, he is now unavoidably on the retraite (289 list, and the King of France permits his coming over, not alone without difficulty, but with wishing him a good journey, through the Duc de Luxembourg, his captain in the gardes du corps.

Adieu, dearest both—Almost I embrace you in dating from Dover. Had you my letter from Trèves? I suspect not, for my melancholy new history would have brought your kind condolence: or, otherwise, that missed me. Our letters were almost all intercepted by the Prussians while we were there. Not one answer arrived to us from Paris, save by private hands. . . .

December 24, 1815. My heart has been almost torn asunder, of late, by the dreadful losses which the newspapers have communicated to me, of the two dearest friends (290) of my absent partner; both sacrificed in the late sanguinary conflicts. It has been with difficulty I have forborne attempting to return to him; but a winter voyage might risk giving him another loss. The death of one of these so untimely departed favourites, how will Madame de Stael support? Pray tell me if you hear any thing of her, and what. . . .

[With the year 1816 a new section of Madame d'Arblay's correspondence may be said to commence in her letters to her son, the late Rev. A. d'Arblay, who was then pursuing his studies at Caius college, Cambridge. It has been thought advisable to be more sparing in publication from this, than from the earlier portions of Madame d'Arblay's correspondence. Without, however, a few of these letters to her son, "the child of many hopes," this picture of her mind, with all its tenderness, playfulness, and sound sense, would scarcely be complete.]

ALEXANDER D'ARBLAY: SOME OLD BATH FRIENDS.

(Madame d'Arblay to Mrs. Locke) Bath, February 15, 1816. Incredible is the time I have lost without giving in that claim which has never been given in vain for news of my own, dear friend - but I have been-though not ill, so continually unwell, and though not, as so recently, in disordered and disorganizing difficulties, yet so incessantly occupied with small, but indispensable occupations, that the post hour has always gone by to-day to be waited for to-morrow. Yet my heart has never been satisfied. I don't mean with itself, for with that it can never quarrel on this subject, but with my pen- my slack, worn, irregular, fugitive, fatigued, yet ever faithful, though never punctual pen. My dearest friend forgives, I know, even that; but her known and unvarying lenity is the very cause I cannot forgive it myself.

We have had our Alexander for six weeks; he left us three days ago, and I won't tell my dear friend whether or not we miss him. He is precisely such as he was—as inartificial in his character, as irregular in his studies. He cannot bring himself to conquer his disgust of the routine of labour at Cambridge; and while he energetically argues upon the innocence of a preference to his own early practice, (291) which he vindicates, I believe unanswerably, with regard to its real superiority, he is insensible, at least forgetful, of all that can be urged of the mischiefs to his prospects in life that must result from his not conquering his inclinations,"- I have nearly lost all hope of his taking the high degree A judged to him by general expectation at the University, from the promise of his opening.

Of old friends here, I have found stationary, Mrs. Holroyd, and Mrs. Frances. and Harriet Bowdler. Mrs. Holroyd still gives parties, and tempted me to hear a little medley music, as she called it. Mrs. F. Bowdler lives on Lansdowne-crescent, and scarcely ever comes down the hill. Mrs. Harriet I have missed, though we have repeatedly sought a meeting on both sides; but she left Bath for some excursion soon after my arrival. Another new resident here will excite, I am sure, a more animated interest ' Mrs. Piozzi.

The Bishop of Salisbury, my old friend, found me out, and came to make me a long and most amiable visit, which was preceded by Mrs. I –, and we all spent an evening with them very sociably and pleasantly.

FRENCH AFFAIRS. GENERAL D'ARBLAY'S HEALTH.

(Madame d'Arblay to her Son.) Bath, Friday, April 2, 1816. ......The Oppositionists, and all their friends, have now a dread of France, and bend their way to Italy. But the example now given at

Paris, in the affair of Messrs. Wilson and Co. (292) that Englishmen are as amenable to the laws and customs of the countries which they inhabit, as foreigners while in England are to ours, will make them more careful, both in spirit and conduct, than heretofore they have deemed it necessary to be, all over the globe. It is a general opinion that there will be a great emigration this summer, because John Bull longs to see something beyond the limited circumference of his birthright - but that foreign nations will be now so watchful of his proceedings, so jealous of his correspondence, and so easily offended by his declamation or epigrams, that he will be glad to return here, where liberty, when not abused, allows a real and free exercise of true independence of mind, speech, and conduct, such as no other part of the world affords.

I am truly happy not to be at Paris at such a juncture; for opinions must be cruelly divided, and society almost out of the question. Our letters all confess that scarcely one family is d'acord even with itself. The overstraining royalists make moderate men appear jacobins. The good king must be torn to pieces between his own disposition to clemency, and the vehemence of his partisans against risking any more a general amnesty. All that consoles me for the length of time required for the cure of your padre's leg is the consequence, in its keeping off his purposed visit. A cold has forced him to relinquish the pump till to-day, when he is gone to make another essay. He is so popular in Bath, that he is visited here by everybody that can make any pretext for calling. I have this moment been interrupted by a letter to invite me with my "bewitching husband" to a villa near Prior Park. He is not insensible to the kindness he meets with - au contraire, it adds greatly to his contentment in the steadiness of a certain young sprig that is inducing him here to plant his final choux; and the more, as we find that, as far as that sprig has been seen here, he, also, has left so favourable an impression, that we are continually desired to introduce him, on his next arrival, wherever we go.

Your kind father, upon your last opening of "All here is well," instantly ran down stairs, with a hop, skip, and a jump, and agreed to secure our pretty lodgings for a year.

THE ESCAPE OF LAVALETTE. THE STREATHAM PORTRAITS.

(Madame d'Arblay to her Son.) Bath, April 30, 1816. The three chevaliers have all been condemned as culpable of aiding a state-criminal to escape, but not accused of any conspiracy against the French government. They are therefore, sentenced merely to three months' imprisonment. (293) Certainly, if their logic were irrefutable, and if the treaty of Paris included the royal pardon with the amnesty accorded by the allied generals, then, to save those who ought not to have been tried would have been meritorious rather than illegal; but the king had no share in that treaty, which could only hold good in a military sense, of security from military prosecution or punishment from the Allies. These Allies, however, did not call themselves conquerors, nor take Paris, nor judge the Parisians; but so far as belonged to a capitulation, meant, on both sides, to save the capital and its inhabitants from pillage and the sword. Once restored to its rightful monarch, all foreign interference was at an end. Having been seated on the throne by the nation, and having never abdicated, though he had been chased by rebellion from his kingdom, he had never forfeited his privilege to judge which of his subjects were still included in his original amnesty, and which had incurred the penalty or chances of being tried by the laws of the land, and by them, not by royal decree, condemned or acquitted.

A false idea seems encouraged by all the king's enemies, that his amnesty ought to have secured pardon to the condemned: the amnesty could only act up to the period when it was granted and accepted; it could have nothing to do with after offences.

I am grieved to lose my respect and esteem for a character I had considered so heroical as that of Sir R. Wilson: but to find, through his intercepted correspondence, that the persecution of the Protestants was to be asserted, true or false, to blacken the reigning dynasty. . . to find this truly diabolic idea presented to him by a brother of whom he speaks as the partner of all his thoughts, etc, has consumed every spark of favour in which he was held throughout the whole nation, except, perhaps, in those whom party will make deaf and blind for ever to what opposes their own views and schemes. I do not envy Lord Grey for being a third in such an intercourse, an intercourse teeming with inventive plots and wishes for new revolutions!

Your uncle has bought the picture of my dearest father at Streatham. (294) I am truly rejoiced it will come into our family, since the collection for which it was painted is broken up. Your uncle has also bought the Garrick, which was one of the most agreeable and delightful of the set. To what recollections, at once painful and pleasing, does this sale give birth! In the library, in which those pictures were hung, we always breakfasted; and there I have had as many precious conversations with the great and good Dr. Johnson as there are days in the year. Dr. Johnson sold the highest of all! 'tis an honour to our age, that!—360 pounds! My dear father would have been mounted higher, but that his son Charles was there to bid for himself, and, everybody must have seen, was resolved to have it. There was besides, I doubt not, a feeling for his lineal claim and pious desire.

REGARDING HUSBAND AND SON.

(Madame d'Arblay to a Friend.) Bath, August 17, 1816. I have been in a state of much uncertainty and disturbance since I wrote last with respect to one of the dearest possible interests of life, the maternal: the uncertainty, however, for this epoch is over, and I will hasten to communicate to you its result, that I may demand further and frequent accounts of your own plans, and of their execution or change, success or failure. All that concerns you, must to me always be near and dear.

General d'Arblay is gone to France, and here at Bath rest sa femme et son fils. (295) There was no adjusting the excursion but by separation. Alexander would have been wilder than ever for his French mathematics in re-visiting Paris; and, till his degree is taken, we must not contribute to lowering it by feasting his opposing pursuits with fresh nourishment, M. d'Arblay nevertheless could by no means forego his intention which a thousand circumstances led him to consider as right' He could not, indeed, feel himself perfectly   sa place without paying his devoirs to his king, notwithstanding he has been put by his majesty himself, not by his own desire, en retraite. The exigencies of the treasury demand this, for all who are not young enough for vigorous active service; but his wounded leg prevented his returning thanks sooner for the promotion with which the king finished and recompensed his services;(296) and therefore he deems it indispensable to present himself at the foot of the throne for that purpose now that he is able to "bear his body more seemly" (like Audrey) in the royal presence. He hopes also to arrange for receiving here his half-pay, when sickness or affairs or accident may prevent his crossing the Channel. Choice and happiness will, to his last breath, carry him annually to France; for, not to separate us from his son, or in the bud of life, to force that son's inclination in fixing his place or mode of residence, alone decides his not fixing there his own last staff. But Alexander, young as he left that country, has seen enough of it to be aware that no line is open there to ambition or importance, but the military, most especially for the son of an officer so known and marked for his military character: and I need not tell you that, with my feelings and sentiments, to see him wield a sword that could only lead him to renown by being drawn against the country of his birth and of mine, would demolish my heart, and probably my head; and, to believe in any war in which England and France will not be rivals, is to entertain Arcadian hopes, fit only for shepherds and shepherdesses of the drama.

MATERNAL ANXIETIES.

(Madame d'Arblay to General d'Arblay.) Bath, October 28th, 1816. Certainement, et très certainement, mon bien cher ami, your beautiful strictures upon la connoissance et l'usage du monde would have given "un autre cours mes idées"(297) were the object of our joint solicitude less singular; but our Alexander, mon ami, dear as he is to us, and big as are my hopes pour l'avenir, (298) our Alexander is far different from what you were at his age. More innocent, I grant, and therefore highly estimable, and worthy of our utmost care, and worthy of the whole heart of her to whom he shall permanently attach himself. But O, how far less aimable! He even piques himself upon the difference, as if that difference were to his advantage. He is a medley of good qualities and of faults the most extraordinary and the most indescribable. Enfin, except in years, in poetry, and in mathematics, il n'est encore qu'un enfant. (299)

Were he so only as to la connoissance, et mˆme l'usage du monde, I should immediately subscribe to the whole of your really admirable dissertation upon the subject in the letter now before me, for I should then sympathise in your idea that a lovely young companion might mould him to her own excellence, and polish him to our wishes; but O, nous n'en sommes pas !! (300) When he is wholly at his ease, as he is at present, with his mother, and as he would soon inevitably be with his wife, he is so uncouth, so negligent, and absent, that his frightened partner would either leave him in despair to himself, or, by reiterated attempts to reason with him, lose her bridal power, and raise the most dangerous dissensions. He exults rather than blushes in considering himself ignorant of all that belongs to common life, and of everything that is deemed useful. Even in mathematics he disdains whatever is not abstract and simply theoretical. "Trouble I hate" he calls his motto. You will easily conceive that there are moments, nay, days, in which he is more reasonable; I should else be hopeless: nor will he ever dare hold such language to you. but it is not less the expression of his general mind. Sometimes, too, he wishes for wealth, but it is only that he might be supine. Poor youth! he little sees 'how soon he would then become poor! Yet, while thus open to every dupery and professedly without any sense of order, he is so fearful of ridicule, that a smile from his wife at any absurdity would fill him with the most gloomy indignation. It does so now from his mother.

A wife, I foresee you will reply, young and beautiful, sera bien autre chose; mais je crois que vous Vous trompez: (301) a mistress, a bride,—oui! a mistress and a bride would see him her devoted slave; but in the year following year, when ardent novelty is passed away, a mother loved as I am may form much judgment what will be the lot of the wife, always allowing for the attractions of reconciliation which belong exclusively to the marriage state, where it is happy.

Nevertheless, I am completely of your opinion, that a good and lovely wife will ultimately soften his asperity, and give him a new taste for existence, by opening to him new sources of felicity, and exciting, as you justly suggest, new emulation to improvement, when he is wise enough to know how to appreciate, to treat, and to preserve such a treasure. But will four months fit him for beginning such a trial? Think of her, mon ami, as well as of him. The "responsibility" in this case would be yours for both, and exquisite would be your agony should either of them be unhappy. A darling daughter-an only child, nursed in the lap of soft prosperity, sole object of tenderness and of happiness to both her parents. rich, well-born, stranger to all care, and unused to any control; beautiful as a little angel, and (be very sure) not unconscious she is born to be adored; endowed with talents to create admiration, independently of the ,clat of her personal charms, and indulged from her cradle in every wish, every fantaisie.—Will such a young creature as this be happy with our Alexander after her bridal supremacy, when the ecstasy of his first transports are on the wane? That a beauty such as you describe might bring him, even from a first interview, to her feet, notwithstanding all his present prejudices against a French wife, I think probable enough, though he now thinks his taste in beauty different from yours; for he has never, he says, been struck but by a commanding air. All beauty, however, soon finds its own way to the heart. But could any permanent amendment ensue, from working upon his errors only through his passions? Is it not to be feared that as they, the passions, subside, the errors would all peep up again? And she, who so prudently has already rejected a nearly accepted pretendant for his want of order!!! (302) (poor Alexander!)

How will she be content to be a monitress, where she will find everything in useful life to teach, and nothing in return to learn? And even if he endure the perpetual tutoring, will not she sicken of her victories ere he wearies of his defeats?

And will Alexander be fit or willing to live under the eye, which he will regard as living under the subjection, of his wife's relations? In this country there is no notion of that mode of married life -, and our proud Alexander, the more he may want counsel and guidance, will the more haughtily, from fearing to pass for a baby, resent them. Let me add, that nothing can be less surprising than that he should have fixed his own expectation of welfare in England. Recollect, mon ami, it is now nearly three years ago since you gave him, in a solemn and beautiful letter, his choice between Cambridge and la compagnie de -Luxembourg, into which you had entered him saying that your position exacted that you should take your son back to serve, or not at all. You have certainly kept his definite answer, from which he has never wavered. And again, only at your last departure, this August, you told us positively that you could not take your son to France at twenty-one years of age with any honour or propriety but to enter him in the army. I would else, you know, have shut myself up with him in some cottage always, merely for the great pleasure of accompanying you.

Alexander, therefore, now annexes an idea of degradation to a residence non-military in France. He would deem himself humbled by the civil place at which you hint, even if you could bring him, which I doubt above all, to submit to its duties. He regards himself, from peculiar circumstances, as an established Englishman (though born of a French father), with your own full consent, nay, by your own conditions. I by no means believe he will ever settle out of England, though he delights to think of travelling.

And such, mon ami, appeared to be your own sentiments when we parted, though they are changed now, or overpowered by the new view that is presented to you of domestic felicity, for Alexander. I have written thus fully, and after the best meditation in my power, according to your desire; and every reflection and observation upon the subject, and upon Alexander, unites in making me wish, with the whole of my judgment and feeling at once, to keep back, not to forward, any matrimonial connection, for years, not months, unless months first produce the change to his advantage that I dare only expect from years.

ADVANTAGES OF BATH: YOUNG D'ARBLAY'S DECREE.

(Madame d'Arblay to Mrs. Locke.) Bath, November 10, 1816. I wish to live at Bath, wish it devoutly; for at Bath we shall live, or no longer in England. London will only do for those who have two houses, and of the real country I may say the same; for a cottage, now Monsieur d'Arblay cannot, as heretofore, brave all the seasons, to work, and embellish his wintry hours, by embellishing anticipatingly his garden, would be too lonely, in so small a family, for the long evenings of cold and severe weather; and would lose us Alexander half the year, as we could neither expect nor wish to see him begin life as a recluse from the world. Bath, therefore, as it eminently agrees with us all, is, in England, the only place for us, since here, all the year round, there is always town at command, and always the country for prospect, exercise, and delight.

Therefore, my dear friend, not a word but in favour of Bath, if you love me. Our own finishing finale will soon take root here, or yonder; for Alex will take his degree in January, and then, his mind at liberty, and his faculties in their full capacity for meditating upon his lot in life, he will come to a decision what mountain he shall climb, upon which to fix his staff; for all that relates to worldly prosperity will to him be up-hill toil, and labour. Never did I see in youth a mind so quiet, so philosophic, in mundane matters, with a temper so eager, so impetuous, so burningly alive to subjects of science and literature. The Tancred scholarship is still in suspense. The vice-chancellor is our earnest friend, as well as our faithful Dr. Davy, but the trustees have come to no determination - and Alex is my companion-or rather, I am Alex's flapper—till the learned doctors can agree. At all events, he will not come out in Physic; we shall rather enter him at another college, with all the concomitant expenses, than let him, from any economy, begin his public career under false colours. When he entered this institution, I had not any notion of this difficulty; I was ignorant there would be any objection against his turning which way he pleased when the time for taking the degree should arrive.

I am now in almost daily hope of the return of my voyager. His last letter tells me to direct no more to Paris.

[After this time General d'Arblay made frequent journeys to Paris.]

PLAYFUL REPROACHES AND SOBER COUNSEL.

(Madame d'Arblay to her Son.) Bath, Friday, April 25, 1817. Why, what a rogue you are! four days in town! As there can be no scholarship—alas! it matters not; but who knew that circumstance when they played truant? Can you tell me that, hey! Mr Cantab? Why, you dish me as if I were no more worth than Paley or Newton, or such like worthies!

Your dear padre is very considerably better, surtout in looks, but by no means re-established; for cold air—too much exertion—too little—and all sorts of nourishment or beverage that are not precisely adapted to the present state of the poor shattered frame, produce instant pain, uneasiness, restlessness, and suffering. Such, however, is the common condition of convalescence, and therefore I observe it with much more concern than surprise - and Mr. Hay assures me all is as well as can possibly be expected after so long and irksome an illness.

"The scholarship is at an end— So much for that!" pretty cool, my friend!

Will it make you double your diligence for what is not at an end? hey, mon petit monsieur?

But I am sorry for your disappointment in the affair you mention, my dear Alex: though your affections were not so far engaged, methinks, but that your amour proper (303) is still more bless, (304) than your heart! hey? However, 'tis a real loss, though little more than of an ideal friend, at present. But no idea is so flattering and so sweet, as that which opens to expectation a treasure of such a sort. I am really, therefore, sorry for you, my dear Alex.

Your determination to give way to no sudden impulse in future is quite right. Nothing is so pleasant as giving way to impulse; nothing so hazardous.

But this history must double your value for Messrs. Jones Musgrave, Jacobs, Ebden, Theobald, and Whewell. "Cling to those who cling to you!" said the immortal Johnson to your mother, when she uttered something that seemed fastidious relative to a person whose partiality she did not prize.

Your padre was prevailed upon to go to the play. We were both very well pleased with H. Payne in certain parts; in some instances I even thought him excellent, especially in the natural, gentlemanly, and pensive tones in which he went through the gravedigger's and other scenes of the last act. But, for the soliloquies, and the grand conference with the mother! oh, there, Garrick rose up to my remembrance with an éclat of perfection that mocks all approach of approbation for a successor.

But you, M. Keanite, permit a little hint against those looks that convey your resentment. They may lead to results that may be unpleasant. It is best to avoid displaying a susceptibility that shows the regret all on your own side! Let the matter die away as though it had never been. Assume your cool air; your "so much for that!" but do not mark a d,pit that will rather flatter than vex. At first, it was well; you gave way to Nature and to truth, and made apparent you had been sincere: but there, for your dignity's sake, let all drop; and be civil as well as cool, if you would keep the upper hand.

PREPARATIONS FOR LEAVING BATH.

(Madame d'Arblay to General d'Arblay.) 1817. .....June 18. I made a morning visit to Mrs. Piozzi, whom I found with +Dr. Minchin, an informed, sensible physician. She was strange, as usual, at first; but animated, as usual, afterwards. The sisters, Mrs. Frances and Mrs Harriet Bowdler, called upon me, and were admitted, for I heard their names in time; and we had much good old talk), that is, Frances and I; for Harriet is ever prim and demure and nearly mute before her elder sister.

June 25. Fixing the last day of the month for my journey, I set seriously to work to hasten my preparations. What a business it was! You have no conception how difficult, nor how laborious, it is to place so many books, such a quantity of linen, such a wardrobe, and such a mass of curiosities, in so small a compass. How fagged and fatigued I retired to rest every night, you may imagine. Alex vigorously carried heavy loads at a time from the study to the garret, but only where he might combine and arrange and order all for himself. However, he was tolerably useful for great luggages.

June 26. We spent the afternoon at Larkhall place, to meet there Maria and Sophy. My dear sister (305) was all spirit and vivacity. Mr. Burney, all tranquil enjoyment—peace, rest, leisure, books, music, drawing, and walking fill up his serene days, and repay the long toils of his meritorious life. And my sister, who happily foresees neither sickness nor ennui, is the spirit and spring of the party.

June 28. I devoted all day to leave-taking visits, for so many houses were opened, and claimed long confabulations, from their rarity, that I had not finished my little round till past ten o'clock at night. Yet of these hosts, Mrs. Frances Bowdler, Mrs. Piozzi, Mrs. Morgan, and Mrs. Andr, were out. Two of the three latter ladies are now in France, and they have written word, that the distress in their province exceeds all they have left in this country! Madame do Sourches has written a similar melancholy account; and Mrs. Holroyd, who received my longest call this morning, read me a letter from Lady B. with words yet stronger of the sufferings in the Low Countries! O baleful effects of "Bella, horrida bella!" I sat an hour also with Mrs. Harriet Bowdler, in sober chat and old histories. She has not—il s'en faut—the exhilaration and entertainment of her clever sister; but there is all the soft repose of good sense, good humour, urbanity, and kindness. One cannot do better than to cultivate with both; for if, after the spirited Frances, the gentle Harriet seems dull, one may at least say that after the kind Harriet, the satirical Frances seems alarming.

But my longest visit was to the excellent Mrs. Ogle, who is the oldest acquaintance with whom I have any present connection in the world. It was at her house I first saw Mrs, Chapone, who was her relation; I visited her, with my dear father, my mother-in-law, and my sisters; though from circumstances we lost sight of each other, and met no more till I had that happy encounter with her at Cheltenham, when I brought her to the good and dear king. My respect for her age, her virtues, and this old connection, induced me to stay with her till it was too late to present myself elsewhere. I merely therefore called at the door of Madame de Sommery to inquire whether they Could receive me sans c,remonie for half an hour in the evening. This was agreed to, and Alex accompanied or rather preceded me to Madame de Sommery, who had her two jolies daughters, Stephanie and Pulchérie, at work by her side, the tea-table spread à l'Anglaise, and four of your théâtres (306) I upon the table, with Alex just beginning "Lido" as I entered. I was never so pleased with them before, though they have always charmed me; but in this private, comfortable style they were all ten times more easy, engaging, and lively than I had ever yet seen them.

INSTALLED AT ILFRACOMBE.

(Madame d'Arblay to General d'Arblay.) Ilfracombe, Devonshire, June 31, (sic) 1817. . . .This very day of our arrival, before Alex had had time to search out Mr. Jacob, somebody called out to him in the street, "Ah, d'Arblay!" who proved to be his man. They strolled about the town, and then Jacob desired to be brought to me. Unluckily, I was unpacking, and denied. He has appointed Alex for a lesson to-morrow. May he put him a little en train!

July 5. I must now give you some account of this place. We are lodged on the harbour. The mistress of our apartments is widow to some master of a vessel that traded at Ilfracombe, with Ireland chiefly. She has three or four children: the eldest, but twelve years old, is the servant of the lodgers, and as adroit as if she were thirty. Our situation is a very amusing one; for the quay is narrow, and there are vessels just on its level, so close that even children walk into them all day long. When the sea is up, the scene is gay, busy, and interesting; but on its ebb the sands here are not clean and inviting, but dark and muddy, and the contrary of odoriferous. But the entrance and departure of vessels, the lading, unlading, and the management of ships and boats, offer constantly something new to an eye accustomed only to land views and occupations.

A CAPTURED SPANISH SHIP.

But chiefly I wish for you for the amusement you would find from a Spanish vessel, which is close to the quay, immediately opposite to our apartments, and on a level with the parlour of the house. It has been brought in under suspicion of piracy, or smuggling, or aiding the slave trade. What the circumstances of the accusation are I know not - but the captain is to be tried at Exeter on the ensuing western circuit. Meantime, his goods are all sequestered, and he has himself dismissed all his sailors and crew to rejoin him when the trial is over. He is upon his parole, and has liberty to go whithersoever he will; but he makes no use of the permission, as he chooses not to leave his cargo solely under the inspection of the excisemen and custom officers here, who have everything under lock and key and seal. He is a good-looking man, and, while not condemned, all are willing to take his word for his innocence. Should that be proved, what compensation will be sufficient for repairing his confinement? He has retained with him only his physician, his own servant his cook, and a boy, with another lad, who is an American. I see him all day long, walking his quarter-deck, and ruminating upon his situation, with an air of philosophy that shows strong character. His physician, who is called here the " doctor," and is very popular, is his interpreter; he speaks English and French, has a spirited, handsome face, and manners the most courteous, though with a look darkly shrewd and Spanish.

THE SPANISH CAPTAIN'S COOK.

But the person who would most entertain you is the cook, who appears the man of most weight in the little coterie; for he lets no one interfere with his manoeuvres. All is performed for the table in full sight, a poêle (307) being lighted with a burning fierce fire upon the deck, where he officiates. He wears a complete white dress, and has a pail of water by his side, in which he washes everything he dresses, and his Own hand, to boot, with great attention. He begins his pot au feu soon after seven every morning, and I watch the operation from my window; it is entirely French, except that he puts in more meat, and has it cut, apparently, into pounds; for I see it all carved into square morsels, seemingly of that weight, which he inserts bit by bit, with whole bowls, delicately cleaned, washed and prepared, of cabbages, chicory, turnips, carrots celery, and small herbs. Then some thick slices of ship ham and another bowl of onions and garlic; salt by a handful, and pepper by a wooden spoon full. This is left for many hours; and in the interval he prepares a porridge of potatoes well mashed, and barley well boiled, with some other ingredient that, when it is poured into a pan, bubbles up like a syllabub. But before he begins, he employs the two lads to wash all the ship.

To see all this is the poor captain's only diversion; but the cook never heeds him while at his professional operations; he even motions to him to get out of the way if he approaches too near, and is so intent upon his grand business that he shakes his head without answering, when the captain speaks to him, with an air that says, "Are you crazy to try to take off my attention?" And when the doctor, who often advances to make some observation, and to look on, tries to be heard, he waves his hand in disdain, to silence him. Yet, when all is done, and he has taken off his white dress, he becomes all obsequiousness, respectfully standing out of the way, or diligently flying forward to execute any command.

SHIPS IN DISTRESS.

July 6. Alex and I went to church this morning, and heard a tolerable sermon. In the evening there was a storm, that towards night grew tremendous. The woman of the house called us to see two ships in distress. We went to the top of the house for a view of the sea, which was indeed frightful. One ship was endeavouring to gain the harbour; the other, to steer further into the main ocean; but both appeared to be nearly swamped by the violence of the winds and waves. People mounted to the lighthouse with lights; for at this season the lantern is not illuminated; and a boat was sent out to endeavour to assist, and take any spare hands or passengers, if such there were, from the vessel; but the sea was so boisterous that they could not reach the ship, and were nearly lost in the attempt. Alex ran up to the lighthouse, to see what was doing; but was glad to return, as he could with difficulty keep his feet, and was on the point of being lifted off them down the precipice into the sea. I never was so horrified as when, from the top of the house, I perceived his danger. Thank God, he felt it in time, and came back in safety. It requires use to sustain the feet in such a hurricane, upon a rock perpendicularly standing in the ocean.

YOUNG D'ARBLAY's TUTOR.

July 7. We have heard that one of the vessels got off; but no tidings whatsoever have been received of the other. It is suspected to be a passage vessel from Bristol to Ireland. I have had Mr. Jacob to tea; I could not yet arrange a dinner, and he was impatient for an introduction. I like him extremely: he has everything in his favour that can be imagined; sound judgment without positiveness, brilliant talents without conceit, authority with gentleness, and consummate knowledge of science with modesty. What a blessing that such a character should preside over these inexperienced youths! Mr. Jacob has aided us to remove. Time is a plaything to the diligent and obliging, though a thief to the idle and capricious; the first find it, in the midst of every obstacle, for what they wish, while the latter lose it, though surrounded by every resource, for all that they want. I had such success that I now write from my new dwelling, which I will describe to-morrow.

July 9. Quelle joie! this morning I receive a welcome to my new habitation, to make it cheer me from the beginning. 'Tis begun June 28th, and finished July 2nd. How propos is what I had just written of time in the hands of the diligent and obliging! yet how it is you can bestow so much upon me is my admiration.

I have not mentioned a letter I have received from Mrs. Frances Bowdler. She tells me of the marriage of Miss — to a Prussian gentleman, and expresses some vexation at it, but adds, "Perhaps I ought not to say this to you," meaning on account of the objection to a foreigner; and then elegantly adds, "but one person's having gained the great prize in the lottery does not warrant another to throw his whole wealth into the wheel." Not very bad English that?

GENERAL D'ARBLAY'S ILL-HEALTH.

(Madame d'Arblay to Mrs. Broome.) Ilfracombe, Post Office, July 23, 1817. .....I have letters very frequently from Paris, all assuring me M. d'A. is re-establishing upon the whole; yet all letting me see, by collateral accounts, anecdotes, or expressions, that he is constantly in the hands of his physician, and that a difficulty of breathing attacks him from time to time, as it did before his journey: with a lassitude, a weakness, and a restlessness which make him there, as here they made him since his illness, unfit for company, and incapable, but by starts and for moments to have any enjoyment of mixed society! I do not therefore, feel comfortable about him, though, thank heaven, not alarmed. And at all events I am glad he tries the change of air. Change of scene also was advised for him by all but he is too kind to find that beneficial when we are separated; and he writes me frequent avowals of seizures of dejection and sadness that reduce him to a state of great suffering. The parting, while he was in a situation so discouraging, was very cruel but Alexander had, and has, no chance of taking a tolerable degree without a friend constantly at hand to remind him of the passage of time. He never thinks of it: every day seems a day by itself, which he may fill up at pleasure, but which opens to him no prospect of the day that will succeed! So little reflection on the future, with so good capacity for judging the present, were never before united.

PARTICULARS OF ILFRACOMBE.

We are very well lodged for pleasantness, and for excellent people. We have a constant view of the sea from our drawing room, which is large and handsome - our bedrooms also are good; but our minor accommodations, our attendance, dinner equipage, cooking, etc, would very ill have contented my general had he been here. The best men, the most moderate and temperate, are difficult, nay, dainty, compared with women. When he comes, if I am so happy as to see him return while we are here, I must endeavour to ameliorate these matters. Ilfracombe is a long, narrow town, consisting of only one regular street, though here and there small groups of houses hang upon its skirts, and it is not destitute of lanes and alleys.

The town part or side Is ugly, ill paved and ill looking: but the backs of the habitations offer, on one side the street, prospects of fine hills, and on the other, noble openings to the sea. The town is built upon a declivity, of which the church is at the summit, and the harbour makes the termination. It was in the harbour, that is upon the quay, that we were at first lodged; and our apartments were by no means without interest or amusement; but just as we were comfortably settled in them, we were told the ebbs and flows, etc, of the tides left occasionally, or brought, odours not the most salubrious. To this representation I thought it right to yield so implicitly, that I sought a new abode, and changed my quarters instantly.

YOUNG D'ARBLAY'S AVERSION TO STUDY.

(Madame d'Arblay to General d'Arblay.) Friday, September 12, 1817. I have so much to say to my dearest friend, that I open my new sheet at the moment of finishing the old one, though I shall not send it for a week - and let me begin by quieting your poor nerves relative to La Chapelle, in assuring you I neglect no possible means to follow, substantially and effectually, your injunctions, though I dare not tell him that you would never pardon the smallest infraction of our new treaty. He is not capable, mon ami, of an exactitude of that undeviating character. To force further solemn promises from so forgetful, so unreflecting, yet so undesigning and well-meaning a young creature, is to plunge him and ourselves into the culpability of which we accuse him. To attempt in that manner to couper court, (308) etc, instead of frightening him into right, would harden him into desperation. His disgust to his forced study is still so vehement, that it requires all I can devise of exhortation, persuasion, menace, and soothing, tour tour, to deter him from relinquishing all effort! The times, mon ami, are "out of joint:" we must not by exigeance precipitate him to his ruin, but try patiently and prudently, every possible means, to rescue him from the effects of his own wilful blindness and unthinking, idle eccentricity. If we succeed, how will he bless us when his maturer judgment opens his eyes to the evils he will have escaped! but if we fail why should we lie down and die because he might have obtained fame and riches, yet obstinately preferred obscurity with a mere competence? Put not Your recovery and your happiness upon such a cast! My own struggles to support the disappointment for which I am forced to prepare myself, in the midst of all my persevering, unremitting efforts to avert it, are sufficiently severe; but the manner in which I see your agitation threaten your health, makes his failure but secondary to my apprehensions! Oh, mon ami, ought we not rather to unite in comforting each other by sustaining ourselves? Should we not have done so mutually, if the contagious fever at Cambridge had carried him off? And what is the mortification of a bad degree and a lessened ambition, with all the mundane humiliation belonging to it, compared with the total earthly loss of so dear an object, who may be good and happy in a small circle, if he misses, by his own fault, mounting into a larger? Take courage, my dearest ami, and relieve me from the double crush that else may wholly destroy mine. Let us both, while we yet venture to hope for the best, prepare for the worst. Nothing on my part shall be wanting to save this blow; but should his perversity make it inevitable, we must unite our utmost strength, not alone to console each other, but to snatch from that "sombre d,couragement" (309) you so well foresee, the wilful, but ever fondly-loved dupe of his own insouciance. . . . (310)

A VISIT FROM THE FIRST CHESS PLAYER IN ENGLAND.

And now to lighter matters. I hope I have gained a smile from you by my disclosure that I lost my journal time for my usual post-day by successive dissipation? What will you have conjectured? That I have consented at last to listen to Mr. Jacob's recommendation for going to the Ilfracombe ball, and danced a fandango with him! or waltzed, au moins! or that I have complied with his desire of going to the cricket-ground, just arranged by the Cantabs and some officers who are here, in subscribing three guineas for the use of a field? Vous n'y êtes pas; (311) for though I should like, in itself, to see a cricket-match, in a field which Mr. Jacob says is beautifully situated, and where the Bishop of Ossory and his lady, Mrs. Fowler, go frequently, as two of their sons are amongst the players; yet, as Jacob evidently thinks our poor Alexander ought not to spare time for being of the party, I cannot bear to quit my watchful place by his side, and go thither without him.

Mais—Vous vous rendez, n'est-ce-pas? (312) Eh bien—to go back to Sept. 2nd. Alexander and I were nearly finishing our evening, tea being over, and nine o'clock having struck, while he was reading the "Spiritual Quixote" (313) for a little relaxation; when Miss Elizabeth Ramsay came to tell me that a gentleman was just arrived at Ilfracombe who begged leave to wait upon me, if I would admit him; and she gave me a card with the name of Mr. Bowdler. Of course I complied, and Alexander was wild with joy at the thought of such an interview, as Mr. Bowdler is acknowledged the first chess-player in England, and was the only man, when Philidor was here, who had the honour of a drawn battle with him: a thing that Philidor has recorded by printing the whole of the game in his treatise on chess. I was not glad to bring back his ideas to that fascination, yet could not be sorry he should have so great a pleasure.

Mr. Bowdler presented himself very quickly, though not till he had made a toilette of great dress, such as would have suited the finest evening assembly at Bath. He was always a man of much cultivation, and a searcher of the bas bleus (314) all his life. He is brother to our two Mrs. Bowdlers, and was now come to escort Mrs. Frances from his house in Wales, where she has spent the summer, to Ilfracombe. I had formerly met this gentleman very often, at bleu parties, and once at a breakfast at his own house, given in honour of Mrs. Frances, where I met Sophy Streatfield, then a great beauty and a famous Greek scholar, of whom the Literary Herald says:—

"Lovely Streatfield's ivory neck, Nose and notions ê la Grecque."

He was extremely civil to Alex, whom he had longed, he said, to see, and Alex listened to every word that dropped from him, as if it would teach some high move at chess.

We had much talk of old times. We had not met since we parted in St. James's-place, in the last illness of my dear Mrs. Delany, whom he then attended as a physician. He stayed till past ten, having left his sister at the hotel, too tired with a sea passage to come out, or to receive chez elle. But he entreated me to dine with them next day, the only day he should spend at Ilfracombe, with such excess of earnestness and Alex seconded the request with so many "Oh, mamma's!" that he overpowered all refusal, assuring me it could not interfere with my Bath measures, as it was a dinner, pour ainsi dire, (315) on the road, for he and his sister were forced to dine at the hotel. He also declared, in a melancholy tone that he might probably never see me more, unless I made a tour of Wales, as -he began to feel himself too old for the exertion of a sea voyage.

The next morning, immediately after breakfast, I waited upon my old friend and namesake, Fanny Bowdler, and sat with her two hours tête a tête, for her brother was unwell, and she is admirable in close dialogue. I had hardly got home ere she followed me, and stayed till it was time to dress for dinner; when again we met, and only parted for our downy pillows. Her strong sense, keen observation, and travelled intelligence and anecdotes, made the day, thus devoted to her, from ten in the morning to ten at night, pass off with great spirit and liveliness: but Alex, oh! he was in Elysium. Mr. Bowdler took a great fancy to him, and indulged his ardent wish of a chess talk to the full; satisfying him in many difficult points, and going over with him his own famous game with Philidore - and, in short, delivering himself over to that favourite subject with him entirely. It will not, however, be mischievous, for Mr. Bowdler's own enthusiasm is over, and he has now left the game quite off, not having played it once these seven years.

THE DIARY CONTINUED.

A COAST RAMBLE IN SEARCH OF CURIOSITIES.

The term for Alexander's studies with Mr. Jacob was just finishing, and a few days only remained ere the party was. to be dispersed, when I determined upon devoting a morning to the search of such curiosities as the coast produced. I marched forth, attended only by M. d'Arblay's favourite little dog, Diane, with a large silk bag to see what I could find that I might deem indigenous, as a local offering to the collection of my general, who was daily increasing his mineralogical stores, under the skilful direction of his friend, -the celebrated naturalist, M. de Bournon.

I began my perambulation by visiting the promontory called "the Capstan"—or rather attempting that visit; for after mounting to nearly its height, by a circuitous path from the town, by which alone the ascent is possible, the side of the promontory being a mere precipice overlooking the ocean, a sudden gust of wind dashed so violently against us, that in the danger of being blown into the sea, I dropped on the turf at full length, and saw Diane do the same, with her four paws spread as widely as possible, to flatten her body more completely to the ground.

This opening to my expedition thus briefly set aside, I repaired to the coast, where there are pebbles, at least, in great beauty as well as abundance. The coast of Ilfracombe is broken by rocks, which bear evident marks of being fragments of some one immense rock, which, undermined by the billows in successive storms, has been cast in all directions in its fall. We went down to the edge of the sea, which was clear, smooth, and immovable as a lake, the wind having subsided into a calm so quiet, that I could not tell whether the tide were in or out. Not a creature was in sight; but presently a lady descended, with a book in her hand, and passed on before us to the right, evidently to read alone. Satisfied by this circumstance that the tide was going out, and all was safe, I began my search, and soon accumulated a collection of beautiful pebbles, each of which seemed to merit being set in a ring.

The pleasure they afforded me insensibly drew me on to the entrance of the Wildersmouth, which is the name given to a series of recesses formed by the rocks, and semicircular, open at the bottom to the sea, and only to be entered from the sands at low tide. I coasted two or three of them, augmenting my spoil as I proceeded; and perceiving the lady I have- already mentioned composedly engaged with her book, I hurried past to visit the last recess, whither I had never yet ventured. I found it a sort of chamber, though with no roof but a clear blue sky. The top was a portly mountain, rough, steep and barren - the left side was equally mountainous, but consisting of layers of a sort of slate, intermixed with moss; the right side was the elevated Capstan, which here was perpendicular; and at the bottom were, the sands, by which I entered it, terminated by the ocean. The whole was altogether strikingly picturesque, wild and original. There was not one trace of art, or even of any previous entrance into it of man. I could almost imagine myself its first human inmate.

My eye was presently caught by the appearance, near the top, of a cavern, at the foot of which I perceived something of so brilliant a whiteness that, in hopes of a treasure for my bag, I hastened to the spot. What had attracted me proved to be the jawbone and teeth of some animal. Various rudely curious things at the mouth of the cavern invited investigation; Diane, however, brushed forward, and was soon out of sight, but while I was busily culling, hoarding, or rejecting whatever struck my fancy, she returned with an air so piteous, and a whine so unusual, that, concluding she pined to return to a little puppy of a week old that she was then rearing, I determined to hasten; but still went on with my search, till the excess of her distress leading her to pull me by the gown, moved me to take her home; but when I descended, for this recess was on a slant, how was I confounded to find the sands at the bottom, opening to the recess, whence I had entered this marine chamber, were covered by the waves; though so gentle had been their motion, and so calm was the sea, that their approach had not caught my ear. I hastily remounted, hoping to find some outlet at the top by which I might escape, but there was none. This was not pleasant but still I was not frightened, not conceiving or believing that I could be completely enclosed: the less, as I recollected, in my passage to the cavern, having had a glimpse of the lady who was reading in the neighbouring recess. I hastily scrambled to the spot to look for her, and entreat her assistance; but how was I then startled to find that she was gone, and that her recess, which was on less elevated ground than mine, was fast filling with water!

CAUGHT BY THE RISING TIDE.

I now rushed down to the sea, determined to risk a wet jerkin, by wading through a wave or two, to secure myself from being shut up in this unfrequented place: but the time was past! The weather suddenly changed, the lake was gone, and billows mounted one after the other, as if with enraged pursuit of what they could seize and swallow. I eagerly ran up and down, from side to side, and examined every nook and corner, every projection and hollow, to find any sort of opening through which I could pass-but there was none.

Diane looked scared; she whined, she prowled about - her dismay was evident, and filled me with compassion-but I could not interrupt my affrighted search to console her. Soon after, however, she discovered a hole in the rock at the upper part, which seemed to lead to the higher sands. She got through it, and then turned round to bark, as triumphing in her success, and calling upon me to share its fruits. But in vain! the hollow was too small for my passage save of my head, and I could only have remained in it as if standing in the pillory. I still, therefore, continued my own perambulation, but I made a motion to my poor Diane to go, deeming it cruel to detain her from her little one. Yet I heard her howl as if reduced to despair, that I would not join her. Anon, however, she was silent—I looked after her, but she had disappeared.

This was an alarming moment. Alone, without the smallest aid, or any knowledge how high the sea might mount, or what was the extent of my danger, I looked up wistfully at Capstan, and perceived the iron salmon; but this angle of that promontory was so steep as to be utterly impracticable for climbing by human feet; and its height was such as nearly to make me giddy in considering it from so close a point of view. I went from it, therefore, to the much less elevated and less perpendicular rock opposite; but there all that was not slate, which crumbled in my hands, was moss, from which they glided. There was no hold whatsoever for the feet.

"I ran therefore to the top, where a large rock, by reaching from the upper part of this slated one to Capstan, formed the chamber in which I was thus unexpectedly immured. But this was so rough, pointed, sharp, and steep that I could scarcely touch it. The hole through which Diane had crept was at an accidentally thin part, and too small to afford a passage to anything bigger than her little self.

The rising storm, however, brought forward the billows with augmented noise and violence; and my wild asylum lessened every moment. Now, indeed, I comprehended the fulness of my danger. If a wave once reached my feet, while coming upon me with the tumultuous vehemence of this storm, I had nothing I could hold by to sustain me from becoming its prey and must inevitably be carried away into the ocean.

EFFORTS TO REACH A PLACE OF SAFETY.

I darted about in search of some place of safety, rapidly, and all eye; till at length I espied a small tuft of grass on the pinnacle of the highest of the small rocks that were scattered about my prison; for such now appeared my fearful dwelling-place.

This happily pointed out to me a spot that the waves had never yet attained; for all around bore marks of the visits. To reach that tuft would be safety, and I made the attempt with eagerness; but the obstacles I encountered were terrible. The roughness of the rock tore my clothes - its sharp points cut, now my feet, and now my fingers - and the distances from each other of the holes by which I could gain any footing for my ascent, increased the difficulty. I gained, however, nearly a quarter of the height, but I could climb no further and then found myself on a ledge where it was possible to sit down - and I have rarely found a little repose more seasonable. But it was not more sweet than short: for in a few minutes a sudden gust of wind raised the waves to a frightful height, whence their foam reached the base of my place of refuge, and threatened to attain soon the spot to which I had ascended. I now saw a positive necessity to mount yet higher, co–te qui co–te, and, little as I had thought it possible, the pressing danger gave me both means and fortitude to accomplish it: but with so much hardship that I have ever since marvelled at my success. My hands were wounded, my knees were bruised, and my feet were cut for I could only scramble up by clinging to the rock on all fours.

When I had reached to about two-thirds of the height of my rock, I could climb no further. All above was so sharp and so perpendicular that neither hand nor foot could touch it without being wounded. My head, however, was nearly on a level with the tuft of grass, and my elevation from the sands was very considerable. I hoped, therefore, I was safe from being washed away by the waves; but I could only hope; I had no means to ascertain my situation; and hope as I might, it was as painful as it was hazardous. The tuft to which I had aimed to rise, and which, had I succeeded, would have been security, was a mere point, as unattainable as it was unique, not another blade of grass being anywhere discernible. I was rejoiced, however, to have reached a spot where there was sufficient breadth to place one foot at least without cutting it, though the other was poised on such unfriendly ground that it could bear no part in sustaining me. Before me was an immense slab, chiefly of slate, but it was too slanting to serve for a seat-and seat I had none. My only prop, therefore, was holding by the slab, where it was of a convenient height for my hands. This support, besides affording me a little rest, saved me from becoming giddy, and enabled me from time to time to alternate the toil of my feet.

A SIGNAL OF DISTRESS.

Glad was I, at least, that my perilous clambering had finished by bringing me to a place where I might remain still; for with affright, fatigue, and exertion I was almost exhausted. The wind was now abated, and the sea so calm, that I could not be sure whether the tide was still coming in. To ascertain this was deeply necessary for my tranquillity, that I might form some idea what would be the length of my torment. I fixed my eyes, therefore, upon two rocks that stood near the sea entrance into my recess, almost close to the promontory, from which they had probably been severed by successive storms. As they were always in the sea I could easily make my calculation by observing whether they seemed to lengthen or shorten. With my near-sighted glass I watched them; and great was my consternation when, little by little, I lost sight of them. I now looked wistfully onward to the main ocean, in the hope of espying some vessel, or fishing-boat, with intention of spreading and waving my parasol, in signal of distress, should any one come in sight. But nothing appeared. All was vacant and vast! I was wholly alone-wholly isolated. I feared to turn my head lest I should become giddy, and lose my balance.

LITTLE DIANE.

In this terrible state, painful, dangerous, and, more than all, solitary, who could paint my joy, when suddenly, reentering by the aperture in the rock through which she had quitted me, I perceived my dear little Diane! For the instant I felt as if restored to safety, I no longer seemed abandoned. She soon leaped across the flat stones and the sands which separated us, but how great was the difficulty to make her climb as I had climbed! Twenty times she advanced only to retreat from the sharp points of the rock, till ultimately she picked herself out a passage by help of the slate, and got upon the enormous table, of which the upper part was my support; but the slant was such, that as fast as she ascended she slipped down, and we were both, I believe almost hopeless of the desired junction, when, catching at a favourable moment that had advanced her paws within my reach, I contrived to hook her collar by the curved end of my parasol and help her forward. This I did with one hand, and as quick as lightning, dragging her over the slab and dropping her at my feet, whence she soon nestled herself in a sort of niche of slate, in a situation much softer than mine, but in a hollow that for me was impracticable. I hastily recovered my hold, which I marvel now that I had the temerity to let go; but to have at my side my dear little faithful Diane was a comfort which no one not planted, and for a term that seemed indefinite, in so unknown, a solitude, can conceive. What cries of joy the poor little thing uttered when thus safely lodged! and with what tenderness I sought to make her sensible of my gratitude for her return!

I was now, compared with all that had preceded, in Paradise: so enchanted did I -feel at no longer considering myself as if alone in the world. O, well I can conceive the interest excited in the French prisoner by a spider, even a spider! Total absence of all. of animation in a place of confinement, of which the term is unknown, where volition is set aside, and where captivity is the work of the elements, casts the fancy into a state of solemn awe, of fearful expectation, which I have not words to describe; while the higher mind, mastering at times that fancy, seeks resignation from the very sublimity of that terrific vacuity whence all seems exiled, but self: seeks, and finds it in the almost Visible security of the omnipresence of God.

To see after my kind little companion was an occupation that for awhile kept me from seeing after myself, but when I had done what I could towards giving her comfort and assistance, I again looked before me, and saw the waters at the base of my rock of refuge, still gradually rising on, while both my rocks of mark were completely swallowed up!

THE INCREASING DANGER.

My next alarm was one that explained that of Diane when she came back so scared from the cavern; for the waves, probably from some subterraneous passage, now forced their way through that cavern, threatening inundation to even the highest part of my chamber. This was horrific. I could no longer even speak to Diane; my eyes were riveted upon this unexpected gulf, and in a few moments an immense breaker attacked my rock, and, impeded by its height from going straight forward, was dashed in two directions, and foamed onward against each side.

I did not breathe—I felt faint—I felt even sea-sick. On, then, with added violence came two wide-spreading waves, and, being parted by my rock, completely encompassed it, meeting each other on the further and upper ground. I now gave up my whole soul to prayer for myself and for my Alexander, and that I might mercifully be spared this watery grave, or be endowed with courage and faith for meeting it with firmness.

The next waves reached to the uppermost end of my chamber, which was now all sea, save the small rock upon which I was mounted! How I might have been subdued by a situation so awful at once, and so helpless, if left to unmixed contemplation, I know not—had I not been still called into active service in sustaining my poor Diane. No sooner were we thus encompassed than she was seized with a dismay that filled me with pity. She trembled violently, and rising and looking down at the dreadful sight of sea, sea, sea all around, and sea still to the utmost extent of the view beyond, she turned up her face to me, as if appealing for protection and when I spoke to her with kindness, she crept forward to my feet, and was instantly taken with a shivering fit.

I could neither sit nor kneel to offer her any comfort, but I dropped down as children do when they play at hunt the slipper, for so only could I loose my hold of the slab without falling, and I then stroked and caressed her in as fondling a way as if she had been a child; and I recovered her from her ague-fit by rubbing her head and back with my shawl. She then looked up at me somewhat composed, though still piteous and forlorn, and licked my hands with gratitude.

THE LAST WAVE OF THE RISING TIDE.

While this passed the sea had gained considerably in height, and, a few minutes afterwards all the horrors of a tempest seemed impending. The wind roared around me, pushing on the waves with a frothy velocity that, to a bystander, not to an inmate amidst them, would have been beautiful. It whistled with shrill and varying tones from the numberless crevices in the three immense rocky mountains by whose semicircular adhesion I was thus immured - and it burst forth at times in squalls, reverberating from height to height or chasm to chasm, as if "the big-mouthed thunder"

"Were bellowing through the vast and boundless deep."

A wave, at length, more stupendous than any which had preceded it, dashed against my rock as if enraged at an interception of its progress, and rushed on to the extremity of this savage chamber, with foaming impetuosity. This moment I believed to be my last of mortality! but a moment only it was; for scarcely had I time, with all the rapidity of concentrated thought, to recommend myself, my husband, and my poor Alexander, humbly but fervently to the mercy of the Almighty, when the celestial joy broke in upon me of perceiving that this wave, which had bounded forward with such fury, was the last of the rising tide! In its rebound, it forced back with it, for an instant, the whole body of water that was lodged nearest to the upper extremity of my recess, and the transporting sight was granted me of an opening to the sands but they were covered again the next instant, and as no other breaker made a similar opening, I was still, for a considerable length of time, in the same situation: but I lost hope no more. The tide was turned: it could rise therefore no higher; the danger was over of so unheard-of an end; of vanishing no one knew how or where—of leaving to my kind, deploring friends an unremitting uncertainty of my fate—of my re-appearance or dissolution. I now wanted nothing but time, and caution, to effect my deliverance.

The threat of the tempest, also, was over; the air grew as serene as my mind, the sea far more calm, the sun beautifully tinged the west, and its setting upon the ocean was resplendent. By remembrance, however, alone, I speak of its glory, not from any pleasure I then experienced in its sight: it told me of the waning day; and the anxiety I had now dismissed for myself redoubled for my poor Alexander. . . .

With my bag of curiosities I made a cushion for Diane, which, however little luxurious, was softness itself compared with her then resting-place. She, also, could take no repose, but from this period I made her tolerably happy, by caresses and continual attentions.

But no sooner had the beams of the sun vanished from the broad horizon, than a small, gentle rain began to fall, and the light as well as brightness of the day became obscured by darkling clouds.

This greatly alarmed me, in defiance of my joy and my philosophy; for I dreaded being surprised by the night in this isolated situation. I was supported, however, by perceiving that the sea was clearly retrograding, and beholding, little by little, the dry ground across the higher extremity of my apartment. How did I bless the sight! the sands and clods of sea-mire were more beautiful to my eyes than the rarest mosaic pavement of antiquity. Nevertheless, the return was so gradual, that I foresaw I had still many hours to remain a prisoner.

ARRIVAL OF SUCCOUR.

The night came on—there was no moon - but the sea, by its extreme whiteness, afforded some degree of pale light, when suddenly I thought I perceived something in the air. Affrighted, I looked around me but nothing was visible; yet in another moment something like a shadow flitted before my eyes. I tried to fix it, but could not develop any form: something black was all I could make out; it seemed in quick motion, for I caught and lost it alternately, as if it was a shadow reflected by the waters.

I looked up at Capstan: nothing was there, but the now hardly discernible Iron salmon. I then looked at the opposite side. . . . ah, gracious heaven, what were my sensations to perceive two human figures! Small they looked, as in a picture, from their distance, the height of the rock, and the obscurity of the night; but not less certainly from their outline, human figures. I trembled—I could not breathe—in another minute I was espied, for a voice loud, but unknown to my ears, called out "Holloa!" I unhesitatingly answered, "I am safe!"

"Thank God!" was the eager reply, in a voice hardly articulate, "Oh, thank God!" but not in a Voice unknown though convulsed with agitation—it was the voice of my dear son! Oh what a quick transition from every direful apprehension to' joy and delight! yet knowing his precipitancy, and fearing a rash descent to join me, in ignorance of the steepness and dangers of the precipice which parted us, I called out with all the energy in my power to conjure him to await patiently, as I would myself, the entire going down of the tide.

He readily gave me this promise, though still in sounds almost inarticulate. I was then indeed in heaven while upon earth.

Another form then appeared, while Alex and the first companion retired. This form, from a gleam of light on her dress, I soon saw to be female. She called out to me that Mr. Alexander and his friend were gone to call for a boat to come round for me by sea. The very thought made me shudder, acquainted as I now was with the nature of my recess, where, though the remaining sea looked as smooth as the waters of a lake, I well knew it was but a surface covering pointed fragments of rock, against which a boat must have been overset or stranded. Loudly, therefore, as I could raise my voice, I called upon my informant to fly after them, and say I was decided to wait till the tide was down. She replied that she would not leave me alone for the world.

The youths, however, soon returned to the top of the mountain, accompanied by a mariner, who had dissuaded them from their dangerous enterprise. I cheerfully repeated that I was safe, and begged reciprocated patience. They now wandered about on the heights, one of them always keeping in view.

Meanwhile, I had now the pleasure to descend to the sort of halfway-house which I had first hoped would serve for my refuge. The difficulty was by no means so arduous to come down as to mount, especially as, the waters being no longer so high as my rock, there was no apprehension of destruction should my footing fail me.

Some time after I descried a fourth figure on the summit, bearing a lantern. This greatly rejoiced me, for the twilight now was grown so obscure that I had felt much troubled how I might at last grope my way in the dark out of this terrible Wildersmouth.

They all now, from the distance and the dimness, looked like spectres: we spoke no more, the effort being extremely fatiguing. I observed, however, with great satisfaction, an increase of figures, so that the border of the precipice seemed covered with people. This assurance that if any accident happened, there would be succour at hand, relieved many a fresh starting anxiety.

Not long after, the sea wholly disappeared, and the man with the lantern, who was an old sailor, descended the precipice on the further part, by a way known to him; and placing the lantern where it might give him light, yet allow him the help of both his hands, he was coming to me almost on all fours - when Diane leaped to the bottom of the rock, and began a barking so loud and violent that the seaman stopped short, and I had the utmost difficulty to appease my little dog, and prevail with her, between threats and cajolements, to suffer his approach. . . .

MEETING BETWEEN MOTHER AND SON.

My son no sooner perceived that the seaman had found footing, though all was still too watery and unstable for me to quit my rock, than he darted forward by the way thus pointed out, and clambering, or rather leaping up to me, he was presently in my arms. Neither of us could think or care about the surrounding spectators—we seemed restored to each other, almost miraculously, from destruction and death. Neither of us could utter a word, but both, I doubt not, were equally occupied in returning the most ardent thanks to heaven.

Alexander had run wildly about in every direction; visited hill, dale, cliff, by-paths, and public roads, to make and instigate inquiry-but of the Wildersmouth he thought not, and never, I believe, had heard; and as it was then a mere part of the sea, from the height of the tide, the notion or remembrance of it occurred to no one. Mr. Jacob, his coolheaded and excellent hearted friend, was most unfortunately at Barnstaple, but he at length thought of Mr. John Le Fevre, a young man who was eminently at the head of the Ilfracombe students, and had resisted going to the ball at Barnstaple, not to lose an hour of his time. Recollecting this, Alex went to his dwelling, and bursting into his apartment, called out, "My mother is missing!"

The generous youth, seeing the tumult of soul in which he was addressed, shut up his bureau without a word, and hurried off with his distressed comrade, giving up for that benevolent purpose the precious time he had refused himself to spare for a moment's recreation.

Fortunately, providentially, Mr. Le Fevre recollected Wildersmouth, and that one of his friends had narrowly escaped destruction by a surprise there of the sea. He no sooner named this than he and Alexander contrived to climb up the rock opposite to Capstan, whence they looked down upon my recess. At first they could discern nothing, save one small rock uncovered by the sea: but at length, as my head moved, Le Fevre saw something like a shadow—he then called out, "Holloa!" etc. To Mr. Le Fevre, therefore, I probably owe my life.

Two days after, I visited the spot of my captivity, but it had entirely changed its appearance. A storm of equinoctial violence had broken off its pyramidal height, and the drift of sand and gravel, and fragments of rocks, had given a new face to the whole recess. I sent for the seaman to ascertain the very spot: this he did; but told me that a similar change took place commonly twice a year - and added, very calmly, that two days later I could not have been saved from the waves.

GENERAL D'ARBLAY'S RETURN TO ENGLAND.

(Madame d'Arblay to a Friend.) Bath, November 9, 1817. Can I still hope, my dear friend, for that patient partiality which will await my tardy answer ere it judges my irksome silence? Your letter of Sept. 27th I found upon my table when I returned, the 5th of October, from Ilfracombe. I returned, with Alexander, to meet General d'A. from Paris. You will be sorry, I am very sure, and probably greatly surprised, to hear that he came in a state to occupy every faculty of my mind and thoughts—altered—thin—weak—depressed—full of pain—and disappointed in every expectation of every sort that had urged his excursion!

I thank God the fever that confined him to his bed for three days is over, and he yesterday went down stairs and his repose now is the most serene and reviving. The fever, Mr. Hay assured me, was merely symptomatic; not of inflammation or any species of danger, but the effect of his sufferings. Alas! that is heavy and severe enough, but still, where fever comes, 'tis of the sort the least cruel, because no ways alarming.

Nov. 15. I never go out, nor admit any one within—nor shall I, till a more favourable turn will let me listen to his earnest exhortations that I should do both. Mr. Hay gives me strong hopes that that will soon arrive, and then I shall not vex him by persevering in this seclusion: you know and can judge how little this part of my course costs me, for to quit the side of those we prize when they are in pain, would be a thousand times greater sacrifice than any other privation.

THE PRINCESS CHARLOTTE'S DEATH.

You are very right as to Lady Murray, not only, of course, I am honoured by her desire of intercourse, but it can never be as a new acquaintance I can see the daughter of Lord and Lady Mulgrave. I have been frequently in the company of the former, who was a man of the gayest wit in society I almost ever knew. He spread mirth around him by his sprightly ideas and sallies, and his own laugh was as hearty and frank as that he excited in others; and his accomplished and attaching wife was one of the sweetest creatures in the world. Alas! how often this late tragedy in the unfortunate royal family has called her to my remembrance! (316) She, however, left the living consolation of a lovely babe to her disconsolate survivor;—the poor Prince Leopold loses in one blow mother and child.

The royal visit here has been a scene of emotion:—first of joy and pleasure, next of grief and disappointment. The queen I thought looked well till this sudden and unexpected blow; after which, for the mournful day she remained, she admitted no one to her presence, but most graciously sent me a message to console me. She wrote instantly, with her own hand, to Prince Leopold-that prince who must seem to have had a vision of celestial happiness, so perfect it was, so exalted, and so transitory. The poor Princess Charlotte's passion for him had absorbed her, yet was so well placed as only to form her to excellence, and it had so completely won his return, that like herself he coveted her alone...... Princess Elizabeth is much altered personally, to my great concern; but her manners, and amiability, and talents, I think more pleasing and more attaching than ever. How delighted I was at their arrival!

THE QUEEN AND PRINCESSES AT BATH.

(Madame d'Arblay to her Son.) Bath, November 9, 1817. We have here spent nearly a week in a manner the most extraordinary, beginning with hope and pleasure, proceeding to fear and pain, and ending in disappointment and grief.

The joy exhibited on Monday, when her majesty and her royal highness arrived, was really ecstatic; the illumination was universal. The public offices were splendid; so were the tradespeople's who had promises or hopes of employment; the nobles and gentles were modestly gay, and the poor eagerly put forth their mite. But all was flattering, because voluntary. Nothing was induced by power, or forced by mobs. All was left to individual choice. Your padre and I patrolled the principal streets, and were quite touched by the universality of the homage paid to the virtues and merit of our venerable queen, upon this her first progress through any part of her domains by herself. Hitherto she has only accompanied the poor king, as at Weymouth and Cheltenham, Worcester and Exeter, Plymouth and Portsmouth, etc.; or the prince regent, as at Brighthelmstone. But here, called by her health, she came as principal, and in her own character of rank and consequence. And, as Mr. Hay told me, the inhabitants of Bath were all even vehement to let her see the light in which they held her individual self, after so many years witnessing her exemplary conduct and distinguished merit. She was very sensible to this tribute; but much affected, nay, dejected, in receiving it, at the beginning; from coming without the king where the poor king had always meant himself to bring her - but just as he had arranged for the excursion, and even had three houses taken for him in the Royal-crescent, he was afflicted by blindness. He would not then come; for what, he said, was a beautiful city to him who could not look at it? This was continually in the remembrance of the queen during the honours of her reception; but she had recovered from the melancholy recollection, and was cheering herself by the cheers of all the inhabitants, when the first news arrived of the illness of the Princess Charlotte. At that moment she was having her diamonds placed on her head for the reception of the mayor and corporation of Bath, with an address upon the honour done to their city, and upon their hopes from the salutary spring she came to quaff. Her first thought was to issue orders for deferring this ceremony but when she considered that all the members of the municipality must be assembled, and that the great dinner they had prepared to give to the Duke of Clarence could only be postponed at an enormous and useless expense, she composed her spirits, finished her regal decorations, and admitted the citizens of Bath, who were highly gratified by her condescension, and struck by her splendour, which was the same as she appeared in on the greatest occasions in the capital. The Princess Elizabeth was also a blaze of jewels. And our good little Mayor (not four feet high) and aldermen and common councilmen were all transported.

NEWS ARRIVES OF THE PRINCESS CHARLOTTE'S DEATH.

The Duke of Clarence accepted their invitation, and was joined by the Marquis of Bath and all the queen's suite. But the dinner was broken up. The duke received an express with the terrible tidings: he rose from table, and struck his forehead as he read them, and then hurried out of the assembly with inexpressible trepidation and dismay. The queen also was at table when the same express arrived, though only with the princess and her own party: all were dispersed in a moment, and she shut herself up, admitting no one but her royal highness. She would have left Bath the next morning; but her physician, Sir Henry Halford, said it would be extremely dangerous that she should travel so far, in her state of health, just in the first perturbation of affliction. She would see no one but her suite all day, and set out the next for Windsor Castle, to spend the time previous to the last melancholy rites, in the bosom of her family.

All Bath wore a face of mourning. The transition from gaiety and exultation was really awful. What an extinction of youth and happiness! The poor Princess Charlotte had never known a moment's suffering since her marriage. Her lot seemed perfect. Prince Leopold is, indeed, to be pitied.

(Madame d'Arblay to Mrs. Broome.) Bath, November 25, 1817......We are all here impressed with the misfortunes of the royal house, and chiefly with the deadly blow inflicted on the perfect conjugal happiness of the first young couple in the kingdom. The first couple not young bad already received a blow yet, perhaps, more frightful: for to have, yet lose-to keep, yet never to enjoy the being we most prize, is surely yet more torturing than to yield at once to the stroke which we know awaits us, and by which, at last, we must necessarily and indispensably fall. The queen supports herself with the calm and serenity belonging to one inured to misfortune, and submissive to Providence. The Princess Elizabeth has native spirits that resist all woe after the first shock, though she is full of kindness, goodness, and zeal for right action.

AN OLD ACQUAINTANCE. SERIOUS ILLNESS OF GENERAL D'ARBLAY.

(Mrs. Piozzi to Madame d'Arblay.) Bath, Thursday, February 26, 1818. I had company in the room when Lady K-'s note arrived, desiring I would send you some papers of hers by the person who should bring it. I had offered a conveyance to London by some friends of my own, but she preferred their passing through your hands. Accept my truest wishes for the restoration of complete peace to a mind which has been SO long and so justly admired, loved, and praised by. Dear Madam,—Your ever faithful, H. L. P. Who attends the general? and why do you think him SO very bad?

(Madame d'Arblay to Mrs. Piozzi.) Bath, February 26, 1818. There is no situation in which a kind remembrance from you, my dear madam, would not awaken me to some pleasure; but my poor sufferer was so very ill when your note came, that it was not possible for me to answer it. That I think him so very bad, is that I see him perpetually in pain nearly insupportable; yet I am assured it is local and unattended with danger while followed up with constant care and caution. This supports my spirits, which bear me and enable me to help him through a malady of anguish and difficulty. It is a year this very month since he has been in the hands of Mr. Hay as a regular patient. Mr. Hay was recommended to us by Mrs. Locke and Mrs. Angerstein, whom he attends as physician, from their high opinion of his skill and discernment. But, alas! all has failed here; and we have called in Mr. Tudor, as the case terminates in being one that demands a surgeon. Mr. Tudor gives me every comfort in prospect, but prepares me for long suffering, and slow, slow recovery.

Shall I apologise for this wordy explanation? No - you will see by it with what readiness I am happy, to believe that our interest in each other must ever be reciprocal.

Lady K- by no means intended to give me the charge of the papers; she only thought they might procure some passing amusement to my invalid. I must, on the contrary, hope you will permit me to return them you, in a few days, for such conveyance as you may deem safe; I am now out of the way of seeking any.

I hope you were a little glad that my son has been among the high Wranglers.

NARRATIVE OF THE ILLNESS AND DEATH OF GENERAL D'ARBLAY.

THE GENERAL'S FIRST ATTACK: DELUSIVE HOPES.

Bolton Street, Berkeley Square. It is now the 17th of November, 1819. A year and a half have passed since I was blessed with the sight of my beloved husband. I can devise no means to soothe my lonely woe, so likely of success as devoting my evening solitude to recollections of his excellences, and of every occurrence of his latter days, till I bring myself up to the radiant serenity of their end. I think it will be like passing with him, with him himself, a few poor fleeting but dearly-cherished moments. I will call back the history of my beloved husband's last illness. Ever present as it is to me, it will be a relief to set it down.

In Paris, in the autumn of 1817, he was first attacked with the deadly evil by which he was finally consumed. I suspected not his danger. He had left me in June, in the happy but most delusive persuasion that the journey and his native air would complete his recovery from the jaundice, which had attacked him in February, 1817. Far from ameliorating, his health went on daily declining. His letters, which at first were the delight and support of my existence, became disappointing, dejecting, afflicting. I sighed for his return! I believed. he was trying experiments that hindered his recovery; and, indeed, I am persuaded he precipitated the evil by continual changes of system. At length his letters became so comfortless, that I almost expired with desire to join him - but he positively forbade my quitting our Alexander, who was preparing for his grand examination at Cambridge.

On the opening of October, 1817, Alex and I returned from Ilfracombe to Bath to meet our best friend. He arrived soon after, attended by his favourite medical man, Mr. Hay, whom he had met in Paris. We found him extremely altered-not in mind, temper, faculties—oh, no!—but in looks and strength: thin and weakened so as to be fatigued by the smallest exertion. He tried, however, to revive; we sought to renew our walks, but his strength was insufficient. He purchased a garden in the Crescent fields, and worked in it, but came home always the worse for the effort. His spirits were no longer in their state of native genial cheerfulness: he could still be awakened to gaiety, but gaiety was no longer innate, instinctive with him.

GENERAL D'ARBLAY PRESENTED TO THE QUEEN.

In this month, October, 1817, I had a letter from the Princess Elizabeth, to inform me that her majesty and herself were coming to pass four weeks in Bath. The queen's stay was short, abruptly and sadly broken up by the death of the Princess Charlotte. In twenty-four hours after the evil tidings, they hastened to Windsor to meet the prince regent and almost immediately after the funeral, the queen and princess returned, accompanied by the Duke of Clarence. I saw them continually, and never passed a day without calling at the royal abode by the queen's express permission; and during the whole period of their stay, my invalid appeared to be stationary in his health. I never quitted him save for this royal visit, and that only of a morning.

He had always purposed being presented to her majesty in the pump-room, and the queen herself deigned to say "she should be very glad to see the general." Ill he was! suffering, emaciated, enfeebled! But he had always spirit awake to every call; and just before Christmas, 1817, we went together, between seven and eight o'clock in the morning, in chairs, to the pump-room. I thought I had never seen him look to such advantage. His fine brow so open, his noble countenance so expressive, his features so formed for a painter's pencil! This, too, was the last time he ever wore his military honours—his three orders of "St. Louis," "the Legion of Honour," and "Du Lys," or "De la Fidélité;" decorations which singularly became him, from his strikingly martial port and character.

The queen was brought to the circle in her sedan-chair, and led to the seat prepared for her by her vice-chamberlain, making a gracious general bow to the assembly as she passed. Dr. Gibbs and Mr. Tudor waited upon her with the Bath water, and she conversed with them, and the mayor and aldermen, and her own people, for some time. After this she rose to make her round with a grace indescribable, and, to those who never witnessed it, inconceivable; for it was such as to carry off age, infirmity, sickness, diminutive stature and to give her, in defiance of such disadvantages, a power of charming that rarely has been equalled. Her face had a variety of expression that made her features soon seem agreeable; the intonations of her voice so accorded with her words, her language was so impressive, and her manner so engaging and encouraging, that it was not possible to be the object of her attention without being both struck with her uncommon abilities and fascinated by their exertion.

Such was the effect which she produced upon General d'Arblay, to whom she soon turned. Highly sensible to the honour of her distinction, he forgot his pains in his desire to manifest his gratitude;— and his own smiles—how winning they became! Her majesty spoke of Bath, of Windsor, of the Continent; and while addressing him, her eyes turned to meet mine with a look that said, "Now I know I am making you happy!" She asked me, archly, whether I was not fatigued by coming to the pump-room so early? and said, "Madame d'Arblay thinks I have never seen you before! but she is mistaken, for I peeped at you through the window as you passed to the Terrace at Windsor." Alas! the queen no sooner ceased to address him than the pains he had suppressed became intolerable, and he retreated from the circle and sank upon a bench near the wall - he could stand no longer, and we returned home to spend the rest of the day in bodily misery.

GLOOMY FOREBODINGS.

Very soon after the opening of this fatal year 1818, expressions dropped from my beloved of his belief of his approaching end: they would have broken my heart, had not an incredulity —now my eternal wonder,—kept me in a constant persuasion that he was hypochondriac, and tormented with false apprehensions. Fortunate, merciful as wonderful, was that incredulity, which, blinding me to my coming woe, enabled me to support my courage by my hopes, and helped me to sustain his own. In his occasional mournful prophecies, which I always rallied off and refused to listen to, he uttered frequently the kind words, "Et jamais je n'ai tant aimé la vie! Jamais, jamais, la vie ne m'a été plus chère!" (317) How sweet to me were those words, which I thought—alas, how delusively—would soothe and invigorate recovery!

The vivacity with which I exerted all the means in my power to fly from every evil prognostic, he was often struck with, and never angrily; on the contrary, he would exclaim, "Comme j'admire ton courage!" (318) while his own, on the observation, always revived. "My courage?" I always answered, "What courage? Am I not doing what I most desire upon earth—remaining by your side? When you are not well, the whole universe is to me, there!"

Soon after, nevertheless, recurring to the mournful idea ever uppermost, he said, with a serenity the most beautiful, "Je voudrois que nous causassions sur tout cela avec calme,—doucement,— cheerfully même (319) as of a future voyage—as of a subject of discussion—simply to exchange our ideas and talk them over."

Alas, alas! how do I now regret that I seconded not this project, so fitted for all pious Christian minds, whether their pilgrimage be of shorter or longer duration. But I saw him I, oh, how ill! I felt myself well; it was, therefore, apparent who must be the survivor in case of sunderment; and, therefore, all power of generalizing the subject was over. And much and ardently as I should have rejoiced in treating such a theme when he was well, or on his recovery, I had no power to sustain it thus situated. I could only attend his sick couch; I could only 'live by fostering hopes of his revival, and seeking to make them reciprocal.

During this interval a letter from my affectionate sister Charlotte suggested our taking further advice to aid Mr. Hay, since the malady was so unyielding. On January the 24th Mr. Tudor came, but after an interview and examination, his looks were even forbidding. Mr. Hay had lost his air of satisfaction and complacency, Mr. Tudor merely inquired whether he should come again? "Oh, yes, yes, yes!" I cried, and they retired together. And rapidly I flew, not alone from hearing, but from forming any opinion, and took refuge by the side of my beloved, whom I sought to console and revive. And this very day, as I have since found, he began his Diary for the year. It contains these words:—

"Jamais je n'ai tant aimé la vie que je suis en si grand danger de perdre; malgré que je n'aye point de fièvre, ni le moindre mal à la tête; et que j'aye non seulement l'esprit libre, mais le coeur d'un contentement Parfait. La volont, de Dieu soit faite! J'attends pour ce soir ou demain le resultat d'une consultation." (320)

PRESENTS FROM THE QUEEN AND PRINCESS ELIZABETH.

On this same day Madame de Soyres brought me a packet from her majesty, and another from the Princess Elizabeth. The kind and gracious princess sent me a pair of silver camp candlesticks, with peculiar contrivances which she wrote me word might amuse the general as a military man, while they might be employed by myself to light my evening researches among the MSS. of my dear father, which she wished me to collect and to preface by a memoir.

Her mother's offering was in the same spirit of benevolence, it was a collection of all the volumes of "L'Hermite de la Chauss,e d'Antin," with Chalmers's Astronomical Sermons, and Drake's two quartos on Shakespeare; joined to a small work of deeper personal interest to me than them all, which was a book of prayers suited to various circumstances, and printed at her majesty's own press at Frogmore. In this she had condescended to write my name, accompanied by words of peculiar kindness. My poor ami looked over every title-page with delight, feeling as I did myself that the gift was still more meant for him than for me—or rather, doubly, trebly for me in being calculated to be pleasing to him!—he was to me the soul of all pleasure on earth.

What words of kindness do I find, and now for the first time read, in his Diary dated 2nd February! After speaking—hélas, hélas!—"de ses douleurs inouies," (321) he adds, "Quelle étrange maladie! et quelle position que la mienne! il en est une, peut étre plus ficheuse encore, c'est celle de ma malheureuse compagne; avec quelle tendresse elle me soigne! et avec quel courage elle supporte ce qu'elle a souffrir! Je ne puis que r,p,ter, La volont, de Dieu soit faite!" (322)

Alas! the last words he wrote in February were most melancholy:— "20 Février, Je sens que je m'afaiblis horriblement—je ne crois pas que ceci puisse ˆtre encore bien long. (323) Chére Fanny, cher Alex! God bless you! and unite us for ever, Amen!"

Oh my beloved! Delight, pride, and happiness of my heart! May heaven in its mercy hear this prayer! . . .

THE GENERAL RECEIVES THE VISIT OF A PRIEST.

In March he revived a little, and Mr. Tudor no longer denied me hope; on the 18th Alex came to our arms and gratulations on his fellowship; which gave to his dearest father a delight the most touching.

I have no Diary in his honoured hand to guide my narrative in April; a few words only he ever wrote more, and these, after speaking of his sufferings, end with "Pazienza!

Pazienza!"—such was his last written expression! 'Tis on the 5th of April. . . .

On the 3rd of May he reaped, I humbly trust, the fair fruit of that faith and patience he so pathetically implored and so beautifully practised.

At this critical period in April I was called down one day to Madame la Marquise de S—, who urged me to summon a priest of the Roman catholic persuasion to my precious sufferer. I was greatly disturbed every way; I felt in shuddering the danger she apprehended, and resisted its belief; yet I trembled lest I should be doing wrong. I was a protestant, and had no faith in confession to man. I had long had reason to believe that my beloved partner was a protestant, also, in his heart; but he had a horror of apostasy, and therefore, as he told me, would not investigate the differences of the two religions; he had besides a tie which to his honour and character was potent and persuasive; he had taken an oath to keep the catholic faith when he received his Croix de St. Louis, which was at a period when the preference of the simplicity of protestantism was not apparent to him. All this made me personally easy for him, yet, as this was not known, and as nothing definite had ever passed between us upon this delicate subject, I felt that he apparently belonged still to the Roman catholic church; and after many painful struggles I thought it my absolute duty to let him judge for himself, even at the risk of inspiring the alarm I so much sought to save him! . . . I compelled myself therefore to tell him the wish of Madame de S—, that he should see a priest. "Eh bien," he cried, gently yet readily, "je ne m'y oppose pas. Qu'en penses tu?" I begged to leave such a decision wholly to himself.

Never shall I forget the heavenly composure with which my beloved partner heard me announce that the priest, Dr. Elloi, was come. Cheerfully as I urged myself to name him, still he could but regard the visit as an invitation to make his last preparations for quitting mortal life. With a calm the most gentle and genuine, he said he had better be left alone with him, and they remained together, I believe, three hours. I was deeply disturbed that my poor patient should be so long without sustenance or medicine - but I durst not intrude, though anxiously I kept at hand in case of any sudden summons. When, at length, the priest re-appeared, I found my dearest invalid as placid as before this ceremony, though fully convinced it was meant as the annunciation of his expected and approaching departure.

THE LAST SACRAMENT ADMINISTERED.

Dr. Elloi now came not only every day, but almost every hour of the day, to obtain another interview; but my beloved, though pleased that the meeting had taken place, expressed no desire for its repetition. I was cruelly distressed; the fear of doing wrong has been always the leading principle of my internal guidance, and here I felt incompetent to judge what was right. Overpowered, therefore, by my own inability to settle that point, and my terror lest I should mistake it, I ceased to resist; and Dr. Elloi, while my patient was sleeping from opium, glided into his chamber, and knelt down by the bedside with his prayer book in his hand. Two hours this lasted; but when the doctor informed me he had obtained the general's promise that he should administer to him the last sacrament, the preparations were made accordingly, and I only entreated leave to be present.

This solemn communion, at which I have never in our own church attended with unmoistened eyes, was administered the same evening. The dear invalid was in bed: his head raised with difficulty, he went through this ceremony with spirits calm, and a countenance and voice of holy composure.

FAREWELL WORDS OF COUNSEL.

Thenceforth he talked openly, and almost solely, of his approaching dissolution, and prepared for it by much silent mental prayer. He also poured forth his soul in counsel for Alexander and myself. I now dared no longer oppose to him my hopes of his recovery—the season was too awful. I heard him only with deluges of long-restrained tears, and his generous spirit seemed better satisfied in thinking me now—awakened to a sense of his danger, as preparatory for supporting its consequence.

"Parle de moi." He said, afterwards, "Parle—et souvent. Surtout Ò Alexandre; qu'il ne m'oublie pas!" (325)

"Je ne parlerai pas d'autre chose!"(326) I answered . . . and I felt his tender purpose. He knew how I forbore ever to speak of my lost darling sister, and he thought the constraint injurious both to my health and spirits: he wished to change my mode with regard to himself by an injunction of his own. "Nous ne parlerons pas d'autre chose!" I added, "mon ami!—mon ami!—je ne survivrai que pour cela!" (327) He looked pleased, and with a calm that taught me to repress my too great emotion.

He then asked for Alexander, embraced him warmly, and half raising himself with a strength that had seemed extinct but the day before, he took a hand of Alexander and one of mine, and putting them together between both his own, he tenderly pressed them, exclaiming, "How happy I am! I fear I am too happy!"

Kindest of human hearts! His happiness was in seeing us together ere he left us his fear was lest he should too keenly regret the quitting us!

At this time he saw for a few minutes my dear sister Esther and her Maria, who had always been a great favourite with him. When they retired, he called upon me to bow my knees as he dropped upon his own, that he might receive, he said, my benediction, and that we might fervently and solemnly join in prayer to Almighty God for each other. He then consigned himself to uninterrupted meditation: he told me not to utter one word to him, even of reply, beyond the most laconic necessity. He desired that when I brought him his medicine or nutriment, I would give it without speech and instantly retire; and take care that no human being addressed or approached him. This awful command lasted unbroken during the rest of the evening, the whole of the night, and nearly the following day. So concentrated in himself he desired to be!—yet always as free from irritation as from despondence—always gentle and kind even when taciturn, and even when in torture.

When the term of his meditative seclusion seemed to be over, I found him speaking with Alexander, and pouring into the bosom of his weeping son the balm of parental counsel and comfort. I received at this time a letter from my affectionate sister Charlotte, pressing for leave to come and aid me to nurse my dearest invalid. He took the letter and pressed it to his lips, saying, "Je l'aime bien; dis le lui. Et elle M'aime." (328) But I felt that she could do me no good. We had a nurse whose skill made her services a real blessing; and for myself, woe, such as he believed approaching, surpassed all aid but from prayer and from heaven—lonely meditation.

When the morning dawned, he ordered Payne to open the shutters and to undraw the curtains. The prospect from the windows facing his bed was picturesque, lively, lovely: he looked at it with a bright smile of admiration, and cast his arm over his noble brow, as if hailing one more return of day and light, and life with those he loved. But when, in the course of the day, something broke from me of my reverence at his heavenly resignation, "Resign?" he repeated, with a melancholy half smile; "mais comme ça!" and then in a voice of tenderness the most touching, he added, "Te quitter!" I dare not, even yet, hang upon my emotion at those words!

That night passed in tolerable tranquillity, and without alarm, his pulse still always equal and good, though smaller. On Sunday, the fatal 3rd of May, my patient was still cheerful, and slept often, but not long. This circumstance was delightful to my observation, and kept off the least suspicion that my misery could be so near.

THE END ARRIVES.

My pen lingers now! reluctant to finish the little that remains.

About noon, gently awaking from a slumber, he called to me for some beverage, but was weaker than usual, and could not hold the cup. I moistened his lips with a spoon several times. He looked at me with sweetness inexpressible, and pathetically said, "Qui?" He stopped, but I saw he meant "Who shall return this for you?" I instantly answered to his obvious and most touching meaning, by a cheerful exclamation of "You! my dearest ami! You yourself! You shall recover, and take your revenge." He smiled, but shut his eyes in silence. After this, he bent forward, as he was supported nearly upright by pillows in his bed, and taking my hand, and holding it between both his own, he impressively said, "Je ne sais si ce sera le dernier mot—mais ce sera la dernière pensée—notre reunion!" (329) Oh, words the most precious that ever the tenderest of husbands left for balm to the lacerated heart of a surviving wife! I fastened my lips on his loved hands, but spoke not. It was not then that those words were my blessing! They awed—they thrilled—more than they solaced me. How little knew I then that he should speak to me no more!

Towards evening I sat watching in my arm-chair, and Alex remained constantly with me. His sleep was so calm, that an hour passed in which I indulged the hope that a favourable crisis was arriving; that a turn would take place by which his vital powers would be restored; but when the hour was succeeded by another hour, when I saw a universal stillness in the whole frame, such as seemed to stagnate all around, I began to be strangely moved. "Alex!" I whispered, "this sleep is critical! a crisis arrives! Pray God— Almighty God!—that it be fav—." I could not proceed. Alex looked aghast, but firm. I sent him to call Payne. I intimated to her my opinion that this sleep was important, but kept a composure astonishing, for when no one would give me encouragement, I compelled myself to appear not to want it, to deter them from giving me despair. Another hour passed of concentrated feelings, of breathless dread.

His face had still its unruffled serenity, but methought the hands were turning cold; I covered them—I watched over the head of my beloved; I took new flannel to roll over his feet; the stillness grew more awful; the skin became colder.

Alex, my dear Alex, proposed calling in Mr. Tudor, and ran off for him.

I leant over him now with sal volatile to his temple, his forehead, the palms of his hands, but I had no courage to feel his pulse, to touch his lips.

Mr. Tudor came; he put his hand upon the heart, the noblest of hearts, and pronounced that all was over!

How I bore this is still marvellous to me! I had always believed such a sentence would at once have killed me. But his sight—the sight of his stillness, kept me from distraction! Sacred he appeared, and his stillness I thought should be mine, and be inviolable.

I suffered certainly a partial derangement, for I cannot to this moment recollect anything that now succeeded, with truth or consistency; my memory paints things that were necessarily real, joined to others that could not possibly have happened, yet so amalgamates the whole together as to render it impossible for me to separate truth from indefinable, unaccountable fiction.

Even to this instant I always see the room itself charged with a medley of silent and strange figures grouped against the wall just opposite to me, Mr. Tudor, methought, was come to drag me by force away; and in this persuasion, which was false, I remember supplicating him to grant me but one hour, telling him I had solemnly engaged myself to pass it in watching. . . .

But why go back to my grief? Even yet, at times, it seems as fresh as ever, and at all times weighs on me with a feeling that seems stagnating the springs of life. But for Alexander, our Alexander!—I think I could hardly have survived. His tender sympathy, with his claims to my love, and the solemn injunctions given me to preserve for him, and devote to him, my remnant of life—these, through the Divine mercy, sustained me.

May that mercy, with its best blessings, daily increase his resemblance to his noble father.

March 20, 1820. (288) M. d'Arblay, who was, it appears, still lame (boiteux) from the kick which he had received from a horse. ED,

(289) Half-pay.

(290) The Comte de Narbonne and Comte F. de la Tour Maubourg.

(291) He had studied mathematics in Paris according to the analytical method, instead of the geometrical, which was at that time exclusively taught at Cambridge.

(292) See infra, p. 387-8. ED.

(293) It is not without pain that we find Fanny, in this letter defending the harsh treatment accorded by the Bourbon king to Lavalette and others of the partisans of the emperor. Lavalette had served Napoleon both as soldier and diplomatist. At the restoration of the Bourbons in 1814 he retired from public life, but on the return of Napoleon he again entered the service of his old master. He was arrested after the downfall of the emperor, tried for treason, and condemned to death. His wife implored the king's mercy in vain, Lavalette was confined in the Conciergerie, and December 21, 1815, was the day fixed for his execution. The evening before that day his wife visited him in the prison. He exchanged clothes with her, and thus disguised, succeeded in making his escape. His safety was secured by three English gentlemen, one of whom, Sir Robert Wilson, conveyed Lavalette, in the disguise of an English officer, across the Belgian frontier. For this generous act the three Englishmen were tried in Paris, and sentenced, each, to three months' imprisonment. ED.

(294) At the sale of the collection, formed by Mr. Thrale, of portraits of his distinguished friends, painted by one of the most distinguished of them—Sir Joshua Reynolds. The collection comprised portraits of Johnson, Burke, Dr. Burney, Reynolds, etc. Reynolds painted two portraits of Johnson for Mr. Thrale. That referred to by Fanny is probably the magnificent portrait painted about 1773, and now in the National Gallery, for which Thrale paid thirty-five guineas. ED.

(295) "His wife and son."

(296) M. d'Arblay had been promoted by Louis XVIII. to the rank of Lieutenant-General. ED.

(297) "Certainly, and very certainly, my dearest, your beautiful strictures upon the knowledge and the customs of the world would have given another current to my ideas."

(298) "For the future."

(299) "He is still but a child."

(300) "That is not our case."

(301) "Will be quite another thing; but I think you are mistaken."

(302) This paragon of perfection, then, was an actual person, whom General d'Arblay was thinking of as a wife for his son! ED.

(303) Self-love.

(304) Wounded. (305) Esther Burney. ED.

(306) Volumes of plays. ED.

(307) Stove.

(308) "Make short work."

(309) "Gloomy discouragement."

(310) "Apathy."

(311) "You are quite mistaken."

(312) "You give it up, don't you?"

(313) An interesting and humorous novel by the Rev. Richard Graves, the friend of Shenstone. ED.

(314) Blue stockings.

(315) "So to speak."

(316) The Princess Charlotte, only child of the prince and princess of Wales, was married at the age of twenty (May 2, 1816) to Prince Leopold of SaxeCoburg. On the 5th of November, 1817, she was delivered of a still-born child, and died a few hours later. ED.

(317) "I have never loved life so much! Never, never has life been dearer to me!"

(318) "How I admire your courage!"

(319) "I should like us to talk of all that with calmness,— mildly,—even cheerfully."

(320) "Never have I so much loved life as now that I am in so great danger of losing it; notwithstanding that I have no fever, nor is my head in the least affected; and not only is my mine] clear, but my heart perfectly at ease. God's will be done! I await the result of a consultation this evening or to-morrow."

(321) "Of his unheard-of sufferings."

(322) "What a strange malady! and what a position is mine! there is one perhaps more grievous yet, that of my unhappy companion— with what tenderness she cares for me! and with what courage she bears what she has to suffer! I can only repeat, God's will be done!"

(323) "February 20. I feel that I am getting horribly weak—I do not think this can last much longer."

(324) "Well, I have no objection. What do you think of it?"

(325) "Speak of me! Speak—and often. Especially to Alexander; that he may not forget me!"

(326) "I shall speak of nothing else!"

(327) "We shall speak of nothing else! my dear!—my dear!—I shall survive only for that!"

(328) "I love her well; tell her so. And she loves me."

(329) "I do not know if this will be my last word—but it will be my last thought—our reunion."

SECTION 27. (1818-40)

YEARS OF WIDOWHOOD. DEATH OF MADAME D'ARBLAY'S SON. HER OWN DEATH.

(Extracts from Pocket-book Diary.)

MOURNFUL REFLECTIONS.

May 17, 1818. This melancholy second Sunday since My irreparable loss I ventured to church. I hoped it might calm my mind and subject it to its new state—its lost—lost happiness. But I suffered inexpressibly; I sunk on my knees, and could scarcely contain my sorrows—scarcely rise any more! but I prayed—fervently—and I am glad I made the trial, however severe. Oh mon ami! mon tendre ami! if you looked down! if that be permitted, how benignly will you wish my participation in your blessed relief!

Sunday, May 31. This was the fourth Sunday passed since I have seen and heard and been blessed with the presence of my angel husband. Oh loved and honoured daily more and more! Yet how can that be? No! even now, in this cruel hour of regret and mourning it cannot be! for love and honour could rise no higher than mine have risen long, long since, in my happiest days.

June 3. This day, this 3rd of June, completes a calendar month since I lost the beloved object of all my tenderest affections, and all my views and hopes and even ideas of happiness on earth. . . .

June 7. The fifth sad Sunday this of earthly separation! oh heavy, heavy parting! I went again to church. I think it right, and I find it rather consolatory-rather only, for the effort against sudden risings of violent grief at peculiar passages almost destroys me; and no prayers do me the service I receive from those I continually offer up in our apartment by the side of the bed on which he breathed forth his last blessing. Oh words for ever dear! for ever balsamic! "Je ne sais si ce sera le dernier mot—mais ce sera bien la derniére pensée—notre réunion."

VISITS RECEIVED AND LETTERS PENNED.

June 18. My oldest friend to my knowledge living, Mrs. Frances Bowdler, made a point of admission this morning, and stayed with me two hours. She was friendly and good, and is ever sensible and deeply clever. Could I enjoy any society, she would enliven and enlighten it, but I now can only enjoy sympathy!—sympathy and pity!

Alex and I had both letters from M. de Lafayette.

June 23. To-day I have written my first letter since my annihilated happiness-to my tenderly sympathising Charlotte. I covet a junction with that dear and partial sister for ending together our latter days. I hope we shall bring it to bear.

With Alex read part of St. Luke.

June 29. To-day I sent a letter, long in writing and painfully finished, to my own dear Madame de Maisonneuve. She will be glad to see my hand, grieved as she will be at what it has written.

With Alex read part of St. Luke.

June 30. I wrote—with many sad struggles—to Madame Beckersdorff, my respectful devoirs to her majesty, with the melancholy apology for my silence during the royal nuptials of the Dukes of Clarence, Kent, and Cambridge; and upon the departure of dear Princess Eliza,' and upon her majesty's so frequent and alarming attacks of ill health.

With Alex read the Acts of the Apostles. . . .

July 8. I have given to Alex the decision of where we shall dwell. Unhappy myself everywhere, why not leave unshackled his dawning life? To quit Bath—unhappy Bath!—he had long desired: and, finally, he has fixed his choice in the very capital itself. I cannot hesitate to oblige him.

August 28. My admirable old friend, Mrs. Frances Bowdler, spent the afternoon with me. Probably we shall meet no more but judiciously, as suits her enlightened understanding, and kindly, as accords with her long partiality, she forbore any hint on that point. Yet her eyes swam in tears, not ordinary to her, when she bade me adieu.

August 30. The seventeenth week's sun rises on my deplorable change! A very kind, cordial, brotherly letter arrives from my dear James. An idea of comfort begins to steal its way to my mind, in renewing my intercourse with this worthy brother, who feels for me, I see, with sincerity and affection.

Sept. 5. A letter from dowager Lady Harcourt, on the visibly approaching dissolution of my dear honoured royal mistress! written by desire of my beloved Princess Mary, Duchess of Gloucester, to save me the shock of surprise, added to that of grief.

Sunday, Sept. 6. A fresh renewal to me of woe is every returning week! The eighteenth this of the dread solitude of my heart; and miserably, has it passed, augmenting sorrow weighing it in the approaching loss of my dear queen!

Again I took the Sacrament at the Octagon, probably for the last time. Oh, how earnest were my prayers for re-union in a purer world! Prayers were offered for a person lying dangerously ill. I thought of the queen, and prayed for her fervently.

Sunday, Sept. 27. This day, the twenty-first Sunday of my bereavement, Alexander, I trust, is ordained a deacon of the Church of England. Heaven propitiate his entrance! I wrote to the good Bishop of Salisbury to beseech his pious wishes on this opening of clerical life.

REMOVAL FROM BATH TO LONDON.

Sept. 28. Still my preparations to depart from Bath take up all of time that grief does not seize irresistibly; for, oh! what anguish overwhelms my soul in quitting the place where last he saw and blessed me!—the room, the spot on which so softly, so holily, yet so tenderly, he embraced me and breathed his last!

Sept. 30. This morning I left Bath with feelings of profound affliction, yet, reflecting that hope was ever open—that future union may repay this laceration—oh, that my torn soul could more look forward with sacred aspiration! Then better would it support its weight of woe.

My dear James received me with tender pity; so did his good wife, son, and daughter.

Oct. 6. My dear Alexander left me this morning for Cambridge. How shall I do, thus parted from both! My kind brother, and his worthy house, have softened off the day much; yet I sigh for seclusion—my mind labours under the weight of assumed sociability.

Oct. 8. I came this evening to my new and probably last dwelling, No. 11, Bolton Street, Piccadilly. My kind James conducted me. Oh, how heavy is my forlorn heart! I have made myself very busy all day; so only could I have supported this first opening to my baleful desolation! No adored husband!

No beloved son! But the latter is only at Cambridge. Ah! let me struggle to think more of the other, the first, the chief, as also only removed from my sight by a transitory journey!

Oct. 14. Wrote to my—erst—dearest friend, Mrs. Piozzi. I can never forget my long love for her, and many obligations to her friendship, strangely as she had been estranged since her marriage.

Oct. 30. A letter from my loved Madame de Maisonneuve, full of feeling, sense, sweetness, information to beguile me back to life, and of sympathy to open my sad heart to friendship.

Nov. 7. A visit from the excellent Harriet Bowdler, who gave me an hour of precious society, mingling her commiserating sympathy with hints sage and right of the duty of revival from every stroke of heaven.

Oh, my God, Saviour! To thee may I turn more and more.

DEATH OF THE QUEEN: SKETCH OF HER CHARACTER. (331)

Nov. 17. This day, at one o'clock, breathed her last the inestimable Queen of England. (332) Heaven rest and bless her soul!

Her understanding was of the best sort; for while it endued her with powers to form a judgment of all around her, it pointed out to her the fallibility of appearances, and thence kept her always open to conviction where she had been led by circumstances into mistake.

From the time of my first entrance into her household her manner to me was most kind and encouraging, for she had formed her previous opinion from the partial accounts of my beloved Mrs. Delany. She saw that, impressed with real respect for her character, and never-failing remembrance of her rank, she might honour me with confidence without an apprehension of imprudence, invite openness without incurring freedom, and manifest kindness without danger of encroachment. . . .

When I was alone with her she discarded all royal constraint, all stiffness, all formality, all pedantry of grandeur, to lead me to speak to her with openness and ease; but any inquiries which she made in our tête a têtes never awakened an idea of prying into affairs, diving into secrets, discovering views, intentions, or latent wishes, or amuses. No, she was above all such minor resources for attaining intelligence; what she desired to know she asked openly, though cautiously if of grave matters, and playfully if of mere news or chit-chat, but always beginning with, "If there is any reason I should not be told, or any that you should not tell, don't answer me." Nor were these words of course, they were spoken with such visible sincerity, that I have availed myself of them fearlessly, though never without regret, as it was a delight to me to be explicit and confidential in return for her condescension. But whenever she saw a question painful, or that it occasioned even hesitation, she promptly and generously started some other subject.

Dec. 2. The queen, the excellent exemplary queen, was this day interred in the vault of her royal husband's ancestors, (333) to moulder like his subjects, bodily into dust; but mentally, not so! She will live in the memory of those who knew her best, and be set up as an example even by those who only after her death know, or at least acknowledge her virtues.

I heard an admirable sermon on her departure and her character from Mr. Repton in St. James's church. I wept the whole time, as much from gratitude and tenderness to hear her thus appreciated as from grief at her loss—to me a most heavy one! for she was faithfully, truly, and solidly attached to me, as I to her.

Dec. 12. A letter from the Duchess of Gloucester, (334) to My equal gratification and surprise. She has deigned to answer my poor condolence the very moment, as she says, that she received it. Touched to the heart, but no longer with pleasure in any emotion, I wept abundantly.

MADAME D'ARBLAY'S SON IS ORDAINED.

Sunday, April 11, 1818. This morning my dearest Alexander was ordained a priest by the Bishop of Chester in St. James's church. I went thither with my good Eliz. Ramsay, and from the gallery witnessed the ceremony. Fifty-two were ordained at the same time. I fervently pray to God that my son may meet this his decided calling with a disposition and conduct to sanction its choice! and with virtues to merit his noble father's name and exemplary character! Amen Amen!

WITH SOME ROYAL HIGHNESSES.

July 15. A message from H. R. H. Princess Augusta, with whom I passed a morning as nearly delightful as any, now, can be! She played and sang to me airs of her own composing, unconscious, medley reminiscences, but very pretty, and prettily executed. I met the Duke of York, who greeted me most graciously, saying, as if with regret, how long it was since he had seen me.

In coming away, I met, in the corridor, my sweet Duchess of Gloucester, who engaged me for next Sunday to herself.

July 26. Her royal highness presented me to the duke, whom I found well-bred, Polite, easy, unassuming, and amiable; kind, not condescending.

QUEEN CAROLINE.

(Madame d''Arblay to Mrs. Locke.) Wednesday, June 7, 1820. . . . All London now is wild about the newly arrived royal traveller. (335) As she is in this neighbourhood, our part of the town is surprised and startled every other hour by the arrival of some new group of the curious rushing on to see her and her 'squire the alderman, at their balcony. Her 'squire, also, now never comes forth unattended by a vociferous shouting multitude. I suppose Augusta, who resides still nearer to the dame and the 'squire of dames, is recreated in this lively way yet more forcibly.

The 15th of this month is to be kept as king's birthday at Court. Orders have been issued to the princesses to that effect, and to tell them they must appear entirely out of mourning. They had already made up dresses for half mourning, of white and black. I should not marvel if the royal traveller should choose to enter the apartments, and offer her congratulations upon the festival.

(Madame d'Arblay to Mrs. Locke.) Elliot Vale, London, August 15, 1820. How long it seems—"Seems, madam! nay, it is! since I have heard from my most loved friend!—I have had, however, I thank heaven, news of her, and cheering news, though I have lost sight of both her dear daughters. . . .

We are all, and of all classes, all opinions, all ages, and all parties, absolutely absorbed by the expectation of Thursday. The queen has passed the bottom of our street twice this afternoon in an open carriage, with Lady Ann (336) and Alderman Wood! How very inconceivable that among so many adherents, she can find that only esquire! And why she should have any, in her own carriage and in London, it is not easy to say. There is a universal alarm for Thursday. (337) the letter to the king breathes battle direct to both Houses of Parliament as much as to his majesty. Mr. Wilberforce is called upon, and looked up to, as the only man in the dominions to whom an arbitration should belong. Lord John Russell positively asserts that it is not with Lord Castlereagh and the ministers that conciliation or non-conciliation hangs, but with Mr. Wilberforce and his circle. If I dared hope such was the case, how much less should I be troubled by the expectance awakened for to-morrow—it is now Wednesday that I finish my poor shabby billet. Tremendous is the general alarm at this moment for the accused turns accuser, public and avowed, of King, Lords, and Commons, declaring she will submit to no award of any of them. What would she say should evidence be imperfect or wanting, and they should acquit her?

It is, however, open war, and very dreadful. She really invokes a revolution in every paragraph of her letter to her sovereign and lord and husband. I know not what sort of conjugal rule will be looked for by the hitherto lords and masters of the world, if this conduct is abetted by them. . . .

The heroine passed by the bottom of our street yesterday, in full pomp and surrounded with shouters and vociferous admirers. She now dresses superbly every day, and has always six horses and an open carriage. She seems to think now she has no chance but from insurrection, and therefore all her harangues invite it. Oh Dr. Parr!—how my poor brother would have blushed for him! he makes those orations with the aid of Cobbett!—and the council, I suppose. Of course, like Croaker in "The Good-natured Man" I must finish with "I wish we may all be well this day three months!"

GOSSIP FROM AN OLD FRIEND, AND THE REPLY.

(From Mrs. Piozzi to Madame d'Arblay.) Bath, October 20. It was very gratifying, dear madam, to find myself so kindly remembered, and with all my heart I thank you for your letter. My family are gone to Sandgate for the purpose of bathing in the sea, this wonderfully beautiful October; and were you not detained in London by such a son as I hear you are happy in, I should wish you there too, apropos to October, I have not your father's admirable verses upon that month; those upon June, I saw when last in Wales could you get me the others? it would be such a favour and you used to like them best.

How changed is the taste of verse, prose, and painting since le bon vieux temps, dear madam! Nothing attracts us but what terrifies, and is within—if within—a hair's breadth of positive disgust. The picture of Death on his Pale Horse, however, is very grand certainly-and some of the strange things they write remind me of Squoire Richard's visit to the Tower Menagerie, when he says "Odd, they are pure grim devils,"—particularly a wild and hideous tale called Frankenstein. Do you ever see any of the friends we used to live among? Mrs. Lambert is yet alive, and in prosperous circumstances; and Fell, the bookseller in Bond Street, told me a fortnight or three weeks ago, that Miss Streatfield lives where she did in his neighbourhood, Clifford Street, S. S. still.

Old Jacob and his red night-cap are the only live creatures, as an Irishman would say, that come about me of those you remember, and death alone will part us, he and I both lived longer with Mr. Piozzi than we had done with Mr. Thrale.

Archdeacon Thomas is, I think, the only friend you and I have now quite in common: he gets well; and if there was hope of his getting clear from entanglement, he would be young again, he is a valuable mortal.

Adieu! Leisure for men of business, you know, and business for men of leisure, would cure many complaints. Once more, farewell! and accept my thanks for your good-natured recollection of poor H. L. P.

(Madame d'Arblay to Mrs. Piozzi) Bolton Street, December 15, 1820. Now at last, dear madam, with a real pen I venture to answer your kind acceptance of my Bath leave-taking address, of a date I would wish you to forget-but the letter is before me, and has no other word I should like to relinquish. But more of grief at the consequence of my silence, namely your own, hangs upon the circumstance than shame, for i have been so every way unwell, unhinged, shattered, and unfitted for any correspondence that could have a chance of reciprocating pleasure, that perhaps I ought rather to demand your thanks than your pardon for this delay. I will demand, however, which you please, so you will but tell me which you will grant, for then I shall hear from you again.

I must, nevertheless, mention, that my first intention, upon reading the letter with which you favoured me, was to forward to you the verses on October, of my dear father, which you honoured with so much approbation. but I have never been able to find them, unless you mean the ode, written in that month, on the anniversary of his marriage with my mother-in-law, beginning:—

Hail, eldest offspring of the circling year,
October! bountiful, benign, and clear,
Whose gentle reign, from all excesses free,
Gave birth to Stella—happiness to me."

If it be this, I will copy it out with the greatest alacrity, for the first opportunity of conveyance.

So here, again, like the dun of a dinner card, I entitle myself to subjoin "An answer is required." . . .

You inquire if I ever see any of the friends we used to live amongst: almost none; but I may resume some of those old ties this winter, from the ardent desire of my son. I have, till very lately, been so utterly incapable to enjoy society, that I have held it as much kindness to others as to myself, to keep wholly out of its way. I am now, in. health, much better, and consequently more able to control the murmuring propensities that were alienating me from the purposes of life while yet living, this letter, indeed, will show that I am restored to the wish, at least, of solace, and that the native cheerfulness of my temperament is opening from the weight of sadness by which I had long believed it utterly demolished. But Time, " uncalled, unheeded, unawares, "-works as secretly upon our spirits as upon our years, and gives us as little foresight into what we can endure, as into how long we shall exist. . . .

MORE GOSSIP.

(From Mrs. Piozzi to Madame d'Arblay.) Penzance, Thursday, January 18, 1821. Dear Madame d'Arblay was very considerate in giving me something to answer, for something original to say would be difficult to find at Penzance; but your letter has no date, and I am not sure that Bolton Street is sufficient. Poor Mrs. Byron, who used to inhabit it, would have enjoyed her grandson's (338) reputation, would not she? had it pleased God to lengthen her life like that of Mrs. Lambart, who died only last week, but a few days short of her expected centenary-as did Fontenelle. You are truly fortunate, dear madam, so was your father, in leaving those behind who knew and could appreciate your merits—every scrap will properly be valued—but those verses belong not to the October I meant. . . .

Mrs. Bourdois and her sisters—all true Burneys—will be angry I don't live wholly at Bath, and their society would prove a strong temptation; but Bath is too much for me, who am now unwilling to encounter either crowds or solitude: I feared neither for three-score years of my life, and earnestly now join my too disinterested solicitations to those of your son, that you will no longer bury your charming talents in seclusion. Sorrow, as Dr. Johnson said, is the mere rust of the soul. Activity will cleanse and brighten it.

You recollect the —'s; Fanny married Sir Something —, and is a widowed mother. The young man, of whom high expectations were formed, took to the gaming table, forged for 5000 pounds, and was saved out of prison by the dexterity of his servant:—a complete coup de th,ftre. That I call sorrow scarce possible to be borne. You saw the story in the newspapers, but possibly were not aware who was the sufferer.

Will it amuse you to hear that "fine Mr. Daniel," as you used to call my showy butler, died an object of disgust and horror, whilst old Jacob, with whose red nightcap you comically threatened the gay dandy—lived till the other day, and dying, left 800 pounds behind him! Such stuff is this world made of!

The literary world is to me terra incognita, far more deserving of the name (now Parry and Ross are returned) than any part of the polar region; but the first voyage amused me most and when I had seen red snow, and heard of men who wanted our sailors to fly, because they perceived they could swim, I really thought it time to lie down and die; but one cannot die when one will, so I have hung half on, half off, society this last half year; and begin 1821 by thanking dear Madame d'Arblay for her good-natured recollection of poor H. L. Piozzi.

ILL-HEALTH OF THE REV. A. D'ARBLAY. DR. BURNEY'S MSS.

(Madame d'Arblay to Mrs. Piozzi.) Bolton Street, Berkeley Square, Feb. 6, 1821. You would be repaid, dear madam, if I still, as I believe, know you, for the great kindness of your prompt answer, had you witnessed the satisfaction with which it was received; even at a time of new and dreadful solicitude; for my son returned from Cambridge unwell, and in a few days after his arrival at home was seized with a feverish cold which threatened to fasten upon the whole system of his existence, not with immediate danger, but with a perspective to leave but small openings to any future view of health, strength, or longevity. I will not dwell upon this period, but briefly say, it seems passed over. He is now, I thank heaven, daily reviving, and from looking like-not a walking, but a creeping spectre, he is gaining force, spirit, and flesh visibly, and almost hour by hour; still, however, he requires the utmost attention, and the more from the extreme insouciance, from being always absorbed in some mental combinations, with which he utterly neglects himself. I am therefore wholly devoted to watching him.

I am quite vexed not to find the right October. However, I do not yet despair, for in the multitude of MSS. that have fallen to my mournfully surviving lot to select, or destroy, etc, chaos seems come again; and though I have worked at them during the last year so as to obtain a little light, it is scarcely more than darkness visible. To all the vast mass left to my direction by my dear father, who burnt nothing, not even an invitation to dinner, are added not merely those that devolved to me by fatal necessity in 1818, but also all the papers possessed from her childhood to her decease of that sister you so well, dear madam, know to have been my heart's earliest darling. When on this pile are heaped the countless hoards which my own now long life has gathered together, of my personal property, such as it is, and the correspondence of my family and my friends, and innumerable incidental windfalls, the whole forms a body that might make a bonfire to illuminate me nearly from hence to Penzance. And such a bonfire might perhaps be not only the shortest, but the wisest way to dispose of such materials. This enormous accumulation has been chiefly owing to a long unsettled home, joined to a mind too deeply occupied by immediate affairs and feelings to have the intellect at liberty for retrospective investigations. . . .

A LAST GOSSIPING LETTER.

(From Mrs. Piozzi to Madame d'Arblay.) Sion Row, Clifton, near Bristol, March 15, 1821. I feel quite happy in being able to reply to dear Madame d'Arblay's good-natured inquiries, from this, the living world. Such we cannot term Penzance—not with propriety—much like Omai, who said to you, "No mutton there, missee, no fine coach, no clock upon the stairs," etc.; but en revanche here is no Land's End, no submarine mine of Botallock! What a wonderful thing is that extensive cavern! stretching out half a mile forward under the roaring ocean, from whence 'tis protected only by a slight covering, a crust of rock, which, if by any accident exploded,

"Would let in light on Pluto's dire abodes,
Abhorr'd by men, and dreadful ev'n to Gods."

Plutus, however, not Pluto, is professed proprietor, 'tis an immense vacuity filled with the vapours of tin and copper, belonging to Lord Falmouth and a company of miners, where sixty human beings work night and day, and hear the waves over their heads, sometimes regularly beating the Cornish cliffs, sometimes tossing the terrified mariner upon the inhospitable shore; where shipwreck is, even in these civilized days, considered as a Godsend.

I am glad I saw it, and that I shall see it no more. You would not know poor Streatham Park. I have been forced to dismantle and forsake it; the expenses of the present time treble those of the moments you remember; and since giving up my Welsh estate, my income is greatly diminished. I fancy this will be my last residence in this world, meaning Clifton, not Sion Row, where I only live till my house in the Crescent is ready for me. A high situation is become necessary to my breath, and this air will agree with me better than Bath did.

You ask how the Pitches family went on. Jane married a rough man, quarter-master to a marching regiment, and brought him three sons: the first a prodigy of science, wit, and manners; he died early: the second I know nothing of: the third, a model of grace and beauty, married the Duke of Marlborough's sister. Peggy is Countess Coventry, you know, and has a numerous progeny. Emily is wife to Mr. Jolliffe, M.P. for some place, I forget what. Penelope married Sir John Sheffield, but died before he came to the title. I dined with them all last time I was in London, at Coventry House. Poor old Davies's departure grieved me, so did that of good Mr. Embry; au reste, the village of Streatham is full of rich inhabitants, the common much the worse for being so spotted about with houses, and the possibility of avoiding constant intercourse with their inhabitants (as in Mr. Thrale's time) wholly lost!.....

DEATH OF MRS. PIOZZI.

May, 1821. I have lost now, just lost, my once most dear, intimate, and admired friend, Mrs. Thrale Piozzi, (339) who preserved her fine faculties, her imagination, her intelligence, her powers of allusion and citation, her extraordinary memory, and her almost unexampled vivacity, to the last of her existence. She was in her eighty-second year, and yet owed not her death to age nor to natural decay, but to the effects of a fall in a journey from Penzance to Clifton. On her eightieth birthday she gave a great ball, concert, and supper, in the public rooms at Bath, to upwards of two hundred persons, and the ball she opened herself. She was, in truth, a most wonderful character for talents and eccentricity, for wit, genius, generosity, spirit, and powers of entertainment.

MRS. PIOZZI COMPARED WITH MADAME DE STAEL.

She had a great deal both of good and not good, in common with Madame de Stael Holstein. They had the same sort of highly superior intellect, the same depth of learning, the same general acquaintance with science, the same ardent love of literature, the same thirst for universal knowledge, and the same buoyant animal spirits, such as neither sickness, sorrow, nor even terror, could subdue. Their conversation was equally luminous, from the sources of their own fertile minds, and from their splendid acquisitions from the works and acquirements of others. Both were zealous to serve, liberal to bestow, and graceful to oblige; and both were truly highminded in prizing and praising whatever was admirable that came in their way.

Neither of them was delicate nor polished, though each was flattering and caressing; but both had a fund inexhaustible of good humour, and of sportive gaiety, that made their intercourse with those they wished to please attractive, instructive, and delightful and though not either of them had the smallest real malevolence in their compositions, neither of them could ever withstand the pleasure of uttering a repartee, let it wound whom it might, even though each would serve the very person they goaded with all the means in their power. Both were kind, charitable, and munificent, and therefore beloved; both were sarcastic, careless, and daring, and therefore feared. The morality of Madame de Stael was by far the most faulty, but so was the society to which she belonged so were the general manners of those by whom she was encircled.

SISTER HETTY.

(Madame d'Arblay to Mrs. Burney.) October 21, 1821. "Your mind," my dearest Esther, was always equal to literary pursuits, though your time seems only now to let you enjoy them. I have often thought that had our excellent and extraordinary own mother been allowed longer life, she would have contrived to make you sensible of this sooner. I do not mean in a common way, for that has never failed, but in one striking and distinguished; for she very early indeed began to form your taste for reading, and delighted to find time, amidst all her cares, to guide you to the best authors, and to read them with you, commenting and pointing out passages worthy to be learned by heart.

I perfectly recollect, child as I was, and never of the party, this part of your education. At that very juvenile period, the difference even of months makes a marked distinction in bestowing and receiving instruction. I, also, was so peculiarly backward, that even our Susan stood before me; she could read when I knew not my letters. But though so sluggish to learn, I was always observant: do you remember Mr. Seaton's denominating me, at fifteen, "the silent, observant Miss Fanny"? Well I recollect your reading with our dear mother all Pope's works and Pitt's "AEneid." I recollect, also, your spouting passages from Pope, that I learned from hearing you recite them before—many years before I read them myself. But after you lost, so young, that incomparable guide, you had none left. Our dear -father was always abroad, usefully or ornamentally; and, after giving you a year in Paris with the best masters that could be procured, you came home at fifteen or sixteen to be exclusively occupied by musical studies, save for the interludes that were

"Sacred to dress and beauty's pleasing cares:"

for so well you played, and so lovely you looked, that admiration followed alike your fingers and your smiles: and the pianoforte and the world divided your first youth, which, had that exemplary guide been spared us, I am fully persuaded would have left some further testimony of its passage than barely my old journals, written to myself, which celebrate your wit and talents as highly as your beauty. And I judge I was not mistaken, by all in which you have had opportunity to show your mental faculties, i.e. your letters, which have always been strikingly good and agreeable, and evidently unstudied.

When Alex comes home I will try to get "Crabbe," and try to hear it with pleasure. The two lines you have quoted are very touching.

Thus much, my dear Etty, I wrote on the day I received your last; but . . . .

November. I write now from Eliot Vale, under the kind and elegant roof of sweet Mrs. Locke, who charges me with her most affectionate remembrances. Perhaps I may meet here with your favourite Crabbe: as I subscribe to no library, I know not how else I shall get at him. I thank you a thousand times for the good bulletin of your health, my dearest Esther; and I know how kindly you will reciprocate my satisfaction when I tell you mine is inconceivably ameliorated, moyennant great and watchful care: and Alex keeps me to that with the high hand of peremptory insistence, according to the taste of the times for the "rising generation" expects just as much obedience to orders as they withhold. If you were to hear the young gentleman delivering to me his lectures on health, and dilating upon air, exercise, social intercourse, and gay spirits, you would be forced to seek a magnifying glass to believe that your eyes did not deceive you, but that it was really your nephew haranguing his mother. However, we must pass by the exhorting impetuosity, in favour of the zealous anxiety that fires it up in his animated breast.

OFFICIAL DUTIES TEMPORARILY RESUMED.

I was kept in town by a particular circumstance—I might say, like the play-bills, by particular desire; for it was a fair royal personage who condescended to ask me to remit my visit to Eliot Vale, that I might attend her sittings for her picture, her two ladies being at that time absent on cong,. You may believe how much I was gratified, because you know my sincere and truly warm attachment for all those gracious personages; but you may be surprised Your poor sister could now be pitched upon, where so much choice must always be at hand, for whiling away the tediousness of what she, the princess, calls the odious occupation of sitting still for this exhibition - but the fact is, I was able to fulfil her views better than most people could, in defiance of my altered spirits and depressed faculties, by having recourse simply to my memory in relating things I saw, or heard, or did, during the long ten years, and the eventful—added one year more, that I spent abroad. Only to name Bonaparte in any positive trait that I had witnessed or known, was sufficient to make her open her fine eyes in a manner extremely advantageous to the painter.

THE REV. A. D'ARBLAY NAMED LENT PREACHER.

(Madame d'Arblay to Mrs. Burney.) February 29, 1823......Thanks for that kind jump of joy for the success of Alex at Lee, and for my hopes from St. Paul's. You ask who named him preacher for the 5th Sunday in Lent: How could I omit telling you 'twas the Bishop of London himself? -This has been brought about by a detail too long for paper, but it is chiefly to my faithful old friends Bishop Fisher of Salisbury and the Archdeacon of Middlesex that we owe this mark of attention; for Alex has never been presented to the Bishop of London.

MADAME D'ARBLAY'S HEALTH AND OCCUPATION.

You still ask about my health, etc. I thought the good result would have sufficed; but thus stands the detail: I was packing up a board of papers to carry with me to Richmond, many months now ago, and employed above an hour, bending my head over the trunk, and on my knees -when, upon meaning to rise, I was seized with a giddiness, a glare of sparks before my eyes, and a torturing pain on one side of my head, that nearly disabled me from quitting my posture, and that was followed, when at last I rose, by an inability to stand or walk.

My second threat of seizure was at Eliot Vale, while Alex was at Tunbridge. I have been suddenly taken a third time, in the middle of the night, with a seizure as if a hundred windmills were turning round in my head: in short, I had now recourse to serious medical help, and, to come to the sum total, I am now so much better that I believe myself to be merely in the common road of such gentle, gradual decay as, I humbly trust, I have been prepared to meet with highest hope, though with deepest awe—for now many years back.

The chief changes, or reforms, from which I reap benefit are, 1st. Totally renouncing for the evenings all revision or indulgence in poring over those letters and papers whose contents come nearest to my heart, and work upon its bleeding regrets. Next, transferring-to the evening, as far as is in my power, all of sociality, with Alex, or my few remaining friends, or the few he will present to me of new ones. 3rd. Constantly going out every day-either in brisk walks in the morning, or in brisk jumbles in the carriage of one of my three friends who send for me, to a tête a tête tea converse. 4th. Strict attention to diet. . . .

I ought to have told you the medical sentence upon which I act. These were the words—"You have a head over-worked, and a heart over-loaded." This produces a disposition to fulness in both that causes stagnation, etc, with a consequent want of circulation at the extremities, that keeps them cold and aching. Knowing this, I now act upon it as warily as I am able.

The worst of all is, that I have lost, totally lost, my pleasure in reading! except when Alex is my lecturer, for whose sake my faculties are still alive to what—erst! gave them their greatest delight. But alone; I have no longer that resource; I have scarcely looked over a single sentence, but some word of it brings to my mind some mournful recollection, or acute regret, and takes from one all attention—my eyes thence glance vainly over pages that awaken no ideas. This is melancholy in the extreme; yet I have tried every species of writing and writer—but all pass by me mechanically, instead of instructing or entertaining me intellectually. But for this sad deprivation of my original taste, my evenings might always be pleasing and reviving—but alas!

DESTROYED CORRESPONDENCE.

(Madame d'Arblay to Mrs. Burney.) August, 1823. What an interesting letter is this last, my truly dear Hetty 'tis a real sister's letter, and such a one as I am at this time frequently looking over of old times! For the rest of my life I shall take charge' and save my own executor the discretionary labours that with myself are almost endless; for I now regularly destroy all letters that either may eventually do mischief, however clever, or that contain nothing of instruction or entertainment, however innocent. This, which I announce to all my correspondents who write confidentially, occasions my receiving letters that are real conversations. Were I younger I should consent to this condition with great reluctance-or perhaps resist it: but such innumerable papers, letters, documents, and memorandums have now passed through my hands, and, for reasons prudent, or kind, or conscientious, have been committed to the flames, that I should hold it wrong to make over to any other judgment than My Own, the danger or the innoxiousness of any and every manuscript that has been cast into my power. To you, therefore, I may now safely copy a charge delivered to me by UP our dear vehement Mr. Crisp, at the opening of my juvenile correspondence with him,—"Harkee, you little monkey!—dash away whatever comes uppermost; if you stop to consider either what you say, or what may be said of you, I would not ,give one fig for your letters."—How little, in those days, did either he or I fear, or even dream of the press! What became of letters, jadis, I know not; but they were certainly both written and received with as little fear as wit. Now every body seems - obliged to take as much care of their writing desks as of their trinkets or purses, for thieves be abroad of more descriptions than belong to the penniless pilferers.

THE PRINCESS AND THE REV. A. D'ARBLAY.

(Madame dArblay to Mrs. locke.) 11 Bolton Street, Nov. 1824. Now then for a more cheerful winding-up. I came from Camden Town very unwillingly,—but Alex was called to Cambridge to an audit, and so I took that opportunity to make a break-up. But the day before I quitted it I received the highest resident honour that can be bestowed upon me—namely, a visit from one of my dear and condescending princesses. She came by appointment, yet her entrance was so quick that Alex had not time to save himself. However, she took the incident not only without displeasure but with apparent satisfaction, saying she was very glad to renew her acquaintance with him. She had not seen him since the time of his spouting, "The spacious firmament on high"—"Ye shepherds so cheerful and gay," etc,—all of which she remembers hearing. Ah—I have never recollected till this instant that I ought to have gone to her the next day! how shocking!—and now that I have the consciousness, I can do nothing, for I am lame from a little accident.—Well!—she is all goodness-and far more prone to forgive than I, I trust, am to offend.

A VISIT FROM SIR WALTER SCOTT.

Although Madame d'Arblay's intercourse with society was now usually confined to that of her relations and of old and established friends, she yet greeted with admiration and pleasure Sir Walter Scott, who was brought to her by Mr. Rogers. Sir Walter, in his Diary for Nov. 18th, 1826, thus describes the visit:—"I have been introduced to Madame d'Arblay, the celebrated authoress of 'Evelina' and 'Cecilia,' an elderly lady with no remains of personal beauty, but with a simple and gentle manner, and pleasing expression of countenance, and apparently quick feelings. She told me she had wished to see two persons-myself, of course, being one, the other, George Canning. This was really a compliment to be pleased with—a nice little handsome pat of butter made up by a neat-handed Phillis of a dairy-maid, instead of the grease fit only for cartwheels which one is dosed with by the pound.

"I trust I shall see this lady again."

MEMOIRS OF DR. BURNEY.

From the year 1828 to 1832 Madame d'Arblay was chiefly occupied in preparing for the press the Memoirs of her father; and on their publication, she had the pleasure to receive letters from Dr. Jebb, Bishop of Limerick, and from Mr. Southey, the poet.

Among the less favourable criticisms of her work, the Only one which gave Madame d'Arblay serious pain was an attack (in a periodical publication) upon her veracity—a quality which, in her, Dr. Johnson repeatedly said "he had never found failing," and for which she had been through life trusted, honoured, and emulated.

DEATHS OF HESTER BURNEY AND MRS. LOCKE. (1835 to 1838.)

Madame d'Arblay's letters were now very few. A complaint in one of her eyes, which was expected to terminate in a cataract, made both reading and writing difficult to her. The number of her correspondents had also been painfully lessened by the death of her eldest sister, Mrs. Burney, and that of her beloved friend, Mrs. Locke; and she had sympathised with other branches of her family in many similar afflictions, for she retained in a peculiar degree not only her intellectual powers, but the warn) and generous affections of her youth.

"Though now her eightieth year was past," she took her wonted and vivid interest in the concerns, the joys, and sorrows of those she loved.

DEATH OF THE REV. A. D'ARBLAY.

At this time her son formed an attachment which promised to secure his happiness, and to gild his mother's remaining days with affection and peace: and at the close of the year 1836 he was nominated minister of Ely chapel, which afforded her considerable satisfaction. But her joy was mournfully short-lived. That building, having been shut for some years, was damp and ill-aired. The Rev. Mr. d'Arblay began officiating there in winter, and during the first days of his ministry he caught the influenza, which became so serious an illness as to require the attendance of two physicians. Dr. Holland and Dr. Kingston exerted their united skill with the kindest interest; but their patient, never robust, was unable to cope with the malady, and on the 19th of January, 1837, in three weeks from his first seizure, the death of this beloved son threw Madame d'Arblay again into the depths of affliction. Yet she bore this desolating stroke with religious submission, receiving kindly every effort made to console her, and confining chiefly to her own private memoranda the most poignant expressions of her anguish and regret, as also of the deeply religious trust by which she was supported.

The following paragraph is taken from her private notebook:—

"1837. On the opening of this most mournful—most earthly hopeless, of any and of all the years yet commenced of my long career! Yet, humbly I bless my God and Saviour, not hopeless; but full of gently-beaming hopes, countless and fraught with aspirations of the time that may succeed to the dread infliction of this last irreparable privation, and bereavement of my darling loved, and most touchingly loving, dear, soul—dear Alex."

DEATH OF MADAME D'ARBLAY'S SISTER CHARLOTTE.

Much as Madame d'Arblay had been tried by the severest penalty of lengthened days, the loss of those who were dearest to her, *one more such sorrow remained in her cup of life. Her gentle and tender sister Charlotte, many years younger than herself, was to precede her in that eternal world for which they were both preparing; and in the autumn of the year 1838, a short illness terminated in the removal of that beloved sister.

ILLNESS AND DEATH OF MADAME D'ARBLAY. (1839-40.)

Madame d'Arblay's long and exemplary life was now drawing to a close; her debility increased, her sight and hearing nearly failed her; but in these afflictions she was enabled to look upwards with increasing faith and resignation. In a letter on the 5th of March, 1839, she wrote the following paragraph, (340) which was perhaps the last ever traced by her pen:—

"March 5, 1839. "Ah, my dearest! how changed, changed I am, since the irreparable loss of your beloved mother! that last original tie to native original affections! . . .

"Wednesday. I broke off, and an incapable unwillingness seized my pen; but I hear you are not well, and I hasten—if that be a word I can ever use again—to make personal Inquiry how you are.

"I have been very ill, very little apparently, but with nights of consuming restlessness and tears. I have now called in Dr. Holland, who understands me marvellously, and I am now much as usual; no, not that—still tormented by nights without repose—but better.

"My spirits have been dreadfully saddened of late by whole days—nay weeks—of helplessness for any employment. They have but just revived. How merciful a reprieve! How merciful IS ALL we know! The ways of Heaven are not dark and intricate, but unknown and unimagined till the great teacher, Death, develops them."

In November, 1839, Madame d'Arblay was attacked by an illness which showed itself at first in sleepless nights and nervous imaginations. Spectral illusions, such as Dr. Abercrombie has described, formed part of her disorder; and though after a time Dr. Holland's skill removed these nervous impressions, yet her debility and cough increased, accompanied by constant fever. For several weeks hopes of her recovery were entertained; her patience assisted the remedies of her kind physician, and the amiable young friend, "who was to her as a daughter," watched over her with unremitting care and attention but she became more and more feeble, and her mind wandered; though at times every day she was composed and collected, and then given up to silent prayer, with her hands clasped and eyes uplifted.

During the earlier part of her illness she had listened with comfort to some portions of St. John's Gospel, but she now said to her niece, "I would ask you to read to me, but I could not understand one word—not a syllable! but I thank God my mind has not waited till this time."

At another moment she charged the same person with affectionate farewells and blessings to several friends, and with thanks for all their kindness to her. Soon after she said, "I have had some sleep." "That is well," was the reply; "you wanted rest." "I shall have it soon, my dear," she answered emphatically: and thus, aware that death was approaching, in peace with all the world, and in holy trust and reliance on her Redeemer, she breathed her last on the 6th of January, 1840; the anniversary of that day she had long consecrated to prayer, and to the memory of her beloved sister Susanna.

(330) *Her departure for Germany with her husband, the Prince of Hesse-Homburg, to whom she had been recently married. ED. '*

(331) *From a Memorandum book of Madame d'Arblays.*

(332) *Queen Charlotte died at the palace at Kew, in the seventy-fifth year of her age, after an illness of six months. ED.*

(333) *At Windsor. ED.*

(334) *The Princess Mary, who had married her cousin, the Duke of Gloucester. ED.*

(335) *Queen Caroline. George IV. was now king, George III. having died January 29, 1820. A brief account of the life of Queen Caroline may be of assistance to the reader. Her father was the Duke of Brunswick: her mother a sister of George II. She was born in 1768, and married her cousin, the Prince of Wales, in April, 1795, A speedy estrangement followed, brought about by the prince's intrigues, especially with Lady Jersey; and, after the birth of their daughter, the Princess Charlotte, a total separation took place. In 1806 a charge of adultery was brought against the Princess of Wales. The charge was declared disproved, but colour had been given to it by the undoubted levity and imprudence of her conduct. In 1813 she went abroad, and spent several years in travelling on the continent. Her behaviour during this period gave rise to fresh charges, from which she has never been entirely cleared. She returned to England, June 6, 1820, came to London, and took up her residence in*

South Audley Street, at the house of her friend, Alderman Wood, one of the members of Parliament for the city of London. Shortly before her return, the king's ministers had proposed to settle upon her an annuity of L50,000 for life, subject to the conditions of her continuing to reside abroad, and refraining from assuming the title of queen. This proposal she instantly rejected. She was received in England by the people with unbounded enthusiasm, to which the general discontent then prevailing questionless contributed. A secret committee of the House of Lords, appointed to examine the charges against the queen, having made their report, the government brought in a bill to deprive her of the title of queen, and to dissolve the marriage. She was defended by counsel before the House of Lords, her leading advocate being Mr. (afterwards Lord) Brougham, The Motion for the third reading of the bill passed (November 10) by a small majority, but the bill was immediately afterwards abandoned by the government. This proceeding was generally considered as tantamount to an acquittal, and was celebrated by illuminations and the voting of congratulatory addresses in all parts of the country. Queen Caroline did not long enjoy her triumph. She presented herself at Westminster Abbey on the occasion of the king's coronation, July 19, 1821, but was refused admission. Less than three weeks later she was dead. ED.

(336) Lady Ann Hamilton, who had formerly belonged to Queen Caroline's household, and had joined her in France, shortly before her return to England. ED.

(337) Thursday, August 17, was the day on which the queen's trial commenced before the House of Lords. ED.

(338) Lord Byron, the poet. ED.

(339) Mrs. Piozzi died at Clifton, May 2, 1821, having survived her second husband about twelve years. ED.

(340) To her niece Mrs. Barrett.

Frances Burney – A Short Biography

Frances Burney was born on June 13th, 1752 in Lynn Regis (now King's Lynn).

Her mother, Esther, was described as of "warmth and intelligence," the daughter of a French refugee, she had been brought up a Catholic.

Frances's father, Charles Burney, was a noted musician, musicologist and composer as well as being a man of letters.

In 1760 the family moved to Poland Street, In London's Soho, giving them an entrée to a wider circle of the cultural elite.

A difficult situation arose in 1766 when Charles Burney eloped to marry for a second time. Elizabeth Allen, was the wealthy widow of a King's Lynn wine merchant and already the mother of three children.

The two families were now merged into one and tensions were always simmering as Elizabeth established her rules in an overbearing way, always with the threat of anger near to the surface.

Her father had always favoured her sisters Esther and Susanna over Frances. By the age of 8 Frances had still not learned the alphabet and couldn't read. Her sisters were sent to be educated in Paris whilst Frances educated herself, reading from the family library, which she then devoured as her ambitions began to take hold. She now also began her own 'scribblings'.

In 1762, her mother, Esther, died and it was a loss that Frances was to feel deeply for the rest of her life.

However, there was one family friend who had spotted Frances's talents. He was Samuel Crisp. He encouraged Frances to write, mainly by requesting frequent journal-letters from her that recounted the family goings-on and also that of her social circle in London.

Frances was fifteen by the time her father eventually remarried in 1767. Pressure was also being exerted for her to give up writing; it was "unladylike" and "might vex Mrs. Allen."

Feeling that she had been improper, she burnt her first manuscript, The History of Caroline Evelyn, which she had written in secret. However, Frances did keep an account of the emotions that led up to this in her diaries which she thereafter continued to write, a practice she kept faith with for 72 years.

Frances was a talented storyteller with a strong sense of character, she often wrote these "journal-diaries" as correspondence to her family and friends, recounting events from her life and her observations upon them. Her diary contains the extensive reading in her father's library, as well the visits and behaviour of the various important arts personalities who came to their home. Frances and her sister Susanna were particularly close, and it was to her that Frances would correspond throughout her adult life, in the form of such journal-letters.

In 1775 Frances received a proposal from Thomas Barlow, whom she had met only once before, and which she recounts amusingly in her journals.

By 1778 Frances Burney was ready to be acknowledged as an author. The publication that year of Evelina or the History of a Young Lady's Entrance into the World, was published anonymously in 1778, without her father's knowledge or permission, by Thomas Lowndes, who, after reading the first volume, agreed to publish it upon receipt of the finished work.

This was a time when having a novel published by a young woman was almost unthinkable. In fact, she had her brother pose as its author. Unfortunately, he was also the negotiator and despite its critical success and praise from such luminaries as Edmund Burke and Dr Johnson she received only twenty guineas.

Its comic depictions of English society and realistic use of accents among the working class brought it to the attention of her father who was at first surprised and then supportive that his daughter had published a novel and enhanced the family's standing. With the books rare use of a female teenage protagonist Frances was already pushing the boundaries of the novel.

It also brought Frances an invitation to the home of patron of the arts Hester Thrale. Here she met Dr Johnson, who would remain her friend and correspondent throughout the period of her visits, from 1779 to 1783. Mrs Thrale wrote to Dr Burney on July 22nd, stating that: "Mr. Johnson returned home full of the Prayes of the Book I had lent him, and protesting that there were passages in it which might do honour to Richardson: we talk of it for ever, and he feels ardent after the dénouement; he could not get rid of the Rogue, he said." Dr Johnson's best compliments were eagerly transcribed in Frances's diary.

Sojourns at Streatham could occupy months at a time, and on several occasions the guests, including Frances, made trips to Brighton and Bath. As with other notable events, these experiences were faithfully recorded.

In 1779, encouraged by the public's warm reception of comic material in Evelina, and with offers of help from Arthur Murphy and Richard Brinsley Sheridan, Frances began to write a dramatic comedy called The Witlings. The play satirised London society, including the literary world and its pretensions.

It was not published at the time as her father and Samuel Crisp thought it would offend some of the public by seeming to mock the Bluestockings, and also their reservations about the propriety of a woman writing comedy. The play is the story of Celia and Beaufort, lovers kept apart by their families due to "economic insufficiency".

In 1781 Samuel Crisp died. Much of her subsequent work, Cecilia, or Memoirs of an Heiress, was written after much discussion with Crisp. The novel was published the following year. Her advance was now £250 and the first edition ran to 2000 copies, the first of several printings that year alone.

The narrative of Cecilia tells of Cecilia Beverley, whose inheritance from her uncle comes on the condition that she marries but keeps the family name.

In 1784 one of her greatest supporters, and her frequent correspondent, Dr Johnson, died. Her promising relationship with a clergyman, George Owen Cambridge, was also over. Frances was 33 years old but she had made a great deal of her life already.

In 1785, thanks to her association with Mary Granville Delany, a woman influential in both literary and royal circles, Frances travelled to the court of King George III and Queen Charlotte. There she was offered the post of "Keeper of the Robes", and a salary of £200 per annum. Frances hesitated. She had no wish to be separated from her family, nor to anything that would restrict her time in writing. But, unmarried at 34, she felt obliged to accept and thought that improved social status and income might allow her greater freedom to write.

She developed a warm relationship with the queen and princesses that lasted into her later years, yet her worries were prophetic: the position exhausted her and left her little, if any, time to write. She was unhappy and her feelings were amplified by a poor relationship with her colleague, Elizabeth Schwellenburg, co-Keeper of the Robes.

But despite writing little in the way of novels she still kept at her journals recounting life at court and the various political and social events.

By 1790, frustrated at her lack of writing, her further failed relationships, and with her health failing she asked to be released from service. The request was granted.

She returned to her father's house in Chelsea, but continued to receive a yearly pension of £100. She maintained a friendship with the royal family and received letters from the princesses until her death.

Between 1790–91 Frances wrote four blank-verse tragedies: Hubert de Vere, The Siege of Pevensey, Elberta and Edwy and Elgiva. Only the last was performed but met with public failure and played for only one night.

The French Revolution which had begun in 1789 brought support from many English literates for the ideals of equality and social justice. It was now that Frances became acquainted with a group of French exiles known as "Constitutionalists", who had fled France and were living at Juniper Hall, near Mickleham, where Frances's sister Susanna lived.

Frances quickly became attached to General Alexandre D'Arblay, an artillery officer who had been adjutant-general to Lafayette, a hero of the French Revolution.

Frances's father disapproved because of Alexandre's poverty, his Catholicism, and his ambiguous social status as an émigré. In spite of these objections they were married on July 28th, 1793.

On December 18th, 1794, Frances gave birth to their only child, a son, Alexander.

The impoverished couple were saved from poverty in 1796 by the publication of her next novel Camilla, or a Picture of Youth, a story of frustrated love and impoverishment. She made £1000 on the novel and sold the copyright for another £1000. This was enough to enable them to build a house in Westhumble; Camilla Cottage. Their life was now happy on all fronts.

Sadly, the news that her sister Susanna and her family were moving to Ireland that year caused her, and her father, some consternation, as did her sister Charlotte's remarriage in 1798 to the pamphleteer Ralph Broome.

Between 1797–1801 Frances wrote three further comedies; Love and Fashion, A Busy Day and The Woman Hater. All were unpublished during her lifetime.

The illness and death of Susanna in 1800 brought an end to their lifelong correspondence. Frances was devastated and only resumed her journal writing at the request of her husband, for the benefit of their son.

In 1801 D'Arblay was offered service with the government of Napoleon in France, and in 1802 Frances and her son followed him to Paris, where they expected to remain for a year. The outbreak of the war between France and England meant their stay extended for ten years. Although the conditions of their time left her isolated from her family, Frances was supportive of her husband's decision to move.

In August 1810 Frances developed pains in her breast. Her husband suspected breast cancer. Through her royal network of acquaintances, she was treated by leading physicians and, a year later, on September 30th, 1811, she underwent a mastectomy performed by "7 men in black". The operation was performed by M. Dubois, the accoucheur (midwife or obstetrician) to the Empress Marie Louise, Duchess of Parma, and widely considered the best doctor in France. Frances was later able to write about the operation in detail, since she was conscious through most of it, anesthetics not yet being in use.

Frances survived, even though she was still in recovery and not back to full health, returned to England in 1812 to visit her ailing father and also to avoid young Alexander's conscription into the French army

In 1814, Frances published her fourth novel, The Wanderer or, Female Difficulties, a few days before her father's death. A story of love and misalliance set in the French Revolution", it criticises the English treatment of foreigners during the war.

Frances made £1500 from the first run, but it did not go into a second English printing, although it met her immediate financial needs.

In 1815 Napoleon escaped from Elba. D'Arblay was then serving with the King's Guard, and he became involved in the military actions that followed. Frances joined her wounded husband at Trèves, and together they returned to Bath, England. Frances wrote an account of this and of her Paris years in her Waterloo Journal, written between 1818 and 1832. D'Arblay was rewarded with promotion to lieutenant-general but died shortly afterwards, in 1818, of cancer.

Frances now moved to London to be nearer to her son, a fellow at Christ's College. In honour of her father she gathered and in 1832 published, in three volumes, the Memoirs of Doctor Burney. The memoirs overly praised her father's accomplishments and character. Always protective of her father and the family's reputation, she deliberately destroyed evidence of facts that were painful or unflattering.

She now lived almost in retirement, outliving her son, Alexander, who died in 1837, and her sister, Charlotte, who died in 1838.

Frances continued to receive many visits from younger members of the Burney family, who gathered to listen to her fascinating accounts and her talents for imitating the people she described. She continued to write in her journals but alas her canon of novels and plays received no further additions.

Frances Burney died on January 6th, 1840.

She was buried with her son and her husband in Walcot cemetery in Bath.

There is a Royal Society of Arts blue plaque to record her period of residence at 11 Bolton Street, Mayfair.

Frances Burney – A Concise Bibliography

Fiction
The History of Caroline Evelyn, (manuscript destroyed by author, 1767.)
Evelina: or, The History of a Young Lady's Entrance into the World. 1778.
Cecilia: or, Memoirs of an Heiress. 1782.
Camilla: or, A Picture of Youth. 1796.
The Wanderer: or, Female Difficulties. 1814.

Non Fiction
Brief Reflections Relative to the French Emigrant Clergy. 1793.
Memoirs of Doctor Burney. 1832.

Journals & Letters
The Early Diary of Frances Burney 1768–1778. 2 volumes. 1889.

The Diary and Letters of Madame D'Arblay. 1904.
The Diary of Fanny Burney.
Dr. Johnson & Fanny Burney by Fanny Burney.
The Early Journals and Letters of Fanny Burney, 1768–1786. 5 volumes.
The Court Journals and Letters of Frances Burney. 4 volumes. (to date).
The Journals and Letters of Fanny Burney (Madame D'Arblay) 1791–1840. 12 volumes.

Plays

The Witlings, 1779 (satirical comedy).
Edwy and Elgiva, 1790 (verse tragedy). Produced at Drury Lane, 21 March 1795.
Hubert de Vere, 1788–91 (verse tragedy).
The Siege of Pevensey, 1788–91 (verse tragedy).
Elberta, (fragment) 1788–91 (verse tragedy).
Love and Fashion, 1799 (satirical comedy).
The Woman Hater, 1800–1801 (satirical comedy).
A Busy Day, 1800–1801 (satirical comedy).

www.ingramcontent.com/pod-product-compliance
Lightning Source LLC
Chambersburg PA
CBHW051531260626
47170CB00003B/878